CAME A CAVALIER

FRANCES PARKINSON KEYES

CAME
A
CAVALIER

JULIAN MESSNER, INC. • NEW YORK

PUBLISHED BY JULIAN MESSNER, INC.
8 WEST 40TH STREET, NEW YORK 18, N. Y.

PRINTED IN THE UNITED STATES OF AMERICA

TO NORMANDY
AND ALL THAT IT REPRESENTS
IN THE PAST, PRESENT AND FUTURE
OF THE ENTIRE WORLD

THIS EDITION OF *Came a Cavalier* IS ESPECIALLY PREPARED FOR BOOK CLUB DISTRIBUTION WITH THE APPROVAL OF THE AUTHOR.

PART ONE

Searching

December 1918–May 1919

"The American Red Cross maintained within our zones a system of 'Line of Communication Canteens,' which furnished refreshments and relief to troops in transit and became a valuable feature of the Red Cross work. The statistical work of the Searchers attached to statistical sections and to hospitals obtained much information for relatives."

—Final Report of General John J. Pershing, Commander-in-Chief, American Expeditionary Forces in Europe, to the Secretary of War, September 1, 1919

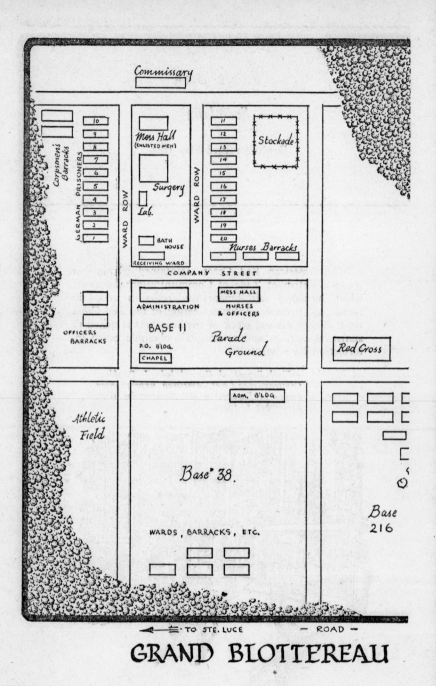

GRAND BLOTTEREAU

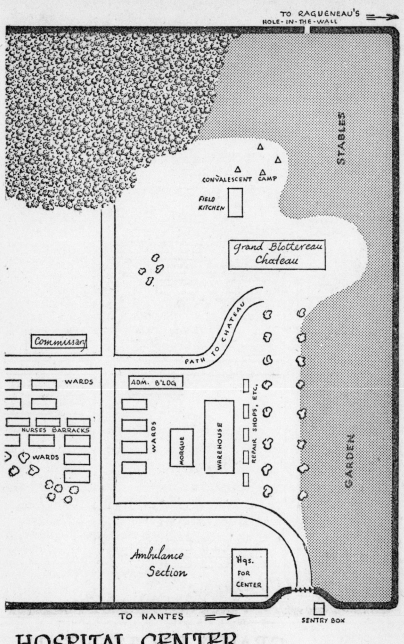

TO RAGUENEAU'S
HOLE-IN-THE-WALL

STABLES

△
△ △
CONVALESCENT CAMP

FIELD
KITCHEN

Grand Blottereau
Chateau

Commissary

PATH TO CHATEAU

WARDS

ADM. B'LDG

WARDS

NURSES BARRACKS

WARDS

MORGUE

WAREHOUSE

REPAIR SHOPS, ETC.

GARDEN

Ambulance
Section

Hqs.
FOR
CENTER

TO NANTES

SENTRY BOX

HOSPITAL CENTER

PART ONE

Searching

December 1918–May 1919

CHAPTER I

"You BETTER DUCK, Miss Galt, here comes your frog!"

"Ye gods, *again!* Why, he can't be, Arkie!"

"Maybe he can't, but he is. He makes damn good time on that bicyclette of his, too!"

Constance Galt, the new Red Cross "Searcher" at Base Hospital 11, did not wait for a second warning. She had been heading towards the tiny office tucked into one corner of the Receiving Ward when the gaunt giant stationed at the intersection of Company Street and Ward Row called out to her; now she turned hastily back, rounded the Bath House, and darted in among the oak trees at the rear. Only these oaks—a small grove—remained of the vast forest which had once extended southward from the Château de Grand Blottereau, near Nantes; the rest had been sacrificed to provide room for three large barrack-type hospitals. As a grove, what remained did not amount to much; as a hiding place, she had more than once found it a convenient refuge.

She did not dislike or misunderstand the solemn boy from Sainte-Luce. She could not help being touched by his devotion, and all his family had been extremely kind to her. Moreover, she realized that time inevitably hung so heavily on his hands in the isolated château where he lived that he would naturally have grasped at any pretext for diversion, even if he had not possessed the adolescent's normal predilection for the unfamiliar, the military, and the feminine. There was absolutely nothing for him to do at Sainte-Luce these days after the Armistice while waiting to be called up, and he looked upon the installation of an American post in the neighborhood as a godsend. Constance was responsible for only part of the encampment's fascination for him. But her office was always his first objective, and his visits were becoming more and more frequent and prolonged; when so many desperately sick men needed her more, she could hardly be blamed for regarding him with mounting disfavor. The sergeant in charge of the convalescent workers, whose native state had prompted the nickname which seemed so curiously appropriate, was only one of several faithful watchmen charged with signaling that the inopportune caller had again arrived.

"Wait up there, Miss Galt! Unless you've got a heavy date at the Supply Depot, I could use a few minutes with you."

Constance came to an abrupt stop, realizing, just in time, that she had almost collided with Captain Duncan Craig, the officer of the day. In her haste and preoccupation, she had not noticed him coming towards her from Ward 17. Now she reddened under his amused gaze.

"No, I'm not hurrying to a date. I was just—— Do you need me in 17? Is Cronin worse?"

"On the contrary, he's better. I've just come from him, and the wound's draining splendidly. He's drowsy too, so he's quite as well off without company. When I said I could use a few minutes with you, I meant just here. Couldn't we lean up against the Bath House and have a chat and a smoke?"

"You know I can't smoke in uniform."

"Well, take it off—unless you'd rather not drop it in this damn mud!" Then as the girl stiffened slightly and pressed her lips together, he added: "There, as you were!— However, I would like to know what you started to say when you told me you didn't have a date, you were just——"

"I was just running away from Robert de Fremond. I've got Arkie and two or three others trained to give me a high sign."

"Do you make it a practice to run away from your gentlemen friends?"

"I don't know why you should think I need to. Anyway, you wouldn't put Robert in that class, would you? He's under twenty, looks over thirty, and acts about ten."

"I wouldn't ordinarily. But in spite of your uncharitable remarks, he really is quite mature, and he's smitten all right. . . . At that, I wasn't thinking of Robert de Fremond when I asked you my question about gentlemen friends."

"Is it in the line of duty for me to answer wholly personal questions?"

The popularity which Constance Galt had so swiftly achieved at camp lay, to a large degree, in her simplicity and her friendliness under almost any circumstances. But as she answered the officer her normally warm and pleasant voice was unaccountably chilly. He regarded her appraisingly, the merriment which had briefly illumined his tired eyes changing to interest. *That girl's got a damn fine figure,* he said to himself. *A little on the thin side, but that's to be expected, with the kind of life she's leading now. A little on the stiff side too. If she could just fill out a little and relax a little. . . . I'd like to see how she'd look in a different kind of dress—a pink one with a tight bodice and a ruffled skirt, like the one Eileen was wearing at the Waldorf the night before I sailed. I don't believe this girl ever had a dress like that and it would do a lot for her. That blue jersey looks good to the patients, I know. No wonder, either, after they've looked at the nurses' gray seersucker day in and day out! But it doesn't look so good to me, even if it is turned up pretty short to keep it out of this everlasting mud. . . . Thank God her cap doesn't hide her hair. I bet it comes below her knees when it's down, and I sure would like to catch her combing it some day. But at that I like her eyes even better. They've got the same clear look as her skin. And they're kind, too. When a man's dying, she's the Searcher I always think of first. I'm mad as hell if some other doctor's had the same thought. But she sure can freeze up, just like she did right now. And I bet there's some reason for it. I bet some man's back of that freezing look she gave me and the way she shut me off. I'd like to know what he did to her. Damn it, I must be loony standing here all this time trying to figure out a thing like that. But I've hit pretty close to the mark. She's trying to make a getaway. I better act quick or she'll be gone.*

"No," he said, speaking almost vehemently. He did not want her to go. "It isn't in the line of duty. And I wasn't trying to be fresh. I was interested, that's all. Let's talk about something else—the de Fremonds, for instance. I don't believe I know how you got acquainted with them in the first place. Would you think I was rude if I asked?"

"Of course not. I was out in the camionette, trying to locate some eggs, and a garrulous old woman with hardly any teeth left told me that she thought maybe if I went to the château, the Countess would help me out. She added that the Countess understood all sorts of languages—even American. Which led me to believe that she herself hadn't understood me very well. Some people don't."

"So you went to the Château Chassay—just like that?"

The Captain was treading cautiously. He decided it was better not to indicate in words that the obvious allusion had not escaped him. His discretion was rewarded. Constance abandoned her attitude of flight and leaned companionably back against the wall.

"Yes, just like that. Arkie drove me over to the village of Sainte-Luce and there was Château Chassay staring us right in the face. The gate to the outer wall was open, and we drove straight through the grounds to the moat and across the drawbridge at the side. I got out and then I just stood and stared—I couldn't help it. Blottereau isn't so different from big gray pretentious houses with mansard roofs that I've seen in suburbs that used to be fashionable before I was born. But this château was. It had a short square central tower and a façade of lovely old rose-colored brick, with stone medallions scattered over it. Some of the medallions had coats of arms on them and others served as frames for the heads of animals— one was a dog and one was a wild boar and two were lions. They looked pretty formidable to me but finally I went up to the door and tugged at the bell pull and there was a clanging sound off in the distance. Presently I heard someone shuffling through a long, cold hall."

"How did you know it was cold before you got into it?"

"I must have found that out afterwards. But it seems as if I'd always known it. Anyway, the door finally opened, and there stood a little old Breton bonne in a fancy lace cap. She was polite, but she was puzzled. She didn't understand me very well either. However, she ushered me into a beautiful little octagonal room facing the front door, and said she would call Madame la Comtesse."

"Was the beautiful little octagonal room cold too?"

"Yes, but she didn't leave me there long. Presently she came back and opened the door into another room at the end of the long hall. There was a huge chimneypiece in it, and a bright fire was burning there. I think I'll always remember how good that fire felt, even after I'm back in Winchester, where we take warm rooms as a matter of course."

"Winchester, Virginia?"

"Winchester, Massachusetts. Do I look as if I'd come 'up from the South at the break of day'?"

"No, now you mention it, I ought to have known you were a New Englander. Should I have recognized the Radcliffe manner too?"

"Certainly not. Nothing so exalted in my life. I went to Tufts. It was not only nearer, it was a good deal cheaper, and I had to think of that, first and foremost."

"I'd like to hear more about the Château Chassay," he remarked, resisting the impulse to voice the last thought and settling himself more firmly against the wall of the Bath House. "Is there anything else about it you think you might remember, back in Winchester, Massachusetts, besides the fireplace?"

"Oh yes. The portraits on either side of the mantel—portraits of the Count's ancestors who were guillotined in the Revolution. Dozens of other portraits too—more than I could count. And the harp in the corner, with most of the strings missing, that belonged to the lady ancestor. And the Chinese chests along the wall. And the lace tidies on all the chairs and sofas, carefully tacked down over the worn places. I was terribly embarrassed when one of the brass hooks on my belt caught in a tidy and pulled it loose. But the Countess wasn't embarrassed. She didn't notice it at all, or if she did, she didn't let on. She went right along talking to me about eggs."

"So she'd shown up by the time you tangled with the tidy?"

"Yes. She showed up very promptly. She made me think of pictures I'd seen of Queen Victoria. She was a little bit of a woman, not at all elegant or beautiful, but more dignified and charming than anyone I'd ever met—and so friendly and helpful. She didn't have any trouble understanding me. She said we'd go right out and look for eggs. She disappeared long enough to put on a plumed hat and a braided dolman, and afterwards she came back and climbed right into the camionette with Arkie and me. She showed us the way to a lot of little towns on the roads back of Sainte-Luce and Thouaré and Mauves and Clermont-sur-Loire. We'd never even known they were there before. We didn't pick up more than three or four eggs at any one place where we stopped, but we stopped at a lot of them. Arkie and I came back to the hospital with a good supply."

The Captain tossed his cigarette into the mud and lighted another, without offering one to Constance this time. Then, slightly shifting his stand, he crossed his arms and leaned against the wall of the Bath House again, as if he found this extremely comfortable. His build made the position natural. He was tall and clean-limbed, more at ease in his uniform than most of the hospital staff, whose bearing generally remained that of the medical man rather than that of the military officer. If it had not been for the signs of strain in his face, this would have had a curiously young look, in spite of its sophistication; his crisp, reddish hair, untouched by gray, enhanced that appearance. He smiled engagingly.

"I've noticed the influx of eggs," he said. "But I didn't know before that you were responsible for it."

"I'm not. The Countess is responsible for it."

"Well, don't let's get into another argument. But I would like to know at what point Robert entered this interesting picture. Did he come climbing into the camionette the next time you went on an egg hunt?"

"No, I never went on any more egg hunts. Once the Countess showed us the way and got things going, Arkie went on those alone. But before we got home that first day, she asked me to come for tea the next Sunday and bring some of the convalescents with me. So I did. And Robert was there. He's her son and he hasn't been called out yet. You know there's another son, named Jean. He was there too."

"You're wrong. I didn't know. This is the first I've heard of Jean. Also too young for military purposes, I presume?"

"Well, he's not quite nine. He's a very nice little boy."

Constance spoke demurely, but the Captain noticed that the pleasant twinkle had returned to her eyes and that the corners of her mouth were twitching slightly. He was pleased beyond all reason at the sight.

"Madame's husband, the Count, was there too," Constance went on. "He has an enormous beard and wears a frock coat. Mostly he stands in front of the fireplace and flaps his coattails while he talks about his ancestors who were guillotined. He says it didn't make any difference, really. He has to fill all the offices that they did. He's the mayor of Sainte-Luce and the justice of the peace; he performs all the civil marriages and he's godfather to all the children."

"Is his conversation wholly historical?"

"No, he talks about other things too. But the Revolution interests me the most, and I'm so busy watching his coattails that I can't listen to everything. I'm terribly afraid they're going to catch on fire."

"And they don't?"

"No, they don't, no matter how much he flaps them around. They never have."

"What do you mean, they never have?"

"I mean they never have when I've been there. But after all, I've only been there three times, so far. Maybe they did before that. And maybe they will yet."

"Are you speaking hopefully or fearfully?"

"Well, a little of both, I guess. Do you blame me?"

The Captain shook his head, laughing, and tossing his second cigarette into the mud, again regarding his companion appraisingly. *She's forgotten she was mad,* he said to himself. "The château isn't the only place you like to go to, is it?"

"It's the only place I've had a chance to go to, so far. Except of course to the dances. I go to one of those every night, even Sundays. That's what's kept me so busy."

"How come I haven't been in on this?"

"I don't mean the officers' dances. I mean the enlisted men's."

"I call that unfair discrimination. What have you got against officers?"

"Nothing. But dancing with enlisted men is an important part of a job like mine. There aren't enough Searchers and Hostesses to go around, so none of us can let up. . . . Besides, no one's invited me."

"Why, you can just go! You don't have to be invited."

"Yes I do. The officers have the nurses to dance with. They don't need us."

"They might want you just the same."

"Then they have to say so. At least as far as I'm concerned."

"All right. I am saying so. I do want you. I'm on duty tonight but I'll call for you next Tuesday around seven-thirty. Meanwhile what about dinner at Ragueneau's? I suppose, absorbed as you are in good works, you haven't been there either."

"No, not yet. But everyone talks about it."

She stood up straight, pulling her short jersey skirt down over her rubber boots. As she did so, Craig noticed that her hands were badly chapped, and that they had a blue look, as if they were very cold.

"Why, you're half frozen!" he said penitently. "I shouldn't have kept you out here all this time."

"Don't worry about that. I haven't felt cold until just these last few minutes. When I first came to France, I was afraid I'd never feel warm again. But I've got used to all of it—the grayness and the rain and the chill that goes straight through to your bones. I honestly don't mind it any more. But if you'll excuse me now, Captain Craig, I think I'd better get back to the office."

"Lord knows how you get through all you do," he remarked. "I don't wonder you think you must get back on the job, if it's ever going to be finished. I'll walk along with you, though, if you don't mind. I'm on my way to the Administration Building myself. Or was, before I was diverted from duty by Daphne in disguise."

Constance smiled, responsively and unreprovingly, but she did not loiter as they rounded the Bath House, and she ran up the steps of her office without looking back. As she opened the door, she saw that she had not overestimated the labors still ahead of her. Her orderly was seated in front of the kitchen table—covered with black oilcloth—which served as her desk. This was piled high with the usual miscellany: notes from the ward nurses demanding the immediate delivery of everything from playing cards and victrolas to mufflers for patients whose heads were cold and "rat cheese" for those with fickle appetites; a scribbled message from an overworked chaplain, telling her that services would be in the Post Office on Sunday and asking her to play the organ; the mail containing the list of the "Missing in Hospitals" which she would have to check against the files in the Sick and Wounded Office before she could go to bed; a sheet of verses from a lovesick lieutenant; and on top of all these a crested envelope, delicately addressed in purple ink.

"Your frog friend waited and waited," Whaley, the orderly, informed her, rising reluctantly from her chair, which he had appropriated during her absence. "But I guess he finally figured you'd been held up somewhere. Of course I couldn't make out much of what the frog had on his mind. You'd think a fellow like that would take pains to improve his mind by learning a little English, now that he's got such a swell chance, wouldn't you? I kind of got the idea he came here to invite you to dinner. Not tea this time, but dinner. Something extra special. Because a cousin of his, fellow by the name of Prism or something nutty like that, is coming to good old Chassay for his leave, and the Countess figured maybe him and you'd enjoy meeting one another."

CHAPTER II

CONSTANCE WAS NOT nearly as indifferent to the crested envelope as her apparent negligence of it had indicated. Her acquaintance with the de Fremonds meant a great deal to her, partly because she found them personally agreeable, and partly because their mode of living intrigued and amazed her. But her very pleasure in the association made her shy about it; she was afraid of seeming to boast of privileges which were more or less exclusive. Moreover, she had a scrupulous feeling of obligation to her work. Leaving the crested envelope still unopened, she turned to the Paris mail, scanning the long sheets that listed the names of men who had been picked up unconscious on the battlefields of the Argonne and hospitalized wherever accommodations could be found for them. She picked up the list, murmured that she would be back, and crossed the road to the Administration Building, where she headed towards the file room, to check the names on her list against those on the cards. Among the names which were vaguely familiar to her, she found six that tallied; in other cases, she found names that were the same, but which belonged to men in different outfits. This meant that she must go to Ward 9, the next to the last in the row, to check with the patients who might or might not be identified, thus involving a further delay before she could get back to her desk.

She left the Administration Building and turned to the right. Long lines of dingy frame buildings, uniform in size and shape, stretched forlornly out on either side of her. She went sloshing on through the mud. The odor of bandages and Dakin solution assailed her nostrils before she was well inside it; then came the general impression of gray walls, gray blankets, and the gray-clad figures of nurses moving among the prostrate forms of hollow-eyed and unshaven men clad in drab flannel pajamas.

Even the few convalescents huddled around the stove at either end of the ward spoke in subdued whispers or sat staring blankly into space. The whole effect was one of unrelieved homelessness and hopelessness.

I mustn't let all this get me down, she said to herself resolutely. *I can't —I won't.* Suddenly she found that the returning thought of the little crested note still lying unopened on her desk helped her so much that she was able to speak lightly to the men sitting around the nearest stove.

"Not fighting tonight, boys? I thought surely I'd find you in the thick of the Argonne Forest if not at Belleau Wood."

The man with the bandaged foot growled helplessly. "What's the use? Rube here—" he jerked his head towards the man with his arm in the splint—"has told the rest of us so many times now it was him did all the fighting at Fismes he's got us whipped down."

"Nonsense, Tony! It would take more than Rube to whip the rest of you down. Wouldn't it, Rube?"

The second man did not growl, but he shrugged his shoulders before answering. "I don't know," he said. "Don't take much to whip some fellows down. Me, I don't give up so easy. It took six of them Jerries to flatten me out."

"What did I tell you, Miss Galt? Maybe some marine can beat him at bragging, but ain't no doughboy can."

"Oh hell, who won this war anyway?"

The question came from the depths of a nearby bed. The occupants of various other cots immediately began to chorus, "The marines! The marines!" But one lone voice, louder than all the others, drowned the rest out.

"The M. P.'s! I tell you it was the M. P.'s!"

Encouraged again, because she had succeeded in rousing the men from their lethargy, Connie walked down the ward towards the nurse, who was feeding a helpless man through a tube, but who looked up with an understanding smile as the tumult began. She nodded pleasantly at Connie.

"Good evening, Miss Galt. I'm glad you've come in. The men are always pleased to see you."

"I like them too. But I can't hang around very long just now. I've got to check on the outfits of two of your patients—Ignatz Warsinski and Aloysius Kelly. Which beds are they in?"

"That's Warsinski right over there, in Bed 18—the man who keeps coughing."

"Is it all right if I give him a lozenge?"

"Well, it can't hurt him any."

Connie reached into the raffia bag habitually slung over her arm, which she kept well supplied with cigarettes, chocolate bars, packaged cookies, and hard candies, though its primary purpose was for carrying notebooks, pads, and pencils. Through long practice she was able to locate the hard candy easily, and approaching the gasping man, she held out a piece.

"Here, try this. It may taste good to you."

He waited for the paroxysm to pass, then extended a wan hand, smiled faintly, and carried the cough drop shakingly towards his mouth. After he sucked it for a moment or two, he was sufficiently relieved to say thank you, and Connie ventured to question him.

"Feel like talking a little?"

"I reckon so, if you got the time to spare."

"That's what I'm here for. Besides, I like to. This is the first chance I've had for a visit with you. What part of the States are you from?"

"Chi. What about you?"

"Not a big city like that. A little place named Winchester—a suburb of Boston. It's very pretty there."

"We got some pretty suburbs around Chi too. Lake Forest. Oak Park. Wilmette."

"I've never seen them, but I've heard of them. You must miss getting out along the Lake. Have you been in France long?"

"Well, it seems long all right. I came across with the Forty-second Division."

"You weren't ever with the Thirty-ninth?"

"No, I stayed right with the Rainbow till I got knocked out."

Another fit of coughing, so violent that it choked him, interrupted him suddenly. Connie waited for it to pass, so that she might say something further to cheer him, though she already knew he was not the Warsinski she was seeking. But the paroxysm went on and on. At last, slipping the box of lozenges into his hand, she rose.

"Here, you keep all of these. I'll come back some other time, when you feel more like talking. Perhaps you'd like me to write a letter for you, too."

He still could not speak, but he managed to nod, and she left him clutching tightly his lozenges. Then she went back to the nurse, who had finished feeding the helpless patient and had gone to the chart room near the entrance, where she was absorbed in her records. This time she did not even look up until Connie spoke to her.

"I'm sorry, Miss Dryden, that one wasn't my man after all. What about the other—Aloysius Kelly?"

The nurse turned in her chair and pointed to the small private room directly across from her office, where only men in the most critical of conditions were placed.

"Kelly's in there," she whispered. "You know what that means. Father Calloran's with him right now. Maybe you'd better wait a few minutes."

"In the private room!" Connie exclaimed in surprise. "Why, I didn't get any notice of it from HQ! There must have been a slip-up somewhere."

"No. He got worse very suddenly. It was his heart. Just this afternoon."

"My, but I'm sorry!—Would you look at his chart and see what his outfit is?"

"Sure."

The nurse reached for one of the charts fastened to small boards and hanging on the wall. "Company K, 110th Infantry," she read.

"Well, that's the way he's entered on my list. But in the office file they have him listed Battalion B, 149th Field Artillery."

"And I'm sure that's right, because that's what's on his dog tag. It doesn't matter much though, any more, what hospital he's in."

The door of the private room opened. Father Calloran came out, closing it quietly after him. The tall priest's athletic build contributed to a powerful presence and under ordinary circumstances, the priest's ruddy face was exceptionally genial. At the moment, however, his expression was grave and his head bent.

"The poor boy went so quickly there wasn't time to call you, Miss Dryden," he said apologetically. And as the nurse leaped up and hurriedly summoned the ward master to call the surgeon on duty, Father Calloran looked at Connie, shaking his head sadly. "I'm sorry you didn't get the word either, Miss Galt," he went on. "I've seen for myself how much comfort you bring to the dying—almost as much as I can. And that helps me too. Now it looks as if we'd have to help each other write that awful mortality letter."

"You can help me, but I'm afraid I can't help you. If I've seen a lot of a man, I have some idea what to say. But I didn't know Kelly at all."

"All right, I'll tell you what we'll say." Father Calloran picked up the chart in his turn and studied it attentively for a moment. "The next of kin's Kelly's mother," he said then. "Well, we'll write that I was with him at the end, that he was conscious while he was receiving the Last Sacraments. That's what she'll want to know. We'll tell her he didn't suffer—at least not to speak of. His record shows he was a good soldier, so we can dwell on that. And we can say the other patients all liked him, and that they're going to miss him a lot. Then we can tell her about the funeral. We'll say that his flag-draped casket was taken to the American Cemetery on a caisson, along with those of four other men who've given their lives for their country. That'll make her feel her boy isn't alone in death and also that she's not alone in her grief either, that she's become one of a great noble company of bereft mothers. We'll say that all along the way between the hospital and the cemetery, the French stopped reverently and stood at attention while the cortege went by, the men with their hats in their hands, the women making the sign of the cross.

"We'll say that the nurse who was with him at the end followed the caisson in an ambulance, and that other American women too were there. You can explain that all the Searchers at the Base attend every military funeral. Then of course we'll say that both chaplains officiated, that a volley was fired by a squad of soldiers and taps sounded. We'll say that the grave was marked immediately with a white wooden cross on which were stenciled her son's name, rank, company, serial number, and date of death, and that later this wooden cross will be replaced by a permanent one made of marble. I think she'd like to know that one of his identification tags was buried with him, and that I hung the other on his cross, having previously copied all statistics for my records. We'll say that little French children will be constantly coming, bringing small bunches of flowers to the cemetery, so that the grave will never be undecorated. And of course we'll say that I offered a Mass for him the day after he died."

"Yes, and I'll come to it, so I can describe it to her. I've no idea what a Mass is like, so I couldn't unless I did come. But I'd be glad to do it."

The priest looked at her quizzically, but answered with great gentleness. "I should like very much to have you come to Mass, Miss Galt—in fact I've already written you, asking if you wouldn't play the organ for me next Sunday morning. Probably you haven't had time to read the note yet—I wrote it just this afternoon. I'll postpone the Mass for Kelly until Sunday. We don't need to mention the day in the letter we write to his mother. We'll simply tell her I'm going to say a Mass for him."

"And you think that'll comfort her?"

"Yes. Yes, I know it will."

Again he regarded her quizzically and spoke gently—so gently that she wanted to ask him why he felt sure of this. But his reference to the note from him which she had not yet seen reminded her of the other still lying unopened on her desk, and she felt impelled to go on; so after asking him to draft a letter and promising to play for him the following Sunday, she bade the priest good night and started for the door. A still stronger impulse, however, forced her back to the group around the stove. The men would take Kelly's death hard, all of them, especially as its unexpectedness had in it a quality of shock; but probably no one would be more seriously affected by it than Carl Bruntz, the soldier whose recovery from his amputation had been so complicated. He had not known beforehand that the leg would have to go; the preliminary examination had not revealed the full extent of the septicemia. But when he had been etherized for further exploration, the discovery had been made that it was a question of either his leg or his life, and the operation had gone forward immediately. The return of consciousness had brought with it abject despair. Bruntz insisted that they should have let him die, that life in such a mutilated form was far worse than death, and he had stubbornly refused to do anything to aid his own recovery. Connie had helped the nurses and doctors fight for him and revive within him the will to live; during this long struggle she had come to recognize his reactions and to feel that he was peculiarly her charge. She went to him now with the air of one seeking co-operation.

"I've just realized that Christmas is right around the corner," she said. "And it doesn't give me a particularly happy feeling. I wonder if some of you wouldn't help me get up a little celebration. I don't know anyone else I can ask to do what I'd really enjoy—having a tree and seeing this place all fixed up with greens. I think I can get a tree, but I wouldn't have time to make ornaments or wreaths. You would, though. Will you do it for me?"

The three convalescents looked first at each other and then at her, without making any immediate answer. Then Reuben Ware, the man with his arm in a splint, spoke rather dourly.

"Where would we get anything to make ornaments out of, in this dump?" he inquired. "Not that we wouldn't just as lief, if we could," he added a little less grudgingly.

"I've made Christmas tree oranaments, time and again, for my kid brothers and sisters," retorted Tony Miglario, the man whose foot was enveloped in big bandages, speaking with some spirit. "I made 'em out of anything I could find. I guess we can find something now."

"I suppose we could save the tin foil from our chocolate bars and cigarettes for balls on the tree," Carl suggested hesitantly. "Or maybe cut stars out of tobacco cans. But we ought to work in some color too, if we could."

"What's the matter with the blue paper around the absorbent cotton?" inquired Miss Dryden. The others had not heard her coming up behind them; now they politely made room for her in their small circle, but Reuben voiced another objection.

"Blue paper ain't bad in its place, but it ain't Christmasy."

Surprisingly, Miss Dryden laughed. "I've been wondering ever since I left Duluth what I could do with the red-flannel petticoat my grandmother gave me for a farewell present," she said. "Now I know. We can have poinsettias on our tree, thanks to good old Grandma."

Reuben Ware looked at her with approval not unmixed with surprise. "Well now, that's not a bad idea, Miss Dryden," he said. It was the nearest approach to praise which had so far passed his lips.

"It ain't at that," Tony chimed in. "I can make the swellest poinsettias you ever seen out of that petticoat of yours, Miss Dryden. You bring it to me tomorrow morning, along with a pair of scissors, and I'll get started right away. We ain't got no time to lose, when you come to think of it."

"If you don't need it all for flowers, I could cut some of it into strips, and we could use them for ribbons to tie the wreaths."

The offer came from an adjacent bed. Almost immediately half the ward seemed to have caught the contagion of the Christmas idea.

"If one of you ladies would get me a red crayon, I could draw real natural-looking bricks on wrapping paper and we could have us a fireplace."

"I've seen something through the window looks a lot like smilax. It was growing on a wall over yonder. If it wouldn't be too much trouble to lug it here, Miss Galt, I could make garlands out of that."

The suggestions were still coming in, thicker and faster all the time, when Connie finally tore herself away and started up Ward Row. This was even gloomier than when she had set out, for the damp drizzle of early evening had been followed by a pelting rain. She turned up the collar of her slicker as high as it would go, thrust her hands into the pockets, and plowed forward through the mud, feeling as if there were no end to this, as if the cheerless walk between the dingy frame buildings grew longer every time she took it.

"You Awk E*rroll* She-car-go Tree*bune!*"

Madame Bonnier, the battered old woman who held the concession for selling papers at camp, was coming along Ward Row, shouting as she came. At first her cry had been utterly unintelligible to Connie, and when this was interpreted to her, she had been solemnly told that the boys from Northwestern bribed Madame Bonnier to pronounce "Chicago *Tribune*" better than she did "New York *Herald.*" Since then she and Madame Bonnier had become fast friends. She was glad to see the bulky form swaying towards her in the dusk, and, as the old newspaper woman came near her, to recognize the ragged maroon sweater which was invariably worn over a variegated collection of other dirty woolen garments. Madame Bonnier was equally pleased to see Connie, and smiled broadly, revealing gums along which a few crooked yellow teeth were sparsely scattered.

"*Bon soir mam'zelle, comment ça va?* You Awk Errol? She-car-go Tree*bune?*"

Connie bought both papers, responded haltingly but feelingly to Madame Bonnier's comments about the "*temps affreux*"—which, however, she could not agree was exceptional—and continued on her way. She began to realize now that she was very hungry, and knew that she must have missed mess by staying so long in the ward; but neither the food nor the surroundings at mess were very attractive. She had often made a meal on chocolate bars and she could do so again. She plodded on and on feeling colder and tireder with every step. As she approached her office, she saw that it was in darkness, and felt guilty because she was relieved that she could have it to herself, knowing that the men who had come to see her must have left it in disappointment.

When unoccupied, the office was always kept locked on account of the supplies, so she was obliged to fumble in the dark for her key; then, putting her bag down on the steps, she wrestled with the padlock and let herself in, batting around to locate the hanging bulb which supplied the only light. After she found this, she stood still for a moment, debating with herself about the oil stove. It was small and smelly, but after all it did give out a little heat. She knelt down beside it and after lighting it continued to crouch before it for a few minutes, adjusting the wicks in the hope of getting the maximum of warmth with the minimum of suffocation. When she had done the best she could, she straightened up again, reached for the shelf where her supplies were kept, and selected two chocolate bars and some cookies. Then settling down in her chair, she opened the crested note and munched contentedly while she read it.

Château Chassay
11 dec. 1918

Dear Miss:
Since a long time we have not allowed ourselves to have no matter what small fete because of the war, but now our parent, Tristan de Fremond, has his permission from Saumur and spends it with us, so we would like to give him pleasure. We are without any serious young girl of good family in the village, however, therefore it would be very gentle on your part if you would dine with us Saturday evening coming, 14 dec., at 20 hrs.

I attend your reply and wish you to accept my most distinguished salutations.

Elise de Fremond

Connie laid down her chocolate bar and reread the letter several times. It puzzled her in places, especially the reference to the parent; she was sure the orderly had said something about a cousin, and the two statements did not seem to fit. Moreover, she was somewhat dismayed at the gravity which seemed to be attributed to her. Perhaps with different clothes on she might succeed in creating an impression of more lightheartedness, she reflected; and gnawing away at her cookies she came to a momentous decision: She would ask for enough time off to go into Nantes and buy a white silk shirt and a swanky cape to go with her dress uniform; both of these were permitted, but neither was issued, and hitherto she had felt she should not indulge in such extravagance. However, girls from Winchester, Massachusetts, were not invited to dine at French châteaux every day. She decided that the investments were justified. She even considered the addition of a velours sailor, currently known as an "undertaker's lid," to her other purchases.

CHAPTER III

"Where have you been all this time, Connie? Out by the rain barrel?"

The question was flung at her gaily from the washroom by her roommate, Gwen Foster, as Connie entered the Red Cross section an hour later. The washroom was directly opposite the front door, beyond the tubular stove which theoretically heated not only the small entryway where it stood, but the two bedrooms on either side of it. Gwen, who was nothing if not casual, was at the moment standing in front of the basin; and as the washroom, like all the other rooms, was devoid of doors, her almost completely unclad condition was plainly visible.

"You better get out of that fetching costume of yours, Connie," she advised. "It looks to me a little on the damp side—no double-entendre intended, so don't start feeling in any special place. Get along to bed. I'll do the toasting." She began to hack slices from a long loaf of French bread. "I can cook the bacon along with the bread."

"Well, it would taste awfully good, Gwen."

"I've got the Vin Sisters, Rouge and Blanc, right with me too, in my own private cellar. Which do you want?"

"I don't believe I want either, thanks. But the bacon will be grand."

"All right, you cuddle down, and I'll fix up a feast on our new Quimper pottery. You look about all in to me."

Gwen continued the preparations for the feast and by the time Connie had settled herself in bed was ready to serve it. She brought crisp bacon and the toasted bread, piled high with butter and jam, on two blue-rimmed plates, decorated with quaint, costumed figures. Then, after giving Connie her share, she poured herself a glass of red wine out of a bottle, which she extracted from behind the army blanket suspended on hooks placed along the edge of a small triangular shelf which served as her clothes closet. Finally she drew up an orange crate and sat down on it, placing her feet on the small keg which stood conveniently near, and took a long drink before she set her glass down on the floor.

"You're making a great mistake, Con," she said. "Take it from me, there's nothing wrong with Sister Rouge. Not that I don't like Sister Blanc too. But somehow she doesn't hit the spot quite the same way."

The sound of approaching footsteps and nearby voices spared Connie from the invited argument on the subject of alcoholic beverages. Gwen cocked her head and listened attentively.

"There comes Tilda," she said, referring to one of the two girls who shared the adjacent room. "She always talks sweet and low, sweet and low, like the wind of the western sea. Just the same, I'd know her voice if I heard it in the middle of the Sahara Desert. And has she a line! One you could hang clothes on!" Gwen paused, not with any intent of malicious eavesdropping, but in keen appreciation.

"'I wonder who's kissing her now,'" she sang under her breath. "Well, we ought to find out any minute now."

Still listening alertly, Gwen took another long drink and bit off a large hunk of toast, which she chewed reflectively. Connie went on eating with quiet appreciation. Presently the front door opened and Tilda Evans came through the hall and limped into the bedroom. She had an exceptionally gentle and pleasant face, but her expression was not as ecstatic as her friends had expected; instead it was resigned. She swung herself up on Connie's cot, kicking off her oxfords as she did so.

"My, but my feet hurt!" she moaned. "A few more nights on those concrete floors and I'll be crippled for life!"

"If your dogs are all that sore, I shouldn't think you would have stood around so long before you made up your mind to say good night to your boy friend," Gwen retorted crisply. "After all, duckboards aren't so easy on the feet either."

"Well, he wanted to kiss me good night and we had to argue that out."

"What for?"

"Gwen, you're impossible," Connie objected. "You know you wouldn't have done it either."

"But I did do it. He put up an awfully good case. That is, at first. Then afterwards I found I didn't give him a thrill after all. I just reminded him of his sister."

Tilda made the remark demurely but drolly. The other girls both burst out laughing.

The front door opened and closed again, this time without an intriguing preamble, and Lois Graham, the fourth member of the Red Cross group, entered the room. She was a tall, spare girl with rather sharp features, ordinarily redeemed by an agreeable smile; but at the moment she was looking distinctly annoyed. She came in without heralding her approach with any sort of cheery greeting, and frowned when she saw the half-empty glass by Gwen's orange crate.

"I do wish you'd cut out that sort of thing, Gwen," she said, her voice registering the same annoyance as her face. "You know how hard I'm trying to curb drunkenness at this camp, and when you bring liquor right into our own quarters, where anyone might see it, that's likely to counteract all the good I can do."

"Stop picking on me, will you, Lois? Now Connie doesn't drink herself, but she leaves me in peace when I get a little central heating inside of me to ward off pneumonia. Anyway this isn't liquor. You talk as if I were swilling cognac around, or sneaking *triple sec* out of coffee cups, the way we have to do at Prévot's, to get by. That glass hasn't anything in it except the pleasant remains of Sister Rouge."

"You may think all that's funny, Gwen, but I don't. I think it's disgusting."

"What's the matter with you anyway, Miss Graham? Did that black sheep you've been herding kick over the bars again?"

As usual, Gwen had hit uncomfortably close to the truth. Lois had been zealously bent on the reform of a certain ambulance driver named James Hewitt, whose ways were beguiling, but whose tastes ran to wine as well as women and song. In her capacity of Hostess at the Hut, armed with hot coffee and generous sandwiches, she had that night awaited his return from a run to Saint-Nazaire; however, in the light of various promises which he had pleasantly but mendaciously made to her, she had been hopeful that the coffee might logically be regarded as a refreshing rather than a stabilizing agent. Her hopes had been rudely shattered. The graceless creature had arrived at the Hut so inexcusably late as to suggest that he might have tarried in unsuitable company, and in a condition which even a girl less strait-laced than Lois Graham might well have regarded as badly intoxicated. Lois's annoyance under these trying circumstances was understandable. The trouble was, Gwen understood it only too well.

This time it was Connie who stepped into the breach. "If we don't settle down pretty soon, we won't get to sleep before reveille," she reminded her companions. "Tilda, as long as you're still up anyway, would you mind taking this precious plate?" Then, seeing that Lois still looked pained and that Gwen still seemed prepared to give battle, she decided that the Quimper pottery did not create enough of a diversion, and decided to try something else. "Do any of you happen to know who Saumur is?" she inquired.

She was rewarded by an outburst much heartier than she had foreseen. "What do you mean, who?" Gwen inquired, amidst the general uproar. "What made you think it was a who?"

Connie had not meant to mention her invitation to dinner. Now she realized that she was caught. "I had a nice letter from the Countess de Fremond this afternoon," she said. "And she told me that a parent of hers had his permission from Saumur to come and visit her. So I wondered——"

"Saumur is the spiffiest thing in the whole French Army. It's West Point plus. Saint-Cyr is the French West Point and after they graduate from there, the cream of the crop is sent on to this Cavalry School. The parent you're talking about probably isn't a day over twenty-seven, and you'll learn about horses from him. Not to mention lots of other things. A liberal education in himself, that's what he ought to be, especially if he's in the Cadre Noir. What else did the good old Countess say in her letter?"

"She said that there was no serious young girl of good family in the village, and so——"

Again the shouts of laughter arose. "And you majored in languages!" Tilda exclaimed. "They must have been dead ones, all right. A serious young girl, my poor child, doesn't mean a girl who doesn't know how to take a joke; it only means one who doesn't purposely take an innocent joke the wrong way—or something like that. The Countess means well bred and well behaved. And heaven knows you're both, Connie. I wish you well with Monsieur Saumur."

"His name's Tristan de Fremond."

"Good God! You're sure it isn't Percy Vere de Vere?"

"Yes, I'm very sure."

Connie was fond of Gwen, but she was beginning to tire of her ceaseless raillery. She wanted to go to sleep, which was exactly what Gwen would have done in her place; but she could not escape from her own code of civility, and now that she had precipitated the subject under discussion, she felt bound to carry on.

"Dinner is at twenty hours," she said. "I haven't got used to figuring time out that way yet, but it means eight o'clock, doesn't it?"

"Dinner! This is the first you've said about dinner! Are you going to *dinner* at Château Chassay?"

"Why yes! Did I leave that out somewhere along the line?"

They were all unmistakably impressed. They were also very much pleased, and their delight was untinged by any touch of personal jealousy. The compliment which had been paid to Connie was a compliment to them all. They began to ply her with offers, just as they had previously plied her with questions.

"I've got some brand new spats," Lois said eagerly. Her chagrin over the ambulance driver's fall from grace was completely swallowed up in her sincere sense of the fitness of things and in her ability to help create this. "They're really awfully good-looking. The color's nice too. Something between beige and pearl-gray. I want you to wear them with your dress uniform, Connie."

"How are you off for vamping liquid? I got a bottle of Quelques Fleurs the last time I went to the Belle Jardinière, and I haven't used more than half of it. You can have all there is left in the bottle, if you want it," Tilda chimed in generously.

"Just you wait. I've got something that will knock the daylights out of all the spats and perfume in France. Lamp this, will you?"

Gwen reached into a box on the shelf that went along one side of the room and took from it a piece of shrapnel, a German pistol, a sergeant's whistle, and several insignia—the castle of the engineers, the rifles of the infantry, even the guns of the coast artillery—all of which she tossed lightly to one side. Then she lifted out a folded white-silk handkerchief, and shook it open to disclose the Star Spangled Banner and the Tricolor in one corner, lovingly crossed and gaudily embroidered. Underneath them ran the inscription A MA CHÈRE PETITE MAMAN.

"A Pennsylvania Dutchy gave me this," she said. "He isn't actually a shell-shocked case, but he's right next door to it, and I guess he isn't much of a student anyway. His French is right in the same class with Connie's. He never knew he was handing out something intended for his dear little mother. He just caught on that this testimonial of international goodwill had some sort of a loving message on it; and being in French, he took it for granted it was meant for a girl friend. Put that in your pocket, Connie, with lots of Tilda's vamping liquid on it, and then take it out just at the crucial moment. It'll make Tristan de Fremond so dizzy he won't ever look at your feet!"

CHAPTER IV

NONE of the other girls was having the evening off, so Connie had her quarters to herself and made good time. Captain Craig smiled his appreciation when he caught sight of her again.

"Very, very nice! Proud to be seen out with you, Miss Galt."

"I asked for time off yesterday and went shopping in Nantes. I haven't had a sailor before. I've just been wearing an 'Orphan Annie' ulster and the 'old oaken bucket' they issued us in New York with my dress uniform."

"Too bad, when the cape and the 'undertaker's lid' are so becoming. But I'm afraid you'd have got snatched away from me if anyone else had seen you in this outfit first, and that wouldn't have suited me at all. Incidentally, I have everything fixed up with Brown, so set your tender heart at rest. Shall we be on our way?"

They walked down the highway, following the outer embankment of the Loire, and turning again, crossed a poplar-lined causeway leading over the marshes to a second elevation directly above the flowing river. No display of lights clarified the approach to the restaurant. But Craig went without hesitation across a paved terrace towards a long low building where a faint gleam shone from the window and, pushing open a massive door at the center, stood back so that Connie could look inside.

It was her first glimpse of a French kitchen, and she gave a little cry of surprise and delight at the scene before her. From the dark beams of the ceiling, shining copper vessels of every description were suspended, and the wall opposite her was covered in the same way. A large rectangular table ran straight across the room, and several women, under the adroit but dignified direction of another who stood by the table, were bustling back and forth between this and the immense fireplace which engulfed one entire side of the room. A huge fire roared beneath the hood, its flames crimson beyond the blackness of the iron utensils in front of it; and from these utensils rose the appetizing odors of simmering soup, roasting meat, and frying potatoes, which mingled with the smell of the herbs hanging from the beams among the copper pots. While she stood gazing raptly at this dazzling sight, a small gray-haired man with a black mustache, ruddy cheeks, and twinkling eyes came forward and, greeting them effusively, invited them to be seated at one end of the long table, which he cleared with a capable hand. Monsieur le Capitaine and his friend must have an apéritif there, he insisted, while they all took counsel together about a menu Mademoiselle would enjoy. The dignified woman who had been directing her helpers now came forward too, and was presented to Connie by the host as Madame Ragueneau. Obviously no introductions were needed as far as Captain Craig was concerned; he began to laugh and joke with the two at once.

"Just think of a young lady being stationed at the camp for four weeks and never taking time off to meet Monsieur and Madame Ragueneau!" he said in a bantering tone. "The minute I discovered this unfortunate state of affairs I took steps to rectify it. From now on, I'm sure she'll be one of your most regular patrons. But I count on you not to give her anything good to eat if she comes with anyone but me!"

Monsieur Ragueneau laughed heartily at this pleasantry, and Madame smiled politely also; but Connie was aware of careful appraisal meanwhile. She tried to say something in her halting French which would express her appreciation of the gorgeous kitchen and the courteous welcome; but she knew she did this inadequately and began to feel slightly ill at ease, in spite of her attractive surroundings. The arrival of the vermouth did nothing to restore her self-confidence; more tactfully but no less steadfastly than Lois, she had so far declined to drink anything of the sort. She picked up her glass and toyed with it, fearing to seem rude if she did not, and at the same time hoping that no one would notice that she had not gone beyond one small sip. She was relieved when she saw that Captain Craig had grasped the situation, and that he was ready to help her out.

"We're both starving to death, madame," he said. "So I hope you'll excuse us if we take our apéritifs along to the table and finish them with our soup. The *pot-au-feu* smells even better than usual tonight—I can't wait to wade into it. After that I think we'd better have the veal with cream sauce, and of course the *frites* with it. Next *petits-pois* with lots of onions. I hope you'll indulge us and let us have the Brie with our salad, because I don't want anything to take away the taste of the Omelette Célestine afterwards."

"Perfectly, monsieur. And to drink? St. Emilion first, as usual, *bien entendu*. And after that—is it to be the Vicomte d'Arblade or the Vouvray?"

"Let's have the Vicomte with us tonight. . . . Shall we go, Connie?"

She had noticed the open door leading from the copper-hung side of the kitchen into a large dining room where a number of persons were eating. Without question, she started towards it. Craig put his hand lightly on her arm.

"We're not going in there. Come this way."

He led her around the great fireplace, and she saw that Monsieur Ragueneau was opening, with considerable flourish, another door which had been inconspicuously shut and which she had not hitherto noticed. It led into a tiny, dimly lighted room, cozy with warmth from the chimney which formed one wall; a table which might conceivably hold four, but which was set for two, occupied almost all the floor space. Monsieur Ragueneau promptly withdrew, leaving Craig and Connie quietly enclosed. Almost instinctively, she felt behind her for the doorknob, and was slightly troubled when she failed to find it; but her manner remained composed, and she spoke in an unruffled voice.

"Don't you think it would be more fun to have our dinner out there with the others?"

"No. If I had, that's where I would have reserved a table. I wanted very much to get a chance to talk with you, and I couldn't do it in the midst of that riot."

"It sounded perfectly peaceful to me."

"The evening's young yet—not by your standards, but by most people's. Someone's sure to get drunk sooner or later and make an exhibition of himself. Just the sort of thing you'd hate. . . . Here, better let me finish that vermouth for you. You don't want to hurt Monsieur Ragueneau's feelings—I could tell that from the way you acted in the kitchen—and he'll be back any moment now."

The words were hardly out of his mouth when there was a discreet knock at the door, and one of the bustling women entered, proudly bearing a small white tureen and a large silver ladle. Close behind her came the host, who proceeded to serve the steaming soup with great ceremony, standing aside with an anxious air after he had filled the plates. Unless she created a scene, Connie could not possibly leave at this point. She accepted the chair that Craig pulled out for her and tasted her soup.

"*Délicieuse!*" she said, turning towards Monsieur Ragueneau, thankful to be able to manage that much reassuring praise, for his expression by this time suggested that if she did not like his soup, life would be hardly worth the living. He immediately relaxed and, remarking that he would fetch the St. Emilion and return in a "*toute petite seconde,*" he hastened from the room with every appearance of restored satisfaction.

"You relax too, Connie," Craig said easily. "You don't mind if I call you Connie, do you? It seems so much more natural." Then, without waiting for a reply, he went on, "Honestly, my intentions are purely conversational. I want you to tell me the story of your life in Winchester, Massachusetts."

"You'd be terribly bored. It was a very uneventful life."

She spoke in a wholly expressionless way, which would have discouraged anyone less interested and less persistent. Craig, however, continued stubbornly.

"Are you the eldest or the youngest of a large family?"

"Neither one."

"The only child of doting parents, then?"

"I'm an only child. My parents are both dead."

"Sorry. I didn't mean to be so crude."

"It's quite all right. They died before I was old enough to remember them, so the question didn't hurt. My great-aunt Bertha brought me up."

"With the efficient help of your great-uncle George?"

"I didn't have any great-uncle George. Or any uncles at all, for that matter. Aunt Bertha was my grandmother's only sister, too, and for your further information she never married."

"So man-hating runs in the family?"

"I don't know that we actually hate them. I think we just test them out and find them wanting."

Her voice was no longer blank. It was edged with uncontrollable bitterness which confirmed the suspicions which she had already roused at the Bath House. But before Craig could press the issue, there was another knock at the door, and Monsieur Ragueneau re-entered, bearing the St. Emilion. As the soup plates were now empty, he removed these himself; but when he went out again, he called in the general direction of the table that Monsieur le Capitaine was now ready for his veal. Considerately Craig waited for the serving-woman to dish this out before continuing his research, which he decided to approach from a different angle now.

"I suppose your great-aunt Bertha lived in a neat white house on Main Street?"

"Yes, she did. She still does. Poison-neat."

"So that you weren't encouraged to bring home large romping groups of your classmates for potluck any time?"

"I think Aunt Bertha would have had heart failure at the mere suggestion. Sometimes the little girl who lived next door came in to play, when we were small children, but she was always sent home before supper; so I was never invited to her house either, and gradually we drifted apart. We did go to Sunday school together, though."

"At the First Presbyterian?"

"No, the First Congregational. There aren't many Presbyterians in New England. The girls who went to private schools were Episcopalians or Unitarians, and the girls who lived on the other side of the tracks were Catholics. But nearly all the people I knew were Congregationalists."

"I see. The solid citizenry. Is your great-aunt Bertha the president of the Ladies' Aid or the Foreign Missionary Society?"

"She doesn't believe in foreign missions. It's the Home Missionary Society. She's a trustee of the library too, and she sees to it that all the books she thinks are evil get kept behind the ones she regards as good. But you mustn't get the idea she hasn't been kind to me. She's shared what she had with me, and that's meant scrimping for her. She encouraged me to go on with my education. Of course I worked my way through college. But she helped. She gave me a home. That meant I didn't have to live in a dormitory, that I had only my tuition to pay."

"I judge you got pretty good marks, too?"

"There was never anything much the matter with them."

"Valedictorian when you graduated?"

"Yes, from high school."

"What about the graduation ball?"

"Oh, I went to it. And I wasn't a wallflower. I don't dance as well as Tilda Evans, but I can follow after a fashion."

"I bet you can. I expect to find out for myself next Tuesday just how good you are. Meanwhile let's get back to your biography. No heart interest whatsoever in the classmate who escorted you to this ball?"

"No, none at all. I think he only asked me because he didn't get the girl he really wanted. I didn't know him very well, then or afterwards. I never ran with the crowd, because I couldn't keep up my end at home. The graduation ball was just an episode."

The bitterness had gone out of her voice. It was blank again. *Well, evidently that knockout blow she had came later on,* Craig said to himself. Aloud, he asked, "All right, let's get back to your scholastic career. *Summa cum laude* from college?"

"I managed that too. I was afraid for a while that it might be only *magna,* but I made the grade after all."

"Why were you afraid? Did you get sick?"

"No, I've always been very healthy."

"Then did you get upset about something?"

"Yes, for a while."

Well, here we are at last, Craig said to himself. *This is when it happened, whatever it was. And I'll find out about it yet. Maybe right now. I'm getting along better than I expected.* He tried to frame a leading question quickly, but this time Connie was quicker still.

"It didn't amount to anything, though. It didn't even last long enough to interfere with my marks in the end. I had two or three good positions offered me. And I didn't consider any of them very seriously. I decided I didn't want to teach."

"So you came overseas instead?"

"Yes, after a while."

"And in the meantime?"

"I didn't do much of anything in the meantime, except help Aunt Bertha around the house. I like housekeeping very much, and it seemed good to take things easy for a while. I was pretty tired when I got through college."

"I should think you might have been after getting that *summa*—not to mention the little episode that upset you."

"I've already told you that didn't amount to anything. Neither did anything else that happened. Now suppose we talk about you for a change. Are you the eldest or the youngest of a large family or just the black sheep?"

"I'm the second son and we're both on the iron-gray side. I think my brother Bob is a shade or two darker than I am. But neither of us is really inky. And neither of us is a wolf in sheep's clothing. . . . What about a little more veal?"

"No thanks. It *is* good, though. . . . Is your father a prominent banker, or does he worthily represent Illinois in the United States Senate?"

"He makes towels in North Carolina. . . . Probably you're wise to leave a little room for the salad. Here it comes now."

The bustling woman was back, beaming more broadly than ever. Craig poured out another glass of the neglected St. Emilion for himself, and leaned back in his chair, sipping it with relish.

"If we don't do something radical about this, the Vicomte d'Arblade will be here before we've drunk it up," he said. "Won't you at least try it?"

"I suppose I'd better. If I don't, you'll probably dispose of the whole bottle yourself, so Monsieur Ragueneau's feelings won't be hurt."

"I might teach you to like it, the way French children are taught. I'll make a half-and-half mixture for you—no, I guess we better start with two-thirds water and one-third wine in your case. There, try that! . . . Want to hear any more biography while you drink it?"

"If your father makes towels in North Carolina, I suppose your mother's a tobacco heiress?"

"That time you guessed right. Or have you begun to identify me? Has the fame of Craig towels and Royal Plug penetrated to Winchester, Massachusetts?"

"Well, after all, we do read the papers there. And those two products are pretty well advertised—both through the regular channels and in the social columns."

"Not turning sour on me, are you, Connie?"

"I'm sorry. I shouldn't have said that. But you shouldn't have brought me to a private room either, and you have been pretty inquisitive."

"Granted. I won't make either of those mistakes again if you'll give me a second chance. But I like you so much I couldn't help wanting to know more about you, and I couldn't help wanting to be alone with you, either. I don't see how any man could."

She played with her Brie in silence. Craig waited a reasonable length of time, and then ventured another question.

"Do I get the second chance?"

"I'm thinking it over. I'm not at all sure I approve of you. But I don't want to say no. I like you too."

She looked up with a sudden smile, from which all the stiffness was gone.

"Suppose we say it depends on your behavior the rest of the evening," she suggested demurely. "I won't do anything to cramp your style, but I'll tell you afterwards whether I like your technique or not. If I don't, this is the end, as real heroines say If I do, I'll go to that dance with you next Tuesday. Is that fair?"

"It's grand. Now I've really got a chance to show my stuff. Let's shake on it."

He stretched out both hands across the little table, and unhesitatingly she put hers in them. Then he began to talk about his brother Bob, and the way other boys had mocked them both at St. Paul's, because of the tobacco and the towels, and what a rotten time they had had at Princeton. That was why he had gone to Chicago to study medicine, he said—he was through with the East and its infernal snobbishness. Presently he was telling her about medical school. More and more conscious of her responsiveness, he finally told her how he had happened to join up with Base 11. But somehow he did not tell her anything about the sort of home the towel king and the tobacco heiress had created for their sons, and he did not mention Eileen.

CHAPTER V

THE DINNER AT the château was very different.

About three o'clock Saturday afternoon, Robert appeared at Connie's office, having this time succeeded in eluding Arkie. After saying *bon jour,* the visitor next lapsed into wistful silence; but Connie, who was by this time accustomed to his solemn ways, made no effort to hurry him.

"My mother asks me to tell you that she will send the carriage for you at half-past seven," Robert said at last.

"Why, how kind of her! But I never imagined she'd do anything like that, so I've already asked Captain Petrie, who is in charge of our Red Cross section, if I could have the touring car to take me, and he said yes, he'd be very glad to send Maurice with me. Maurice is Captain Petrie's own driver. I'm afraid that I couldn't very well tell him now that I don't want the touring car after all."

She spoke with genuine disappointment. She had been proud and pleased at the thought of going to the château in the touring car, which was reserved for the most important missions; but it could not compare in glamour with a carriage sent forth from a château. Her regret was so obvious that a gleam of sympathetic understanding actually brightened Robert's impassive face.

"No, that would not be correct. But perhaps you might suggest to Captain Petrie that the carriage would bring you back, if that would not seem to you a lack of delicacy."

"I think it's a grand idea. I've been a little worried for fear Captain Petrie might need the touring car himself later in the evening. And then I wouldn't have known exactly what time I ought to tell Maurice to come for me."

Robert seemed to consider her reply satisfactory, but proffered no remark in return. The silence which characterized his calls descended on the office, but as the visitor seemed to have no intention of leaving, Connie decided that possibly she might venture a few questions.

"I understand that there are to be other guests at the dinner," she said. "Would you tell me something about them? Perhaps I could be better prepared for conversation if you did."

"Two of my mother's friends are coming out from Nantes—Madame Helle and Madame Carpentier. They are both very nice ladies. Madame Helle is a widow who is very fond of cats. She keeps one in every room. Each has its own basket, adorned with a ribbon which matches the one tied to its collar. She has a nice little house on the rue de Gigant, and gives dinners herself, quite frequently. She has a good cook and the war does not seem to have affected her in any way. My mother thought that possibly if you made her acquaintance she might also ask you to dinner. Madame Carpentier is generally there with her; they are very intimate. My mother thought if you visited occasionally on the rue de Gigant, it would make a little diversion for you."

"Your mother is very kind," Connie said again. She spoke with genuine gratitude. However, her primary interest was not in the ladies from Nantes, and Robert, having made the longest speech she had ever heard him deliver, had now lapsed back into silence. "Are these to be the only other guests?" she inquired.

"No, Monsieur le Curé is coming also. However, he is very deaf, and generally he does not try to enter much into conversation."

There was another long pause. Connie, who had been toying with a paper-cutter, flung it down.

"And your parent from Saumur?" she asked desperately.

"Tristan? I did not mention him, because he will be staying at the château for a visit, so naturally he will be present at the dinner."

"What is his rank? Perhaps it would be convenient if I knew before-hand how to address him."

"He is a captain of cavalry—a *cuirassier.*"

"I'm not sure I know what that means."

Robert looked at her in mild astonishment. "It means Tristan belongs to the heavy artillery," he explained. "Tristan is very well made, and only tall men of athletic build can become *cuirassiers.* Also it is desirable that they should be natural horsemen as well as trained riders, for they have the largest and most powerful mounts—generally Norman *demi-sangs,* which are a cross between English purebreds and the *race normande.* Tristan has been familiar with these since childhood—indeed horses have always been his great passion, and this has no doubt contributed to his advancement. He is very young to be a captain."

"I'm awfully glad you told me, because otherwise I might have made a bad break in front of your cousin. . . . Is Captain de Fremond still in active service? Was he at the front all through the war?"

"Yes, he is still in active service, or rather he has just returned to duty at Saumur, where he is *officier instructeur d'équitation* in the Cadre Noir; and he was in the war from the beginning. He took part in the victorious *course à la mer,* directly after the First Battle of the Marne. You have heard about the *course à la mer,* haven't you?"

"I must have, but I don't seem to remember it. Tell me about it."

"It was the race with the Uhlans which was run almost the way a game of checkers is played. It saved our Channel ports from the Germans and England from invasion. Tristan was in the first division to reach Dix-mude."

"How exciting! What happened next?"

"Afterwards it was less exciting for a long while. The cavalry fought with the infantry much of the time, still keeping their horses, however. These were left at the rear, in charge of one cavalryman, while four other cavalrymen went forward in rotation. Then in the Somme offensive, the cavalry began fighting again as a unit, coming up behind the tanks and replacing our regular infantry, which was very tired by that time. It also helped in the replacements of the Fifth Army when the English withdrew, stopping a gap left by its absence. A single platoon of thirty-two cavalry-men defended a sector eighteen kilometers wide by going round and round in a circle for twenty-four hours on end, thus creating the effect of an entire division. It was a very clever ruse."

"And your cousin was one of the thirty-two?"

"Yes. He was also one of those sent to the rescue of Reims after the Second Battle of the Marne, when the Germans broke through at Epernay, after being repulsed everywhere else. The cavalry went forward eighty kilometers during one night, but when it reached Epernay the infantry had already been annihilated and the cavalrymen took over. They hid in the hedges and joked with each other about choosing cozy coffins. *En effet,* only twenty-four out of a hundred were still uninjured when General Lyautey finally arrived by automobile and told them they had saved Epernay."

As Robert went on and on, Connie gazed at him with increasing atten-tion. This was not only because she found his recital both enlightening and exciting; it was also because she had never imagined that he would be able to talk either so fluently or so graphically, and the discovery filled her with amazement

"Fortunately Tristan's wounds were slight, though at first his condition seemed more serious than it really was. The surgeons feared above all the reopening of an old wound. This did not happen, but he was sent from the front-line hospital at Châlons-sur-Marne to a base hospital. When he was taken out of the train, he discovered he was in Lisieux, which is his own *sous-préfecture.* He thought he must be delirious, because he heard bells ringing all around him. But they were ringing for the Armistice. It was the eleventh of November."

"What a wonderful story, Robert! I can't thank you enough for telling it to me."

"There is nothing to thank me for. I am very pleased to talk about Tristan. We are all very proud of him, because he has been decorated twice. And we are very thankful because he has made such a swift recov-ery. He gives part of the credit for this to Sœur Thérèse de l'Enfant Jésus. He has a great devotion to her, like so many of the military. Personally I think his rapid convalescence was due largely to happiness—happiness because the war had ended and happiness at being home again. Tristan is very fond of his home."

Connie wanted to ask about the nature of Tristan de Fremond's duties at Saumur, for neither the term *"officier instructeur d'équitation"* nor that of "Cadre Noir" meant anything to her; she also wanted to ask when and where he had been decorated, and why he should have been devoted to Sœur Thérèse de l'Enfant Jésus, whoever this was. But the thought that she was behaving almost as inquisitively as Captain Craig deterred her. Besides, she did not want Robert to form an exaggerated idea of her interest in his cousin. She rose and held out her hand.

"I hope you'll tell me more war stories the next time you come to camp," she said. "In just these few minutes you've given me a better idea than I ever had before about what the French have done. But I'm afraid I must ask you to excuse me now. I have to make the rounds of the wards before I dress, and sometimes I'm unexpectedly detained. It was good of you to come. Please tell your mother how much I appreciate her offer of the carriage."

Robert had also risen, with obvious reluctance, and now he raised his arm and permitted his hand to dangle from it. Connie succeeded in taking this and he said, *"Au revoir, mademoiselle,"* in a voice from which all animation had suddenly gone, but still he made no move towards the door. It was not until Connie had wished him good-by three times that he went slowly down the steps and remounted his bicyclette. Connie picked up a notebook and pencil and ran quickly in the opposite direction from the one he had taken. Sometimes Robert changed his mind after he had already started for home, and came back.

This time luck was with her; although several nurses were awaiting her with lists and requests, they all said that the supplies could be brought the next day, and none of the requests represented emergencies. Connie had devoted the morning to letter-writing, and upon being assured that none of the patients was worse, she felt that her visit to the wards could very well be superficial now. The plan for a Christmas celebration had extended far beyond Ward 9; wherever she went she saw men busy with scraps of tin foil and colored paper, and they hailed her to show her the progress of their work. She returned to her own quarters gratified and thankful that her chance idea had brought about so much good cheer.

Gwen was waiting for her, with the companionable purpose of helping her dress; but when she came back from the washroom, she found that her friend was examining, with eager interest, the new identification bracelet, which Connie had just taken off for the first time.

"Say, when did you change the old lead tag for this neat article?"

"Thursday night."

"I'll say you kept it pretty well hidden. I thought I'd seen you pulling down your sleeves two or three times, for no good reason. But look, wasn't it Wednesday you did your shopping in Nantes?"

"I bought my new sailor and my new shirt then. But my funds don't run to silver bracelets. If they had, I'd have got one right away. I've sort of envied the rest of you yours."

"So this was a present? Along with all those nice dingle-dangles?"

Gwen held the bracelet up to the light, critically examining the small charms that hung from it. All the girls enthusiastically collected little ornaments of this type as pendants for the slender silver bracelets which they substituted, as rapidly as possibly, for the heavier ones made of dull metal that were merely a matter of issue. The acquisition and addition of charms had become something of a fad, and Gwen's own bracelet was already jingling with them. But she had neither the caduceus nor the head of Duchess Anne nor the cross of Lorraine now under observation.

"I'll say Duncan Craig has good taste," she remarked, handing back the bracelet with obvious reluctance. "What I can't understand is, why you wanted to hide this."

Connie did not offer to explain. She knew that the silver chains and their attendant charms were given and accepted generally and very casually; they had no intrinsic value, and since identification bracelets of some description were required, they might well be considered an indicated accessory to a uniform. But privately, she still regarded any kind of a bracelet as an article of jewelry, and jewelry, according to the code which Aunt Bertha had severely interpreted, was something no gentleman ever gave to any lady unless they were formally engaged. When Craig had pressed a little box into Connie's hand as he said good night, telling her he wanted her to have a small souvenir of an evening which had been very happy, at least for him, she had not visualized a memento which would be quite so personal. But she knew she would only magnify its importance to her if she attempted to return it, and secretly, in spite of her doubts as to its propriety, she was very pleased with it. However, her pleasure was still intermingled with a slight feeling of guilt, and she was too shy to express either sensation.

"Me, I'd have been showing this off." Gwen continued, unabashed by her roommate's diffidence. "You needn't say you know that without being told, though."

"I won't. I won't stop to say anything just now. Good night, Gwen."

"Oh, we'll be having another little chat later on. All the rest of us are planning to sit up so that you can tell us about the party."

Without commenting on this gregarious plan, Connie went out of the barracks and saw, to her surprise, that Maurice and the touring car were already drawn up just outside. She had expected to walk over to the Hut to get the motor, and she had been rather dreading the ordeal, since a numerous company would inevitably have forgathered to watch departure.

"Good evening, Maurice. I suppose you know where we're going?"

"No, Captain Petrie he say take mademoiselle wherever she likes."

"I am going to the Château Chassay."

The "touring car" which was held in such reverence was only an open five-passenger Ford, painted khaki color, and identified by the Red Cross on each side. Maurice had already nonchalantly opened the front door from within; but upon hearing the magic words "Château Chassay" he made haste to alight and opened the rear door with an appropriate gesture. Connie settled down in the back seat with a feeling of pleasurable relaxation until they reached the courtyard of the château.

In front of her the bulk of the château loomed dark and formidable; she had not seen it before by night, and in the moonlight it took on aspects at one and the same time more romantic and more redoubtable than in the daytime. The water in the moat was like a sheet of black onyx, inexplicably mirroring silver; the central tower rose, strong and square, to meet the spangled sky that curved down around it. The rosy bricks had taken on the sheen of pink luster, and the stone animals plunging from their medallions were menacing and eerie. Over the doorway the motto beneath the coat of arms stood out with startling intensity, *"Aspera Non Terrent."* All in all the sight held her both overawed and entranced. Doubts of her adequacy in such surroundings, which had assailed her from the beginning, were now multiplied and intensified, but these were permeated with delighted astonishment at her opportunity.

The great door swung open, and the old Breton servant was revealed, bowing and smiling; she would take mademoiselle's cape and hat for her, she said, extending a gnarled hand, and Connie was immediately forced to make the first of the decisions to which she had known she would be unequal. It was not customary for any girl in uniform to remove her headgear; in a way, it would be a breach of etiquette for her to take off her "undertaker's lid"; and yet she sensed that in another it would be an even greater mistake to keep it on. She unpinned the velours hat slowly, smoothing down her coiled braids, and again acted under the old bonne's directions: Mademoiselle would find Madame la Comtesse in the drawing room; would Mademoiselle be pleased to enter?

As the Countess came forward to meet her, Connie saw that most of the other guests had already assembled. The Count, in his customary place before the fire, was talking to a comely little woman of noticeable chic, whose black hair was beautifully dressed and whose black eyes snapped and sparkled. On the farther side of the room, a younger but less striking lady was painstakingly conversing with a very deaf priest. Robert and Jean, left to their own resources, were whispering rather aimlessly to each other. The "parent" was nowhere in sight.

Having greeted her youngest guest cordially, the Countess presented her to the two ladies from Nantes, and made a more or less thwarted effort to present the priest to her. Connie was glad that she had learned the names of Madame Helle and Madame Carpentier beforehand, as she found the murmured sound of them almost unintelligible; the priest she could fortunately address as Monsieur le Curé in any case. Introductions over, the Countess made room for Connie on the small sofa where she herself had been sitting and explained the absence of the honor guest.

"Our parent's train was unfortunately very late. But he has at last arrived and is now making his toilet. He will join us in one small minute. He hastes himself all the possible. Ah! He here is!"

The door from the hall opened again and the missing relative entered the room with an air of agreeable ease. Indeed, it was his complete lack of self-consciousness that impressed Connie even more forcibly and immediately than his striking color and his fine carriage; under the same circumstances, she herself would have been overcome with embarrassment. He murmured, *"Toutes mes excuses,"* as he bent respectfully over the hands of the Countess, Madame Helle, and Madame Carpentier in turn; but he did not sound in the least confused or hurried as he said it. To Connie he merely bowed, very formally, before shaking hands, first with the Count, next with the curé, and finally with his two young cousins. Then he rejoined the Count by the fireplace and entered into facile conversation with him.

Connie's amazement increased as she considered Tristan de Fremond. Certainly he was extremely handsome. His hair and his eyes were both dark brown, and the glow in his cheeks burned its way through bronzed skin. The lines of his chin and his cheekbones were noticeably clean-cut, but his mouth redeemed them from severity; though it was firm, it was full-lipped, and a slight smile played around it even when it was in repose. Connie found it harder and harder to keep her mind on what the Countess was saying to her. But this was not only because the good-looking young officer in his gold-braided uniform of "horizon" blue was such an arresting figure; it was also because his conduct seemed so extraordinary. She had never seen a man kiss a lady's hand before, but she could not understand, if he began his greetings in such a manner, why he should not continue them in the same way; she was even slightly disappointed because he had not. She was equally puzzled because he now made no attempt to talk to her. At the social functions she had attended at home it was almost an unwritten law that the younger guests and the older ones should be divided into two distinct groups, and that if a girl had been invited to a party for the special benefit of a young man, he should devote himself almost exclusively to her, whether he was especially attracted to her or not. The old bonne came to announce that Madame la Comtesse was served, and with the same ease that he had shown upon entering the room, Tristan de Fremond approached the Countess and offered her his arm, again bowing formally to Connie. Then he and his aunt stood aside while the Count led Madame Helle towards the dining room, followed by the curé with Madame Carpentier, and Connie with Robert. Jean at this point unobtrusively disappeared, and the party of eight sat down to dine.

The table was covered with monogrammed damask, and the napkin which Connie unfolded, also of monogrammed damask, was almost as large as the tea cloths she had been accustomed to seeing. Beyond the snowy oval of the table the dimness of the room closed in; she had only a vague impression of heavy carved furniture standing around the walls and ancestral portraits hanging above this. Only one of the portraits, depicting a heavy man gorgeously robed in scarlet, emerged from the encircling gloom. A large soup spoon of crested silver, with an equally large matching fork and an ivory-handled steel knife lay at each place, and this was further marked by a bewildering array of wine glasses, and a small horizontal bar which was even more perplexing. Connie was still puzzling over this glass bar when the tureen was borne in and the Countess began to ladle out the soup. An unrecognized white fish, served with boiled potatoes and a bright yellow sauce, followed the soup after a leisurely interval; and when the fish in turn was removed, Connie realized that she had made her first serious mistake and also learned the purpose of the little glass bar. She had left her big crested fork on her plate; all the others had propped these up on their slides in readiness for the next course!

The older bonne brought her another fork, which clattered as it was placed against her clean plate, to her intense embarrassment; it seemed to proclaim her unfamiliarity with French ways. Her mouth grew drier and drier and she instinctively reached for a glass, only to discover that no water had been served; the white wine in the goblet she had grasped tasted so sour to her that she could hardly swallow it. Her discomfiture was the more acute because she was becoming increasingly aware of her linguistic inadequacies. Seated between Monsieur le Curé, whose deafness precluded any small talk, and Robert, who had never acquired the art of it, she was more or less marooned in any case; but the glowing portrait seemed to suggest the possibility of at least one topic of conversation, and she seized upon this.

"That's a wonderful picture opposite us, the one of the man in red. It seems to shed radiance over the whole room. Has it a special story?"

Robert glanced at the portrait and answered without enthusiasm: "That is a cousin-german of my maternal grandmother, who was an Italian," he said. "Jules Gabrielli, Prince Cardinal."

"A prince!"

"Yes," Robert answered carelessly. "Of course he became a Prince of the Church when he was made Cardinal, but he was a prince anyway. There have been several Cardinals in the family. One of them, Raphael Riario Sforza, was elevated to that position when he was only seventeen.

"Of course there have been Popes in the family too. One of them was painted by Titian and we have a replica of this painting. Perhaps you would like to see it after dinner. I believe it is considered a fine picture, but my favorite is the portrait of Cardinal Sforza's sister-in-law, who married a Medici *en secondes noces*. She was a beautiful blonde lady with lovely long braids something like yours, and in the picture she wears a soft blue dress which is very becoming to her. I should think the same shade might also be very becoming to you, even more so than the bright blue of the jerseys you wear at camp, though I think that suits you very well also."

"I'm glad you like it. . . . I did wear pale blue too, a good deal, before I was in uniform all the time."

"Then after you are out of it again, I hope you will have an evening dress like Catherine Sforza's in both cut and color, and wear it when you come here to dinner."

Connie was almost speechless with amazement, both at the degree of taste and observation which these remarks indicated, and at the casual way in which Robert referred to various princes and potentates, and she lapsed into awed silence. Neither Robert nor the curé seemed disposed to break this and she did not feel equal to making a second attempt herself; instead, she sat very still, hoping that in this way she might at least follow the drift of general conversation. However, this was unfamiliar in subject as well as in tongue, and it went forward at a pace as rapid as the service was slow. Tristan de Fremond was directly across the table from her now, between the Countess and Madame Helle. She watched him under lowered lids as he turned impartially from one lady to the other, obviously pleasing and entertaining both. Then she realized that, in addition to this adroit management, he was also creating an opportunity to glance in her direction from time to time, and she decided that having observed her first faux pas, he was now watching to see what others she would make. In her confusion she knocked over her wineglass, and a wide crimson stain spread rapidly across the snowy cloth.

After that, things went from bad to worse: she clung to her fork only to do it too long this time; with the dessert others, much smaller, were provided. She ate her fruit, clumsily and messily, with her fingers; everyone else manipulated, with great delicacy, the new fork and the small knife that accompanied it, peeling and slicing the fruit before taking small discreet bites at it. Their grace in doing this equaled the skill with which they had previously removed petal-shaped leaves from an edible green cone and dipped them in drawn butter before sucking off the lower portions. Connie's attempts to copy these manipulations were worse than useless. Butter dripped from her fingers, sliding in rivulets up her arms and dropping on her dress; she chewed at the leaves, found her mouth full of cactuslike fibers, and gave up. By the time the Countess gave the signal to leave the table, her sense of enchantment was completely gone; she was more miserable than she had been at any time since coming to France.

When the assembled company returned to the drawing room, the Countess sat down by a small table near the fireplace and began to pour coffee from a Sèvres pot into delicate little cups. Connie, retreating as far as possible, remained at the rear of the group surrounding the hostess, whom Tristan de Fremond was capably engaged in helping. But when the ladies from Nantes had been served, he unexpectedly appeared at Connie's side, bearing two cups and offering her one of them

"I hope I have prepared this to your taste," he said pleasantly. "I have put in it one small piece of sugar, but no milk and no cognac. Was that correct?"

"Yes, just right. I mean, quite correct. Thank you very much."

She was ashamed to find that her fingers were trembling as she took the cup from him. His formal but accurate English had come as another shock; she had assumed, without any special reason for doing so, that he could not speak it. Without appearing to notice her agitation, he drew up a chair and sat down beside her.

"My aunt has been trying to tell me about your work at the hospital near Grand Blottereau," he said. "I am very much interested. However, she has not succeeded in making the nature of it clear to me. She says you are not a nurse, but I think she must be mistaken."

"No, she's right. I'm only a Searcher."

"Yes, that is the term she used and which I did not understand. I do not think she does either, but she has hesitated to ask for an explanation. Now as for me, I do not hesitate. Perhaps not enough." The slight smile which played around his fine mouth deepened. "If the question is not indiscreet, would you be so kind as to tell me what does that mean, a 'Searcher'?"

"It means a girl who's come to Europe under the direction of the Red Cross, and who's been sent to any sort of a hospital center, with the primary purpose of getting information from the wounded."

"Ah, that is very interesting. But still I do not quite understand. Just why should you trouble wounded men by asking them questions?"

"Because they are the only ones who can help in the way that's most needed. They've usually been the last to see the others who are still missing in action, and whom we need to locate, dead or alive. Just the other day, I talked with a patient who was wounded by the same shell that killed a man on either side of him. These two men had been listed as missing in action, but until then no one knew when or how. Now the Central Bureau at Tours has the necessary information."

"And you supplied it?"

"Yes, I supplied it."

"Now all this is beginning to penetrate my thick head. I can see that you are rendering a very important service."

"Getting such information is the most responsible part of my work," Connie went on, much encouraged. "But there's another part that is very closely connected with it. That's the attempt to locate the missing in hospitals. I've had good luck doing this too. . . . Then there's the Home Communication Service."

"I'm afraid you'll have to explain that also."

"I write letters for the men who can't do it for themselves, to let their families know how they are and where they are. Some of these letters are very sad. Of course the mortality letters are saddest of all."

"Mortality letters?"

"Yes, the letters supplementing the official notice that a man's dead. They give all the little details that can't go into the notice. It's terribly hard to tell a man's widow or his mother such things, and we know they're going to be much harder for her to read. But she's entitled to the information, and we hope that some day, when the first shock is over, these letters will be a comfort to her."

"They will be, naturally. The idea is one of great delicacy. I can see that only a woman could render such a service to another woman. But all this must be very depressing to a young girl like yourself."

"It would be, especially as I have to go to all the funerals too, if there weren't brighter sides to it too," Connie replied. She had never heard the word "delicacy" used in such a connection before, and it struck her as singularly apt. "Some of the letters the men send home are fun to write. For instance, the ones where the soldiers tell their best girls all the terrible things that are going to happen if they've been keeping company with sailors."

"Best girls? Keeping company?"

Connie explained, smiling. Tristan de Fremond smiled too and reached for her cup.

"You will drink some more coffee, will you not? I find I am still very thirsty. I am going to ask my aunt to refill these, and then I am coming back for further enlightenment about Searchers and soldiers and for additional enlargement of my vocabulary."

He walked over to the fireplace and spoke in a low voice to the Countess as she refilled the cups. She looked across at Connie a little doubtfully, then she smiled and nodded. Tristan de Fremond came back and sat down again, lighting a cigarette and settling more deeply into his chair.

"I believe you are really very happy in this work of yours," he said. "Is that correct also?"

"Yes. I'm happy to think I'm being of service. I never was of use to anyone in real need before, and I believe I am now. It's a wonderful feeling. And I'm happy in being with girls who are doing the same sort of work I am. They're very friendly girls. I never had such good friends before, either."

She was amazed to find how easy it was to talk with him. Instead of resenting his questions, as she had resented Duncan Craig's, she was pleased and touched by his interest. She felt that she would like to tell him all sorts of things, things about which he had not even asked, but which she was sure he would want to know, from the way he had acted already, and which she wanted to have him know.

"I would like to have you tell me about these friends of yours," he said, almost as if he had read her thoughts. "Are they Searchers also?"

"Two of them are," she answered, and began to tell him about Tilda, who had been to Farmington and made her debut at Sherry's and become a member of the Junior League, but who was very simple in all her tastes and very natural in all her ways, just as if she hadn't been born with a silver spoon in her mouth. Next she told him about Gwen, who came from the Far West and was very free and easy, but who had the kindest heart in the world. Gwen worked at the Convalescent Camp, instead of in the wards like Tilda and Connie, and gave most of her time to the Home Communication Service. The men were just crazy about her and no wonder. Lois Graham was not a Searcher, but a Hostess. She came from the Midwest, and Midwesterners were different from the girls who came from the Coast. Lois had very high principles, and Gwen admired these, and said she wished she could keep as good order in the tents as Lois kept at the Hut. But the two didn't always agree, and sometimes Connie herself found it hard to decide which one was right. But she was very fond of them both, and she had learned a lot from them both, too.

She stopped short, suddenly embarrassed by the fear that she was saying too much. After all, Tristan de Fremond was a total stranger. She had never seen him in her life before. Perhaps she would never see him again. And then she realized this would be a terrible disappointment, that she wanted very much to see him again.

"I am becoming more and more interested every minute," Tristan de Fremond was saying, and his voice showed that he was speaking the truth. "But I find I also need a great many more explanations. Farmington? The Junior League? The Coast? The Midwest? I do not know what any of that means. If you will excuse me, I will get myself a glass of cognac and drink it while you tell me. You will not join me? Well, that will be all the better from my point of view. It will leave you freer to talk."

He rose and poured a small quantity of amber liquid into the bottom of a large tulip-shaped goblet which stood among others around a decanter on a nearby table. Then he came back, cupping the goblet in his hands and burying his nose in it. Afterwards he drew a deep breath of appreciation.

"Very nice," he said. "I am glad to see that my uncle has kept his excellent cellar in spite of the war. The Pouilly was superb at dinner, was it not?" Connie wondered if he was referring to the sour white wine on which she had choked and was thankful that he went on without really seeming to expect an answer. "But still, the very best cognac is not comparable, in my opinion, to the fine old Calvados which we have in my country. . . . Now begin again, if you please, mademoiselle. Sherry's, what is that? Does it have anything to do with the preferred drink of those misguided Spaniards who are not fortunate enough to make either cognac or Calvados in their country?"

"No," Connie said laughing. "It's a very famous establishment in New York that started as a small restaurant, named for the man who founded it. Now it has large suites available for balls and receptions; rich people who haven't room enough in their own apartments use these a great deal for coming-out parties. Most New Yorkers live in apartments nowadays, you know."

"I did not know. As you proceed I am appalled at the extent of my ignorance."

"Then perhaps I'd better not proceed. Anyway, I'd like to stop explaining long enough to ask you a question. I'm a lot more ignorant than you are. What is Calvados and where is it made?"

"Calvados is a very strong apple brandy. It is made in the department of Normandy that has the same name. My branch of the family has always lived in Normandy. But now that I am the only one left, I generally come to Chassay for my leave instead of going to my own château."

"You have a château too!"

"A very small one—not an important one like this. Are you interested in châteaux?"

"I've never seen one before I came to Nantes. Now I've seen two—Grand Blottereau and Chassay. I'm interested in those—I'm very much impressed. I'd like to see a great many more."

"Then I hope some day you will come to Malou. It would give me great pleasure to show it to you. I am sorry to say that since my parents died it has been closed most of the time, and this has given it a cold, empty look. I was an only child and my nearest relative is a nun, so there is no one to go there now. But in the spring, when the apple blossoms are in bloom, the surrounding countryside is very beautiful. You should enjoy seeing that at least."

"I'd enjoy it all. I do hope I can go to see it."

She spoke with earnestness, almost with eagerness; but it was not only the prospect of going to Normandy and seeing another château which made her do this. *He's all alone in the world too,* she was saying to herself. *Perhaps that's what's given me such a fellow feeling with him. Perhaps all orphans have something special in common. He must have been lonely a lot. He must feel as if he'd missed a great deal that can't ever be made up to him. . . .*

"I shall count on your coming," Tristan de Fremond was saying, and he too was speaking earnestly, almost eagerly. Then his tone changed to one of unconcealed regret. "Madame Helle is rising to say good-by. That means the party is breaking up. And as yet I have learned nothing about the Junior League or the Far West or any of the other matters on which I required enlightenment. Perhaps you would have liked to hear more about the various products and attractions of Normandy, too."

"Yes, I should have. I'd have liked it very much."

"Then there is nothing to do, under the circumstances, but to create a way of continuing this conversation on some future occasion, when I trust it will not be subject to premature interruption."

He had risen, bowing and smiling. The bow was not a stiff little acknowledgment of her presence; instead it was a gracious and deferential salutation. As to his smile, Connie was finding this increasingly charming every time it illumined his face. They moved across the drawing room together, and again the Countess looked at Connie a little questioningly but very cordially.

"Madame Helle has suggested that since she and Madame Carpentier must pass directly by you on their way to Nantes, you should descend in their carriage," she said. "If this arrangement is agreeable to you, we will still hope that you will give us the pleasure of putting ours at your disposition on the occasion of your next visit to Chassay. . . . Madame Helle also suggests that perhaps you would dine at her house on Monday night and go to the opera afterwards. She would like to see you again, and the performance is to be *Carmen,* which is always enlivening. We shall all be going from the château, and therefore you will not lack for interpreters. Also we will pass by and take you with us, so the expedition thus arranges itself with every facility."

"Madame Helle's very kind. I'd like very much to go back to the camp in her carriage, and to have dinner with her Monday night too. I've never heard *Carmen* and I've always wanted to. I'd like to have all of you come to the camp too," she went on, gathering courage. "I can't offer you a wonderful dinner, or anything else wonderful, I'm sorry to say. But we do have good movies every night. Would you come to the movies Tuesday or Wednesday," she added hastily, remembering the officers' dance and her engagement with Craig. "If you haven't any other plans for Wednesday——"

None of them had any other plans for Wednesday, they would all be charmed to come to the cinema at the camp. The farewells for the night took place amidst chorused expressions of appreciation for the evening which had just passed, and of anticipation for the pleasant evenings ahead. But again Tristan kissed the hands of the ladies from Nantes and only bowed to Connie.

All the girls were waiting up for her, as Gwen had warned her they would be. They were feasting on lobster salad.

"What was he like? Did he need a shave and smell of other things besides soap?"

"Did the women all have on dowdy black dresses and big diamond earrings?"

"Was the dining room cold as Greenland's icy mountains?"

"Did you have to use the same fork for every course? I meant to warn you beforehand you'd better look around after the fish and see if all the other guests weren't putting theirs on little glass slides."

"I wish you had, Tilda," Connie said feelingly, disregarding the questions. "And why didn't you warn me about those queer vegetables that look like pineapples and taste like cactus?"

"Artichokes? You don't mean to say you'd never eaten artichokes before?"

"Hush up, Gwen. You probably wouldn't have known how to eat them yourself if you hadn't come from the great State of California—I'm sorry, Connie. Did you slip up on anything else?"

"I slipped up on everything I possibly could. Just the same, the evening had several redeeming features."

"All on Tristan de Fremond's face?" inquired the irrepressible Gwen.

"No. But he has a very nice face. And incidentally he didn't need a shave or smell of the things you have in mind, Gwen. His uniform was immaculate and he looked grand in it. His manners are a little queer, but he's got a very pleasant smile and very cordial ways."

"What do you mean, his manners are a little queer?"

"Well, he kissed everybody's hand but mine—I mean every *woman's* hand of course—and when he got around to me he just bowed."

"But Connie, you're not married! Frenchmen don't kiss young girls' hands—at least well-behaved Frenchmen don't. I take it this Captain of yours *is* well behaved?"

"Oh, very! But he isn't my Captain, Tilda."

"You may add him to your collection yet. You made a good beginning Thursday night," Gwen interposed. "Did he see you home?"

"Of course he didn't, Gwen. That's another thing nice Frenchmen don't do in associating with serious young girls like Connie."

"Good Lord, there's hardly anything left for a nice young Frenchman to do, according to you, Tilda! How come you know so much about them anyway?"

"Well, a good many French missions came to the United States with the idea of persuading us we ought to enter the war," Tilda answered demurely. "Some of the younger missionaries had other ideas too. I can't say I made a collection of them, but I did see something of them in the course of their American travels. . . . Of course this isn't the first time I've been abroad either," she added as an afterthought. "As a matter of fact, I've been to Saumur myself. I went there to a *Carrousel*—one of those marvelous shows they put on at the Cavalry School every year about the end of July. I never saw such riding in my life. Just wait till you see this new beau of yours on a horse, Connie, riding with spurs but no stirrups, and doing fancy stunts like the *croupade* and the *cabriole* and the *courbette*. I give you my word I was so fascinated by them that I almost decided—— But you see the trouble with my own beau was——"

"We'd like very much to hear your life story some other time. This time it's Connie who ought to be telling us all. We haven't even found out yet what Percy Vere de Vere really looks like."

"You'll see him for yourself Wednesday night," Connie informed her. Now that Tilda had so unexpectedly restored her self-confidence, she found she could dwell with unmixed satisfaction on her pleasant conversation with Tristan de Fremond instead of on her own shortcomings. After all, he had talked to her for a long time; he had said he wanted to do so again. He had even invited her to visit his château in Normandy, and he had accepted her own invitation with alacrity.

"He's coming here to the movies then," she went on, with mounting assurance. "He and all the rest of the family too, of course. And I'm going to Nantes with them Monday. To dinner and the opera. One of the ladies whose hand he kissed invited me. She didn't have on a dowdy black dress either. She was just as smart as paint. I might also say, before you try to drag it out of me, Gwen, that the reason I didn't ask them for Tuesday instead of Wednesday is because I'm going to the officers' dance with Captain Craig that night. I accepted his invitation before I met Captain de Fremond."

She walked away from them towards the washroom, unbuttoning her jacket as she went. Her friends looked at each other in astonishment and Gwen gave a long whistle.

"Our little Connie is a changed woman," she said. "If Craig and de Fremond can do all that to her in two evenings, there's no telling what the next few weeks will bring forth."

CHAPTER VI

A GOOD DEAL happened in the next few weeks.

After the Sunday morning services in the Post Office were over, Connie waited to have a few words with Father Calloran. He removed his vestments, which he necessarily did without either privacy or ceremony, standing beside the portable altar and laying them over the back of the collapsible chair; then, readjusting his blouse and picking up his cap, he came forward, again a familiar figure to her.

"I wanted to tell you, Father Calloran, that I've enjoyed playing for you very much."

"In spite of the way the organ acted up? I couldn't help hearing the usual dying wheeze at the end of every hymn."

"Yes, in spite of that. Doc Anderson was so much help with the singing that I didn't mind the way the organ behaved. Besides, he kept pulling stops in and out at just the right moment, and that helped too. But when I said I enjoyed being here, I really meant that I enjoyed the services. I thought they were very impressive."

"In what way especially? It would interest me to know."

"Well, especially in their symbolism."

"So you were able to follow the ordinary of the Mass?"

"Yes, Doc shared his prayer book with me when I wasn't playing. And even when I couldn't look on, I understood what you were saying a good deal of the time."

"Then you must be an excellent Latin scholar. It isn't easy for anyone unacquainted with the liturgy to do that."

"Oh, but I've always liked Latin. I studied it all through high school and college, and I took part in two or three of the Latin plays. Since then I've gone on reading it by myself. I hope it's going to help me with my French. I thought I knew that pretty well too, but I'm finding out that I didn't."

"It'll probably come to you quite soon. Learning to speak a language you've only read before is something like climbing a long, hard hill. When you are halfway up, it seems as if you'd never get to the top. Then suddenly you're over it."

He nodded pleasantly and made a slight move in the direction of the door. Then, realizing that the girl might well have had a special reason for awaiting him besides wishing to tell him that she had enjoyed the service, he stopped and waited in his turn. He was certainly very hungry. But from the look of her, she had something on her mind that was more important to her than breakfast was to him.

"Father Calloran," she said hesitatingly, "there's a question I'd like to ask you, if I may. When you're told that a—a person has a 'special devotion' to a—well, to a saint, just what does that mean?"

"It means that person has, or believes he has, great reason for gratitude because of graces or other benefits received and tries to show his gratitude through reverence and piety—perhaps in material ways like offerings or acts of charity as well."

"I see. Thank you very much." She paused as if she thought she ought to find this much information adequate, yet failed to do so. "I asked because I heard that a young French officer had special devotion to Sister Theresa of the Child Jesus," she went on, in a rush of confidence. "The friend who told me said the young officer was like 'many of the military' in this respect. It was all very confusing to me, and at the same time it roused my curiosity. Since then I've met the young officer, and he didn't strike me as being pious at all. Not that he wasn't just as nice as he could be. . . . And then I haven't the least idea who this Sister Theresa is either. So I'm still confused."

"Anglo-Saxons and Latins don't always define or exemplify piety in just the same way," Father Calloran observed. "Not to mention Catholics and Puritans. I think you'll understand the differences better when you've been away from New England a little longer and met a few more agreeable French officers and—if you feel like it—played for me a few more times and stopped to chat with me afterwards. Anyway, don't worry about these differences, whatever you do—they're usually superficial rather than fundamental. As for Sister Theresa, I'll give you a book about her if you like—one she wrote herself, for that matter. It's sweeping the world right now, and you're not the only one who's puzzled about it. She led a very quiet life and she died very young. It doesn't seem, on the face of it, as if she'd had much to offer suffering mankind. But what your friend told you was true: the military do have a great devotion to her, and they're by no means alone in this."

"Thank you, Father Calloran. I do understand much better already. And I'll be glad to play for you next Sunday, if you want to have me."

Usually Connie had some time to herself on Sunday and looked forward to it eagerly through the week. But now she was anxious to make up for her special leave on Wednesday, and for the evenings devoted to her own amusement instead of to dancing at the Hut. Two such evenings were already behind her, three were immediately ahead of her, and this constituted a record. But instead of feeling guilty over it, as she would have a few weeks earlier, she realized, with slight surprise, that the rigidity of her former schedule, which had kept her constantly tense, had also precluded her from doing the best of which she was capable. She had been steadily gaining in self-confidence through experience ever since her arrival at the camp. Now that she was working under less strain, she was able to spread more good cheer.

She went straight from the Catholic service at the Post Office to the Protestant service at the Hut, where she played the piano in the auditorium; then, after a brief stop for checkers in the game room, she replenished her supplies and hurried on to the wards. It was night before she knew it, and for the first time she fell into bed with a sense of accomplishment rather than one of depression. Monday was equally full and equally rewarding; when the de Fremonds' carriage came for her in the evening, she was watching for it at the gate, satisfied with her day's work and blithely anticipating another outing.

She did not have long to wait. Promptly at the appointed hour, the old-fashioned landau came into sight, its little lanterns gleaming on either side; the heavy wheels rolled evenly along over the cobblestones, and the horses' hoofs made a cheerful clatter. As the coachman reined in his pair, the paneled door opened and revealed the cloaked figure of Tristan de Fremond.

"How nice to see you again!" he said in a pleased voice, stepping down. He did not bow from a distance this time; he came rapidly forward and took Connie's hand. "However, you look almost as military as the sentinel standing there!" he said, glancing from Connie to Arkie long enough to return the latter's salute, which lacked the complete impassivity Connie hoped for rather than expected. "I trust you will be able to relax from your responsibilities during the evening."

"I've begun to already," she answered. "In fact, they haven't seemed half so heavy, any of the time, since Saturday."

She would have liked to tell him, then and there, how much easier everything had seemed to her since she met him; and her regret because this was neither the time nor the place to do so was instantaneously swallowed up in the amazing sensation that it would have been superfluous in any case, because he seemed to know it already. He had released her hand almost immediately after taking it; but now he had put his own under her elbow and was guiding her gently towards the carriage and helping her up the steps leading to its cushioned interior. The touch was

44

so light that she could hardly feel it; and yet it had the same reassuring effect as his presence.

"That is because you had a chance to talk about them, those responsibilities," he said, and she knew he really meant, *That is because you told me about them. . . .* "Eh bien!" Here are my aunt and uncle, waiting to greet you in their turn!"

The Count and Countess, esconced in the rear of the landau, welcomed her cordially. How did it go this evening? Would she be well there, *en face?* Then they would put themselves en route. She took the indicated place on the small seat opposite them, instinctively moving over to make room for Tristan by the door. He shook his head, smiling.

"Please stay where you are," he said. "My saber would discommode you if you were at my left. And I should be most uncomfortable also."

I did know that much, she said to herself. *It's in my little book,* French Daily Life— *"A gentleman always seats a lady at his right; any failure to do so is at best a grave oversight and at worst, a deliberate insult." But I forgot. I guess I'm just fated to do the wrong thing.* However, the conviction brought none of the misery which Saturday's mistakes had aroused; she was too glowingly grateful for the tactful way in which Tristan had worded his reminder. He closed the door, slipped across to the other side, and after adjusting his saber sat down. "The night is very frosty," he said, tucking a carriage robe snugly across his knees and hers. In the narrow space, these inevitably touched. But obviously the contact was accidental and not premeditated; it was unmarred by the slightest suggestion of pressure. This, Connie tried to tell herself, was the reason she did not try to draw away. Then, because she was too honest for such pretense, she admitted to herself that this brushing of his knees against hers was as pleasant as the feeling of his fingers on her arm; and now that she had warmly acknowledged the greetings of the Count and Countess, it seemed natural to talk with their nephew again.

"I told you Saturday night that some of the letters I write for the soldiers are very amusing," she said. "I think I got off one of the funniest yet today.

"This boy's right arm was broken and in a cast. That was why he couldn't write, you see. He was from a little town in the mountains near Wellsville, in West Virginia, and he was sending his Croix de guerre to his girl at Bethany for a present. The letter was to tell her how he had won it going into a Boche dugout in the Argonne, where he captured a major and two captains singlehanded, after having the bones in his right arm splintered by a bullet. It was quite a story—the way he wanted me to tell it to her."

"That is easy to understand. But what I do not understand is what was so very funny about such a gallant matter."

"Well, that was it. He won the Croix de guerre in a dice game, and his arm was broken when the Ford car he was cranking backfired. I'm afraid I should have refused to let him perjure himself like that, but I didn't really have the heart to do it. I—I even added the part about the French general kissing him on both cheeks. He'd forgotten to put that in."

Tristan was delighted with the story. He threw back his head and laughed, showing very handsome white teeth as he did so, and then he painstakingly translated it for the benefit of his uncle, who during its first recital had been looking at the others in a kindly but bewildered way, and who now joined heartily in the general merriment. Much encouraged, Connie told another story, which, with a good deal of prompting from Tristan, she managed to translate haltingly herself; and when the Count and Countess both complimented her on the remarkable progress she had been making with her French, she launched into a few conversational ventures on her own initiative. By the time they reached the rue de Gigant, everyone was in high good humor. Connie's first story was repeated again, for the benefit of Madame Helle and Madame Carpentier; and without any mishaps whatsoever she herself made friends with all her hostess's cats, duly admiring their ribbons and baskets, steered her way unwaveringly through a delicious dinner, walked to the opera house, and took her place, again by Tristan's side, at the rear of Madame Helle's *baignoire.*

The opera house at Nantes usually provided an agreeable social experience rather than a distinguished musical production, and the evening's performance of *Carmen* was no exception to the rule; but Connie could find no flaws in the ponderous prima donna, the aging chorus, or the faded settings. Again she had been transported to a new realm of enchantment, and she did not seek to identify its magic elements. Between the acts, various visitors came to the box, among them a younger brother of Madame Carpentier's, who suggested that Captain de Fremond and Mademoiselle Galt might join his sister and himself for a stroll and a *citronade.* The invitation was accepted with alacrity and, as far as Connie was concerned, with mounting pleasure when the four sauntered back and forth, glasses in hand, after a vain attempt to secure a small tin table. But the foyer was stuffy and crowded and the drink tepid and syrupy; in an aside, Tristan spoke disparagingly of both.

"Don't take this as a fair sample of French opera. Wait till you hear *Faust* in Paris, and go out for a look at the grand staircase and a *coupe de champagne* during the *entr'acte.*"

"I hope I won't have to wait too long—I haven't seen anything of Paris yet. Thirty or forty of us got in there late at night, after a terrible Channel crossing and a long, hard train trip. We kept getting sidetracked to let troops go by."

"Yes? And then?"

"Then Red Cross trucks were waiting at the Gare du Nord to take us off and distribute us here and there. Gwen and I drew a dingy little hotel on the rue Saint-Hyacinthe, and spent nearly all the next day standing in line at the Hôtel de Ville getting identity cards. I never knew before it could take so long to do so little."

"And this is the extent of your Paris impressions?"

"Not quite. I was there three days before I got sent to Nantes, and of course I managed to get around a little after I was finally released from the Hôtel de Ville. But everything I'd looked forward to seeing was covered with sandbags, and all the street lamps were painted blue. I'd heard for years about the *Ville Lumière*—the sparkling fountains on the Place de la Concorde and the long jewel-like strings of lights on the bridges. I suppose I ought to have known they wouldn't be there in wartime; but the mental picture went back so far I didn't. The dinginess and the darkness were a shock and a disillusionment."

"We will hope you have no more of those in France. Someday you will see the gay little boats flitting up and down the Seine like fireflies, and the moonlight shining on the *grandes eaux* at Versailles, and the sun streaming through the stained glass in the Sainte Chapelle. Then you will forget all about those first disillusionments."

"I almost have now, just hearing you talk."

Tristan glanced about him. "Madame Carpentier and her brother seem to have been momentarily claimed by other acquaintances," he remarked. "I have not seen them for several minutes now. Shall we go out on the portico for a little? At least the lights of the Place Graslin are on again, and though that is not much to look at compared to what you hoped to see in Paris, it may at least convince you that darkness is not our natural element."

Connie had not even noticed the desertion of their hosts. She followed Tristan's lead willingly and stood behind him between two of the great Grecian columns, looking out past the Hôtel de France to the Court Cambron; then her eyes traveled slowly towards the left and rested on the lights in front of Prévot's restaurant. Tristan watched her fascinated gaze with faint amusement.

"Prévot's is a very pleasant place," he said. "Of course it is even more agreeable in summer, when one can sit at a little table on the sidewalk. But the interior of the restaurant has a certain *cachet* too. If you were only married, I could suggest that we walk across the Place and have a *fillette de Muscadet* and some *petits beurres* between the acts."

"If I were only married! Why then, of course, I couldn't go with you! It wouldn't be right. But since I'm not——"

She stopped short, her expression as bewildered as her words. The look of amusement on Tristan's face changed to one of something very like tenderness.

"When in Rome——" he began. Then he stopped for a moment, weighing his words. "You do not necessarily have to do what Romans do," he went on slowly. "But you should at least become acquainted with their customs, so that you will understand their strange ways. I should like very much to have you go with me to a restaurant, just as you would go with one of your own countrymen—not only for a glass of wine and a biscuit between acts, but for such a dinner as one can get only in Nantes—*brochets au beurre blanc* and *caneton à la nantaise* afterwards. A meal like that is always an experience in itself; it is doubly delicious when shared with the right company." He paused, and Connie wondered why the thought of savoring such dishes should have so sobering an effect upon him. "I shall not invite you to dinner at Prévot's," he said at last, still more slowly, "any more than I shall permit you to ride at my left in a carriage—and for the same reason. But I want you to know that in this case the invitation which is withheld means far more than the one which might be extended."

"Thank you very much for explaining to me," Connie said in a low voice. She knew that her response was entirely inadequate. If Tristan de Fremond had been her algebra teacher, and had patiently clarified a problem which should not have perplexed her in the first place, she could hardly have spoken more mechanically. Yet how could she say, "You have made me very, very happy by what you have just told me"? There was no reason why she should have been so happy. The man beside her was a foreigner and a stranger. She had only seen him once before in her life, and when the Christmas holidays were over, she would probably never see him again. Why should it matter whether he invited her to dinner or not? Or if it did, for some unaccountable reason, certainly she should not tell him so the second time they met! It was disturbing enough to attach so much importance to his words, without confessing to such disturbance.

"Come," Tristan de Fremond was saying quietly. "We must rejoin Madame Carpentier and her brother, so that we may be in time to give the impression that we have been everywhere searching for them, before they begin looking for us. Also that we may be in time to hear Carmen's definition of love. That is still another question on which it is well to get various viewpoints."

CHAPTER VII

The opera at Nantes proved a very poor preparation for the officers' dance, because Connie kept making comparisons between the two and the dance came off a poor second.

When she returned from the wards to her quarters on Tuesday night, she again found Gwen there before her, but this time her lively roommate did not have the same appearance of lying in wait as on some previous occasions. She was seated on her faithful orange crate, putting on a pair of fresh stockings with the air of preparing for some festivity herself. She looked up with a wink.

"You needn't think you're the only one who can wangle bids to the officers' dance," she announced triumphantly. "Me, I got one from the C.O. himself."

"I didn't wangle mine, whatever you did," Connie answered with slight asperity. She did not begrudge Gwen the invitation, but she felt some justifiable doubts regarding the manner in which it had been obtained, not to mention a few qualms about the keenness with which her roommate was sure to observe her throughout the evening.

"Well, there are ways and ways," Gwen retorted. "You probably got your bid because you began by acting as if you didn't give a damn anyway, and then by hedging and hedging before you came right out and coyly consented. All that was sure to make a hit with the conquering Craig, because he's been so everlastingly run after that he enjoys making a little effort himself for a change. But that wouldn't go down with the C.O. at all, and I don't have much time to waste, anyway. I say 'Sure, you bet, what time will you come for me?' Only this time he can't come, because he's the host. I got to get myself over that long perilous route to the good old ballroom, unless you and your boy friend will let me tag along with you."

"Of course we'd be delighted to have you."

"Maybe you think you're telling the truth, but just the same, I'm looking forward to seeing Craig's face when he lamps me."

Gwen laughed wickedly. Deciding that perhaps it was safer to make no rejoinder to this disquieting statement, Connie broached a different subject.

"I'd like to wear my new oxfords. But I'd get them so muddy it would spoil them, and besides, they wouldn't be fit to dance in by the time I got to Blottereau."

"You poor sap, don't you know anything?"

"I don't know as much as you do. Remember you got to camp first because I was laid up with the flu in London."

"Yes, I did have three weeks' jump on you. . . . Anyway, you wear your rubber boots and carry your oxfords—at least your boy friend carries them for you. 'Sunny France, thy name is mud!' Then when you get to Blottereau you sit down on a bench conveniently placed just outside the ballroom, and he pulls off your rubber boots and puts on your oxfords. But poor Craig will have to hitch across the floor from you to me, because he has two pairs of shoes to put on. That'll spoil some of the effect of the knight errantry."

Connie listened with increasing disquietude to Gwen's prattle. Craig would be almost sure to think that she herself had engineered Gwen's invitation in order to avoid being alone with him; it would be hard to convince him that this was not the truth, and meantime his attitude was sure to be resentful. She did not wish to seem overeager to appease him, and on the other hand, she wanted him to believe she had played fair; she did not feel equal to the rather delicate task of steering a middle course between two extremes of action.

"Say," Gwen remarked suddenly, "wouldn't you like to ask that crowd from the château here for dinner tomorrow evening, before the movies? The rest of us were talking about it last night while you were out playing around with them, and we thought maybe you'd like to throw a party yourself, to show you weren't a sponger. After all, they've had you up at their place quite a lot now. Of course we couldn't offer a baronial hall and a lot of fancy food served in courses, like your French friends; but I could fix you up pretty well at the field kitchen, and they ought to be glad to settle for steak sandwiches. After all, it's a long time since they've had any white bread."

"Why, Gwen, that's awfully kind of you! As you say, we can't offer them the same things they give us, but they may like our things just because these *are* different. I'll send Sam up to Château Chassay with a note the first thing in the morning."

"We'd really have liked to give you a surprise party. But we figured that might be kind of hard on the de Fremonds—they might try to hurry through an early snack before they came down to camp, and then they wouldn't have any room for steak sandwiches. On the other hand they might tell all the servants to stay up for them, so they could eat after they got home, which they couldn't after I get through feeding them. Besides, I was sure you'd want to ask Craig if we had a party and tonight will give you your best chance."

"You're right about the de Fremonds, but you're wrong about Captain Craig. I don't want to ask him to the party."

"For the love of Mike, why not? I shouldn't think you'd want Tristan de Fremond saddled with a lot of extra girls. The whole bunch is planning to come to this shindig, you know."

Connie had not considered this angle, and fresh doubts now rose in her mind. Instead of having everything agreeably settled for her, as it had been on the previous night, she was herself being called upon to pass on one vexing question after another. Before she could decide what to do, she heard a knock on the door and ran to open it. Duncan Craig stood on the threshold, smiling engagingly.

"I've come to claim the promised reward for good behavior," he announced.

"Sh-sh-sh!" Connie whispered, miserably aware of Gwen's cocked ears. "My roommate's going with us."

"The hell she is! I didn't think you'd try to cheat like that, Connie."

"I didn't cheat. Major Haynes invited her himself and of course he couldn't come for her."

"Well, can't she get herself over there?"

"She suggested that, but I didn't think you'd want her to. I said we'd be glad to have her go over with us. I thought you could make quite a grand entrance with two girls and that you'd enjoy doing it."

Craig looked at her searchingly for a moment, then he laughed. "All right, Connie, you win," he said. Then he called, in the general direction of the bedroom, "Come on, Gwen, you devil! What's keeping you?"

"Just putting on the finishing touches."

She dipped into the corridor, her red curls bushing out under her cap and her freckled face enlivened by a wide grin. "You're a great one to talk about devils," she said. "You could give the poor old boy all sorts of pointers. Here, take our shoes."

She handed him the two pairs of oxfords, tied together by the laces. He slung a pair over each shoulder, and with a mock bow offered each girl his arm.

"*Embarras de la richesse,*" he said. "Or to quote even more aptly—

"'How happy I could be with either,
   Were t'other dear charmer away.'"

The dance was already in full swing when Duncan Craig entered the great octagonal ballroom, still with a girl on either arm. But Major Haynes was watching for Gwen's arrival, and after greeting all three cordially, swept her quickly away. Craig made another mock bow to Connie.

"This is mine, I believe? Or am I mistaken about that too?"

"No, this time you're right. Really, Captain Craig, I couldn't help it. I would have if I could."

"All right, I believe you. Stop worrying. I know Gwen and her tricks pretty well. And you couldn't lie if you tried to—it just isn't in you. . . . I thought we were on first-name terms though, since Thursday. What's the meaning of this formality?"

"It still seems more natural to call you Captain Craig, that's all. Perhaps I'm a little overpowered by all this elegance."

"Which elegance?" he asked.

"Why, this ballroom's a great deal more elegant than the Hut! You know that." She looked admiringly from one of the great stone fireplaces to the other, and then towards the long windows leading to the terrace. "Remember, I haven't seen it before. This is the first time I've danced on a parquet floor too, and I appreciate that after all the miles I've traveled over hard, gritty concrete. I can manage without the crowd and the confusion in the Hut too, and I like dancing longer with the same man."

"Now, I really *am* pleased."

"I mean, it bewilders me to be snatched away by one almost as soon as another has grabbed me. That everlasting whistle gets on my nerves."

"Foiled again. You led me to hope that the reason you liked dancing longer with the same man was because that man happened to be me."

Connie did not answer. The "knight errantry" had been even more trying than she expected. His first efforts to get her boots off had been unsuccessful, and she had been forced to keep bracing herself against the wall back of the bench, in order that Craig might get hold of them better; then at last they fairly flew off, so fast that she could not get her skirts down. Her slim legs, encased in sheer clocked stockings, were very, very pretty, and Craig looked the appreciation which he did not voice while he cupped her heel with his left hand and drew the shoe on with his right. As the shoe slipped firmly into place, his left hand apparently slipped also; at all events it was far above her ankle when he released her. Now his dancing had the same daring character. He not only held her even closer than the current vogue sanctioned; he had also pressed his cheek against hers almost immediately. There was no denying that he danced beautifully, and her love of music alone would have made his accomplishment a pleasure and a challenge. But while she danced with Duncan Craig, she kept thinking of Tristan de Fremond: placing her carefully at his right on the little folding seat in the barouche; tucking the robe about her so that she would not be cold; drawing away from her slightly so that she would not be crowded or confused; explaining why he did not ask her to slip away for Muscadet and *petits beurres;* saying so lightly that she must listen to Carmen's definition of love. . . .

"So it wasn't?" Craig persisted, pressing her hand.

"Wasn't what?" Connie asked, coming back to the present with a start.

"Wasn't that you especially liked dancing with me. Are you in a trance or something? You wouldn't mind changing partners right now, since you could do it without a whistle?"

"No, I wouldn't mind. Of course you do dance beautifully. But——"

"But I don't keep my distance? And you prefer perfect gentlemen who do?"

"No. I mean yes. I guess I mean first no and then yes, don't I?"

She laughed, and the tension between them eased. "Fox trots weren't invented for perfect gentlemen—or perfect ladies either!" Craig told her jestingly. "Forget about your high-school hops, or whatever it was you were thinking about just then, for a few minutes, will you? Perhaps we could really have some fun if you did. Once you get the swing of this you'll do better. But what I'm really waiting for is the moment I get you into a tango. . . . Hello there, Cris, what do you want?"

He had been tapped unmistakably twice before he turned his head. A fresh young lieutenant, recently discharged from the Officers' Ward, was trailing after them with the obvious intention of cutting in. Craig, having disregarded this as long as possible, ended by relinquishing his partner with obvious reluctance.

"If I'd known you were going to play such mean tricks on me, I'd have kept you in bed a couple of weeks longer," he told the junior officer, with a wink. "I might even send you back there, you know. . . . Well, behave yourselves, you two. And don't let Cris get away with anything you shut me out on, Connie. Remember, I'll be watching you both from the side lines."

The interloper regarded Craig's retreating figure with unconcealed annoyance and, after a moment's hesitation, decided that he might give tongue to this. He himself had never seen Connie at a dance before, but he had liked and admired her from the first moment that she had come into the Officers' Ward; offhand he would have said that she was the last girl he would ever have expected to find with Craig. Since she had given the doctor her first dance, he must have been her escort; but Cris Henderson did not believe she made a practice of going out with Craig, and something in her expression seemed to reflect his own resentment.

"Who does that old sawbones think he is, anyway?" he growled. "I thought he was never going to look around, and I've got just as much right to cut in as he has to dance with you in the first place. . . . Haven't I?"

"Yes, of course. . . . I'm glad to see you out, Lieutenant Henderson. I didn't think when I got that pinochle deck for you that you'd be ready to lay it aside quite so soon."

"Lay it aside nothing. I'm taking it with me to Coblenz Thursday. I understand little treasures like that are hard to find in the Rhineland, and I've been winning *beaucoup francs* ever since I got it. I believe you've brought me good luck, Miss Galt."

"If you're not leaving till Thursday, perhaps you'd like to come to a little party my roommate's giving for me tomorrow evening."

"Gwen Foster? If I know her, she's got her crowd together already. I wouldn't want to butt in."

"You wouldn't. I know she'd be glad to have you. So would I. You see, this is really my party, so Gwen's told me to invite men—the extra ones, I mean. The dinner was planned in the first place as a compliment to the de Fremonds, who've been awfully good to me. They've got a cousin visiting them now, a French captain of cavalry. I know he'd enjoy meeting some American officers."

"And you think a front-line officer might provide some welcome relief from a bunch of medicos? Well, perhaps for the honor of the service I ought to accept—especially as I'd be tickled to death."

He did not seem to expect any answer to his question about the "bunch of medicos," and Connie did not volunteer any. But she knew he had been thinking of Craig when he asked it, and as the evening wore on she gave more and more thought to Gwen's advice. She noticed that Craig asked Gwen to dance almost as often as he asked her, and from all appearances they were having a hilariously good time together. Gwen not only danced cheek to cheek as a matter of course, she managed at the same time to keep up her end in an exchange of slightly off-color stories. When Craig came to get Connie for coffee and doughnuts, he was still laughing over Gwen's latest contribution so heartily that Connie decided Gwen was perfectly capable of taking him off her hands the next evening too. So, rather diffidently, after they had settled themselves and their refreshments on the stairway she broached the subject of the party and the reasons for giving it. Craig listened without comment until she actually asked him to join it.

"If I come, do I sit above or below the salt?" he inquired at length.

"I don't know just how the saltcellars are arranged in field kitchens. I rather think that they are on a shelf and that you reach."

"You know what I mean, Connie. Don't hedge. I told you before you're no good at that sort of thing. Are you asking me because you'd enjoy having me, or because you'd enjoy having me keep Gwen busy?"

"Do you usually analyze invitations?"

"No, not usually. But this time my pride's a little touched and my curiosity's considerably aroused. I can't help feeling that you're not trying to dodge poor Robert's dashing cousin quite as persistently as you always dodge him. In other words, this is one time when you don't seem to be running away."

Connie took a long swallow of coffee and set her cup down on the stairway beside her. Afterwards she brushed the sugar from the doughnuts carefully off her fingers. Then she looked Craig squarely in the face.

"You're right," she said. "This time I'm not running away. I don't need to. Do you want to come to the party or don't you?"

He would be glad to come to the party, Craig told her a little dryly, and during the last dance, which was a waltz, he behaved with almost Victorian circumspection. He did not argue either when Connie said it would really be easier for her to put on her rubber boots herself, because she was used to doing it and knew just how they went; they were sort of tricky. She proved her point by getting into them with great dispatch and dexterity and felt much better afterwards. The walk back to the barracks was also unmarred by any disturbing incident. Now that Major Haynes had been relieved from his duties as a host, he was presumably looking after Gwen himself; at all events, she did not accompany the others, and Craig made light and impersonal conversation, without seeking to loiter or to offer importunate caresses. Reassured, Connie slackened her pace a little as they approached the rain barrel, her mood softening. After all, she did not want to act like a prude or a tartar, she told herself, almost reproachfully, looking at Craig's wholly expressionless face. It was only—it was only——

"What's that noise?" Craig asked suddenly.

"What noise? I don't hear anything."

"Listen for a minute and you will. Someone's crying."

They stopped short, just beyond the rain barrel. It was normally very quiet around the camp at this hour, and any unusual sound easily penetrated the silence. Almost instantly Connie caught the murmur of subdued sobbing which Craig had immediately identified.

"Something must have happened to upset one of the girls!" she exclaimed. "I never knew any of them to cry before. You'll excuse me, won't you? I must find out what the trouble is right away."

"Of course you must. I'll wait here for a few minutes, to make sure it isn't sickness."

The quarters were in complete darkness when Connie hurried in. She switched on the hall light, then stood still and listened again. The sobs were coming from the rear room, shared by Tilda and Lois, and presently, as her eyes grew accustomed to the dimness, Connie saw that Tilda was not there and that Lois, still fully dressed, was curled up on her bed with her face buried in her pillow. Connie went quickly over to her and knelt down beside her, putting one arm around the huddled shoulders.

"Lois!" she said tenderly. "What's the matter? Are you in pain?" And as Lois shook her head slightly, without raising it or answering, Connie remembered the errant disciple whom her friend had been trying so hard and so vainly to reform. "That awful ambulance driver hasn't come in drunk *again,* has he?" she asked with swift solicitude. "Don't take it so hard, Lois, please don't. You've done everything you could, really you have. Anyone else would have given up long ago. The man's past redemption, that's all."

Lois suddenly sat up, drawing a long breath to swallow her sobs, and mopping fiercely away at her face with her silk handkerchief. "Don't you dare talk that way about him, Constance Galt," she said belligerently. "He's a very fine person, underneath. I've always known it; I've always been sure he'd come out all right in the end. Only he's never had anyone to bring forth his good qualities before."

"But Lois——"

Lois rose from the bed and stood before Connie accusingly. "James Hewitt has done me the honor of asking me to marry him!" she announced. "And I have accepted him. He has explained everything that happened the other evening to my entire satisfaction and we are formally engaged. I hope that in the future you will speak more respectfully of my prospective husband."

"Oh Lois, I'm terribly sorry! I mean I'm terribly glad! That is, I'm sorry I said the wrong thing and I'm glad you're happy. You are happy, aren't you?"

"Of course I'm happy. I'm gloriously happy," Lois answered with dignity. "What a silly question to ask! Did you ever hear of a girl who had just become engaged who wasn't gloriously happy?"

"But if you're so happy, what made you cry like that?"

"I was crying for joy, of course. Didn't you ever cry for joy, Connie?"

"No," said Connie rather shortly, "I never did. Don't let's talk about me, Lois, let's talk about you. Are you going to announce your engagement right away? Is there going to be a *wedding* at camp? Honestly, I'm so excited I don't know what to do."

In her excitement, which was quite unfeigned, she completely forgot Duncan Craig, who was still standing by the rain barrel. He waited for half an hour and then, as the sobs had long since stopped and the animated voices within gave no evidence of illness, he walked slowly away. Before he went to bed that night, for the first time in over a week he wrote a long letter to Eileen.

CHAPTER VIII

It was so late when Gwen got in that Lois and Tilda were both asleep, and Lois had entrusted Connie with the task of telling the great news to her roommate.

"Wouldn't you rather tell her yourself?"

"Yes, of course. But it's two o'clock now and after all, I have to be on duty at seven-thirty. I can't imagine what Gwen's doing out until such an hour."

"She's probably gone to Midnight Mass."

"That doesn't last two hours. Gwen's going to get into trouble one of these days if she doesn't watch out."

With this dark prediction, Lois turned out her light and relaxed into virtuous and contented slumber. Tilda, who had been as surprised as Connie at Lois's news, had nevertheless received it with characteristic and becoming amiability, and saying she would want to hear more about James in the morning, had also gone to sleep. When Gwen finally let herself in, with admirable caution, around three, Connie was the only one waiting to receive her.

"Gwen, what do you think?" she whispered. "Lois is engaged."

"Stop stringing me. Right now I'm too tired to take a joke."

"I'm not stringing you. She's engaged to James Hewitt."

"Connie, I just told you I'm dead on my feet."

"And I told *you* I'm not joking. When I came in I found her crying, so I started to sympathize with her. I told her the miserable wretch wasn't worth her tears. And she flew at me like a tiger. She says no one's understood him before. She says she's gloriously happy."

With considerable vehemence, Gwen began to swear while Connie, mindful of the lacking doors, tried hard to quiet her. But Gwen's profanity was followed by a spirited charge.

"And I suppose you and Tilda, like a couple of boobs, fell on her neck and said b-bless you, my child."

"Well, what else could we do?"

"You could have told her she was a damn fool. You could have told her to run like a rabbit while she still had time, if she couldn't act with any more sense than one."

"If she loves him——"

"Lois has got her first real thrill, the poor simp, and she thinks that's being in love. It's nothing but thwarted nature taking revenge. Lois is a healthy adult female who never knew before she was anything but a modest, well-educated girl with high temperance principles. I suppose Jim Hewitt's the first man who ever gave her a good hard hug and kissed her till her lips stung."

"Well, I should hope so, Gwen."

"Well, I shouldn't. I know just what she's letting herself in for. Me, I could handle a roughneck like Jim because I'm a roughneck myself—that is, I could if I were in love with him, and believe me, I know the difference between the real thing and nature's little tricks. But Lois has been a lady about thirty years too long. It's too late now for her to stop being refined. If I weren't dead on my feet, like I've said twice already, I'd wake her up and tell her so right now. But I'll do it the first thing in the morning instead."

"Oh Gwen, please don't!"

"Shut up. I don't want to talk about it any more."

Gwen dropped into bed and gentle little snores soon proclaimed her complete oblivion. Connie tossed and turned most of the night, worrying about Lois, worrying about Gwen, worrying—after she tardily remembered him—about Duncan Craig. When she finally drifted off, it was to sleep so soundly that she did not hear the morning bugle; but eventually she was awakened by the sound of angry voices in the hall.

Gwen and Lois were quarreling, quarreling bitterly and without restraint. Gwen was calling Lois an inhibited old maid who had suddenly gone haywire; Lois was calling Gwen a common tart. After this exchange of insults and others in like vein, each vehemently informed the other that the camp was not large enough to hold them both and threatened dire results if there were not an immediate demand for a transfer.

Lois was not through voicing her grievances. "I never thought you'd side with Gwen against me," she said, following after Connie. "I thought I could count on you, whatever happened."

"You can count on me. So can Gwen. I'm not taking sides with either of you. I'm trying to see both sides. There *are* two sides, Lois. After you've cooled off a little, you'll be only too ready to admit it. You'll be sorry you lost your temper. At least, you've said often enough that's one of the tests of a lady—whether she can keep hers when everybody else flies into a rage."

Connie jammed her cap down over her braids and picked up her slicker. Decidedly the day was getting off to a very poor start. She was short of sleep, she was upset about Craig, and she was distressed by her friends' quarrel. Her head ached and so did her heart.

"I've simply got to get started, Lois," she said from the door. "Shan't I say, as I stop by the Hut, that you're not feeling well this morning? Then you won't be expected."

"Thanks, Connie. It's nice of you to think of that. And of course you'll say I won't be coming to the dinner this evening. I'm sorry to miss your party, but under the circumstances, I can't very well help it. If I feel better by evening, I'll try to be on hand for the movies, though. I'd like very much to help you welcome the de Fremonds."

"And I'd like very much to have you. It wouldn't seem the same to me if you weren't there. . . . So long, Lois."

"So long, Connie. And you're right—I shouldn't have lost my temper. I *am* sorry."

So she had really scored at last, Connie said to herself, by her reference to a lady's proverbial self-control; the realization gradually eased her heartache, just as the hot coffee at the Hut had relieved her headache. But when she reached her office she found Gwen sitting on the steps, her knees crossed and one rubber-booted leg swinging back and forth. Her eyes were still blazing with anger and her mouth was grim.

"Don't say it!" she snapped. "What would it prove? I know exactly what you're thinking anyway and I'm damn glad I got all of that out of my system. I'm not going to take anything back and I'm not going to kiss and make up either. If you want to be a little white dove of peace, that's all right by me. But you better go coo somewhere else."

"I wasn't thinking of starting another argument."

She went on up the stairs and unlocked the door of her office. Gwen followed her. At the threshold Connie turned.

"I was planning to write that note for Sam to take up to the château before I went over to the wards," she said. "But I guess we'd better call the party off, hadn't we? Of course Lois isn't coming, and I'm sure you're not in the mood for it, any longer. To tell you the truth, I'm not either. So that would leave just Tilda, and she won't care, one way or the other."

"But you've already invited Craig and Henderson! They told me so!"

"Well, I can write notes to them, saying the party's postponed. I was going to write Captain Craig anyway, at the same time I wrote the Countess. I owe him an apology. He and I heard the sound of crying as we came up to the quarters last night, and he promised to wait and find out if someone were sick. Then afterwards I forgot all about him, I was so taken up with Lois. He probably stood out by the rain barrel for ages."

"But I don't want you to call the party off! I *am* in the mood for it.

I'm dying to meet the de Fremonds, and I've got everything all organized. Besides——"

Connie had already seated herself at her desk and was reaching for her stationery. Gwen leaned over her impetuously.

"What are you going to do, Connie?"

"I'm going to write to Captain Craig."

"You're not going to tell him the party's off, are you?"

"I'm sorry, Gwen. I don't feel like coming to a party tonight any longer. And I wouldn't want to bring the de Fremonds into an atmosphere that was bristling with antagonism. They might get the idea the camp was always like that. However, there's no reason why you and Tilda shouldn't have Craig and Henderson to dinner without the rest of us, is there?"

"Of course there is! Craig would say I was playing a trick on him, just as he did last night. It's you he wants to see. He's simply nuts about you, Connie!"

"He can't be. He hardly knows me."

"But he is! Oh Connie, please be a good sport! Write him a nice note saying how sorry you are you forgot about him last night and that you'll try to make up for it this evening! Get Sam started up to the château with that note to the Countess!"

Connie picked up her pen again. Gwen stood over her, watching her anxiously, until both notes were written and Connie had handed them over for her to read. After Gwen had scrutinized them carefully, she gave Connie a swift kiss.

"Atta girl!" she said affectionately. "Don't you bother with these any more, Connie. I'll take them right along with me and get them into good hands."

Gwen went out of the office cockily, carrying the two notes, and at the same moment Whaley, the orderly, came in whistling "Smiles" and carrying the current "List of the Dying." His cheerfulness represented no real lack of heart; most of the men whose names appeared on the paper had been at the camp a long time, and the listing represented nothing new or startling. Connie took the paper from him and ran over its contents with the swiftness of long practice and no expectancy of shock. But a name she had never seen before detached itself from those with which she had long been familiar, and suddenly leapt out at her.

"Theodore Roosevelt Lee!" she exclaimed. "Ward 3—— Why, everyone was all right when I went there yesterday afternoon! And I never heard of this man before! I must get over right away!"

She dashed across the road and arrived, still panting with haste, at the entrance to the ward. Miss Kleb, the nurse in charge, was in her office sorting medicines and glanced up calmly as Connie came rushing in.

"Is this man Lee in the private room already?" Connie demanded, still panting.

"Twenty—twenty-one—twenty-two," Miss Kleb said aloud. She was counting "C.C. pills," and she did not seem especially pleased at the interruption. "What Lee?" she inquired, making a neat pile of her treasure.

"Why, Theodore Roosevelt Lee!" Connie exclaimed.

"Oh, him!" Miss Kleb responded, still without agitation. "No, he's not in the private room. He's in the fourth bed on the left. You can see him right from here."

Glancing in the designated direction, Connie beheld a huge Negro, his head—inky against his snowy pillows—bent over the game of solitaire in which he was completely engrossed.

"He doesn't look very sick to me," she said.

"Why, he isn't! He's got a bad cold, that's all."

"But he was on the list of the dying Whaley just brought me!"

"Don't tell him that or he *will* die. Go along and see him if you want to though."

Connie went down the ward towards the bed occupied by the namesake of heroes.

"Good morning," she said pleasantly. "How are you feeling today?"

The Negro put a red seven on a black eight, and after wiping his nose with the back of his hand looked up with a cheerful grin.

"Pretty good, thank you, ma'am," he replied. "Ah did get me a misery in mah head, out in all dis rain dey has here, but Ah's feelin' a sight better now Ah's in a good warm bed."

"Is there anything I can do for you?"

"No'm, thank you. Ah's got about everything Ah needs, right here."

"Wouldn't you like me to write a letter for you?"

The Negro forgot his game and brightened perceptibly.

"Yes'm, if you say so."

Connie, extracting her pad from her raffia bag, waited for further information. As none was forthcoming, she asked another question.

"To whom shall I write?"

"Anybody you say, ma'am."

"Well, you'd like a letter to your wife, wouldn't you?"

"Lawdy, miss, Ah ain't got me no wife."

"What about your mother, then?" Connie asked.

"She daid."

"Well, your father?"

"Never had none."

"And you didn't have any brothers or sisters either?"

"Yas'm. Ah has a sister."

"That's fine. Let's write to her then. What's her name?"

"Her name Miz' Frozena Paine."

"And her address?" Connie inquired, writing busily.

"She live right by de railroad track."

"Yes, but what street? What town?"

"I thinks dey calls it Railroad Street. But anyway everybody in Greenville know Frozena."

"Greenville? What state?"

"Yas'm, hit in de States."

"But *which* state? There are lots of Greenvilles in the United States. Is the one where your sister lives in Mississippi? Or South Carolina? Or North Carolina?"

"That's right, North Carolina."

"And you'd like to tell her that you're getting along finely, that everyone here at camp has been awfully good to you, but that you're looking forward to seeing her soon?"

"Yas'm, I reckons that would be all right."

Connie began the letter, her zeal for good works considerably dampened by the exhausting effort of securing vital statistics from Theodore Roosevelt Lee. The Negro, instead of resuming his interrupted game, sat staring into space, his cheerful grin gone, his expression becoming more and more wistful. At last he spoke hesitantly.

"Does dey have real things growing in de woods over here, like us does at home?"

Connie's moving pencil stopped. "What kind of things, Lee?"

"Pretty things, like holly."

Connie's heart contracted. Before she could answer, the Negro went on, no longer with hesitation, but with eagerness.

"Christmas time at home, me and Frozena, us used to go out in de woods, cutting down little holly trees and stripping de branches offen big ones. Den us used to go up and down de streets, ringing white folks' doorbells and asking 'em, 'Doesn't you all want a pretty holly tree to hang your Christmas gifts on? Doesn't you want pretty holly branches to put on your chimneypieces?' Us made right smart money dataway. What holly us had left over, us take to de A.M.E. church and give it to de preacher for de Sunday school."

"And you were wondering whether I could get you some holly for the ward?"

"Yes, ma'am, dat's just what I was a-wondering. Ain't never wrote no letter before. Don't seem to come natural. But holly where I could see it—boy, dat'd be something!"

Connie put the pad back in her raffia bag. A vision of the red berries dotting the woods around Chassay, and the tall waxen-leaved trees bordering the inner wall of the courtyard, rose before her eyes.

"I think I can promise you some holly, Lee," she said. "I think I know exactly where I can get some. It does grow here. In fact, two kinds. One kind has lots of red berries, just like ours, but it has white borders on the green leaves, too."

"Sho nuf?"

"Yes, sure enough." And now she saw not only the trees brightening the forests and flanking the walls. She also saw Tristan de Fremond helping her pick the holly that was to assuage the homesickness of the Negro who could not go with his sister into his own woods to gather it, or offer it for sale to his own white folks or give it to his preacher for the colored Sunday school.

CHAPTER IX

THE DE FREMONDS accepted the invitation to dinner with the same alacrity they had shown in accepting the invitation to the movies. But it was not until the evening was drawing to an end that Connie had a chance to speak to the Countess about the holly.

Though she met the party from Château Chassay at the gate, conversation was brief and general on the way to the office at the Convalescent Camp, where Gwen and Tilda, Craig and Henderson, were all waiting for them. Then they went on to the field kitchen—a huge square tent, its cooking equipment on rollers, with a long plank table running down one side and K. P.'s serving from this. As Gwen's party approached, the mess sergeant drew her aside and spoke to her in a stage whisper.

"The boys have set up a special table for you and your friends," he told her, jerking a thumb towards one corner of the tent. "Go up and get your grub, same as usual, but don't bother to take your plates back. Red'll clear away for you."

The group filed up to the counter, where bean soup was ladled out to them from large caldrons. Carrying the agateware bowls containing this delicacy with great care, to avoid spilling it, they moved cautiously across the ground to the designated "table"—some planks spread across sawbucks—and took their places on the benches at either side of this. Gwen, as hostess, seated the table to suit herself, without too much regard for protocol; she put Tristan at her right and Craig at her left, the former with Tilda on his other side and the latter coming off a poor second with Robert, who, because of Lois's absence, became an extra man. Opposite her were the Countess, Henderson, Connie, and the Count. Tilda attempted a surreptitious remonstrance with this arrangement, but Gwen silenced her quickly and effectively. This was her party, wasn't it? All right then, she would run it. When Tilda had one herself, she could do the same. . . .

Connie was also aware of the unconventionality of the seating, and chagrined that the Countess should have been placed by a junior officer, with no one at all on the other side; but there was nothing she herself could do to remedy the situation either, except to redouble her efforts to converse agreeably in her halting French with the Count. To her relief, he showed no signs of taking umbrage over his slighted importance, but evinced the keenest interest in his primitive and unfamiliar surroundings, and kept up a rapid-fire comment on everything that was happening. Red removed the soup bowls with a swagger, and swung the steak sandwiches expertly into place, much to the Count's delight. Big china mugs filled to the brim with steaming coffee, which was sweetened from inexhaustible sugar bowls, made their appearance before the sandwiches had been displaced by chocolate pudding; and pickles, jam, butter, and extra bread remained all the time on the plank table within easy reach. Cigarettes and chocolate bars added to this general effect of abundance; and since the service was speedy and the movie schedule inflexible, Connie's resourcefulness in small talk was not overtaxed. Red had hardly slammed down the last plate when Gwen said she hated like all get-out to hurry them, but they must get a move on if they really wanted to see the show; and she forthwith bade them good night, adding it was just her luck that she couldn't get over to the Hut herself, but that she knew they'd be all right in Tilda's lily-white hands, not to mention Connie's little brown ones.

While Gwen was talking, Tilda had slipped quietly over to Craig, and now she managed to murmur, under cover of the general polite leave-taking, that she hoped to goodness he would do something about the Countess. He shook his head, frowning slightly.

"I'm not going on either."

"Oh yes you are! Gwen's got away with enough for tonight! The old gentleman was really having a grand time, and of course the Countess wouldn't let on that she wasn't too. But you know as well as I do what she must think of the way she was shunted off in a corner. Gwen didn't even bother to talk across the table to her. She was much too busy with you and the 'parent.' You're coming to the movies with us. It isn't only a question of what the de Fremonds must be thinking. Don't you know Connie's mortified to death?" Tristan quickly took his place beside Connie.

"Dinner in the field kitchen was most interesting," he said agreeably. "I am very much impressed with your army food. This is the first time I have eaten at an American mess, and incidentally this is the first time in four years that I have eaten white bread."

"I'm afraid you're more impressed with American food than American manners."

"I'm much interested in those too. As I told you the other evening, we French have our own way of doing things. Why not the Americans also? I found the young ladies on both sides of me very entertaining, each in a different way. Remember, you had prepared me, very ably, for their outstanding attributes. I can now see for myself that Mademoiselle Foster has great driving power and Mademoiselle Evans great tact. Those are almost equally fine qualities."

"Yes, they are," Connie agreed gratefully. Again she was amazed by the ease with which Tristan de Fremond was able to relieve her mind, and looking up at him she saw that he was regarding her with the same grave expression as on Monday night.

"But if you will permit me to say so on such short acquaintance, there is another quality which is finer still. I think the English word for it is singleheartedness. Now both Mademoiselle Foster and Mademoiselle Evans, with all their merit, have also ulterior purposes. If I am not mistaken, Mademoiselle Foster uses her strong will to gain her own ends, as well as to push through her work, and Mademoiselle Evans smooths over every situation because she herself finds disharmony unpleasant rather than because she wishes to put others at their ease. But what you are doing, or trying to do, is for the good of others. Perhaps you make mistakes. Nevertheless I am sure you are always unselfish and always sincere."

"But I make so many mistakes that I get terribly discouraged."

They were already approaching the Hut, where long lines of men, most of them more or less visibly disabled, were waiting outside for the second show. They were laughing and talking among themselves, and several hailed Connie with unfeigned pleasure, while others merely nodded, grinning sheepishly, as she came by. Tristan slackened his pace.

"But I cannot believe you make many serious mistakes. If you did, the men would not like you so much. And they do, you know. They would be very pleased if you would stop and speak to them now. You are going to, are you not?"

"All right, if you wouldn't mind."

She had nothing special to say to any of them, and the shyness which so frequently beset her overcame her now; she did little more than return their friendly greetings. But Tristan, with his customary ease, asked questions on his own initiative and answered, with open responsiveness, those which were put to him. It was not until the doors of the Hut opened, disgorging the first-show audience and signaling that the long lines outside should begin to move in the direction of the auditorium, that he took his unhurried leave of the last inquirer and followed Connie's lead inside. Lois, looking rather pale and wan, but completely composed, was waiting to welcome them and conduct them to the "box" which had been reserved for them. This was merely a railed-in platform at the rear of the hall, supplied with three rows of benches, on the first of which the Count and Countess had already been installed with as much ceremony as conditions would permit. Lois now seated herself between them, not without some anxious glances in the general direction of the audience at large, whose behavior she feared might not be sufficiently decorous to show proper respect for the illustrious French guests. The other members of the party took their places rather haphazardly in the rear, but this time it was Craig who managed to slide in beside Connie, effectively pinning her between himself and the wall.

The canvas curtain on the stage was drawn aside, and the title of the movie, SHE WENT TO THE CITY, flickered across the screen. In an unbelievably short time, an innocent and hapless heroine, who had left her rural home and her stalwart suitor for the more enticing pleasures of the wicked metropolis, had fallen into the clutches of a ruthless villain and was completely in his power. Her predicament quickly called forth stamping and catcalls from the audience, to a degree which justified Lois's worst fears, but her important guests were far too preoccupied themselves to be aware of her concern or of the unseemly behavior on the floor. The Countess was leaning forward entranced, her hands ecstatically clasped; the Count, carefully balancing his tall hat on his knees, was sitting with his chin thrust forward and his beard outspread, ejaculating, *"Oulala Oulala!"* in a vehemently audible voice. He did not relax or subside until the final rescue; then, as the canvas curtain rolled into place again, he leapt up and began voicing his enthusiastic thanks for the evening's entertainment. Lois responded disparagingly.

"I'm sorry it wasn't better. We often have very good movies, and I was hoping we might have one of the very best tonight. Do come again some other time."

With one voice, all four de Fremonds told her they would be only too glad to do so. They assured her that no spectacle could possibly have pleased them more, and the Countess included Lois in her usual invitation to Connie for the following Sunday. Mademoiselle Evans would be most welcome also, the Countess added, turning graciously in the direction of Tilda who, as usual, had made a very favorable impression. No mention was made of Gwen, whose absence might plausibly account for the omission, though the others realized only too well that she herself was to blame for it, and Connie longed to put in a good word for her. She tried to catch up with the Countess as the party from the château moved towards the gate, but Craig was now leading the way with the two guests of honor, and Connie had fallen behind again with Tristan.

"Do you think there'd be time now to tell you what I started to say when we were going to the hall?"

"Of course. Or if not, we can always create it."

Again he slackened his pace, and with decreasing tension, Connie told him about the homesick Negro from North Carolina. Tristan listened without comment or interruption until she had completely finished. Then he spoke quickly and cordially.

"And of course you would like to get some holly from our park for this poor forlorn creature? Probably the kind that grows in the courtyard also? My aunt would be almost confused that you should think it necessary to ask. The only reason she has not offered it would be that she did not know of the need. But come, we will tell her right away."

In a few swift strides he caught up with the others and, speaking in rapid French, repeated Connie's little story. The Count and Countess nodded understandingly at intervals during the recital, throwing out an occasional expression of sympathy. Tristan had hardly finished when his aunt turned to Connie.

"When would it suit you to get this holly?" she asked.

"Any time would suit me. That would be in line with my work, you see, so I wouldn't have to ask permission, and if Arkie isn't free to drive the camionette, I'm sure Sam could arrange to. But I don't think I should gather it too long before Christmas. Would Saturday afternoon be all right?"

"Perfectly. At three in the afternoon? We shall expect you then. Again thanks, dear Miss Galt, for a most delightful evening."

It was the Countess who spoke. But as Tristan took her hand, Connie knew, without the telling, that he would be waiting for her in the woods. And though Craig made no reference to either Tristan or the holly as they walked back to her quarters, she realized that he knew it too.

CHAPTER X

She saw him as soon as the car turned into the great iron gateway leading from the highroad to the woods encircling the courtyard.

A few pines and hemlocks were scattered through the more abundant oaks and beeches, but for the most part the trees were bare, except for a few copper-colored leaves which clung persistently to their limbs and rustled in the winter wind; so his bright blue uniform stood out vividly, framed by gaunt branches. He was obviously watching for the car and as it approached he saluted gaily and sprang forward across the crackling underbrush.

"Good afternoon," he said, opening the door of the camionette and giving Connie his hand. "It occurred to me that I might be of help in getting the holly. I have brought both a large knife and a small hatchet with me, and I have investigated the sources of supply. There are several little trees which I think could be used just as they are for decorations, and many more that can furnish some boughs. Some of them are the kind which have the leaves with white borders. Shall we go and have a look? . . . I take it for granted you have brought useful implements with you also," he added, turning pleasantly to Arkie. "We will have to see which of us is the better woodchopper."

Arkie had experienced a slight pang at the sight of the spruce young officer, whose presence seemed to indicate that he himself might be left cooling his heels in the camionette while the others explored the woods in a leisurely way; consequently, the reference to woodchoppers came as a great relief to his mind. He jumped out of the camionette grinning, and proceeded to draw from its recesses some knives and a hatchet of his own, which Tristan, to Arkie's further gratification, volubly admired, saying that his own poor tools would suffer by comparison. A short dialogue ensued, in which both men agreed that the American Army certainly had the best of everything at its disposal; then Connie was drawn into the conversation, and all three set off together in a direction which Tristan signified, where they would find the holly trees best suited to their purpose.

The first of these was near at hand—a beautiful straight little tree with luxuriant glossy foliage and quantities of scarlet berries; but Tristan suggested that perhaps it would be better to go farther, and get that on the way back. It was very pleasant walking through the woods, for though the air was crisp, the sun was shining with unaccustomed brightness and came filtering through the trees, making lozenges of light on the low-growing vines and thickets. Besides the holly, there was an immense amount of smilax, and many of the oaks were laden with mistletoe; a recent windstorm had blown down one of these and it lay directly across their path. Connie turned back and looked at it thoughtfully after Tristan had helped her over it, but just then he called her attention to the poignant note of an unfamiliar bird, and while she was questioning him eagerly about it, they left the fallen tree behind them.

Tristan finally paused in a grove where several tall holly trees were clustered. This would be the best place, he thought, to begin their gathering, and for some moments he and Arkie busily cut branches while Connie sat on a stump watching them. Then they all picked up as much as they could carry and began moving back to their starting point. Arkie must be used to the woods, Tristan remarked, to make such good progress. Anyone who was not found underbrush hard going. Arkie, swelling with increasing pride, strode forward faster than ever, explaining as he went that his native state was a great one for forests and that it would be too bad if he didn't know how to get around in them. Then, pausing briefly for breath and observing that Connie, though doggedly keeping up with her two male companions, was obviously finding this difficult, he made a suggestion.

"I reckon the woods ain't much in Massachusetts though, where Miss Galt comes from," he said. "You're dead right, Captain—a person that hasn't got the trick of it can get tuckered out mighty quick walking in 'em. We went a far piece too before we turned around. Why don't you sit down on that log and rest yourself awhile, Miss Galt? If you'll just pile your holly on top of what I'm carrying, I can take your load right along with mine. After I get those into the truck I'll clip off that cute little tree we saw the first thing and look around for one to match it. Then I'll start back for more branches and we can meet somewhere along the way. Just take your time."

"I am getting a little tired. But I don't like to hold up the procession. Won't you go with Arkie, Captain de Fremond?"

"Certainly not! I am sure that was not at all what our friend had in mind, was it, Sergeant?"

"You bet it wasn't!" Arkie answered with emphasis. "Here, I can take all that the three of us has got so far, easy enough. That's the idea, Captain, pile it right up!"

Looking more or less like an animated tree, Arkie resumed his triumphant march. Tristan lighted a cigarette and sat down beside Connie on the fallen oak which Arkie had designated as a log.

"My good opinion of the sergeant as a woodsman is increasing by leaps and bounds," he remarked. "Did I dream it, or has this particular tree some special attraction for you? I thought you were studying it rather carefully when we passed it before."

"I noticed how much mistletoe it has on it. I couldn't help wondering whether your aunt would mind if we cut some of that too."

"She would certainly be delighted if you would rid all her trees of it. It is a terrible parasite. Why should you wish to cut it?"

"We use mistletoe for Christmas decorations too—in a rather special way."

"What is the special way?"

"We hang bunches of it in places where people are bound to pass under it—doorways between rooms, for instance. And if a man meets a girl in such a doorway, it is considered quite all right for him to kiss her, even though they're not engaged."

"I see. Such meetings are, of course, always wholly accidental?"

"Oh, of course!"

The elusive smile she found so alluring had come into play when he asked his question, and his eyes began to twinkle. She answered rather demurely, but afterwards she looked up and laughed. Tristan laughed too.

"I know now what is meant by a happy accident," he said. "And I never did before, though I shall have to confess that this time you have not startled me by presenting a strange custom to my attention. We have this same pleasant form of Christmas celebration in France, and incidentally it seems to me one that is ideally adapted to strengthening the *entente cordiale* between our two countries. . . . But your sick soldiers—how could they benefit by a decoration of the kind you describe?"

"Well, they're not all bedridden, you know. And then of course there are the corpsmen and the doctors."

"Oh yes, of course. . . . By the way, I found the doctor who was at your party last Wednesday quite intriguing."

"Yes, he's generally considered very attractive."

"But I should imagine that mistletoe might be rather superfluous in his case. I believe that, like your friend Mademoiselle Foster, he goes after what he wants in a very direct manner."

To her intense annoyance, Connie realized that she was blushing, and this annoyance was increased by her certainty that Tristan had not failed to observe the blush. She shifted the subject.

"I'm glad you mentioned Gwen, because I've been wanting to ask another favor. Your aunt very kindly invited both Lois and Tilda to come with me tomorrow to Château Chassay. But she didn't ask Gwen. The others spoke of their invitations, not realizing she didn't have one too. Gwen's feeling very badly about it. Of course I don't want to be presumptuous. But if perhaps it was just an oversight——"

Tristan extinguished his cigarette with rather elaborate care. "Since you are yourself so sincere," he said slowly, "I am sure you would prefer that I should also be candid. It was not an oversight. My aunt liked both your friends very much. But Mademoiselle Foster failed to make a good impression. I hope you will not take it too much to heart, and that Mademoiselle Foster will not do so either. In some ways my aunt is a very conservative person. I pointed out to her that Mademoiselle Foster, like Mademoiselle Graham, had been her hostess, whereas Mademoiselle Evans, though she added greatly to the décor, had taken no active part in the evening's entertainment. My aunt admitted this, but insisted that Mademoiselle Foster had been so remiss in her manner of dispensing hospitality that she was not entitled to the courtesy of a return invitation. I am very sorry. I have never known Aunt Elise to take such a stand before, and I am quite powerless to change it."

"You mean the Countess is so offended because she wasn't properly seated that she won't ask Gwen to the château?"

"Not at all. I know she was surprised because my uncle was not placed at Mademoiselle Foster's right hand, a courtesy my aunt naturally took for granted would be accorded him instead of some younger man. She is very simple in some ways, but very proud in others, and I do not believe that any slight would make much impression upon her pride. In this case she would simply have put it down to a lack of savoir-faire. But unfortunately she gathered—I do not know just how you would express it—in French we would say it this way: she gathered that Mademoiselle Foster is not a serious young person."

"Oh, but the Countess is wrong! I do know your expression! It was—explained to me quite recently. And she's doing Gwen an injustice, honestly she is!"

Connie spoke with great earnestness. She was appalled to gather from Tristan's speech that Gwen's high-handed ways had led her into the Countess's bad graces. Tristan regarded her gravely.

"I will tell her what you have said," he answered slowly. "I do not think she realized that you yourself would be so much distressed. She has a very high regard for you and I am sure she would not willingly cause you pain. I will see if it will not be possible to dispatch an invitation to Mademoiselle Foster this evening. It would be quite logical, besides being absolutely true, to say that Aunt Elise expected to see her again, and Mademoiselle Foster may gather from this that she would have been asked later. Besides, allowances should certainly be made for her, in my opinion. Not only because she is an American, but because any young girl so greatly *éprise* should be excused for neglecting everyone except the object of her affections."

"I don't think I understand what you mean."

"But surely, Mademoiselle Galt, it must be evident to everyone that Mademoiselle Foster is very deeply in love with that engaging young doctor whom we have both agreed is so attractive, and that he is at least receptive to her attentions."

"Oh no! She can't be! He isn't! Why——"

She stopped, blushing more deeply than ever, her head whirling with confused thoughts, her heart in a tumult. Her denial had been spontaneous and sincere, but the words were hardly out of her mouth when she began to doubt her own veracity. Varied memories came crowding in upon her: Gwen's reference to her own meeting with Craig by the Bath House, which she now realized might have been jealously rather than casually observed; Gwen's adroitness in making a third when they all went to the officers' dance; the intimacy of her attitude during it; the untimeliness of her return after it; Gwen's references to Craig; Craig's references to Gwen —*I know her, and all her tricks. She's a devil;* his reluctance to leave her and go to the auditorium. All these recollections and many others now seemed to dovetail together, confirming Tristan de Fremond's impressions. But if he were right, why then——

"You seem to be very much surprised," Tristan de Fremond was saying. "And in the face of your astonishment, I am reluctant to be indiscreet. But there are reasons why I hope you will pardon me for asking if you had

68

grounds for believing that Captain Craig might have other interests?"

"I think probably he has a good many. He rather strikes me as being that kind of a man. Not that I know him very well."

The reply came so quietly and so quickly that it gave the effect of complete detachment and mild reproof. Though Tristan de Fremond realized that this self-possession was only skin-deep, he did not fail to pay it the tribute it deserved.

"What an excellent answer! You must have a great gift of evaluation. Now you do not know me very well either. Do I strike you in the same way?"

"Oh, I think you have numerous interests too! But I believe they are more varied than Captain Craig's. You are very fond of horses, for instance. I doubt if Captain Craig knows one end of a horse from another."

"I see. The sad result of too much concentration elsewhere."

Again their eyes met and again they laughed together, the momentary strain between them instantly easing. Tristan leaned over the tree trunk and began to hack away at a mass of mistletoe.

"We must get to work on this so that it will be ready for the excellent Arkie to take on his next load," he observed. "But I am going to put a price on my own labors. I am also much chagrined at my failure to receive a certain invitation which I covet, and I shall take things in my own hands and boldly ask for it. Surely the man who provides the mistletoe has a right to observe its effectiveness, it not actually to test this! I insist on coming to your Christmas party."

CHAPTER XI

Everyone agreed that the mistletoe added immeasurably to the holiday decorations. There was no lack of this, for in addition to the clusters from the fallen tree, which Connie and Arkie took back to camp in the camionette, a huge two-wheeled cart, heaped high with it, arrived on Christmas Eve from the château, and thanks to Arkie was passed through the gate and trundled up to the very door of her office. The blue-smocked peasant who delivered it brought no note but said, with a sweep of his broadbrimmed hat, that he had been told Mademoiselle would understand—which she did. Arkie appeared while she was vainly striving to cope with it, and offered his services.

"Looks to me like you've got enough of this stuff now to give everyone a kissing chance. But Whaley'll never get it put around by himself. I'm off guard duty now till tomorrow, so I thought I'd come along and give him a hand. Where do you want us to start?"

"With the wards, of course. I think you'll have enough left over for the Hut and the ballroom and the mess halls too. And don't you dare forget the nurses' barracks either! But couldn't you put big bunches on top of all the stretchers and take them along right now?"

"Sure we can!" Arkie said heartily. "Get going there, Whaley!"

With Connie helping, the two noncoms quickly added the mistletoe to the stacks and started off. She stood watching them, thankful to see the transformed stretchers put to such a pleasant purpose, but so weary with attempted well-doing that her relief was untinged with exultation. And she still had a hard evening ahead of her. She had been accompanying a group of corpsmen who were members of Father Finn's Paulist Choristers, during their rehearsal of the Gregorian chant they were to sing at Midnight Mass, and in the course of these rehearsals she had extracted a promise from them that they would also sing carols in the wards; but the promise had been contingent on one from her that she would go with them. They would be along at any moment now, and so would Tristan de Fremond.

He had again brought up the subject of another invitation to camp at his aunt's Sunday tea, and in response to his repeated request, she had suggested the Christmas Day dance at the Hut. At first he had fallen in with this idea very readily. Then she happened to mention the carols, and he had said that if he were obliged to make a choice, he would rather go with her to the wards. She suspected that later he would persuade her that he should take in the dance after all, and that the most adroit way of achieving two visits was to dwell first on Christmas Eve. Fate had unexpectedly intervened to ease the strain at the quarters, for Lois had been suddenly ordered to Savenay before she could even ask for a transfer. Gwen had helped efficiently—almost too efficiently—with the hurried packing, and no fresh hostilities had broken out in the midst of the confusion which attended it, which was not a little to Gwen's credit, for Lois was complacent almost to the point of smugness over the fortuitous turn events had taken. The two had even embraced, stiltedly on Lois's part and with elaborate carelessness on Gwen's, before Lois climbed into James Hewitt's ambulance and disappeared bag and baggage.

Connie assented to the arrangement Tristan suggested and now she was waiting for him, wishing she were not so tired, wishing she were not so involved, wishing above all, that she had never happened to meet Duncan Craig by the Bath House. . . .

He had been waiting for her at her office when she returned from Château Chassay on Sunday, with the proposal that this would be a good evening for them to have their delayed dinner at Le Petit Saint-Jean. Wondering if she were fated always to be waylaid by someone more or less unwelcome, when she was going up her own steps—and what she could do about it if she were—she had declined the invitation on the ground of being too busy to accept it, what with preparations for Christmas and all. He had then suggested the evening of the twenty-sixth instead. Well, she was afraid she would be pretty tired the evening of the twenty-sixth, after being up practically all night on the twenty-fourth and dancing practically all day on the twenty-fifth. So she thought perhaps——

"Come clean, Connie. I've said that before, but evidently it needs repeating. What's eating you now? I behaved all right the night of the movies, didn't I?"

"Yes, at the movies."

"But not at supper? Don't tell me I can actually get a rise out of you just by talking to another girl!"

The anger which was so rarely roused surged through her now. "Of course not!" she answered indignantly. "You weren't over and above polite to our French guests, though."

Craig retorted, speaking angrily too: "You and Tilda both seem bent on making me over. I'm quite aware that the Junior Leaguer and the learned collegian are qualified to give all sorts of pointers on usages in polite society. But it's barely possible that they're superfluous in my case and that I acted the way I did because it darned well suited me to, not because I didn't know any better. Remember, I haven't any special reason for wanting to impress a noble French family."

"And remember I haven't any special reason for wanting to dine with you. Good night, Captain Craig."

She had practically shut the door in his face, but the ungracious gesture had not given her even momentary satisfaction. She was ashamed of her rudeness and resentful because Craig had been able to provoke her to anger. Most of all, she was again deeply chagrined by the consciousness that she lacked savoir-faire.

The problem of Gwen's attitude towards Craig and his towards her also became more and more vexing the more Connie pondered it. She was increasingly disposed to believe that Tristan de Fremond had analyzed Gwen's feelings correctly; but she could not clear the air by a direct or even an indirect question on the subject, and apparently she was to be given no time to size up the situation by deliberate observation. Unconsciously and involuntarily she herself had succeeded in attracting Craig, and he would continue to make life difficult for her until he succeeded in rousing an answering spark.

In her perplexity and discouragement, she thought not only of Tilda and Gwen but also of Lois. At least Lois had known what she wanted and how to get it; these two salient facts stood out inescapably amidst the welter of lesser ones. James Hewitt might be unworthy of her love and she might be misguided in bestowing it; but she had achieved her purpose, and she had shown courage as well as determination in doing so. Once Connie had known what she wanted too, but where Lois had achieved, she had failed. Sitting weary and despondent at her desk on Christmas Eve, waiting to make her rounds of the wards, she wondered if among the many she would see lying mutilated and helpless there would be even one whose sense of futility could be more complete than her own. . . .

She jumped up to answer a knock at the door, brushing away two large, obtrusive tears as she did so. Tristan de Fremond was standing in the entry, his gold-braided cap and black gauntlets in one hand, the other already extended to take hers. His blue-cloaked figure detached itself from the shadows as he stepped forward into the unshaded light of the bare bulb which hung from the ceiling.

"*Joyeux Noël!*" he said. His voice was earnest rather than gay, and there was a ring to it which made Connie feel that this was not merely a casual greeting but a sincere expression of hope that her Christmas really would be joyful. "I am a little early, I think— I hope you do not mind?"

"No, I'm glad to see you. Won't you sit down? The others will be here in just a few minutes." She sat down herself and handed him a small package. "Meanwhile, what about a carton of American cigarettes for a Christmas present? After all, you gave me a cartload of mistletoe!"

"I should be delighted to have the cigarettes," he said, accepting the little package. "But is it then an American custom to exchange presents at Christmas time?"

"Yes. Isn't it a French custom too?"

"No, we exchange them on New Year's Day. Christmas with us is wholly a religious celebration. Even those of us who go to church once or twice a year would never dream of missing Midnight Mass."

"And I'm going to Midnight Mass for the first time in my life tonight! Father Calloran hasn't anyone else to play for him, so he's asked me to do it."

"You play, then? You did not tell me that before, only that you loved music. And now it appears you are yourself a musician! Why, you are a young lady of many talents!"

"Indeed I'm not. Just before you came I was thinking——"

"Yes? What were you thinking?"

"About what a failure I am."

Her answer came like a willing confession to an understanding listener, but she could not keep her voice from trembling as she made it.

"A failure?" Tristan's words rang out warmly again, this time with surprise as well as sympathy. "If you imagined that, even for a moment, it must be because you are unhappy about something else and did not think clearly. Perhaps some other time you would tell me what it was. Not now, because, as you said, the others will be here at any moment and confidences are always best when they can be unhurried. But meanwhile I should like so much to hear you play. I am persuaded that you do it beautifully. Would you let me stay on and go to Mass here? Or would that be trespassing too much on your time?"

"It wouldn't be trespassing on my time. I'd like very much to have you stay. But won't the others at the château be waiting for you?"

"No, because I said I might go on into Nantes, to the cathedral. The others are all going to the village church. . . . That's settled, then—I'm staying. Listen—isn't that the choristers coming now?"

More conscious of sound than she, he had caught the first strains of approaching music, with the tramp of advancing feet. The corpsmen were coming down Company Street, singing as they came. Their triumphant song echoed through the encircling stillness of the camp:

> "'Adeste fideles,
> Laeti triumphantes;
> Venite, venite in Bethlehem,
> Natum videte Regem angelorum.

Still singing, the corpsmen marched around the corner of the Receiving Ward and halted under Connie's window. Then the song ceased and there was a gentle tap on a lower pane. Connie stepped over and threw open the window.

"We'll be right out, boys!" she called to them gladly. And did not realize until afterwards that she had spoken for Tristan as well as herself and that until this moment no one else had known that he was going with them.

The corpsmen accepted Tristan's presence without awkwardness and with no visible surprise. The news of his stay at the château, and its effect on their favorite Searcher, had already leaked out, and some of them had seen him sitting in the "box" at the performance of *She Went to the City* and had been favorably impressed with his appearance. One of them, somewhat more sensitive than the others, had even been slightly concerned that a visiting French officer of such obvious distinction had not been provided with more suitable entertainment, and had been conscious of a passing wish that on some other occasion this might be provided. Now such an opportunity was apparently offered. The corpsman in question stepped up briskly, extending his hand, and all the others followed suit, voicing their welcome.

"Pleased to have you with us, Captain." . . . "The men in the wards will be mighty glad to see you, sir. They're tickled to death with their holly and mistletoe, and the word's got around you sent it to them."

The leader, Doc Anderson, turned to Connie.

"Any special place you want to start this show, Miss Galt?"

"If you don't mind, I'd like to begin with Ward 9, because that's where the idea for this celebration originated. Carl and Tony made the first ornaments out of tin foil and red flannel, and that got all the others started making things too. . . . Then somewhere along the line I want to take in Ward 3 so that Captain de Fremond can see Theodore Roosevelt Lee in all his glory—he's got a regular hedge of holly around him! I know that isn't the logical way to go, but just the same——"

"Who the hell wants to be logical on Christmas Eve? Come on, let's get going!"

The speaker, Howard Callahan, met with a ready response; he had a persuasive personality as well as an angelic voice. Immediately the corpsmen swung into line, with Connie and Tristan bringing up the rear, and marched down Ward Row at a rapid clip, lustily singing "Angels We Have Heard on High." They had just reached the *Gloria* refrain when they arrived at Ward 9, and they entered it still singing with great gusto, swinging down one side of it and halfway up the other before they came to a halt by the Christmas tree which stood in the center. Scarlet poinsettias nestled in its branches and silver balls hung from them; its base was swathed in snowy cotton and its top was crowned with a tin star. Though the tree formed the focal point of the decorations, all the others

73

were worthy of this: at the further end of the ward stood the fireplace made of wrapping paper, its "bricks" realistically crayoned on. Festoons of smilax hung in long loops around every wall, and sprigs of holly and mistletoe were fastened to the headboards of all the cots.

The walking patients had deserted their usual posts by the two stoves, and instead were gathered around the tree and the fireplace, with bits of holly stuck in their bathrobes. Even the bed patients had added this festive touch to their dingy gray pajamas, and nearly all of them were propped up on their pillows. Not to be outdone by her charges, Miss Dryden had wreathed her cap and apron with holly, and as the choristers approached the tree she gaily saluted each in turn. Then as the song came to an end and the hearty applause rang out, she swung her arms wide and beat her hands together in the typical manner of a cheer leader.

"Come on now, boys—all of you together! Let's show these corpsmen they're not the only ones who have voices!"

The cheering rose to a roar, which did not subside until Doc Anderson, who was leading the choristers, gave the signal for silence. Then, in the strange hush which follows a tumult, came the strains of "Once in Royal David's City." It was not until these died down, amidst scattered shouts of "More! More!" that Connie managed to present Tristan to Miss Dryden and to identify him as the donor of the holly and the mistletoe. The blithe little nurse quickly clapped her hands again, calling for attention.

"Hey, you men, listen! Here's the gentleman who sent us all our best decorations, Captain de Fremond. What do you say to that?"

"What's the matter with the Cap'n?" Reuben Ware shouted surprisingly, waving his uninjured arm. Instantly the chorus crashed out a reply.
"*He's* all right!"

"*Who's* all right?" demanded Reuben.

"The Captain!" roared the ward.

"Speech! Speech! Spee——" The demand came from Warsinsky. He strangled as he made it, and the final syllables were swallowed in a cough. But he continued to make insistent motions with his hands. Miss Dryden turned appealingly to Tristan.

"I don't know whether you feel like it or not. But they'd all be awfully pleased if you would."

"Then of course. Not that I am certain I can say the right thing. But I can try. . . ." He stepped slightly aside from the group around the tree, and began to talk slowly and carefully, turning first in one direction and then another so that he would not seem to address any one portion of the ward to the exclusion of the others. "I thank you for your welcome," he said. "But I assure you that as an outsider I consider that I am much privileged to attend this American celebration as your guest, through the kindness of Miss Galt. Also I am happy to know that the little present I was able to make to you, acting for my aunt, has added some cheer to this Christmas you are spending so far from your homes and which is inevitably lonely for you on that account. On future Christmas Eves, when you are in your own country, I hope you may look back on the one you have spent in mine without too many regrets, for the French people have been honored in being your hosts, and have tried to do what little they could to let you know that these are their sentiments." He paused and smiled. "I have said that all very badly," he observed apologetically. "I am a soldier, not an orator, and you all know the difficulties which beset the one who attempts to take the part of the other. Besides, my English is limited. But not, believe me, my goodwill!"

"Say, that was a swell speech!" Tony had come limping up to Tristan, and was now gazing at him in unabashed admiration. "Course you didn't talk like an American woulda done, but just the same, it went over big. . . . Whad'ya think of my flowers?" he continued, pointing a proud finger towards the red-flannel poinsettias. "Keen, ain't they? The whole thing was her idea"—here he jerked his black head in Connie's direction —"but we all done what we could to carry it out."

"You did wonders, Tony," Connie said warmly. "You and all the others too. I'm coming back tomorrow to look at everything in detail. But I'm afraid I have to take Captain de Fremond away now. I see Doc Anderson making signs that we ought to be getting along, and I know we must stop in the private room to see Reed before we leave the building."

"You mean some patient who is dangerously ill?"

"Yes—a dreadful case of septicemia."

In pathetic contrast to the cheerful convalescents propped up in the ward, Reed was lying on his back, the bedclothes almost flat above his emaciated form. With an obvious effort, he turned his head slightly towards his visitors, his sunken eyes lighting and a wan smile briefly illuminating his pale face.

"Hello!" he whispered. "I've been hoping you'd come in here too."

"We'd have come here no matter what else we had to skip. You really know something about music. What do you want to hear most?"

" 'It Came upon a Midnight Clear.' "

The choristers sang it from start to finish. Then, as they began moving towards the door, Connie saw that Reed was making a feeble gesture with one hand, as if he were trying to stop them. She leaned over and spoke to him gently.

"I'm terribly sorry, Reed. But they have to go to so many places!"

Mutely, he turned his head away again, with a sigh of resignation. But Doc Anderson had seen both gestures. He made a signal to stop and his tone was unmistakably forceful.

"It's our rule to give one encore to an evening. We wouldn't think of breaking it. What's your choice, pal?"

" 'I Saw Three Ships Come Sailing By.' "

Again the choristers sang the carol through. Long before they reached the final glad refrain, Connie felt a lump in her throat and realized her eyes were overflowing.

> " 'The Virgin Mary and Christ were there,
> On Christmas Day, on Christmas Day.
> The Virgin Mary and Christ were there,
> On Christmas Day in the morning.' "

She raised her hand to brush away the tears and, with clearing vision, saw that other bystanders' cheeks were also wet. Some of the singing voices were growing husky too.

> " 'And all the bells on earth shall ring,
> On Christmas Day, on Christmas Day,
> And all the angels in Heaven shall sing,
> On Christmas Day in the morning.' "

The song came to an end and this time Reed did not try to stop the singers as they moved towards the door, treading with quiet footsteps. His eyes were serene and the smile had come back to his wan lips. He looked perfectly at peace.

"One more session like that, Connie, and your Paulist Choristers won't hold out through the evening," Doc Anderson said to Connie while they were going down the steps leading into the Row. "They all know Reed's been a church singer himself and they all know just how far gone he is now. . . . Well, I bet the Virgin Mary and Christ *will* be there to welcome him, and all the angels sing. He's the sort that has it coming to him. . . . Look, we must be getting along. Did I understand you to say you'd like to go directly from here to Ward 3 without stopping anywhere else?"

"Yes, if you don't mind."

"Not at all. As we agreed before, Christmas Eve's no time to be logical."

"You don't mean to tell me you're going to pass up my ward while you're down at this end of the Row!" Their progress had suddenly been halted by the unexpected appearance of a tall, red-haired nurse, who bore down upon them from the opposite direction, determination in every line of her face and figure. "I've been watching for you ever since I saw you go into Ward 9," she went on accusingly. "I thought you might try to pull something like this! But I'd have you know my Jerries like Christmas music too, and I don't propose to have them left out of this show!"

"Well, boys, what do you say?"

Doc Anderson had turned and was looking questioningly from his fiery assailant to his choristers. There was a long pause. Then Howard Callahan spoke with unwonted seriousness.

"Well, after all, boys, you know it *is* Christmas Eve."

"Well, come on in, everybody. My Jerries can hardly wait to see you."

There could be no possible doubt of this. Since the choristers themselves had not entered this ward in the middle of a song, no delay in applause was indicated, and the shouting and clapping began at once. Moreover, the visitors had hardly finished their performance when the patients staged one of their own. The sound was at first so soft that it was hard to believe this came from over a hundred throats. But presently it swelled and strengthened, rising in exquisite harmony. The Germans were singing their traditional Christmas hymn as it had first been sung in the snowbound Bavarian village of its simple and touching creation:

> " 'Stille Nacht, heilige Nacht!
> Alles schläft, einsam wacht
> Nur das traute hochheilige Paar.
> Holder Knabe im lockigen Haar,
> Schlaf in himmlischer Ruh,
> Schlaf in himmlischer Ruh.' "

"I have to hand it to those Boches, they do know how to sing," Howard Callahan muttered, turning to Tristan de Fremond as the last notes died away. "There isn't anything the matter with the song itself either. But under the circumstances it seems to me we ought to be singing your Christmas carol somewheres along the line too."

"But we're going to, Howie!" Connie exclaimed quickly. "During Communion at Midnight Mass! You can't have forgotten that!"

"No, I haven't forgotten that. But I thought we might sing it before then too, so the Captain could hear it."

"I should be delighted to hear it twice, of course. I could never hear it too often. But I shall be at the Mass, in any case."

"Oh, if you're staying on——"

Callahan shot a glance at the Frenchman, his voice betraying his surprise. Tristan answered imperturbably.

"Yes, unless I should be intruding. But Miss Galt has been good enough to assure me that I would not."

After the group had reached the Hut, Connie found a "pretext" for remaining there, for serving everyone who came and dancing with everyone who asked her, for doing anything that would keep her away from Tristan until Mass began. Even after the services had started, she was still disquieted; when the time for Communion came, her fingers fumbled over the keys and her eyes filled with tears as she played the ancient hymn which had been written in a Paris barroom and raised to the glory of a Christmas carol revered throughout France:

> " 'Oh holy night, the stars are brightly shining.
> It is the night of our dear Saviour's birth. . . .' "

The choristers sang steadily on, in spite of her faulty playing; the worshipers, Tristan among them, approached the altar rail. Her vision cleared, her mind steadied itself. She found the strength to pray. . . .

She was still praying when Tristan came and stood quietly beside the little organ, waiting for her to look up. The makeshift chapel had emptied fast; even Father Calloran, after one swift glance in the direction of his organist and the man beside her, went quietly away. Connie lifted her head at last, and met Tristan's eyes gazing steadfastly into hers. And suddenly she was not unhappy any more or afraid of anything in the world.

CHAPTER XII

By MID-JANUARY THE Sunday-afternoon visits to Château Chassay had become almost a matter of routine. Just before Christmas the Countess had told Connie to bring half-a-dozen convalescents "without further ceremony" every Sunday about five, and she had done this. Then, after she had ceased to expect any more of the little crested notes, one was delivered to her, not by Robert, who had finally been called up, but by the younger of the two Breton bonnes.

Dear Miss—Connie read with comparable surprise—
Would you well come to tea with my husband and myself in all intimacy this next Sunday instead of bringing with you the soldiers who are in train to get well? We would fix another day so there would be no danger that these would have a deception, but it is understood that you are only on Sundays free and this is a case of urgence. Please make all our excuses to the young men and explain that we will expect double the usual number the Sunday after. In attending you will be very gentle to permit us a small conference with you alone. We shall send the carriage for you at 16½ hours unless you tell Solange that would be an inconvenience for you.
Please accept as always my affectionate salutations.
Elise de Fremond.

Connie read the note through twice, rapidly the first time, slowly the second. Then she looked up and nodded to the bonne. "Please tell Madame la Comtesse it is *bien entendu,* Solange," she said, though actually she did not understand at all, and only replied in this way because she was able to phrase that much French. As a matter of fact she was a good deal puzzled and a little troubled. She could think of no possible reason why the Count and Countess should wish to speak to her privately, least of all on a matter of "great urgency." For all she knew, that expression might be as misleading as the word "parent"; however, she decided that this time she would not try to probe into strange meanings with her friends' help.

Although she had been to Château Chassay so frequently, she had not seen Tristan de Fremond since she had parted from him by the rain barrel after Midnight Mass. The walk between the makeshift chapel and her quarters had consumed a scant ten minutes, and the first part of the short distance had been covered in silence. She was still under the spell of the magic moment when she had looked up and met his eyes, and he apparently was absorbed in regarding the heavens. At last he drew a long breath and stopped, putting a detaining hand gently on her arm.

"Look!" he said in a rapt voice. "The stars *are* brightly shining—that is not just a line in a Christmas hymn, it is a literal fact. After all the rain and mist of the last weeks, the skies are clear. And it is very still. This really is a silent night, there is no doubt of that, and somehow it seems like a holy one too. The strange feeling that it is has been growing on me every minute, while we have walked along."

"It has on me too," Connie whispered.

"And I have been thinking of something else that is very strange too—the similarity of the words in the Germans' song and in our own—'Silent night, holy night, all is calm, all is bright. . . .' 'Oh holy night, the stars are brightly shining.' Do you in your country also have one that is something like that too?"

"Yes, very like. It was written by a bishop in my own state, a man who was greatly beloved and respected by persons of all creeds. It begins:

" 'O little town of Bethlehem,
How still we see thee lie!
Above thy deep and dreamless sleep,
The silent stars go by.' "

"You see! Many different kinds of people, in many different countries, are moved by the same thoughts, in the same way, at a time sacred to all of them. Your hymn was written by a great prelate, ours scribbled by a lonely wastrel, the Germans' composed by a village choirmaster and a parish priest striving together to overcome the handicaps of a broken-down organ. We all celebrate the birth of the Prince of Peace as our supreme festival. And yet we go on from generation to generation striving against each other, killing each other. It is very sad. . . ."

He drew another long breath and this time it ended in a deep sigh. Then he looked down at her and smiled.

"That is a great way for a soldier to talk, is it not?" he asked. "Or when it comes to that, for any man to talk after giving the greeting of 'Joyeux Noël!' . . . "Good night, dear little Searcher. And good-by. May you find less and less weariness and more joy with the coming of the new year!"

So she would not see him again, after all, she realized lying awake in the darkness. But the consciousness brought no new sadness with it, and no wonder as to the reason. To have danced with him on Christmas Day, to have chatted with him in his aunt's drawing room, even to have walked with him in the quiet forest, would have marred the memory of that midnight meeting and starlit parting. They had been perfect and complete in themselves, and she reverted to them over and over again in her thoughts, her fears assuaged, her hopes high, her needs met; meanwhile she threw herself wholeheartedly into her work and it absorbed her as never before.

Immediately after Christmas, when going through the Officers' Ward in a routine way, she stopped by a young lieutenant's bed, merely because it was the first one she happened to pass; he was apparently well on the way to recovery and seemed in good spirits. She entered into casual conversation with him and for some moments they talked quietly about trivial matters; then, feeling that others required her presence she nodded and said she would be on her way. "And good-by if I don't see you again," she added. "I suppose you'll be starting home any day now." She had hardly pronounced the word "home" when a terrible change came over his face; he uttered a piercing shriek and began to twist violently about; then his right arm shot out in the direction of his bedside table. But Connie was quicker than he was; she had seen a razor blade lying uncovered, seized it before he could reach it, and thrown it on the floor; then, leaning over him, she grasped his wrists, speaking to him soothingly. She managed to hold him alone until the occupant of the next bed had leaped to her assistance, and the ward nurse and orderly had reached the madman's bedside. Between them they had pinned him down by the time the ward surgeon came hurrying in, though his struggles continued until he was quieted by a hypodermic. When he sunk into a merciful stupor and been carried away to a private room, Connie turned apologetically to the patient who had helped in the first emergency.

"I didn't know he was a shell-shock case. If I had, I never would have mentioned his going home."

"He hasn't shown the slightest sign of shell shock before. If he had you may be sure a razor would have been taken away from him. And besides, I couldn't have helped noticing something, with his bed right beside mine. He's been coming along fine, as far as I could see, except that he didn't want to get up, and there wasn't any earthly reason why he shouldn't just on account of the little scratch he'd got. Don't you worry for fear you did the wrong thing—no one could have foreseen a fit like that, and most girls would have been petrified with fright when he threw it. Instead you thought quick and acted quick. . . . See here, you're not hurt yourself, are you? That looks to me like blood on your dress."

Connie glanced quickly down at the blue jersey and to her surprise saw red smudges on the skirt. With increasing astonishment she regarded her hand to find that both her thumb and forefinger were gashed.

"I guess I did cut myself a little, but I hadn't even noticed it, in the midst of all this excitement. Perhaps I'd better run along and find some iodine."

"You won't have to run far. In fact, this is one of the times when you better not run at all. And that's an order from the O.D. Come right on into the office."

She turned to see Duncan Craig standing in the adjacent doorway and though aware that the flush which she always found so annoying was already flooding her face, answered imperturbably.

"I'm sorry to have you bothered with it. I'm sure it doesn't amount to much. But just as you say, of course."

He stood aside for her to pass into the cubicle where the surgical supplies were kept and drew out a chair for her beside the one wooden table. Then, seating himself on a stool opposite her, he reached for her hand.

"Let me have a look at this. I want to see how deep those cuts are."

"If they'd been very deep, I'd have noticed them sooner, wouldn't I?"

"Probably. But it's just as well to make sure before I begin swinging iodine around."

She let her hand lie limply on the table while he made his examination and did not flinch when he finally cleaned out the cuts. He laid down the swab and looked at her in his usual quizzical way.

"We'll have to give that a few minutes to dry. We might talk in the meantime."

"All right. What would you like to talk about?"

"I might say first of all that both the nurse and the surgeon are very loud in your praises. They say that if it hadn't been for you that poor devil might have cut his wrists a darn sight worse than you cut your fingers."

"It's very kind of them to praise me. But I don't feel I really deserve it."

"Neither do I. I don't think Red Cross workers ought to go around driving men crazy. It seems to me that form of activity is becoming a regular habit with you. Of course your victims react differently at first, but they give each other ideas just the same. The next thing you know I might be trying to slash my throat."

"Would you have to keep hacking away at it? Couldn't you make one of those nice clean cuts surgeons like to talk about?"

"I might. Or I might ask you to take a hand and help polish me off instead of helping to save me. You're pretty good yourself, when it comes to cutting."

"I consider that a compliment. Like a good surgeon, I pride myself that I never do it except as a last resort. . . . I think the iodine's dry now, don't you?"

"No, not anywhere nearly. Besides, there are several things I'd like to say about two practices allied to the one we've been discussing—namely, cutting in and cutting out. I'm not feeling very friendly these days to either Cris Henderson or Tristan de Fremond. Each of them spoiled an evening for me."

"I'm sure they'd both be deeply distressed to hear it. But at that I didn't get the impression those evenings were spoiled for you."

"Because I was cutting up with Gwen—to go on still further with the allied practices? Why, that was just an attempt to salve a sore heart and hide its hurt under a devil-may-care attitude! You know that, don't you?"

Connie felt the iodine, assuring herself that it really was dry. "Did you want to put a bandage on this before I leave?" she inquired.

"Yes, and while I'm doing it I'd like you to answer my question."

She let her hand lie limp again while he went on with his ministrations. Then as he failed to free it when the bandage was wholly in place, she made an attempt to withdraw it.

"I'd like to go now, Captain Craig, if you don't mind," she said coolly. "You've finished doing what you brought me in here for."

"Oh no I haven't! I've been determined to thrash things out with you ever since you slammed the door in my face, and so far you've managed to avoid me. But now you've played right into my hands—not purposely,

I'll admit, but you've done it just the same. I don't suppose you'll go so far as to cry for help if I detain you a few minutes longer."

"No, I shan't go that far. But as I reminded you the first time we had a private conversation, it isn't generally considered in the line of duty for an officer to confront a subordinate with wholly personal questions. And as I'll remind you now, at the risk of being bromidic, there's a kind of conduct defined as being unbecoming an officer and a gentleman."

He released her hand abruptly and jumped up, pushing back his stool. She saw that for the second time she had infuriated him; but this time she had managed to keep completely cool herself, and before she reached the doorway he caught up with her and spoke with no trace of anger in his voice.

"I apologize," he said earnestly. "You're right again, Connie. I shouldn't have taken advantage of your injury to keep you in here. When it comes to that, I shouldn't have behaved the way I did at the dance, or the movies either, and I ought to have admitted that before, when you tried to talk to me about it, instead of rushing off in a rage. But I'm ready to admit it now. If I say I'm sorry, can't we stop quarreling? I don't want you to quarrel with me all the time. I want you to like me."

"I was beginning to. And then——"

"And then I made a fool of myself. And after that a still worse fool. I know. But I really do have some redeeming qualities." He was speaking more and more persuasively, almost pleadingly, and though he had never before failed to win his point when he brought such pressure to bear, he could see that he was making almost no headway with Connie. "There isn't some other reason why you're avoiding me, is there?" he asked on sudden impulse. "One that I don't know about?"

"I'm not sure whether you know about it or not. But I thought perhaps there was a reason, one we've never mentioned, why you and I ought not to see too much of one another. If you can't guess what it is, I can't tell you. I might be mistaken anyhow."

He looked away, and for a moment he seemed to be considering something which gave him concern, and which he too hesitated to mention. Then he turned back to her, his face clearing. "You're not by any chance thinking about Gwen, are you?" he asked, almost gaily. "Why, bless your heart, Gwen doesn't mean a thing on earth to me!"

"And it isn't possible that she might think she does?"

"No, it isn't. Not by the wildest stretch of the imagination." And as he saw that Connie still hesitated, he added quickly, "I don't mean a thing to Gwen either, if that's what's on your mind. Being you, I suppose it might be. I was even more of a fool than I realized not to think of that before." He was looking at her with greater and greater admiration every minute. "You certainly are a loyal little soul," he said wonderingly. "I hope Gwen appreciates you. She ought to be mighty proud to have you for a friend. I would be. Well, I've told you that before. But I'm telling you again. I'm telling you it would mean the world and all to me. And I'm telling you too that as far as Gwen Foster's concerned there's no reason on earth why you shouldn't be. On my word of honor, Connie."

She returned his steady gaze, her doubts gradually vanishing, her resentment gone. It was not until long afterwards that she wondered whether he had really emphasized Gwen's name in speaking, or whether she had only imagined it.

He did not make the mistake of trying to detain her any longer, or of suggesting definite times for further meetings. But the next day he wrote her a brief note telling her he thought he better have another look at her hand—not that he believed there would be any complication, but of course there was always the slight danger of an infection. He would be in the operating pavilion from five to seven, he said, and perhaps she would drop in between those hours. . . . It was nearly seven when she reached there, for she had been subject, as usual, to unexpected delays: a soldier whose papers were lost, and who therefore could not be discharged, appealed to her for help; he had just heard that his only child, a little girl three years old, was in a critical condition following a mastoid operation, and he was nearly frantic with worry. Connie could do nothing to help locate the papers, she was obliged to tell him, regretfully, but at least she could have the latest news cabled through Red Cross channels, and with this assurance he went away, somewhat comforted. He was just leaving the office however, when Jim Hewitt came into it. The erstwhile reprobate was taking his engagement to Lois very seriously; he seemed to regard it less as an affair of the heart than as a challenge to a nobler way of life. Now that he was beloved by a lady, it behoved him to become a gentleman; but he was somewhat puzzled as to ways and means of accomplishing this end and hopeful that Connie might enlighten him. She was obliged to listen long and patiently to his story and to choose her words carefully in making tactful suggestions.

Just as she was about to leave her office, the lastest edition of *The Stars and Stripes* was brought in and dumped down in front of her, and she knew she must distribute the papers through the wards before she did anything else. She could not deprive the men of the pleasure they took in their paper, or even delay this. Starting out with the heavy package under her arm, she met Madame Bonnier, who stopped her reproachfully as she hurried past with only a nodded greeting. Mam'zelle always used to buy both the You Awk Er*rol* and the She-car-*go* Tree*bune;* would she not buy one little paper today? Madame Bonnier drew her maroon sweater more closely around her ample, untidy person and shivered. Connie bought both papers and laughingly indicated her own bundle before she hurried on again.

"See, I'm delivering papers too. We're colleagues."

She left Madame Bonnier not only placated but delighted. However, all this consumed so much time that Craig was scrubbing up after his last operation when she finally reached the pavilion. He greeted her with undisguised relief.

"Hello there! I was beginning to lose hope—not that I really thought you'd back out, this round, but of course I couldn't help wondering."

"I'm sorry. It's just the same old story. I never know when I'm going to be held up or why or for how long."

"And of course you'd never tell anyone to get the hell out of there when you wanted to make a getaway from the office yourself. Well, never mind, as long as you finally did come. Let's have a look at that hand."

He snipped the bandage apart, unrolled it expertly, and examined the cuts with care. "They're coming along all right, but they're pretty deep at that," he said. "Do they hurt much?"

"Only when I try to use my hand. It's awkward having it tied up."

"No sharp shooting pains going up your arm?"

"No—just a little local soreness."

"You're a good soldier yourself, Connie. Your pretty little ears would burn if you knew all the nice things I've heard about you today."

He reached for fresh supplies and began to use them. Connie laughed a little ruefully.

"I told you before I didn't deserve those nice things. If that razor had been a gun, I might not have snatched at it so quickly."

"I should hope not. It might have gone off and then there really would have been trouble."

"Yes, I know. But that wasn't what I meant. I meant I'd have dreaded the noise it might make so much I'd have shrunk instinctively from touching it."

"You'd have dreaded the noise so much?" Craig repeated incredulously.

"Yes. Ever since I can remember loud sudden noises have done something queer to me. The first time I went to a birthday party I burst out crying when all the other children began to pull their snappers. I was finally sent home, still in tears and more or less in disgrace. You can just imagine how long it was before I had another invitation! And Fourth of July was really a hideous ordeal for me. I used to stay in my room with my head buried in my pillow, but still I couldn't altogether shut out the sound of the cannon crackers. Of course all the boys in the neighborhood took a malign delight in setting them off under my window."

"And you've never outgrown this phobia?"

"No, never. If anything, it's grown worse. I couldn't help wondering what I'd do if I got anywhere near the firing line in France. Of course I didn't know when I volunteered that the war'd be over almost as soon as I landed."

"But in spite of your horror you went ahead and volunteered just the same?"

"Oh yes. I had to do that—something made me. So I had to take a chance on the noise, and hope and pray I'd find some way to stand it or even overcome it. But I don't know. . . . After the captain of the *Grampion* told us, on the way over, that in case a submarine was sighted, the siren would sound three sharp blasts, I kept listening for it. I didn't waste any time worrying about what might happen if a sub did actually hit us, but I dreaded hearing those blasts."

Craig laid down his scissors and put away his gauze. "What you've just told me is extremely interesting to me, both as a physician and as a friend," he remarked. "I'd like to talk to you about it a little longer—a good deal longer in fact. But it's after seven-thirty now and I'm starving to death. Will you hit me over the head with your one good hand if I tell you that, no matter what you think to the contrary, I am convinced the long-awaited moment has now arrived for our dinner at the Petit Saint-Jean?"

Laughingly, she had agreed with him and they had gone into Nantes together, not only that evening, but on New Year's Eve as well. Feeling as she did about noise, the Hut would be no place for her that evening, Craig reminded her; it would be the scene of an ungodly racket until the wee small hours. She knew that in this instance at least he was not stressing one point to gain another, and readily fell in with his suggestion for a tête-à-tête dinner at a quiet restaurant. When he ordered a *fil"ette de Muscadet* and *caneton à la nantaise,* he noticed that she lapsed into temporary abstraction, and that afterwards she seemed to show an un-wonted degree of interest in the menu. Would they have *petits beurres* too, she inquired? And were those funny little fish really *brochets?* But there was nothing in her attitude which suggested intentional withdrawal, and except for her few trivial and natural questions, she followed his conversational lead throughout the leisurely and delicious meal, sipped without objection the wine he ordered, and lingered without urging over the coffee and cordial. When these were finally finished too, he asked her casually, whether she would feel like dropping by the Officers' Club to have a dance or two and see the New Year in, she agreed, still without pressure; and she drank a toast with the others. Though she did not share Gwen's predilection for Sister Rouge and Sister Blanc and could not distinguish fine vintages from poor ones, as Tilda did with such care, the severity of her attitude towards "the cup that cheers" had relaxed considerably, and the amenity of her mood had not changed when he said good night to her at her own door.

"We had a pretty good time, didn't we?"

"Yes, wonderful."

"And we've got lots more like it ahead of us, haven't we?"

"I hope so."

"I hope so too. And it won't ever be my fault again if we don't." He paused, giving weight to his last words. "You can give me a very happy new year, Connie. Will you?"

"I'll try."

"That's all I need to know—for now. Good night, Connie."

"Good night—Duncan. And Happy New Year!"

After the departure of Lois for Savenay, Gwen had moved in with Tilda, leaving Connie in sole possession of the room which the two had formerly shared. Tilda, it appeared, was dependent upon the company of a roommate to ward off homesickness in her more depressed moments; and though Connie had not previously realized that Tilda had moments of such deep depression, she herself had been secretly pleased at the proposed rearrangement, having always minded the lack of privacy more than any other phase of camp life. She entered her quarters on New Year's Eve to find them completely deserted and delightfully quiet. Gwen must be still at Blottereau, Tilda still at the Hut, she realized; and glancing at the little clock on the wooden shelf, Connie saw that it was only two and knew that the other girls would not be in for at least another hour. Then she caught sight of a square white box, tied with gauze ribbon, which was lying on her bed, and hurried to open it, gladder than ever to be alone, since her solitude freed her from questioning eyes.

The light, folded papers within the box parted to disclose a big bunch of purple violets, encircled with glossy leaves and confined with a tasseled cord of green silk to which a small envelope was attached. She regarded this envelope with no feeling of curiosity, conscious only of mild surprise because the flowers had not reached her in time to wear that evening, and because Craig had not mentioned them. Then, almost mechanically she withdrew the enclosed card, and read the superscription with startled eyes:

Before long the woods at Chassay will be full of violets instead of holly and I hope we may gather many of them together. Meantime I send you this small bunch to let you know of these hopes and to bear with it the repetition of one I have already expressed—that all your sorrows may be lightened and all your joys doubled in the coming year.
Faithfully yours,
Tristan de Fremond

She gazed at the little card with increasing joy and wonder, all the rapture of Christmas returning to her in a strange joyous rush; then, sitting down on her bed, she picked up the violets and buried her face in them. They were deliciously cool and fresh, and she drew in deep breaths of their fragrance before putting them down beside her on the bed, and, still touching them with one hand, turned the little note over and over with the other. At last she replaced the violets in their box, and set this on the suitcase which served as a bedside table; but she left the cover off and the papers parted, and frequently during the night she leaned over to smell them again, and to reread the note with the help of her flashlight. She did not sleep very much. She did not want to. If she had slept she would have missed many moments of unexpected gladness.

In the morning she pinned the violets to her uniform, and wore them throughout New Year's Day; but she did this rather self-consciously, first because a bouquet was such an unaccustomed ornament that it made her feel conspicuous, and later because she found that it was the object of so much general interest and comment. Some of the remarks made to her were sly and some were broad, but almost universally they hinted at Craig as the donor; when he himself saw them, he looked rather fixedly, first at Connie and then at the flowers, though he did not mention these either immediately or in the course of their numerous meetings afterwards. Meanwhile he gave her several presents himself: a little silver ermine and a Breton fleur-de-lis to add to the charms on her bracelet—he

86

had meant to give these to her on Christmas Day, he said, but at that time they were not speaking. They laughed together at the idea that they had been so silly and she handed him the bracelet so that he could add the new charms; then he fastened it on again for her. The next night he brought her two pairs of buckskin gloves; and a beribboned basket of *petits fours* from the best *pâtisserie* in Nantes, a tea cloth of Breton lace, and some pretty pottery to use with it, all followed each other in rapid succession.

Connie was pleased with these presents and showed it; but she could not wholly suppress a feeling that they might not have been either as numerous or as costly if Tristan's offering had not come first, and none of them moved her as much as the violets. When she wrote to Tristan thanking him for these, she tried to tell him how much they had meant to her; and when she did not receive a letter herself acknowledging hers, she wondered once or twice whether she had perhaps erred in saying either too little or too much. But as she sat fingering the note that Solange had brought her and trying to solve, unaided, the mystery of its contents, she did not connect it in any way with her New Year's present. And the mystery was still unsolved the following Sunday when she descended from the old-fashioned landau at the entrance to Château Chassay, and the older bonne admitted her to the long, cold corridor.

CHAPTER XIII

THE DRAWING-ROOM door swung open, disclosing the Count and Countess at their usual posts in their accustomed setting, with a cheery fire burning and an inviting table already prepared for tea. The porcelain, Connie noticed, was not the same she had seen used for tea before; this was a very beautiful Sèvres service, reserved, she would have supposed, for great occasions. The Countess was wearing several very beautiful rings and some fine laces that Connie had never seen before, and it seemed to her that her hostess's manner had changed too: if anything, it was more cordial than ever. On Connie's arrival, the Countess had kissed her on both cheeks for the first time; but now that she was serving the tea, she somehow made a ceremonial of this usually simple rite, though she still chatted with her accustomed friendliness. She had just had a letter from Robert, she said; he was finding the *caserne* at Vannes rather bleak, but on the whole, everything was going well with him. . . . She had been into Nantes the day before, and had found Madame Carpentier very happy over her husband's unexpected return. . . . Madame Helle was also in a state of considerable excitement, for a very different reason: Ninette, her most magnificent Persian, had just given birth to five beautiful kittens! The conversation went on and on without giving the slightest clue to the "urgent matter" which the Countess had written she felt impelled to discuss. It was not until Solange had been summoned to clear the tea table—another unprecedented formality—and had left the room, closing the door carefully after her with her broad foot, that the Countess came over to the little sofa where she had installed Connie and, sitting down beside her, took her hand and pressed it gently.

"My dear," she said, looking at the girl, her eyes suffused with kindness, "my dear Constance—you will, I hope, permit that I shall now call you Constance?"

"I'd like very much to have you. I've been wondering for a long time why you didn't."

"We are perhaps old-fashioned in our ways," the Countess said with a slight sigh. "It does not come so easily to us, using the Christian names of persons we have known only a short time. However, in your case, it is of course different. . . . You have perhaps guessed what it is, the matter of urgency which indicated this small conference?"

"I'm sorry. I haven't the slightest idea. I've been rather worried since I received your note. I hope nothing is wrong?"

"No, no, nothing is wrong. I regret to have caused you anxiety."

"It would perhaps be well if we should explain at once," suggested the Count.

"Yes, yes. We must not, in effect, delay."

Constance waited expectantly. The Count and Countess, having agreed that it was time to come to the point, exchanged glances without saying anything further for several minutes. Then the Countess sighed again, not as if she were really distressed, but as if she felt a sigh appropriate under the circumstances.

"I believe our parent, Tristan de Fremond, informed you that he is an orphan?" she said at last.

"Yes. He told me so the first time I met him. I was very sorry to hear it. You see I'm an orphan myself. So I know how hard it is to be without a father and mother."

"You have our sympathy. We had indeed gathered that this was your situation, from Tristan. It seems you and he exchanged confidences."

"Perhaps we did. Why yes, we must have. But I haven't thought of it in just that way before." With her usual annoyance when this happened, she realized that she was blushing. "I believe I did tell him I was brought up by a great-aunt," she ended lamely.

"Yes, and Madame this great-aunt, it would appear, lives at a vast distance from Europe, in North America, and has never visited France or become acquainted with French customs. Tristan felt that under the circumstances, it would perhaps be better if we should speak to you directly, instead of addressing ourselves first to Madame your great-aunt."

"You wanted to get in touch with Aunt Bertha about something?"

"Since we are Tristan's nearest parents, it is of course entirely proper that we should speak for him. But it would be more proper if we could address first Madame your great-aunt, and then, if we secured her consent and approval, talk with you."

"My dear Elise, I fear you are still not making this important matter clear to our guest."

Connie looked gratefully at the Count. Her bewilderment had now reached the stage where she was not only deeply puzzled but exceedingly nervous. However, she felt she must apologize for her density.

"I know I'm terribly stupid. But I don't understand a single word you've said to me so far. I mean I don't see what connection Aunt Bertha has with——"

"Our parent, Tristan de Fremond, has requested that in his behalf we should ask for your hand in marriage."

The tardy statement was certainly not lacking in clarity. But it had almost the force of an unexpected blow. Connie recoiled as if she had been suddenly struck by a hand hitherto extended only in kindness.

"Oh no!" she exclaimed. "You can't mean that! . . . You're—you're joking."

"My dear Constance, I assure you that it is not the custom in France to jest on questions of such a nature."

For the first time, a slight stiffness had crept into the Countess's tone. But having administered her mild reproof, she went on, this time speaking slowly and patiently, as if she had begun to recognize the need of great tact and gentleness.

"I must ask your pardon. I knew there was a difference in our customs, but not that it was so very great. Neither did I realize that Tristan's request would so completely amaze you, since it was evident from the very first that he regarded you with great respect and admiration and that soon he also felt an even greater tenderness for you."

"But I didn't know he regarded me with respect and admiration from the first! I saw him looking at me that night at dinner when I kept making mistakes——"

"You kept making mistakes?" the Countess repeated, bewildered in her turn. "But what mistakes, my dear Constance?"

"I didn't save my fork, I didn't know how to eat artichokes, I knocked over my wineglass."

The Countess laughed comfortably, then patted the girl's hand. "And you thought Tristan was looking at you critically because you did not save your fork, and so on? He was not thinking of forks, I assure you. His eyes were fixed upon your hair. He told me, after you left that evening, that he had never seen such beautiful hair. And from there he went on to mention various other ways in which you compelled his attention— oh, not all in the same speech, *bien entendu!* But little by little. My husband and I both realized before his permission was over that he was very much *épris*. And you were not conscious of it at all?"

Connie's blush deepened. "I have heard the word '*épris*' before, but I'm not sure I know exactly what it means," she said hesitantly. "If it just means finding that someone's unusually congenial, liking someone a whole lot—why, yes. I suppose I did realize he felt that way about me —after a while. But if it means being seriously in love—thinking about marriage—— No, I never imagined that for a moment!"

"My dear child, when a young man like Tristan becomes attached to a young girl like yourself, it is always a serious matter. He does not allow himself to think of her except in terms of marriage." Again a slight stiffness had crept into her manner. But as she went on, she spoke with regret rather than reproof. "Evidently there are shades of meaning which are not quite clear to either of us, due to differences of language as well as of customs. However, I assure you that when I said Tristan was *épris*, I did indeed mean that he regarded you with the utmost devotion and that he hoped you might return this feeling. Were these hopes then vain? Were you not drawn to him in the least?"

"Yes. Yes, I was drawn to him," Connie said candidly. "I liked looking at him too. He's very attractive, I don't need to tell you that. And I enjoyed talking to him. I find it natural to tell him things I don't ordinarily speak about. I didn't know why, I didn't try to analyze it. I just found it was."

"Now that is all very well," said the Countess encouragingly, patting Connie's hand once more. "You do not dislike him, that is already something."

"I don't see how anyone could possibly dislike him," Connie said, taking heart and speaking with increasing candor. "I didn't know he respected and admired me—that is, in the way you say—but I certainly respect and admire him. There's something about him that commands respect and admiration. And—trust. Not many men make you feel, first of all, that you can trust them. At least I've never known many that did."

"But my dear Constance, if Tristan has already commanded your respect and admiration and confidence, why should you cry out as you did when I told you that he desired to marry you?"

"Because it was such a shock. I never thought of anything like that in connection with him."

"I fear that I was very maladroit in my approach to the subject. I have already told you how sorry I am for that. I should have prepared you better. But now that the shock is over, you will give favorable thought to this declaration, will you not?"

"I'm terribly sorry, but I don't see how I could."

"Now, now!" said the Countess, repeating her comforting gesture. "You do not need to say, 'Yes yes, I well wish to marry him, this same day,' if you would not; but you can say you would well think of it."

"But that wouldn't be fair if I knew all the time I was going to say no in the end."

"But why should you be so certain that in the end you would say no? Are you then so sure that our parent could not give a young girl happiness?"

"No, it isn't that. I should think he could make almost any girl happy. I've—I've been very happy in his presence, every time I've seen him."

"*Alors,* if you have already been happy in his presence knowing him slightly, why can you not believe that you might be still happier knowing him better? You have said yourself that he commands sentiments of admiration. It is true. He has a very estimable character. Not that he has failed to commit his little follies, like any normal young man. But there have never been any entanglements, and that phase is far behind him now. There is no reason for fearing that you would not have his entire devotion."

"It isn't that either. I wish I could explain better. But I can't."

The Countess turned towards her husband, hoping for help.

"Perhaps we should dwell for a few moments not only on Tristan's attachment to our guest, but on some of his more material qualifications," the Count said practically. "To be sure, he is not wealthy, but he has a competence. And a title."

"A title!"

"Yes. Titles are not generally used in the French Army by officers below the rank of general. Nevertheless, it is a very old and honorable one. And there is every reason to suppose that someday he will be a general. He is very young to be a captain. And his position in the Cadre Noir carries with it enormous prestige. In itself it is a mark of distinction. You have gathered that, have you not, mademoiselle?"

"Yes, I've gathered that. Not that I know exactly what the Cadre Noir is and does. Everyone seems to take it for granted that of course I must, and I haven't liked to ask too many questions. But even without understanding, I'm sure I couldn't help to maintain its prestige. I wouldn't know how. I'd be afraid to try. And as for a title——"

"The Cadre Noir constitutes a special section in the Cavalry School at Saumur," explained the Count, interrupting her gently but firmly and making no immediate reference to the fears she expressed. "As a unit, it is concerned with the history of military equitation and with all questions pertaining to this high art, of which it is the faithful guardian, conserving its character of exactitude, intrepidity, and elegance—all this in accordance with the most exalted French traditions, as interpreted by the greatest masters, whose methods have been carefully codified. It is commanded by an officer known as the *écuyer en chef* or *instructeur en chef d'équitation*—titles which are rather difficult to present idiomatically. The literal translations are 'Chief Squire' and 'Chief Instructor of Equitation.' The rank of *écuyer en chef* is never lower than that of *commandant* and it may be as high as that of colonel; colloquially he is very generally known as *le grand dieu*—the great god. This will give you some idea of the enormous respect, not to say reverence, with which he is regarded. Under him he has eleven *officiers instructeurs d'équitation*— *écuyers* and *sous-écuyers*—who are colloquially known as *les dieux*. Tristan is one of the *écuyers*. Again I find it hard to give you a literal translation. However, perhaps you are beginning to grasp the general idea."

"Yes, I'm beginning," Constance said falteringly. "But——"

"The officers of this special unit normally wear black," the Count went on relentlessly. "Hence the term Cadre Noir—Black Staff. You have not seen Tristan in this uniform because it has not yet been resumed since the war. But it soon will be, and I asure you it is very striking. Moreover, its resumption will serve to differentiate further between the officers of the Cadre Noir and the other officers of the school, making the formers' unit seem more exclusive than ever. Because the latter, who are in charge of all other types of military instruction and who are naturally far more numerous, are *not* resuming the gray-blue uniforms which originally caused them to be designated as the Cadre Bleu. They will merely have insignia with gray-blue backgrounds. But I am sure the Cadre Rose will remain unshorn of all its delightful adornments."

"The Cadre Rose?" inquired Constance, wondering how many cadres the Count would insist upon talking about. For a long time she had wanted to learn more about the mysterious and exalted Cadre Noir; but instead of being grateful to the Count because he had finally enlightened her, she was becoming almost resentful because he would not permit her to escape.

"The charming ladies who are married to the officers at the school, or closely related to them," the Count announced, beaming. "Among whom you will certainly be one of the most charming of all."

"I certainly shall not. Oh, I don't mean to sound so ungracious, Monsieur de Fremond! But I can't marry your nephew."

The Count and Countess looked at each other silently. The Count now stopped stroking his beard and retreated to his accustomed place by the fire, where he again stood flapping his coattails, his kindly countenance overcast. His wife made a slight signal indicating sadly that she hoped he would try to help her further, but he shook his head sadly back and forth and then cocked it slightly to one side, as if the better to hear what this strange young American would say next.

"You have another attachment yourself?" the Countess persisted patiently, abandoning hope of her husband's assistance. "Another obligation perhaps?"

"No, I haven't any other attachment or obligation. I told you I couldn't explain. I am very much touched by your parent's proposal, very much honored. But I must ask you to tell him that I can't think of accepting it."

"Then you must give some good reason for declining to do so. Tristan would not consider any that you have so far mentioned as having merit. He would simply say that you must inevitably come to care for him in the end, since you already like him so much, and since you do not think of any other suitor with a greater sense of obligation or with more tenderness. And he would add that as far as the question of time is concerned, he is entirely at your disposition. Indeed, I am sure that he will consider it to your credit that you did not give an immediate answer in the affirmative. It shows a certain delicacy which he will appreciate."

"I'm afraid I still haven't given you the right idea. I'm not being coy and I'm not trying to turn things over in my mind." With a desperate sense of being at bay, Connie cast about for some objection that would put an end to the Countess's pleading. Then she had a sudden inspiration. "Captain de Fremond would take it for granted that his wife would have a dowry, wouldn't he?" she asked. "I haven't a cent."

"*Tiens!*" said the Countess, in a tone of great surprise, looking at her guest with unconcealed curiosity. "Your poor parents then had no time to make proper provision for you before they left you an orphan? They were perhaps killed together in a railroad accident while you were still an infant?"

"No, they died about two years apart—my father of pneumonia, and my mother of cancer. They were both sick a long time, and their illnesses used up all the money there was—it wasn't much. Anyway, it isn't customary for American girls to have dowries. At least, I never heard of one who did."

"*Tiens!*" said the Countess again. Obviously Connie's latest disclosure was the most amazing of any that had been made throughout the whole fantastic afternoon. "Tristan will of course be surprised," she went on thoughtfully. "And his surprise will be tinged with regret. Not on his own account. To be sure, a cavalry officer is always put to greater expense than one in any other branch of the service and a wealthy wife, under such circumstances, can always be of great help to her husband. But I do not need to tell you that there are no mercenary motives back of Tristan's declaration, and he has always been satisfied to live with great simplicity, aside from the maintenance of his horses. But he would wish his wife to have every comfort, and I am afraid that will not be possible with only his *rentes*—how do you say, income? Yes, that is it—with only his income to live on. He would like very much to retire from the Cadre Noir as soon as he may properly do so—and spend all his time at his château. He is very fond of Normandy and of the type of country life he can enjoy at Malou. You might find it a little *monotone,* but on the whole I do not think it would be distasteful to you, and such a mode of living is not too dull. Yes, with care, I think you could do very well on Tristan's *rentes* if you lived at Malou. Or if you objected to his retirement, and he remained in the cavalry, then he would still have his salary. And *voilà! Tout s'arrangera!*"

The Countess beamed benignantly at Connie. Having settled this point satisfactorily, to herself at least, she seemed to feel that there was nothing further to discuss. Connie sought for some fresh objection.

"I wouldn't want to live on my husband's income if it weren't customary for a wife to do that in this country," she said. "And I certainly wouldn't want to stand in the way of his having proper equipment for his position, or of his retirement, if he felt the time had come for that. Having a dependent wife might make just the difference—between being able to live comfortably on his income and being obliged to go on with the grind to earn more money, I mean. Besides, I've just thought of another difficulty even greater than the one connected with money, and that's the question of religion. Have you forgotten that I am not a Catholic?"

"Have I forgotten? But my dear child, this is the first I have heard of it, so how could I forget it? Are Catholics then nonexistent in your country, like dowries?"

"No," Connie answered, suppressing an almost hysterical inclination to laugh. "They don't come in quite the same category. As a matter of fact, there are a good many Catholics in the United States. But in the part I come from——" She stopped abruptly. She could not very well tell a countess who lived in a château, and who numbered princes and potentates among her relatives, that in certain circles of Winchester, Massachusetts, Catholics were not considered among the socially elect. "My people have always been Protestants," she ended rather feebly, "my people and all my friends."

"My dear Elise, you have always said yourself that the Edict was unnecessarily harsh and that some of the Huguenots came from quite acceptable families," the Count reminded his wife, putting in a word for the first time in a long while. "This is perhaps an opportunity to prove to ourselves, in a practical way, that the days of intolerance are over."

"Ye–es," the Countess murmured rather vaguely. Then, gathering her forces again, she turned to Constance and spoke with resolution, as if determined to put an end to a troublesome question at once. "Yes, the days of intolerance are over," she agreed. "Nevertheless, you understand, of course, that all your children would have to be brought up in the Church. You would be obliged to promise that, formally, in writing, before the marriage ceremony could take place."

"I'm afraid I couldn't agree to anything like that. I'm afraid I'd feel that was something my children ought to decide for themselves later on. That is, if I had any—of course, perhaps I wouldn't." She was coloring again, but this time she was less conscious of her blush, because she was otherwise preoccupied. "So you see that settles it. I couldn't marry a Catholic under such conditions," she said earnestly. "Besides, I don't believe mixed marriages can be successful, even if there isn't any question of children. I think there must always be a danger of friction between the husband and wife on questions of religion."

She rose, almost triumphantly. Never had she entertained such a kindly feeling for the Catholic Church as in this moment when it seemed to be offering her escape. But her triumph was short-lived.

"Tristan would never permit friction to arise between himself and his wife. He is far too tactful," the Countess told her, rising also. She did not speak indignantly; but in spite of her measured tones, Connie knew that her hostess felt she was herself unjustified in disparaging her suitor by such a reference. "And the Church is very wise," the Countess went on. "Without wisdom, it could not have endured nearly two thousand years. I think you could count on it to solve your problem, if you would only permit this. After all, it has solved many others."

She paused, sighing more sadly than she had done before; then she smiled, rather uncertainly. "However, that is neither here nor there," she said. "Now that we have made the indicated first approach we shall have to let Tristan plead his own cause—which no doubt he will do at his first opportunity. I am sorry, very sorry, for his sake and a little for yours, that we have failed so signally. It is not every day that a young girl inspires in a young man of fine principles the feeling you have awakened in him. And I know that Tristan's attachment to you is sincere and strong; he will find it hard when such sentiments have been inspired to learn that they are not returned. As for my husband and myself, we were ready to welcome you into our family with open arms. So we have our small disappointment too."

Connie tried to answer, but she could not, because of a strangling in her throat. She was very close to sobs.

94

"You would like to go back to the camp now, would you not?" the Countess asked quietly, without appearing to notice her guest's agitation. "I will ring and have the carriage brought around at once. And I shall count on you to remember that next Sunday you are to bring double the usual number of young men who are in train to get well. We shall try to make a real fete of the occasion."

Her essential kindness, like her essential dignity, was impervious to bafflement. Only a really great lady, Connie knew, would, or could, have responded in such a way to the refusal of a strange and obscure girl to accept the welcome and the alliance offered by an old and noble house. Again she struggled for speech, and this time she succeeded in voicing what was in her heart.

"I do think I'd better go back to camp now," she said. "I'm grateful to you for understanding. But I can't go without telling you how grateful I am for—for everything else too. Your—your good opinion of me. Your willingness to take me into your family. You can't know how much that means to me. You see I've never had a family, and to think I could have been almost like a daughter in your home——" She stopped for a moment, overcome by the knowledge of all she was renouncing. "But it wouldn't be fair," she said. "I—I couldn't cheat like that. I'll try to explain some day. To you—and to your nephew."

CHAPTER XIV

DURING THE NEXT few days, the impression that something was wrong with Constance Galt became more and more general at Base 11.

The first person to notice this, strangely enough, was Father Calloran; returning Sunday evening to the makeshift chapel for a stole which he had left there among his other vestments after Mass that morning, he was amazed, when he switched on a light, to see the little Searcher sitting on a rear bench, in an attitude of deep dejection. She jumped up instantly and, after a startled exclamation, stammered an apology.

"Why, Father Calloran! I had no idea you'd be coming back here in the evening! And perhaps I shouldn't have come myself."

"Of course you should have, if you wanted to. I'm not going to stay—don't let me disturb you. I had an emergency call for a confession and I needed to get my stole. But that's under my hand right now."

He picked it up and turned again towards the door, nodding without further comment. It was Connie who felt impelled to speak again.

"I wanted to be alone and I couldn't think of any place but this. I knew it would be open and empty, and the friends who share my quarters drop in and out of my room all the time—of course you know there aren't any doors. Generally I'm very glad of their company, because I'm fond of them both. But tonight I didn't feel like talking. There was something I had to think over."

"My dear child, there's no reason why you should try to justify your presence here. Or to explain it, unless you want to. At least not to me. Priests are reared in the tradition of a Church which believes in keeping its doors open at all times, not only for those who wish to worship, but for those in need of prayer and meditation. Stay here as long as you like."

He put his hand lightly on her shoulder, smiling reassuringly, and as he did so he saw that there were undried tears on her cheeks.

"And don't hestitate to let me know if I can be of any help to you," he added quietly. Then he switched out the light again and went on his way. After hearing the urgent confession of an agitated penitent who had suddenly sought him out in his own quarters, he wandered back to the chapel, less with the idea of replacing his stole than in finding out whether the distraught girl was still there. She was not, and she made no effort to get in touch with him afterwards.

Connie had broken a dinner engagement with Duncan Craig Sunday on the ground of a bad headache, and she was so obviously upset that he took his disappointment that evening not only philosophically but sympathetically; however, when she continued her excuses, his temper got the better of him and they quarreled again. Tilda and Gwen meanwhile found her so unresponsive to all friendly overtures that they took offense and ceased to make these, and a barrier, so real that it seemed tangible and visible, rose between the two rooms. Connie no longer needed to seek solitude; she had it without the asking. Then a letter arrived which she had half hoped and half dreaded to receive, absorbing her thoughts completely.

Ecole de Cavalerie, Saumur
26 January, 1919

My dear Constance:
I am so sorry to learn from my aunt that a certain visit you made her proved painful to you. I see now that it would have been better if I had spoken to you before I left Château Chassay, in such a way as to prepare you for a definite declaration later. However, please believe me when I tell you that it would have been far easier for me to speak than to remain silent. I have loved you almost from the moment we met, and nothing in the world—except, of course, the accomplished fact—could make me so happy as your promise to become my wife. I thought to do you honor by courting you according to our customs; instead of this I have succeeded only in distressing you, and I believe needlessly. I still venture to hope that in spite of this first error of judgment, for which I ask your forgiveness, I shall eventually succeed in making you believe that you could find happiness in my suit and still greater happiness in the fullness of my love. At all events, I know you will not deny me the opportunity of trying to convince you of this and, with such an end in view, I applied for special leave as soon as I heard from my aunt. I have finally obtained it for next Sunday, 2 February, and shall therefore leave for Nantes on that day, proceeding immediately to the camp, which I should reach about the middle of the afternoon. I shall then come to your office in the confident expecta

*tion of a kind reception and a fair hearing. In the meantime, please accept
the assurance of my entire devotion.*

Toujours à vous,

Tristan de Fremond

Contance glanced at the calendar. The postmark on Tristan's note was January 27, and this meant that it had been three days en route; even if she answered immediately, her reply would not reach him before he left Saumur. Besides, she did not feel equal to replying immediately. In spite of the formality with which he had written, Tristan's words were extremely moving to her; she could not bring herself to respond indifferently when she was so greatly touched. But neither could she give him the encouragement which alone would satisfy him. She went mechanically on with her work, but she could not help dwelling more and more on her own problems and when Sunday came, she acted with unaccustomed firmness in clearing her office of all inopportune visitors. Tristan's arrival found her in sole occupancy of it, though this result had not been achieved without a struggle; and when she opened the door for him, only her quick color betrayed her lack of inner composure.

"Won't you come in?" she asked gravely. Then, realizing that this was inadequate, she added, "I'm glad to see you again."

"Not half as glad as I am to see you," he answered, entering quickly and closing the door after him. "Especially as your reception indicates that I am to have a chance to plead my own cause."

"I didn't see how I could refuse you that. Anyway, you didn't give me time to answer your letter."

"Perhaps I planned it that way. Would you think I had been very unfair if I admitted to you that this was so?"

"No. But I don't want to be unfair either. I did feel you had a right to talk to me yourself, because you seemed so sure that would make a difference, and because you apparently hoped so much that it might. But before you begin I think I ought to tell you that it won't. I'm terribly sorry. But I know that in the end I'll have to give you the same answer that I gave the Countess."

"Suppose we do not worry about the end just now. Suppose we begin by thinking about the beginning. And suppose you leave the intervening time to me—remember my family motto!" His smile had such a contagious quality that Connie's gravity was not proof against it; she smiled faintly in return. "But this office does not seem to me the best place for a confidential talk of any kind," Tristan continued, glancing about him. "Since the French method has failed, and today we are to try courtship à *l'américaine,* would you go for a walk with me? To Orvault perhaps, if you have not already been in that direction? We would reach it by cutting across country and going through some lovely lanes with high banks topped by *fagot* trees. And we would have an objective—there is a curious crossroads *calvaire* at Orvault which I wish very much to show you—a large *calvaire* that surmounts a little chapel and has curved steps going up to it on either side. I do not think that this walk would be too long for you to take without fatigue, but of course we could stop and rest whenever you wished. It is unseasonably mild today, almost like spring. You would not be cold if we sat down on a big stone somewhere."

"You mean we'd talk while we rested?"

"I should most certainly do so, yes. But you need not say anything in reply unless you feel like it. I am not going to try to wring a confidence or a promise from you against your will, you may depend on that."

"I do depend on it. And you make the walk sound very attractive, Tristan."

Quite easily and naturally she had called him for the first time by his Christian name. He immediately grasped the significance of this, though she did not.

"Well, that was rather the idea," he said almost lightly. "At least it was very definitely the hope."

As if there were nothing more to be said on the subject, she reached for the cape lying over the back of her unused chair. Tristan took it from her gently and placed it over her shoulders, with a gesture indicative of a caress; then they went out of the office together and headed at once towards the gate, where Arkie, who had just come on duty, saluted, grinning broadly.

"How're you, Captain? Nice to see you back. Taking to the tall timber again?"

Tristan returned both the salute and the smile, but, plainly puzzled, appealed to Connie for enlightenment. "Just what does he mean by that, the good Arkie?" he asked under his breath. "My manual of conversation said nothing about taking to the tall timbers." And when Connie explained, laughing a little in spite of herself, Tristan laughed too.

"No, Sergeant, I suggested a cross-country walk instead of the woods this time," he said. "I want to show Miss Galt the *calvaire* at Orvault."

"I've been there myself. It's a mighty pretty little place. But it's a far piece from here, so it wouldn't surprise me if you'd be kind of late getting back. Well, good luck to you anyway!"

Connie had expected that their route would take them immediately into the fields of which Tristan had spoken; instead he turned first in the direction of Nantes and they went as far as the outer boulevard before they branched off into the country. Then, with surprising suddenness, the tree-topped banks of little lanes closed in around them. They met a few white-coifed women, a few old men in loose black smocks, and here and there a team of huge, plodding oxen or a couple of dogcarts blocked their progress; but the tension of the workaday world slackened almost instantly, and soon its manifold discordances seemed innocuous and remote. The lanes, leading into each other, wound peacefully on and on, their high banks hiding even the few scattered cottages along the way; and finally one sloped down towards a small stream spanned by a rustic bridge with seats on either side. Tristan and Connie stopped almost simultaneously.

"This is the place you meant, isn't it?"

"It is one of those I had in mind. But there are others farther on, if this does not please you for any reason."

"It pleases me very much. I'd like to stay here for a little while."

She put her hand to her throat, loosening her cape, and again the gesture with which Tristan took it from her suggested a caress. He spread it carefully over one of the rustic seats and they sat down, side by side, facing each other silently. The small stream, rippling along over the smooth stones imbedded in the underlying sand, made a soft sound, but there was no other. Connie drew a deep breath.

"Tristan," she said in a low voice. "I told you before that I wanted to be fair. I told your aunt so too. I don't see how I can be, except in one way. I think I have to tell you why I can't marry you."

"I want to have you, if it would in any way relieve your mind. But otherwise there is no reason why you should."

"You think so, because you don't understand. Perhaps you won't anyway, but I must try to make you."

"I believe I shall always understand, Constance, whatever you tell me, and also when you tell me nothing at all. You must do whichever will make you happier."

"It isn't going to make me at all happy to tell you what I'm going to. It's going to be very hard. But in the end it would be harder still if I didn't."

"I have already begged you to think less of the end and more of the beginning. Can you not do so?"

"No—no—I can't. Because we'd always have to face the end sometime. Wouldn't we?"

"Yes. Sometime. But not until we were well prepared for it."

"You say that because you're trying to spare me. But you can't."

"Very well. However, you might let me try. You assured my aunt that your affections were not engaged elsewhere—at least that they are not at present. Perhaps they have been sometime in the past."

"Yes. They have been. I went to a coeducational college, and I fell very deeply in love with one of my fellow students."

"A coeducational college, that is one to which young men and young girls both go?"

"Yes. And we don't use the term 'college' the way you do. It isn't a preparatory school. It's an institution of higher learning. A college may be part of a university or an entity in itself, but it has university rank."

"I see. So you went to a coeducational college when you were about eighteen and——"

"Eighteen or nineteen is the average age, but I'd skipped some grades, and I wasn't quite seventeen when I entered. You see, I'd never had many interests except my lessons, so I tried to make them take the place of other things, and in a way I succeeded. I got very good marks myself, and sometimes I was able to help my classmates get good marks too. Quite a number of them got in the habit of asking me if I wouldn't try, and I was always very pleased when I could."

"Of course, because it is natural for you to want to help. As natural as breathing."

"That wasn't the only reason," Connie said doggedly. "I was glad to be helpful, of course, but I was gladder still to feel that I wasn't altogether an outsider. You see, I didn't take part in sports, I didn't belong to clubs, I didn't go to dances—nothing like that. I lived at home, with my aunt, and commuted—I mean I just went back and forth to college for classes. I was working to pay for my tuition, and I managed to do that, so my education wasn't a burden to my aunt. But I couldn't manage the extra-curricular activities too. They take a lot of time and a lot of money. This meant that the only kind of companionship I had came from my good marks. Do you understand so far?"

"Yes, only too well."

"All right. You see now that I wasn't as disinterested as you thought I was. I hated being left out, and I snatched at the only chance I had to get in. Besides, I was terribly proud of my marks. I'd start envying some other girl her good clothes and her basketball letter and her wonderful dates, and then I'd think, 'Well, anyway, I got an *A* in Latin II and she flunked out.' Afterwards I'd feel smug and self-satisfied. I wouldn't be sorry for myself any longer, but I wouldn't be sorry for her either. I was a horrid girl, and I deserved everything that happened."

"I am sure you were always a very lovely girl and that it was the other one who was horrid. I think she probably boasted about all these things she had which you did not and hurt your feelings very much, that it was only afterwards you tried to comfort yourself by thinking of your good marks. I am sure you never talked about them. I am also sure you are trying to blame yourself for what was actually someone else's fault."

"Tristan, you must get rid of these ideas you have about me. . . . Anyway, one afternoon when I was coming out of the library, an upper-classman who was sauntering along alone stopped and asked if he couldn't carry my books for me. Probably you don't know, but in the United States that's very often one of the first steps in what you call courtship. I was so surprised and excited that I dropped half of the books while I was trying to hand them to him. You see, he was one of the most important persons in college—a fine athlete and a wonderful dancer. Besides, his people were the social leaders of Medford. I didn't suppose he even knew me by sight. So when he suddenly suggested—— Well, of course we stooped over to pick up the books at the same time, and knocked our heads together, and then we got to laughing and talking, and the next thing I knew we were both on the streetcar bound for Winchester. Aunt Bertha saw us coming up the walk together and she recognized this man from his pictures. He'd been fullback on the Tufts team that beat Harvard, and you can just imagine what that meant! Oh no, you can't either! Of course this is all Greek to you!"

"Please, Constance, go on with your story just as you were telling it. A little of it is Greek to me, as you say, but most of it is quite clear. It is much better that you should say things in your own way."

Connie looked down at her hands, which until then had been lying idle in her lap, and began to clasp and unclasp them. When she looked up again, she saw that Tristan had shifted his position a little, and realized that he had done this on purpose, in the hope that it might make the hard telling easier for her if she were not facing him directly. A rush of gratitude swept over her.

"Well, Aunt Bertha asked him to come in and presently she invited him to stay for supper," Connie explained. "That was another shock, because she'd never done such a thing before. He accepted as if he were very much pleased, and when I started out to help her, just as usual, she opened the door from the sitting room into the parlor and told us to stay in there while she got things on the table. She said supper would be ready in just a few minutes. It was, too, though I'll never know how she did it. She got out all the best china that I'd never seen used but once or twice before, and made biscuits and creamed chicken and opened a jar of strawberry jam."

"I can see that it must have been a delicious supper," Tristan observed helpfully. "So good that no doubt the fortunate young man wanted to come again very soon, for another such supper. . . . By the way, would it not be easier to talk about him if you gave him some sort of a name, no matter what?"

"His name was Eugene. But of course no one called him that. Everyone called him Gene."

"His name was Eugene, but everyone called him Gene," Tristan repeated thoughtfully. "That is the usual *petit nom*—how do you say, nickname—for it?"

"Yes," Connie said, answering the second question first. "I've known lots of Eugenes, and every last one of them was called Gene." It was clear that she attached no special importance to the name, and felt no special sentiment for it. "Aunt Bertha did invite him to supper again, and he came. Presently he began to come without being invited. There was always a place laid for him. Aunt Bertha liked him a lot too. She was tickled to death when he stopped calling her Miss Slocum and started calling her Aunt Bertha himself.

"One evening he stayed so long that I finally told him I'd have to get to work. You see, I was tutoring high-school pupils who'd got behind with their lessons because they were sick or stupid, and I always had a lot of papers to correct the last thing at night. Tutoring was one of the ways I earned money. I never charged anything for the help I gave the girls I knew in college, because if I had, I'd have lost that sense of companionship which meant so much to me. But I did charge younger boys and girls whose parents could well afford to pay me, and I got good prices too. I don't know what I'd have done if I hadn't."

"You would have found something else to do. You would have been resourceful."

"I did find other things to do. I played the organ in church, and I sold magazine subscriptions to people who didn't want them, and I made cakes and sandwiches for rich people's parties. But none of these things began to bring me in as much money as the tutoring. So the time came when I simply had to get at those papers, and I told Gene that. Then he laughed and asked if I couldn't correct them in the parlor just as well as in my bedroom, and I said why yes, I guessed so, and went and got them. He sat beside me and smoked while I worked on them. There wasn't an ash tray in the house, but he said he could use a saucer just as well. I went out to the pantry and got one for him, and he followed me, and then he put his arms around me and kissed me."

Connie raised her hand and passed it slowly over her forehead, shielding her eyes. But she could not hide her lips so easily and Tristan could see that those were trembling.

"The next time he came I had the saucer on the table all ready for him to use, and the papers all laid out so that I could start working on them. He smoked for a while and then he drew up a straight-backed chair and sat down beside me at the roll-top desk, pulling a paper of his own out of his pocket. He laughed a little in the jolly way he had, and put his arm around me again; then he said very casually he'd heard I was simply a whiz at calculus, but that he'd never been able to make head or tail of it —that he was a darn sight better off with a football under his arm or a dance floor under his feet than he was with a book in his hand any day. I took the paper and looked at it, and the problems were awfully simple, really. I put the other papers aside and spread his out and in a few minutes everything was cleared up. He seemed so grateful I was ashamed. It was such a little thing to have done for him and he had done so much for me."

"You felt he had done you a favor because he offered to carry your books and accepted your hospitality and kissed you in the pantry?"

"I told you that you wouldn't understand, Tristan. You have, more than I expected. But now you've stopped."

"No, I have not stopped. I only wanted to be quite sure. Because it seems to me you had done *him* a great favor in permitting him to carry your books and inviting him to supper in your home and accepting his embraces. It seems to me that any man so favored would be very much honored."

"Well, if it seems that way to you, I can't explain. Perhaps I better stop trying. Only I want to finish saying all this, now that I've started."

"And I want to have you. Let me see if I cannot do better about understanding. Was it because you really felt that this Eugene was a person of great importance, and you were not, that you considered that he had done you a favor?"

"Yes," Connie answered eagerly. "Yes, that's it. He *gave* me importance. When other girls heard he was coming to see me they felt entirely different about me. Men too. I began to have other callers. There's a Bible verse about the one whom the king delighteth to honor; probably you don't know it, because Catholics don't read the Bible, but——"

"I believe the passage to which you refer is in the Book of Esther," Tristan remarked briefly, without troubling to refute the charge. "So this Eugene was regarded as a kind of king at Tufts College, and as soon as the rumor spread that he appreciated your fine qualities, others who had hitherto been blind to these suddenly discovered them also. Well, that has happened before, of course, and doubtless will again, in other places besides the Holy Land and the State of Massachusetts. But did this football hero confine his attentions to those he could pay you privately?"

"Oh no! At least not for long. He gave me tickets to all the games. Of course he couldn't take me himself, because he was always in the field. But Aunt Bertha went with me. She hadn't even seen any kind of collegiate sport and she was almost as thrilled as I was . . . And then he began asking me to dances. You can't imagine what it meant for a girl like me to walk into a fraternity dance with Gene Clayton."

She did not realize that inadvertently she had spoken his full name; she was absorbed in her story now and she went on with it rapidly.

"I had to have pretty clothes then—I just had to. All the other girls wore coonskin coats to football games, and I found a store that would sell me one on the installment plan at a great discount. It had been made to order and then sent back because it didn't fit. I watched for out-of-season sales to buy party dresses, too. I was lucky, being able to walk right into models that had been marked down. But I had to borrow money to pay for them just the same. I borrowed it from the bank and Aunt Bertha helped me. She put up her Tel. & Tel. and her Pennsylvania Railroad stock for security. She had just a little in each, but she borrowed as much as the bank would let her. And when that wasn't enough, I started charging for the college tutoring I did as well as the high-school tutoring. After that I did lose the sense of companionship with other girls which had meant so much to me. But it didn't matter any more, because I had Gene's. And he was never ashamed of the way I looked when I went out with him. He never needed to be."

Again she paused, but this time, instead of shading her eyes with her hand she looked Tristan proudly in the face.

"I told you he made me an important person too," she said. "I was considered the most important girl in college by that time. I was leading all my classes and winning debates and playing solos in concerts and getting the best parts in plays. I finally joined some clubs and I was elected to office in two of them. And of course I became a sorority member too. It was a wonderful feeling to be such a success in every way after all the years when I felt I was a failure in everything except my lessons. But you mustn't think it was just a sense of satisfaction that made me happy. I was happy because I was head over heels in love with Gene Clayton and because I was sure he was head over heels in love with me."

"Yes, Constance, I did understand that. I understand it fully."

"We went to all the dances together, we went skating in the winter and swimming in the summer. Gene's mother asked me home for Sunday dinner and took me into Boston in her limousine to symphony concerts and matinees. And Gene kept on coming to supper at Aunt Bertha's and taking little papers out of his pocket while I was correcting mine. After a while he began coming every night and he brought books with him as well as papers. He was studying terribly hard—so hard that he didn't have time to go to many dances any more. But I didn't mind. I loved getting ready for him—cooking good things for him to eat and putting flowers in the college colors on the dining-room table. I loved being alone and quiet with him in the parlor. I loved the feeling that I was helping him and that he depended on me."

"But all that is quite as it should be. That is how most young women feel about their first loves."

"I'm only telling you about that to explain why I trusted him so completely. To me, anything he did was right. It never occurred to me to doubt him. And when he asked me to help him with his term paper in American history, I was only too glad to do so. We looked up the references in the library together and I drew the charts for him because he laughed and said he was too clumsy. As a matter of fact, I practically wrote the paper. About all he did was to copy it. And he received a top grade. The paper was read as the best one turned in by the class. And when I heard about it from one of the other girls, because he didn't tell me, it made me feel happy and proud to think I had helped him. I was prouder than I'd ever been before in my life. I was humble and grateful and every night I went to bed filled with rapture at the thought that the man I loved needed me."

"That he needed you or that he wanted you?"

"Both. One as much as the other. But that was a good question, Tristan. It shows you do understand—a lot. Well, we went out less and less, and we worked and—made love more and more. Then finally one night when Gene met me outside the library, where I was waiting for him, he said he wasn't coming home with me after all, because he had to meet the manager of the football team unexpectedly about a very important matter. Of course I was disappointed, and the evening seemed awfully empty, but I wasn't hurt—not until he'd made the same sort of excuses three or four times. Then I began to wonder if I'd hurt *his* feelings, and I asked him. He passed it off very lightly. He said of course not, and the next night he did come to supper and he did make love to me afterwards. But later on, when I asked him if he had anything special on his mind, he said no, he didn't want to work any more. I thought he meant just that night. I didn't mean to badger him or run after him, honestly I didn't, Tristan. But I thought I'd misunderstood. I thought I *must* have. And finally he told me the truth."

"And that was?"

"All he had been trying to do was to assure his acceptance at West Point. You see, he had received an appointment from his Congressman. But unless he made an outstanding college record of credits, he would have to take a mental examination for Academy entrance, in addition to the physical one—principally mathematics and English. And of course in such an examination he couldn't get help. He couldn't—cheat. So he had to make good grades at Tufts, especially in American history, because the professor who taught that subject was very strict and did not give especially good grades, and if he got a low grade in that subject, that would pull down his general average. And he had to have a really excellent term paper to get a good grade. So——"

"So it was really on your term paper that he managed to get into West Point?"

"Yes. That was the worst of it. And when I realized that, I realized something else too: that I'd connived with dishonesty. Until then I'd never thought of it that way. I'd only thought I was helping Gene as I'd helped lots of other students who weren't good at their lessons. Well, not quite the same way. Before that I'd done tutoring for money and I'd done it for companionship, and this time I was doing it for love. But I hadn't taught Gene anything about American history. I had only helped him to cheat—and the reason I didn't realize at the time how abominably dishonest it all had been was because I was so desperately in love. If that's what falling in love can do to a girl—if it can make her lose her sense of values, her standards of integrity, not just about the man she loves but about everything, why then——"

"Why, you poor child! No wonder you are so terribly afraid! You are the soul of honor and you cannot bear to feel that ever again—— But you should not be afraid. You must not be. You have not lost your sense of values or your standards of integrity. There is not a man on earth who could make you do that. Gene Clayton never touched your soul. He never even knew you had one."

"That doesn't make any difference," Connie said doggedly. "Maybe I didn't lose them, entirely, but I certainly lost sight of them. I'm never going to risk that again."

"You will never need to. Any man who is worthy of your love will help you guard them."

"A man like you might want to. But how do I know what I'd do myself? I don't. You don't either. It won't do any good for you to say you do because I don't believe it. I *can't*."

She bowed her head and there was a long silence. Tristan did not try to argue with her. But at last he reached over and took her hand, holding it quietly in his own while he waited for her to go on.

"He went away," she said at last. "He went away without even coming to say good-by to me. Afterwards I wrote to him—I wrote two or three times. Of course I know now that was a great mistake. I was only thinking I loved him so much life wasn't worth living without him."

She stopped, choked with sobs. Tristan continued to wait quietly.

"I thought too, that I must have failed him in some way, without knowing it, that if I hadn't he couldn't have left me after—after——"

That sentence she could not finish. She looked up appealingly, met Tristan's steady eyes, and bit her lips to stop their quivering. Presently she succeeded. "At last he did write to me. He said he'd hoped I wouldn't force him to—*force* him to—— That the—the affair would just come to a natural end. But since I seemed determined to nag him, he thought he'd better tell me the truth straight out. From the very beginning—from that first day when he asked to carry my books—he'd been intending to do exactly what he did do. I mean he'd been intending to see if I could get him through those examinations. He'd taken them once before and failed. And this was his last chance. He couldn't get the appointment to West

Point unless he could pass them this time. The reason he didn't tell me all that at the outset was because he was afraid he'd hurt my vanity—my *vanity!* He said he thought I wouldn't like the implication that I was a grind, that I wasn't good at anything else.

"He said it was always easier to get on the right side of a girl by making love to her, that if she didn't actually have a harelip and an ugly disposition a man got some fun out of it himself. And then of course it was very important to make the whole thing as 'hush-hush' as possible because there'd be such a terribly heavy penalty if he were found out cribbing like that. *If he were found out!* That was all that mattered to him. It didn't matter whether it was right or wrong, whether he'd done something dishonest and made me do something dishonest. . . . He ended up by saying he hadn't expected me to take our little affair—he used that expression again, 'our little affair'—so seriously. He'd rushed other girls, and they never did. It was too bad I hadn't been able to give and take the same way. He wished me the best of luck."

"Constance—my very dear Constance—I beg of you not to weep like that."

She was crying uncontrollably now, and not only uncontrollably, but unashamedly. It was not worth while to suppress her tears any longer; it did not matter whether Tristan saw them. He knew the whole sordid story now. It was not until she realized how much distress her abandonment to grief and shame was causing him that she made an effort to compose herself and speak calmly and collectedly.

"You understood all that—well, most of it. So now you'll understand the rest. You'll understand what it was like, finishing out my college course as the girl Gene Clayton jilted—the girl who didn't have sense enough to know from the beginning that all he wanted was to pick her brains. I couldn't just sink back into oblivion again—he'd put his mark on me too plainly for that. Perhaps it was the best thing in a way. It made me set my teeth and go on, do or die, until I graduated at the head of my class. It made me work like a galley slave to pay back the money I'd borrowed and do it in record time. It made me jump at the chance of coming to France and trying to see if I couldn't be of some use in the world after all. But it did something else to me too. It frightened me and froze me up. I can't let myself go any longer. I'm afraid I'll make a fool of myself again. I can't even bear to have anyone touch me. It affects me just the way a raised hand affects a little whipped dog."

"But Constance darling, you have 'let yourself go,' as you call it, with me. You have talked with me freely, from the beginning. You have never shrunk away when I touched you."

"But don't you see I thought you were different? You were just courteous and quiet and friendly and—reassuring somehow. You didn't try to make love to me, the way most men do as soon as they have the least chance. I thought you didn't want to and I was glad of it. I didn't *dream* you wanted to. How could I? If I wasn't good enough for Gene Clayton, how could I imagine you'd think I was good enough for you? I'm not. That's another reason I can't marry you."

"You were a great deal too good for Gene Clayton, darling. That was just the trouble—or a large part of the trouble. But after all, this is not a question of goodness in any case. It is a question of love. I have loved you from the first moment I saw you, as I have told you before, and he never loved you at all. I doubt if he ever loved anyone but himself or whether he ever will. Surely you are not going through life denying that love can exist simply because you were misled by the first man who spoke of it to you! That would be like a traveler who saw a mirage in a desert and therefore lay down to die instead of seeking the next oasis!"

"I don't deny it exists. I've felt its existence. But the feeling's gone."

"The mirage is gone. The reality remains. I have told you repeatedly that I love you and want you for my wife. Do you refuse to believe me?"

"You've compelled me to believe you. I know that your love is a reality. But I couldn't be your wife unless I loved you too."

"I am not urging you to marry me immediately. For the moment I was only trying to convince you how greatly I desire to marry you. I am not even asking you to give me your love. I am only begging you to receive the assurance of mine. Surely you do not feel that you can never accept affection in any form, from anyone?"

She tried to answer with candor and calmness.

"I want what we usually call affection very much, and I'd rather have yours than anything else in the world. But that wasn't what you meant, was it, when you first talked about love?"

"It was a very important part of what I meant when I talked about love, and I believe we do understand the same thing when we speak of affection. Do you not mean by that tenderness, trust, a feeling of harmony and ease in another's presence, the impulse to share experiences and exchange opinions, to impart confidences?"

"Yes, Tristan, that is just what I mean."

"Then you have made me very happy by telling me you want my affection more than anything else in the world. And I am sure that I do not need to add that your desire is fulfilled." He looked down at her, his face suffused with fondness. "I may add that you have made me not only very happy but very hopeful," he went on. "Because I believe that since you have wanted that, someday you will want more. When that day comes, my happiness will be complete."

He rose, holding out his hand. "Come," he said. "Let us now go on with our walk and find the *calvaire* that we set out to see."

CHAPTER XV

February 9, 1919

Dear Tristan:
Thank you for your nice letter of the fourth and for the beautiful camellias which came last night. I wore some of them to church this

*morning and to your aunt's tea this afternoon, but there were so many
I arranged the rest in bowls, which I managed to get from the mess hall.*

*Of course I was very much surprised that you had written to Aunt
Bertha telling her you wanted to marry me, and simply staggered when
the Countess told me she had done so too, suggesting that as soon as
civilians were allowed to cross the Atlantic, Aunt Bertha should come to
Château Chassay for a visit. I have written her myself, and I can't help
hoping my letter will go through faster than yours and the Countess's,
so that the poor old lady won't have too much of a shock. I've already
explained to you that it isn't usual in the United States for a young man
to propose to a girl through her family. He thinks if he proposes to her
he's done quite enough. And very often he doesn't actually propose to her
until they've seen a good deal of each other. Don't you remember what
I told you that first time we talked about "best girls" and "keeping company"? Well, after a young man has "kept company" with his "best girl"
for a while, they begin to have an "understanding." The understanding
is that some day they'll be married, and eventually he tells her that's what
he wants. But generally she doesn't worry while she's waiting for him to
put it into words.*

Connie laid down her pen. The first part was all right. But as she considered the last sentence, grave doubts and bitter memories began to assail
her. She crossed out the last sentence in the paragraph, realized that the
erasure did not wholly conceal the words, barred them a second time, and
surveyed the untidy result with dissatisfaction. She would have to start all
over again. She took a fresh sheet and began to rewrite the mutilated
paragraph.

Connie looked out of the office window and there was a patch of bright
blue sky. She was not sure whether she was pleased to see the blue sky
or not. Duncan Craig wanted her to go for a long walk with him that
afternoon, and somehow, since she had been to Orvault with Tristan de
Fremond, she associated outings in the country with him, though this
association was sadly wanting in logic: she had taken a dozen outings
with Duncan to the one with Tristan. But for Duncan she would have
seen only a small part of that lovely countryside which was fast becoming
almost as familiar to her as her own.

He came jauntily into the office, a red heart-shaped box under the crook
of his left arm, a funny little frilled nosegay in his right hand, and grinned
broadly in response to her startled expression.

"You don't meant to tell me that no one else has remembered that this
is Valentine's Day? Well then, for once I've got the edge on all your other
admirers, and I'll just say in passing that they must be slipping." He
placed the gaudy box on the table in front of her and handed her the
nosegay with a mock bow. "Carry this along and stick it in your sailor
when we get into the country, will you?" he said, still jestingly. "It's a
long time since I've walked out with a girl wearing a flower-trimmed hat,
and it'd sure look good to me for a change."

"Where are we going today?"

"Over on the other side of the river. It's pretty country, and I think you might get some amusement out of trying to talk to some of the people. They've picked up a few words of English from our men who've been stationed there, and they mix these words right in with their own queer brand of French. The result's darn funny sometimes."

"I should think it might be. Do we take the middle bridge?"

"Yes. We'll go straight ahead in the direction of Goulaine."

Except for its medieval fortress, Goulaine itself proved no different from many other villages in the same vicinity. Its small gray houses were clustered around a small gray church, its inn was named the Cheval Blanc. At the moment when Duncan and Connie passed through, its one street was almost deserted, and no opportunity arose to test its inhabitants' strange patois.

Connie stopped near the doorway of the house which she and Duncan had been approaching, suddenly aware that he had stopped already, and that he was talking to the red-cheeked, white-capped old woman who had answered his knock. He was speaking in French, and Connie caught the words *"rhum chaud"* and saw the woman look questioningly from him to herself, and then, after a moment's hesitation, nod and smile, opening the door wider.

"It's all right," Duncan said, turning to Connie. "Come on in."

They stepped over the threshold into the typical kitchen of a Breton cottage which obviously served every purpose, and sat down at a table near the glowing hearth. The housewife herself had disappeared, and apparently her menfolk, if she had any, were still in the fields, for there were none in evidence, and though Connie and Duncan could hear children chattering in the distance, they did not appear either. Minutes passed, and still the peasant woman did not return. At first Connie felt too comfortable and relaxed to question this absence, but eventually she began to feel puzzled too.

"Where do you suppose our hostess is all this time?"

"Probably getting something extra special out of her *cave*. You'd be surprised at the good stuff some of these peasants keep tucked away."

He spoke contentedly, almost drowsily. It was clear that the coziness and the warmth of the quaint little kitchen had affected him too.

"C'est prêt, monsieur, 'dame."

The peasant woman had come back. She was standing by a small, inconspicuous door in the rear bobbing a curtsey, smiling more broadly than ever. But she had no tray in her hand, and evidently she expected them to come with her instead of intending to serve them in the kitchen. Connie and Duncan arose, still hardly more than half roused and not without reluctance; the firelight on the hearth, the shadows on the wall, the perfect quiet, the sense of shelter and intimacy, had all been very pleasant. When they reached her side, the peasant woman turned and began to mount the worn and crooked steps of an outside stairway. When she reached the top, she threw open another door, ushering them through it.

" 'Um chaud," she said proudly and, going out, shut the door after her.

Daylight had still prevailed in the fields when they went inside, but the overhanging eaves had obscured the small stairway, and after Connie stumbled once on the uneven steps, Duncan had put an arm around her to steady her. Now, still half-embraced, they stood blinking before the flames of another fire, newly laid this time, which crackled cheerily under the hood of a chimneypiece which was a mere triangle in one corner. They were in a tiny, raftered room, so low-ceilinged that it was possible to stand upright only in the center. The wooden shutters of the two dormers had been carefully closed, and only the crackling fire gave the room its radiance, though a single candle stood in readiness for use on a bedside table. A carved armoire, huge and secretive, covered one side of the room; the bed, also huge and carved, was the only other piece of furniture. A mountainous red eiderdown billowed above its framework.

"What in hell——" Duncan began. Then suddenly he laughed. "Remember what I told you, Connie? That these people have learned a few English words and mix them right in with their French? When I asked that woman for a 'rhum chaud,' she thought I was doing the same thing, that what I said was a 'room chaud'—not a hot drink but a warm room! We've found the quaint colloquialism we were looking for, all right!"

"Well, now that we have found it, suppose we start back to camp again. I think it's high time."

She spoke slowly and distinctly, her voice flat and expressionless. Though his arm was still around her waist, she had managed to detach her real self completely. Duncan swung her around, forcing her to face him.

"Look here," he said furiously, "if you think I engineered this, you'd better think again. I had no more idea of what that woman was up to when she left us than you did. I'm telling you the truth, and I want you to tell me, before we go out of this room, that you believe me."

"All right. I believe you. Now let's go."

He dropped his arm and turned towards the door. Then he turned again, his back to it.

"Listen, Connie," he said. "Listen, darling." The anger had gone from his voice, and something else had come into it, something she had never heard there before. "I want you. I want you terribly; I have for a long time—ever since that day I met you in the grove. But I swear I didn't plan this. It wouldn't mean a thing to me to take you by a trick, against your will. You'd have to want it too. I can't bear to have you speak to me like that. Because I don't just want you, I love you. I have almost from the beginning. Not quite. I'll tell you the truth about that too. But when we were in the surgery together, something happened to me. I realized what it would do to my life if I could have your loyalty and devotion, the kind you've given Gwen, only more than that—the kind you'd give a man if you cared for him enough to marry him. Since then I've loved you with all my heart and soul. For God's sake tell me you believe that too, and say it as if you meant it!"

His earnestness was almost as overpowering as his passion. No matter how hard she tried to remain unmoved, Constance could not do it. No resentment, no rage, was proof against such a plea as this. Her sense of outrage streamed away from her, leaving in its wake a strange, bewildered excitement. Involuntarily she stammered out the question she had not meant to ask.

"Then why—if you don't just want me, if you really love me, why——?"

"Why haven't I asked you to marry me? I was a fool not to clear things up for you long ago. I've been a fool right along, as far as you were concerned. Well, I've admitted that before. What I ought to say is just—I've been a fool."

"You told me on your word of honor that as far as Gwen was concerned there wasn't any reason——" Connie began falteringly. Duncan interrupted her.

"It isn't a question of Gwen," he said. "It's a question of Eileen."

"Eileen?"

"Yes. You don't know her, you never heard of her, you've never seen her. I wouldn't mention her name if it could mean anything to you. She lives in New York. She's very beautiful."

He lingered over the last words. Connie waited a minute for him to go on and when he did not do so, she asked a question, with great gentleness.

"You're engaged to her, aren't you, Duncan? I know that lots of men over here are engaged to girls back home, and they think now they've grown away from those girls. But they haven't really. When they get back themselves——"

"Engaged to her? No, I'm not engaged to her. She's married already."

"But if she's married already, then it's hopeless, isn't it?"

"Are you really as innocent as you sound, Connie, or are you just pretending?"

"Pretending what?"

"That you haven't guessed I'd been Eileen's lover for a long time before I came away."

"But you can't love Eileen and me both!"

"No, I don't love you and Eileen both. I love you. I've never loved Eileen the way I love you, Connie. I've never loved any woman this way before. But I did love Eileen, in a different way, once. I told her I loved her. I told her so a great many times. We'd have got married if we could. We intended to some day."

"You mean there'd have been a divorce?"

"We didn't discuss it definitely. I think Eileen's husband would have given her a divorce, if she'd insisted. He isn't altogether a bad chap when he isn't drunk. But he's drunk most of the time. And when he sobers up, he's sorry for what he's done under the influence. Her husband's much older than she is, too. Drinking the way he does—well, we never put that into words either, but of course we couldn't help thinking about it. . . . Perhaps a divorce wouldn't be necessary. Perhaps it would save a lot of trouble and scandal if we just waited. I hadn't forgotten my parents' divorce, I didn't want to go through anything like that myself. Not that this would have been so bad. But it would have been bad enough. Divorce is a dirty business, however you look at it."

"Does—does Eileen care about you? You said you've given her to under-stand that you and she would be married sometime, that you hoped you could be. Would—wouldn't it hurt her a lot if she thought you had gone back on her?"

"I think it would hurt her," he said steadily. "It would hurt her pride a lot, anyway. It would be a body blow in that respect. I don't think it's ever occurred to Eileen that a man who'd been her lover could ever want an-other woman more than he wanted her. . . . I suppose she does care about me, after a fashion. Of course she cares about a lot of other things too."

"What sort of things?"

"Oh, money and position and all that. Of course she'd have plenty of money anyway, but I'm not so sure about the position. The Social Regis-ter. The Colony Club. Just the right friends. Her entry at the Horse Show. Her box at the Metropolitan. But she'd never be reconciled to ostracism from her own set, she'd never be satisfied to live anywhere except in New York or Paris. It couldn't be all for love and the world well lost, the way it could for you, Connie, if you cared enough and if you could leave the world behind with a clear conscience."

"I see. But no matter what else she cares about, if she cares for you most——"

"I think she does, in her way," he repeated. And the stillness of the room closed in on them again. At last Duncan Craig got slowly to his feet. "There isn't anything more to say, is there?" he asked quietly.

"No. I'm sorry, Duncan, but there isn't."

CHAPTER XVI

"Lieutenant Tyson will see you now, Miss Galt."

The Red Cross worker who acted as Lieutenant Tysons secretary held open the door leading from the outer office to the inner sanctum, and Connie rose from the bench where she had been sitting for the last half-hour to cross the room. She had not the slightest idea why the personnel officer had sent for her.

"Hello, Connie! I see you're next."

Tilda was coming out of the open door, a strange expression on the pretty face which was normally so noncommittal. Connie's anxiety imme-diately increased.

"Why, hello! Did he send for you too? What's wrong?"

"Go ahead in and you'll find out. I mustn't hold you up now."

As Connie entered the inner sanctum, she saw that Lieutenant Tyson was standing by the window, with his back to her, and he did not turn immediately, although he did not seem to be looking at anything in par-ticular and must have heard her come in. At last he wheeled slowly.

"Good afternoon, Miss Galt," he said. "Won't you sit down?"

He seated himself on one side of his desk, motioning towards a chair on the other. For a moment he fidgeted with some papers lying before him. Then he cleared his throat and smiled rather wanly.

"I suppose I should have been prepared for what was coming, but instead of that, it's rather a blow. I've just had word that all Searchers are being recalled to Paris. You are expected to report there within a week and await transportation home."

"Oh—I thought I'd done something wrong!"

The words came tumbling out involuntarily. Then her relief was instantly engulfed in consternation. How could she tear herself away like that from an incompleted task? How could she readjust her whole way of living with such suddenness? How could she leave without even seeing Tristan?

"If no one ever did anything worse than you have, the world would be a pretty good place," Tyson was saying, rather dryly. "I've yet to receive a complaint about you, after all these months. I'm sure you'll be glad to hear that and I'm glad I can tell you so. It's nice we've got something to be happy about, isn't it? Taken by and large, I'm not feeling especially cheerful right now, and I don't suppose you are either."

"No. No, I'm not. . . . Is there any special thing I ought to do first?"

"Yes. First of all, check your list against the hospital files to make absolutely sure all indicated mortality letters have actually been written. If they haven't, clear them up at once. Then give me a signed statement saying that part of your work is entirely in order."

"Why, I know it is! Isn't everyone's?"

"I'm not so sure," he answered, still more dryly. "Next make certain that all information secured while searching has been put into final form and mailed to Paris. I know you can't always keep it typed up as you go along."

"I have it typed through last week. Since then the men have been coming in and going out so fast that I've concentrated on getting the information rather than on putting it into final form. But I'll straighten things out right away."

"Good. After you've finished that, start in on your supplies. Make a complete inventory of everything you have on hand, and turn it over to me as soon as you can."

"I haven't many supplies left. It won't take me long to make the inventory. But what about my records?"

"Sort them according to subject and tie them into bundles. Label the bundles "Constance Galt, Searcher, Base Hospital 11, Grand Blottereau" and leave them stacked in your office. I'll have them crated and sent to Red Cross Headquarters in Paris."

"They are sorted, after a fashion. I've kept them on the supply shelves. I don't think it will take me long to get those in order, either."

"So much the better. HQ hasn't given us much time to do all that's expected of us."

He looked out of the window again. Connie waited for him to go on, outwardly composed, inwardly perturbed. Though she had managed to accept them in a matter-of-fact way, she knew that the orders she had just received actually represented an enormous amount of work. She would need to give it her undivided attention in order to get it all done within a week; and it would be hard to keep her personal problems wholly in abeyance. At this very moment, when she should have been thinking about typed lists and bundled reports, she was wondering how Aunt Bertha, who had expected her to remain abroad indefinitely, would receive the news that she was coming home almost immediately. With a good deal more agitation, she was wondering how she would reconcile Tristan to the idea of her impending departure from France. . . .

"This dingy old place doesn't look so bad, now that the flowers in the window boxes are out," Tyson was saying irrelevantly. "I always did like petunias. . . . I'm sorry I'm the one to give you marching orders, I'll miss you when you're gone, and if I don't ever see you again it won't be my fault. That's all, Miss Galt. Good afternoon."

"Good afternoon, Lieutenant Tyson. And thanks a lot for what you've said. I appreciate it."

Connie decided to go back to her office.

Craig came. "May I come into your office and have a smoke?"

"Of course, if you don't mind being neglected. Lieutenant Tyson told me, about an hour ago, that all Searchers were being recalled and that I'd have to be ready to leave within a week. That means I've got to pitch right in and not lose a minute."

Craig gave a long whistle. "Surprises are certainly coming thick and fast around here today! You say *all* Searchers? That means the other girls too —not just you?"

"Yes, I met Tilda coming out of Lieutenant Tyson's office just as I was going in. I haven't had a chance to talk to the others yet, but I know it will be a shock to them too."

"No doubt. But perhaps not quite as much of a one as it is to you. At least I don't suppose they all have the same international complications."

He looked at her half jestingly, half tenderly, and she managed to return his smile. Since St. Valentine's Day, their attitude towards each other had changed completely, and the fact that this change had been practically painless to Connie was due largely to Craig's tact and understanding. The day after their poignant experience, he had written her a letter which she still treasured and which she knew she always would: they had closed a door after them, he said, and they had both agreed that they could never again cross its threshold; but in the course of his life, which was longer than hers, he had learned that for every door closed behind, another opened ahead—or anyway, that it could if the will and the purpose were there to set it ajar. He hoped and believed that he and she would both find many such doors ahead, and that some of these they might find together. At least he thought it was worth while trying, and if she were willing, he would do his best to help her. The letter needed no answer; if she would just follow his lead when they met, he was sure everything would be all right. And he was, as always, devotedly hers. . . .

She had taken him at his word, and had left the letter unanswered; and though she felt shy the first time she saw him after receiving it, this shyness was swiftly dispelled. His manner was so natural and so friendly that she could not remain self-conscious in his presence; and from then on, though he never sought her out, neither did he seem to avoid her. On the surface, their present relationship was one of easy, almost merry camaraderie; but it had an underlying current of strong and tender feeling. Now, as Craig knelt on the floor of her office tying into neat bundles the files which Connie rapidly sorted, she drew comfort from his support and was happy in his helpfulness.

Owing to a combination of handicapping circumstances, Tristan had been able to leave Saumur only twice since the day he had taken Connie to Orvault—the scarcity of officers resulting in frequent Sunday duty, the urgency of trips undertaken to reassemble equipment, the inopportunity of visiting princes and other potentates. But on one of these occasions Connie had returned from Château Chassay so entranced with having been rowed round and round the moat that she could not keep her reminiscent pleasure to herself; and on the other the Count and Countess had given a dinner in her honor which included all her special friends. In both these gestures Craig had been quick to see that only her own hesitation prevented her acceptance as the daughter of the house, and also to recognize the caliber and persistence of his rival. Furthermore, he knew that though Connie had not seen Tristan de Fremond lately, she was writing him regularly and receiving frequent letters and gifts in return. Some of the gifts had been small enough to conceal: the tiny medals in the form of bells and flowers from the famous Balme factory at Saumur, and the exquisite miniature painted from the picturesque portrait of Jeanne Delamare, founder of the Sisters of St. Anne, showing her in a wide hood and still wider sleeves. Others, comprising a variety of well-chosen books, quantities of flowers, and an occasional small flat hamper of Saumur's famous sparkling wine, were so much in evidence that they could not be overlooked, while the attraction which the Post Office obviously held for Connie was very different from the mild interest with which she had regarded it when letters from her Aunt Bertha were the only ones she had special reason to expect. Craig could not help drawing his own conclusions, and he was wise enough to realize that if he himself were out of the running as a suitor, his best chance to retain the standing of a favored friend lay in generosity of both speech and action.

He and Connie walked over to the Administration Building now, and turned in to the little cubicle where she had gone so often to send her wired reports to Paris Headquarters. Johnston, the corporal who acted as telegrapher, looked up from the keys on which he was busily ticking out a message and extended his hand for the typed form he expected to find ready for him.

"How are you, Connie? I'm way behind with my messages for the first time in weeks. But I'll get yours off, Connie. Hand it over here."

"It isn't written yet. Wait just a second."

He shoved a sheet of paper across to the edge of the table, and she leaned over, writing:

DE FREMOND
ÉCOLE DE CAVALERIE
SAUMUR
ALL SEARCHERS BEING RECALLED ORDERED TO REPORT PARIS WITHIN WEEK AND AWAIT TRANSPORTATION HOME WILL ADVISE EXACT DATE DEPARTURE NANTES WHEN INFORMED MYSELF

CONSTANCE

She handed the message to the telegrapher, but instead of reading it through as usual with the swiftness of long practice, he looked up, with a surprised whistle at the end of the first sentence. "Well, what do you know!" he exclaimed. "That's news to me, bad news too. I'm going to miss having you around. . . . This is of course an official message, Miss Galt?" he concluded, with mock formality.

"Oh, but of course it isn't! It's—it's very personal! I entirely forgot I shouldn't send a personal message from here, I was so upset. . . . And you didn't remind me, either!" she said accusingly, turning to Craig.

"I confess to great negligence. On the other hand, I thought you wanted to get this special message off right away, and I figured that maybe the Corporal here would help you out. I wasn't wrong, was I, Johnston?"

"Bet your life you weren't, Captain. You can count on me. This'll be in Saumur before bedtime."

"Duncan's outside. He wants us to come to dinner with him at Ragueneau's."

"What, all three of us at the same time? He can't be running true to form any more. I've thought for a long while the poor old boy was slipping, but I didn't know it was as bad as this."

"Well, shall I tell him you're not interested? He's waiting to find out what you want to do."

"Who said I wasn't interested? I'd be a lot more thrilled, as far as Duncan Craig is concerned, if he'd drop this pose of his and strut his regular stuff again. But I'm interested in him, whatever he does. I've tried to get that across to you several times now. Besides, I've got to eat somewhere, and it might as well be Ragueneau's as anywhere else."

On either side of Ragueneau's the chestnut trees were in bloom, a mass of pink at one end and of white at the other, while over the lattice work of the terrace, wisteria hung in pale-purple festoons. After the long gloomy winter, all this spring lushness seemed doubly beautiful, doubly welcome.

As the dinner progressed, the girls dismissed their own problems long enough to question Craig about his own possible plans. He thought the whole hospital center would be closing down in another month or so, he said; but he hadn't decided yet whether he'd go back to the States when it did.

"When I do get back to New York, Tilda, I'll give you a ring and see if we can't get in an evening at the Waldorf. . . . I don't know about the

Folies Bergères, Gwen—it all depends on whether I can get leave myself while you're in Paris. . . ."

He saluted in an offhand manner and sauntered out of sight. Connie unlatched the door and went straight to the tubular stove, which she knew would need tending after her long absence. The fire was almost out, and for the next few moments she gave it her undivided attention. When she finally dusted off her hands and turned towards her bedroom, she saw that Gwen was blocking her way.

"Look here," she said sharply. "I thought a while back, that you had laid off Duncan Craig, like I suggested you might. You don't want him yourself, that's plain enough. You've fallen for that Frenchman, as hard as you can fall for anyone—not that I'd call it very hard. You haven't got it in you to take a real tumble for a man. You're the kind of girl who figures no man on God's green earth is good enough for her to marry, but who doesn't want to turn one loose for someone else. And who doesn't mind snatching one away from another girl either."

Tilda had gone straight to her room when the three girls came in, bent as usual on keeping out of trouble. But for the once her sympathies had outstripped her abhorrence of scenes. She came back into the hall and put her hand on Gwen's arm, paying no attention when Gwen tried to shake her off.

"You know good and well Connie didn't snatch Duncan Craig away from you," she said calmly. "If he made a few passes at you before she came, it was only because he had nothing else to do and you were only too glad to help him while away his time. She did divert his attention, *without* knowing it, but in this case it was a great deal more like rescue work than snatching, if you ask me. And the previous object of his affections wasn't a girl named Gwen. It was a girl named Eileen."

Connie gave a slight gasp. Gwen snorted angrily.

"What are you talking about? There isn't a girl at this camp named Eileen."

"I didn't say she was at this camp, did I? She's on Park Avenue right this minute—my mother mentioned her in the letter I got this morning. This lady friend of his has got a husband already. But the affair's been going on so long you might almost say it was more or less legalized. I'm quite sure Craig feels he has a definite obligation there."

"How come you know all this?"

Tilda shrugged her pretty shoulders. "Eileen and I came out the same time," she said. "We've always run with the same kind of people. She married before the end of her debutante year, and she's lived in the same apartment house with my family ever since. I've seen a good deal of her, first and last, and she likes to talk. I'll say this for Duncan, he's always been a model of discretion, as far as this affair goes. But I used to see him in the elevator every now and then. Sometimes he had a cute little girl with him—a cute little girl with reddish hair."

"*Reddish hair!*" Gwen echoed angrily. "What are you driving at, Tilda Evans? Lots of people have red hair, haven't they? I have myself. What does that prove?"

"Nothing. Nothing at all. I just mentioned it in passing. She has reddish curls and an awfully trick way of looking at you from under her lids. A smile you didn't forget, too." Tilda went on talking quietly and Connie listened, sick at heart. Tilda was talking about a little girl with reddish hair and a trick way of looking at you and a smile you couldn't forget—a little girl who was protected by the name of her mother's husband and his unassailable position, and who must be thus protected at all costs. A great wave of pity welled up in Connie's heart. For the first time she realized that for all his charm and talent and money, Duncan Craig had never been happy, and that now he never would be. His wretched boyhood had culminated in the degradation of his parents' divorce. He had failed to pursue his profession with the perseverance and in accordance with the standards which might have made him a great doctor. And through his own folly he had forfeited his freedom to marry the woman he really loved and give his own name to his firstborn child.

"I used to see him at big parties too, once in a while," Tilda was continuing. "He told me when I first got here that I looked familiar somehow, and asked if we hadn't met. I said I didn't think so, and he didn't pursue the matter. Naturally I didn't either. But if you think I'm not telling you the truth, you are making an awful mistake."

"Did you know this too?" Gwen demanded, wheeling around on Connie.

Connie glanced at Tilda beseechingly, and though she did not answer, the look was a giveaway.

"And you turned him down because of this bitch in New York?" Gwen said scornfully. Then, without waiting for an answer, she rushed on: "So now you're going to be a sister to him, and he's going to fight it out along those lines if it takes all summer? I'm beginning to see the light—all kinds of light, in fact. I know he's wasting his time as far as you're concerned, whether he knows it or not, the poor boob, and I'm going to get busy right off. I'm not going to let any bitch stand in my way, whatever you did, and with three thousand miles between this Eileen and Duncan Craig I'll have an easier time of it. Since he saw her, he and I have been through a war together, and that gives us something in common already that he and she never had, something that's meant a lot in our lives. That won't be the only thing either. When you get down to rock bottom, he and I belong to the same breed, and in the long run that counts more than anything else. I see how he feels about her and I don't like him any the less for it either. But all the same, I know how I feel about him, too. You don't know what it's like to love a man so hard it hurts, Connie. If you did, you wouldn't blame me for going out to get him."

"I'm not blaming you," Connie said very quietly, and went into her own room, wishing as she had never wished before that there were a door she could close after her.

The personal packing came last. Connie made a neat pile of half her heavy underwear and her more dilapidated sweaters; these, as well as her rubber boots, would be going to Madame Bonnier. In another neat pile she put the rest of the underwear and her woolen socks and pajamas; these would go to the French cleaning woman employed in the barracks. She wished there were something personal and pretty she could give to Madame Helle and the Countess, but both thought and searching failed to bring such gifts to light; she would have to content herself with getting candy from the commissary. But as she went through her collection of programs, cards, and notes, she found that she wanted to keep them all. She paused in the midst of her packing to look them over before tying them neatly together in packets.

An envelope addressed in Aunt Bertha's handwriting floated down on her lap, and she opened it and reread the letter inside. It was the one her aunt had written her after being informed of Tristan's first proposal. (Connie had not mentioned the later ones.)

Winchester, Mass., March 1, 1919

My Dear Constance:

I have received your letter telling me about the Frenchman who wants you should marry him, and also letters written by this Frenchman himself and by a lady who says she is his aunt, though why his aunt should bother to write me is something I do not understand.

Of course this news was considerable of a shock to me as I presume you realize. Brought up in the good Christian way you were, I never would have believed you could give a thought to a foreigner. You must have encouraged him some too or he never would have proposed. I will say this for him, he didn't lose any time telling you what his intentions were, and telling me too and getting his aunt to tell me. He made a thorough job of it and no mistake. His aunt even asked me to come and stay with her. But of course that isn't to be thought of. At my age I couldn't leave Massachusetts to go to a foreign country where the people have peculiar customs and where they can hardly talk the king's English. The way things have turned out I guess it would have been a good deal better if you hadn't gone either. Anyway I'm glad you had sense enough to put this young man in his place, and I hope that is the end of the matter, so I don't see that anything more needs to be said on the subject. I give you credit for not being so silly as to change your mind.

We have had a hard winter, the flu has been very bad and there have been several deaths among the neighbors but not those who would be most missed. The church needs shingling, and we have had both a chicken-pie and an oyster supper to raise money for it, but labor is so high that we didn't have enough, after all our trouble. Lots of people are complaining about the scarcity of help, but I am thankful to say that I am still able to do for myself and not dependent on having a hired girl clutter up my nice clean kitchen. We have been short of coal too. So the house has been kind of cold, but spring must be coming on because I saw a robin in the backyard yesterday when I went out to hang up the dishcloths. The cooky jar and the cake box are both still empty all the time, but I am hoping it won't be long now until I can get enough white flour to bake me one batch of biscuits. I am certainly good and tired of seeing Mr.

Hoover's picture hanging in my pantry over a long list of things he doesn't want I should eat. I don't see what business he has to meddle anyway. I guess he got these ideas of his living abroad so much. America is good enough for me and I hope it will be for you from now on. I should judge you'd got your fill of foreigners and that you would be coming home before long. I shan't be sorry to see you back.

Your affectionate aunt,
Bertha Slocum

Connie replaced the letter in the envelope, laughing a little and sighing a little as she tied it up among others with her gauze ribbon. Then she reread the note that had come in from Tristan that morning in the wake of a telegram acknowledging hers.

Ecole de Cavalerie, Saumur
12 May, 1919

Dearest Constance:
   The Frenchman proposes, but the American Army disposes. The news in your telegram was certainly unexpected, but I believe it was less upsetting to me than it was to you. Haven't I kept telling you that I wanted to show you Paris in the spring? And now it appears that I'm to have that pleasure! Knowing something of military methods, I can't believe that your transportation to the States will be forthcoming immediately. Before your next orders come through we should have plenty of time to talk over plans—and make them. Above all, don't worry. I'm sure everything is coming out all right, and I am counting on your assurance that you'll wire me again as soon as you know exactly when you're leaving Nantes.
   I'm writing in haste to catch the post so this is very brief, but every line in it is written with love.
   Toujours à toi,

Devotedly,
Tristan

Connie slid this letter in beside Aunt Bertha's, then removed it from the packet and put it in her breast pocket. She had already sent the promised wire, saying she was leaving Nantes that evening, and the sorting and packing were now done. She and Gwen and Tilda were going straight to the train, Arkie sang out that they had better step on it, because the train was already in; Sam had rushed ahead with the luggage and was trying to hold down three seats. They rushed too, with Arkie shoving them towards a compartment identified by Sam's anxious head sticking from the window. Then they were boosted and hauled aboard, and Sam and Arkie were both back on the platform waving and shouting, and the train was moving out of the station. . . . .

The train was heaving itself into a station, and the crowded corridor began to seethe with frantic passengers before the jerky stop came; then the confusion increased as those who were getting off collided with those who were forcing their way on. The door slid open again, disclosing a black-clad figure, and a tall erect man slipped inside, closing it swiftly after him.

"*Il n'y a pas de place,*" Connie began, in her improved French. Then the man turned and she stopped suddenly, her words drowned in a little cry of amazement and joy.

"*Il y a de place pour moi, chérie,*" Tristan de Fremond was saying, and she was in his arms.

CHAPTER XVII

"How on earth did you find me?"

"How on earth could I help it? I knew when your train left Nantes, I knew Saumur was on its route and that it stopped here, and I knew you'd be in a first-class carriage. There aren't so many of those nowadays that they're hard to locate. I saw you instantly through the corridor window. . . . Good evening, Gwen. Good evening, Tilda. What a pleasant little reunion we seem to be having!"

Without releasing Connie, he held out his hand to the others and they both welcomed him delightedly.

"Talk about being Johnny-on-the-spot! Why, you could give lessons to almost any Yank, Tristan!"

"Well, after all, Saumur's his natural habitat. It isn't so hard to wander down from the Cavalry School to the station, especially with strong incentive."

"You don't mean to say you expected to see him, Tilda!"

"It wasn't much of a shock to me. But it's not any less a pleasure because it wasn't a surprise," Tilda said with her usual blandness.

"I bet you didn't expect to see him in those clothes, though! How come, Tristan?"

"The Cadre Noir's got back into its own uniform at last, that's all. What do you think of it?"

Gwen reached up and slid back the silk shade covering the dim little light. Disclosed in the traditional black costume of the cavalry's crack unit, the young officer cut an even more distinctive and elegant figure than he had in his horizon-blue. The three girls expressed their admiration, openly though variously.

"Now that's what I call the cat's whiskers!"

"And it isn't full dress, either, is it, Tristan? You wear white breeches then, don't you?"

"I can't believe anything could be more stunning than all black!"

While Connie was speaking, she was shaken by the now familiar jerk which presaged departure. She went on still more excitedly. "Tristan, you'll have to hurry! The train's beginning to move. I'll wire you tomorrow where I'm staying."

Tristan laughed and drew her closer to him. "I've no intention of hurrying. I'm going along too. And I've arranged for all three of you to stay with friends of mine, unless you'd rather not. Some very good friends of mine, the Bouviers, who have an *haras*—that is to say, a stud farm—near Lisieux, also have a pied-à-terre in Paris. The family consists of a young couple, Jacques and Stéphanie, who are in the country just now, with their baby, and Jacques' mother, who is still in town. I've been in touch with them all since I first heard from you. Madame Bouvier *mère* would be delighted to have you and the other girls come to her house in the Faubourg Saint-Germain, and I think you'd like it better than a hotel—it's a charming old place and she's a very charming lady. Then Jacques and Stéphanie are counting on having us stay with them at the *haras* when we go to inspect Malou."

"It all sounds wonderful—so wonderful that I hate to make any objection, because that would seem unappreciative. But Tristan, it also sounds as if——"

"As if what?"

"As if you thought everything were all settled. And it isn't. It can't be. I have no idea yet what the Red Cross is going to do with me, but there's an order against demobilization of women in Europe. If that holds, I'll have to go back to the United States anyway whenever I'm sent. That might be next week, or it might not be for months, if I were transferred. Gwen thinks we could get into another branch of service if we wanted to. She does and Tilda doesn't. I haven't decided yet. But anyway, I couldn't stay on in France as a civilian."

"You could if you married a Frenchman, darling."

"There would be all kinds of red tape about that too. I'd be glad to visit your friends and to see Malou—if it doesn't bind me to anything."

"Nothing but to let me go on leading you towards realities. One of these is that every normal woman wants and needs a home. And you've never felt that you had one, in the real sense of the word. Isn't that true, Constance?"

"Yes," she said slowly. "It is true. Aunt Bertha's always been kind to me, according to her lights, but her house hasn't seemed——"

"And besides, it's hard for two women to make one by themselves, with no man to help them. I believe that in Malou you'd find the home you've longed for. And in it there'd be a man whose greatest desire was to help you. At least promise me that you will think of it in that way."

"I have, already. But I can't marry you just for a home. Or for any of the other things you can offer. It wouldn't be fair. I've tried to explain that too. Unless I were marrying you for yourself——"

Tristan laughed softly. "But you might even do that, in the end! Perhaps I dare to say at this point that you seemed rather glad to see me tonight, and that so far you haven't drawn away from me. I've had my arm around you for more than an hour now. Doesn't it feel natural for you to have it there, after all, darling?"

"Yes," Connie admitted, "it does. Don't take it away, Tristan."

"Such an idea never entered my head. And now that so much is satisfactorily settled, why not try going to sleep with your head on my shoulder?"

He smiled down at her so tenderly that she could not help returning the smile with equal tenderness; responding to the pressure of his hand at her waist, she leaned back. Then, finding that her head rested against one of the epaulets she had so greatly admired, and that this was stiff as well as shining, she slid a little further down in his embrace. The fine black broadcloth of his military coat was soft against her cheek, and, as she nestled closer to it, she was aware of the virile frame beneath it. With such comfort and such support, the last need of bracing herself against the movement of the train was gone. Gradually her tired body relaxed, her soothed senses responded. A delicious drowsiness stole over her, and she drifted off into profound and peaceful slumber.

"Your friend Miss Foster has just left here, Miss Galt. She is being transferred to the Graves Registration Service and she will have two weeks' leave. After that she'll be sent to the Argonne. I think the same arrangement could be made for you. But I should need to have an immediate answer."

"By 'immediate,' do you mean this afternoon?"

"No, but certainly within the next four or five days. There will be few opportunities for transfers and many requests."

Miss Benedict, Chief of Home Communication Service in France, apparently was a woman who always made wise decisions without delay.

"And if I don't take advantage of this opportunity?" Connie asked hesitantly.

"Then your name will go on the sailing list at once and you will await transportation home in Paris."

"May I ask how long a wait I should probably have?"

"It might be a week and it might be a month. My guess is that it would be somewhere between the two." Connie rose. "Thank you very much, Miss Benedict. I would like a few days to think it over. But I'll be in again early next week and let you know what I've decided."

She went out into the bright spring sunshine, which gave added luster to the statue of Jeanne d'Arc on the Place des Pyramides and penetrated the arcades of the rue de Rivoli. She would have liked to loiter a little in front of the inviting shop windows, where every sort of trinket was displayed, or on a bench in the Tuileries Gardens, where she could watch the children rolling their hoops around the gay flower beds; but she decided to stick to her decision of going straight back to her own room, where she would have no distractions while considering her problem. She found Tilda still in bed, propped up on large square pillows and looking extremely satisfied with her lot in life.

"I've had two baths," she informed Connie, "and luncheon on a tray— Russian salad and sweetbread patties and coffee éclairs. Our hostess has been in to see me, and speaking of chic, wait till you see her! But the best thing about this whole establishment is the bed. I don't know that I'm ever going to get out of it again, except to take more hot baths. . . .

123

What news did you get at Headquarters? Of course Gwen hasn't come back yet and won't, until dinnertime, so I haven't heard a thing."

"Gwen's been offered a transfer to Graves Registration and she's taken it. I've been offered one too, but I haven't decided yet."

"I should think it would be terribly sad working in those military cemeteries. You better come along home with me."

"I think perhaps I had better. If I do, I'll be demobilized as soon as I get there, and I don't know how long I'd be tied up if I went with Graves Registration. I'd sort of like to feel I could go on to something else if I wanted to."

"Such as?— Or don't you want to tell me?"

"Yes, I'd like to tell you. The time's come when I feel I've got to talk to someone who'd understand." She sat down on the bed and Tilda took her hand.

"Are you trying to decide what to do about Tristan de Fremond?" Tilda asked gently.

"Yes. He asked me in January to marry him—or rather he had his aunt and uncle ask me. Then after I said no, I couldn't possibly, he came and asked me himself. I said no again. I didn't want to marry anyone when Tristan first proposed to me. It was Tristan himself who changed my feeling about that, in a general way. But still I didn't see how I could marry him. Not that I haven't liked him, better than almost anyone I ever met, from the beginning. But I didn't dream he was in love with me."

"Did you begin to realize that you could marry Tristan de Fremond? Not that you *would* but that you *could,* that you were falling in love with him in spite of yourself?"

"Yes. Yes, I did realize it. I do realize it. But it's still a question of could and not would. He promised not to hurry me, and I know he'd have kept his promise if those unexpected orders of ours hadn't come in. Now he wants me to go to Normandy with him right away to see Malou—his château. He seems possessed of the idea that once I've seen this home of his, I won't find it so hard to make up my mind. He hasn't asked me to promise anything. He's only asked me to go."

"And you're hesitating over that?"

"Not because I wouldn't enjoy going. But I'm afraid if I did, he'd get the idea that the visit was conclusive. And it wouldn't be."

"I wouldn't worry about that if I were you. I'd go to Normandy with him tomorrow, if that's what he wants. It'll be a beautiful trip right now, with the apple trees all in bloom. Of course I don't know about Malou, but that's probably pretty nice too. And I don't believe Tristan's wholly self-seeking in urging you to take this trip. I think he knows it'll mean a lot to you, in all kinds of ways."

"Yes, it would mean a lot to me in all kinds of ways. But Tilda, there's still another reason why I'm hesitating. I don't know how to do things in the grand manner. My people have always been poor. I'd never even been out of New England until I came abroad. I've always had to save up just to go into Boston, and the only way I got as far as the White Mountains was to be a waitress at the Crawford House. Now if it were you, that would be different. You've got all the qualifications I haven't."

"All except beauty and character," Tilda said quietly. "Don't look so startled, Connie. You *are* beautiful. I'm just pretty. And there's an awful lot of difference, let me tell you, between being beautiful and being pretty."

Tilda pressed Connie's hand and released it. Then she pushed back the covers and swung her pretty legs over the side of the bed. Connie looked at her in renewed surprise.

"What are you going to do?" she inquired. "The last I heard you were never going to get out of that beautiful bed again."

"That was before you told me about this invitation to Lisieux," Tilda retorted, fumbling in her bag for fresh underwear. "I'm going to get into my clothes as fast as I can, and take you out to buy some of your own. *Real* clothes! We won't have as much time as I'd like before the shops close, but with your figure, we can do a lot in a little while. If you think I'm going to stand by and see you go off with Tristan de Fremond with nothing but that uniform of yours, you don't know me as well as you ought to. In fact, I hope by the time Tristan gets here for dinner tonight you'll already be looking a little less tailored and a little more tender. Don't try to talk back to me. Just give me a free hand for the next few hours!"

CHAPTER XVIII

"I'm afraid you'll find the first part of the trip dull. But farther on the landscape's very pleasant. We have the Seine in sight most of the way between Mésierès and Mantes, and again briefly near Bonnières, before we leave it entirely. Personally, I always like to ride along beside a river."

"Yes, so do I. But I'm not finding the trip dull, Tristan, not any of it. I'm enjoying every minute."

Constance spoke with complete sincerity. From the moment that she had seen her beautiful new bags stowed away in a funny little army car which Tristan had managed to borrow, and stepped into it herself, she had felt a sense of joyous relief, not only from the burdens and responsibilities of the last few months, but also from the problems and disappointments which had so long beset her. To start off like this, on a fine spring morning, equipped with lovely new clothes and bound for unknown country and strange sights, with a dashing young officer for her guide and companion and a fabulous stud farm as her destination, was the gladdest and maddest adventure of her hitherto restricted life. She drew in long breaths of happiness, and leaned luxuriously back, lifting her face to the sunshine.

"At last I'm seeing all the things I wanted to see for so long. You're showing them to me, Tristan."

"I'm sharing them with you. That's better. Of course I'm sorry that the Paris sight-seeing we planned had to be confined to one evening; but perhaps we can work in more next week, after we get back from Normandy. This trip couldn't have been put off. . . . Look, that's the Pavillon Henri IV ahead of us now—we're just coming into Saint-Germain. We could have an early lunch here, if you like—the restaurant's very good. But I was really aiming at the Grand Cerf in Evreux. That's my favorite stopping place, partly because it's about halfway between Paris and Lisieux, and partly because I have a certain sentiment for Evreux. I went to the Jesuit school there and spent some very happy years in the old town."

"Then let's go on to Evreux, by all means. It's much too early to eat anyway, isn't it?"

"It's never too early nor too late either, if you're in the mood, as a Frenchman usually is, and if a good place presents itself, as it usually does in France. But we'll save Henri IV for another time."

They began winding their way through the narrow streets of countless gray villages. As they neared Pacy, the villages were more scattered, the rolling countryside more peaceful and pleasant; increasingly a certain softness and stillness came creeping into the air. When the funny little car suddenly backfired, the report, seeming louder than it was because of the all-prevailing quiet, came as startlingly as a close and unexpected gunshot. Constance seized Tristan's arm, and could not wholly suppress a slight scream, though she quickly bit her lips to stop it.

"Why, what's the matter, darling?" Tristan asked anxiously. "You didn't really think someone was trying to pick us off, did you?"

"No—no. At least, I didn't think at all. It's just that I can't seem to stand any loud sudden noise. I'll be all right in a minute."

"Nothing has happened to upset you? Nothing but that harmless little backfire?"

"No, nothing, Tristan. Really! I'm terribly ashamed of being so silly. But ever since I was a baby——"

Briefly, she outlined the symptoms of the phobia which, a few months earlier, she had described to Craig, while Tristan listened with interest and solicitude. Then he dismissed the subject with a grave comment.

"Now I am doubly thankful that the war was over with before you arrived in France. You would have suffered merely at the sound of airplanes overhead. The bursting of shells and bombs, even in the distance, would have been anguish for you. Well, let us rejoice all that is over now, forever. France will show you only her smiling face and you will hear only the sound of her laughter. And it is high time you tasted of her abundance. I am sure you need food and drink to restore and refresh you. Fortunately, we are almost to Evreux."

Connie watched Tristan guide the queer little car expertly through a further succession of narrow winding streets, and bring it skillfully to a stop in front of a high wall whose very blankness had a beckoning quality. Then, as he took her hand to help her out and led her through a grilled gateway into a spacious courtyard, flanked by façades of mellow brick and dominated by the great stone stag which formed its central ornament, her errant musing came to an abrupt end in a spontaneous exclamation of pleasure.

"What a charming place! And from the street you'd never even guess it was here. But surely all this space isn't taken up by a restaurant!"

"No, the restaurant's attached to a very good hotel—or the hotel's attached to it, whichever way you choose to put it. Of course we French think the restaurant's the most important part, just as you Americans think the plumbing's the most important part. I've never stayed here myself, because it's such an easy run to Lisieux, and I'm always in a hurry to get on. But when I was at the Jesuit school, my relatives who came for special exercises invariably stopped at the Grand Cerf. . . . Here comes the *maître d'hôtel* now. I hope nothing's happened to the Riesling they used to have here. . . . It's warm enough to eat outside, don't you think so?"

It was plenty warm enough, Constance agreed heartily, and she sat down, basking in the sunlight, while Tristan discussed details in the menu and talked over old times with the delighted waiter. A checked cloth, which Tristan assured her was only the first of hundreds like it which she would soon be seeing, was quickly spread over a little tin table; and presently a beautiful golden wine and an unbelievable variety of hors d'œuvres, temptingly set forth in little shell-shaped dishes, were placed before them. As they ate and drank, with healthy appetite, Tristan began to talk about their prospective hosts.

"Perhaps I should tell you a little more about the Bouviers before we actually descend upon them. Stéphanie is the only daughter of the Marquis and Marquise de Vallerin. They had I don't know how many sons, and finally this one little girl, so of course she was the darling of the family. Her father, a real grand seigneur, is the director of the great Haras du Pin, the government-owned stud farm founded by Louis XIV, which has always had a man of high rank and distinguished record at the head of it. To me it is one of the most arresting institutions in France. The Grand Monarch's own architect designed the buildings, including the director's château, and these cover as much ground as a good-sized village, and are as much of an entity. Then there are acres and acres of park and forest besides, intersected with bridle paths and drives which are in constant use. One of these days you and I will go riding in them."

"I don't know how to ride, Tristan."

"That is one of the first things I am going to teach you."

"Over this week end?"

"No," he said nonchalantly, "some time in the future. There is no special hurry and we don't need to fix a date. Now you have diverted me with your jest about learning to ride over a week end. Where was I? Oh yes, I was saying that the Haras du Pin is a magnificent institution. Many of the horses we use at Saumur come from Le Pin, so it has long been my pleasant duty to go there a good deal, and I have known Stéphanie and her family from childhood. In fact, it was I who invited her to her first *Carrousel*. And how does she reward me? By falling head over heels in love with my best friend!"

"Was that a great blow to you?" Constance inquired, quietly sipping her golden wine.

"It would make a much better story if I could say that it was, wouldn't it? But alas! I am that most disillusioning type of Frenchman, existing in fact rather than in fiction, who reaches the advanced age of twenty-eight before really succumbing to love! No, I was only joking—I mean in referring to Stéphanie, not in my latest statement, which was made in deadly earnest." He paused long enough to look at her fondly over his own wineglass, then went on with his story. "Stéphanie made her debut in Paris the spring before war broke out," he said. "And she had a *succès fou*—that is, she was a great beauty and a great belle. But as far as all her eligible suitors were concerned, they might just as well never have existed. Nothing would do but she must wait for Jacques Bouvier to come home from the war, and when he returned a *grand blessé,* that made no difference either."

"From the way you say 'all her eligible suitors' it sounds as if the man she married wasn't one of them."

"No, he wasn't. That is, not in the usual sense of the word, though he's one of the finest fellows in the world. But you see, he belongs to the bourgeoisie and Stéphanie to the *haute noblesse* on both sides of the family; so it was natural for the de Vallerins to wish their only daughter to make the same sort of an alliance that they themselves and all their forebears had. Then there was another reason: both Jacques' maternal grandparents and one of his paternal grandparents were Jews, and the de Vallerins misprized them for racial and religious causes, in addition to all the others."

"You don't mean to say that our hostess in Paris is a Jewess!"

"Yes, I do. I'm not astonished that it didn't occur to you—you would think of her only as a strikingly handsome brunette. But her father was an enormously wealthy international banker, Abel Solomon. Indeed, it is his money that has made possible the maintenance of that charming pied-à-terre where you have been staying. It is also his money that has facilitated the transformation of an out-at-the-elbow *domaine* into one of the finest stud farms in a region that is famous for them. Incidentally, Abel Solomon was a great patriot and a great philanthropist as well as a great financier. But that did not prevent the de Vallerins from considering Stéphanie's marriage to his grandson a mésalliance, especially as Jacques' paternal heritage, in addition to being partly Jewish, is in no way outstanding. He looks like his father, Guy Bouvier, who was a Breton, a blond, and a Catholic, and who became a man of considerable substance in Saint-Malo. But Guy's mother was the daughter of a Jewish shopkeeper who married the owner of a small fishing fleet."

"So that it really required courage for her to persist in marrying him?" Connie inquired thoughtfully.

"Yes, great courage. Of course she should never have been forced to suffer such an ordeal. But old prejudices die hard sometimes, even when they are founded on injustice and ignorance. However, Stéphanie has had her reward. I do not believe there is a happier woman in all France today, or a more passionately devoted husband. And if she had given in to her parents, she would undoubtedly be married now to some man who delighted in the beauty of her person without sensing the splendor of her soul and whom she would therefore instinctively elude, herself remaining unfulfilled."

As if enough had been said on this particular subject to give it due weight, Tristan attacked with great vigor the Châteaubriand which had now been set before him, making no remarks except in praise of the superlative food until his plate was empty. Then he picked up the thread of conversation while eating his cheese.

"Of course the Haras de L'Abbatiale, where we are going, is only one of many around Lisieux," he said. "You will go to various others in the course of time, I hope. But there is only one Stéphanie de Vallerin, only one Jacques Bouvier, and only one Mark Mullins."

"Mark Mullins?"

"Yes. Another luxury that would have been impossible without Grandfather Solomon's money. He is a Yorkshireman and one of the most famous stud masters in the world. The blooded stock in his care is worth at least a million francs, possibly more, and he has a very lively sense of his responsibility. What is more, he really loves his horses, and to hear him talk about the foals, you'd think they were children. In a sense they *are* his children—he hasn't any of his own. He also claims that he is slightly deaf, but the only time he doesn't hear what you say to him is when he is engrossed in drinking terribly strong tea and reading the "Edition Sportif" of *Paris-Turf*."

"You make him sound like quite a character, Tristan."

"He is quite a character. Incidentally, among the other talents, he has a genius for handling his grooms—his boys, he always calls them. He has thirty or so under him. I'm not sure of the exact number."

"Thirty grooms! On one place!"

"Yes, at least that many. And there are twenty gardeners—or anyway there used to be before the war."

"Now I'm beginning to get overpowered again."

"There is the *grand manoir,* where Jacques and Stéphanie and their baby are installed. Then there is the *petit manoir,* which is kept ready at all times for Madame Bouvier *mère*. But as you might guess by looking at her, Paris is more to her taste than the Vallée d'Auge. Next in line is the guest house, to which I shall probably be relegated, and commodious quarters for the various grooms and gardeners, not to mention the famous Mark Mullins. By the way, the name L'Abbatiale comes from the house, somewhat apart from the others, that was once the residence of an abbot, and which has now been divided into quarters for the head gardener and his assistant."

"Don't tell me any more, Tristan. I simply can't take it all in. I'm even beginning to have fresh doubts as to whether I can face so much grandeur."

"Then I had best get you into the car again, before you have a chance to go back on me! And here I was planning to tell you about my own neighbors too! Well, I can do that as we go along, when I am sure you cannot escape. . . . *Jules, l'addition, s'il vous plaît!*"

With as much urgency as if his jesting words had been spoken in earnest, Tristan drew back Connie's chair, guided her through the court-yard, and helped her into the car. But once they were in it, he did not talk much after all, or press her to do so. Instead, he quietly observed her unconcealed pleasure in the countryside through which they were passing, making only an occasional illuminating comment or answering a delighted question. The character of the landscape was gradually chang-ing again; it was fresher, more verdant, lovelier in every way than it had been during the earlier part of their ride. Hillsides sloped gently away from the valleys through which the road wound, and all along it were orchards in full bloom. The houses had lost their universal monotone of gray, and revealed a variety of picturesque half-timbered styles; in the gardens opening before these, roses grew in reckless profusion. Cocks as well as crosses surmounted the steeples of village churches, and calvaries marked the crossroads and towered above the hedgerows with increasing frequency.

At last the road took a sudden, twisting plunge between a tiny chapel on one side and an undulating orchard on the other, and beyond these Connie caught an enchanted glimpse of spires and squares and streets. A small city, lightly veiled with mist, nestled in the declivity below. Connie looked up at Tristan with a rapt exclamation, and he answered the question she had not asked.

"Yes," he said, "that is Lisieux. Breath-taking, is it not, when you come upon it from the heights in that unexpected way?"

He steered the car to the side of the road and brought it to a stop. "You would like to sit here and enjoy this lovely panorama for a few minutes, I am sure," he said. "Our little Carmelite Sister made Lisieux famous. But to me it has always had a strange, supernal quality—perhaps on account of the mist. I hope you will visit the grave of Sœur Thérèse with me some day—I often go there in pilgrimage. It is such a peaceful place, that green hillside above Lisieux which looks down on all the loveliness of our Vallée d'Auge. The Carmelites' graves are marked only with white crosses, but from each mound white roses spring, as if to defy death. I would like you to have a rose from the grave of Sœur Thérèse to press in your book of devotions."

"I don't use any book of devotions," Connie admitted. "At least, I always carry a Bible around with me, as a matter of habit, but I don't read it very often any more. Aunt Bertha brought me up to read a chapter every day, going right straight through from start to finish, and then beginning all over again. But you wouldn't want me to put a rose from a Carmelite nun's grave in the King James version of the Bible, would you?"

"Why not? I should think that might be a very useful place for it. And speaking of Sisters and such, how would you like to stop and see my cousin Marie Aimée? The Bénédictine Abbaye is right on our way to the *haras*."

"The Bénédictine Abbaye?"

"Yes. The convent where Sœur Thérèse was educated and where she made her first Holy Communion. Marie Aimée is a member of the Benedictine Community there. I am almost sure I told you about her before. She is related to me through my mother's family, and except for the de Fremonds in Nantes, is the only cousin I have."

"You may have told me about her before, but if you did, it didn't register, at least for long. You've given me so many surprises, Tristan, and you jump so quickly from one thing to another, that you keep me confused. I'd just begun to get used to the idea of——"

"Of being engaged to me?" Tristan interrupted eagerly.

"No, no! That is, not—not exactly. But at least I'd begun to recover from the shock of your proposal, and the way you made it, when you began to spring another set of surprises on me. Take today for instance: You come and carry me off in an army car, you fill me full of food at a famous inn, you tell me I'm going to visit at a place where there are thirty grooms and twenty gardeners, you show me Lisieux from the top of a high hill, you talk about gathering roses from a nun's grave, and now you want to take me to a convent to see a strange cousin!"

"And you've loved every minute of it, now, haven't you?"

"Ye—es. But best of all, I've loved just riding along through the country. That doesn't appall me as much as the rest of it. Incidentally, I'm thankful that you've stopped saying 'Is it not?' and 'Does it not?' again. You did that all the time you were talking about the cemetery and that's one of the things that still disturbs me most—having you talk to me in such a formal way."

Tristan laughed. "You'll have to forgive me," he said. "You see, it's still a way that comes most easily to me, because that's the way I was taught to speak English. So when I'm very much in earnest, I lapse, quite unconsciously, into stiffness. I'll keep on trying to do better, though. Do we call on my cousin, or don't we?"

"Of course, if you want to."

He set the car in motion again, and they went on down the hill, turning just before they reached the foot of it, from the broad boulevard on which they had approached the city, first into a succession of steep, narrow streets, where the high, half-timbered houses seemed to meet almost overhead, and then into a series of squares, all full of business and bustle, especially the one flanked by the graceful Gothic cathedral. Tristan stopped the car and helped Connie out beside a tall building with a severe, gray façade that curved away from the bend of a noisy, crowded street.

"Here we are at the old *pensionnat*," he said. "It's been used for a hospital during the war. Now I believe there's a plan afoot to remodel it into a hostelry for aged gentlewomen in modest circumstances. A few such are already sheltered in the building that's always called the *vieux bâtiment*. That distinguishes it from the new ones that are only two or three hundred years old. There's another entrance to the Abbaye, but I like this best—or perhaps I should say I like my first welcome to come from Gertrude, the lay *portière* who also cooks for the old ladies."

While he was talking, he began tugging away at an iron bell pull, not unlike the one at Château Chassay, and a bell tinkled somewhere off in the distance, just as it did there. Then, from some still unseen but nearer place, came the sound of bolts being drawn, of heavy inner doors creaking on their hinges, and of felt-shod feet shuffling hurriedly forward. Lastly, on the door leading into the street a wooden panel slid away from a grilled opening so tiny that Connie had not even noticed it before, and between its frets a timorous face and a pair of cautious eyes were revealed. Almost instantly there was an incredulous squeal of delight, and the outermost door swung open, disclosing the bent, gray-clad figure of a little old woman, whose obvious delight completely transfigured her meek face and apologetic bearing. Tristan seized her by the shoulders and kissed her resoundingly on both cheeks.

"*Tiens,* Gertrude, how goes it, then? Let me have a good look at you!" he exclaimed. "Why, you get younger and better-looking every time I see you! But I also observe that you are still intent on keeping wolves away from your precious flock! I thought you would never open that door! Of course I am a suspicious character and you would do well to beware of me. But shame on you for making a beautiful young lady wait! One who has never visited a convent before, and who had a bad enough idea of them already! What is she going to think now?"

"But, Monsieur le Capitaine, how should I know it was you? Or that you would bring a beautiful young lady with you after all the years that you had come without one? Besides, I made all possible haste!" the old portress protested, twisting about to gaze at him with adoration.

"Well, is it because you have half killed yourself with hurrying that you have no breath left to invite us in?"

"Oh, Monsieur le Capitaine, *je vous demande pardon!* But you gave me such a turn that I do in effect forget my manners. Come in then, quickly. Mère Marie Aimée will be transported with delight at seeing you—and you too, of course, mademoiselle."

The last was added politely, but obviously as an afterthought, as the old portress closed the great outer door and shuffled ahead to set the inner one further ajar. In doing so she revealed a spacious, grassy courtyard, ornamented with trees and flowers and bisected by a broad gravel path lined with linden trees.

"If Monsieur, 'Dame will repose themselves for a small second, I will go and ask whether Mère Marie Aimée may receive them," Gertrude suggested timidly.

She shuffled off again, this time in the general direction of the chapel. Tristan indicated a rather dilapidated seat under the lindens.

"Here is your chance to rest after all the excitement you accuse me of causing you," he suggested. "This bench may not provide the best possible means for repose, but it seems to be all there is in sight. And perhaps the so-called *calme monastique* will help out."

"As a matter of fact I really don't feel as tired as I did before we came in. . . . What is that wonderful old building used for?"

"That is the *vieux bâtiment* I was telling you about. The bakery, the bookbindery, and the cobbler's shop are also located in the *vieux bâtiment.* Not that I have ever seen them, of course."

"Do the nuns bind books and make shoes?"

"Yes, Benedictines lead a very active life. They milk cows and raise vegetables and do exquisite needlework, and they manufacture the best liqueur in the world. Certainly you must have known about the liqueur, because it bears their name!"

"I knew about it, but somehow I didn't ever associate it with nuns!"

"I see you still have a lot to learn about the contemplative life. I must persuade Marie Aimée to let us have some Benedictine to take away with us. And now I see that Gertrude is signaling to us that we may come in."

The old portress, still nodding excitedly, was standing near a door at the chapel side of the courtyard, and as Connie and Tristan came up to her, she led the way. Into a building of delicate design and exquisite proportions, they were ushered by a *sœur tourière,* who greeted Tristan with the same unabashed delight which Gertrude had revealed. The *sœur tourière,* having offered them two straight-backed chairs on one side of the grille which divided a large, paneled parlor in two, bowed herself out again, leaving them alone. Again Connie ventured a whisper.

"I think these grilles are horrible," she said. "They make me think of a prison."

"They won't if you remind yourself that they are to keep the world out, not to keep the nuns in," he replied in a normal tone of voice. "Remember that this seclusion has been eagerly sought and hard-won. It took as much courage and determination for Marie Aimée to come here as it did for Stéphanie to marry Jacques. Ah, here she is now! By the way, you don't need to whisper any longer."

There was certainly nothing suggestive of a whisper in the nun's glad exclamation of welcome. She came rapidly across the space intervening between the rear of the room, where she had thrown open a door which formed an integral part of the paneling, and the farther side of the grille which Connie and Tristan were facing from the front. The flowing black of her garments accentuated the grace with which she moved, and the white wimple which framed her oval face intensified its clear color. Even before Marie Aimée reached them, Connie was aware of a striking resemblance between Tristan and this cloistered cousin of his. She had the same splendid eyes, the same glowing cheeks, the same irresistible smile; indeed her very voice rang in the same way.

"Tristan, how good it is to see you—and how glad I am you have brought this lady with you!" she exclaimed, immediately including them both in her joyous salutation. "I have never doubted your safe and happy return. Of course you have been constantly in my prayers and somehow I felt sure that these prayers would be answered. But even confidence in your safety is not as satisfying as seeing you in the flesh."

"I am grateful for the prayers and I too have no doubt that they helped. But I'd also like a kiss."

"Now, now! You know very well that we cannot embrace! However, this is such a special reunion that I am going to slip my fingers through the grille and take yours in mine."

Suiting her action to her words, she managed to thrust her white finger tips forward in such a way that he could grasp them with his strong brown hands, and holding them firmly, he gazed at her with the same tenderness which her own look revealed. Connie was instantly aware that the harmony between the seasoned soldier and the cloistered nun was one of curiously kindred spirits, that their close physical likeness was only a small part of their essential resemblance. She was even surer of this when Tristan began to speak of her to his cousin.

"This lady I have brought to see you, Marie Aimée, is a young American whose name is Constance Galt," he said. "She has been attached to an American hospital near Nantes, doing fine work there, and has just been released. At the moment, she is wondering what she will do next. I am hoping very much that she will decide the next step should be towards marriage, and that eventually I shall be fortunate enough to become her husband. She knows the de Fremonds of Chassay well—indeed it is to them that I owe the joy of meeting her. But I wanted you to welcome her into the family too."

"Which I do, with all my heart and soul."

The nun withdrew her fingers lightly from her cousin's and turned to Connie. The expression of her winsome face was very sweet, and her splendid eyes were thoughtful.

"I hope it has not been too much of an effort for you to make this visit, which means so much to me, mademoiselle," she said. "It is perhaps the first time you have been to a convent?"

"Yes."

"And you are not yourself a Catholic?"

"No."

"Then I am afraid you have found some aspects of your visit strange or even startling."

"I have, a little," Connie confessed.

"They will seem less strange and startling the next time, and soon they will not seem so at all," Marie Aimée assured her, speaking still more gently. "You see I am venturing to hope you will come very often to visit me in the future. Meanwhile I shall pray that you will be guided to make your decision in the way most pleasing to God, and that this way may also prove to be the one which would give great happiness to my cousin. And why not, since marriage stands high among God's own sacraments? . . . You are taking Mademoiselle to see Malou, Tristan?"

"Yes, tomorrow. We are on our way to L'Abbatiale now. Have you yourself seen anything of the Bouviers lately, Marie Aimée?"

"Yes indeed. Stéphanie brings the baby to visit me every week or so. She is a beautiful child, quite the convent darling."

"And Jacques?"

"He comes too, but not so frequently. After all the *haras* must have his first attention. . . . Will this be your first visit to a stud farm, mademoiselle?"

"Yes, the very first."

"This *beau cousin* is not confusing you too much, is he, with all these strange impressions? A first visit to a convent and a first visit to a stud farm, both the same day! *Voyons,* Tristan, that is crowding things too much!"

"I know, but I have to crowd them now, because if I don't, she'll be gone."

Again the nun looked thoughtfully at Connie, and she told the girl in a grave voice that she would pray for her. "And I believe you will enjoy the *haras* very much, and that will make up to you for finding the Abbaye forbidding," she went on. "The horses are very beautiful, and of course at this season the little foals are all out in the green pastures with their mothers. It is a lovely sight."

While she was speaking, a bell began to ring and she rose. Again Constance was poignantly aware of the supreme grace with which she moved and the loveliness of her face.

"That is the summons to vespers, so I must leave you," she said. "And probably you should be on your way to L'Abbatiale yourselves by now, in any case. I depend on you to give my most affectionate greeting to the Bouviers. And thank you again for your visit."

Constance watched her intently as she crossed the paneled parlor and opened the disguised door. Instead of watching Marie Aimée, Tristan looked at Constance.

"Well?" he said when the nun had disappeared, his voice betraying a slight amusement that was so often mingled with its tenderness.

"Well, of course you're right. She's more than beautiful, she's radiant. She makes me feel happy and serene because she's so happy and serene herself. And somehow she seems to belong to all this, and all this to her. I don't mind the grille so much now that I've seen her behind it. She must have been very brave to go on as she has. Did the man she cared about die in some especially dreadful way?"

Tristan laughed. "I'm the only man Marie Aimée's ever cared about, and of course that was as a cousin, almost as a brother, not as a lover. She still cares about me just as much as ever, for that matter. The Church doesn't frown on family affection. On the contrary it regards this as highly salutary to both body and soul."

"Then why——"

"I'm afraid I'll have to shatter some more delusions. Contrary to popular Protestant belief, the unhappy termination of a love affair isn't the usual reason for entering a convent."

"What is the usual reason?"

"The conviction that it offers the only true vocation. Not for everyone of course—there are vocations in the world as well as in the cloister. But for the person seeking it. To that person it represents great joy, just as marriage does for another—to Stéphanie, for instance. It is not a sacrifice in the usual sense of the word, much less is it an inadequate compensation for something more precious that has been lost. It is the supreme fulfillment."

They had come to a sign reading Haras de l'Abbatiale with a small black arrow pointing enticingly to a hedged byroad which took them deeper and deeper into green and quiet countryside. This was to all appearances totally uninhabited; but eventually they came upon a low, thatched building with a sign which designated it as a café, and across the road from this, white fences suggested some kind of a private enclosure. Tristan turned in at a picket gate and guided the car between two long rows of stalls which were apparently not in full use at the moment. Then he nodded from the stalls towards a neat building, rather nondescript in character, which stood beyond them.

"I know where I am now," he said. "I haven't been here since the beginning of the war, and of course there have been some changes. Besides, everything probably is not—how do you say?—running on all cylinders just yet. But I am sure the harem is further on, and that this is the male department of the *haras*. Those stables we just passed are the colt foals', where they are put as soon as they are weaned, and these are the stud master's quarters just over here. Mark Mullins has a *bureau*—I mean an office—downstairs, right beside the prize stallion's stall, and upstairs a very cozy housekeeping apartment. In that way the stallion is never left unguarded day or night. Of course he has his special groom too—the *étalonier,* who is devoted to his charge, and whose only duty is to care for him. But it is just as well that the stud master should also keep a watchful eye on Saladin."

"Is he dangerous?"

Tristan smiled. "No, he's very gentle. But he's also very valuable. He's a beautiful creature, and he's never been beaten in a race yet, though he's run in all the classics—the Grand Prix, the Prix de Jockey Club, the Arc de Triomphe, and I don't know how many more. That makes his offspring very valuable too, so it's highly important to safeguard and continue the strain. I believe his service charge alone is twenty thousand francs."

"His service charge?"

"Yes. For covering a mare." And noticing that she still looked puzzled, his smile deepened. "I see that your Aunt Bertha must have neglected to include the phraseology which is considered good usage in the animal kingdom when she was giving you the inevitable little lecture on the facts of life," he observed. "But Stéphanie will make up for that deficiency in short order. You may find her almost alarmingly outspoken, but your alarm will pass under the influence of her charm. Well. . . . Tomorrow I will bring you back here to show you Saladin's manège and paddock, and present you to His Majesty, unless Jacques insists on doing so himself. But now, as I've said before, I think we should not linger."

The fields had begun to take on a landscaped look, the trees were less scattered, and the gravel road, bordered by rosebushes in full bloom, wound its way through clumps of shrubbery to a fork where one arrow was marked FERME DE L'ABBATIALE, and the other MANOIRS ET JUMENTERIE. Here Tristan turned abruptly to the right, and the luxuriant growth about them, parting suddenly, revealed an immense quadrangle. It was open at one end and surrounded on three sides by long, low stables roofed with beautiful purple and green tiles and divided into brightly painted box stalls; these were enclosed at the bottom, but stood open at the top and were thus flooded with afternoon sunlight. A clock tower dominated the large central section, which faced due south, and on the further side of the greensward, only slightly apart from the quadrangle, were half a dozen attractive half-timbered houses, partially concealed by plane trees. As the car swung up to the lawn, a young woman in a white dress who was sitting beside a perambulator in front of the largest house snatched a baby from its carriage and came running over to meet the visitors.

"You can drive all the way!" she called. "The road comes right up to the houses now, Tristan!" But apparently she could not wait for him to take the designated road. Instead she rushed across the greensward and then jumped up and down with impatient joy, bouncing the unprotesting baby about while Tristan was stopping the car. When he opened the door and got out, laughing, she tossed the baby into his arms and threw her own about his neck.

"*Mauvais sujet,* we thought you were never coming!" she cried in a glad voice, kissing him on both cheeks with as much spontaneity as he had shown in kissing the old portress. "Only four years since you were here? Nonsense, it is half a lifetime! And remember I was not here then, so what good did that visit do me?" She released him from the embrace, which he had returned with as much heartiness as his handicapped position would permit, and held out her hands to Constance. "I must give you a kiss too!" she exclaimed, suiting her action to her words. "We are so happy, my husband and I, that Tristan has brought you to us. Jacques has been watching for you both all the afternoon, and now of course, just at the wrong moment, Mark had to call him away. But he will be back almost as soon as we reach the house. We can all get into this car together, can we not? Give me back my beautiful treasure, Tristan. A superb infant, is she not? There, it is just as I thought—we could not be better!"

Somehow they had all squeezed into the little army car and Tristan had it in motion again. They had not covered the short strip of road that still separated them from the group of picturesque Norman houses before Connie had decided that this was the most attractive young woman she had ever seen in her life. Stéphanie Bouvier had all Gwen's vivacity, but she also had a distinctive charm in which Gwen was totally lacking. Her thick black hair was brushed away from a fine forehead, her glowing cheeks curved down to meet a beautiful white throat, her bare arms complemented strong and shapely hands. She was wearing no jewelry except one huge emerald ring, and at first glance, her white dress appeared wholly unremarkable, wherein lay its consummate art; it outlined her generous bosom, small waist, and long, tapering thighs with Grecian simplicity. Nor had Stéphanie spoken with exaggeration in referring to her baby as superb; the child was a replica, in miniature, of her mother.

"What is your baby's name?" she asked Stéphanie, wishing she dared to take the child into her arms.

"Margot. It suits her, I think. She is really a love. But I see you are discovering that for yourself. Therefore you will not be annoyed because her father and I adore her so openly. . . . About Jacques, Tristan. He is terribly mutilated, of course. I believe you are prepared for that. But perhaps I should warn you once more, because, though he gives no sign, he cannot help being correspondingly sensitive."

Tristan nodded without answering. They had already reached the largest house, and two impeccable servants had emerged from it—a maid wearing a black-silk uniform and a cap with long streamers, a man in a red-and-black striped waistcoat and an immaculate and enveloping apron. Without awaiting intructions, they fell upon the baggage, removing it adroitly from the car, which the man then drove away with a flourish while the maid disappeared with the smaller bags. Stéphanie, hoisting her baby over one shoulder, turned questioningly to Connie.

"Do you wish to go to your room at once, or will you come with me first to see the paddocks, before the mares and foals come in for the night?"

"I'd like very much to go first to the paddocks," Connie answered promptly, remembering the hint Tristan had dropped. "I'd still have time to freshen up before dinner, wouldn't I, after we got back?"

"But certainly. We never dine before eight. Let us be on our way then. . . . Ah, here comes Jacques at last!"

Two figures had emerged from a central door in the clock tower at the farther end of the quadrangle. One was a small, spare man, who carried himself so erectly that he gave the effect of stiffness, and who was dressed in whipcord breeches, a leather coat, and polished riding boots; he carried a crop in one hand, and tapped it against his boots while he talked. The other man, who was much taller and who was wearing tweeds, was on crutches, which he manipulated skillfully though one leg was gone almost to the hip and one arm to the elbow. For a moment they remained so deep in conversation that they did not even look away from each other; then the man on crutches glanced across the greensward and caught sight of the group near the house. He gave a hearty shout, waved first his remaining arm and then a crutch, and began covering the intervening space at a surprisingly rapid rate; the other man disappeared inside the stable. As the cripple came nearer, Connie could see that his face was scarred and his body twisted. She also saw that Stéphanie was looking towards him with shining eyes.

"Come, let us hurry and meet him halfway!" Stéphanie said. She already had a winged look, and while neither Tristan nor Connie loitered, she had reached her husband long before they caught up with her and had met him with a fond embrace, though she could not have been parted from him more than an hour or so. Tristan waited until they showed some sign of being willing to separate from each other; then he went forward himself, hailing his old friend.

"*Eh bien, mon vieux! Nous voilà enfin! Comment ça va?*"

"*Bien, toujours bien!*" the cripple responded, detaching himself sufficiently from his wife and child to wring Tristan's hand and nod cordially to Connie. As he did so, she was again aware of an arresting personality, very different from his wife's, but no less magnetic. His thick, wiry hair must once have been almost copper-colored, but it had turned prematurely white, and the whole effect was now sandy, and inexplicably attractive; the long furrows in his lean cheeks deepened as he smiled; and his eyes, which had warm amber lights in them, crinkled around the corners. Far from being a drained or bitter face, it was one of amazing vitality and buoyancy. "What bad chance not to be present when you arrived, after all these years!" he went on, skillfully adjusting his position to profit by the arm which Tristan had flung around his shoulder. "Of course it would have to be just at that moment Mark would call me to say that Tarte à la Crème, one of our best mares, was in labor difficulties. But now I think all is well again, and she has a fine colt foal too. You will wish to visit our maternity ward later, I hope—it is the most recent improvement at L'Abbatiale, the result both of my own best efforts and Mark's. But first for a good drink while we fight the war all over again! I take it the apéritifs are in readiness, Stéphanie?"

"Of course. Go back to the house with Tristan, and Miss Galt and I will join you later on the terrace. She wants to see the foals before they come in. . . . What I meant was 'I know you want to be alone with your friend for a little while,'" she added in an undertone to Connie, watching the two men as they moved away, already deeply in talk. "It is a hard thing for women to learn, is it not, how superfluous they are at a meeting of old comrades? No matter how much they are beloved, they must wait, at such times, for their turn."

Connie, having already decided that Stéphanie knew far more about men than she would ever find out, made no direct reply

"Perhaps we had better avoid the pharmacy just now, since Tarte à la Crème has so recently dropped her foal," Stéphanie suggested. "But Jacques is right—I think you will find it interesting to visit later on. But come, this is the way to the paddock."

To Connie's great relief, Stéphanie skirted the pharmacy, leading the way through a narrow path to a great, green pasture enclosed by a high white fence, where half a hundred beautiful mares, some bay and some chestnut, were peacefully grazing, each with a little foal beside her. "A lovely spectacle, is it not?" Stéphanie asked, hitching Margot higher over her shoulder, as if she wished to be sure the wide-eyed baby were also enjoying the scene. "I bring Margot here every day, that she may enjoy this too. I want her first consciousness, next to that of me and naturally of her father, to be of horses. And I think it will. Presently I shall begin carrying her in front of me on my saddle. Meanwhile, she will learn to know all our stock by sight."

"You really think so?"

"But certainly. How can I doubt it? You would see that if those foals and all those mares should be separated, and then all put back together again, each foal would know its own dam. Not one would make a mistake. Should I then believe that my own beautiful child is less intelligent than a foal?"

"Of course not," Connie said hastily. "But you see, Madame Bouvier, I've never had a chance to come to a place like this before. I don't know anything at all about horses."

"You will learn," Stéphanie said kindly. "And of course you will wish to do so as quickly as possible, for Tristan's sake. Unfortunately he has never been able to afford an *haras* of his own. Nevertheless, as you have doubtless already heard, horses have always been his great passion—that is, until very recently," she added archly. "Now we understand he has another, and high time too. There is great need for a chatelaine at Malou, as you will see for yourself."

Again Connie took refuge in silence. Stéphanie sank easily down on the ground, unbuttoned her white dress, and laid her baby against her full breast. Margot nosed eagerly about for a moment, then caught at the nipple, and began to nurse in deep drafts, noisily and contentedly. "So far I am a great success as a brood mare, according to Jacques," Stéphanie said proudly. "I conceived at once, I went full time without complications, I gave birth and am now giving suck as normally and easily as possible. It only remains to be seen whether I can continue in the same way. We are enchanted with Margot, of course; but after all, no man's mind is really at rest until he has begotten at least one son. I hope that by this time next year Jacques may be reassured."

"You're thinking about another baby already?"

"But how could I help it, knowing Jacques' necessity? Because he has suffered and lost so much, it is even greater than most men's. He needs not only constant proof of my loyal and lasting love, but constant proof of his own enduring virility."

Stéphanie asked the question and made the statement as simply as if she was saying that he was hungry and thirsty. "Perhaps my feeling about all this is stronger because I have lived most of my life where mating is the universal rule and fecundity the universal aim," she said slowly. "I have never been happy when I was away from my horses. Their laws are mine too, and it seems suitable for me to speak of human beings in the same way I speak of them. I think you shrank a little when I said I was a good brood mare. But I am proud I can say that—remember I told you only those worthy of future champions are chosen for their mothers! We seek to transmit nothing but the finest strains."

"I believe I see what you mean now. I confess I didn't before."

"As a matter of fact, I could speak of being 'full' or 'empty' just as naturally and just as proudly, though I suppose such expressions would shock you too."

"They don't exactly shock me. It's just that they're so unfamiliar I hardly grasp them."

"We say a mare is 'empty' when she has broken at the end of the season without conceiving again. We say she is 'full' when the service has been successful. And there is such a beautiful term for such service. But you do know that, of course?"

"Is it—covering?"

"Yes—then you had heard it already."

"Not until today. Tristan used it today and I didn't understand. He smiled and said he would explain, but of course I shouldn't have needed an explanation. It was very stupid of me not to realize at once——"

Stéphanie stretched out the strong, brown hand on which the great green stone glittered and took Connie's quietly but firmly in hers.

"Of course you are not stupid," she said. "Tristan has told us that you are very learned for so young a lady. In fact he said so much about it that I was almost afraid to meet you."

"Why, you couldn't have been!" Connie exclaimed. "*I* was afraid of meeting *you!* Tristan had talked to me about you too, of course. And I thought from what he said I would be very ill at ease here. Instead of that——"

"I shall tell Tristan just what I think of him for frightening us about each other, all to no purpose. However, little harm has been done, because I am not afraid any more either. You see, you do not give the effect of learning—you are very sweet and gentle and very, very pretty. I understand quite easily Tristan's new passion which has turned his thoughts away at last from the *haras* he could not have." For a moment Stéphanie's dazzling smile illumined her lovely face. Then this grew grave again. "This knowledge of yours, it is there I know, although it does not show too much," she said. "But does it perhaps lack balance? Has it come too much from books and buildings and not enough from living creatures and green fields?"

"Yes, I am afraid it has," Connie said in a low voice.

"Then could you not learn from the others too? I believe Tristan hoped you would if you came here. So let me try to help you. We speak of 'covering,' yes. And every time I hear that said, I think of all the different meanings it may have. Not that the act of mating is shameful, for any of God's creatures—surely only evil minds and prudish spirits would try to make it seem so! It is natural and wonderful in itself, still more so in its secret and mysterious promise of perpetuation. But to cover—that also signifies to shelter, does it not? To protect? To encompass? All that besides physical union!

"When Tristan told you I would explain," she said softly, "I am sure he knew I would think of all these different meanings. I am sure he knew I would tell you, from the fullness of my heart, that my own happiness comes through the knowledge that I am encompassed by my husband's love."

CHAPTER XIX

For a long time after she had gone to bed that night, Constance lay with her cheek pillowed on her arm, looking out at the square of sky framed by her casement window. The sky itself was sapphire-colored and starlit, and a window box full of bright flowers formed a fragrant border at the base of it. But Constance was not looking at the sky, or drinking in the perfume of the flowers; she was reliving the day, from the moment she had stepped into the little army car early that morning to the moment when she had said good night to Tristan at the door of the guest cottage.

She was sitting on the grassy slope at the paddock's edge, watching Stéphanie as the young mother nursed her beautiful baby, and hearing the happy young wife declare that her cup of joy was full because she was encompassed by her husband's love. . . .

From then on, it was of this encompassment, in its varied manifestations, of which Constance had been most aware. She and Stéphanie had remained near the paddock until the "boys" had come to take the mares and their foals into their stalls for the night, and Connie had watched them going in glad and graceful procession from their green pasture to their big box stalls, strewn with golden straw. Afterwards they had gone on to the *grand manoir*, reaching it as the tall clock in the hallway struck seven. From the drawing room beyond came the vigorous rise and fall of male voices, and a hearty laugh rang out above the tinkle of ice. Stéphanie paused with her hand on the doorknob, and shook her head, smilingly.

"I think it is still too soon for us to break in," she said. "After all, they have not had a chance to visit each other since the *course à la mer*. In any case, you would probably like to see your room now."

She went lightly up the stairway, her baby, who was now fast asleep, carried with loving care, and stopped before a door which stood lightly ajar. As she pushed it farther open, the rosy draperies, soft rugs, and carved furniture of an exquisitely appointed room were disclosed. Bowls filled with the same sort of top-heavy red roses which Connie had seen in the driveway were scattered about, the windows were open above their flower boxes, and the mingled fragrance of blossoms and fresh air pervaded the room. But a cheerful fire was burning under a marble mantel, so there was comforting warmth too, and Connie expressed her grateful pleasure.

"You can't imagine how good that fire looks to me. I've been so cold in France that I've wondered, over and over, if I'd ever feel comfortable again. Even now, though it's warm in the sun, when there is any, it's cold out of it, especially indoors and in the evening."

"Yes, I know. Tristan had warned us that you were finding our French climate and our unheated houses very trying. We shall try to make you more comfortable here than you have been so far. Ah, I see that Simone has unpacked for you, as I was sure she would have. What a charming gown! And how perfectly it must suit you!"

Stéphanie laid the sleeping baby down on the bed, picked up the dinner dress of soft blue crepe which was spread out on the rosy counterpane, and draped it with expert fingers over Connie's oxford-gray uniform, continuing to express her admiration as she did so. Then she put the dress down again, reclaimed the baby, and nodded in temporary farewell.

"I think I told you, dinner is at eight—or rather we take an apéritif then, and dine as soon as we feel like it afterwards. Come down whenever you wish, of course. But perhaps you would like this hour to yourself. By the way, no one else uses your bathroom. . . . Would you care to kiss Margot good night?"

"Oh, I'd love to! And I'd like the hour alone very much too. It *has* been a very full day, though I've enjoyed every minute of it."

Constance stooped over to kiss the baby's soft forehead, ringed with damp, dark curls, and involuntarily her lips strayed beyond the dimpled cheeks and came to rest in the creases of the warm little neck. Then she found that she did not want to take her mouth away; the impulse to go on kissing this beautiful little creature, to prolong the rapture of feeling the petal-like skin, was almost overpowering. Stéphanie seemed instantly to divine her desire.

"You would like to take her in your arms for a minute, too, would you not?" she asked gently. "Oh, not that way! Have you never held a baby before?"

"No, I never have."

Constance knew her voice sounded stifled as she answered, and she hoped Stéphanie would think this was because her face was again half buried against Margot's neck; but she did not really believe that Stéphanie was so easily deceived. She held the baby out to its mother, and turned away, her eyes brimming.

"*Voyons,* you must not allow yourself to be distressed at showing how you feel," Stephanie said kindly. "To take a little child in your arms for the first time, even if it is not your own child—that is the sort of experience which we call *très émotionant.* It is a mistake to suppose that only the first kiss of love can give a sensation that is moving in the same way. Besides, you are very tired. You should rest a little before you come downstairs, and drink a cup of hot tea. I will send you some at once. And do not have the dinner hour at all on your mind. We are never too much bound by time here at the *grand manoir.* It is only in the stables that it is necessary that everything should march with precision."

Stéphanie went out, closing the door quietly after her. Connie crossed over to the chimneypiece and stood looking down at the cheerful little fire until Simone appeared with the promised tea, drawing a small table up beside a low padded chair and inquiring solicitously if there were anything else she could do for Mademoiselle. No, there was nothing, Connie said briefly; she did not feel like talking just then, or even having anyone else in the room with her. But the tea refreshed her. She filled her cup a second time, ate two of the *madeleines* which were also on the tray, and smoked a cigarette. Then she went into the bathroom, sprinkled scented salts in the tub, turned the water on, and slowly began to undress.

Up to then, there had been no chance to change from her uniform after all. When Tristan arrived at the pied-à-terre the evening before, it was with the announcement that he had made reservations at Voisin's and had seats for *Faust* afterwards. Acting on Tilda's suggestion, Connie would have put on civilian clothes for a quiet dinner at Madame Bouvier's house; but she could not wear these at a restaurant and at a place of public amusement, or, on leaving Paris the next day, in an army car. She had been disappointed at the delay in trying the effect of the new dinner dress and the other lovely things she and Tilda had chosen together; but now she was glad that she would be wearing many of these for the first time in the house that belonged to Stéphanie and Jacques, with only Tristan for a fellow guest. She lay at leisure in the tub for a long while, luxuriating in the scented water; then, still moving slowly, she dried herself with thick, soft towels, powdered herself all over, and began to put on her new garments with the same delightful lack of haste: a thin crêpe-de-chine "teddy," delicately embroidered; a silly little corset, made mostly of ribbon; fine silk stockings; silver slippers. Then she seated herself at her dressing table, took down her hair, and unplaited the braids; presently it was swirling all about her in a cloud of gold. She spread it over her shoulders like a shawl and amused herself by sitting on it; finally she rebraided it and coiled it around her head, pinning it firmly into place but permitting little tendrils to escape over her temples, so that the effect was unrestrained. Finally she unstoppered a tiny bottle of perfume, sniffed in long breaths of it, and dabbed it behind her ears. Now she was ready for the new dress with its matching slip. It went on easily over her head, without disarranging her carefully dressed hair, fell into place above her breasts, around her waist, across her hips. It was soft to the touch, and she stood fingering it for a minute before she looked at herself in the glass. The mirror reflected a vision that was wholly strange to her: a slim, golden-haired girl delicately dressed in pale blue, femininely lovely, utterly desirable. . . .

She waited until the clock in the hallway had struck eight before she started down the stairs, her happy mood tinged with uncontrollable but not unpleasant shyness. It was so long since her neck and arms had been bared in public that she was acutely aware of their exposure now that she had left her own bedroom. And never in her life had she owned a dress like this one; even if a uniform had not so long been her only wear, this unaccustomed elegance, this costly simplicity, would have made her self-conscious. While she was still hesitating on the landing, the drawing-room door was flung open and Stéphanie came out. She was still wearing white, but this time her dress was entirely sleeveless and cut in a V which came almost to her high waistline. A second great emerald, twice the size of the one that glowed on her finger, hung from a fine gold chain which encircled her neck. Compared to her costume, the one which Connie wore was the epitome of reserve.

"Oh, how wonderful you look!" Stephanie exclaimed. "Tristan will never be happy to have you in uniform again after tonight. Tristan, did you ever see such a transformation?"

She seized Connie's hand and drew her impulsively towards the drawing room. As Tristan sprang forward to meet them, Connie saw that he, too, had been transformed. Previously she had thought that nothing could exceed in smartness the uniform which she had first seen him wearing on the Paris train; but now that white breeches had been substituted for black ones and that he had put on all his orders and decorations, he cut an even more dashing figure. He came quickly up to her and put his hands on her shoulders.

"Why, the word 'wonderful' only half expresses it!" he cried enthusiastically. "You should have said miraculous, Stéphanie! Let me turn you around, chérie, so that I can look at you from all sides. This is the sort of dress Robert was talking about when he said you could look like our portrait of Catherine Sforza if you really gave yourself half a chance!—Oh yes, I overheard, and he was right!—Three guesses, Jacques—is this blue marvel a creation of Worth or Paquin, or our former comrade in arms Lucien Lelong?"

"It might be any one of the three, because I suspect that a great deal of heartfelt care went into its adjustment," Jacques replied, smiling. "You have often said yourself, *mon vieux,* that the manner in which a dress was cut did not count for half so much as the manner in which it was worn. But there! We are perhaps taking it too much for granted that Miss Galt desires to be treated like one of the family. You are acting towards her with no more ceremony than you do towards Stéphanie, Tristan. . . . Please be seated, mademoiselle, and let me try to make up for Tristan's bad manners by an exhibition of my own, which are notoriously worse."

She took the indicated seat beside him, already feeling more at ease, and by the time they had finished their apéritifs she had forgotten that her sleeves came only halfway to the elbow, and that her neck was bare below the collarbone. Her host continued to chat with her, lightly and agreeably, until dinner was announced. Then he led her into the dining room, seated her at his right, and for a few minutes pursued the pleasant conversation which was addressed primarily to her. Next, adroitly, he steered it into more general channels. And it was Tristan, not he, who eventually diverted it to their own favorite subject.

"Are you going to start racing again, Jacques?"

"I am indeed."

"Have you anything good enough to engage for the Gold Cup at Ascot?"

"I hardly aspire to the Gold Cup, but I might get a long distance handicap with Reine Iseult, if the handicapper isn't too hard on me. She's a beautiful bay, and I've great expectations of her staying powers. I've thought of her in another connection too—how would you like her for a wedding present? If she turns out good enough, she might be the foundation of your own *haras.*"

"You're not serious, are you, Jacques?"

"Of course, if you're serious about getting married, and any girl in her senses can be persuaded to take you seriously."

This time it was Jacques who looked laughingly towards Connie. She laughed too.

Before the evening was over, Tristan was drawing sketches designed to show the possible adaptation of his commons to a stable for Reine Iseult and her progeny.

Lying awake in the darkness, her cheek pillowed on her arm, Constance went on looking unseeingly at the square of starlit sky above the flowering window box. Instead she seemed to see Stéphanie with her baby at her breast again, humming a last lullaby before she tucked the little girl into her cradle for the night. She seemed to see the expression on Jacques Bouvier's face as he watched his wife bending over their child, waiting for her to leave the cradle and come to him. Then Stéphanie's as she straightened up and hurried across the room. After that the last light went out in the room of Connie's vision, and she could see no more; but she knew that the time for which Stéphanie had waited with such contented tranquillity was come, that her husband was wholly hers now and that she was indeed "encompassed" by the fullness of his love. And with the knowledge came the happy thrill of her own restored femininity and the strange, sweet poignancy of her own awakened desire. . . .

At last a faint, distant sound penetrated her tingling consciousness. Presently she realized it must be coming from footsteps moving quietly, almost stealthily, across the lawn, and afterwards from a nearer movement which rustled the shrubbery. Before she had time to be frightened, she heard Tristan softly calling her by name.

"Constance! Are you asleep?"

"No—is anything wrong?"

"Of course not. But I want to say good night to you. Can't you put on a dressing gown and come to the window?"

Simone had spread the new shell-pink negligee over a chair with the same solicitude she had shown a few hours earlier in spreading the blue dress over the counterpane. Connie leapt out of bed and wrapped the negligee over her filmy nightdress, slipping her bare feet into the little feathered mules that stood near by. Then she hurried to the window. There was no longer any fear in her heart, only a feeling of such amazed delight that she could not put it into words. Instead she tried to quiet it with chiding.

"Tristan, you must be stark, raving crazy! What will Stéphanie think if she finds out?"

"She won't find out. She and Jacques sleep on the other side of the house. And you may be very sure they're not thinking of you and me just now, or of anyone in the world except each other. But even if she did find out, she wouldn't be at all surprised or at all shocked. You don't suppose she really expected me to let you go with just that little casual good night at the guest-house door, do you?"

"Of course she did. Anyway I did. It's perfectly absurd for you to come back here. At this rate, you'll start serenading me in a minute!"

"I shall indeed. I have a very good repertory of love songs. Please tell me which you prefer—

> " 'Les beaux jours
> Sont si courts,
> Amoureusement,
> Garde moi
> Près de toi,
> Tendrement.' "

—he chanted softly. Then shifting air and meter, he went on—

> " 'Jusque toi mes chants dans l'ombre
> Montent doucement.
> Tout se tait, la nuit est sombre,
> Viens près d'un amant.' "

"Tristan! I didn't know you could sing!"

"There are so many things you don't know about me yet, *chérie!* Because you don't give me a chance to teach you."

"On the contrary, you've given me more lessons today, directly and indirectly, than I can possibly take in. Incidentally, your examples of women who've achieved happiness because they had the courage of their convictions haven't been lost on me. But I think you're being absurd now. What difference does it make whether you say good night to me at the guest-house door or out there on the lawn?"

"I wasn't thinking of staying indefinitely on the lawn. There are trellises all over the side of the house and I'm a very good climber."

"Tristan, you wouldn't!"

"Why not?"

"You know very well why not."

"I don't see why you shouldn't kiss me good night It would make a very pleasant ending to a pleasant day."

She looked down at him without answering. The moonlight was playing strange tricks on his black-and-white uniform, on his dark hair and up-lifted face. Suddenly she found she could not chide him any longer, even in jest.

"Wouldn't it?" he insisted.

"It might. But——"

"Haven't you felt yourself that the way we said good night was rather inadequate? Haven't you been wishing, just a little——? Connie, Connie, you know you have! I'm coming. All you have to do is to lean out of the window over the flower box."

She heard a rustling in the shrubbery again, and then the creaking of a wooden trellis. In another instant his head and shoulders were level with her own. The window box still separated them, but only by its width, and Tristan leaned easily across this. Their lips touched, parted, touched again, and the second time clung together. Then he drew away from her before she wanted to have him and looked at her with laughing eyes.

"What is more," he said lightly, "you and I could be just as happy together as Jacques and Stéphanie if I could only make you believe it. And we could have a beautiful baby too. Only ours would be a boy. Good night, darling."

CHAPTER XX

A LITTLE NOTE was lying under a crimson rose on the breakfast tray which Simone brought in response to Connie's tardy ring the following morning. She read it quickly.

Dearest—

You are a terrible sleepyhead. Jacques and Stéphanie and I have all been to Mass, and besides asking for many minor favors, have fervently prayed that your Puritanism may be overcome, whatever happens to your Protestantism. Now we have eaten an enormous breakfast, tout à fait à l'anglaise, *and are planning to walk over to see Saladin as soon as we have comfortably digested it. I hope you will feel like joining us, at least before we leave Mark Mullins's quarters. Then you and I could start for Malou from there. The sun is shining and the army car is rearing to go. As for me, I can hardly wait to tell you again how much I love you.*

Toujours à toi,
Tristan

Connie looked up from the scribbled sheets to see that Simone's eyes were fastened on her with that look of rapture which any love affair, even one which must be enjoyed vicariously, invariably inspires in the Gallic soul.

"Please ask the others not to wait for me," Connie said. "But tell them I will join them in Monsieur Mullins's quarters as soon as I can."

"Bien, mademoiselle."

She herself was sure that wherever Stéphanie and Jacques were at that moment, she would find Tristan waiting for her when she went down. She wanted to make haste, but she was healthily hungry, and her coffee and brioche were delicious. Then she could not resist the temptation of taking another bath, and her hair, as usual, required patient handling. It was over an hour before she finally went downstairs, dressed in another brand-new outfit. But there was no trace of impatience in the greeting which Tristan gave her as he emerged from the drawing room and came forward to meet her.

"At the risk of being repetitious, I must again tell you how lovely you look!" he said, eying with enthusiasm her soft tan wool dress and the loose wrap she carried over her arm. "You certainly know how to choose the colors which suit your own coloring best! I think we shall have to adopt fawn and azure for our *haras.*"

"I couldn't have chosen so well by myself. Tilda helped me. You know you said when I came downstairs last night that I looked like the portrait of Catherine Sforza. Well, the idea that I might occurred to Tilda at the dressmaker's, and I fell in with it because Robert had already put it into my head, as you know. Then she pointed out that this wrap, being reversible, blue on one side and tan on the other, would do for both daytime and evening wear until I could get another. She seemed to think I ought to have another eventually."

"Of course you should. Tilda is a very discriminating person. Let us walk along and join the others. I have the car down at the outer gate already. Incidentally, I hope you slept well?"

"Very well, thank you."

He asked the question casually and she answered it demurely. He made no reference to his gallantries of the night before, nor did he suggest or attempt an embrace as they took the road leading to the "male department." No one was in sight when they reached this, so Tristan led the way through Mark Mullins's empty office to the stallion's stall, where

Stéphanie, Jacques, and Mark were already standing in attitudes of admiration, while Raoul, the *étalonier,* stroked Saladin's beautiful dark bay coat. Then, holding the bridle lightly in both hands, the proud keeper turned the stallion slowly around, so that the graceful curves of his neck would be revealed, and the morning sunlight play over the superb muscles of his back and loins. He showed no inclination to be refractory; but as he walked to and fro, he tossed his head about and seemed impatient for swifter and more vigorous action. Involuntarily, Connie shrank back towards the rear of the stall, and Mark Mullins regarded her with thinly veiled contempt.

"You haven't got any call to be afraid, Miss Galt," he said curtly. "This horse has just the same temperament he had in his racing days, and that's a good one. You can pat himself yourself, if you like."

Such a caress was the last thing on earth Connie desired to give; but she could feel not only the stud master's derision, but Tristan's disappointment and Stéphanie's surprise at her shrinking. So she advanced in a rather gingerly fashion and extended a timid hand. Then, finding that the feel of the velvety neck was unexpectedly pleasant, and that the stallion did not seem to resent or even notice her attention, Connie went on patting him with an increasing show of courage. However, she was definitely relieved when the *étalonier* opened the door of the stall and led Saladin towards the paddock. The animal was no sooner released than he began to move with a splendid free action, breaking quickly into an easy gallop.

"*Dieu,* what a beautiful mover!" Tristan exclaimed, turning to Mark Mullins, who had come forward and was standing by the paddock gate, his eyes beaming behind his horn-rimmed glasses.

"Yes, his action's like his temperament—it hasn't changed since his racing days," Mark Mullins responded, with another scornful glance at Connie. "He's a very free-going horse. Never has needed any persuasion to do the necessary work for general health."

As if conscious of admiring glances and remarks, Saladin continued to gallop joyfully around his paddock for some moments. Then, with a final toss of his head, he slowed into a ramble and from that relapsed into quiet grazing, paying no further attention to his visitors.

Tristan put his hand lightly under Connie's elbow.

"Good-by, Mark—that's certainly a world beater you have out there, but it isn't a bad thing to vary one's interests and pursuits occasionally, as I'm rather tardily finding out. . . . I'll take time to go through my commons today, Jacques, and let you know about the possibilities of a stable worthy of Reine Iseult. . . . Don't wait dinner for us, Stéphanie, if we're late. We may very well be."

He was already moving through the yard as he spoke, steering Constance along beside him. But once they were in the car by themselves, he seemed content to let matters drift, as he had the afternoon before. They traversed most of Lisieux without stopping, then turned east on a highway which Connie had not seen before, and from which innumerable smaller roads branched off. In an unbelievably short time they had left both city and suburbs behind them and seemed already deep in the heart of a countryside even lovelier than the one they had seen the day before.

It was hilly and for the most part open, with great expanses of meadow sweeping up and down; but every now and then the fields merged into forests, where the sunlight slanted in through the tall trees and lay in bright, scattered patches on the sheltered ground. All sorts of flowers enlivened the landscape: the fields were dotted with buttercups and daisies, Queen Anne's lace and red clover, with here and there a scarlet square of poppies; the orchards were a mass of apple blossoms, ranging from snow-white to pale pink, the roadsides lined with flowering thorn, elderberry, and chestnut trees in full bloom. But to Connie the fresh verdure seemed even more beautiful than the flowers; never before had she seen such striking shades of green, deepening from jade to emerald and back to jade again. The grass, close-cropped by grazing herds; the ferns which curled like plumes above carpets of moss; the spreading leaves of wild strawberries and periwinkle; the ivy twining tree trunks; the lofty foliage on the waving branches—all these had united in lavish contribution to create the verdant symphony. Connie turned a glowing face to Tristan.

"You didn't half prepare me for it! The Breton spring was exquisite, but it can't compare with this in richness. I never imagined anything *could* be so green. How can it be?"

"I think it's the climate—the rains which come so quickly and frequently, alternating with the sunshine. We've been lucky so far this morning, with only one short shower. But we're likely to get half a dozen more before the day's over. The sun in Normandy is like a very shy lady —she keeps withdrawing, she veils her pleasing face whenever she can. But when she's persuaded to reveal it, the sight has a quality of magic. You should feel very much at home with a lady like that, Constance."

"Perhaps I should. But if the Norman verdure is the result of the Norman climate, isn't that like another sort of lady too? The sort who weeps easily and often, for a purpose?"

Tristan laughed. "I'm afraid so. But you'd feel less at home with her, Constance. You'd have to learn to endure her without impatience, and that might take a great effort on your part."

As he spoke, the delicate blue of the sky was suddenly obscured by pearl-gray clouds and rain slanted across their path, in the same way that sunlight had slanted a moment before. It was cool and delightful, and fresh fragrance seemed to rise from the ground as it fell. The glow in Connie's face deepened under its dampness, and Tristan, stopping the car, took one hand off the wheel and stroked the cheek nearest him lightly with one finger.

"You don't know how much rosier you look already," he said. "That's something else our Norman climate does—it makes nice red cheeks. Have you noticed the children we've seen? They're all as ruddy as apples. But your skin's different, Constance—different and lovelier. More like the apple blossoms."

"Last night I found out you were a singer, Tristan. Now I'm beginning to think you're a poet. What else are you, besides being a soldier?"

"I'm a lover. At least I'm a suitor that wishes beyond anything in the world that he might be. A lover and a husband at one and the same time." With his finger tips he began tracing petaled patterns on Connie's cheek and finally drew a whole flower. Then he let his arm slide down over her shoulder, and leaning forward, kissed the center of the design his finger had described. *"Chérie,"* he murmured, with his lips still against the soft skin, *"chérie, si tu savais seulement combien je t'aime, tu ne te retirerais pas autant."*

"I do know, Tristan. I'm beginning to think I love you too, that I can't help it. I don't mean to withdraw, really I don't. Certainly last night——"

"Yes, last night, for the first time, I felt that you still would have been willing to have me stay when I left you—perhaps even glad."

"I would have been glad. I wanted you to."

"Then, darling, why is it that this morning——"

"Because it's still too soon to decide definitely."

"I do not see why. You permit me to kiss you now."

"Only once in a while!"

"Yes, to be sure, only once in a while. But I know even that much is a favor you would not accord lightly, any more than I would seek it lightly from you."

She did not answer, but sat with her hands loosely clasped in her lap, looking away from him and gazing again at the landscape as they drove on.

Eventually Tristan turned aside to allow the passage of a high wooden cart, drawn by a huge gray horse and driven by a blue-smocked peasant. Under the immense canvas hood which covered the cart, Connie saw three or four flaxen heads bobbing up and down, and presently these came more boldly into view, revealing the driver flanked by numerous progeny, all with cheeks as red as those Tristan had so recently described, and large wondering blue eyes. Their unabashed stares were rather disconcerting to Connie; and though their father nodded respectfully to Tristan, he too turned a curious gaze on her, obviously puzzled by her appearance on this unfrequented road. Tristan was quick to sense her discomfiture and to ease it.

"We are coming to our own driveway right away now," he said. "I'm going to complete my turn and swing into the avenue just as soon as the cart gets by." And as this clattered off over the crest of the hill, he set the car quietly into motion again. "Look ahead of you," he said. "No, not down the road. Down that *allée.*"

She followed the sweep of his hand towards a long avenue lined with ivy-twined hemlocks, which transected twin apple orchards where sheep were grazing under the trees. There was no hedge between the hemlocks and the orchards, so she could see the blossoms in all their abundance as the car went slowly down the slope of the avenue towards the great iron gate at the end of it. They had almost reached this when a little boy appeared suddenly on a bypath running at right angles from it through a grove which lay beyond the orchard. He was leading a tiny mouse-colored donkey, with two shining milk pails dangling over its side, and a smaller child, dressed in a peaked hood and double-breasted coat of pale-blue wool, seated on its saddle. Connie drew a quick breath and put her hand on Tristan's arm.

"This isn't real!" she gasped. "Any of this! It can't be. I'd begun to think so on the road and now I'm sure of it. Hansel and Gretel don't spring into sight like that except in fairy tales."

"Let's hope not. Hansel and Gretel were German children. These are little Normans and just as real as I am. They are the gardener's children, and they were both born on the place. So was their father and so was their grandfather. . . . *Pierre, ouvre-moi la porte, veux-tu bien?"*

The elder child nodded with a cheery *"Tout de suite, monsieur."* Then he let go the bridle and ran quickly forward. The gate swung slowly and creakingly on its hinges and the car passed through it into a large circular area enclosed on either side by long thatched outbuildings which curved around it, and at the end by a small château towards which it sloped and which curved away from it. Apple trees in full bloom were scattered, apparently at random, through this area, giving it an effect of openness lacking in the more closely and precisely planted orchards through which they had been passing; but this pleasing effect was somewhat marred by the condition of the grass, which was nowhere cut or tended, and in places deeply furrowed by heavy cartwheels; over it wandered goats, cows and fowl of every description. Disregarding the obtrusive presence of these creatures, Connie gazed raptly past them at the turreted crescent of stone and brick which rose beyond.

"Oh, Tristan, why did you say Malou couldn't compare with Chassay? It can! It does!"

"Do you really think so?"

"Yes, really. It's smaller, but I like it even better. It's more impressive, approached from the front this way instead of from the side like Chassay. And it has two turrets, with those intriguing pepperpot tops, instead of just one square tower!"

"It hasn't got a fine outer wall like Chassay, or water in the moat, or well-kept grounds and gardens. This courtyard's a disgrace. I must speak to Bernard about it. But I suppose, with no one but his father to help him, the poor fellow's had too much on his hands. And then it's a long time since anyone has shown any interest in keeping up appearances."

"I don't care. I still think it's even more charming than Chassay. Somehow it's more homelike too."

She sprang out of the car, her eyes still on the building before her. Then linking her arm in his, she pressed forward with unconcealed eagerness. Obviously the state of the courtyard had not proved disillusioning to her; in her preoccupation with the château, she was still hardly conscious of its inappropriate surroundings. Tremendously relieved by this attitude, and thrilled by the spontaneity with which she had taken his arm and the tone of her voice as she had said "homelike," Tristan forgot his own momentary disturbance and began to talk gaily and confidently.

"That's Bernard standing by the drawbridge right now, bowing and scraping. He's a good fellow, really, even if he doesn't keep his livestock in the *bassecour,* where it belongs. You'll help me persuade him he ought to, won't you? Look, the little stone turrets you admired, on either side of the drawbridge, are identical, but the two wings beyond are entirely different. The shorter one, on the left, made of brick, is François I."

"I'm afraid that doesn't date it exactly, for me. I've warned you that French history isn't my forte."

"You'll pick it up in no time, especially if you'll consider reading aloud to me, long winter evenings. . . . Oh well, François I is early sixteenth century—that is, he was born in 1494, but he didn't become king until 1515. He shines in the reflected glory of his court painters, his architects, his silversmiths, his mistresses, and the Field of the Cloth of Gold; but he was really quite a person himself too. You'd enjoy getting better acquainted with him, especially if I helped you."

"Oh, I knew that much about him, and incidentally, quite a little about Benvenuto Cellini and Diane de Poitiers, believe it or not! I even knew that Leonardo da Vinci died in his arms. But I'm a very poor chronologist. Is the longer, half-timbered wing Louis XII or Henri II?"

"*Touché!* However, we call half-timbered construction *colombage* in Normandy. We can read up on that during those long winter evenings that are ahead of us too, if you like. But suppose we go on now and return Bernard's salute. Incidentally, do you mind if I say you're my fiancée when I present this *brave homme* and the house servants? It really would be the most suitable thing to call you, under the circumstances."

"But I'm not. I haven't promised anything. And you promised me——"

"I know. But couldn't you be my fiancée just this one day? Or my *future,* if you like that better? If I only thought you *were* my future, Constance, I wouldn't ask for anything else!"

They were almost up to the drawbridge. When they first began to talk about medieval architecture, Tristan had stood still, with her arm securely tucked under his, giving her a chance to survey the picturesque example which confronted them. Now he was hurrying her along towards the smiling gardener, who was waiting beside the outer gate of the drawbridge, and Constance could already see that the inner gate was opening also, disclosing one of the house servants at attention. She could even catch a glimpse of a red-tiled floor and massive oak armoires, surmounted by shining brasses, standing against white walls. She had to answer in some way, however rashly.

"If it has to be one or the other, I think it better be fiancée. *Future* sounds—well, so terribly comprehensive, the way you put it. I understand what you mean when you say you have to call me something suitable, under the circumstances. But it's just for today, remember."

"Very well, fiancée for today. Nothing *future* about it just now. We can talk about that later. Haven't I said from the beginning that we shouldn't worry too much about endings? . . . *Eh bien, Bernard, comment ça va? J'ai l'honneur de vous présenter à ma fiancée, Mademoiselle Galt, qui est venue nous rendre visite en Normandie.*"

"Nous sommes heureux comme tout de vous revoir, mon capitaine, et surtout dans des tels circonstances. Mes hommages, mademoiselle. J'espère que votre future demeure sera complètement à votre goût."

The jovial peasant was beaming from ear to ear. He shook hands with them both, talking rapidly and excitedly, and swung the gate still further open. Tristan laughed.

"You see, Constance, it's inevitable, that word! You better give up trying to escape it. Well, here is Léon, waiting to welcome us too." And when a second exchange of greetings, similar to the first, had taken place, he went on, "Now for a tour of your—— All right, *chérie,* I won't say it again! I did promise. First, this little square hall we are entering is what we call the fort. That is what it was called four hundred years ago by the first Tristan de Fremond, when men-at-arms were constantly stationed in it, and knights rode their horses straight through it to a central court. The crescent-shaped building you see now is only half of the original château, which once formed a hollow circle. The inner court has now ceased to exist, unfortunately, but to us the fort is still the fort. We have avoided changes whenever we could—unlike Americans, who make them whenever they can!"

Bernard had followed them into the fort, and now stood eying them, exchanging whispered remarks with Léon while both awaited further orders. Tristan turned to them with a gesture of dismissal.

"I'll get out to the commons sometime later in the day, Bernard, but I don't know exactly when. Go on with your regular work, and I'll find you, wherever you happen to be. Mademoiselle will want to see the kitchen garden, I'm sure, and I've a wonderful surprise for you connected with the stables, so we'll need to give those special attention. That's all for now. . . . I'm going to take Mademoiselle over the house before we have luncheon, Léon, and I think we'll save the kitchen wing till the last. That'll give Blondine lots of time to perfect her luncheon. I'll call her if Mademoiselle needs anything. Otherwise we'll see her later on."

"Bien entendu, mon capitaine. She would have been with me to greet you and Mademoiselle, but you were a little advanced of what she expected. She had not yet changed her dress."

"You'll find out that's chronic," Tristan remarked as the caretaker disappeared in the wake of the gardener. "Blondine has never had time to change her dress. Of course she should have been at the door too. I'm sorry. I hope you don't mind."

"You keep forgetting, Tristan, that I'm not used to retinues. I wouldn't even have thought of Blondine and her slackness if you hadn't mentioned her."

"Two or three peasants don't constitute a retinue, I'm sorry to say. I'd like to give you a corps of well-trained, efficient servants, like those at L'Abbatiale. I'd like to give you everything in the world you want and need to make you happy."

"I don't want or need a corps of well-trained servants to make me happy, Tristan. If I had to choose—I mean if there were any reason why I should—I think I'd rather have the kind that lets animals wander through the courtyard and never starts to dress on time than the kind at the *haras*. I'm sure I'd feel more at home with them."

This was the second time she had used it, that word "home." He looked lovingly down at her, his mounting desire tempered by tenderness.

"I think it's about time I kissed you again," he said. "If I understood right, you are now willing I should do so—once in a while. It's quite a long while since the last time."

"Why, no it isn't! It can't be more than an hour!"

"It seems like an eternity to me. And after all, you have at last officially become my fiancée—for today. My American fiancée. I'm sure that generally American fiancées are a great deal more co-operative than you are."

"Tristan, as I kept telling you last night, you're absurd."

"And as I've kept telling you, I'm in love. Isn't every man who's in love a little absurd? If he isn't, I think he ought to be. I think there must be something wrong with him if he isn't. And with every girl who isn't too. . . . There, that's better. Now let's look over this house of ours together."

With his arm around her waist, he opened the door into a small entryway at the left of the fort, which led to a paneled parlor both paved and walled in gray and hung with quaint pastel portraits. A carved mantel, made of dark veined marble, dominated the farther end of the room; a large mirror surmounted this, and a silent gilt clock, sheltered by a *silène* and two matching ornaments, stood on the mantelshelf. The fireplace had been closed in, except where it provided an opening for a small porcelain stove. Tristan went over to this and put his hand on it.

"Just as I feared!" he said. "I gave orders beforehand to have a good fire going, and I know this is Blondine's idea of one. But the stove is barely lukewarm. Sit down for a minute, Constance, and I'll put some more wood on."

He pressed her waist and took his arm away from it. Connie seated herself on one of the small stiff sofas near the fireplace and watched him wrestle with the stubborn little stove. She wanted to help him, but she was afraid that an offer to do so might come under the head of those unsuitable gestures of which there seemed to be so many in France, and after a time, as he was getting no results whatever, she became afraid that her gaze might be adding to his discomfiture and permitted this to wander around the room. It was certainly very formal. The pastel portraits nearly all depicted persons with powdered wigs, the gentlemen in scarlet uniforms with high collars, the ladies in brocade dresses with stiff bodices, and even the children posed in solemn attitudes, holding prim flowers or little wooden birds. In striking contrast to these was the superb painting of a woman whose dark ringlets fell in disordered profusion over her shoulders, and whose wide-sleeved dressing gown of royal blue parted to reveal a shift so sheer that the color of her delicate skin and the complete outline of her beautiful breasts were fully revealed beneath it. Tristan, looking up from his labors, observed Connie's half-fascinated and half-horrified expression and offered a laughing word of explanation.

"Our only unconventional family portrait," he informed her. "The strange part of it is that, as far as I know, the lady's conduct was exemplary. She was not a king's favorite, as you seem to be unjustly suspecting, but the highly regarded consort of my most illustrious ancestor. Why she chose to be painted in such complete déshabille, and why he chose to let her, is a family secret so old I'm afraid we'll never guess the answer to it at this late day."

Tristan resumed his futile efforts with the stove, and Connie continued to glance discerningly about the room. Under the portraits were ranged glassed-in cabinets containing quantities of small porcelain coffee cups and various other fragile objects which did not seem to have been put there for any particular purpose besides ornamentation. Most of the furniture was equally useless, and none of it could possibly have been called comfortable. Moreover, the room was not as clean as it should have been; dark marks showed around the latches and on the jambs of the door, and the windowpanes were clouded under their complicated covering of lace and brocatelle. It was musty too, as if it had not been aired in a long time; and its mustiness mingled with its chill. But in spite of its depressing atmosphere, Connie realized that it had basic beauty, and unwillingly she began to see it not as it actually was, but as it easily might be: with the wonderful woodwork and the wonderful tiles scrubbed to shining cleanliness, and the floor partially overlaid with a jewel-colored rug. With the fireplace unstopped again, and a bright fire burning behind well-polished andirons on the hearth, under a gaily ticking clock. With the windows washed and the curtains drawn back to form a drapery and not a veil. With a few of the coffee cups and a little of the bric-à-brac deleted and something with more meaning substituted for them. With a few books and a few flowers scattered over the tables. . . . It would not take her any time at all to transform this room. She could do it in a few days. She would love doing it.

"Please let me help you," she said, rising abruptly and going over to the hearth. She could not bear sitting idly on the stiff sofa any longer, conjuring up visions which she found it harder and harder to resist, while Tristan continued to wrestle with the stubborn little stove. And as Tristan protested, she went on: "I know all about stoves, of every kind and description. If I hadn't before I left Winchester, I would have after Base Hospital 11! It won't take me but a minute to get this one going."

"I'll call Léon. That's what I ought to have done in the first place. But I wanted to keep on being alone with you. I can do anything with a horse, but a stove is something else again."

"Please don't call him. I—I want to keep on being alone with you too. There! That's beginning to burn already! But if you hate stoves, Tristan, why don't you get rid of them? Why don't you open up this beautiful fireplace and have big wood fires in it?"

"They wouldn't give enough heat in really severe weather. You don't know yet what our Norman winters are like. Why, you think it's cold now, in May!"

"Well, does that horrid little thing give enough heat?" Connie inquired scornfully, pointing to the offending stove. "I'm sure it doesn't, and besides, if you'll forgive me for saying so, it's an eyesore. Is there any reason why you shouldn't have central heating in this château? There's a cellar, isn't there?"

"Yes, of course there's a cellar—that's where the dungeons used to be. It has a beautiful groined ceiling, which is quite an architectural feature in itself, though of course the purpose of such vaulting was to give the best support, not to provide the most beauty. It also has an excellent *cave,* full of fine vintages. The château's been used so little, for such a long time, that they have gone right on mellowing. There's plenty of room for a heating plant—I don't suppose there's any reason why there shouldn't be one, except that heating plants are pretty expensive."

"Too expensive for you to afford?"

"Not if I went without something else," he said, after a moment's thought during which he resolved to make no additions to the vintage wines, and silently revised his estimate for improving the stable. "I've told you frankly, Constance, I'm not rich. But yes, I could afford central heating for Malou, if you think we ought to have it."

"I think you ought to have it."

"I don't need it just for myself. I never live here. I never shall live here alone. I explained that to you, too."

"Yes, I know. . . . Are we going to look at the rest of this château, or are we going to stay here?"

"You've made it so warm and pleasant I'd like to stay here. I can see just what you'd do to this room if you lived at Malou." And as Connie muffled a startled exclamation, he laughed and said: "Did I read your mind? That's another thing any lover ought to be able to do. But you're right, we'd better look over the rest of the house, or the déjeuner will spoil—Blondine's much too discreet to call us. There's a small salon on this side of the fort that I think you'll like better than this large one. Come, let's have a look at it."

He led the way back to the little entry and opened a second door, on the left, which Connie had not previously noticed, disclosing a semicircular room so small that there was hardly room to pass between the tall carved bookcases rising against the inner wall and the big flat-topped desk standing beside the one window. But it had all the cheeriness the formal parlor lacked. Two deep, well-worn chairs, covered with crimson plush, were drawn up in front of the tiny corner fireplace, and outmoded family photographs were scattered companionably about. There was even a wicker workbasket, with a faded ribbon bow on one side, which stood open on a little table, revealing neat rows of spools and a plump, punctured pincushion. Tristan looked at Connie with an inquiring smile.

"Oh Tristan, I do like it better! I like it a lot!"

"I thought you would. This was my mother's private parlor—the other was for company. My father's office was in the wing on the other side of the fort, which is one room deeper than this one. But he hardly ever used it except for transactions with his male employees and similar business. Instead he sat at that big desk, attending to accounts and correspondence, and my mother sat beside him, sewing. This room is so small that the fireplace *could* heat it, so it was always warm and cozy. In the evenings, after the day's work was done, they moved over to those two big chairs, and my mother knitted while my father read aloud."

"It sounds awfully pleasant. Did you sit here with them?"

"Sometimes. But they were very sufficient to themselves. I know they loved me dearly and that they didn't mean to be selfish. Besides, I started away to school very young, and I was never much at home after that—I went straight from Evreux to Saint-Cyr and from there to Saumur. Of course I had a horse here and went riding and hunting a good deal anyway, during my vacations. But I think I was always a little lonely."

"When you said perhaps you'd read aloud to me evenings and teach me more about French history, were you thinking of your father and mother, and the happy hours they had together in this little sitting room?"

"Yes, of course."

He seemed about to add something else, and this time she thought she read his mind, that he wanted to say: *But if we had a little boy, he'd have his place here too. The room's very small but it's not too small for that. Our little boy wouldn't be lonely, he wouldn't have to go off riding in the woods with only his horse for company. We'd have him with us a lot, outdoors and indoors too. And besides, he'd have brothers and sisters to play with.* She was sure that this was what Tristan wanted to say because it was what she wanted so much to say herself, and because she was more and more conscious of the harmony between their thoughts. But she still shrank from admitting that it existed, and she asked a wholly commonplace question.

"Is that curved surface by the mantel the inside wall of one of the little towers I admired so much?"

"Yes, and the space between the two walls serves a very useful purpose. It's a *cabinet de toilette.* Would you care to explore that by yourself?"

"Not right now, thanks."

For the first time that day she spoke a little coolly. The frank attitude of the French towards certain bodily functions was still offensive to her; even the most cultured and refined persons seemed to have this—even Tristan, who she had begun to think was so nearly perfect. And now Tristan was looking at her, not with concern or tenderness or adoration, but with amusement.

"*Voyons, chérie,* are you annoyed with me because I mentioned a *cabinet de toilette* to you? Or because I asked whether you would care to explore that by yourself? You have come with me alone to see my home, which I hope will be your home too, you have said you would be my fiancée—oh, nothing promised beyond today, *bien entendu,* but for that long at least! Then surely you do not expect me to show you only the parlor, you do not expect me to talk only of desks and workbaskets and reading aloud! Even friends can face all the natural intimacies, of whatever kind, or else they would not really be friends. And we are much more than friends already. You know that, you admit it, don't you?"

"Ye–es. But the mention of what you call 'natural intimacies' doesn't come as easily to me as it does to you. You were brought up to talk about them. I wasn't."

"Then this is another point on which we must try to establish better international understanding. Meanwhile, shall we explore the interior of the other tower together? That has a staircase in it. Americans talk about staircases, don't they?"

"Yes, they talk about them and they love to explore them. Is this a winding staircase, Tristan?"

"It certainly is. It couldn't possibly have been built otherwise. Why do you ask? Have winding staircases a special interest for you?"

"Yes, symbolically. There's a quotation I've always liked very much— 'All climbing to high places is by a winding stair.'"

Tristan considered it for a moment. "Yes, I can see why that would appeal to you. And it appeals to me too. I believe we are going to climb to high places together, Constance. But it may well be by a winding stair. I have told you from the beginning that the ascent would not be easy. But I know we can make it, if you will only trust yourself to me. However, before undertaking this symbolic ascent, let us make the real one. I'm sorry that we cannot do it arm-in-arm, because the stairway is too narrow. If you would excuse me, I will go ahead of you and show you the way."

The second floor proved to follow the same general plan of the first, with a succession of rooms in the wings which curved away from a square central hall on either side; but in character and decoration these upper rooms were quite different from those downstairs. Their walls were covered with *toile de Jouy* stretched between oaken panels which matched the carved furniture, while the wall patterns were repeated in the draperies and upholstery; the whole effect was quaint, delicate, and indescribably charming, and the faint mustiness was not unpleasant, as it had been in the parlor, but suggestive of some elusive scent distilled from the flowers of an old-time garden. Again, Connie found that involuntarily she was visualizing the château as it might look after it had been aired and cleaned and inhabited; one of the picturesque chintz patterns seemed to her exceptionally suited to a guest room, another for a nursery; and she was especially intrigued with the two recesses which formed respectively a small dressing room and an alcove for a beautiful bed on either side of the fireplace. Tristan made another teasing comment.

"I'm sure you're wondering why there isn't modern plumbing in that dressing room instead of an old-fashioned washstand."

"Well, there could be, couldn't there? But as it happens, that isn't what I was thinking of."

"What were you thinking about, *chérie?*"

"Will you promise to behave if I tell you?"

"Haven't I always been a model of discretion?"

"You were at the beginning. But lately you've been backsliding. And last night you lapsed very noticeably." Their eyes met and they laughed together. "I was thinking that if I lived here, this is the room I'd like for mine," she admitted.

"For *yours?*"

"Well—for ours."

"That's better. I agree with you. It has more *cachet* than any of the others. Also the largest bed."

"Do—would we have to leave that big crucifix over the bed?"

"No. Not if you would rather have it elsewhere in the room."

She could not tactfully tell him that she would greatly prefer it should not be there at all, and she decided not to say that she thought the portrait of the beautiful ancestress who had been painted en déshabille would look wonderful over the fireplace. So she asked another question instead.

"Are there more rooms over these?"

"Only an unfinished attic and the servants' quarters. But there could be several little dormer rooms very easily, if we needed them, just as there could easily be central heating and modern plumbing. Are you planning for a very large family, or a great deal of company, or both?"

"I wasn't planning for anything."

"You shameless little liar! You've done nothing except plan all the morning."

"Well then, I think it would be very nice to have company. Not too much. Just enough to make not only our neighbors but our friends who live at a distance feel they were welcome in our home, in the same way we'd hope they'd make us welcome in theirs. So we'd need several spare rooms. Otherwise we'd be cramped by our house guests, and we'd feel we were imposing when we visited them, and that would be too bad. Because we'd want to go to Paris and elsewhere in France too, occasionally, so we wouldn't grow self-centered and provincial. But I don't think that going places and seeing people, here or elsewhere, would be essential to our happiness. I think we could be perfectly contented at Malou indefinitely, and by ourselves."

"I don't know that we'll have to make such an effort towards creating improved international relations after all. You couldn't have expressed my own ideas about having company and making visits better if you'd tried. But what about the family?"

"There isn't any family to consider, except Aunt Bertha, is there? I don't believe we could possibly persuade her to come to France—you should see the letter she wrote me when she heard you'd proposed! Just the same, I'd like her to feel she was welcome any time, that a room she could call her own was always ready for her."

"*Bien entendu.* But I wasn't thinking of Aunt Bertha when I spoke of a family and you know it."

"All right. I'd like to have one. I'd hope for a baby right away, wouldn't you, so we could be sure? I feel a good deal as Stéphanie does about that. And if it were a boy, as you said it surely would be, then of course I'd hope he'd have a little sister, a few years younger."

"So far so good. I've always liked families that began with a boy and a girl too. But then I've always liked a repetition, in the same order. However, I'll agree to stop with the first girl, conversationally, if you'll let me remind you that it's *well* over an hour now since I've had a kiss."

This time he got it without argument, and after a moment they went gaily down the winding stairs and started on the last lap of their inspection tour. A series of folding doors, which had previously been closed and which now stood wide-open, led through the fort to the right wing, accentuating its length, and framing a huge fireplace which dominated the farthest wall. On either side of the hearth, silhouetted against the flames, a big black cat lay asleep, its tail curled around its feet. Connie repeated the startled question she had asked when she saw the children emerging from the woods.

"Are those real?"

"Of course they're real."

"I don't believe it."

"All right, I'll show you! Minette! Froufrou!"

The cats roused simultaneously, and two pairs of great green eyes blinked solemnly in the direction of the intruders and then languidly closed again. Otherwise the contented felines did not deign to notice a disturbing presence. But Blondine, who had been occupied at the side of the kitchen, and therefore invisible from the court, now came shuffling forward, wiping her hands on her blue apron and making little clucking sounds. Evidently she had still not taken time to change her clothes, for her felt slippers were full of holes and her woolen dress covered with spots; moreover, the almost toothless condition of her jaws gave a weird, gaping look to her wide smile of welcome. However, her eyes were merry and shrewd and her ruddy, wrinkled face shone with good nature.

"But we are glad to see you again at last, Monsieur le Capitaine! We were beginning to be afraid you had abandoned us forever."

"You know I'd never do that, Blondine. I've been delayed because I didn't want to come alone this time, and it's taken me a long while to persuade Mademoiselle to come with me. But here we both are at last. And you have no idea how hungry we are!"

"You must put yourselves at table immediately. Everything is prepared. If Mademoiselle will be pleased to enter."

The old bonne stood back deferentially. But instead of starting forward immediately, Connie looked appealingly at Tristan.

"Couldn't we eat in the kitchen, beside that lovely fire?"

"Blondine would be horrified at the mere suggestion, and so would Minette and Froufou. But you can still see the fire from where you'll be sitting. And I think you'll like the dining room too. It is *tout à fait normande,* just as the bedrooms are, and you admired those. Now—tell me if this isn't pleasant?"

He drew out one of the heavy oak chairs which were placed around the refectory table, and seated her with ceremony. Yes, Connie said, looking from the dark beamed ceiling to the massive sideboard, and from the red-and-white checked tablecloth to the red-and-white-checked walls, this room was charming too. Did they call this sort of check shepherd's plaid, and was it another characteristic of the region, like the *toile de Jouy?* It was much *more* characteristic, Tristan hastened to assure her; she would find the *toile de Jouy* all over France. But this check—*Norman* plaid, not shepherd's plaid, please!—was really typical of this countryside. Had she forgotten that he told her in Evreux she would see it over and over again? Of course it came in other color combinations, but never more than two at a time, and one of these always white. Personally he was a little sorry that none of the bedrooms had checked walls.

"We could have those in the dormer rooms, if we decided to fix them up, couldn't we?" Connie asked so spontaneously that she could not stop herself.

"We could. We will. I can see that this forlorn old château is going to be the envy of all who see it, in no time. I'll give you a year to transform every part that needs doing over, and to reanimate every part that already has its own charm, as this does—well, perhaps two years, if that baby you're going to have right away, to make sure, takes up too much of your time at first. Look, I'm afraid I'm going to be jealous of him if he comes too soon. I want you all to myself for a while. Well, we'll talk about that some more by and by. It's a very provocative subject and we might get so absorbed in it that we neglected Blondine's feast."

He bent over to kiss her again, lightly this time, but also without asking permission. Then he sat down himself, moving silverware from a place at the opposite end of the long table to another at right angles from where she was sitting and pleasantly near her. There were two carafes, one filled with water and one with red wine, on the table, but Tristan pushed both aside and reached for a copper-bound wooden jug, filling first Connie's goblet and then his own with clear, russet-colored liquid that foamed as he poured it.

"At Malou we drink cider with meals and Calvados after them," he said. "Do you remember our first meeting, Connie, when you asked me what Calvados meant and where it came from?"

"Yes, very well. I remember everything about that meeting—including all the faux pas I made."

"Please forget about those. Please only remember that a man who had been through four years of hell suddenly seemed to see the gates of a terrestrial heaven opening for him at last!"

His hands closed over hers again for an instant, then moved slowly back towards his glass. He raised this and touched it to hers, looking intently at her. *I love you, Constance,* his eyes said, *I love you with all my heart and soul. I've loved you from the very first, but I knew you had to find out that love could heal instead of hurting before you could be ready for anything except gentleness and tenderness, so I tried to be patient. I knew you couldn't face passion then. But you can face it now, you can accept it, you can return it. You don't know it yet yourself, but I know it. You've betrayed in a hundred different ways that you're ready for it. Please believe me, darling. Please don't resist me any longer, please come to me quickly and gladly. If you'll only do that, I'll fill your whole being with rapture. I'm not pleading just for myself, I'm pleading for you too. . . .*

"Tristan, you said you wouldn't until afterwards——"

Again his thoughts had come to her like words. She was not even aware that the words themselves were still unspoken.

"You're right, darling. But afterwards——"

Later she confessed that if he had taken her in his arms then and there, she would never have known that she had not eaten. She was already so close to forgetfulness of every material thing that she no longer heard the murmuring fire, or the shuffling footsteps of Blondine, she no longer smelled the fragrance of savory food, she no longer saw the massive silver-laden sideboard or the gay red-and-white-checked walls. But Tristan, like a true Norman, was far more of a realist; the world would never be well lost for him, no matter how deeply he was in love, for he would see no reason why it should be. Surely, he would argue, love and life should and must go forward together, if both were to achieve perfection; and food and drink stood high upon the register of life's good things. He was, and always would be, a hearty trencherman. When Blondine came in carrying an omelet finely flavored with young green chives and mixed with crou-tons fried in fat, he divided it evenly and attacked his own portion vigor-ously, meanwhile talking with enthusiasm about practical plans for the improvement of Malou. *Poulet de la Vallée d'Auge* came after the omelet and received the same appreciative treatment from him; so did the arti-chokes, the salad, the Liverot, and the immense strawberries encircling a mound of whipped cream. By the time these were reached, he had begun to talk about the people who were to be their neighbors, whom he wanted Connie to meet as soon as possible: Monsieur le Maire, whose cozy little house stood just over the next rise of land; Monsieur and Mademoiselle de Lavarande, whose *manoir* was reached by the same side road; the Bourdels and the Duchesne-Fournets who lived at La Monteillerie and Cambrai, the two châteaux nearest Malou, both much larger and more elaborate than this was. But when Blondine had withdrawn for the last time, after serving the coffee, he rose and went to a tall, narrow armoire in the corner and, unlocking it, took from it two tiny glasses of etched crystal and the most extraordinary bottle Connie had ever seen. It was deeply encrusted with earth, and the neck, all of a yard long, curved slightly at the end to meet a cork capped with a miniature silver pitcher. As Tristan tilted the bottle, the lid of this tiny pitcher opened, and a dark, rich liquid came gurgling out of it into the etched glasses. Tristan set the bottle down on the floor near his chair, which it overtopped, and still standing himself, raised his glass.

"We've had the cider, now it is time for the Calvados," he said. "No feast here is complete *sans trinquer*—without a solemn toast." He turned the glass slowly around, so that it would catch the light, and the liquid in it seemed to come alive. "This is more than fifty years old," he said, "and every year of the fifty has added to its value and its power. The bottle that holds it is never taken from its hiding place except on the greatest occa-sions—betrothals, weddings, christenings. My grandfather toasted his bride in it and my father his, each knowing the beloved worthy of the toast and the toast worthy of the beloved. Now, with this same joyous knowledge, I shall drink to you!—Madame la Baronne de Fremond, Chatelaine of Malou, and my own liege lady!"

He raised his glass still higher and began to drink, slowly and sparingly, savoring each drop. Then he set his glass down and looked at her.

"Aren't you going to drink too?"

"I thought it wasn't customary if the toast was in your honor."

"It isn't. But you can propose a toast in your turn, and drink then."

His eyes were inviting her, urging her, caressing her. She twisted the glass, her fingers trembling a little.

"And when you start to drink, do it slowly, as you saw me doing just now," he said. "This ancient Calvados kindles a fire."

"It—it was kindled already, wasn't it, Tristan?"

"Yes, it was kindled already. Our minds met almost as soon as our eyes, the first time we saw each other. And then our spirits. That is the way it should be, darling. The physical yearning should come last, not first, if love is to be lasting. But it must come in time to make love complete between a man and a woman. And it has come. Long ago for me, only recently to you. We do not need the Calvados, as you say. But still, it is a symbol of an old Norman custom. It would make me very happy, Constance, if you would drink to me."

"Then—to the Baron de Fremond—Lord of the Manor—and of my heart!"

She tried to look steadily up at Tristan, to speak to him again. But her eyes misted over and she was suddenly stifled by sharp, ecstatic pain. Then Tristan took the goblet from her unresisting hand and she was in his arms, with her face lifted to his kisses and her breast locked against his in an embrace which beatified as it bruised and healed while it hurt.

"I want to take you out on the terrace, darling. You haven't been there yet. We'll sit and look out on the valley and plan for our wedding."

They had gone back to the fort at last, and Tristan was opening the doors that led from this to the gallery beyond. "Look, darling," he said. "Did you ever see anything more beautiful in your life?"

One arm was still around her. With the other he made a sweeping gesture. Beyond the terrace, an open bank, framed on either side by thick foliage, plunged suddenly downwards to a rolling pasture and where the brilliant grass was shadowed here and there by clusters of pointed firs and graceful beeches. Only the narrow silver ribbon of a winding stream seemed to divide this intimate pasture from the wide, unbroken stretches of the Vallée d'Auge. If there were roads, the greenery had engulfed them; if there were buildings, these too had been concealed in the valley's deep embrace. On the farther side of the valley, a second slope, rising more gently than the one flanking the château, was studded with neat orchards planted in rows of restful precision, which reached to the quiet skyline. Gazing at the scene spread out before her in such spaciousness and silence, Connie was struck again, as she had been that morning, by the endless variety of rich and brilliant verdure in which the countryside abounded. But now she saw this in far greater expanse than the view from either the hedged highways or the woodland roads had at any time permitted. Around and about her were nothing but an emerald earth and an azure sky meeting in exquisite harmony.

"Did I lead you to expect too much? Or is it as beautiful as you hoped?"

"As I hoped! It's beautiful beyond anything I ever saw or imagined."

While she was speaking a glow so brilliant that the very trees were gilded in its reflection overspread the sky. Then as the sun sank slowly, long bands of rose and amethyst, shading into each other, began to stretch across the horizon, and instead of fading, only moved and changed. The amethyst turned to pearl at the north and turquoise at the south; the bands of rose widened and separated, blowing away like feathers; soon they were merely pink wisps of cloud overhead. Lights began to twinkle in the distance, revealing houses previously hidden; but sheltering stillness continued to enfold the valley. And suddenly, above the lingering rose, a great star glowed in solitary splendor. Brilliant as the young moon, and far more beautiful, it spread its glory over earth and heaven alike. Beneath its rays the light mist rising from the valley turned to silver, and the sapphire of the sky grew luminous. Connie gazed at it in rapt astonishment.

"Oh, Tristan, look! I never saw such a beautiful star before either!"

"Of course you have. You've seen that same star hundreds of times before."

"I have? Where? When?"

"Wherever you've been. Whenever you've looked at a clear evening sky. It's Venus, you know."

"Then the difference is that I never saw it shining over this valley before and that I never saw it with you. I thought, walking back from Midnight Mass——"

"Yes, darling, I did too."

"So first we saw the Christmas stars together and now we're seeing the star of love together—I've discovered them with you. You've *revealed* them to me. Not only the stars but their meaning. You've given me a complete and perfect revelation of a new heaven and a new earth. This"—her eyes again sought the valley—"is part of the revelation. But this"—she raised her lips to his again—"is what made it possible for me to see it in all its glory."

PART TWO

Finding

July 1939–August 1944

"And Ruth said. Entreat me not to leave thee, or to return from following after thee: For whither thou goest, I will go; and where thou lodgest, I will lodge: Thy people shall be my people and Thy God my God:

"Where thou diest, will I die, and there will I be buried: the Lord do so to me, and more also, if aught but death part thee and me."

RUTH 1:16–17

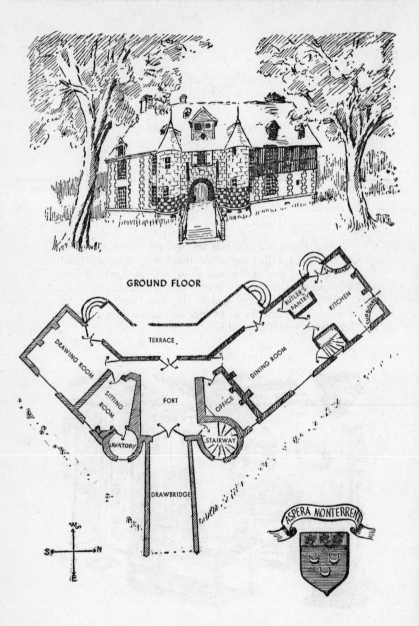

GROUND FLOOR

CHATEAU DE MALOU

(after its restoration by Constance and Tristan De Fremond)

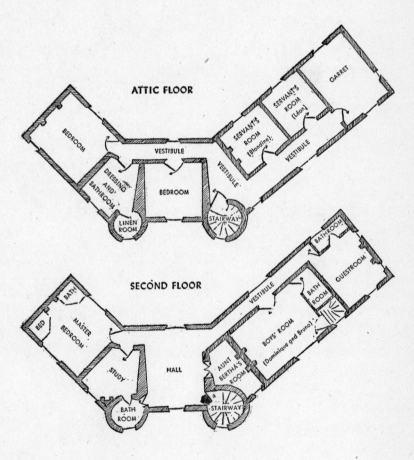

ATTIC FLOOR

BEDROOM

VESTIBULE

DRESSING AND BATHROOM

BEDROOM

LINEN ROOM

STAIRWAY

VESTIBULE

SERVANT'S ROOM (Blondine)

SERVANT'S ROOM (Léon)

VESTIBULE

GARRET

SECOND FLOOR

BED

BATH

MASTER BEDROOM

STUDY

HALL

BATH ROOM

STAIRWAY

AUNT BERTHA'S ROOM

VESTIBULE

BOYS' ROOM (Dominique and Bruno)

BATH ROOM

BATHROOM

GUESTROOM

PART TWO

Finding

July 1939–August 1944

CHAPTER XXI

CONSTANCE DE FREMOND sat on the terrace at Château Malou, facing the Vallée d'Auge, her hands folded tranquilly in her lap, her eyes fixed dreamily on the peaceful scene which for twenty years had epitomized the harmony and happiness of her married life.

The day had been a busy one, like most of her days. But now everything was in readiness for the anniversary celebration into which she had put so much time and effort. She had just been over the château from attic to cellar, checking on the last detail of its perfect order and its pleasing decorations. Except for the kitchen, from which the bustling Blondine had swiftly driven her, it was quiet throughout. Bruno and Aunt Bertha were both in their rooms, the boy as usual absorbed in a book, the old lady dressing with the childlike vanity of the aged. Tristan had not yet come in from the commons, and the house guests had not yet arrived. Nick, who frequently found the longest way round the shortest way home, was going to L'Abbatiale before coming to Malou from Saint-Cyr; Constance could count on procrastination from him until Margot was ready to accompany him, and she was glad, at the moment, to be free from the girl's volcanic presence and to relax in the assurance that her other dinner guests would be still later in arriving.

Her health had never been better; but she seemed to tire a little more easily and quickly than when she had plowed endlessly through the mud at Grand Blottereau, stood for hours by the bedsides of wounded men, returned to her office for the preparation of endless reports, danced far into the night, and still risen at six the next morning ready and eager for the day's work. After all, twenty years did make a difference. It was all very well for Tristan to say she did not look a day older than when they were married, for Nick to insist she was mistaken for his sweetheart, and for

Bruno to add she was taken for his sister. Her mirror was kind to her also. Her figure had rounded a little, but only enough to give it the curves it had lacked and needed in her youth. The few white hairs which had crept in among the golden ones only gave her crown of glory a different luster, and her soft skin was still unlined. Marriage and maternity had given her bloom, maturity had only added to its mellowness and charm. But Constance knew that though time had treated her so leniently, its passage had taken as well as given. She still had abundant vitality; but she needed intervals of solitude and tranquillity such as this to assure its continuance. Tristan recognized this need of hers and safeguarded it, as he had recognized and safeguarded every other, from the beginning. It was not wholly by chance, she knew, that she had this quiet hour to herself. Somehow, somewhere along the line, by saying just the right word or doing just the right thing, he had secured it for her. . . .

Her happy thoughts went back to the first evening when they had stood on this terrace together, watching the rising of the evening star above the setting sun. With the practicality permeated by fine feeling which was so essential a part of his character, he had made wise and loving suggestions for their immediate plan of action: she was to decline a transfer to some other branch of Red Cross service and accept the alternative of awaiting transportation home in Paris. Meanwhile, their engagement must of course be formally announced, so that he would have the unquestioned right to spend every moment of possible leave with her, as her declared and recognized fiancé. He would give her an engagement ring at once. In fact, he would give her two, if that would be agreeable to her. One was very old; it had been handed down in the family for he did not know how many generations. That was the reason he would like her to have a second one which would be all her own. Because when her eldest son fell in love, he would have a right to ask her for the ancestral betrothal ring and he would probably do so. But no one except herself would have a right to the other. . . .

Constance fingered both rings thoughtfully now, turning them so that their jewels would catch the sunlight. The ancestral ring was dominated by an enormous sapphire, encircled in diamonds and set in heavy embossed gold. Tristan had given it to her the same night that he told her about it, extracting it from the wallet where he said it had been wearing a hole for six months because it had taken her so long to make up her mind, and he was determined to have it ready the moment she finally did so. She had worn it on the third finger of her left hand until she was married, and then she had shifted it to her right hand, because it was too large and heavy to slip easily over a wedding ring. Indeed, she had never worn any other ring with it, because its magnificent effect would have been marred if she had. And she had never taken it off, except when she was bathing and when the ring itself required cleaning, since that first magic evening on the terrace. Tristan had warned her that constant immersion in water would injure the ancient setting, and that the ring must periodically be taken to a famous jeweler who would give it professional care while she waited. She had always been glad that it was not necessary to leave it with this expert, with whom she made an appointment before-hand and who gave the ring immediate attention. Her hand did not feel natural without it; it was always the first thing she picked up from her dressing table after her bath. She would miss it very much when Nick took it away from her. But after all, there would be no need to worry about that for a long time yet. Nick was only nineteen, and he had never looked at any girl except Margot Bouvier, who laughed at him and re-minded him constantly that she was more than a year older than he was, which to all intents and purposes meant that she was ages older, because she was a girl and he was a boy—a mere child really! Margot knew very well that Nick was no child, and Constance knew it too; still, she felt that the beautiful betrothal ring was safely hers for a long time yet. And after she had twisted her own engagement ring, a band of alternating sapphires and diamonds which fitted easily over her wedding ring, back and forth for a few minutes, she returned to twisting the other, because its immense central sapphire caught and held the sunlight so much better. . . .

They would have some wonderful spring days and evenings together, Tristan had told her that first time on the terrace, when he had given her the ancestral ring. And during the periods when he was inevitably absent, she would be assembling her trousseau, with Tilda's help. She had an-swered a little doubtfully.

"I'm afraid I can't have much of a trousseau, Tristan. Clothes like these" —she glanced down at the soft tan wool—"and that blue dress I wore last night seem to be very expensive, though you wouldn't think it to look at them."

"Oh wouldn't I? *Haute couture* is another thing I know more about than you apparently suppose. But talk to Tilda about a trousseau, anyway. I think you'll find her very helpful. Of course I hope you'll wear my mother's lace. It's really exquisite and I want you to be the most dazzling bride Winchester, Massachusetts, has ever beheld."

"Winchester, Massachusetts?"

"Certainly. Where else would you be married? French missions are crossing the Atlantic now in droves. If I can't manage to get attached to one of them, I might as well resign from the Army at once as superfluous. And if I can't slip away from Washington long enough to see the beauty spots of New England, accompanied by my blushing bride, everything I ever learned about maneuvers must have been wasted on me. Afterwards we'll go back to Washington together. I understand it's rather warm there in summer, but that's the kind of climate you've been clamoring for."

"But Tristan, I'm not sure Aunt Bertha could give me the sort of wed-ding you have in mind. I'm not sure she'd want to, even if she could. I'm not sure I'd want to have her, either."

"Well, ask Aunt Bertha anyway. I'll ask her too. I'll tell her it means a great deal to me. I'm willing that the wedding ceremony itself should be private and very simple—in fact, for a mixed marriage, it would be better that way. But I want the reception to be the last word in dignity and ele-gance. I want to invite the other members of my mission and all the mem-bers of the Embassy staff to it—I shall ask the Ambassador to be my best man and I hope you'll ask Tilda to be your maid of honor. I want you to invite all the girls you could never ask home to supper when you were a child, all the classmates who snubbed you in college, all those 'social leaders' of Medford. I want the invitations to read, 'Miss Bertha Slocum requests the pleasure of your company at the marriage reception of her niece, Constance Galt, and Captain Tristan de Fremond, *Officier Instructeur d'Équitation, à l'École de Cavalerie à Saumur.'* And I want the visiting cards you order engraved 'Le Baron et la Baronne de Fremond.' "

Afterwards, everything happened exactly as he had wished and planned: on her return to Paris she told the redoubtable Miss Benedict that she was not applying for a transfer after all. She electrified Miss Benedict's chagrined secretary by saying she was going to marry a Frenchman, adding rather maliciously that he did not suck in his soup or sop up his gravy with his bread. She tried briefly to locate Gwen, who had already left the maisonette, without telling anyone where she was going, when Connie returned from Lisieux; and failing to do so, agreed with Tilda that there was no use in worrying about Gwen, who could certainly look out for herself, and wrote the runaway at headquarters, where she would inevitably report before going on to the Argonne.

She consulted Tilda about a trousseau, and Tilda was "helpful" to the last degree, asking, almost indignantly, whether Connie had so much false pride that she would not accept a wedding present from her maid of honor, and stating, conclusively, that in this instance the trousseau *was* that wedding present. She shopped with Tilda and went sight-seeing with Tristan through ten enchanted days; and then, abruptly, came the orders sending her back to the States for demobilization, and she and Tilda embarked on the *France* with about twenty other Red Cross workers and had a delightful passage home.

So there she was, actually back in Winchester early in June, and a cable from Tristan was waiting saying that everything was arranged about the mission, that he would be in the States himself before the first of July, and would she please cable back the date which would suit her best for the wedding? She had meant to broach the delicate subject of the reception by slow degrees to Aunt Bertha, and to lead up to the still more delicate subject of a Catholic marriage ceremony with even greater caution. Now there was no time for these conciliatory measures. The idea of the reception Aunt Bertha swallowed, to use her own subsequent words, hook, line, and sinker. She would admire to show the neighbors and that college crowd and all those Medford snobs what was what. Of course the house was pretty small, but she had always known they would find a use sometime for the double doors between the parlor and the sitting room, even if they were terrible for draughts. She guessed this was the time; throwing the rooms together, there would be a lot of space, and folks didn't come all at once to a reception, same as they did to a missionary meeting, except for a few old gossips who were afraid they'd miss something.

Of course this Frenchman wouldn't expect her to serve intoxicating liquor? At that point, Constance decided it was best to be slightly indefinite, and when the Ambassador sent six cases of Moët et Chandon, with his compliments, and Aunt Bertha had been persuaded to sample the contents of one bottle, she declared she couldn't see that champagne was much different from ginger ale, except better. She supposed it wouldn't do to hurt this gentleman's feelings when he had been so thoughtful; it was plain he was a good provider. She would as lief have a fruit punch at the reception, and Connie could put some of this sparkling stuff into it, if she had a mind to. . . .

When it came to a question of the Catholic ceremony, however, this was another matter. War raged between Connie and Aunt Bertha, Connie declaring it didn't make a bit of difference to her, but it did to Tristan, and she was going to get married the way Tristan wanted. Aunt Bertha declared, with equal vehemence, that the Reverend Thaddeus Ingersoll, pastor of the First Congregational, would perform the marriage service or there would not be any. The engraved invitations for the reception were already ordered, and all Connie's feminine acquaintances, who had never made friendly gestures in her direction before, were giving her "showers" and flocking to the house to see her trousseau and rapidly arriving presents; and still the battle continued. Then Connie bethought herself of Father Calloran and took the bold and extravagant step of calling him by long distance, one morning when Aunt Bertha was out doing the marketing.

She had received a letter from him, soon after her own demobilization, saying he was back in the States himself sooner than he had expected, and that he hoped they might keep in touch with each other. He had heard of her engagement, through Captain Craig, just before leaving Grand Blottereau, and he wanted to send her his best wishes. He had thought ever since Christmas Eve that something like this might happen, and he was more than glad that it had. Captain de Fremond had made a most favorable impression upon him. If there were anything he could ever do to be of service——

Evidently the present difficulty was exactly what he had in mind when he said this. At all events, he appeared with surprising swiftness in the wake of Connie's telephone call, and after exchanging a few reminiscences, both grave and gay, about Grand Blottereau with her, addressed himself adroitly to Aunt Bertha. He perfectly understood her position, he assured her; almost anyone in her place would feel the same way. But perhaps she had not quite grasped how Captain de Fremond felt: there had been many sad and disgraceful cases of unprincipled young men who called themselves good Catholics, but who were unfortunately nothing of the sort, that consented to a Protestant service, and even welcomed it, because they did not regard it as sacramental, or to put it more bluntly, as binding. Captain de Fremond wanted to make sure that no one could put such a construction on his attitude; he was marrying a girl of fine character and high principles, and he intended that his respect for her should be unmistakable. Father Calloran did not hammer away on these lines; presently he began to talk to Connie about their common friends again. So Tilda was to be her maid of honor! And did she hear from Gwen?

Aunt Bertha suggested tartly that he had better stay to supper and after he had taken his unhurried departure she gave a slight snort as she started, with Connie's help, to wash up the dishes.

"Well, he talked me into it," she said. "He's got a way with him, like a lot of those Irish. You can't say but what they're pleasant and persuasive, whatever else you say about them. And I guess, when you come down to it, he's right about this Frenchman you're so bound and determined to marry. The young man did tell you his intentions, straight off the bat, and there's never been anything crooked about them, as far as I can see. Maybe this notion of his about getting married by a priest has some sense to it. Anyhow I'm not going to say anything more against it. You can fix up the parlor for the ceremony the way you're a mind to. I presume you want this Irish Papist should officiate?"

Yes, that was just what she wanted, Connie said. Father Calloran had undertaken to speak to the pastor of St. Mary of the Angels in Winchester, and explain the special reasons for her choice; it seemed this was not an unusual procedure, that it would not be considered discourteous. Aunt Bertha sat up late at night, sewing on the lavender silk which she herself was to wear at the wedding, and several times Connie caught her surreptitiously looking over the presents which were being assembled in the double spare room.

Tilda came over from New York a week before the wedding, and without aggressiveness or presumption quietly smoothed out all harassing complications. The florist, who had hitherto resisted every suggestion for decoration which ran counter to his own, was soon—figuratively speaking —fawning at her feet and accepting her verdict that lilies made a more effective background for an altar than potted palms. The caterer, who had insisted that cold salmon and boxed wedding cake could not possibly be included in the price Miss Slocum was prepared to pay for a wedding breakfast, decided that they could be, after all. Tilda declined to subscribe to the theory that "hired help" was impossible to find; within twenty-four hours of her arrival, a neatly uniformed maid was answering the telephone and the doorbell and waiting on table, and another, slightly less elegant but no less competent, was making beds, washing dishes, and mopping floors. At the very end, Tilda even persuaded Aunt Bertha, whom she herself addressed as Aunt Bertha from the beginning, to accept the services of the caterer's wife, who, she discovered—though no one else had ferreted out this fact—was a blue-ribbon cook in her own right. Tilda listed the presents, which were now coming in by the dozen, handled society reporters and photographers, whose appearance on the scene amazed Constance and gratified Aunt Bertha, and arranged a party of her own at the Chilton Club—of which, it now devolved, she was an out-of-town member—that brought the wedding preparations to a triumphant close.

The guests at this party included not only the official group from Washington, which was even larger and more distinguished than Tristan had predicted, and several young Boston blue bloods of both sexes, whom it appeared Tilda had known for years, but another guest who, at least as far as Constance was concerned, was the most unexpected of all. While Tilda was unpacking after her arrival from New York, she paused long enough for a cup of tea and a surreptitious cigarette in the single spare room, and inquired, in her usual absent-minded way, whether Constance had heard from Duncan Craig lately.

"Why, no! Have you?"

"Yes. As a matter of fact, I've seen him."

"Seen him!"

"Yes, he came home too. He didn't go with the Army of Occupation or join a commission to the Balkans after all. While he was hesitating, just as you did, about whether to take a transfer or not, he heard that Eileen's husband had died. So he didn't hesitate any longer. He accepted immediate demobilization."

"But if her husband's only just died, Duncan wouldn't marry her right away, would he? You've said he's always been so careful about appearances! Wouldn't he wait at least a year?"

"I suppose he'd have waited as long as she asked him to. But she didn't wait at all. She'd married someone else before he got here."

"Oh, Tilda, she hadn't!"

"Yes, she had. I think, as a matter of fact, that Duncan had been out of the running ever since he was sent across. Eileen likes a lover nearer than three thousand miles off."

"But if Eileen's married again——"

"Yes, that's just it. It left Duncan at loose ends and he took it pretty hard. Especially as I gather there might have been a chance for him, as far as you were concerned, if it hadn't been for Eileen."

"Yes, there might. But I'm glad it didn't happen. I mean, I'm glad as far as I'm concerned. It would have been a mistake, Tilda, and this isn't. I know it took me a long time to decide, but now I'm surer every day that I decided right. . . . Does this give Gwen a chance, do you think?"

"I don't know. After all, Gwen's three thousand miles away now. She went to Graves Registration because she thought Duncan was going with the Army of Occupation."

"Not just on that account, Tilda. Please be fair. But what—what about the little girl you used to see in the elevator, the cunning little girl with red hair?"

"Oh, she's with Eileen of course—she couldn't be anywhere else, could she? A great heiress she is, too. Her father—ahem! Eileen's first husband —left her several cool millions, besides all the money he left Eileen."

"Then he never suspected——"

"I don't know what he suspected. Anyway, that's what he did. . . . Look, Connie, what would you think of asking Duncan to the wedding? I believe he'd be awfully pleased."

"Why, I did ask him! I addressed the invitation to him at Grand Blottereau, but it will get back to him in course of time."

"I'm not talking about an engraved invitation that will catch up with him a month or two from now. I'm talking about a wire asking him to *come.* I need a host for my party at the Chilton Club. Duncan makes a very good host."

"Well all right, Tilda, if you think I better."

Guests were still arriving when Tilda signaled to her that she must leave the receiving line because it was time for her to change her dress, and Duncan Craig was still preoccupied with other guests who had been there a long time already. As she slipped through the crowd, her veil falling over her face again, her bouquet again in her hands, she saw him raise his punch glass to salute her; but she did not have a moment to talk with him alone. She was hurrying out of her bridal white and into her blue traveling suit; she was stamping her feet into patent-leather pumps and picking up her patent-leather purse; she was standing at the top of the stairs, waiting to throw her bouquet; she was running down them to the sound of cries that Tilda had caught it; she was being showered with rice on the doorstep; she was racing across the sidewalk on Tristan's arm and cameras were clicking all around them; she was in the car with him and they were off, headed towards a blue lake nestling among white mountains. . . .

Shutting her eyes now, Constance could still see that little lake nestled among the mountains, its blue water drawing its clarity from their snows; the memory of it had remained poignant and splendid throughout the years. But the green valley that lay beneath her, the quiet hills rising beyond it, held memories which were infinitely beautiful too. And not only memories. She did not need to look back into the past to find happiness; she was happier now, she thought, than she had ever been before. She could rejoice not only because she had found the one man in all the world whom she wanted for her lover and her husband, but because she had kept him; not only because she had conceived children he had begotten, but because she had borne and reared his sons to approaching manhood; not only because, having been lonely all her life, she had found communion at last, but because she had created a home from a cold and empty house, filling it with warmth and loveliness and joy.

Its transformation had not been as immediate or as complete as Tristan had hoped and intended. While they were staying beside the little lake, he had not consulted her about any change of plan; indeed, among all her memories there was none of any intrusive problem during that idyllic interlude. But after they reached Washington, he had spoken to her seriously about their future.

"The Commandant at Saumur is very averse to my idea of prompt retirement. He thinks I ought to wait fifteen years."

"Fifteen years!"

"Not fifteen years from now. Fifteen years from the time I entered Saint-Cyr. That isn't so very far off. At the end of that time I'd be entitled to a *retraite proportionale,* as it's called, and that wouldn't be at all *mal vu.* I'd be retired as a reserve officer on half pay, probably with higher rank than I have now."

"And in the meanwhile——"

"In the meanwhile we'd be most of the time at Saumur. But we could spend the summer vacation at Malou, and the incidental holidays. Also an occasional week end."

"But you wanted to live there all the time!"

"Yes, I did. I still do. But after all, I'd be only thirty-three when I retired. So, considering the law of averages, I still ought to have a good many years of life at Malou ahead of me."

"Then you're staying in the Cadre Noir after all?"

"Yes, unless you'd rather I didn't."

If he had suddenly told her that he wanted to stay in Patagonia or Tibet, at that stage, or almost any stage, she would joyfully have agreed that it was the best thing to do; and as matters turned out, she was enchanted with Targé, the strange and beautiful hillside habitation which fortuitously became available. So it was not in an orchard-ringed Norman château, but in one set high among vine-covered rocks forming the *coteau* between Saumur and Montsoreau that Constance and Tristan created their first home.

Tristan did not mind going to the mess to drink a few toasts, even if that did bring him home late to dinner. But these banquets which kept him up half the night, these "baptisms" which kept him out all night, were something else again. He was not going to any more of them. Did she need to have him tell her why?

No, she did not need to have him tell her why, she answered.

"I'm glad you feel like that. Because if we should have a long separation, the feeling would comfort you and sustain you."

"But since you don't want to be separated from me at all——"

"No, I don't want to be separated from you at all. But something might force us apart."

"You don't mean another war, Tristan? Why, there couldn't be another war! I've heard you say yourself, dozens of times——"

"I know. Don't let's talk about separations. Don't let's think about them. Don't let's talk at all. And let's think only of how happy we are, here together."

He drew her closer to him, and she put her arms around his neck and pressed his face down against her own. She had been a responsive bride from the beginning, for the ardor of his approach to her had been mingled with such tenderness and understanding that it disarmed all resistance, and the result of her trustful self-abandonment had been rapture in the full experience of love. She had never failed to make him aware of her joy in receiving him. But the embrace in which she clung to him now was much more than a joyous reception; it was an expression of her own spontaneous passion, of her own overwhelming urgency. The very thought of separation had impelled her to seek complete and immediate union. She finally drifted off towards peaceful slumber as the first light of dawn began filtering in through the closed shutters of her quiet room.

CHAPTER XXII

It was in this same room that her firstborn came into the world on the Easter Sunday following their marriage.

Constance had been wonderfully well throughout the period of her pregnancy, and her well-being, combined with the manifold demands of her new life, caused her to regard her condition casually, though joyously. It did not seem worth while to see a doctor while she was in Washington, because she would be leaving there so soon—a specialist expected to take care of you from the first moment to the last. Then there was no time to see one during those first weeks in Saumur, when she was hunting for a house and settling one and getting acquainted. Finally, after Christmas, she came down with a hard cold, and it seemed natural to suggest that the physician who took care of her then should continue to do so. He did not appear concerned about her, then or later; but when he was summoned late in the evening of Good Friday, he took Tristan aside after his first examination.

"I think I should prepare you, Monsieur le Capitaine. Perhaps I should have done so before, but after all, Madame was then already enceinte, so what was the use? She does not have the best build for childbearing, being very narrow through the hips. Her labor is likely to be prolonged."

"You don't mean to say you think there's danger?"

The doctor shrugged his shoulders slightly. "There is always danger. We call childbirth a natural function, and so it must have been once. But civilization has changed all that. I have every hope that Madame will come through her ordeal superbly. However, I repeat, her labor is likely to be prolonged and she is not built for childbearing. As to the first, you must help me decide whether to tell her that she has many hard hours ahead of her—you know her temperament better than I do. As to the second, you can discuss that with her later—or not, as you see fit."

"I think it's always easier for her when she knows what she's facing. I think you better tell her."

"Pardon, Monsieur le Capitaine, I think you better tell her."

It was not until afterwards, of course, that Constance knew the details of this conversation. And they had faded from her mind long since, together with other details of that first confinement, mercifully dimmed by time. But she would never forget how Tristan had come to her bedside, taking her hand lovingly in his.

"Dearest, try not to resist the pain. The doctor says it will be harder if you do. And he says you need to save your strength all you can."

"Because it's going on like this a long time?"

"Yes, because it's going on a long time. Only it won't be like this. It will be worse. But you have the courage for it."

It was Friday night. She was suffering, but she did have the courage for it. It was Saturday morning, and her courage was leaving her, but Tristan went on telling her that she had it. It was Saturday noon, and she was in anguish; she could still hear him talking to her, but she did not pay attention to him any more. It was Saturday night, and she was in agony. She could not bear it any longer, no one could bear it and live. But it was midnight again, and still she was alive, and still she was descending farther and farther into this bottomless pit of torture. She heard the doctor saying, in one of those whispers more audible than ordinary speech, that they should have sent for a specialist from Paris, that they should have at least taken the patient to a clinic, but it was too late for all that now. It was a high-forceps case and he was not an experienced surgeon; however, Madame would never give birth to the child by herself. And at last came the chloroform, for which she had begged so long in vain, and long, long oblivion. . . . And then church bells ringing in the distance, and a shrill wail near her and Tristan's face wet against her own.

"It's Easter Sunday, darling, and we have a beautiful boy. Keep very still, you're going to see him presently. I think we ought to name him Dominique, don't you?"

Certainly he should be named Dominique, she whispered, between tears of mingled weakness and joy, as she lay listening to those jubilant bells and that thin little wail. Then presently she drifted off into deep, deep slumber, more profound than any she had ever known, and when she woke again it was growing dark, and it was very quiet; the nurse had brought the baby and put it against her breast. It lay there, incredibly small and helpless, incredibly bone of her bone and flesh of her flesh, incredibly fruit of that gorgeous passion flower which she and Tristan had plucked together. When he came back and sat beside her bed again, gazing down at her with adoring eyes, she lifted her head proudly above her son's and spoke to her husband.

"It won't be so hard the next time, Tristan. I've always heard it never was with the second one. Don't think that I'm afraid. . . ."

No, she had never been afraid, thank God, of anything or anyone since she had married Tristan. And he had held the memory of those dreadful days and nights longer than she. But he could not hold it forever, since present passion is always stronger than past suffering. But the next time he had sent her to Paris, away from him, and Bruno was born in the American Hospital, and it was easier because the specialist had no old-fashioned ideas about saving anesthetics for the last. He had no patience, either, with various other ideas, and spoke his mind plainly on various subjects to which Constance had no wish to listen. She went back to Saumur and to Tristan, trying to pretend she had never heard him. But afterwards she could not pretend any longer. The first great grief of her married life came with the birth of her third child—dead. And after that the greater grief of knowing that she could never conceive again.

So they had not achieved their family of four after all, she and Tristan, and sometimes there was a little ache in her heart when she saw Stéphanie and Jacques surrounded by their many sons and daughters. But it never lasted long, because Tristan still meant more to her than any child could have, and because Nick and Bruno would have filled any mother's heart with joy. They had been four and two, respectively, when Tristan's *retraite proportionale* had been approved; so they had grown up at Malou, typical Normans, hearty, red-cheeked, strong-limbed. Nick was the handsomer of the two, with all his father's old dash and spirit. It had been taken for granted that he would follow in his father's footsteps; and now he had almost completed his second year at Saint-Cyr, and was going to Saumur when the fall term began. Bruno was quieter, strangely studious, instinctively devout; he had just graduated with high honors from the Jesuit school in Evreux, where his father and grandfather had gone before him, and had received a scholarship for the Sorbonne. Constance had never confessed, even to herself, that she loved one better than the other. But though the strain of mysticism certainly did not come from her, in Bruno she saw more of herself, in Nick more of their father; and it was inevitably in the reincarnation of her own lover that she felt the most vital joy. In like measure, Tristan himself had a tender place in his heart for Bruno; but the real worshiper of both boys was Aunt Bertha.

It was Tristan who had first urged her to come to France, pleading a cause to which she could not turn a deaf ear; Constance had failed to recover her strength after the birth and death of her third child. For the first—and, as it proved, for the only—time her health was seriously impaired; an operation might be necessary. At all events, a long period of rest was indicated. And here they were on the point of leaving Saumur and moving back to Malou for good! In the brief summer vacations during the past five years, they had talked about the changes they would like to make. Tristan had been quick to carry out his intention of teaching Constance to ride, and she had proved an apt and enthusiastic pupil; the long, leisurely canters which they took over the place not only familiarized her with the property, but created an ideal opportunity for uninterrupted conferences about its possible improvements. In the evenings, as they sat together in the *petit salon* they drew plans and made estimates; but the actual improvements had never advanced very far. Now at last the time had come when Constance could devote herself in earnest to modernizing and beautifying her home, and this would be a distraction to her during her convalescence. But with two noisy, active little boys to care for also, she would certainly overtax her strength unless she were relieved in many ways. She would find it especially hard to maintain the high standards of housekeeping which Aunt Bertha had taught her unless there were constant supervision of the French servants, who, Tristan was bound to confess, were not strong on scrubbing. And before much of anything else was done to Malou, it must be thoroughly cleaned up!

Constance always insisted, laughingly, that it was the last part of the appeal which brought Aunt Bertha grimly to France. She might have poohpoohed Connie's "female troubles," she might have said the improvements were a "needless expense," and she must have almost certainly regarded with alarm the prospect of two noisy small boys who would inevitably track mud into the house, bellow for food between meals, and develop croup or earache in the middle of the night. But she could not resist the temptation to "house-clean" a château! So she rented the house on Main Street to careful tenants of good moral character and bought a tourist ticket on the *President Harding,* determined to remain not only American but Republican until the last possible moment. When her baggage was opened for the inspection of the customs officials at Le Havre, these officials were bewildered to find that it was largely filled with washing powders, commercial cleansers, and disinfectants of every sort and description; and she presently divulged to her amused niece and nephew that she had a vacuum cleaner and an electric washing machine in the hold.

All these products of American zeal and industry were promptly put into use, and Malou emerged from Aunt Bertha's efforts in a state of spotlessness never before achieved in the four hundred years of its history. But having once got it clean, she declared that she did not propose to let it deteriorate to its former deplorable condition; she saw nothing to do but to remain and keep it in order. She said nothing about keeping the little boys in order, though from the moment of her arrival she had soused them thoroughly with soap and water every day, besides scrubbing their hands and cleaning their nails before every meal. In fact she did not mention them in any way, and they had long since escaped from her physical ministrations, whereas the house had not. But Constance and Tristan both knew that her thwarted maternity had been assuaged at last, and that the love she gave these adopted children of her old age was the most powerful and poignant emotion that had ever come into her life.

After Aunt Bertha had been at Malou for two years, the careful tenants of good moral character had written that they would be glad to buy the house on Main Street, and she had surreptitiously cabled her acceptance of their offer. Then she had returned to Winchester to give personal attention to the details of the transaction and to supervise the removal of the furniture. She had realized a tidy sum from the sale, for real estate was booming during the postwar period and the little house was well located; and with the augmented income which she received from it, she insisted on "paying her own way" at Malou to a more substantial degree than previously, though from the beginning she had stated curtly that she did not propose to be beholden to anyone for her keep. Some of her household equipment she had given to the Home Missionary Society; the rest she had brought with her when she came back to France. She had taken the little room over Tristan's office for her own, stubbornly refusing to accept the much larger one at the end of the right wing which he and Constance both urged her to accept; and this little room was soon incongruously crowded with the black-walnut "set" which had been her mother's, while a few similar pieces found their way, much to her gratification, into the newly created guest rooms on the third floor. Her own sheets and towels, her own china and silver, were installed in armoires set apart for them. The linen she kept for her own use; the china and silver were kept for special occasions when she was proud to share them with the corresponding equipment of Malou, occasionally calling attention to the fact that she did not have modern trash either.

She learned to speak French with a remarkable degree of grammatical correctness, though she never acquired a good accent or accepted idioms; and, with the years, she became a more and more respected member of the community. She did not change her mode of dress, her manner of speech, and least of all her Puritanical viewpoint; but this independence of action and thought gave no offense, either in the nearby village of Norolles, or in the larger circles of Norman town and country life into which she was gradually drawn. On the contrary, it won her recognition as a "personality."

Connie could not imagine Malou without Aunt Bertha any more, and she was thankful that she did not have to. At first she and Tristan had felt impelled to suggest from time to time that perhaps Aunt Bertha would like to go home for a visit. She had begun by answering rather vaguely that now the house on Main Street was sold, she did not know exactly where to aim for. Then finally she had inquired if Malou was not her home. She had presumed it was. After that nothing more had been said on the subject and the presence of this spry, vigorous old lady had permitted Constance to become and remain the Mary rather than the Martha of the household. Since this was what Tristan wished, it was what she wished also. Nevertheless, her days were never idle; the effect of well-ordered tranquillity, which was now one of Malou's outstanding characteristics, had not been achieved by accident. The "modern improvements" she had found so lamentably lacking at first had been added one by one; the attic story had been finished off to provide two extra guest rooms and improved servants' quarters; the cellar had a neat store closet for preserves of every sort besides its dusty *cave* full of sound wines. But Constance had given the château far more than sanitation and convenience; she had given it distinction through elimination, restoring its erstwhile dignity and elegance by clearing it of the clutter which obscured its finest features. She had let in air and sunshine, sweeping away its mustiness; it was bright and inviting, the cherished abode of an American woman who had brought to it all her skill of housekeeping and knowledge of homemaking, both permeated with her love; but at the same time it was also more than ever the worthy domain of a Norman nobleman.

Through the open door of the fort leading onto the terrace, Constance heard the faint rumble of a motor in the courtyard, and sat up more alertly, to listen for further sounds. Perhaps the first of her guests were already arriving; if so, she should go to welcome them. But no voices came floating across the drawbridge, and though momentarily footsteps seemed to be coming in her direction, these died away again. Probably it was someone who had come to see Tristan, and who had been hailed from the commons. The conversion of these into a more modern dairy, garage, and stable had gradually taken place at the same time as the improvements in the château itself, and the quarters for the gardener and other employees on the place had also been bettered, as the number of these had increased.

Jacques Bouvier had more than made good his promise of starting a stud for Tristan as a wedding present: he had sent not only Reine Iseult to Malou, but with her three other beautiful mares—Princesse Lointaine, Duchesse Anne, and Comtesse Monique—in charge of Mark Mullins's best "boy," Martin Dublaix. Bernard and Martin had taken kindly to each other from the beginning, and without any formal understanding that he was to remain, Martin had stayed on and on. The Queen, the Princess, and the Countess all foaled the following spring, and the next year the Queen produced a colt foal which was given the name of Heir Apparent, and which almost immediately showed great possibilities. When fully grown, he was a gorgeous creature, bay like his dam, well coupled-up, deep through the girth, with beautifully balanced shoulders, good quarters, and a straight hind leg. His performance on the track soon justified his promise; as a two-year-old he won the Critérium de Maison Lafitte and the Grand Critérium at Longchamps; as a three-year-old he won the Poule d'Essai des Poulins and the Prix Lupin, and at the end of his third racing season when he won the Grand Prix de Paris and the Prix de l'Arc de Triomphe, Tristan was offered 10,000,000 francs for him.

Tristan was most unwilling to part with the beautiful bay, but the offer was far too substantial to dismiss. It made possible not only the enlargement of the stable, but greater financial ease all along the line. The improvements inside the château which meant so much to Constance were facilitated by the sale. The number of mares at Malou was increased from four to ten, and Mark Mullins, who had always taken a personal pride in the establishment, sent over a second "boy," Benoît, who had been trained as an *étalonier;* for the time that a stallion could be added and mares brought in from outside for breeding, had now arrived. Bernard's elder son, Pierre, who had opened the gate for Constance the first time she came to Malou, was fast developing into a satisfactory groom; and the younger son, Michel, though he spent much of the time with his father and grandfather in the dairy and garden, was not infrequently found helping in the stable too. Martin remained year after year, growing constantly in power and prestige. Malou would never attain the splendid stature of L'Abbatiale as a stud farm; but it had developed naturally and pleasantly, it had prospered continuously, and it had filled a long-felt want for Tristan. Everything that made him happy made Constance happy too. She never begrudged him the time that he spent in his stables, or the companionship he found there. Apparently he was enjoying such companionship now. . . .

The steps were coming closer again, and this time Constance recognized them. No one but Nick walked in that swift, springing way, as if he had wings on his feet. But if Nick were there, then Margot would be too—they would be laughing and talking together, and her ridiculous high-heeled, toeless sandals would be keeping step with his polished boots. Constance rose, realizing in any case it was high time she put an end to her reverie and checked again on party preparations. Then, before she could cross the terrace and enter the house through the fort, Nick himself came out to greet her.

She thought that she had never seen so gay and gallant a figure. The tight, strapped red trousers of the Saint-Cyriard, though less elegant than the white breeches of the Cadre Noir, were even more striking; the black tunic was equally so. Though Nick so greatly resembled his father, he was more slightly built, and his extreme slenderness, while it carried with it a suggestion of supple strength, gave him an even smarter carriage than Tristan's. His head was bare, and the sun shining on his black hair made it glisten like lacquer. His teeth were dazzling against his full red lips. He had a more sensuous mouth than Tristan's, and the smile which played around it was more mocking; but it had the same quality of charm. He caught her around the waist and kissed her on both cheeks.

"*Tiens, maman,*" he said gaily. "If I didn't know better, I'd say you were just old enough to be preparing for your wedding, not the twentieth anniversary of it! But where would that leave me? Still floating cherubically among the clouds, waiting for the midwife angel who brings baby angels down to their earthly parents, I suppose! And that wouldn't suit me at all! I never have cared for fleecy clouds and fluffy wings and scraps of ribbon floating precariously over an otherwise exposed person." Both boys were bilingual, but Nick never uttered a word of English if he could help it, and when he did, it had the same stilted form as Tristan's when she had first known him, so Constance never urged it. His fast-flowing, often flippant French became him infinitely better; and since he persisted in calling her *maman,* instead of *ma mère,* also in the French fashion, there was another reason for preference. *Maman* might pass, even from a boy nineteen years old; but "mamma," to her, sounded silly except from the lips of a very small child. "Sit down again, won't you?" he went on, pushing her gently back in her chair. "I want to have a little talk with you. It's usually the other way around, isn't it? The parent, male or female, seeks to have a little talk with the offspring, ditto, in order to inform him or her about the facts of life, several years after said offspring has become thoroughly acquainted with them."

"Nick, stop talking nonsense!" his mother said dotingly. "Where's Margot?"

"Coming along later, with all the others. I tell you I want to have a little talk with you, so I came on ahead. Margot agreed with me that it might be better, since she is the subject of the proposed conversation."

"I don't believe there's time for a serious conversation just now," Constance said evasively, half rising. "I suppose you think when twenty people are coming for dinner and a hundred or more afterwards that arrangements just take care of themselves. But I was just getting ready, when you came——"

"To go and bother Blondine. And to shift the place cards again—which latter will give you a chance to admire that gaudy Capo di Monte dinner service from the Craigs. Next you want to peek in on all the other presents and make sure no rose petals have fallen from the vases onto the carpet in the *grand salon.* I know. But there's really plenty of time. Mrs. Craig said she couldn't be ready to leave L'Abbatiale for at least an hour, and the Bouviers won't start without her. And did you ever know

Monsieur le Député or Monsieur le Curé or Monsieur le Maire to stretch their ideas of punctuality to the point of arriving less than forty minutes late?"

"No," Constance confessed, sitting down again. "All right, Nick. What is this about Margot?"

"Just that I want to marry her directly after the Triomphe. If Saint-Cyr had only closed earlier, I'd have liked to have the wedding on your anniversary. But better late than never!"

"Better *late!* You're a great one to talk about marrying late. Why, you're barely nineteen years old!"

"I was nineteen on the fourth of April; this is the first of July," Nick reminded his mother. "Not that I am trying to call attention to the very narrow margin of propriety by which I entered this wicked world. I will, however, call attention to the fact that Margot was twenty on the sixteenth of March."

"You don't need to call attention to that either. In fact, I shouldn't think you'd want to. You know very well that I don't consider it wise for a young man to marry a girl older than himself, even if——"

"Even if she's otherwise exactly the sort of girl his parents had planned to have him marry! Which in this case she isn't! Why don't you say it, *maman?*"

His gay voice was suddenly edged with anger. Constance stretched out a soothing hand and herself spoke very gently.

"No, Nick. That isn't what I started to say. I started to say, even if he'd reached a suitable age himself. I'm not trying to disparage your sweetheart, darling. She's a beautiful girl, and her parents are my dearest friends. If you were twenty-eight at this stage, or even twenty-five, and Margot were three years younger——"

"But I'm not and she isn't. We can't alter the facts that I'm nineteen and that she's a year older than I am—or the fact that for three years now every other man she's met has been trying to get her away from me and that I've had to stand back and take it!"

"But Nick, be reasonable. There couldn't be any question of another man taking her *away* from you when she didn't *belong* to you. I know she's very popular, I know she's had an enormous amount of attention. But that's natural, that's what every normal girl longs for and ought to have before she finally decides. She can make a much wiser decision if she's met a number of men."

"I don't care a hoot in hades whether her decision is wise or not. I want her to decide on me. She has, practically, at last. But I don't dare give her time to change her mind. I want to put a stop to all this attention. If she really did belong to me there couldn't be any question of having her taken away from me. I'd quietly but quickly kill anyone who tried."

The boy was speaking in deadly earnest now. His mother looked at him numbly, wondering what she could say to him next. When he first came out on the terrace, he had tossed his feathered shako on the balustrade, and springing up there himself, had sat swinging the shapely legs encased in the red trousers and shining boots, smoking a casual cigarette.

Now he had jumped down, knocking over his shako as he did so, and stood beside her almost menacingly. She found herself retreating under his furious gaze.

"Don't you want the dynasty to go on?" he demanded. "The de Fremonds have lived in this place four hundred years and we can trace our family tree back a good deal farther than that." It might have been her fancy, but she thought, as he spoke, that he looked at the great sapphire glowing on her right hand, the symbol of betrothal for so many centuries. "And now how many of us are there left?" he went on fiercely. "Just Bruno and me, in the direct line!".

Constance was aware of a slight sense of reprieve. Nick still spoke with bitter intensity, but, though he did not seem to realize it, there was a comic undercurrent to his tragically passionate mood. It was fantastic that he should seize on the pretext of saving a "dynasty" to make a foolhardy marriage at the age of nineteen. Fortunately he could not do so without her permission and Tristan's—for that she could and did thank the conservative law of the land which precluded the marriage of minors without their parents' consent. She had experienced a slight twinge of conscience when she denied his accusation in finishing a sentence for her. It was true that she had intended to end it by saying, *even if he's reached a suitable age himself*. It was also true that Margot was a beautiful girl and her parents Connie's dearest friends; Connie readily admitted both facts. Nevertheless, Nick had picked her mind, which, like his father, he often did. She had not meant to *say, even if it's the sort of girl his parents planned to have him marry*. But she had not been able to help *thinking* this.

Margot Bouvier was not the sort of girl she wanted Nick to marry, quite aside from the disadvantage of that superfluous year. She was headstrong and oversexed; her mother's high courage and frank delight in conjugality were caricatured in her. She wore extreme styles and reveled in near-nudity; her evening clothes lacked even shoestring straps over the shoulders, and her bathing suits—if "suits" they could possibly be called—actually caused raised eyebrows at Deauville. Her make-up was equally obnoxious; her toenails as well as her fingernails were painted blood-color and were as freely exposed; her eyebrows were plucked and her eyelashes mascaraed; her cheeks were rouged and her mouth grotesquely enlarged with gaudy lipstick—Constance could see impudent streaks of her favorite "blend" smeared across Nick's face now.

Margot had been leading him around by the nose ever since he was a child—Nick and every other male, old or young, who came within the range of her rapacious vision, and without doubt she would continue to cast her spells and deride her victims for years to come. Decidedly, Constance did not want her for a daughter-in-law. She did not consider Margot Bouvier a suitable wife for her elder son or a desirable mother for her grandchildren. And that Nick should insist he must marry Margot partly with these grandchildren in view was the most ridiculous of the many mad propositions he had impulsively laid before her in the course of his life.

"Just Bruno and I in the direct line," he was repeating now. "And Bruno doesn't count."

"Nick, what do you mean by saying such a thing as that about your brother?"

The two boys had always been extremely devoted. Different as they were, their tastes and talents complemented each other without clashing, and each admired in the other the qualities which he himself lacked. Constance had never heard Nick speak disparagingly of Bruno before, but now he shrugged his shoulders as he did so.

"Bruno doesn't want to get married, so you'll be spared a second match which won't please you. But perhaps the alternative won't please you either. He wants to be a priest. I suppose it was impossible to expose the de Fremonds, with their strong religious streak, to the Jesuit influence from one generation to another without having it take effect sooner or later."

"He wants to be a priest!"

Constance had not even heard the latter part of Nick's speech. If he had suddenly struck her in the face, she could not have recoiled with more horrified amazement. Having shot his bolt, the boy spoke a little more gently.

"He meant to tell you himself, very soon. But he was afraid it might upset you, and he didn't want to spoil your anniversary. Well, I didn't want to upset you or spoil it either, but I had to do something to make you see my side. Bruno doesn't want to go to the Sorbonne. He doesn't care a rap about the scholarship, except as an honor that might please you and *papa* and make things easier for you financially. He wants to go to the seminary in Bayeux, starting right in this fall. Personally, I hope you'll let him. He'd make a wonderful priest, just the kind the Church needs—and the world. He ought to have been named Dominique, not me. It would have suited him a lot better. He really is the 'Sunday child that's full of grace.'" Nick switched into English as he quoted the old proverb with the ease that came from his complete mastery of two tongues. Then he went on, speaking in French again. "Oh, I know all about the symbolism of Easter, and how you and *papa* felt when you heard the bells ringing after you'd nearly died—almost the same way he'd felt when he heard them ringing after *he'd* nearly died, at the end of the First World War."

"The *First* World War? But, Nick, we're not going to have another world war! That was averted at Munich! It isn't more than six months since France and Germany signed a 'good-neighbor' treaty!"

Nick laughed. Constance had never heard him laugh like that before. Even as she listened she prayed that she would never hear him do so again.

"Oh yes!" he said. "Munich was to give us peace in our time—by selling out Czechoslovakia. And now we're going to reap what we sowed. We'll be sold out ourselves—by the same statesmen, so called, who did that. Our own statesmen. Do you really think Daladier is worthy of dictatorial powers, *maman?* He's much more interested in his next rendezvous with

189

Madame Crussold than he is in the fate of France! But he has those powers, you know. The Chamber voted them to him in March, the day after Great Britain recalled her Ambassador to Berlin, a week before Chamberlain pledged Britain *and* France to fight for Poland in case of aggression! And not content with that, we've agreed to protect Rumania and Greece against attack! We've bowed to Japan's blockade of our concession in Tientsin! And at the same time we're speeding up our military preparations—at least we're doing it as fast as the new labor laws will let us, which isn't any too rapidly. Where do you think all this is leading, if it isn't to war? Or haven't you thought?"

"Yes, I've thought," Constance faltered. "That is, somewhere in the back of my mind I've known there was danger. And I haven't forgotten that awful week last fall when partial mobilization was ordered, and I thought your father might be called out. But since then there's been a lull, a sense of reprieve. . . . Besides, those of us who saw the war of '14 were sure it was the last, that it had to be."

Nick laughed again. "Has *papa* talked to you about this lately?" he asked sardonically. "No, I suppose not. I suppose *papa* has been like Bruno, bent on letting you celebrate your anniversary in peace. *In peace!* The lull you're talking about is over, *maman,* the reprieve's ended. If you'll only listen, you'll hear the tom-toms beating already. Before you know it, the world will be on the march again. Are you going to let me marry Margot before I'm killed or aren't you?"

CHAPTER XXIII

IT WAS TWO months before the formal declaration of war came, but from that awful moment on the terrace when Nick shattered her sense of security and destroyed her happiness, Constance knew that her son had spoken the truth and that she must listen to him. She had put both hands to her face, as if to ward off a physical blow, at his curt announcement about Bruno. Afterwards she had dropped them in stupefaction. Now she stood before him clenching them tightly together, trying to find in them a proof of her power of self-control.

"Nick," she said. "Nick my darling." She stopped, swallowed hard and went on. "Don't speak to me like that, don't think of me like that. I haven't tried to escape from realities. One of the first things your father taught me, one of the things I'm most grateful to him for teaching me, was that it's realities which count, not mirages. But the most precious realities of my life have been my husband, my home, my—my sons. I've been less conscious of others, perhaps, because my horizon's been bounded so perfectly and completely here at Malou. I hadn't willfully shut my eyes to the possibility of war, but they've been fixed on other things. You're right, of course. I've been very heedless. I'm grateful to you for your warning and your rebuke. I needed them."

"All right. I'm glad you admit it. But that still doesn't answer my question."

He stooped over and picked up the fallen shako. As he did so, Constance remembered the traditional reason for the white cock feathers at the top of the *cassar* which rose so jauntily in front of it, and the red ones at the bottom—the latter allegedly had been dipped in blood. Again she swallowed hard.

"About Margot? Naturally there's only one possible answer to that, darling, now that you've explained, and of course the explanation shouldn't have been necessary. Not that I think for a moment you won't come back safe and sound. But if your father will give his consent——"

"He's already given it. I stopped to speak to him before I came out here to find you."

So that was the explanation of the footsteps which had first approached and then retreated, before bringing Nick to her side! He had gone to Tristan and they had talked together, less as father and son than as two male adults who understood and respected each other's viewpoints. Afterwards he had paid her the empty tribute of asking her consent to an arrangement which she could hardly prevent if her husband approved it. When a man wanted a mate, he did not need his mother; when men went to war, women were left behind. . . .

"I'd like to have the engagement announced at dinner tonight," Nick was saying. "Yes, I've also spoken about that to *papa*, and of course to the Bouviers. They all thought it was an excellent idea, that this anniversary was a most propitious occasion." There was no doubt about it, this time he was certainly looking at the ancient betrothal ring. Constance drew it slowly off her finger and dropped it into his hand.

"Then you will want to give Margot this tonight too, of course," she said gently. "My dear boy—nothing on earth means more to me than your happiness. I can't believe—I won't let myself believe—that this will be short-lived. But I can tell you this: If I had lived only a week with your father and afterwards had been blessed by your birth, I should have felt that God had been very good to me in giving me so much happiness. I know Margot would feel the same way. All the brides chosen by the men of your race have been greatly blessed." She lifted her face for his kiss, and momentarily they stood embraced, both too much moved to speak. Then she freed herself, and went on with an effort at lightness. "I will tell your father that you have spoken to me," she said. "Though I suppose he knows this already. And I think I had better tell Blondine too, unless you have forestalled me in that quarter also. She should be putting extra champagne on ice without delay. Since we are going to drink two toasts instead of one at dinner we shall need a double quantity."

Like the terrace at Malou, the kitchen had never lost its charm for Constance. Often, the last thing at night before starting upstairs to bed, she went to the threshold of the great folding doors and looked into it with a deepening sense of appreciation and well-being. At that hour it was orderly and empty; Blondine and Léon, and their young assistants,

Nicole and Denis, had finished their labors and gone to their attic rooms by this time; only the perennial black cats remained dozing in front of the fire which still glowed though it no longer flamed; the bustle, the clatter, the noise, which prevented the quiet contemplation of the kitchen's attractions, had all ceased, and Constance could dwell at ease on the details which continued to fascinate her: the black crucifix standing between the brass lanterns and candlesticks on the chimneypiece, underneath the guns placed crosswise on large wooden pegs. The deep drawer below the raised hearth, which formed a capacious receptacle for warming plates and platters. The inserts of blue-and-white tile on either side of this drawer. The band of matching tile encircling the ledge of the ancient *potager* which stood upright like a stove, and provided both the flat surface on which vegetables could be slowly simmered, and a deep interior, which at other times served as a fireless cooker.

As she approached the kitchen after her talk with Nick, all sorts of magic savory smells were wafted towards her; and when she entered it, and saw again the prodigality of the current preparations, she realized that it had never given her so strong a feeling of abundance, security, and brightness. The long table, the *potager,* and the hearth were all crowded with good things. The sun was shining and the flames leaping; the pots and pans were gilded by a dual radiance, and the faces and figures of the busy servants were bathed in it. Even the great green eyes of the big black cats seemed to glow with unaccustomed brilliance; and Blondine stopped short in the midst of an order she was shouting to Nicole, and gave her mistress a beaming smile.

"All marches well. Madame la Baronne must not disturb herself. Nevertheless I am pleased that she should glance about her. Look at those trout! And those ducks! And at this vast cake on which the last decoration has just been placed. Superb, are they not?"

"They are indeed. But then I never doubted that they would be. I only came to say that some more of the Heidsick '28 must be put to cool because——"

"And as if I had not done it already! He came, that one, to tell me his good news himself! And now at last perhaps I shall soon be seeing the *landiers* put to their proper use, and prepare the *bouillon de la mariée* to some purpose!"

While she was speaking, Blondine pointed a stubby red finger towards the fireplace with an air of smug satisfaction. Besides the ordinary andirons, called *chenets,* with which it was equipped for the support of its logs, two immense supplementary andirons stood in front of it on either side, surmounted by covered earthenware vessels which the topmost part of the framework was formed to uphold. These supplementary andirons were known as the *landiers,* and the casseroles they upheld, though sometimes used for less important purposes, were traditionally designed to contain the brew of beef offered to a feudal bride the morning after her marriage. Blondine had hopefully prepared this brew for Constance on the occasion of the latter's first visit to Malou, with the same lusty anticipation she had felt in making up the alcoved bed with hand-woven sheets and blankets. She had never entirely recovered from her disappointment because neither the bed nor the bouillon had been used. She had intimated as much, in a grumbling way, more than once, and had only shrugged her shoulders at the patient explanation that the visit in question had marked an engagement and not a marriage. At last it appeared that she believed her disappointment was to be assuaged. Constance felt it would not do to let her build her hopes too high only to have them fall.

"Perhaps you will, Blondine. But I don't know that Monsieur Nick is going to bring his bride here to stay. Anyway I'm sure they'll be taking a wedding trip somewhere first."

"*N'importe*. They will be taking their *lune de miel* in France, a civilized country, not among the Indians and bandits who dwell on the other side of the Atlantic. And it will be of brief duration, just long enough for them to get used to the sight and feeling of each other, *en déshabille*. And afterwards he will surely bring her here. The day after the wedding, or a few weeks later—that much difference does not affect the efficacy of my bouillon! But when the *jeune mariée* comes to this château only after months and months, her clothes already bursting at their seams—what credit do I then get for my brew?"

Constance laughed and left the old cook, momentarily cheered by the spectacle of the teeming and radiant kitchen and by Blondine's exuberant expression of good nature. She found Tristan in their room, already dressed for the evening, when she reached it. He came forward quickly, and put his arm around her.

"So Nick's been—what was it Gwen used to call such a proceeding? Shooting off his mouth?" he said.

"Yes. He told me all three pieces of bad news, almost in the same breath."

"Three?"

"That Bruno wanted to be a priest, and he himself wanted to get married, and that the world would be at war again before I knew it."

"And you put all those items in the same class? I admit that the last is bad, but I believe that Nick's timing is exaggerated. France and Germany may go to war with each other, but I doubt if it will be before you know it."

"If they do go to war, that'll mean, won't it——"

"Yes, inevitably. The reservists will be called out at once. But don't let's think about that tonight, Constance, don't let's talk about it. Let's only think that this is our wedding anniversary and that we've had twenty years of happiness together. Let's tell each other nothing can take those away from us, no matter what happens next year or next month."

"That's what I have been doing. With the result that Nick considers me an escapist."

"Never mind what Nick thinks. Let's think to suit ourselves tonight, even if it meets with our eldest son's disapproval." He smiled in the winning way which had lost none of its charm through the years and went on: "So much for the last item you mentioned. As to the other two, I don't consider them bad. It's perfectly natural that Nick should want to get married."

"At nineteen? To a girl older than himself? And that girl Margot Bouvier?"

"Yes, under the circumstances. Nick's been in love with Margot a long time, and it's been very hard for him to see other men constantly hovering around her. He's got something of a temper, I don't need to tell you that, and like most hotheaded people, he's got a strong streak of jealousy in him too. It would be harder for him if he pictured her receiving all kinds of attentions that he didn't actually see. I don't blame him for trying to make sure she doesn't have them."

Constance laughed, not very happily. "Margot doesn't strike me as exactly the kind of girl who'd go into retreat, married or single, with a war going on," she said dryly. "Now if it had only been Ghisèle——"

Ghisèle was the girl who came third in the Bouviers' stop-step family, a brilliant boy whom they had rather defiantly named Abel, after his Jewish grandfather, being second. Everything about Ghisèle was satisfactory. She was two years younger than Nick, she was gentle and lovely, and she had always been deeply devoted to Constance. Though she and Bruno had been thrown together more than she and Nick, this was only because Nick was too much engrossed with Margot to be conscious of Ghisèle's greater suitability as a companion, no matter how tactfully his mother tried to call this to attention. But Constance was certain that Ghisèle secretly adored Nick, and that it would have taken only a sign from him to make her his sweetheart and his slave.

"I knew you'd say that, sooner or later," Tristan remarked good-humoredly. "And of course it would have all the obvious advantages. I suppose that was the trouble—the advantages were almost too obvious to be alluring. Yes, Ghisèle would have been 'just the wife for Nick' if he had only wanted her. But he didn't. He doesn't. And if things turn out the way Nick intends, Margot will go into a 'retreat,' as you put it, whether she wants to or not. Nick puts it differently. He's plenty plain-spoken about hoping to leave her pregnant, and he wants to bring her to Malou as soon as the honeymoon's over. Didn't he tell you that?"

"He talked about carrying on the de Fremond dynasty, and I gathered he would be pleased if there were prompt prospects of a son and heir. He didn't say anything quite as bald as you just have. He didn't say anything about bringing her to Malou, either. I hope very much that he won't. Young married couples are much better off by themselves."

"Yes. But as Nick visualizes this situation, it won't be a case of a young *couple*. It'll be a case of a young wife left behind while her husband goes to war. And he's paying you a great compliment, Constance, in wanting to leave her with you instead of her own mother. That may have been another thing he said more plainly to me than to you. He wants her to be in your care—her and the baby, when it's born."

Constance bit her lip, looking away. She could see the winter closing in, with Tristan and Nick both gone and both in danger while Margot remained rebelliously imprisoned at Malou, with Aunt Bertha and herself as unwilling and resented keepers and no one but Blondine pleased with the arrangement. The prospect filled her with consternation.

"I know you don't approve of Margot," Tristan went on. "But that's normal too—hardly any woman approves of her daughter-in-law at first. I might say in passing that very few girls feel warmly drawn to their mothers-in-law, either. I don't believe Margot's looking forward to the winter any more than you are, Constance. But you've got to say this for her: she's consented to it. That must mean she loves Nick more than we've given her credit for. She wouldn't have promised to marry him at all if she didn't. And she wouldn't have agreed to the laws he's laid down if she didn't love him a good deal."

"No, I suppose not," Connie remarked, trying not to speak grudgingly. "But after all I don't see why she shouldn't love him. I should think he could make any girl fall in love with him very easily. He's the type that seldom seems to have much difficulty in that direction."

"Exactly. Though he has had plenty of difficulty with Margot—just as I did with you. Well, he's won her over, and if he can, you can. After all, Margot's got lots of good stuff in her. I don't see how she could help having, with the parents she's got. She'll be beautiful too, when she's washed off a few layers of make-up and put on a different kind of clothes —all of which she doubtless will do, in the course of time. She's going through a special phase just now. Most girls seem to, at one time or another—most boys too, for that matter. I think Stéphanie's really been very wise to let this phase run its course. And as Stéphanie doesn't 'view with alarm' I don't see why you should."

"Probably I shouldn't. And evidently that dismisses item number two, but not number three. You're the most persuasive person in the world, Tristan, I've known that for a long time now. But even you couldn't convince me that you're pleased because Bruno wants to be a priest."

"No, dearest, I can't say that I am. But only because there are just the two boys, as Nick pointed out. If we'd had half a dozen children, like Stéphanie and Jacques——"

"Or if we'd had just three! If that poor little baby we lost——"

"Yes, that would have made a great difference," Tristan said slowly. "A third boy—then I believe Malou might have been safe." For a moment he seemed sunk in thought, and he did not try to dissemble its gravity. Then he looked up, smiling again. "But I still believe it is, Constance. Not because of our sons. Because of you. . . . Don't resurrect an old grief after all these years. And don't try to stop Bruno. You can't, any more than you can stop Nick. You don't need him anyway. You don't need either of them. You can go on alone."

If he had said, "You and I can go on together, without the boys," she could have believed him, she could have accepted his challenge with hardly a pang. When he said, "You can go on alone," she protested, her heart turning over in her breast. But she could not continue to discuss the future which suddenly showed so menacing a face; the present was shutting in on her with its inappropriate demands. She could hear cars driving up, someone was tapping at the door, the telephone was ringing. Why, of all possible times, should this have to be the one when the house was full of people, when she must watch the service, play the part of a serene and gracious hostess, welcome her son's bride?

Tristan had picked up the receiver. *"Allo, allo,"* he was saying pleasantly. "All right, Stéphanie. Yes, I know how long it takes her. As a matter of fact, I think perhaps it will be just as well all around if we're a little later than we planned in starting. . . . Well, you know—this dual celebration. . . . Yes, wonderful." He turned away from the telephone to see that Constance had opened the study door, and that it was Aunt Bertha who had knocked, arrayed in the latest creation which she had "whipped up" with the help of her faithful Singer sewing machine.

"Land's sake, Constance Galt, haven't you got into your party clothes yet? Those relations of Tristan's that have put themselves out to come all the way from Nantes are crossing over the drawbridge right this minute!"

"You go down with Tristan, Aunt Bertha—thank goodness you and he are both ready! Say I was unexpectedly delayed, say something happened—heaven knows that would be true enough! Listen, have you seen Nick? If you haven't——"

"You go ahead and get into those party clothes of yours, Constance Galt, and don't waste time asking idle questions. Of course I've seen Nick. But I wasn't a mite surprised at his news, whatever you were. I've got eyes in my head, and I can still see out of them, thank the good Lord!"

Aunt Bertha turned away from the study door with her characteristic slight snort, and Constance hurried back into her bedroom, slipping out of her afternoon dress and flinging it down with unaccustomed carelessness on the alcove bed. It was inexcusable that she should not have been ready to welcome the de Fremonds; the Count and Countess were both getting on in years, it represented a real effort for them to take a journey and pay a visit; and they had done this to please and compliment their nephew and his wife. In a sense, it was even more of a compliment that both their sons had come with them.

Well, Aunt Bertha would see them safely to their rooms and explain about Nick, and they would understand, Constance thought gratefully, stooping over to buckle her slippers, and feeling doubly grateful that since the de Fremonds filled all available guest rooms, she had taken advantage of Stéphanie's suggestion that the Craigs should stay at L'Abbatiale instead of Malou. The *grand manoir* and the *petit manoir* were both crowded to the gunwales in these days, but the guest house was always available, and the Craigs had stayed there before—in fact, a fast friendship had sprung up between them and the Bouviers. They were all pleasantly engaged in renewing it now.

It was a good thing that she was able to dress so quickly and that she could do it without assistance, Constance said to herself. She took one swift look at herself in the mirror and smoothed her wedding dress into place. She took pardonable pride in the fact that it still fitted her without alterations, and having been made to wear with old lace and old jewels, it had escaped the fantastic curtailment of the postwar period. For once she could consider her own achievement and her own appearance without a passing pang as she thought of Tilda, who could not possibly have arrayed herself for an anniversary celebration in fifteen minutes, and whose husband indulgently remarked that she was a fine figure of a woman, which, crudely interpreted, meant that she was a little too heavy. Tilda could not possibly have squeezed into her wedding dress, and since it had represented the height of style in the autumn of 1919, its presentation now would be nothing short of grotesque in any case. She would arrive exquisitely turned out, but this flawless effect would represent prolonged preparation, under the ministrations of an experienced maid.

Tilda was certainly the last word in elegance and style. But why not, with nothing to do but make herself look lovely, and with thousands and thousands of dollars to spend on her clothes every year? Besides all that money of her own, more than she knew what to do with, there were the Craig millions, on which she could have drawn at will if Duncan had not invariably made it a point of forestalling her every possible vagary, as if to compensate for the singlehearted devotion he had never given her. She said herself, in her bland, droll way, which had grown a little more languid with the years, that he bought her a new necklace every time he was unfaithful to her, and that presently she would have so many pearls that she would look like the pictures of Queen Margherita of Italy.

As she hurried from her bedroom through the study and the upper hall, Constance wondered whether she dared mention the fact that she had unexpectedly heard from Gwen, who had just arrived in France too. Gwen had wired her congratulations on the anniversary, having previously sent from Spain, in anticipation of the porcelain wedding, the first and one of the most beautiful presents Constance had received: the exquisite figurine of a dancer, whose rosy neck and arms emerged from the same snowy frills of incredibly fine "lace" which also formed the skirt billowing above her slim ankles and poised feet. Constance had been enchanted with this gift, which she knew must have cost a small fortune, and which no one but Gwen would have discovered in an obscure place like Vitoria— just where in Spain was Vitoria?—or managed to dispatch, undelayed by customs duties and undamaged by careless handling.

Constance would have liked to show her appreciation by inviting Gwen to Malou for the celebration, but Tristan had agreed with her that this would not be wise, since the Craigs had already arrived at L'Abbatiale when Gwen's wire came in. After all these years, Gwen had never forgiven Tilda what she called her treachery—a charge which Tilda blithely disregarded. Exactly how it had happened that Tilda and Duncan were married a few weeks after Tristan and Constance went to Saumur, neither of them ever learned. But when the news of the marriage reached France, Gwen had come pelting down from Château-Thierry, arriving unannounced, thwarted and enraged, at the picturesque château of Targé of which they had just taken possession. Incoherent with tears and fury, she had stigmatized Tilda as a false friend, a snake in the grass, a worse bitch than the unknown Eileen; and when Constance tried to reason and remonstrate with her, the result was a still more passionate outburst.

"Don't you try to stand up for her, Connie Galt! I was unfair when I said you'd snatched Duncan away from me. But I'm not being unfair now."

"Yes you are, Gwen. How could Tilda 'snatch him away from you' if he didn't belong to you?"

"That's what I'm trying to tell you, only you won't listen. He *did* belong to me."

"Gwen, he gave me his word of honor——"

"Yes, I know he did, and when he said that, he wasn't lying to you either. All he'd done, before you came to Blottereau, was to make a few passes at me, just as Tilda said. We'd had some pretty hot times together, but we hadn't gone the limit, or anything like it. Duncan's first idea seemed to be that of course we would; but when I told him I hated to pull a bromide on him, but I really wasn't that kind of a girl, no matter how much I looked and even acted like one, he said well, naturally, that settled it. I never fooled myself by trying to pretend I'd won any great moral victory, though. I knew he really didn't care enough to keep on trying to make me. He'd taken me out on the town, and it had been fun while it lasted, but he didn't much mind calling it all off right there. And when you appeared on the scene he wanted to forget all about it. The only time I got anywhere with him was that night at the officers' dance when you got his goat by acting prissy. I thought maybe I was getting somewhere again then. And I wanted to. I wanted to a lot. Because I'd been crazy about him from the beginning. I hadn't turned him down because I didn't want him. I'd turned him down because I didn't want him that way."

"Of course you didn't. And I wish you wouldn't be sarcastic about 'a great moral victory,' Gwen. Because——"

"Who's telling this story? I didn't get anywhere after all, because presently you began to thaw out, and Duncan gave me the cold shoulder again. The cold-shouldering went right on all the time we were at camp. Perhaps you remember that the last night we went to dinner at Ragueneau's, I said something about a date for the Folies Bergères, and Duncan brushed that off. He said he'd have to let me know later, that he wasn't sure whether he could get leave. I knew he'd try to get a Paris date with you. And you don't need to answer that one, because he told me himself. He asked you to go to the Opera with him and meet some French friends of his and you said you'd be glad to. But when he got up to Paris, you'd gone off to Normandy with Tristan. Duncan took me to the Folies Bergères after all. We went to a couple of night clubs after the show and did the usual amount of drinking and dancing, and then Duncan took me back to my hotel and went up to my room with me. He didn't ask whether he could or not; he just came. And believe me, I didn't try to stop him. Of course I'd hoped something like that would happen when I left the Bouviers' and went off on my own. But I'd never dared hope it would be that easy. Or that it would all seem so natural—so inevitable. Not just something I wanted more than anything in the world, but something that had to be."

The tears and the fury and the incoherence were all gone now. Gwen was speaking with an intensity that was the more moving because there was not a tremor in her voice.

"Of course the next morning he realized—well, that I'd never gone to bed with a man before. And he said he was sorry if—— And I told him not to be a damn fool, that I wasn't sorry, that I'd never been so happy in my life. He knew I meant it, and there weren't any more references, direct or indirect, to violating a virgin. After all, the virgin might have been unwise, but she certainly hadn't been unwilling. Anything else but.

"We went to a lot more shows and a lot more night clubs, but we didn't happen to run into anyone we knew and we didn't need anyone else along to have fun. We had lots of fun, everywhere we went. And then we'd go back to that dingy little old hotel and make love. Only the hotel didn't seem dingy to me. It seemed like the most beautiful place in the world."

Involuntarily, Constance thought of the little blue lake nestling among the white mountains, and knew that to Gwen the memory of this small, third-rate hotel in Paris would always be the same as the memory of the lake to her.

"I said another thing that night at Ragueneau's," Gwen went on. "I said Duncan and I had been through a war together, that we had something in common he and Eileen had never had, something that meant a lot in our lives. And I said that when you got down to rock bottom he and I belonged to the same breed, and in the long run this counted more than anything else. I believed that, Connie. I believed it with all my heart and soul. And so I believed that those days and nights in Paris meant just as much to Duncan as they did to me. It wasn't just wishful thinking. I didn't see how they could help it. I thought that by and by we'd be married. Not that he'd ask me to, exactly. That he'd just say we were going to be. As soon as he could cut the red tape that makes it so hard for any Americans to get married in France. I suppose that if I'd really been smart, I'd have said I was going to have a baby and that would have settled it. But I thought too much of him and too much of myself to pull that old gag. It wouldn't have meant a thing to me to have him marry me because he felt he had to. And anyway, I thought he'd want to. As much as I wanted to have him. When I went to Château-Thierry, I thought I'd be seeing him within a few weeks. I would have, too, if Eileen's husband hadn't died. Duncan was all set to join the Army of Occupation when that happened. So he went back to the States instead, and there was Eileen married to someone else and Tilda lying in wait for him."

"But, Gwen, Tilda didn't know——"

"That's just it, she did know. I dropped in at Madame Bouvier's one day when Duncan was busy about his transfer. I realized I'd been pretty rude, running off the way I had, and anyhow, I wanted to know how you'd made out at Malou. You were sight-seeing with Tristan, but Tilda was in bed, between baths, and we got to talking and I spilled the whole story."

"Well, I can understand that. I talked to her about Tristan when I really didn't know how I felt about him myself."

"I don't doubt it. But you see she didn't happen to want Tristan herself. And she did want Duncan. I think she made up her mind to get him just as long ago as I did. Only she knew how to go about it better. Not just to get him, but to keep him. That is, I suppose she thinks she can keep him because she's married to him. I bet she doesn't. I bet he's unfaithful to her before they've been married a year. I hope he is. It'll serve her right, the damn snake in the grass, the dirty bitch."

The raging tears had begun to fall again, the furious speech was once more incoherent; then suddenly Gwen collapsed completely. Constance put her to bed and sent for a doctor, who shook his head gravely and said it was evident that the poor young lady was suffering from a severe nervous breakdown, and that she must have complete rest and quiet. For several weeks she lay in one of the quaint dormer rooms flanked by the *coteau,* and during this time Connie strove in every possible way to show sympathetic understanding, though it was hard for her to put this into words. Gwen was not ashamed of what she had done; she gloried in it. She was still passionately in love with Duncan Craig, and placed the entire responsibility for his dereliction on Tilda. Under these circumstances, Connie could not logically make a comparison between her own reaction to her first great emotional experience and her friend's, or classify Craig as the same sort of cad as Gene Clayton. On the other hand, though ready to admit that Gwen loved Duncan as much in her own way as she, Connie, loved Tristan, it was self-evident that Duncan had not cared for his inamorata as Tristan cared for his wife, and any reference to this would be both futile and cruel. Wisely, because she did not know what to say she said little or nothing, and Gwen, recognizing the reasons for her silence, was soothed by it and grateful for it. She had not exaggerated in saying she did not care whether she lived or died when she came to Targé; and she had always given the de Fremonds credit for getting her back on her job in a state of restored health and complete self-control. But though she did not seem to resent their continued friendship with the Craigs, they had not succeeded in changing her opinion of Tilda, then or later, and she herself had never married.

After winding up her work with Graves Registration, in a way that won much merited praise, she had written some stories about her wartime experiences which had brought her immediate recognition as a keen observer and a vivid narrator. "The White Whale" was a merciless satire on the vain and vapid women who had cluttered a scene otherwise distinguished by efficient and devoted service. "Street of the Bossy English" took advantage of the current nickname for rue Boissy d'Anglais to make some good-natured cracks about British confrères. "Hot Water at the St. James" was the hilarious description of passing her room key through many hands in order that all her friends might take advantage of the bathing facilities she alone was fortunate enough to possess; "Lanterns at Domremy" was a moving account of the village illumination celebrating the feast of Jeanne d'Arc.

From the first rung marked by these stories, she had climbed higher and higher on the journalistic ladder, and was now universally recognized as one of the leading commentators on world affairs, especially those which were notably unsettled. She made light of every discomfort and danger, priding herself that she could go anywhere a man could go and do anything a man could do, besides "smelling out" a war halfway around the world and six months off. . . .

So that was why Gwen was in France now! She had been there the previous summer, she had written brilliant and biting articles about the Munich Conference, and then she had taken a Dutch plane to Java and spent the winter in the Orient, somehow getting back to Spain just in time to see Franco march victoriously into Madrid. Constance, who had managed to retain both Gwen's friendship and Tilda's through the years, by tactfully avoiding all discussion of their mutual animosity during the course of visits carefully arranged to prevent collision, had followed some of the earlier dispatches. But lately she had not kept up with them. Now she suddenly knew as she ran down the circular stairs that Gwen had not come to France, like Tilda, because she thought it was safe to do so, but because she was sure it was not. . . .

There was no time to think about Gwen at the moment, either from the angle of her ancient feud with Tilda, or from the far more disturbing viewpoint of her present descent upon France. Like Nick's headstrong conduct and Bruno's grave decision—not to mention the imminence of war!—these must be dismissed from her mind when she entered her drawing room and while she presided at her dinner table. The beautiful presents sent to her on the occasion of her porcelain wedding had been tastefully arranged in the little sitting room where she and Tristan spent so much time together, and as she reached the threshold of this on her hurried way to greet her guests, Tristan came forward to meet her, his face lighting as he looked at her.

"Dearest," he said tenderly, "you won't believe this, but it's true: You're twice as beautiful tonight as you were twenty years ago and I love you twice as much. Come in here a minute. I've got a present for you. I didn't give it to you upstairs, because we'd talked so long already I didn't dare delay you any longer. But everything's under control. The de Fremonds haven't come down yet. Incidentally, they understood perfectly why you didn't meet them in the fort, and Aunt Bertha covered herself with glory, as usual. None of the other guests has turned up. We've got this moment to ourselves."

He drew her across the room, and picking up a tiny velvet box from his desk, put it in her hand. Then he stood back watching her as delightedly as a young lover making his first great gift to his sweetheart and awaiting her joyous exclamation of surprise. Constance did not disappoint him. She pressed the spring on the front of the little box, her fingers trembling with excitement, and as the lid flew open, she gave a glad, incredulous cry. Imbedded in the satin lining lay the splendid, sparkling replica of the ring she had given Nick that afternoon.

"Here, let me put it on for you," Tristan exclaimed, snatching it swiftly away from her and seizing her right hand. "There—that's better! It didn't look natural to me without a ring, and it didn't feel natural to you without it either, did it? I realized that it would be only a question of time before Nick would demand the other, and I wanted to have one all ready for you that no one could take away from you, and would be your very own. So I ordered this made a long while ago, and I've kept it hidden, waiting for the right moment to give it to you. I'm glad that moment came today, aren't you? No, don't try to say anything now. We'll have another chance tonight after everyone's gone, and you can thank me then, in the way I like best. I hear someone coming now."

It was the first contingent from L'Abbatiale—Stéphanie, Jacques, Ghisèle, and Abel. They had decided to come in sections, Stéphanie announced gaily, partly because Tilda was still dressing and partly because they thought the effect might be overpowering if all seven of them arrived at once. It was a good thing this was a grown-up party, that all the young fry were not coming too! They would have needed a couple of camionettes!

She turned to include Aunt Bertha in her affectionate greeting as she went on talking. Like Constance, she had been kindly treated by the years. Both of them looked younger than Tilda, who had never borne children, whose life had been far less burdened with manifold responsibilities, and who had not experienced the need for the careful financial management which alone had permitted Constance to reach her desired ends at Malou. But recently Stéphanie's beauty had begun to take on a more maternal quality. Jacques was increasingly crippled, and she gave him the same fostering care that she lavishly bestowed on Adrien, her last-born; since this youngest son's birth, Jacques had become less her lover and more her child. Constance, with Tristan's ring on her finger and the last words he had spoken in their little sitting room still lingering like music in her ears, knew that for all the fullness of their friends' lives, hers and her husband's were more abundantly supplied from that wellspring of rapture which for the others was subsiding into a quiet pool of contentment.

"Well, I take it you and Connie have decided, like Stéphanie and myself, that since Margot and Nick have taken the bit in their teeth, we may as well let them jump the hurdle?" Jacques was saying to Tristan, and Tristan was laughingly assenting. Constance would have liked to put in a word too about the engagement. But she saw that Ghisèle was trying to speak to her, and that as usual, the gentle, self-effacing young girl was standing aside for others. What an exquisite little creature she was, Connie thought for the hundredth time, kissing Ghisèle's cheek fondly. She was holding a little package, wrapped in white tissue paper and tied with pink ribbons, in one small hand; now she offered this package to Constance, whispering to her adoringly:

"I didn't want to put my present with the others. I wanted to give it to you myself, because I love you so much, Aunt Constance."

All the young Bouviers called Constance and Tristan aunt and uncle. But presently Margot would be calling them something else. If it had only been this lovely child instead!

"How sweet of you, *chérie,* and how like you! Remember, I love you very much too. I'm sure your present is charming, probably something I've wanted very much for a long time. I must see what it is, right away. . . . There, I'll have to wait after all!"

The de Fremonds from Nantes were entering the room in a body. The Countess, Constance knew, was nearly twenty years younger than Aunt Bertha, but she was more stooped than the spry little New Englander and she gave a greater effect of fragility. The two were very good friends; as soon as the Countess had embraced Constance and extended her cordial congratulations to Nick, she and Aunt Bertha retired together to a small corner sofa, and engaged each other in agreeable conversation. The Count's beard was as wide-spreading as ever, though it was now snow-white, and he still retained his habit of standing in front of a fireplace and flapping his coattails.

His sons had changed more than he had. Jean had chosen to follow in his father's footsteps as a country squire, and at twenty-nine was already relieving the Count of some of the heavier duties incumbent on this position. He did not seem to find these burdensome; he spoke of them as if he enjoyed them, with a twinkle in his eye, and his manner was debonair. Robert was still grave, but the solemn youth, articulate only when his interest was really roused, had developed into an eloquent statesman, speaking with such fluency and grace that his speech seemed the natural flowering of years which had been thoughtful as well as silent. He was now a member of the Chamber of Deputies, belonging, like most of the landed gentry around Nantes, to the Conservative party, whereas the representatives from the city proper were nearly all Socialists. The year before, he had protested vigorously against the desertion of Czechoslovakia by the French and indeed against the entire policy of appeasement, maintaining that this sacrifice of good faith, far from averting disaster from France, would only make the day of reckoning the more terrible when it came.

He was speaking in much the same vein now, and though his remarks were primarily addressed to the local Deputy, Monsieur Juneaux-Chagnon, Constance saw that Bruno and Abel were both enthralled listeners. Even his Socialist friends, Robert was saying, who had found excuses for Hitler's aggression the year before, would be hard put to do so now. The Führer had been false to every promise he had made to Chamberlain, just as he had been false to all previous promises. Instead of contenting himself with the Lebensraum which Czechoslovakia provided, he was now stretching out rapacious hands towards Poland; and it was not really Lebensraum that he wanted, it was the triumphant satisfaction of crushing and destroying, of proving that his evil power was invincible. This time France could not bargain and temporize, whatever England did; and England, Robert believed, was roused at last. If Poland were attacked, or even threatened, France and England would rise to defend her.

"But can they, Monsieur de Fremond?" Abel asked intently. "We had a debate at the Sorbonne last week, and the winner made the point that England and France couldn't defend Poland, no matter how much they wanted to. He quoted figures to show how inadequate all their defenses were—their air forces, for instance. So——"

"So this boy who won the debate thought they shouldn't even try? They are bound by solemn treaty, you know. Poland is their ally."

"Yes, that's what the loser said. But the winner said we had to be practical, and the judges agreed with him."

"I'm afraid the judges were not very practical themselves, Abel. You may be very sure that if Poland were overrun while France and England stood mutely by, they would be the next victims."

"They may be anyhow, mayn't they?"

"Yes, they may be anyhow. But meantime they will at least have got their armies into the field and their warships cleared for action. I have no delusions about their weakness; I am afraid I know more sad statistics than this young debater whom you seem to admire so much. But wonders have been done before—I might almost say miracles have been wrought —when men fought in a righteous cause with little but their faith and their courage to support them."

Robert de Fremond moved slowly away with Monsieur Juneaux-Chagnon at his side. For a moment or two they talked together in lowered tones; then they joined another group. The two boys continued to talk about Poland, Abel's voice and manner becoming more and more excited. He was very blond, like his Breton grandfather, but there was an air of intensity and of vehemence about him that bespoke another strain. Constance liked him even less than she liked Margot. His scholastic record was brilliant; evidently his mind, though facile, was shallow; and how ill-mannered he seemed, entering into an argument with a man like Robert de Fremond! Constance looked from him to Bruno with a contracting heart, rejoicing in the difference between the two. Bruno's sensitive face flushed a little as he talked, and the resemblance to Marie Aimée, long so elusive, suddenly seemed inescapable. Yes, Constance could see what Nick meant when he said that the Church—and the world—needed priests like Bruno. All those strong spiritual traits which had never failed to strike her as contradictory to Tristan's more earthy qualities seemed logical in his son. And they were blended with that complete integrity, that "singleheartedness," which Tristan had always told her was the finest part of her own heritage, and of which she had striven so hard to be worthy. . . .

The bishop, who seldom attended social functions, was making his august entrance, encircling the room majestically so that the guests, in sequence, could kiss the episcopal ring, but tactfully turning his hand over when he reached Aunt Bertha, to let her touch his finger tips instead. It was getting very late. If they did not sit down to dinner presently, they would not be through before the additional guests, invited for the reception, began to appear. These were coming not only from Lisieux, but half a dozen adjacent villages besides. It was not easy to gauge the time of arrival within a few minutes, from such distances.

Tilda, who knew about the reception, should have taken this difficulty into consideration, and if she did not do so of her own accord, Duncan should have reminded her. After all, doctors were obliged to have some sense of punctuality. Not that the exigencies of his profession troubled Duncan very much. His early practice had been one of great promise, and he had made a brilliant record during the war. But after his marriage he had gradually drifted into the role of a fashionable physician, maintaining palatial offices, limiting the number of his patients, and charging fantastic sums which he did not need for the services which he rendered without effort. His mobile manner of life, his long luxurious vacations, the indulgent levity of his attitude towards his wife, were all part of the same picture. . . .

There, they were arriving at last, a car was stopping, steps were crossing the drawbridge, voices were ringing through the fort. Nick glanced at his father, who nodded and smiled, then at his mother, who had no choice but to do the same. But it struck her that in going out to meet Margot, Nick would, automatically, also be the first to welcome the Craigs. It was as if he had already begun to exercise the privileges of a host. . . .

The last guests were finally in the drawing room. Tilda was wearing a moonstone-colored satin, perfect with her pearls, to which, Connie instantly noticed, several superb new strings had been added since her last visit. Her supplementary jewels had obviously been chosen with a view of highlighting the pearls, just as her make-up was skillfully blended with the ash-blond of her hair. The whole effect was studied, artificial, and regal. As she advanced, emanating elegance and costly scent, she managed to include the entire company in one comprehensive smile; but her greeting to her hostess was one of unfeigned warmth and affection.

"Darling, wasn't it wonderful that we could get here? Another sailing and we would have been too late. And there was nothing to be had until the last minute, absolutely nothing! As it was, we had to take two horrid little cabins on Deck B, no parlor, no veranda. But I wouldn't have missed being here tonight for anything in the world. It was worth the trip just to see the château as we came up to it, all lovely and lighted. And of course we're tremendously excited over Nick's news! As for you—Connie, how do you ever do it?"

"How do I ever do what?" Constance protested laughingly, returning her friend's embrace. But she knew—knew that Tilda, who had "everything," was envying her Malou, envying her Nick, envying her the figure which could adjust itself to a twenty-year-old wedding dress, envying her most of all—though this was the one jealousy she did not voice even indirectly—Tristan's unswerving devotion.

Constance turned her face toward her son and his sweetheart. There was no change in Nick since that afternoon, except that now he seemed even more assured and defiant. The girl beside him had the same look of arrogance and audacity. Every extreme in dress to which she had previously been addicted paled in comparison to that of her present costume.

She was wearing scarlet tulle, made as usual without shoulder straps, and cut so low that her young breasts were only half concealed by the heart-shaped bodice. Her full skirt was ankle-length and below it her bare slim feet, inadequately encased in scarlet sandals, shone with the same dazzling whiteness as her neck and arms. Her lips and nails had been extravagantly colored to match the dress and the sandals, and her curly black hair fell loosely over her shoulders, unconfined except for a scarlet flower stuck impudently above each ear; it had the tossed and tumbled look suggesting the locks of a suddenly roused sleeper, or even of a reveler unexpectedly released from a bacchanal. Looking at the girl, knowing that she must be welcomed before the assembled company as Nick's prospective bride, Constance struggled against the vision which confronted her of Margot Bouvier as the future chatelaine of Malou. And in this same instant she knew that only the infinitely greater catastrophe of Nick's death could avert the realization of her vision.

CHAPTER XXIV

FIVE WEEKS LATER, with great state and splendor, Dominique de Fremond and Marguerite Bouvier were married in the Cathedral at Lisieux.

In accordance with the universal French custom, the invitations were sent out in the joint names of the bride's parents and the groom's parents, and all marched together in the cortege: Margot first, escorted by Jacques, Constance next, escorted by Nick, and Stéphanie third, escorted by Tristan. The beadle of the Cathedral, gorgeously attired in crimson and gold, and carrying his mace with an air of supreme importance, preceded the procession; the bridesmaids, the flower girls, the groomsmen, and pages made up the main body of it; and in their wake came an impressive number of relatives near and distant. The de Fremonds from Nantes, learning that a family wedding was to follow close upon the anniversary celebration, had been persuaded to stay on for the second ceremony. The de Vallerins from the Haras du Pin had been joined by various other members of their family, and it was Aunt Bertha's proud privilege to have an aged prince of the blood for her escort. The Bouviers were apparently legion in number, and numerous Solomons also put in their appearance, rather unexpectedly, for though they had of course been invited, it had somehow been taken for granted that only Madame Bouvier and Madame Solomon would come. All in all, when seated, the cortege completely filled the choir; it was necessary to place even such intimate friends as the Craigs, who had also stayed on without much urging, in the nave, which was likewise crowded to the last row; and as it was impossible to squeeze all of the witnesses into the sacristy at once, they were obliged to enter it in relays, after the Nuptial Mass, in order to sign the register.

The bishop, who had graciously consented to officiate, had been unaccountably detained, so that he was nowhere in sight when the cortege arrived in the choir, and the bridal armchairs were necessarily put into use even before the Mass and the sermon. The situation, awkward and inexcusable at best in Constance's eyes, would have been doubly so if the young couple had been obliged to stand while waiting. Suppressing a sigh of relief, she saw them take their places with the utmost composure and sit quietly side by side, as if the wait were entirely inconsequential, and as if not the slightest embarrassment were involved by their formal and public position. Nick adjusted his saber with precision, but did not shift it a second time; his silver epaulets caught the light of the flickering candles, but his shoulders were still. Margot's court train and her long lace veil had both been carefully draped over the back of her armchair by Ghisèle, who, from the side, kept a watchful eye on these to see that their flowing folds were not disarranged by any slight change of position. But her vigilance was unrequired: Margot, the restless, the impatient, the headstrong, was as still as a statue.

When the bishop finally arrived, in full pontificals, fifteen minutes late, she still had not moved a muscle; and as she accepted Nick's hand and rose, approaching the altar rail with him, she did so with unhurried grace, Ghisèle again arranged her sister's lace as the bridal couple knelt, forestalling the possibility that it might catch on Nick's spurs when the two rose; Margot herself seemed oblivious of any potential contretemps. The same dignity and composure marked her bearing throughout the long sermon and the rest of the elaborate ceremony, and when she finally turned and came down the aisle on Nick's arm, under the crossed sabers which made the traditional *voûte d'acier,* Constance was startled at the expression on her face. She had gone to the altar with this veiled, but Ghisèle had now rearranged the lace so that it only framed her forehead, and her look was one of triumphant gladness, all the effrontery and insolence were gone from it. Her lips were parted in a happy smile, and this seemed to embrace everyone whose glance she caught. The very strains of the recessional resounding through the Cathedral seemed to draw their impetus from her unabashed joy.

Once outside, the cortege stopped on the Cathedral steps, to be photographed in couples and in groups. Then the bridal car, profusely decorated with orange blossoms and white-satin ribbons, streamed away towards the rue de Caen. When the third car, in which Constance was riding, reached the Abbaye, she was amazed to see that only the one directly in front of her, conveying Stéphanie and Tristan, was going ahead, and that Nick was giving Margot his hand to alight from theirs. Constance looked at Jacques with an astonished question.

"They're stopping to see Marie Aimée, of course. She's been looking forward to this visit for weeks. In fact it wouldn't surprise me at all if the Prioress permitted all the nuns to assemble in the *grand parloir,* so that they can see Margot's bridal finery and Nick's new full-dress uniform. After all, Margot's been their special pet ever since she was born. Stéphanie and I brought her to the Abbaye directly after her baptism, so that they could admire her christening clothes, and she herself insisted on coming here directly after her first Holy Communion, so that they could admire her bonnet and veil and her first long dress. What could be more natural than for her to come now, after this third great sacrament?"

"It would seem more natural to me if it were primarily a question of a great sacrament and not of becoming clothes."

"But isn't it proper to honor a great sacrament with suitable garments? I don't see anything inconsistent about that!"

"No, of course you wouldn't. . . . It would also seem more natural to me if it had been Ghisèle who wanted to come, though I still think it's rather extraordinary to interrupt a wedding cortege in order to visit a cloister. And it's so out of character, in Margot!"

"Not in the least. You don't fully understand us yet, Connie, after all these years. Not that it matters much when you're so fond of us—and we of you. But you better be prepared for some more extraordinary procedures before the end of the day. Margot's decided to have the cortege make the rounds of the stables, according to the local custom at the Haras du Pin. Only instead of having a *palefrenier* escort the bride and groom from stall to stall, Mark Mullins is going to do it. And you'd better be prepared for some pretty broad jokes when we reach the *haras du monte*. Traditionally, all sorts of pleasantries are permitted on such an occasion. I don't think Nick and Margot will stay at the Abbaye long; they'll be too eager to get on with the rest of the program. On the other hand, they wouldn't have thought the day complete without that visit."

Jacques was right on all points. He had hardly finished giving Constance a detailed description of the marriage customs at the Haras du Pin when the bridal car shot past them, its horn blowing, its white ribbons fluttering in the breeze, its orange blossoms scattering by the roadside. By the time their own car had reached the great quadrangle, Margot and Nick were already stationed, impatiently waiting to begin their tour, with Mark Mullins, decorated whip in hand, beside them, and Stéphanie and Tristan standing laughingly behind them. Presently the cortege had reformed, this time accompanied by a band of hunting horns, whose proud players had come up from the Haras du Pin for the purpose; with the bride and groom leading the procession, this made the rounds of the stables, including the stallion's. All had been swept and garnished, all had been decorated with boughs and blossoms.

Margot's magnificent train and veil, less carefully upheld than in the Cathedral by her attendant pages, whose interest was now wandering to the colts, emerged unsoiled and undamaged from the tour; and her retorts to the "pleasantries" were apt, witty, and entirely unembarrassed, though, as her father had foretold, some of the jokes were certainly very broad. Constance saw him watching his eldest daughter with an expression of fond pride which deepened the furrows in his cheeks and the elusive smile which played around his lips. The amount of walking he had done that day must inevitably have been very hard for him; but he carried it off triumphantly, himself so completely ignoring his crippled condition that no one else was uncomfortably aware of it.

"A great girl, my Margot," he said exultantly. "Perhaps you haven't discovered it yet, Connie, but you will, someday. No, don't try to protest. I can see how she'd rub you the wrong way very often now. But she won't when you and she get used to each other." Constance would have liked to tell him that Tristan had said much the same thing, but such a statement would have been an admission that it had been called forth. "She's getting a fine boy, too, I know that already," he went on pleasantly. "Of course they're both a little on the wild side. But they'll be all the better mated for that—doves and hawks don't belong in the same nest. . . . Well, this seems to be the end of the procession. We'd better see what's being offered in the way of a wedding breakfast."

Two immense striped marquees had been put up in the quadrangle, one obviously prepared for dancing later on, the other already set with a huge table in the shape of a hollow square. To this table Jacques now led Constance, putting her at his right and seating himself at the right of Margot. Constance had of course been to many wedding breakfasts in France by this time, just as she had been to many Nuptial Masses, but she had never seen one prepared on so splendid a scale as this "lunch." ("On every other day in our lives, your lunch is our breakfast," Tristan had told her laughingly years before. "But on the greatest day of all, what you call a wedding breakfast becomes a lunch for us French!") As usual, the lunch was limited to the members of the two families, and to such contemporaries of the bridal couple as had taken part in the cortege, all other friends being invited to a later reception. Even so, numerically it was imposing and gastronomically it was a marvel. Course followed course, while endless toasts were drunk and endless speeches of felicitation delivered; and through it all Margot's happy smile never faded, her bearing never lost its mingled ease and elegance, her flow of apt and witty small talk never flagged.

More cars began to drive up, a signal that the lunch must finally come to an end and the reception begin. Surreptitiously Constance glanced at her wrist watch and saw that it was nearly five o'clock. But if anyone else were tired, if anyone else felt that a celebration which had already lasted for six hours might logically be drawing to an end, there was no sign of this. The bridal couple opened the dance in the second marquee, where a stringed orchestra was alternating with the hunting horns to provide the music; then they returned to stand with their parents and receive the steady influx of guests for another two hours. By that time, everyone who was expected had apparently arrived, and they themselves returned to the dance floor. Nick danced with all the bridesmaids, with all the flower girls, with all Margot's female relatives old and young, while Margot was similarly occupied with the corresponding male contingent. Finally, when it was nearly ten o'clock, and the lights of Japanese lanterns were beginning to flicker and twinkle through the late dusk, Nick came and bowed before his mother.

"You've saved this last one for me, I hope?" he said whimsically.

"I wouldn't have dreamed of giving it to anyone else," she answered, trying to match his lightness of tone.

He put his arm around her waist, and they whirled off together. Nick was a wonderful dancer, but Constance had always been a good dancer too, and gave an illusion of youth on the dance floor; she knew that Nick was proud of the way she moved and looked, proud to have people see him leading out his mother in this final dance before he left with his bride. His eyes were very bright and he laughed and joked with her as they swung about, and finally, when the music stopped, he bent his head and kissed her, holding her close against his heart. . . .

Then, half an hour later, he and Margot were gone. Jacques had given Margot a smart little runabout for a wedding present, and she and Nick came pelting down the stairs of the guest house, where they had gone to change their clothes, and leapt into the car and drove away. It all happened very fast at the end. But Constance had time to see that Nick's eyes were brighter than ever and that there was a new ring to his laugh. Also that Margot, smartly but very simply dressed in old-rose tweeds, looked quite as lovely as she had in her satin and laces and that her face was even more radiant than it had been in church.

During the next few weeks, the vision of Margot's radiant and transfigured face rose constantly before her mother-in-law. The progress of the bridal couple was reported only by a succession of gaudy post cards briefly announcing their arrival at some fashionable watering place, or their departure from this. Dinard, Biarritz, Pau, Hyères, and Juan-les-Pins were all heralded in this way; then came a wire saying they were so enraptured with Monte Carlo that they would stay there until Nick's leave was up. Neither he nor Margot, it was evident, had desired an uninterrupted solitude à deux: instead they had both been determined on a "last fling" and they were certainly having a gay one. But in the midst of this mad whirlwind of pleasure, they were indubitably managing to give vent to their passionate love for each other, all the more vehemently, perhaps, because they were doing so spasmodically, in supercharged and artificial settings.

For some weeks the intervening period was strangely quiet. The wonderful weather, exceptionally balmy and beautiful, added to the impression that nothing could be seriously wrong in a world where one day of mellow sunshine followed another in quiet succession. The crops were abundant, and harvesting took its industrious but unhurried course. The woodchoppers who moved seasonally from one estate to another came as usual to Malou, and stacked up the carefully cut wood in great piles throughout the forest. Early in August both the French and the British sent military missions to Moscow, but the failure of these did not become apparent until Russia and Germany signed a mutual trade agreement a fortnight later and even then it did not seem to spell inevitable disaster. Ciano's meeting with Ribbentrop and Hitler at Berchtesgaden might be reasonably regarded as "just another conference"; Germany's demand for the return of Danzig a gesture which did not necessarily threaten France any more immediately than his similar claim on the Sudeten a year earlier.

Tristan was spending a good many hours close to the radio, reading the daily papers with unusual thoroughness, and making and receiving more long-distance telephone calls than he usually did; otherwise he continued his normal round of activities at Malou. He and Constance had always kept joint accounts, and he had always insisted that she must be thoroughly conversant with the details of his management of the land and of the commons. It was their habit to go over these accounts together every month; according to their custom, they did so early in August.

Everything was in admirable order. In spite of the extraordinary expenditures in connection with their anniversary celebration and Nick's wedding, their bank balance showed a comfortable margin of safety. From the earliest years of their marriage sums had regularly been set aside to care for such contingencies. Constance had always known in which strongbox Tristan kept his will, his certificates of life insurance, and all such other papers as she might need "in case anything happened." He did not remind her of its location when they checked over accounts. But he did go through all the outbuildings with her, reminding her that from now on, the stables and dairy, as well as the château itself, might at any time become her responsibility.

Immediately after the wedding, Tilda and Duncan had gone to Deauville. Soon the Craigs would be heading for Scotland, but in the meantime they had arranged to spend a few days at Malou. This meant that Bruno had moved his books into Constance's study, and was sleeping on the day bed there, so that Duncan could have the room which the two brothers had shared before Nick's marriage. The Craigs, it had long since been made clear, never voluntarily occupied the same one, and the third-floor guest chambers were being transformed into a sitting room and bedroom more adapted to Margot's special needs and tastes. Therefore no other arrangement had seemed feasible for the Craigs; but this was peculiarly welcome to Constance, since it made the long serious talks she wanted to have with Bruno seem less premeditated. Inevitably they were thrown together a great deal more anyway, and she improved every possible occasion of discussing the future with him. None of these opportunities seemed more propitious than a long, lazy afternoon in late August.

"Why don't you plan to stay at home this winter, Bruno? After all, you're a year younger than most of your classmates. You could still catch up with them if you waited."

"Normally. But Nick's already reminded you, Mother, that these aren't normal times. If I waited a year, there isn't a chance that I could finish at the seminary before I'd be called out. If I start in right away there's *just* a chance that I could."

"The war may be over very quickly—always supposing there actually is a war. The experts seem to agree that it couldn't be a long one."

"They reached the same agreement in August, '14, didn't they, Mother? . . . Anyway my regular military service would still be ahead of me, even if there weren't a war."

Bruno turned back to the letter he had been writing. Constance sewed in silence for a few minutes. Then she spoke persuasively again.

"It doesn't seem possible that the opening of the hunting season is only a week or so off. I'm rather glad of it. I don't know when I've felt so much in the mood for riding in the woods. Only I don't like to go alone."

Bruno laid down his pen. "I'll ride with you as much as you like during September, Mother. And I can get home for an occasional week end afterwards. I think Nick reminded you of that too. It's just the riding you really like anyway, isn't it? You've always said the best part of hunting was the music of the *trompes de la chasse* and I've always agreed with you."

"Beg pardon, Madame la Baronne. Some young ladies are at the door, asking if the château is open to tourists."

"Well, you told them, of course, that it is not?"

The interruption could hardly have been less opportune. In another half hour Constance might have made some headway with Bruno, or so she thought. She spoke to Léon with unaccustomed sharpness.

"Yes, Madame la Baronne. But they continued to ask if an exception could not be made in their case. One of them said she had heard of Malou from an old friend of her mother's, who, it appears, was once also a friend of yours—a Madame Heweet if I well comprehended the name."

"Then in that case—— If the young ladies are still here at teatime I'll invite them to stay for it and we'll have it on the terrace."

"*Bien entendu, Madame la Baronne.*"

The old servant shuffled away. Constance rose reluctantly.

"I don't suppose you feel like coming with me, Bruno? They're probably typical college girls, 'doing' Europe in three weeks, for the first time."

"They won't eat me, will they? I'll be glad to come down, Mother, as soon as I finish this letter I was writing."

Constance went down the corridor to the big guest room, where Tilda was installed, and found her friend extended on a chaise longue, wrapped in a dressing gown of old-rose brocade, and leafing through a fashion magazine.

"From what Léon tells me, it appears that tourists have penetrated to our peaceful stronghold. One of them claims to know Lois. I haven't seen them yet, but I'm going down now. I thought I'd tell you about the invasion, in case you'd rather have tea in your room."

"Many thanks, Connie. Of course I would. I don't feel equal, this nice warm day, to the exertion of a sight-seeing tour."

Constance nodded understandingly. She still heard from Lois on rare occasions, and she knew that Tilda did too; but she had not kept in the same close touch with Lois as she had with Tilda and Gwen. The Hewitts had achieved "the nice little bungalow in a suburb of Philadelphia" for which they had hoped and planned during their engagement; but their means had never permitted them to enlarge either this modest dwelling place or their own horizons.

"Would my presence be of material help, or otherwise? If it would, I'm perfectly willing to organize a Cook's Tour."

While the other two were speaking, Duncan had lounged in from the boys' room. He made his suggestion casually and agreeably.

"Considering your invariable success with young ladies, I'd be delighted to have you undertake the tour. I'm feeling almost as lazy as Tilda. Come down whenever you're in the mood."

"I'm in the mood to come now, with you."

He made the remark in the same offhand way in which he had spoken before, asked Tilda if there were anything he could do for her before he left, and waved his hand in a smiling salute. But when they reached the end of the corridor, his manner changed.

"What do you mean, my 'invariable success'?" he asked heatedly. "It hasn't been invariable by any means, and you know it."

"I wasn't weighing my words, I was just making polite conversation. You know *that*. . . . Duncan, I've been watching for a chance to tell you—I'm afraid there may be a collision, after all these years when I've succeeded in avoiding it. Gwen's in France too. She's wired me three times, but she never gives me the least idea where I can send a wire in return. She may show up here any day."

"Still turning the topic adroitly to Gwen after all these years, eh, Connie? Well, it's just as futile as ever. I don't care a hang whether Gwen comes to Malou or not, except that I don't see just where you'd put her right now that you're reserving the third floor for the bride and groom. It's Gwen who's always raised the rumpus—you know *that!* Tilda never raises rumpuses. You know that too."

They were nearing the foot of the circular staircase. From the adjacent office they could hear the radio going at full blast.

"The Soviet Embassy in Paris declines to either confirm or deny the rumor that Russia and Germany are on the point of signing a ten-year non-aggression pact. Nevertheless the rumor persists, strengthened by the news that Foreign Minister von Ribbentrop has arrived in Moscow."

"What is that going to mean, Duncan? If they do sign it, I mean?"

"Tristan will tell us at dinnertime—sooner if he thinks there's anything to tell. No use bursting in on him now—you know he likes to hear those programs through in peace. Besides, the sooner you receive your tourists, the sooner you can get rid of them."

The "tourists" had foregathered in the drawing room and were engaged in inspecting it with enchanted interest when Duncan and Constance came in. Three of them were fresh and alert, good-looking in a somewhat nondescript way, and serviceably rather than stylishly dressed. The fourth girl was much more striking. She had on a beautifully tailored gray suit and a perky little gray hat trimmed with a russet-colored feather which matched her smooth shoes, her smart handbag, and incidentally, her crisp auburn hair. The others looked a little shy and shamefaced at being caught in the careful examination of the cabinet; but this girl came forward without embarrassment, extending her hand and speaking naturally and pleasantly.

"I do hope we're not intruding, Madame de Fremond," she said. "Doris knows your friends the Hewitts, and when she told Mrs. Hewitt we were going to make a tour of the famous Norman inns and châteaux, she said she was sure you wouldn't mind if we stopped by Malou. This is Doris —Doris Milton. And this is Barbara Bailey and this is Helen Shields. We were all at Bryn Mawr together, and now Doris is studying for an M.A. and Barbara and Helen both teach domestic science. I don't do anything important at all, but when I heard what the others were planning for the summer, I thought it would be fun if we made the trip in my car. I *do* drive! By the way, my name's Eileen Callender. I left that out somewhere along the line, didn't I?"

"It's much too pretty a name to leave out," Constance said cordially. "Of course you're not intruding. I'm very glad to see you all." Now that she was actually confronted with these young Americans, she found she could say this with real sincerity. She made the rounds of her visitors, shaking hands with them all and presenting Duncan in a comprehensive introduction. "This is my friend Dr. Craig, who's visiting at Malou just now. He's been here a great many times, so he knows the château well, and he's very kindly offered to help organize a Cook's Tour. In a few minutes my younger son Bruno will join us too, so I believe you'll be well looked after. What would you like to do first? You're in the drawing room now, as of course you gathered, and you entered through the old fort, which we still call by its original name. The dining room's on the other side of it. I can show you that and the kitchen both, if you like. Of course you've found out by this time that the kitchen's very often the most attractive room in a Norman house. . . . By and by we'll have tea on the terrace."

"Oh, I'm sure everything will be just wonderful." . . . "Really, Baroness, it's too sweet of you." . . . "Do tell us who all the lovely ladies are in these portraits!"

The three nice nondescript girls were all bubbling over with gratitude and enthusiasm. The fourth, who was so outstanding among the others, instead of peering excitedly at the curiosities in the drawing room and giving little squeals of delight, looked fixedly at Duncan Craig for a moment and then walked quickly over to him.

"It must be imagination, but I have the strangest feeling I know you already," she said. "My mother had a friend named Dr. Craig who used to come to the house a good deal when I was a very little girl. I was very fond of him—in fact, I used to call him Uncle Duncan. Of course that was years ago. We moved to Philadelphia and lost track of him. It couldn't possibly have been you, could it?"

"Just possibly it might have been. Was your mother Mrs. Edwin Callender before she remarried?"

"Why yes! Then I wasn't mistaken! Oh, I'm awfully glad to see you again!"

With the obvious pleasure in the unexpected recovery of an old friend, the attractive girl attached herself to Duncan Craig. Constance stole one glance at him, and then looked away appalled. His ruddy color had faded suddenly, his loose, sensual mouth had tightened, his whole face was stricken. He was responding adequately and evenly to the girl's animated observations, but this correct and controlled manner did not lessen Constance's feeling of consternation. What would be the eventual outcome of this disastrous chance encounter? Now that Craig, whose marriage had been childless, had accidentally come face to face with this charming young creature, of whom any father might well be proud, would he consent to lose sight of her again? If Tilda changed her mind and decided to come downstairs after all, what would happen then?

"You see, originally the château enclosed an open court, and what you see now is only half of a complete structure," she heard herself saying as the group paused in the fort. "The carts and horses came through here to the other side until fairly recently, as the French understand the word recently—say until a hundred years ago." Doris, Barbara, and Helen responded with gratifying laughs to the unremarkable jest; Eileen smiled appropriately too, but she was not really impressed, and after all there was no reason why she should be; she had probably been to France half a dozen times already, and seen any number of châteaux.

"I feel like such a drone beside the other girls," she was saying to Duncan Craig. "They're all taking this trip in deadly earnest and I'm just enjoying it. I'd like to do something worth while too. But somehow I haven't hit on the right thing yet."

"Well, give yourself time. Perhaps the right thing will come to you."

They were on their way to the dining room now, and from Tristan's office the radio was blaring loudly.

"The D.N.B. announces from Berlin that a non-aggression pact has been signed between Russia and Germany. Count Robert de Fremond, making an impassioned speech in the Chamber of Deputies, bitterly denounces this pact."

Apparently no one except herself heard the radio. Eileen Callender, with the instant recognition of a kindred spirit, was deep in a conversation with Duncan Craig which had nothing to do either with the historical features of the château or the volcanic state of the world. The other three girls were listening with absorbed enchantment to Bruno, who had now joined the group, and who had taken charge of them with competent gentleness. His arrival had lessened Constance's sense of tension; he seemed so serene and content that she drew immediate comfort from his presence, and this feeling of respite continued after the sight-seeing had come to an end and the group went out on the terrace, where the tea table was already invitingly laid. The young visitors' enthusiastic attention now switched from architecture, interior decorating, and quaint kitchen equipment to the view, the garden, and the brioches. . . .

"I think we have more visitors, Mother. I just heard a car drive up. I'll go and see who's in it."

Bruno did not stubbornly decline to talk English, like Nick, and he did not refuse to call Constance "Mother"; in fact he said himself that he considered it a word of far more beauty and significance than "maman." Constance nodded gratefully and watched his retreating figure with adoring eyes. She was thankful that Tristan had turned off the radio, not only because it was a disturbing element in itself, but because its silence was in a measure reassuring. If the news had continued to be menacing, Tristan would have kept it on. She was not disturbed by his absence from the terrace. He always joined her for tea when they were entertaining formally, but he regarded its service as a social practice rather than an occasion for inviting refreshment. Probably he did not even know the young Americans were there. . . .

"It's Miss Foster, Mother. I told her I was sure you'd want her to come right out on the terrace, but she saw the other car and she said I'd better ask you first."

"Gwen? I'll go to meet her, Bruno. Did you tell your father?"

"No, but I will."

"Oh, Madame de Fremond, it isn't *Gwendolyn* Foster, is it? Mrs. Hewitt told us she was back in France, and I've been just *praying* we'd run into her somewhere. I think she's simply marvelous. I read every syllable she writes."

Constance briefly assured her excited visitors that the new arrival was indeed the famous columnist. She had risen and started across the terrace in swift acknowledgment of Bruno's announcement; but before going out to welcome Gwen, she stopped beside Duncan, who was still so absorbed in Eileen that he did not appear to have heard.

"Duncan, Gwen's here."

"Yes? What? Oh well, you said she was likely to turn up any time. . . . And so you decided to go to college instead of making a formal debut?"

He had already turned back to Eileen. Constance went quickly on to the fort. Gwen, trim, alert, vital as ever, was standing just inside the doorway.

"Hello, Connie! Well, you see I got here. But I can't stay. I've got to go straight on to Paris. I didn't want to drive right past the place, though. Who's outside?"

"Some college girls Lois sent here—one of them knows her. And, Gwen, another's Eileen Callender."

"Eileen Callender?"

"I forgot you never knew her last name. Of course I didn't either until an hour ago. Then if you'd seen Duncan's face——"

"Duncan's! So he's here too!"

"Yes. He's out on the terrace talking to this girl now. She's perfectly lovely, Gwen."

"What about Tilda?"

"Tilda's having tea in her room. She said she didn't feel like bothering with a lot of tourists. Perhaps you and I better go up to my study, Gwen. Bruno can take charge very well and we'll be ever so much quieter there. If you've only got a little time——"

Gwen laughed. "You haven't changed much underneath, have you, Connie? I've only got about half an hour. But you can bet your bottom dollar I'm going to spend that on the terrace."

She was already halfway across the fort. Constance tried, vainly, to detain her.

"Gwen, you won't—you won't——"

"Don't worry. I'll behave. But if you think I'm going to miss a chance like this, after all these years——"

She had already stepped out on the terrace. Doris, Barbara, and Helen, feeling that her arrival gave the culminating touch to their most thrilling European experience, responded a little awkwardly, a little bashfully, to her offhand greeting. But Gwen was used to playing the celebrity now and she did it extremely well; almost instantly she put them at their ease. Then, breezily, she turned towards the others.

"Why hello, Duncan! Imagine finding you here! Isn't this just like old times? Especially as you seem engrossed by a charming feminine companion! How do you do, Miss——?"

"I'm Eileen Callender, Miss Foster. I hope you won't mind if I tell you I think it's a very great privilege to meet you."

Her unaffected sincerity, so different from the gushing incoherences of the others, was very appealing. Gwen drew up a chair beside her and sat down.

"So the gilded youth reads the newspapers nowadays? It didn't used to. . . . Connie, haven't you got anything stronger than tea? I could do with a good stiff drink."

"We'll have to see what the *cave* can supply. But Bruno doesn't seem to be back. Duncan, will you see what you can find for Gwen?" Connie asked. Eileen Callender leaned forward towards her questioner.

"Oh, but I'm hardly gilded at all! I've just been telling Dr. Craig. . . . Not that I'm doing anything important, like the other girls." Again Eileen outlined their plans and purposes. "I'd like to, though. It seems as if there ought to be something I could do."

"Have you ever tried to write?"

"Yes, for our college paper, and some of my teachers encouraged me. I liked it, too. But my mother thinks the idea of my being a writer is silly."

"I don't see why. That's all I had ever done when I began writing from the Argonne. At least it wouldn't do any harm to find out whether you could make the grade, and I've got a suggestion. The rattleheaded secretary who was waiting for me in Paris took fright at the way things are going over here and headed for home. I don't suppose you'd care for her job?"

"You don't suppose—— Miss Foster, you're not serious?"

"I'm deadly serious. I can tell just by looking at you that it shouldn't take you long to learn the ropes. If you'll come with me to Paris tonight, I can promise you that you'll be doing something 'important' from now on. But all you'd have to do at the moment would be to transfer your baggage from one car to the other."

In a chorus the others declared that Eileen must not miss a chance like this, that it was simply too wonderful for words. Connie swiftly suggested that of course it *was* a wonderful opportunity, but that perhaps Miss Callender should take time to think it over and decide if she was really qualified; but Constance was completely drowned out. Eileen herself said nothing immediately. Instead, she sat studying the bag in her lap and drawing her gloves back and forth through her hands until Duncan Craig returned with whisky and soda and cracked ice on a little tray. He had brought two glasses. As he set the tray down on a small table beside Gwen, Eileen looked up at him and spoke eagerly.

"Miss Foster's just offered me a job. She says I can go right on to Paris with her tonight. I think perhaps this is what I've been waiting for, without knowing it."

"It's very kind of Miss Foster. But I'm afraid you'd find the work most exacting. And you don't know stenography, do you?"

"Well, I'm not an expert, but I have taken a short course in speed writing. I was elected secretary of the Junior League in Philadelphia and I thought——"

"You see, Duncan."

Gwen reached over, added another jigger to one of the glasses he had been filling, and took a long drink. Duncan Craig did the same. Afterwards he set down his glass with a slight bang.

"Perhaps I shouldn't attempt to advise you on such short acquaintance, Miss Callender, but I really think you'd be much wiser and much happier if you'd go on with the trip you planned to take with your friends."

Involuntarily, Constance and Gwen looked at each other, the same thought in the mind of each. The words were formal and correct enough. But to them the tones seemed to say plainly, "As your father, I forbid you to have anything to do with this mad scheme." The illusion was so complete that they could hardly believe the others were oblivious of their feeling.

"I suppose I should. But——"

"I'll be staying at the Meurice. You can reach me there or through the American Embassy. Why don't you think it over tonight and wire me in the morning, if Dr. Craig's warning makes you hesitate now?"

"No, it doesn't, not really. Or at least, only because I'm afraid I wouldn't be good enough——"

"Mother, Father'd like to see you for a minute. It's rather urgent. I'm sure your guests will excuse you."

Bruno was standing in the doorway, his expression still gentle and composed. As he finished speaking, the bell in the nearby village church began to toll. Then two others, more distant, rang out in unison with it. Suddenly the quiet valley was resounding with echoes. Constance clutched her son's arm.

"Bruno——"

"He's upstairs, Mother. I know he'd rather tell you himself."

Constance ran through the fort and up the circular staircase. The sound of the bells followed her as she mounted. The door of her study stood open, and looking through it to the bedroom beyond, Constance could see Tristan, dressed in a plain khaki uniform. He was bending over a suitcase he was strapping. But he straightened up at her approach.

"Dearest," he said, and stopped. Then he put his arm around her. "I could have called you sooner, but I thought perhaps it would be easier for both of us this way. The *affiches* are up already. I went over to the village as soon as I heard on the radio that the non-aggression pact between Russia and Germany was signed."

"The *affiches?*"

"The notices of the general mobilization. Of course the bells will announce it too." Again he paused and for a moment the room was still, except for the sound of those tolling signals rising from the peaceful valley. "I must be on my way before a gendarme hauls me out in the middle of the night."

"You're going *now!*"

"Yes, Bruno's driving me to Caen, where I have to report. Constance—don't stand in the way of his going to the seminary. It's what he wants to do and what he thinks he ought to do. It doesn't open for six weeks yet, so you'll have him with you that much longer anyway. He'll do everything he can to help you get ready for the winter. And he won't be far off—after all, it only takes two hours to go between here and Bayeux. In case of need you can summon him, and I'm sure the bishop will let him come to you. But you won't try to stop him, will you, Constance?"

"No," she said in a low voice.

"You won't be alone, even after he's gone. You'll have Margot. Nick's probably saying good-by to her right now too—she may have to come back to Malou alone. I don't know exactly what his orders would be, but quite likely he's on his way to join a regiment already." Tristan stopped for a minute, but he did not try to say anything more about Nick. "And you'll have Aunt Bertha," he went on with an effort. "I've talked to Aunt Bertha already. I asked her if she didn't think she'd better leave while it was still safe. All she said was 'I'm not aiming to go,' but you should have seen the withering look she gave me! Of course later on American citizens may be forced to leave. You'll know what's best to do for her if they are."

"Yes," Constance said in a still lower voice.

"But don't forget—you're French now yourself. Of course if you'd married me two years later, you could have chosen your citizenship. But I like to think your decision would have made it the same as when you had no choice."

"You know it would have. I wouldn't have taken advantage of a law that could have separated us, ever."

"I did know it, but I wanted to hear you say so. France is my country and I'm off to fight for it. It's our sons' country too. One of them must be starting off now to fight for it, just as I am, leaving his bride while they're still on their honeymoon. The other one will be in the fight before it's over —don't begrudge him the time he'll have at Bayeux, Constance, it'll be short enough. And France is your country as well as theirs and mine. You'll be staying here, at Malou, while we're off fighting. Promise me you won't leave it, Constance. Promise me you'll save it for us."

"I promise."

"Promise me something else too. Promise that no matter how hard things get, you'll never lose courage. I don't believe they'll be too hard. You'll have plenty to eat, for a long time anyway. You'll have plenty of wood. Not that it's easy to keep warm with nothing else, but it can be' done. You'll be much better off than you would be in a city—it's a comfort to me to remember that. And besides, remember you've taken the de Fremond motto for your own, that difficulties don't daunt you any more. Promise me that no matter what happens you won't lose hope. Don't despair if you hear I've been taken prisoner. I'll escape. Don't believe it if you're told I'm dead. It will be a false report. I'll come back to you, darling. I swear I will. Tell me you believe me."

"I—believe—you—Tristan."

"That's what I wanted to hear you say. All I needed to hear you say. I'm going now, dearest. Don't come with me to the door. That would only make it harder for both of us. Don't try to go back to your visitors. You'd break down if you did. Aunt Bertha's gone to them already. Lie down a little while. That'll give you a chance to pull yourself together. Besides, I've put a small present on your pillow. Oh, nothing much! I couldn't get you another real present so soon after the ring. But I saw this bagatelle in a shop window on the rue Pont-Martin the last time I went into Lisieux and I thought it might amuse you, and please you, and give you a message from me after I'd gone. I was sure, you see, that I'd be going."

He glanced towards the bed, and following his look she saw a wisp of something blue against the rose of its covering. But her eyes were misting and she could not see it very clearly. It did not matter. She would look at it after he was gone. What did anything matter except that he was going, that he was leaving her, that nothing in the world was worth having without him?

"Good-by, dearest. Remember, you've promised."

"I'll never forget. Good-by, Tristan."

She went over to the window to watch him leave. *I ought to have something to wave,* she thought, with that strange reversal to trivial things that characterizes great moments, and instinctively she felt for her handkerchief. But she must have dropped it somewhere, she did not have it tucked inside her blouse as usual. After fumbling blindly for a moment, she remembered the wisp of blue lying on the bed and ran to get it. She waved it until the car had disappeared among the trees, and saw Tristan's answering signal; then she spread out the wisp of blue and looked at it.

It was made of chiffon, and in one corner of it the miniature figure of an astrologer was embroidered above the legend, "These are your stars." Scattered over the filmy surface were constellations variously captioned— "Star of the Shepherds"—"Star of Happiness"—"Star of Love"—"Star of Souvenirs"—"Star of Hope." Looking at the handkerchief through misty eyes, Constance knew that Tristan had trustfully thought that each of the little embroidered stars would have a special meaning for her: that she would think of the first stars they had watched together the night before Christmas at Grand Blottereau, and of Venus rising in all its splendor above the radiance of a far-flung sunset seen from the terrace. Since that first visit to Malou, they had shared many stars of happiness. Now, for a long while, there would be only the remembrance of joyous times to help through the hard ones; but he was relying on her to hold fast to that precious memory, and meanwhile to keep her eyes firmly fixed on the star of hope for the future. Even the color of the little handkerchief was symbolical; this was the shade Tristan had always best loved to see her wear, the one in which he would look forward to seeing her again, at the war's end. There was to be no mourning crape for him. . . .

Moments slipped by and still Constance continued to stand at the window, thinking of all that the handkerchief represented. Eventually she saw Doris, Barbara, and Helen, politely accompanied by Aunt Bertha, appear on the drawbridge and walk over to Eileen's car. The girls' voices were raised in excitement, and Constance could hear them all plainly. It had been simply *perfect,* they were saying, but they were a little afraid they had barged in at the wrong time. The Baroness had been sweet, they would never forget her, they hoped she would have nothing but the best of news from her husband and her son. And they thought Eileen was just right to snatch at the wonderful opportunity Miss Foster was giving her; it really was the chance of a lifetime! Yes, they themselves would go straight to the American Express and see about passage home. They promised. Probably about a hundred thousand other people would be doing the same thing, but after all they did have round-trip tickets, and they didn't care where they bunked. It would really be rather a lark.

They were still chattering and exclaiming when Gwen and Eileen and Duncan came out too, and Eileen's baggage was transferred from her own car to Gwen's. They all shook hands with him and with Aunt Bertha, and climbed into their respective cars and drove off, Gwen and Eileen in a composed, matter-of-fact way, the chatter and laughter of the others punctuated by little shrieks. Constance could still hear these, mingling with the tolling of the bells, as the cars swung out through the orchard and disappeared in the long driveway.

She closed the window, and turned away from it. The evening was still balmy and beautiful, but she thought perhaps if the window was shut, she would not hear the church bells quite so plainly. She was still holding the blue handkerchief, and now she decided that she would tack it to the wall somewhere, as if it were a service flag, so that she could look at it frequently and easily. It was unthinkable that she should put it to ordinary use; and if she laid it away in her drawer, she would not have before her the constant reminder of Tristan's thought and Tristan's message. She looked about her, thoughtfully searching the best place for it, and finally decided to put it above the footboard of her bed, opposite the crucifix, which had never been removed from above the headboard after all. There she would see it the last thing at night and the first thing in the morning, and it would be as a standard for her.

She spread it out on the rose-colored counterpane again, and went to her desk to get the tacks and the small hammer which she always kept in one of its lower drawers. As she opened this, she was conscious of another sound beside the tolling of the bells, which after all she had not been able to shut out. Someone was knocking at her door.

At first she tried to pay no attention. The only person whom she would willingly have seen just then was Bruno, and Bruno could not possibly return for another two hours. This was no time for anyone to intrude upon her with some trivial household demand, some insignificant message, or the announcement of some other inopportune visitor. Without answering, she located the tacks and the hammer and closed the drawer of her desk again. As she did so, the door of the study opened slightly and Duncan Craig spoke to her.

"Please let me come in, Connie."

"I'm sorry, Duncan. I didn't think of its being you. I thought it was one of the servants. Come in, of course."

Something in his voice had already warned her that she must not refuse. She went forward to meet him, still holding the hammer and the tacks. Then she saw the expression on his face and laid them down, her own anxiety and her own grief momentarily submerged in sympathy for him.

"I know you've had a terrific shock, Duncan," she said gently, putting her hand on his arm. "But try not to take it like this. Try to think that perhaps——"

"I've always known Gwen would get even with me sometime," he said dully. "Things like that catch up with you—you've got to expect it. But I thought she'd try to do it through Tilda. I thought I'd know how to handle it when she did. I never thought——"

"But you heard what they all said—that this was a great opportunity for Eileen. She's had a rather purposeless life so far, you'd have to expect that, with—well, with the sort of mother she had. She's wanted something better, she's been searching for it. If you could just forget that it's Gwen who has given her this opportunity, if you could just think of it as a chance to see and record history in the making with a famous journalist——"

"She'll be killed," Duncan said, speaking more dully than he had before. "In this war, reporters will be killed, you'll see."

"Oh, I can't believe that! Not women, anyway."

"Women were killed in the last war. And Gwen'll ask for it. You know that. She's not afraid of anything in the world. You know that too."

"Not for herself. But that's partly because she doesn't feel she has much to live for. Gwen didn't care about being famous, Duncan, she never hoped or planned to be a great journalist. All she wanted was——"

"You don't need to go into all that again. Whatever she wanted twenty years ago, all she's wanted since then is to get even with me. Now at last she's done it."

"You won't go home yourself, will you, Duncan? There'll—there'll be a terrible need for doctors before long."

"You're right, I ought to be able to find some way to make myself useful—a damn sight more useful than I've ever been since the last war. Besides, I'll be able to keep better track of Eileen if I'm over here and can see what that she-devil Gwen Foster is up to. I'll attend to a return passage for Tilda, the first thing in the morning."

"There's still a chance, isn't there, that there won't be a war? After all, the reservists were called out last year."

"Yes, and if there'd been a war then, Germany would have been just that much less prepared. England and France too, of course. No, this time

it's the real thing—the realest thing that's happened in a long time. . . .
Would you mind telling me what you were doing when I came in? Somehow I don't associate you with a hammer."

"I was going to tack up a handkerchief over my bed. Tristan gave it to me for a farewell present."

"A handkerchief for a farewell present!"

"Yes, but a very special kind of handkerchief. Would you like to see it?"

"If you'd like to show it to me."

She walked over to the bed and got it. He inspected it carefully and then he smiled faintly. "Yes, I see. . . . You've been very happy with Tristan, haven't you, Connie?"

"Divinely."

"You've made him divinely happy too. Those things have to be mutual to work. There, that sounds like something I've said to you, or you've said to me, before. . . . There *is* a tie between us."

"I never doubted it. But not the strongest tie, Duncan."

"Perhaps not. A mighty strong one, just the same."

He reached over and took her hand, and she did not draw it away from him. They did not talk any more, but sat for a long time, side by side and hand in hand, looking into the fire.

Stretched out at ease on the chaise longue in the big guest room, Tilda sipped her tea and leafed through her magazine. The country was all right for a little while, she reflected with a yawn, but after a time it began to get dull. Nothing ever happened.

CHAPTER XXV

CONSTANCE WOKE to a sense of silence, strangeness, and vacancy.

Instinctively, before opening her eyes she stretched out her arms—and found them empty. She and Tristan had been parted so little during the twenty years of their marriage that she could not remember having slept alone since the birth of her third child; the alcove bed had always been one of shared slumbers, shared confidences, and shared raptures. Without Tristan, it seemed not only untenanted but unreal.

Tristan had always been an early riser, and it had been their invariable habit to take their morning coffee in this room together. He rang for the *petit déjeuner* when he rose, and by the time he had shaved and showered and was partly dressed, Nicole had brought it in and set it down on a small table beside the bed. Constance sat up among the pillows to drink her coffee, and Tristan drew up a chair beside her and served them both from the small table, chatting companionably while he did so, and stopping long enough afterwards to smoke a cigarette before he went out to the fields and the orchards and the commons. Actually, this light early breakfast took very little time to consume, but it was so unhurried and so cozy that it took on the aspects and the proportions of a leisurely meal. Constance now rang the bell herself, and waited what seemed an interminable period before Nicole appeared, suspiciously red-eyed, bearing a solitary cup and one lone croissant on her little tray. Constance accepted the tray with a brief word of thanks and placed it on her lap. It did not seem worth while to have the little table set up for one cup of coffee and one croissant. Nothing seemed worth while. As instinctively as she had stretched out her arms, she listened for the sound of cheerful whistling above the sound of running water, and waited for the bathroom door to open and for a tall figure, wrapped in a dressing gown, to come out of it and approach her smilingly and buoyantly. When he was in especially high spirits, he sang the refrain of a gay little ditty by Pierre Dudan:

"On prend l'café au lait au lit,
Avec des gâteaux et des croissants chauds.
Prendre l'café au lait au lit,
C'que ça peut être bon, nom de nom!—
Par la fenêtre on entend
Les cloch's des vach's dans les champs.
Olio lé, viv'le café au lait!"

Only the morning before Tristan had been singing this song as he came out of the bathroom. Now, the surrounding silence seemed to deepen while the sense of emptiness increased.

Constance ate and drank with her eyes fixed, as much as possible, on the star-spangled handkerchief which she had tacked up at the foot of the bed the night before, and it was not until she had nearly finished the breakfast she ate with so little appetite that she noticed an envelope tucked under the plate which had held the croissant in such solitary state. Tardily pulling the envelope out from under cover, she saw that it was addressed to her in Tilda's well-known hand, and the note inside was characteristic of the writer. She was sure Connie did not want any more farewell scenes just now, Tilda wrote, which, being interpreted, meant that Tilda herself did not want to risk one which might be marked by any sentiment or sorrow. Besides, to be practical, not a moment should be lost in securing return reservations to the United States; the next thing anyone knew, the steamship companies would be putting total strangers in the same cabin. So she and Duncan were getting an early start. They were going to the Ritz. She would write again from Paris. She was sure Connie would have nothing but the best of news from Tristan and Nick. . . .

Constance put the note back in its envelope, feeling relieved rather than otherwise at this particular turn of events. She did not want guests at Malou just then, even guests who were old friends, and though she was genuinely sorry that Duncan Craig was distressed, she did not feel that he really had much cause for serious concern. Whereas in her own case——

She rose and dressed hastily, realizing that the sooner she was doing something useful, the sooner she could quiet her turbulent anxiety. But first she would stop for another talk with Bruno. Not that she would say anything further in an attempt to dissuade him from going to the seminary at Bayeux, now that she had promised Tristan she would not do so; but a talk with Bruno always gave her a sense of steadiness and support. In that respect, he was far more like his father than Nick. She went into her little study, where he had been sleeping lately, expecting to find him absorbed as usual in a book, and the study was empty too.

Unaccountably alarmed, she hurried through the upper hall to the right wing, and through the open door of the big room which Bruno had shared so long with Nick she saw him quietly replacing the various personal possessions which had been dislodged in order to provide more space for Duncan Craig's—his hound Chess dozing peacefully in the shaft of sunlight streaming in through the east windows. Bruno was the only de Fremond to whom a dog meant more than a horse; but he and Chess—named Winchester in honor of Aunt Bertha's "home town," but nicknamed for the sake of convenience—had been inseparable companions for years. Chess was remarkable neither for his breeding nor his appearance—in fact, his lineage was unknown. Bruno had picked him up as a puppy, on a roadside where he was lying mangled and abandoned; and he had never entirely recovered from a crippled state, in spite of the tender care lavished upon him. But he was extremely intelligent, and though his primary devotion was to Bruno, he was not essentially a one-man dog. Secondarily but unquestionably, he also belonged to the entire family and the entire family to him. He now wagged his tail joyously at the approach of the chatelaine and Bruno looked up with his pleasant smile.

"Hello there! I thought I'd get moved back right away, so that I'd be all ready to ride, or do anything else you'd like, later in the day. It seems good to be in here again. I'm very fond of this old room—not that it's quite the same without Nick."

"I was frightened for a minute when I didn't find you in the study. I felt as if I'd lost you too."

"You'll never lose me, Mother."

"Your father said the same thing. But I feel lost without him, and I shall without you."

"You'll get used to having Father gone before I'm gone too. . . . By the way, Aunt Bertha said not to worry about meals, that she'd map out a plan with Blondine for simplifying them, and show it to you later. Of course the simplifying process will be all the easier with a small family. I think Aunt Bertha's in the kitchen now, so you don't need to bother about going there, unless you want to. You and I can get outside right away. I suppose everything's ready for Margot upstairs, in case she turns up?"

"Yes, I think so. Of course I'll put fresh flowers around later on. I don't imagine Margot will think of letting us know exactly when to expect her, if she is on her way."

"Probably she won't be able to. All the wires are bound to be terribly crowded these next few days. . . . Did you plan to go to the stables this morning? I'll be glad to come with you if you did."

As a matter of fact, Constance had no such definite plan; but the suggestion was logical, and besides, she felt increasingly that anything that represented escape from the house, which seemed more and more silent and empty the more she saw of it, would be extremely welcome. Outside the blue sky was only slightly veiled with fleecy clouds, the ripening apples already hung in clusters from the sturdy trees, and the areaway resounded with the cheerful noise of calves and poultry. But at the entrance to the stables, Martin met her with a troubled face.

"Madame la Baronne knows that I shall do my very best. And I do not complain. How could I with all the suffering, worse than my poor pains, that lies before us? But I am not as young as I was, and that cursed rheumatism catches me more and more often, every winter, laying me flat. And with all the others gone——"

"All the others gone!"

"But of a certainty, Madame la Baronne. It is possible that Benoît will not be retained. He is nearly forty-five himself, that one, and not too solid either. But as to Pierre and Michel, hearty both of them, there is not a chance that we shall see them again until the war is over, and then only if it is the will of the good God. Naturally all three left at the same time as the Commandant. They did not come to make their farewells, hesitating to disturb you during those last hours when the Baron was at home and when you had besides several guests at Malou. But they did not doubt you knew they would be leaving and that you would wish them Godspeed."

Constance looked from the old groom to her young son without answering. Evidently Bruno as well as Martin had taken it for granted that she realized only the aging, the very young, and the disabled would remain unaffected by the order for mobilization. Tristan must have taken it for granted too, since he had not mentioned it. He had told her that somehow she should manage to get enough food and enough fuel from the place, *at least for the present,* but he had referred to no minor difficulties. He had expected her to cope with those as a matter of course.

"Yes, naturally," she said at last. "I understand, Martin. I mean, I understand why Benoît and Pierre and Michel didn't come to say good-by, and I understand about the difficulties you're facing with the stables too. Have you any solution to suggest?"

"Perhaps Madame la Baronne would consider sending some of the mares to L'Abbatiale. Many of the 'boys' there are of a certain age, like myself. I believe there will be enough of them left to carry on the work in the *haras,* after a fashion. Of course in the gardener's department there will have to be economies. All the trees can hardly remain ringed around with flower beds, as heretofore." Martin paused for a moment, smiling rather wryly. "But Monsieur Mullins will see to it that in his province somehow things arrange themselves. It is his way to do so. . . . I could continue to look after four mares, as I did at the beginning, in spite of those twenty extra years on my poor back. Perhaps even five or six mares," he added, with thoughtful pride. "And possibly Bernard and Léon could help me, not to mention Denis, who has been left to us on account of his bad eyes. After all, the women can do the field and garden and dairy work as well as the housework."

"Yes, naturally," Constance said again. "I believe your idea about L'Abbatiale is a good one, Martin. I'll think it over and let you know later."

"As Madame la Baronne wishes."

He turned away, and Constance knew that he had gone back to the hopeless task of trying to do everything in the stables when no one remained to help him. She looked at Bruno again.

"I think I'd better talk to Lise and Aylette before I go back to the house."

"Yes, I believe they'll be expecting you."

Neither Martin nor Benoît had ever married; each maintained modest bachelor quarters, Martin beside the "harem," Benoît near the stallion's stall. But Bernard and Pierre, and their respective wives, Lise and Aylette, were more commodiously installed; both the space over the garage and the space over the riding horses' stables had been converted into up-to-date apartments in the course of the general restoration at Malou. Bernard and Lise and their younger son, Michel, as well as Bernard's childish old father Joseph, lived in one of these, Pierre, his wife Aylette, and their little daughter Lucie in the other. Lise was already well past middle age, but she was still vigorous, and she regarded hard work as her natural lot in life. Constance felt the chances that she would rise to an emergency were better in her case than in that of Aylette, who was of a less hardy type.

Like Martin, Lise met her visitors at the door of her quarters, but with a less troubled countenance. "One sees that Martin has been talking of difficulties already!" she exclaimed with cheery contempt. "*Voyons,* Madame la Baronne, you and I have been through one war already. We learned to turn our hands to this and that before, we can do so again. My bit of cooking—what is that to keep me occupied? I have done half the work in the dairy and half in the kitchen garden these many years already. Well, I can do it all if needs be, with such help as Aylette and the old one can give me. He is out puttering among the cabbages now, happy as a lark, while he mumbles curses on the Germans, whom he imagines to see advancing as he saw them in '70—for he has been through more wars than you and I, Madame la Baronne! And Aylette is at the *lavoir,* doing the washing for all of us. Not that she thought to offer. But then the young wives of today, what can one expect of them? They are still untried. They will all learn, Aylette among them. Little Lucie can learn too. At five, she should be already washing the dishes, and doing much besides that is useful. Has Madame la Baronne herself been to take a turn in the kitchen garden of late? Well, she should go this very morning. The air is fresh, it will restore her."

Constance had never felt the same vital interest in the grounds that she did in the château, probably because she had had far more natural aptitude for interior decorating than for making things grow outdoors; even Tristan admitted that in spite of her many qualities, she did not have "green thumbs." Largely to please him, she had taken charge of the small plot of ground on the ledge of the steep descent directly below the terrace, where roses and dahlias grew in such profusion; but she secretly preferred gathering these flowers to tending them, and she had never attempted the supervision of the far larger area behind the stables and garages where a much greater variety of flowers grew alongside the abundant vegetables. As she entered it now, she wondered how she could have disregarded it so long, for it was a lovely place.

High brick walls, surmounted by peaked red tiling, enclosed it, and along these walls were espaliered boughs laden with peaches and pears. Close beside the walls, to give them greater warmth, lay wide berry beds, already covered with straw; and next to these were the brick walks which surrounded the long, orderly rows of vegetables, inviting enough in themselves, and rendered doubly so by the manifold bloom of the flowers scattered among them—roses and dahlias even larger and more luxuriant than those growing back of the terrace; multicolored gladioli and snapdragon at the height of their bloom; chrysanthemums which revealed, so far, only the small tight buttons that would later expand into magnificent blossoms. A row of potted plants, mostly gorgeous crimson and purple fuchsias, bordered two sides of the walk; at one end of the garden an array of silvery milk pails, neatly ranged, lay open along the length of an immense wooden table; and diagonally across from this was the ancient *lavoir,* formed by one of those pools, or *mares,* esteemed in Normandy as far superior to running water for supplying water to irrigate a garden and to facilitate laundry work.

This *lavoir,* farther back, narrowed into a merry little brook, and was unprotected from the elements except by a peaked red roof, yet for centuries all the washing at Malou had been done there. Constance was sure that Blondine still secretly preferred it to the modern laundry in the beautiful vaulted basement, and that she felt cheated because this robbed her of long garrulous afternoons with Lise and Aylette. The younger woman was working there now, as her mother-in-law had said she would be, her shapely back bent over the sloping slab against which she was rubbing the heavy linen that, intermittently, she also pounded with a large paddle. Constance went up to her and spoke to her kindly.

"Lise tells me you're taking over all the laundry work, Aylette," she said. "I want you to know how much I appreciate this. And we'll probably be seeing a good deal of each other from now on. I've just decided that I ought to be able to manage taking care of this garden, with your grandfather's help, as well as of the little one back of the château. That'll leave your mother-in-law freer for the dairy."

The girl looked up from her labors without an answering smile. "I didn't have any choice but to take the laundry over," she said sullenly. "Maybe you don't know it, Madame la Baronne, but my mother-in-law's a hard one, and she's always hated me. She had other plans for Pierre. If I could, I'd take the kid and go to my own people in the North. But the Boches might get there before I did, so I guess I'll have to stick it out here and if I don't work I'll get beaten. Nicole is lucky. Mère Bernard can't touch her—yet."

"I'm afraid Nicole doesn't think she's lucky. She looked as if she'd been crying when she brought me my breakfast this morning. She and Michel are very fond of each other, aren't they? I'm sorry they couldn't have been married before Michel had to leave."

Aylette shrugged her plump shoulders. In a blowsy way she was rather handsome, and the movement disclosed more clearly the shape of her full breasts, already scantily concealed by the shoddy fabric of a dress that was too tight for her.

"You may come to the château to do the washing whenever you like, you know, Aylette. When it begins to grow cold, you'll find the heated basement much more comfortable than this open *lavoir*. And Blondine will show you how to use the electrical machine. It makes the work ever so much easier and lighter."

Aylette shrugged her shoulders a second time and picked up her paddle. Her manner had lacked respect ever since she came to Malou, but it had never been actually impudent before. *A lot you know about work,* her attitude seemed to say. *You'll come out here for an hour or two, on pleasant days, and putter around for a while. But someone else will do the spading and fertilizing, the real planting and weeding and raking, everything that might soil your hands or tire your back or make your clothes smell bad. I've seen your sort at what you call work before.* Constance wanted to tell Aylette that she had worked hard as a girl too, that she did know what work was, that she could and would prove this. But she realized it would be futile to attempt an explanation. She went back to Bruno, who had been talking to old Joseph, his arm around little Lucie, his dog at his feet, while she herself was at the *lavoir*.

The next few days passed without exciting or disturbing incidents. The household settled down to a simplified routine, which released Léon and Denis entirely for out-of-door work and gave some to each woman besides. The transfer of the stallion and shortly afterwards of six mares and their colts to L'Abbatiale was achieved without undue difficulty, thanks to the efficient co-operation of Mark Mullins and the elderly "boys" he had left.

Bruno had evidently been right about the choked mails and wires, for no messages came through, even from Tristan, and the radio furnished prompter and more concise news than the long-delayed daily papers, which went into countless editions and flaunted extravagant headlines, but after all revealed very little. Hitler and Henderson were exchanging communiqués, mostly on the subject of Poland. Great Britain and France were speeding up mobilization. But the final declaration of war still hung fire. . . .

With the stubborn determination of proving that she was equal to hard work, Constance spent endless hours in the kitchen garden, resting occasionally on a bench drawn up beside the table where Lise ranged the shining milk pails, but returning to the château only after long periods of backbreaking labor. On the third day which she spent in this way, she saw the little Renault runabout Jacques Bouvier had given Margot for a wedding present parked in front of the drawbridge as she came through the orchard. She hastened forward and found Margot already installed on the terrace, drinking vermouth and eating sandwiches, while she talked excitedly to Bruno, pausing occasionally to pat Chess. She was wearing the tweed suit which was so becoming to her, but it had already lost the look of freshness and smartness which distinguished it when she started on her honeymoon, and her blouse was rumpled, her hair even more disordered than usual, and her hands grimy.

She rose civilly enough at her mother-in-law's approach, kissed her dutifully if casually on both cheeks, and after sitting down again, glanced at her with sufficient frequency to make a show of wishing to include her in the conversation. But it was obvious that the girl found it much more natural to address most of her remarks to Bruno. Nick, it appeared, had left her in Monte Carlo ten days earlier in response to a telegram telling him to report at the Cavalry School immediately. He had taken the first train out, and she had packed up their things and started for Saumur alone, driving early and late; but she had not been able to make any sort of time, because all the roads were blocked with troops and trucks and tanks.

Sometimes she had been obliged to drive half the night before she could find any kind of a room to sleep in. It was not as if she knew anyone in that part of France who would take her in out of friendship. How would she ever know anyone in Lyon or Nevers? She had just smoked cigarettes and gone on. Then she had been in Saumur, staying at a badly overcrowded hotel, just four days when Nick and all the rest of his promotion had been ordered off to join some regiment, she didn't know which or where, and she had taken to the road again. Yes, she had gone to L'Abbatiale long enough to say hello, and she had tried to telephone from there, but she could not get the call through; it was pretty silly, wasn't it, that short distance? She would like to go back there again the next day, if nobody minded, because she had seen only about half the family, and anyhow, she had been too dog-tired to visit much. She was dog-tired now. She would like another drink and another sandwich, and then, if they would excuse her, she would get out of her filthy clothes and tumble into a hot bath and a real bed, neither of which she had so much as seen since she left that wonderful Hôtel de Paris in Monte Carlo. . . .

She did not wake up until the following noon, and then, very naturally, she wanted to start back to L'Abbatiale directly after lunch. It also seemed perfectly natural, since she had such a late start, that she should desire to spend the next night there, and then for thirty-six hours she shuttled back and forth between the two places. She continued to be civil to Constance, but her attitude was one of withdrawal rather than approach, and her first excited volubility and craving for companionship were succeeded by long periods of comparative silence and an inclination to shut herself up in her own rooms. Constance tried, religiously, to make the girl feel welcome and at ease; but she herself was handicapped by her own physical exhaustion and mental anxiety. Now that war was actually declared, her forlorn hope that some last-minute miracle might avert this was gone. She knew that if Tristan and Nick were not already in danger, they soon would be, and with redoubled determination she devoted herself to the task of safeguarding Malou's resources, as far as this lay within her power.

Gradually she abandoned her efforts to establish a more intimate and harmonious relationship with her daughter-in-law, deciding that time would probably prove the most helpful factor in their mutual adjustment. It was not until she came in unusually late from the garden to learn from Bruno that Margot had not been seen or heard from since going upstairs after luncheon, and that she had not answered when he called her to tea, that Constance became really concerned. She did not like to seem curious or intrusive, but at last she decided that she could not wait any longer, that she must go to Margot's room and see if by any chance the girl was ill. Above the second story, the circular stairway was unlighted, and evidently someone had turned off the switch from the top, so that she could not put it on again. She groped her way along in the obscurity, which, next to noise, she had always hated more than anything in the world, her fingers reaching eagerly towards the switch. When they found it and she snapped the light on again, she felt better. But her vague impression that something was amiss still persisted.

She went along through the vestibule, snapping on more lights, and calling softly to Margot as she went. There was no answer. She knocked at the door of the first dormer guest room, which Nick had decided should be the bridal chamber, since the second, having a fireplace, made the more desirable sitting room of the two. There was still no answer. Constance opened the door and switched on another light. The room was empty. She went on to the sitting room and repeated the process, with the same results.

On the attic floor the tower ended in a large closet with a sharply pointed roof, providing excellent storage for linen; but it lacked height except in the middle and any means of ventilation other than the door leading into it, and therefore was not adaptable for a bathroom. The room over the study seemed the logical alternative; and with the amount of space which this allowed, Constance had achieved a very attractive dressing room as well. The door of the dressing room was the only one she had not so far tried in the course of her present search. She did so now, and she found it locked.

"Margot," she called again. "Margot my dear, is anything the matter?"

There was no immediate answer, but Connie was certain she heard sounds of stirring. She called again. This time the answer came, irritably, almost impudently.

"You don't always assume something's 'the matter,' do you, madame, when you find a bathroom door locked?"

"You're not ill?"

"No, of course I'm not ill. I'll be out in a few minutes."

"I'll wait and go downstairs with you."

"There's no reason why you should."

Nevertheless, Connie did wait. She stood in the corridor a long time, listening to Margot as the girl moved around the dressing room making vague sounds which ceased altogether for moments at a time. Then at last she came out wearing nothing but a black chiffon nightgown and banging the door after her.

Even in the dim light of the vestibule Connie could see that she had been crying. For the first time since her arrival at Malou, Margot's face was extravagantly made up, but the hastily applied rouge did not hide the ravages of the tears underneath. Her mouth was set in a hard line and her eyes were desperate and angry.

"My dear," Constance said gently, "I know it's very hard for you to be left alone like this, so soon after your marriage. I should have felt just the same. But I want you to believe that I do understand that I'll do everything in my power to make you as contented as I can under the circumstances. Perhaps you'd rather not come down to dinner tonight? In that case, I'll send a tray up to you."

"I'm not coming down to dinner, but you needn't bother to send a tray up to me. I don't want anything to eat."

"My dear, you must eat. I know that's hard, too, when you're unhappy. But——"

"Don't tell me I ought to be eating for two. That would be simply the last straw."

The girl's voice was bitter now as well as hard. She leaned against the door which she had slammed behind her and confronted her mother-in-law.

"Since you've been so determined to track me down and drag me out, I suppose I may as well tell you what's the trouble," she said. "When Nick left me to join his regiment, he went off in a rage because things hadn't turned out the way he planned. And then I saw red too, because it wasn't my fault. So we quarreled. We were both too furious to say good-by. And that was such a lousy way to have a honeymoon end that I get mad again every time I think of it. That's all the trouble with me. I'm mad clear through."

"Nick was angry because things hadn't turned out as he planned?"

"He wanted to be sure before he left that I was going to have a baby. Well, he wasn't sure. On the contrary, he was sure I wouldn't. At least he was sure I wasn't going to have one nine months and ten minutes after I was married, the way you and *maman* did. I knew that was what he wanted and I thought he had it coming to him, under the circumstances. I'd have been glad if it had. But I'm not God."

"Margot dear——"

"I think he might have been a better sport about it. He didn't need to act as though he thought it was my fault. He might have said, well, he'd probably be getting leave, sooner or later, we'd have another chance. He shouldn't have intimated that if he'd married Ghisèle instead, everyone would have been better pleased."

"Margot, Nick loves you dearly, he couldn't have done that."

"Well, he didn't say it in so many words! But that was what he meant. And of course I'd lost my temper too, by that time, so one thing led to another. It wasn't news to me, anyway, that you all liked Ghisèle better. She's a lot more your type. And she probably would have conceived the first time she ever got into bed with a man. She's that type too. I told Nick he could divorce me, if he wanted to, that I'd make it perfectly simple for

232

him, and then he could marry Ghisèle afterwards. Oh, I know he couldn't marry in the Church, but I don't think that would matter much to him. I really think that would be the best plan all around. If there's still time, of course, before he gets killed. Anyway I don't see any use in my staying on at Malou. The whole point was to keep me out of harm's way while I was waiting for the spring arrival of the heir to all the de Fremonds. Well, there isn't going to be any spring arrival, and I don't like staying here any better than you like having me. So I might just as well go where I can enjoy myself and leave you in peace. If you want to know what I've been doing up here all by myself, I'll tell you. I've been packing. If you don't mind, I'm going on with it now."

This interview left Constance terribly shaken, especially as Margot put her threat of departure into execution the very next morning, despite the earnest plea, in which Bruno and Aunt Bertha both joined, that she would reconsider, or at least wait a little longer before deciding that she could not possibly be contented at Malou. A move to L'Abbatiale would not have mattered so much either. Constance was generous enough to concede that Jacques and Stéphanie might be able to handle their difficult daughter better than she could, and even perhaps that they did not find Margot difficult at all. She herself had felt from the beginning that Nick was unwise in persisting that Margot must come to Malou, but she had not expected the girl's recoil from it to be so violent or to take so defiant a form. Margot did not even go to L'Abbatiale to say good-by to her parents. She jumped into her little Renault and drove straight to Paris, where Madame Bouvier *mère* received her coolly at the pied-à-terre in the Faubourg Saint-Germain and ordered her to go home again. Margot's retort to this order was an even bolder challenge to authority. She went straight to the enormous house on the Avenue Foch where her great-grandmother Solomon, the widow of the famous financier, lived in solitary splendor, and stubbornly stayed on there.

Madame Solomon also tried to remonstrate with the girl and to point out the error of her ways. But the old lady was feeble and lonely; a young and vigorous presence brought life and laughter to the gloomy house which it had lacked for a long time; after a few days the protests of Madame Solomon ceased. Triumphantly, Margot wrote to her parents, to Constance, and to Nick that she was having a wonderful time. Nobody in Paris seemed to be taking the war too seriously and everyone was giving marvelous parties and it was great to be in on them. All the girls whose husbands and fiancés had gone to the Front were singing a new song, *"Je t'attendrai la nuit et le jour, je t'attendrai toujours,"* but they were doing an awful lot of this faithful waiting at night clubs. She had met a number of her old flames and they were all eager to take her out on the town; a lot of them were still left to do it. She supposed they were assigned to some special type of work that kept them in Paris, but if so, they were vague about it. Margot was vague about it too. . . .

The possibility that Nick might be baffled in his heart's desire for a child had occurred to Constance in the beginning, but she had not dwelt on it, less because she was deliberately trying to evade an issue than because she was so much more gravely concerned about his safety and his father's. Now she was pierced with the poignancy of her son's disappointment and horrified at the results of his bride's reaction to it. She did not believe that he had started the quarrel which was still raging when he and Margot parted; he must have had extreme provocation to reach such a degree of rage and to make such unjust charges. But indubitably his sense of bafflement must have heaped fuel on the flames. He had foreseen the probability of death's approach and prepared for it; but he had not visualized the possibility that he himself might not pass on the torch of life before it was too late.

Letters were coming through to Malou from him now, brief, infrequent letters, suffused with smoldering anger still. Clearly, he felt that his mother was partly to blame for his bride's rebellion, with which, he stated curtly, he would deal himself when he first got leave, or even received a transfer, which he hinted might occur before long, though naturally he could give no indication either of his present or his future whereabouts.

Golden crops were being gathered into ancient barns, russet-colored apples were being crushed in the old mill, and the foaming cider was being stowed away in the cellar. Constance tried to oversee all such work, besides getting the garden in order for the winter, and she was so healthily exhausted when night came that usually she tumbled into bed as soon as she and Aunt Bertha had eaten their supper. It was only when a letter from Tristan revived poignant memories of their shared happiness that she lingered on the terrace in the mystic starlight, dreaming of the hours that they had spent there together. Her other letters she scanned hastily in the rare moments when she rested on the garden bench or while she was walking through the woods to check and recheck the fuel supply. She was getting a good many from the Front these days. Duncan Craig had joined a French Red Cross Ambulance Unit there, and wrote vividly of his experiences. The aimlessness and desuetude which had stultified him for so long had given way before the quickening of his interest and the drive of his activities. But he was still unsatiated, still seeking more intensive and exciting fields of endeavor, and still, obviously, furious with Gwen and anxious about Eileen, who occasionally wrote in high spirits themselves.

They had remained in Paris only long enough after the outbreak of war for Gwen to make preparations for going to Poland. She, perforce, approached this via Italy, Yugoslavia, and Rumania, every frontier to the northeast being already closed; and she could make no arrangements to take Eileen further than Rome, as visas beyond there were available only to duly accredited journalists. Eileen had never been to Rome before and she was enchanted with it. She did not in the least mind when Gwen hurried off to Cernauti and, between sight-seeing expeditions, wrote a little piece herself about riding through the narrow side streets of Rome in an open victoria, late at night, and what she had noticed while doing it—the strange effects of light and shadow on the façades of old churches, the old palaces that had turned tenements, the little groups of people clustered around doorways and sitting in front of small tables at sidewalk cafés, the echoing fragments of stray songs, and clear notes swelling from an accordion.

She had been afraid it was just tourist stuff, but Miss Foster said no, it was good, and sent it off for the editor of *This Month* to see. Gwen's own articles were very different—terse, ruthless, describing without exaggeration the horrors she had witnessed and revealing her unswerving determination to make these real to her readers. The recital was a grim one, but with her purpose fulfilled and her Polish articles filed, Gwen consented to a stopover in Milan on the way back to France. She was all in, she wrote Connie from Paris; she would have to take things easy for a few days before starting off on another jaunt. She had a hunch that she might go to Finland later on; but before that she wanted to get up behind the Maginot Line. She was peeling an eye and girding up a loin before she attacked the stuffed shirts at the Foreign Office on the subject. If Connie had any bright ideas about cracking the Quai d'Orsay, she, Gwen, would be pleased to hear them. . . .

Connie had no bright ideas and in replying she urged Gwen to give up her own, and to send Eileen back to the United States, even if she would not go herself. Wouldn't Gwen admit there was such a thing as pushing your luck too far? No one and nothing could stop Gwen, of course; but Eileen ought to be stopped, and Gwen could do that.

The answer to this letter came from Eileen herself, and the tone of it was as reproachful as was consistent with courtesy. She had never done anything in her life which meant as much to her as that trip to Italy; nothing would induce her to lose the chance of having other experiences like it, unless she found she were handicapping Miss Foster in her work. And Miss Foster had been good enough to say that far from being a nuisance, she had been a help. Once or twice she had noticed little things Miss Foster had overlooked because Miss Foster was naturally preoccupied with big things. Miss Foster had been pleased when Eileen mentioned these items, and had actually used them in her pieces. They had heard from the editor of *This Month* and he had accepted her own little article and had asked her to submit others. She was just as pleased as Punch about it and Miss Foster was too. Incidentally, she had an idea herself as to how they might get up near the Maginot Line. She knew that nice Dr. Craig was somewhere in that vicinity, and she had written him asking him if he could not possibly arrange it. She believed he was the sort who would be resourceful about arranging things. He had written her several times since they met at Malou. That was how she happened to have his address. . . .

At the bottom of Eileen's letter Gwen had scrawled, "For God's sake, let the poor kid alone. She's coming along fine—will anyway if the rest of you will keep your damned hands off her." But even without this warning, Constance would not have remonstrated further about Eileen. However, the letter troubled her, in more ways than one. She did not for a minute think that Craig could arrange the trip to the Maginot Line, or that he would even if he could; but the very fact that he and Eileen were corresponding seemed ominous. So did the fact that she herself had heard nothing from or about Tilda. . . .

In a way, the most reassuring of all the letters that came through at this period were those from Bruno. With his usual sensitivity, he had contrived to make the parting with him early in October as painless as possible; and every evening he wrote to his mother, posting the letter before he went to bed. She did not receive the letters with the same regularity, but she knew that he had written them, and the knowledge was in itself a solace and a support. Autumn was closing in now, the days were growing short and gray, the leaves were falling from the trees and sweeping across the drab ground, blown by a bitter wind. Constance was busy, she was well, she found relief in hard physical labor and release in the sound slumber which followed after it; she could look towards the winter with the assurance that her household would not go either hungry or cold, as her husband had predicted that she would be able to do; and as week succeeded week and still no alarming news came from the quiescent battle line, her anxiety became less trenchant and acute. But the radiance which had illumined her life for so long was nearly all gone from it. The letters from Bruno, the knowledge of his nearness, his spirituality, his constant love, supplied such rays of it as were left.

He came home for *Toussaint,* as he had promised her he would, and they had three happy days together. He talked with her at length about Nick and Margot, easing her pain for her firstborn, and bespeaking her tolerance for the willful girl. He spoke reassuringly of his father's chance for continued safety. He praised her industry and accomplishments and joined her as much as possible in the work she was doing. He went to church with her and rode with her through the woods. Then he was gone again, and this time, for all his tenderness, the parting was harder than it had been before and had in it a greater quality of finality. After he had gone, his mother waited for his first letter with an eagerness which she could not control. She could no longer comfort herself with the assurance that if it did not come one day it would the next.

And then it came.

Centre Préparatoire, Rambouillet
November 15, 1939

Dearest Mother:

I am not sure whether I did right in not telling you when I was home what I am going to write you now. But if I made a mistake, I hope you will forgive me, for I did not want to cloud our happy days together by giving you a fresh anxiety.

I have not gone back to the Seminary nor am I planning to return. Not because I was unhappy there or because my superiors were dissatisfied with me. Not because I have ceased to feel that my vocation is the priest-hood. But because, after a great deal of thought and even more prayer, I have decided that I should interrupt my preparation for it. As long as I believed that Nick would follow in Father's footsteps at Saumur, I had no qualms. But ever since Nick left for the Front without ever entering the School of Cavalry, I have had doubts. I have felt that something would be unfinished, something which should have been completed and which might have been glorious if Father's work were carried on.

So, after making inquiries and securing the permission of my superiors, I have entered one of the training centers which have been hastily organized in order to prepare young civilians who previously had no idea of having military careers to enter the Cavalry School at Saumur. Besides this one at Rambouillet there is one at Montaubon and still another in Algiers. When we get to Saumur we shall be classed as E.A.R.—Élèves Aspirants de Réserve—or prospective reserve officers, and the few old officers who are still left there, with the addition of a few younger ones who will be recalled from the Front to reinforce them, will be our teachers. According to present plans, we shall stay where we are for about six months and at Saumur for another six months before we are sent to the Front ourselves. But of course no one can plan with any degree of certainty in these days.

I am working very hard, but I am very happy and I am also completely at peace, both with God and with myself. I feel sure, as sure as I have ever been of anything in my life, that I have done right in coming here. So I hope you will not be angry with me for doing so. I am writing to Father by this same mail explaining, or trying to explain. Please, Mother, try to understand, and please believe that I love you very much, and that I would not willingly cause you pain. But there are some things that are even more important than sparing the feelings of a person you love, and what I am doing is one of them, or at least it seems that way to me.

Devotedly your son,
Bruno

P.S. Next to you and Aunt Bertha and Margot, I miss Chess. Perhaps when I go to Saumur we can find some way for me to take him with me.

CHAPTER XXVI

THE PERIOD BETWEEN All Saints' and Christmas was barren, dreary, and seemingly interminable at Malou. The only news which broke the monotony was the surprising disclosure that the coveted trip to the Maginot Line had become a reality for Gwen and Eileen. Craig had not only arranged it, through certain high powers with whom he stood in well, but had acted as their escort during the course of it, work at the hospital to which he was attached being practically at a standstill because of the lack of casualties. Obviously he had ceased to beat his head against a stone wall, as far as Eileen was concerned.

Compared to the dreary weeks which had preceded them, the holidays passed with incredible swiftness. Tristan, Nick, and Bruno all obtained Christmas leave and their presence brought with it a renewal of vitality and courage. To be sure, as far as Nick was concerned there was also a renewal of turbulence. After a month with the Ninth Regiment of Dragoons at Epernay, he had been sent to the Saar—disclosures which he was now able to make in person, though his whereabouts had necessarily remained unrevealed in his letters; then he had been recalled to Saumur for maneuvers at Fontevrault, and on his way south he had stopped off long enough in Paris to wrest Margot from her luxurious quarters at Madame Solomon's palatial residence on the Avenue Foch and the frivolous company she was keeping. She had left Paris most unwillingly. She would much rather have had Nick with her at the night clubs, where she was still singing *"Je t'attendrai toujours,"* than to have gone with him to Saumur, which she characterized as a "sixth-rate town," and though he had succeeded in dragging her away from her lighthearted companions and the places they frequented, it was clear that she resented this. Apparently her reunion with him had been marked by as much dissension and violence as their parting; and though some sort of a peace had been patched up between them, this was obviously due more to the fact that, in spite of herself, Margot found Nick irresistibly attractive and exciting than to any change of attitude or behavior on his part.

The announcement that he was going back to Fontevrault from Malou, after his Christmas leave, to join the Second Cuirassiers of the newly created Light Armored Division did not help matters either. It appeared that the young officers assigned to this post for further training were to be stationed in the village itself this time, instead of in Saumur, as they had been during maneuvers, and they were still to be allowed to have their wives with them, since Fontevrault was out of the so-called "military zone." Nick proposed to get some kind of a room in the village, install Margot there, and spend his (extremely limited) spare hours with her. The rest of the time she would have to spend alone, or in the company of other young women similarly placed. Margot did not hesitate to say that Saumur had been bad enough in the autumn, but at least while there she had been able to stay in a reasonably comfortable hotel, where there were a few kindred spirits, whereas she could imagine nothing more cold, dreary, lonesome, and generally uninviting than Fontevrault in midwinter, and that Nick would have to club her into unconsciousness before he could get her there. To such declamations Nick replied nonchalantly that he was very good with a club and let it go at that. But generally either Tristan or Bruno managed to put in a soothing word or change the course of conversation; and since neither of them appeared unduly concerned about the bridal couple, Constance managed to submerge her own disquietude in happier thoughts.

This was the easier because in many other ways things were going better at Malou than they had since early fall, and because the observance of the holidays brought with it so many thrilling preoccupations. Benoît had already been released from the army, because of his physical disabilities; but these disabilities were not sufficiently severe to prevent him from lightening Martin's labors, and the aged groom went about these more cheerily now that his old comrade was there to help him. Michel was home too, making the most of his brief *permission;* he not only worked early and late, but he took advantage of his leave to marry Nicole, and everyone at Malou and on the surrounding estates and farms united to make their wedding a festive occasion.

They were married in the parish church, directly after the civil service in the *mairie* across the road from this. The bells which had tolled so mournfully for the August call to arms now rang out joyfully through the frosty air, for the strong old bell-ringer bent over almost double in her efforts to give them a heartier sound. Everyone went merrily from the church to the little general store near by, which served as telephone exchange and *bureau de tabac,* and—on such an occasion as this—in lieu of a café, and the bride and groom were toasted in good sound cider; and finally everyone returned to Malou, where long tables were spread in both dining room and kitchen and a gigantic feast prepared. To be sure, the peasants sat at one table and the gentry at the other; but they talked and joked and toasted back and forth, and when the time came for dancing, Tristan himself led out the bride. And everyone felt so happy and so carefree, what with the good fare and the good company and all, that for a little while the war and all it stood for were forgotten.

And then came Christmas Eve and Midnight Mass and all the *charitons* —those men of goodwill and good standing in the community pledged to alleviate suffering and sorrow—stationed in the choir stalls of the parish church, holding their great staves upright and wearing the vestlike crimson and gold *chaprons* reserved for the greatest occasions. And after Midnight Mass came the *réveillon,* with turkey at two in the morning instead of two in the afternoon, as it would have been in Winchester, Massachusetts, but otherwise, as Aunt Bertha said with satisfaction, not so very different after all. And all of the children and not a few among their elders firmly believed that the cows and the sheep were all murmuring together and would continue to do so until dawn, for such was their privilege on Christmas Eve because creatures of their kind had once stood around the manger of the Christ Child.

Of course there was also the Christmas tree, with presents on one side of it for the family and on the other for their faithful retainers. And there was carol-singing in both church and château, and a second *réveillon* on New Year's Eve, and everyone or nearly everyone was very happy.

The traditional festivals of Christmas and New Year's, and the wedding with its attendant lusty commotion, roused everyone from the sense of tedium and dreariness which had been increasingly hard to shake off during the dull, drab weeks before the holidays, and gave impetus to further efforts to relieve the monotony. But in spite of valiant endeavors to maintain these after the men of Malou had gone away, the women who were left behind found they were sinking back again into their former state of apathy. The very absence of war news, which at first had given them such a sense of reprieve, finally became a nerve-racking endurance test. How much longer was this "phony war"—this *drôle de guerre*—to go on, accomplishing nothing, leading nowhere, but meanwhile dividing families and disrupting all normal existence?

The invasion of Finland by Russia, and the eventual capitulation of that plucky little country, roused mingled feelings of indignation and admiration. But Finland was a long way off. Try as they might to do otherwise, the waiting women could not but regard it objectively, and the same was true, though to a lesser degree, when Germany invaded Denmark and Norway. The resignation of Daladier as premier of France did not seem especially portentous; his leadership had been neither compelling nor distinguished. Quite possibly Reynaud might do better. It was not until the Netherlands, Belgium, and Luxembourg were suddenly overrun that danger began to seem real, near, and personal. But Nick was home again now on his second leave, and Margot was with him. For Nick's mother, their provocative presence served temporarily to minimize and deviate the pressure of imminent trouble from without.

Inevitably, the fury with which they had parted from each other at Monte Carlo and rejoined each other in Paris had abated; but Margot had neither forgiven nor forgotten Nick's inexcusable behavior and unjust accusations on both occasions, and her own conduct had done nothing to promote repentance on his part. He had succeeded in getting her to Fontevrault and in keeping her there throughout his two months' training course. But no sooner had he finished this and been sent to the Belgian border than she herself had returned to her great-grandmother's house and stayed there until he wrested her from it and dragged her to Malou a second time. From the scornful allusions which she made to her residence in the renowned but isolated village, Constance gathered that her attitude there, from start to finish, had been one of undisguised contempt. Every time Margot spoke of the quarters she had shared with Nick, she referred to "a horrid blank little house where it was so cold you had to blow on your hands to get them warm and could see your breath while you did it."

But after all, it was not Margot's attitude towards Fontevrault that gave Nick's mother the deepest and most poignant concern, it was Margot's attitude towards Nick. The very air was electric in their presence, partly with the still smoldering anger which neither took the trouble to conceal, and partly with their equally unassuaged desire. Try as she might, Constance could not dismiss the vision of their almost savage attitude towards each other. Except at meals, she saw very little of them, for they spent most of their time in their own quarters; but the consciousness of the drama unfolding there was too strong to dismiss. As clearly as if she could really hear them, she knew they were quarreling again, hurling fantastic charges and countercharges at each other. As surely as if she could really see them, she knew that Margot was further infuriating Nick by resisting and repulsing him, because her open resentment still prevailed against her secret yearning. And Nick's mother was equally sure that the boy himself did not hesitate to act ruthlessly if the resistance were prolonged or frequent.

There must be moments, of course, when Margot was caught off guard, through drowsiness or surprise, or when her own clamoring senses were too strong for her. At such times her union with her husband might still approximate an act of love. But for the most part it was only an act of passion, unredeemed by tenderness or devotion. Any day, Margot's rebellion might take the form of sudden and complete desertion, if Nick did not mend his ways. Any day, Nick's violence might take a still more unforgivable form than it had already, if Margot did not mend hers. They were the victims of a vicious circle, and they had forged its links themselves.

The certainty of all this troubled Constance as she dwelt upon it, and through the dark watches of her own lonely nights she sought vainly for some solution which might heal the breach between her elder son and her daughter-in-law. She tossed and turned hour after hour, thinking about Tristan, thinking about Bruno, but thinking most of all about Nick and Margot, striving against each other in the chamber above her own. . . .

It was because of this lonely and anxious wakefulness that she was the first to hear the noise of shouting and of a knocker resounding through the hushed house, suddenly shattering the silence of the night. . . . She switched on the light, sprang out of bed and ran to the window, answering the summons. She did not need to be told what it meant. This was what had happened before, not to her, but to many other women. When there was no time for the *affiche* or the radio to send out a call to arms, the police had gone in the dead of night to wrest men from their beds and send them back to battle. The police were at Malou now, for Nick. The German advance must have reached France. It might already have caught Tristan. But she could still thank God that it would never harm Bruno. . . .

She ran down the stairs, throwing her dressing gown about her as she went. The shouts and pounding had ceased when she called from the window. No one else, apparently, had heard them, for no one else was hurrying to the fort with her. She drew back the bolts and turned the huge key in its massive lock. The great outer door swung slowly open, and she saw that the *maire* himself, a man of formal and precise bearing and great integrity, was standing on the drawbridge. He bowed gravely, almost rigidly, and stepped inside.

"My regrets, Madame la Baronne. I come with bad news. . . ."

"I know. Just what——?"

"The Germans have taken Sedan."

"Sedan!"

"Yes. History repeats itself. Sedan has marked a fatal turning point for France once before. My father was killed there, madame, in 1870. Now perhaps my nephews——" He checked himself. "Will you be so good as to call the Lieutenant at once? And tell him, for me, that he must leave immediately?"

"Shall I also say that you are waiting for him?"

"Unfortunately I must visit four other houses in the vicinity, taking a similar message. I could return, but as the Lieutenant has, I believe, other means of getting to the station——"

"Of course. Perhaps you will stop by the commons and call Benoît as you go by."

"It is understood, madame. *Au revoir—et courage!*"

He was gone, swallowed up in the darkness that lay beyond the heavy door. Constance hurried up the stairs again. When she reached Aunt Bertha's room, she paused briefly; it would be a bitter blow for the old lady to wake in the morning and find that Nick had gone without a word of farewell to her. On the other hand, Nick himself hated any kind of leave-taking and required that these should be kept to a minimum; this was a time when Nick's wishes, more than any others, must be considered. Constance went on up the second flight of stairs without knocking, but when she reached the dormers, she turned first in the direction of the servants' rooms, and tapped on Blondine's door. The old cook answered instantly.

"Yes, Madame la Baronne, I come."

She appeared almost as soon as she had answered, and Constance saw that she was fully dressed, as if she had lain down prepared for such a summons. "They have come then, the evil tidings?" she said calmly. "I have awaited them for these three nights now. I have heard the hoot owl in the woods. Strange that I did not hear the *maire's* knock when it came. But then, with my hearing what it is now, and this room at the back of the house . . . There will be coffee for Monsieur Nick by the time he is dressed and packed, madame. In my kitchen everything is already in readiness."

She lumbered off, clumsily but quickly, and presently the stairs were creaking under her heavy tread. Constance went back down the corridor to the room Nick and Margot had chosen for theirs. As she paused before it, she could hear the murmur of their voices.

It was not the angry murmur she had heard so often, either in reality or in her tormented imagination. Neither did it seem to strike any note of haste or shock, as it certainly would have done if Nick and Margot had heard the *maire's* summons and Nick were already hurrying to answer it. There was no sound of anyone stirring, only the harmonious mingling of whispers. And from this vague, almost voiceless speech, soft words detached themselves from time to time, making themselves heard through the very force of their meaning. "I do love you, Nick, I always have, I always will. I'm sorry I ever said I didn't. I'm sorry I ever acted as if I didn't." . . . . "I know, darling, I understand. It was my fault, all my fault. But from now on——" "You're not kissing me hard enough, Nick, you're not holding me close enough. No, of course you don't hurt me. You couldn't. Nothing could hurt me now, nothing, nothing! Oh Nick, don't ever let me go again." . . .

Constance took her hand from the knob and retreated, covering her ears, shutting her eyes. She could not stand outside that closed door an unwilling eavesdropper on words which were in themselves a seal of love; still less could she invade a chamber where at last two warring natures were reconciled, and where a mystical union of spirits had finally beatified a union of the flesh. For long moments she stood still, literally incapable of action, almost incapable of any coherent thought beyond the one that centered on those young lovers locked in each other's arms. Then with desperate resolution she forced herself to go forward again.

"Nick," she called softly. "Nick darling." There was no answer and she went nearer and called more insistently. "Nick, Nick!" Still no answer came, so she opened the door a crack and spoke into the darkness. "Nick, please answer me. Nick, you must answer me." Then at last she heard a responsive sound coming from the depths of the darkness into which she had called so long and so vainly. But it was not Nick's voice. It was Margot's—soft, smothered, still tinged with unquenched ecstasy.

"Yes—yes. What is it? Someone is calling you, Nick."

"It's Mother. I've been sent to get you, Nick. Sedan has fallen."

"What? What's that about Sedan? Say it again!"

"The Germans have taken Sedan. The *maire* has been here with a summons. You have to leave at once."

"Oh Nick, not *now!* You can't leave now! Not after——"

It was a cry of anguish straight from a stricken soul. Constance heard her son answer his wife soothingly and encouragingly, but she could not distinguish the words. Again there was a low murmur, and this time it was followed by vague rustling sounds. Then Nick turned on the light.

He was already out of bed and he already had on a bathrobe over his pajamas. He gave the effect of being almost completely clothed as well as completely collected, and without saying another word he walked over to a suitcase and began to fling his possessions into it. Margot sat up in bed, her black hair tumbling over her white shoulders, her lacy nightgown open over her beautiful breasts. Both of them seemed to have completely forgotten an alien presence. For a moment or two Margot looked fixedly at Nick without making any sound, her lips trembling visibly, her eyes overflowing. Then she brushed back the tears and, slipping from the bed, went to her husband's side.

"I could pack for you while you dress," she said. "That will save you time."

Margot did not come downstairs to see Nick drive away. Constance was sure that he had asked her not to, just as his father had made the same request of her. She herself watched the car out of sight, and then she turned back towards the kitchen. The nights were still very cold, or at all events she was very cold. She would get herself some coffee before she went back to bed. She had made a pretense of drinking some with Nick, but it had been a pretty poor pretense. Now she would take a big, hot cupful.

Blondine was still stirring around, snuffling rather suspiciously, but making a considerable show of industry. She poured out the coffee for her mistress, and Constance sat down at the long kitchen table to drink it, instead of taking it into the dark, deserted dining room. The fire on the kitchen hearth was burning brightly and the black cats were all dozing in comfort before it. Blondine continued to busy herself in the same vicinity. At last Constance looked up and asked, rather aimlessly, what she was doing.

"Madame la Baronne should not have to ask," Blondine replied tersely, and as she spoke she stopped sniffling and lifted the earthen cover from the casserole surmounting one of the great iron *landiers*. A fragrant smell rose from it, and when Blondine dipped a long-handled spoon into the depths of the vessel and began stirring its contents, the delicious odor grew stronger and more savory. "I am preparing the *bouillon de la mariée,*" she announced. "This broth will be at Madame Nick's bedside in five minutes, and within another five it will at least be warming her vitals and restoring her strength. She needs it now as she never did before, and who knows? Perhaps at last it will do something else for her."

Margot did not go away from Malou again except to visit her parents at L'Abbatiale. She did not talk much for the first few weeks after Nick had gone, but she showed no signs of restlessness or discontent, and presently she asked if there were not something she could do to be useful, and was assigned special tasks, just as the others had been. She performed some of these rather awkwardly at first, because she was unaccustomed to any kind of work, but she was industrious and she learned readily. Before long she had become very efficient. Like Constance, she needed to be busy, because the news that was coming through was now getting worse and worse. But Constance never saw her lips tremble again, or tears flowing from her eyes.

Early in June she came to tell her mother-in-law that she was almost sure she was going to have a baby, but that she thought she had better wait a week or two before writing Nick about it. She wanted to be *absolutely* sure so that there would be no chance that he might be disappointed.

The letter was never written and Nick never knew that he had begotten a child. For while Margot and Constance were still talking joyously about the prospective baby the *maire* came to tell them that Lieutenant Dominique de Fremond had been killed at Dunkirk.

CHAPTER XXVII

IT WAS A beautiful warm evening, and Constance and Margot were sitting out on the terrace, watching the sunset before going in to get the latest news on the radio. This had been very bad for days now, and it was bound, almost inevitably, to be worse. Paris had been bombed and the government had fled from it. The Germans had begun a new offensive on the Somme. Then they were only thirty-five miles from the capital. They had crossed the Marne. Then they had crossed the Seine. Italy had declared war on the Allies. It was almost certain that tonight they would hear that Paris had fallen. The French kept retreating, and Aunt Bertha went around muttering that they had lost their gumption, while Constance and Margot, with diminishing success, tried their best to deny this. Their spirits were very low, their hopes fading fast. But the valley still lay shimmering in the mellow light, the trees on the embankment were still gilded by its rays, the Touques was still a ribbon of gold twisting among the radiant fields. The only sound was the note of a wood dove calling to its mate, and the evening star shone in all its glory. The Vallée d'Auge had the same aspects of eternal beauty and eternal peace as when Constance had first seen it, twenty-one years before.

"Don't you agree with me, madame, that it would be better to wait another week or two before telling him?"

"Yes, probably. It seems too bad that he should have to wait, even a day, for such good news. But as you say, it is too early to be sure, and perhaps you shouldn't risk disappointing him. This means more to him than anything else in the world, Margot—except, of course, your love."

Constance had risen and put her arms around the girl, kissing her cheek fondly, when Margot told her about the baby. They were still standing embraced when Blondine came out on the terrace, the ruddy color gone from her face. The first thought that struck both Constance and Margot was that she must suddenly have been taken ill.

"What is it, Blondine? Is something the matter?"

"Monsieur le Maire is calling, Madame la Baronne."

"Then tell him we shall be very pleased to see him. And suppose we offer him some strawberries with crème Chantilly along with the coffee and Calvados."

"He will not be remaining today for refreshments, Madame la Baronne. Will you receive him here or in the *grand salon?*"

"Why, here! It is far too beautiful an evening to go indoors."

Blondine turned and lumbered off, wiping her nose with the back of her hands as she went. Margot looked at Constance, alarm leaping into her big dark eyes.

"Something dreadful has happened!" she cried. "Something dreadful, and Blondine knows what it is already!" She rushed towards the door leading into the fort and met the *maire* on the threshold. "Which one is it?" she asked, clutching his arm.

The *maire* came forward slowly. He was wearing the somber costume reserved for official visits of condolence and carrying a tall silk hat in one black-gloved hand. He cast a pitying glance at Margot, but he addressed Constance.

"It is the Lieutenant, Madame la Baronne."

"Wounded?"

"Killed."

She put her hand out blindly towards the balustrade and then leaned against it, seeking support. Everything had gone dark around her, and this dark world seemed to be swirling. But she managed to ask two other questions, her voice sounding as if it belonged to someone else and as if it came from a great distance.

"Where? How?"

"At Dunkirk. As yet I do not know how. There has been a general flight to England, accompanied by terrible slaughter. Both the British and the French are in full retreat. The first official communiqués—those that are sent to me for transmission to bereaved families—are very brief. But within a short time, a few days or a few weeks at the most, you will receive letters from some of the Lieutenant's surviving comrades and probably from a superior officer, giving you further details. Meanwhile you may be very sure, however, that your son has died a hero's death. . . . Your son, madame," he repeated, still addressing Constance, "and your husband, madame," he added, glancing again at Margot. "I hope this knowledge may be of some slight consolation to you in your great grief. And I offer you both my heartfelt expressions of sympathy."

"He didn't know," Margot said in a dull voice. She did not look at the *maire* as she spoke; she simply gazed vaguely into space. "If I'd written him right away, he might have got the letter before he was killed. And I didn't. Because I wanted to be sure."

"My daughter-in-law had hopes of being able to send my son some very good news," Constance explained, meeting the *maire's* eyes, in which bewilderment was now mingled with pity. "But she delayed, because she wasn't sure that her hopes had foundation. Naturally now she regrets——"

"It isn't fair," Margot said again, her voice even duller than before. "It isn't fair he should have been killed without knowing. He was sure from the beginning that he would be killed. He faced that. What he couldn't face was fearing the family mightn't go on at Malou. That all this would be lost to someone else. Perhaps to the enemy." For the first time she loosed her hold of the *maire's* arm and wheeled slowly around, until she had faced every aspect of the château and the landscape visible from the terrace. "It isn't fair," she repeated. Then she walked away from the others and disappeared inside the fort.

"It would perhaps be better that the poor young thing should have a little time alone, in which to recover," the *maire* said, in a voice of compassion. "And you, madame, you must repose and collect yourself. I will not intrude any longer on your sorrow. Besides, I have, alas! other messages of a similar nature to deliver. The last time I saw you I was going from house to house summoning these poor young men to go out to battle. And now I must go from house to house saying that Death himself has summoned them. I am too old to fight myself, and this is my task in the war, so I must not shirk it. But I ask you to believe it is a hard one."

He was gone, his spare somber figure swallowed up in the deepening shadows in the fort, just as it had been swallowed by the darkness of the drawbridge on the night when he came to send Nick to his death. Constance sat down, bowing her head over her clenched hands, trying to pray, resolved not to weep. Presently she must go inside to give the necessary directions. . . . But directions for what? There could be no funeral, and hence there could be no preparations for one. Soon a Memorial Mass would probably be celebrated for Nick and for the other young men whose families the *maire* was now visiting, each in turn. But there was nothing she could do about that now, or that she need do at any time—the *maire* and the curé, between them, would make all arrangements. She did not even need to tell anyone that Nick was dead; Blondine would have done that for her already. And soon—all too soon—the men of Malou who were still there only because they were too old to fight, and the women of Malou, both old and young, would seek her out and offer their sympathy, and urge her, according to their own dispositions, to rest, or to be brave, or to give way to her grief, because that was what would make it easiest to bear in the end.

They in turn would be followed by all the neighbors, and all the acquaintances of the de Fremond family who, in one way or another, could reach Malou in the midst of the confusion now reigning in France. The French set great store by visits of sympathy. But to Constance these represented a hideous ordeal. She did not want to see anyone just now, not even Jacques and Stéphanie whom she loved so dearly; she could not respond to anyone just now. She wanted to be alone, exactly as Margot had wanted to be alone, and by her own desolation she could measure the depth of her daughter-in-law's. But Margot still had the hope of her firstborn, and she, Constance de Fremond, had lost hers. She opened her eyes for a moment, and then she closed them again, smothering a cry. Because, for a moment, it had not seemed as if she were alone after all. It had seemed as if Nick were with her again, the sun shining on his sleek black hair, the mocking smile playing around his mobile lips, the red and black of his gay uniform accentuating the slender grace of his figure. And the feathers of his *cassar* were white at the top, but red at the bottom—because they had been dipped in blood.

The Memorial Mass for Nick and the three other young men of Norolles who had been killed at Dunkirk was celebrated at the parish church four days later. The chief sensation of which Constance was aware when it was finished was one of overwhelming fatigue. Margot's magnificent example of self-control had helped her to maintain her own, and she had not broken down at any point throughout the long ceremony or during the numerous visits of condolence which, as she had foreseen, followed each other in quick succession. She was still able to speak and act calmly, and even in her rare interludes of solitude, she remained composed. But she had reached the point where she was incapable of any further activity. She admitted this to Aunt Bertha as they went up the stairs together after returning from the church.

"I think I'll lie down for a little while, Aunt Bertha. I don't believe there's any reason why I shouldn't. As far as I know, there's no one I need to see and nothing I need to do just now."

"There's no one you need to see and nothing you need to do until you feel like it. I'm coming right along with you to your room to help you off with your clothes. You haven't lost your gumption, like the French, thank goodness. But you're all tuckered out."

Never, since she was a little girl, had Aunt Bertha made an offer of personal service to her. Instinctively, because this offer seemed so out of character, Constance protested.

"Why, Aunt Bertha, I don't need any help to undress! No one has ever helped me undress, except the few times when I've been ill and once when I fainted."

"You're not so far from fainting now. I'm coming along with you."

Constance did not attempt any further protest. Her exhaustion had reached a point where speech was almost as difficult as movement.

"Don't you try to argue with me any more, Constance Galt, and don't you try to walk a step further, either. You sit right down in that rocker and let me start getting you out of your clothes. That headgear you've got on is enough to weigh anyone down, just in itself."

Constance had never approved of the heavy mourning in which French-women swathed themselves indefinitely after the loss of relatives near and far; but she had realized that her appearance at a Memorial Mass for her son would seem to lack respect for the dead if she did not wear a long black veil, at least on this occasion. Aunt Bertha had gone to Lisieux to buy the veil, along with other indispensable articles of somber wearing apparel, and had draped it herself over a small black hat which Constance already possessed, while Stéphanie had busied herself with Margot's needs. Stéphanie had taken it for granted that her daughter would wear conventional widow's weeds, and had procured them from Caen, since the rapid advance of the enemy and the corresponding flight of refugees had made a trip to Paris impractical. But none of them had dwelt on the significance of this advance and this retreat. Inevitably, during these last tragic days, their thoughts were centered on Nick, who was dead, and on Margot, who must go on living. . . .

Aunt Bertha removed the heavy veil and the hat to which it clung, placing them carefully on a nearby table and smoothing her niece's hair with a gentle hand. Then she knelt down beside Constance and unbuckled the straps with which her shoes were fastened over the instep. As she did so, Blondine, whose principal occupation of late had been the announcement of visitors, appeared apologetically on the threshold.

"*Je demande pardon, Madame la Baronne, mais ce n'est pas Monsieur et Madame Bouvier. Ce sont trois Allemands!*"

Terror was written in every line of Blondine's faithful face. Constance slipped from Aunt Bertha's ministering hands and sprang up with a small incredulous cry.

"*Germans! At Malou!*"

Aunt Bertha had also risen at Blondine's announcement and, with some determination, she now pushed her niece back into the armchair. "You stay right where you are, Constance Galt," she commanded. "I've been expecting this, quite some time, and I guess I'm capable, without anyone's help, of telling three Germans what I think of them, forcing their way into a house of mourning like this. Don't you act like a frightened rabbit either, Blondine. Those three Germans aren't going to eat you. They like their women younger and tenderer, from what I hear."

Aunt Bertha restrapped the shoe she had been loosening, again admonishing Constance to lie still, then she strode from the room, snorting as she went. In the fort, she found three German officers looking about them with polite though undisguised interest. The door was open into the dining room, revealing its inviting interior. Aunt Bertha's first action after reaching the bottom of the stairs was to close this door with something very like a bang.

"What is it you want?" she demanded, turning.

At her approach, all three Germans had put their heels together with a click, bowing from the waist down with a suddenness and swiftness which suggested the pressure, by some unseen hand, of a hidden spring in a mechanical doll. Then two of them had ceased looking about them to gaze at her instead, not with discriminating observance, as they had been inspecting the house, but with a fixed and glassy stare. The third saluted, in formal military fashion, and with rather more expression in his face than the others addressed her politely.

"Do I have the honor of addressing the Baronne de Fremond?" he inquired in excellent French.

"You do not. The Baronne de Fremond isn't going to see anyone today, even her best friends."

"Ah! I should greatly regret to disturb her. But I fear I must ask her to receive me. Perhaps you would be kind enough to tell her that Colonel von Reden is calling, accompanied by his aide-de-camp, Lieutenant Nolte, and by Captain Reinwald."

"I just told you she can't see anyone. She isn't able to."

"Do I gather, madame, that she is seriously ill?"

"She's all tuckered out. She's kept up better than I ever expected her to, but now she's tuckered out. I don't aim to have her disturbed."

As she often did in moments of great excitement, Aunt Bertha had switched from her careful but laborious French into the New England colloquialisms which were natural to her. Colonel von Reden did not seem in the least disconcerted by this change. He continued to speak as calmly and courteously as before, but he now shifted to excellent English.

"I have perhaps the honor to speak to a relative of the Baronne de Fremond?" he hazarded.

"I'm her great-aunt. Bertha Slocum. Miss."

"Thank you. I had hardly expected to have the pleasure of meeting any Americans in or about Lisieux just now, Miss Slocum, except of course, the Baronne. I have been looking forward very much to meeting her. . . . Would it be indiscreet if I inquired how you happened to disregard the admonition given last autumn by the American consular and diplomatic officers that all nationals should immediately return to the United States?"

"I don't know as it's any of your business. Germany isn't at war with the United States."

"Nothing could be farther from our thoughts. My question was prompted wholly by friendly interest. I apologize if it was indiscreet, and immediately withdraw it. However, at the risk of seeming insistent, I fear I must ask you to have some member of the household announce me to the Baronne, since you do not wish to do so yourself. If I am not mistaken, she married Commandant de Fremond before that peculiar regulation entitled the Cable Law went into effect. Therefore she was not empowered to choose whether she would retain the citizenship with which she was born or adopt that of her husband's country. Consequently, she is now legally a Frenchwoman."

"I never said but what she was."

"No. But you said she could not receive us. And I fear I must point out to you, with the greatest regret, that while Germany is not at war with the United States, and of course never again will be, she is at war with France. In fact, now that we have marched into an undefended Paris and that Marshal Pétain has asked for an armistice, it is not, perhaps, premature to say that France is to all intents and purposes already a conquered nation. At all events, it is to a large degree an occupied nation. It is necessary that we should discuss with the Baronne such aspects of this occupation as may affect Malou. It may interest you to know that the neighboring château of the Monteillerie has already been selected as temporary Staff Headquarters of the Third Army Corps."

"It doesn't interest me, but it doesn't surprise me either. The Sadi Carnots aren't at the Monteillerie. After all, they've got six or seven châteaux and they can't be in them all at once. The de Fremonds are different. They don't have so much property, but they look after what they've got. You can't walk right into Malou without so much as saying by your leave, the way you did at the Monteillerie."

"It was not my intention to do so. That is exactly why I wish to confer with the Baronne."

"You seem to know a lot about my niece and her family. Maybe it won't be news to you that her son Dominique was killed at Dunkirk."

"I shall offer her my heartfelt condolences and I hope she will feel moved to offer me hers. I lost both my sons in the same battle. . . . I believe the Baron and Baronne de Fremond have still another son?"

"Yes, at the Cavalry School in Saumur."

"Saumur? Now that is very interesting. Our advance is expecting to reach Saumur by tomorrow, or the day after at the very latest. But perhaps it would be just as well if we did not mention this to the Baronne. We would not wish to cause her any needless distress. And now, my dear Miss Slocum, if you will be so kind——"

"I've told you twice I'm not going to say to that poor grieving woman——"

"Then I shall be forced to announce myself. Excuse me. I am extremely sorry."

He stepped quickly to one side. Aunt Bertha, with equal speed, darted in front of him and stood before the stairs, blocking his way. Without roughness, but with inescapable firmness, he took her by the shoulders, much as he might have handled a stubborn child, and removed her from his path. Then he went on up the stairway, his two subordinates at his heels. Having reached the top, he paused for a moment, glancing in both directions, necessarily uncertain as to which would take him most quickly into the presence of the chatelaine. While he hesitated, Aunt Bertha caught up with him, snorting with baffled rage.

"If you're bound and determined to force your way into my niece's privacy, I can't stop you," she said indignantly. "I haven't got the strength to wrestle with a man of your build. Not that I ever presumed I'd have to. Men don't wrestle with women where I come from. But there's no reason why you should go prying into every nook and corner of the house with the excuse that you're looking for the Baronne. If there's any decency at all left in you, maybe you'll knock."

"Certainly. And I assure you, Miss Slocum, that the Baronne will be treated with the greatest respect. I regret that my attitude towards you should have seemed lacking in this, but you gave me no choice."

He bowed again, and knocked on the indicated door. Instead of saying "Come in," Constance opened it herself. Then she stood on the threshold, her black-clad figure vividly outlined against the golden afternoon light, her wreathed hair reflecting its radiance, while she silently appraised the man who confronted her. Though well over six feet tall, he was so superbly proportioned that his height was not, in itself, overpowering; and nothing in his countenance remotely suggested brutality. His color was fresh rather than ruddy, his eyes a cool clear blue, his smooth thick hair a brighter gold than her own; his features and the outline of his face were remarkably clear-cut, his head proudly set on his shoulders. A formidable array of orders and decorations extended across the smooth surface of his beautifully tailored uniform, which fitted his fine figure as if this had been poured into it. Looking past him to his companions, Constance could see that they were unremarkable copies of their superior officer; they were both tall, both blond, both stiff, and both profusely decorated. But they lacked the undeniable distinction of their leader, whose survey of his unwilling hostess had been quite as thorough as her own. He saluted, and the two officers behind him bowed from the waist at exactly the same minute.

"Baronne de Fremond? My name is Gerd von Reden," he said courteously. "I am desolated to disturb you. But it is imperative that I should acquaint myself with the facilities of your château, and I have assumed, I hope not mistakenly, that you would prefer to show these to me yourself, rather than to have me make my investigations independently."

"You mean that Malou has been requisitioned?"

She spoke icily, without any acknowledgment of his salutation. He answered with redoubled deference.

"Not in the sense which I believe you mean, Baroness. There is no question of asking you to leave this charming place, or even of disturbing you materially. But I shall trespass on your kindness by requesting you to accommodate a few guests, and naturally it will be necessary for me to know how many you could conveniently receive, and in what manner."

"You must have already learned from my aunt that I am not voluntarily receiving anyone at present. You have forced yourself upon us, in spite of everything she could do to stop you. I don't suppose we shall be any more successful in stopping you from quartering anyone here that you please."

"I repeat, Baroness, that I am desolated to seem intrusive. As soon as I have the necessary information, I shall not disturb you any further and neither will anyone else—at least for the present. Would you be kind enough to tell me how many guest rooms you have?"

"Only one."

As he asked his first question, Gerd von Reden had taken a small neat pad from his pocket, and stood with the attached pencil poised for writing. He now pressed this against the topmost sheet of the pad, and without otherwise moving it, looked at her in polite astonishment.

"Only one, in this large house?"

"We did have three. When my elder son married, two of these were put at the disposal of him and his bride. My daughter-in-law is occupying those now. I hope she is resting at the moment. She has just returned from a Memorial Mass offered for her husband."

"I see," Gerd von Reden said. He did not add any other comment. Instead he began to write, in a small careful hand. "And the room which your elder son had previously occupied?"

"He shared a room with his brother, to whom this still belongs. Then my aunt lives with me, as you must have already gathered, and naturally she has a room of her own. We also have several old servants who live with us. My own bedroom is on the farther side of this study."

"It would not, of course, be feasible, then, to convert your study into a guest room to be occupied by strangers. But in case a certain amount of adjustment were indicated, your aunt and your daughter-in-law could occupy it, could they not, thereby releasing their own quarters? And—excuse me, I do not say it to give you pain—the room your sons shared—that must be available now?"

"I suppose you might call it 'available.' It's empty."

For the first time, she turned her head away. Gerd von Reden went on writing in his little notebook.

"This wing must be reserved for your use and that of the ladies living with you. The wing on the other side of the hall contains exactly——?"

"Three bedrooms. The others, the ones we set aside for my elder son and my daughter-in-law, are dormer rooms on the floor above."

"And how many bathrooms are there altogether?"

"Three, of normal size. There's also a very large dressing and bathroom combined on the dormer floor, and a tiny converted closet on one side of my fireplace. Then there's a downstairs lavatory."

"I see the American influence has been at work," Gerd von Reden remarked, permitting his solemn expression to relax in a slight smile. "No doubt the central heating system is equally alien and equally thorough."

"We have found it very satisfactory. I imagine you would too. Provided you have anything to burn in it."

"We shall try to deal with that detail. . . . Thank you very much, Baroness. Now that you have supplied me with this valuable information, I think I may spare you the inconvenience of inspecting the house today. I am sure nothing you have told me is misleading." His cold blue eyes met hers for a moment, and then he turned briefly away, involuntarily accepting the indignant rebuke which he saw in her face. "No, of course not," he went on, rather hastily. "And may I add that, from the little I have seen, the château is as charmingly appointed as it is conveniently equipped." He stressed the words *from the little I have seen* and paused again; but this time Constance looked away herself, without acknowledging the unmistakable hint. "It will, however, be necessary for me to see the stables," Gerd von Reden continued. "You have accommodations for how many horses?"

"Horses!"

"Yes. I believe there is a widespread idea among our enemies that horses have outlived their purpose in war. But we make very extensive use of them. Not, however, to form crack cavalry units with such slogans as 'Be Elegant,' I assure you. Primarily, the horses are used in the infantry, to draw the heavy carts transporting both provisions and ammunition. I think these carts, which we call *Lastwagen* and which I believe the French call *fourgons,* will soon be quite a familiar sight on your Norman countryside. They are not unlike your local cabriolets, except that they are low instead of high and have four wheels instead of two." He began this speech in a tone of consummate sarcasm and continued it as if he were doing his hostess a great favor by enlightening her as to the differences between *fourgons* and cabriolets, and as if these details should be of supreme interest to her. Constance answered with a degree of irony which matched his own.

"And you bring the horses which draw your *fourgons* all the way from Germany?"

Colonel von Reden gave a slight cough. As if it were violently contagious, Captain Reinwald and Lieutenant Nolte immediately did the same.

"Not always. Sometimes we are fortunate enough to find them in France. You said you had accommodations for how many?"

"I don't think I said. Normally we have ten or twelve mares in our small *haras,* and four or five riding horses, in an entirely separate stable."

"Normally?"

"Yes. When our *étalonier* and younger grooms were called out, we sent most of the mares and the stallion away, because we did not have a sufficiently large staff to care for them at Malou."

"Then you have a certain number of empty stalls?"

"Yes, at the moment."

"And you have considerable pastureland? During the summertime, a fairly large number of horses could be pastured at Malou, could they not?"

"No, because we have cattle and sheep also. We have only enough pastureland for our normal number of horses."

Colonel von Reden continued to make entries in his neat little notebook. "Believe me, I wish to spare you all possible inconvenience, Baroness," he said at length, replacing the pencil in a small loop at the side of this, "as well as to show you every courtesy. But perhaps you will allow me to remind you that you have now twice used the word 'normal,' and that however much we may both regret it, these are not normal times in France. An army has already marched into an undefended Paris, and is in complete possession of that beautiful city, which, I assure you, will be governed with the greatest correctness and efficiency. A campaign for improving its sanitary conditions—what I believe Americans would call 'a thorough cleanup'—has been planned long in advance and will immediately be put into effect."

"You say an *'undefended Paris.'* Do you mean to tell me that no effort whatsoever was made to stop your advance?"

"None whatever. Paris was voluntarily declared an open city, and we paraded through it with the same ease that we parade up and down our own Siegesallee and Unter den Linden. Happily for us, times have changed since Gallieni saved the day for the French by organizing the taxicabs of Paris and sending out reinforcements to an army which was almost annihilated. There are no Gallienis in France at present."

Constance looked away, not trusting herself to speak, while Aunt Bertha muttered something more to the effect that the French seemed to have lost their gumption.

"No later than tomorrow, possibly by nightfall today, Marshal Pétain will ask for an armistice," Colonel von Reden continued. "We shall of course grant this, after a sufficient interval to give the question weight. The war is over, Baroness, as far as France is concerned."

"I don't believe it! Paris isn't France! A few regiments may have surrendered, a few civilians may have been cowed. But that isn't the French Army! That isn't the French people! They'll both fight on and on, the way they did before."

"You are of course entitled to your opinion, Baroness. I can see that you have formed a great attachment—shall I say even a great admiration? —for your adopted country. It would be unfortunate if you should suffer a sad disillusionment. Which brings me to the point of saying I do not need to trespass any longer upon your solitude. I will glance through the commons as I leave the estate, but it is not in the least necessary that you should accompany me to them. I shall endeavor to give you notice before the guests I am sending you are due to arrive. However, I am sure you will understand if this notice is brief. I suggest that your daughter-in-law and your aunt vacate their quarters as promptly as possible, so that there may be no last-minute confusion. I think that is all, Baroness."

"Just a minute. If the war is over, as you say, my husband and my younger son will be coming home very shortly. Then we should require the same amount of living space as before. Very soon we should require more. My daughter-in-law is expecting a child."

"If the Baron returns, you and he would share a room, would you not? And your younger son, I believe, has not yet completed his studies and therefore should be at home very little in any case. Surely in a great house like this, a young man could find a 'shakedown' almost anywhere—to borrow another of those expressive American terms which I learned from the Army of Occupation after the last war. As for your daughter-in-law, she could certainly go to her own parents for her confinement. Unless I am entirely misinformed, the palatial establishment founded by the late Abel Solomon has almost unlimited space in it. And we have no present plans for its occupancy. Its location does not render it convenient. I am very much afraid, Baroness, that I shall have to ask you to accept the arrangement for living space which I have already outlined."

Once again he bowed profoundly. But before he did so, Constance noticed a different glitter in his piercing blue eyes; suddenly their coldness seemed contagious as, a little earlier, his cough had been, and this time the contagion included her. She noticed that both Captain Reinwald and Lieutenant Nolte were looking at her with frozen expressions, and she herself shivered with new dread, all the more sinister because it was undefinable. The invasion of her home, the misappropriation of the stables and pasture land, she could understand and therefore face. But this reference to L'Abbatiale as "the palatial establishment of the late Abel Solomon" had a sinister implication, and her heart contracted as she heard it. But her voice remained cool and calm.

"My aunt, Miss Slocum, will go with you to the commons, since you feel it is necessary that you should visit these," she said. And lifting the veiled hat from the table where Aunt Bertha had placed it, she walked away and closed the bedroom door after her.

Throughout the conversation which had just taken place in the study, Aunt Bertha had stood aside, silent except when she muttered something about gumption, her arms folded across her gaunt bosom, a grim expression upon her plain face. Later, as Constance watched from the window where she had looked down on so many glad arrivals and ominous departures, she could see Aunt Bertha, still silent and still detached, stalking ahead of the three officers in the direction of the stables. In a way, the thought of the encroachment there was almost as painful as that of their presence in the house; Constance would be less able to control it, partly because she could not watch it so well and partly because it was less essentially her province. Benoît and Martin would do their best, she knew, to keep the usurpers within recognizable limits; but the type of men sent there would be very different from those quartered in the house, and her own faithful retainers would lack mastery over them. With Tristan at home, the problem would have been entirely different. Tristan not only had the habit of authority, but a rare talent for it. He did not need to resort to presumptuous measures or evil innuendoes to enforce it. It became him, naturally and graciously.

Well, if the invaders had told the truth about Paris, he might very possibly be there soon again, his very presence a mainstay and a safeguard. Mourning for her dead son, grieving for a fallen France, Constance could still cling to the hope which he had told her to hold, a hope which now seemed to promise fulfillment sooner than she had foreseen. If an armistice should actually be sought the next day, it might well be signed within a week. Inside of a month, at the very most, Tristan could be back at Malou. . . .

She was still standing at the window, and still dwelling, with resurgent confidence, on the future, when the three German officers rode away. Having watched them out of sight, she continued to gaze fondly towards the double crescent enclosed by the commons, forming the slope towards the château where the last of the apple blossoms still fluttered from the trees. While she did so, she heard the approach of a car, and even before she saw this recognized it from its sound. Only one person in Calvados drove a car which sounded like that, and this person was Mark Mullins. Anyone else would have relegated such a noisy antiquity to the scrap heap long before. But Mark Mullins delighted in its raucous progress. He insisted that it announced his arrival as effectively as a hunter's horn, and in one sense he was certainly right. With the first smile which she had been able to summon since hearing of Nick's death, Constance went down to meet him.

He came across the drawbridge with his usual jaunty step, tapping his whip against his riding boots as he moved along. He had changed surprisingly little in twenty years. He was a little grayer and a little leaner, the furrows in his cheeks were deeper, and he blinked more continually behind his huge horn-rimmed glasses. But he was as spry and as droll as ever. At the moment his expression was more solemn than usual, befitting a visit of condolence. At the same time, he did not give the effect of being as greatly downcast as Constance would have expected, knowing his adoration of Nick. She was speedily enlightened as to the reason.

"I thought to get here sooner, I did indeed," he told her, wringing her hand and blinking at her from behind his glasses. "I wanted to be at that service this morning, and I thought I could make it too. But the roads are that crowded with refugees I was just inching along, a good part of the time. The things those poor folks are taking with them! Birdcages and music boxes and wax wreaths and glass cases and I don't know what all besides. As if it would do them any good to clear out of their houses! Much better if they'd stayed and looked after them, say I. The Huns will be getting to them presently, and the dirty thieves couldn't help themselves to so much if the proper owners were on hand."

"I understood, of course, that there must be some good reason why you didn't get here for the Memorial Mass. But it's strange no one else spoke of having so much trouble bucking the refugees."

"Land, lady, I'm not talking about those back roads between Lisieux and Norolles! They've kept clear so far, and they'll go on keeping clear, except for a few stray fools blocking them here and there, because they're off the beaten track. I'm talking about the national highways, like the main trunk line to Nantes."

"You've been to Nantes?"

"Well, next door to it, as you might say. To Saint-Nazaire. I've been taking quite a few quiet little trips, right along through the spring. I haven't gone around blabbing about them so much. Not that I'm distrusting you, Baroness, or anyone else at Malou, mind. But the less said about things like that to anybody, the better. I'm only telling you now because I want you to know how it happened I wasn't here to do honor to that poor lad of yours."

"I'd be very happy to have you tell me. But don't let's stand here on the drawbridge. Let's go out to the terrace and sit down."

"I take it very kindly that you should invite me, Baroness, a day like this. I won't keep you long."

He followed her through the fort, still tapping his boots with his whip as he went. But when they reached the terrace and were both seated, he laid the whip carefully down beside his cap and leaned forward, blinking rapidly and speaking with unsubdued excitement.

"My eyesight isn't so good, Baroness, you know that. But it isn't so poor, either, but what I could see the Huns would be humping right along, once they got going. So I started to do some humping too. Every time there's been a boat leaving Le Havre, there've been four or five of our mares and foals aboard. But a week ago I figured I wasn't moving fast enough or getting off enough stock at a time. So I set off to Saint-Nazaire with twenty of the pretty creatures."

"Twenty!"

"Yes, ma'am—I mean yes, Baroness, twenty. And I got every one of them onto the *Champlain*. The rumor's going around this will be her last voyage before the Huns take her over, and if that's true, and I guess it is, I had a case of now or never on my hands. The frogs were starting to take down the gangplank when number twenty was stepping across it. But he made it all right. A fine colt, Cluny, by Trumpeter out of Petronille; you'll remember him, I make sure. I pointed him out to you myself, a few days after he was dropped, and I said to you then, 'Baroness, there's a colt that's going far.' I didn't figure when I said it, though, that he'd be going as far as the States."

Mark Mullins chuckled and then checked himself, realizing that this was neither the time nor the place for an unseemly exhibition of mirth. Nevertheless he continued his story with unabated satisfaction.

"And when I got back to L'Abbatiale this morning, I find all the family already started off to the services for the poor lad, and I have to snatch a shave and a clean shirt before I can strike out again myself. So I cut along upstairs to my quarters and make haste, and when I come down again, what's the sight that meets these poor old eyes of mine? A German colonel, or maybe he's a general, but anyway about seven feet tall, with bright yellow mustaches waxed down sharp as needles at their long ends, and the chest of a whale with more badges on it than the Lord Mayor of London ever had to his name."

"A German colonel has been here today too," Constance interposed. "With two other officers. They'd hardly left when you arrived."

"Is that so?" inquired Mark Mullins. "They must have taken the road to Le Breuil and gone on to Lisieux that way, whereas I came straight to Norolles. But maybe I'll be meeting them yet, and if I should, I'll know what to say to them too. Be that as it may, when I came up to him my visitor was twirling those waxed mustaches of his with one hand, and in the other he was holding a big sheet of paper with a lot of typing on it. 'My good man,' says he, very pompous. 'I have here a complete list of all the thoroughbred brood mares of L'Abbatiale, at which I should like to have a look, as I have plans for them.' . . . 'My good sir,' says I, very plain, 'I'm afraid that it will be impossible for you to see them just now, whatever these plans of yours may be, as they are nearly all off for a little swim, which I thought might be good for their health in this fine summer weather. . . . Unless of course, sir,' I adds very respectful, 'you should care to plunge into the Atlantic and swim after them.'"

Again Mark Mullins chuckled, and though he managed to do it more soundlessly this time, the chuckle was even deeper than before.

"A madder man you would never wish to see in a month of Sundays," he observed gloatingly. "But what can this German general do about it? Nothing but take himself off, foaming at that dirty mouth of his and muttering words which I cannot understand, not speaking German, thank the good Lord for his mercies. America isn't in the war, and it's to the States those horses are headed, bound straight for the Craigs' fine place in Kentucky. I don't doubt that they'll have the best attention there, not for a moment. And that means all the best mares and foals you sent me from Malou, Baroness, when your boys were called out, as well as all the best of our own stock. . . . Well, I'll be going to tell Martin the good news, now that I've told it to you. It'll relieve the poor fellow's mind, and I don't doubt that he has enough on it right now."

"I'm sure he'll be very glad to see you, just as I've been. Thank you for coming, Mr. Mullins. And thank you for telling me your wonderful story. It's helped a lot. More than anything that's been said to me since —I mean these last few days."

CHAPTER XXVIII

THE FATIGUE WHICH had overwhelmed Constance after Nick's funeral persisted for days. She did not give in to it, as both Aunt Bertha and Margot urged her to do; but the more she struggled against it, the more exhausted she became. Then late one afternoon, when she had spent a large part of the day in preparing for the detachment of Germans, whose unwelcome arrival at Malou might be expected at any minute, she suddenly fainted away in the large guest room. When she came to herself, she dimly realized that she was lying on the chaise longue, and that a man in uniform was sitting beside her. As her vision cleared, she saw that this was Duncan Craig.

"Your faithful personal physician, arriving most opportunely," he remarked, without preamble, as casually as if he had seen her the day before. "Lie still, Connie, till I tell you it's all right for you to get up and walk as far as your own room, with my assistance. What are you trying to do, kill yourself? You're going to take a strong sedative if I have to hold your nose to make you swallow it, and stay in bed for the next three or four days if I have to stand over you with a club to keep you there."

"I don't even want to move—it seems so good just to lie still and look at you," she said gratefully, stretching out her hand. "Just the same, I'd like to hear—well, everything you can tell me."

"All right. I don't know why my recent personal history should give you much of a shock. It's no news to you that there's nothing more I can do on the Western Front, because you know there isn't any Western Front left. Now of course the Ambulance Unit has been disbanded. I haven't got out of uniform yet because I haven't been able to locate my other clothes. My suite at the Ritz—or rather the suite I thought was mine—is now occupied by a Junker general. The expression of his aide-de-camp becomes even blanker than usual whenever the subject of my missing wardrobe arises."

"I know all about that blank expression. . . . Where are you staying?"

"Well, I thought perhaps you'd let me stay here for a few days. Lately I've just been knocking around in Paris, sleeping anywhere I could—all my friends there are in about the same boat I am. For personal reasons, I don't want to leave France just now. So I'm going to offer my services to the government, as soon as there is any kind of a government I can offer them to."

"You know what a godsend it would be to have you here, Duncan, as long as you can stay. . . . Did you have some definite type of service in mind?"

"Yes. There's bound to be some sort of a setup for war wounded. I thought I might get a job as a consulting specialist, which would take me from one hospital to another. I'd have a good deal of freedom of action that way. . . . Look, don't let's talk any more about me. Or about you either, right now. You've had a knockout blow, Connie. I know how well you've stood up under it. But I'm going to bend all my energies, for the next week or so, to seeing that you don't stand up any more. We'll have lots of time to visit while you lie in bed and rest."

It was partly the strong sedative he gave her, no doubt, that made her relax at last; but it was even more his comforting and reassuring presence. He did not offer her condolences or ask her questions; but his unexpressed sympathy encompassed her. She realized that Aunt Bertha must have told him the little they themselves knew about Nick's death, and divulged that they had received no news from either Tristan or Bruno and that Margot was expecting a child; but his knowledge of all this was revealed gradually, almost incidentally, as he and she spoke of other things. He divined that it was easier for her, at first, to talk about his interests than her own anxiety and grief; and though he did not volunteer much information, he responded readily enough when she questioned him.

"You've told me that you wanted to stay in France for personal reasons, Duncan. Did you mean on account of Eileen?"

"Yes. She's in England right now, but God knows how long she'll stay there. She was in Paris when it fell, and what she feels about the French won't bear repeating—not to you anyway. She spent most of the winter in Rome—she's been crazy to get back there ever since she was there before. And you probably know that Gwen flew to Finland in January and went all over the place, even to Rovaniemi."

"I never heard of Rovaniemi. Where is it?"

"It's the capital of Lapland. I never heard of it myself until I read Gwen's article about it. I hate to say so, but now I feel as if I'd been there. I can feel the sting of that Arctic cold and see the Laps moving clumsily around through the snow with their lanterns."

"Why do you hate to say it, Duncan?"

"Well, you know how I feel about Gwen. But I've got to admit she can write. She's writing better and better all the time. Perhaps you'd like to see some of her articles. Eileen's been sending me carbon copies of them. Also carbon copies of her own. She's trying to write herself. She's had all of two pieces accepted and only six turned down, thus far, so she's greatly encouraged."

"She should be. And you're almost beside yourself with pride. Which *you* should be. I'd love to see the articles, Duncan. Gwen's and Eileen's both. Perhaps you'd read some of them aloud to me."

"Glad to."

She was not so exhausted now, and she picked up her neglected knitting while he read to her. Inevitably the close, quiet companionship evoked memories of countless evenings when Tristan had read to her in their little sitting room while she sewed, and the memories brought poignant longing with them. But this companionship evoked memories too, and looking back she realized that nearly all of them were happy. As Craig had once reminded her, there was a tie between them also. Recognizing its strength, she ventured to ask him further questions.

"You said I knew how you felt about Gwen. Don't you feel any more kindly to her than you did last summer, Duncan? After all, she's not only given Eileen a great opportunity. She's made her very happy."

"Yes. I've got to admit that too. Eileen's going places on her own someday, thanks to the push from Gwen. I can see that. And she'd never have been satisfied to keep on with the society racket year after year, like her mother and Tilda. And she's grown very fond of Gwen. She doesn't call her Miss Foster any more. She calls her Aunt Gwendolyn, which tickles Gwen almost to death. Well, I suppose I have to hand Gwen something. Not that I like doing it yet."

Had the last word slipped out unintentionally, Connie wondered, or had Duncan dropped it on purpose, to let her see, without eating his previous words, that his attitude had changed already and that he was well aware it might change further? She hazarded another question, more intimate still.

"I've never heard a word from Tilda, Duncan, since the day you and she left here last August. Is she all right?"

"Yes. I believe so. Not that I've heard very much or very often myself. Letter-writing never was one of her strong points, you may remember—it requires too much effort. And then there's nothing certain about mail getting to and from the States these days, except through official channels."

"I imagine Tilda could make use of official channels, if she wanted to."

"Yes, I guess she could. But she might have to make an effort to do that too."

"It makes me feel badly to hear you talk about Tilda that way, Duncan."

"Sorry. But aren't you getting a little *difficile,* Connie? You don't like the way I talk about Gwen, you don't like the way I talk about Tilda, you won't let me talk about—well, we'll skip it. Suppose we talk about Margot for a while. That ought to be safe. And pleasant. You're happy over the prospect of a baby, aren't you?"

"Yes, very—if everything will only go all right!"

"Of course everything will go all right. Margot'll have her baby the way Stéphanie had all hers—easy as falling off a log. I've looked her over, and she's in fine shape. If it'll make you any easier though, I'll try to get back here and make you another visit around the first of February."

"Of course it would make me feel easier. Of course it would mean everything to have you here."

"All right. Count on it then."

He took a small notebook out of his pocket and scribbled a date in it. "Possibly I may get back before. I don't know yet how confining this job I'm after will be. Or even whether I'll get the job, of course. But I'll keep in touch with you as well as I can. I think our Teuton visitors may make that a little complicated, but I'll manage—there's bound to be some kind of an Underground before long. I suppose though, since you're on the right road again, that I ought to be getting back to Paris pretty soon."

He rose, stretching himself in a leisurely way, and glanced around the room. His gaze fixed itself on the starry handkerchief at the foot of the alcove bed.

"I helped you tack that up, didn't I, the day Tristan left?" he asked thoughtfully. "You've never taken it down since, I suppose."

"No, never. It's the first thing I see in the morning and the last thing I see at night."

"'Ad astra per aspera,'" he said. "You always manage to reach the stars somehow, Connie, and to hold onto them. . . . How about trying your feet again a little tonight? As your personal physician, I think you could do it all right. In fact, I should advise you to start getting around a little again. I know you want to be up and doing when the Huns get here, and I suppose they'll be along almost any day now. I'd like nothing better than to help you receive them. But I know I ought to be getting back to Paris."

As a matter of fact, it was nearly two months after this that Colonel von Reden came back to Malou. When he returned, he arrived without previous announcement, and he brought with him, in addition to his aide-de-camp, another lieutenant, an adjutant, and eight men besides his orderly. Captain Reinwald had evidently been assigned to duties elsewhere. At all events, he did not appear, nor was he mentioned.

Colonel von Reden took possession of the boys' room for himself and of Aunt Bertha's room for his aide-de-camp, Lieutenant Nolte. The other lieutenant, whose name was Leinmeister, and the adjutant, Koppin, were installed in the large guest room, whose last invited occupant had been Tilda. The eight men were domiciled in the commons, half of them with Lise and Bernard, and the other half with Aylette. Von Reden's orderly, Klietsch, was also assigned to Aylette, on the ground that she had more room available, since she and little Lucie could sleep together, whereas Lise and Bernard also had to provide for old Joseph.

At first, all the officers used Tristan's little *bureau* as their office, but one morning Constance entered the dining room to find that most of their working equipment had been moved in there. Leinmeister and Koppin were both seated at typewriters, busily tapping away, and Nolte was standing between two tall steel files, sorting and interchanging their contents. The old family portraits had been removed from the walls, and maps were tacked up in the places thus vacated. The dining-room table was piled high with official-looking documents, and it was flanked on either side by a flat-topped double desk. When she appeared in the doorway, von Reden, who was engaged in scrutinizing one of the documents with which the dining-room table was piled, immediately arose and saluted politely.

"It appears that we shall be required to handle a far greater volume of administrative work at Malou than we had originally expected," he said, in a voice which indicated that he took it for granted this explanation would be entirely satisfactory. "Therefore, henceforth I shall use Commandant de Fremond's *bureau* as my private office, and my assistants will work here. We effected the change of equipment during the night, after you had retired. I hope you were not disturbed? I personally supervised the moving of the furniture, and kept cautioning my men to make as little noise as possible. Did you hear them?"

"No, I didn't hear them. May I ask where you have put the de Fremond portraits?"

"Certainly you may ask. You only forestall an explanation I was about to offer. They have all been placed, with the greatest care, in the attic. I also supervised this removal personally, and saw to it that cloths were wrapped around each one to protect it, and padding stuffed between two when one overlaid the other in being propped against the eaves. Would you care to inspect the results? I feel rather proud of them, and I should be pleased to accompany you."

"No thank you, not at the moment. I take it you have also made arrangements for the service of meals elsewhere?"

If he noticed the sarcasm in her voice he gave no sign of this. Instead he continued to speak with studied courtesy.

"Certainly, Baroness. Now that unforeseen circumstances have forced us to convert your charming dining room into a temporary office, it will obviously be impractical to keep on using it in the way for which it was originally designed. Besides, the procedure of serving two sets of meals, one after the other, has seemed to me inefficient, not to say unsatisfactory. In the first place, it has obliged you and your aunt and your daughter-in-law to eat earlier than you normally would, and it has obliged my assistants and myself to eat correspondingly later—a trifling inconvenience, of course, but after all we become creatures of habit, especially as we grow older, do we not? Besides, the preparation of meals in sequence consumes much more time than preparation simultaneously, and contributes to the perpetual disorder in any kitchen, but especially one which—if you will permit me to say so—is not keyed to a schedule of rigid punctuality and economy in any case. I have therefore arranged that you and Miss Slocum and Madame Dominique de Fremond should in future have your meals—with the exception, naturally, of the first breakfast, which will be served, as usual, in your private apartments—in the small salon, and that my assistants and myself will be served at the same time in the large salon. I am sure the logicality of this arrangement cannot fail to impress you."

"I'm afraid it doesn't. I'm afraid I'm more impressed with the fact that I'm required, simultaneously, to give up my dining room and my drawing room. That will leave me very much restricted."

"Restricted! I beg you to reflect, Baroness, that you still have undivided occupation of your upstairs apartments! And that I did not anticipate, as I warned you on the occasion of my first visit. I told you then, quite candidly, that I should be obliged to ask your aunt and your daughter-in-law to share these with you. Yet only your aunt has been so far dispossessed. And I gather that Miss Slocum's removal to Madame Dominique de Fremond's apartments was quite as much due to her own choice, and yours, as to the desirability of having my aide-de-camp in a room adjoining mine."

He made the statement, which was entirely true, in a tone suggestive of reproach. When it became evident that the bridal suite would not be requisitioned after all, at least for the time being, Aunt Bertha had announced, with her usual brevity, that she was going to sleep in Margot's dressing room and not in Constance's study. Constance had gravely agreed with her that perhaps this would be the best arrangement, and beyond saying that she would have the day bed moved upstairs, had made no further comment. Margot had made no comment either, and had voiced no objection. The possible reasons for the wisdom of such a move had never been mentioned, then or later. Now Colonel von Reden's manner made it clear that he saw in them a basis for resentment. But for once he did not remind his hostess, as he had so many times previously, of his pride in the fact that his conduct and that of all his associates was so completely correct.

"I recognize that more work will be entailed by service in the two salons than in the dining room," he went on, "because of the greater distance from the kitchen. Of course my orderly will continue to serve my associates and myself. But it has occurred to me that it would be well to have Aylette assist Nicole. I trust this will be agreeable to you."

"It wouldn't be agreeable at all. Aylette has had no training as a house servant. Besides, with five soldiers quartered with her, she has all she can do as it is."

"Her mother-in-law can arrange to feed them with the others. That will leave her with only the chamber work to do, which should not be too onerous. Believe me, it would be much the best plan, Baroness."

She did not attempt to argue with him. It would not only have been quite futile in any case, but she felt it beneath her dignity to enter into a discussion with a man towards whom she felt such resentment. She turned away from the dining-room door and walked across the fort to her little sitting room; the furniture had already been rearranged, to permit the installation of a center table. Tristan's desk, which she had been given no opportunity of emptying, was gone from its position by the window, and one of the armchairs which had previously stood by the hearth had been wheeled into its place. The other armchair was missing. She had no choice but to return to the dining room and make an effort to reclaim Tristan's possessions. Von Reden was still seated at the center table sorting documents.

"I find that you've removed my husband's desk from my private sitting room. The drawers are full of his personal papers. At least they were last evening. I shall have to ask you what's become of them."

"Certainly, Baroness. In this instance I did not merely supervise a piece of work, I did it myself. The papers have all been placed in cartons, and each carton has been labeled, 'Contents of top drawer, left' . . . 'Contents of middle drawer, right,' and so on. I am sure you will find them in perfect order. The cartons have been placed with the portraits, in the attic. Again let me suggest that you check over these belongings of yours, in my presence."

"But the drawers were locked and I have the key."

"Fortunately I also had a key which fitted the lock, so I was not obliged to disturb you," von Reden said pleasantly. "And let me assure you that Baron de Fremond's desk will have every care. I intend to reserve it for my own personal use."

"But you're already using the one in his *bureau*."

"I'm turning that over to Lieutenant Nolte. We have managed to install the desk from the sitting room in the office also. Of course it makes us very crowded, but it proved possible. Let me repeat, Baroness, your husband's desk will have every care."

"I'd like very much to have the armchair that's been removed put back in the sitting room. That was also my husband's. Besides, without it, there's only one left in the room. I can't offer an armchair to even one caller and still sit in one myself. We'd have to sit in those high stiff chairs you've put around the center table."

"A table makes a very pleasant center for a group. I do not need to remind you that it is quite generally used as such, in France as well as in Germany."

"It isn't in America."

"I thought you prided yourself that you were now a Frenchwoman, Baroness. I also thought it probable that you would be having fewer visitors in the future than in the past, and that those you did see you could receive in your study. After all, as I reminded you before, your daughter-in-law still has her private sitting room where she can see the members of her family, though I imagine they will be coming here less as time goes on also. The armchair was sent to Aylette's quarters, which were lacking in comfort, if you will permit me to say so. However, if you make an issue of the matter, I can order it brought back."

"I certainly do make an issue of it. I do not propose to have your soldiers lounging in my husband's armchair while they smoke their dirty pipes and drink their vile beer and tell their filthy lying stories."

She was beside herself with rage, far too angry to weigh her words or curb her tongue. Von Reden did not even appear to notice her fury. He spoke quietly to Lieutenant Nolte, who was still sorting files.

"You will have the armchair which was in the sitting room of the Baroness brought back immediately, Lieutenant. Replace it in the quarters with one of the armchairs from the room I am now occupying."

"My dead son's! Never!"

Von Reden laid down the document he had continued to hold, straightening the pile so that the latest paper would fit precisely on top of it, and spoke with an air of great patience. "Perhaps you will make a suggestion yourself, Baroness? The needlepoint love seat from the large drawing room perhaps? Or one of Madame Dominique de Fremond's recent selections? My own choice would have led me in the latter direction, but I understood that you were bitterly opposed to having her disturbed in any way."

"I am bitterly opposed to having her disturbed in any way. I am also bitterly opposed to having you misappropriate any of the furniture from this château in the way you are suggesting."

"The Baroness is not willing that our men should have any sort of an easy chair in which they can relax after their day's labors, Lieutenant Nolte. You will act accordingly. You will also make a note of the fact."

Colonel von Reden bent over his documents as if these now required his undivided attention after an unnecessarily disturbing interruption. For the second time, Constance turned away from the dining room, now almost as angry with herself as she was with the Colonel. She had allowed herself to be drawn into an argument after all, when for weeks she had succeeded in avoiding this, and she was sure that von Reden was secretly gloating over his success in finally provoking one. He must be even more triumphant because he had aroused her to wrath. Ever since his arrival she had managed to be as outwardly cool and collected as he was himself, even when she was seething inside. He might even act in retaliation. "You will make a note of the fact, Nolte," he had said, in referring to her refusal to permit Tristan's armchair, or any substitute for it, to be used in the commons. And after all, what did Tristan's armchair matter, now that he was no longer there himself to sit in it, by her side, reading aloud while she sewed, evening after evening? What did the battered chairs from the boys' room matter, now that they were not there to tumble over these together, or to sink into their depths for one last satisfied, animated review of the day's happenings before they dropped off to sleep, side by side? What did anything matter, now that Tristan was gone and Nick and Bruno were both dead?

Somehow she had managed to hold fast to the hope that Tristan would sometime return, somehow she had managed to face the certainty that Nick would not. But she still flinched from the knowledge that Bruno was lost to her forever as from a physical blow. She never spoke of it, and as far as possible she acted as if she never thought of it. She now paused at the open door leading to the drawbridge, trying to calm her spirit and to decide where to go and what to do next. The dull ache of loneliness and longing, which had gradually supplanted the first piercing pain of Tristan's absence and the boys' deaths, had never lessened, and it kept her restless and edgy, all the more so because she strove, generally with success, to conceal this endless misery.

She felt that for the moment she could not go back to her own room, from which she had just come, and where the void left by the absence of those she most loved was still almost unbearable. All the rest of the house, except Margot's suite, was now pre-empted by von Reden and his minions —a glance at the drawing room, which had certainly also undergone "rearrangement" by this time, would only increase the rage and resentment which the sad sight of the little sitting room had aroused. As for Margot, Constance tried to intrude on her as little as possible. The girl's active antagonism against her had long since abated, like hers to her daughter-in-law; they had, in a certain sense, become allies. But they had not become intimates, and Constance was walking warily, lest Margot should suspect that her condition was being used as a pretext for supervision or interference, and she had not yet spontaneously suggested that she would like to have her mother-in-law spend more time with her.

The commons offered as little helpful distraction as the château. Lise, whom she had always found cheerful and congenial, had both her house and her hands so full that any interruption was an imposition. Aylette had shown herself so increasingly insolent and hostile that Constance actually went out of her way to avoid encounters with her, though chagrined that an ignorant, coarse-grained young peasant should have the power to cause her such discomfiture, and deeply concerned because little Lucie, for whom Constance felt genuine affection and concern, could not be wrested from her unworthy mother and placed where she could be surrounded with fostering care and tenderness.

As for the stables, Constance had never gone to those since the day when von Reden had informed her that the remaining mares had been "removed." The stalls were filled with hacks of various descriptions, and Martin and Benoît fed these jaded creatures and kept their quarters reasonably clean. But the "boys" went about this work in surly silence, which had deepened since the day they learned that Mark Mullins, as an Englishman, had been sent to an internment camp at Caen. They knew that without him L'Abbatiale, though still unmolested, had lost its moving spirit, and the desolation which had descended on the older *haras* deepened that of its offshoot. The cheerful sounds of whistling and shouting, which Constance had always associated with the stables, were long since stilled.

While she stood hesitating before the drawbridge, Chess came padding quietly across it and stopped beside her. Then he walked sedately through the door, turning, when he was halfway across the drawbridge, to regard her with beseeching eyes, as if to remind her that it was time for their customary walk about the place. Well, after all, she might as well follow him. She went with him up the grassy slope, then on through the arched passage which divided the commons and led into the kitchen garden. Then she stopped, looking across the neat rows of vegetables interspersed with flowers to the quaint *lavoir*.

As usual, Aylette was ensconced beside it. But she was not washing. All the soiled linen she had brought from the château and the commons had been loosely bunched and bundled together to form an untidy couch, slightly raised at the top to simulate a bolster, and on this disorderly bed Aylette was reclining, with her hands behind her head and her knees crossed. She looked relaxed, satisfied, and completely evil. Beside her, looking equally at ease, equally content, and equally depraved, was seated one of the German soldiers quartered in the commons. As he caught sight of the great dog approaching in front of the chatelaine of Malou, the soldier sprang to his feet, straightening his tunic and reaching for his cap, meanwhile muttering something hastily under his breath. Aylette smoothed first her hair and then her skirt, bringing the latter down below her knees, which she now uncrossed. The smoldering rage which Constance had been trying so hard to subdue flamed into fury again.

"Behr, get out of this garden," she said in a voice she hardly recognized as her own. "You too, Aylette," Constance went on as the soldier slunk away, still muttering and still fumbling at his clothes. "You may leave the linen here. I will send someone else to get it."

"Pardon, Madame la Baronne. It all requires washing."

"So I see. I doubt if any linen at Malou has ever been so greatly in need of cleansing. But I will have it washed in the laundry—that and all the linen used on the place hereafter. Your own duties in that direction are ended."

"As Madame La Baronne wishes."

She was on her feet now, and her eyes, as impudent as her speech, were meeting the chatelaine's without apology or abashment. She walked out of the garden, still swinging her hips.

CHAPTER XXIX

When bruno went to the seminary at Bayeux, he had parted from Chess ruefully but resignedly; after all, he came home frequently over the week ends, and he had his dog with him then. When he went to Rambouillet, the question of taking Chess with him naturally could not arise, because he made his preparations secretly. But when he left for Saumur, he announced that Chess was going along.

"Dogs aren't allowed at the Cavalry School, are they?" his mother inquired doubtfully.

"I spoke to Father about that at Christmas time. He said that theoretically they weren't. Then he laughed and added that occasionally they appeared, in a rather mysterious manner, and that he'd never heard of one being shot to rid the premises of it, or of anybody being disciplined because a dog seemed to be particularly attached to some special person. In the case of a student living in a dormitory, the arrangements would naturally be complicated. But Father didn't think they were insurmountable. I don't either."

So Chess and Bruno went off together, to the obvious satisfaction of both. A few days later, Bruno wrote his mother that just as he and Father had thought, everything had been very easy to arrange. He had not tried to push his luck by keeping Chess in the dormitory too long; he had immediately begun to make inquiries about someone who would give his dog a good home, in a place where the poor creature wouldn't have to be kept more or less surreptitiously, or shut up alone for hours while his master was at classes or off on maneuvers. Among the persons of whom he made these inquiries were the Barrau sisters, who ran that wonderful inn at Gennes which she and Father had told him so much about; and they had suggested just the right person.

The person the Barraux suggested was Monsieur l'Abbé Souillet, the curé of Milly-le-Meugon, a little village about six kilometers from Gennes, and Bruno had gone at once to see him. Bruno didn't suppose Mother had ever been to Milly because, after all, it was a very small, unimportant place, and there would be absolutely nothing in the normal course of events to take her there. But this Abbé was a personality. He knew everything there was to know about the vintage wines of the region, he read Greek for pleasure, and most of the daylight hours that he could spare from his parish duties he put into the cultivation of lilies. He had an immense garden back of the rectory, twice as large as the one at Malou, and —if Mother didn't mind having Bruno say so—twice as well developed. Monsieur le Curé didn't seem to think a dog would do much harm in the garden—after all, there was a big courtyard too, so Chess could stay there most of the time when no one was around to watch him. The matter had been settled then and there, over a bottle of the best Faye d'Anjou he had ever tasted; and Chess was now learning about lilies while he, Bruno, learned about military tactics.

Long satisfactory letters continued to come for a month after Bruno had gone to Saumur, and they were reinforced by frequent telephone calls, which, though necessarily briefer, gave Constance the glow of happiness that came from hearing his voice. He had not been able to telephone from Bayeux and Rambouillet except when he could get off long enough to go to a public telephone booth; but at Saumur the school telephone was available to the cadets, within reasonable limits, and Bruno went on using it after the letters began to grow shorter and vaguer in character. Constance guessed that there must be a reason for this increasing haziness and eventually she became certain of it.

"I can't talk but a minute," he said when he called her one evening. His *"Allo, Allo!!"* had been as cheery and ringing as usual; but as he continued he spoke with unwonted intensity. "The lines seem to be rather crowded tonight; it's taken me quite a while to get through. Everything going well at home?"

"Yes, darling. How's everything at Saumur?"

"Fine. This is a great place. A great school. I can't be glad enough I came. Those standards I wrote you about—they're getting higher and higher. The next time you write Father, tell him so for me, in case I shouldn't have a chance."

"All right, I will."

"I guess that's all for tonight. Give my love to everyone. But remember I love you best."

There was a buzzing and a crackling on the line and then it went dead. Constance hung up the receiver feeling sure that he would not try to talk to her again, probably that there would be reasons why he could not.

During the next few days she kept closer than ever to the radio, listening in vain for the word "Saumur." During this interval, Stéphanie, who was worried about the health of Madame de Vallerin, went down to the Haras du Pin to see her parents, and took advantage of the opportunity to do some errands in nearby Alençon. She returned to L'Abbatiale reassured about her mother, but deeply concerned over other conditions, and came straight to Malou, telling Constance about them even before she went upstairs to see Margot.

"You'd be surprised to see how many refugees there are on the main roads. People are just pouring out of the northern cities, and of course there are bound to be some fifth columnists among them. No one can get in and out of the big towns without a pass any more." She paused for a moment. "I heard at Alençon that in Saumur the cadets are charged with examining such papers," she went on. "Also with looking out for parachutists. The E.A.R. are stationed on all the bridges, with twelve-hour watches for each brigade. That seems awfully long to me. I also heard that one of the brigades has adopted the slogan 'Be Elegant' for its device," she ended with a slight smile.

Constance managed to smile too. "Apparently the cadets are running true to form," she said. "Both with their twelve-hour watches and their new slogan, I mean. I realized that some radical changes must be taking place at Saumur. Until just a little while ago, Bruno wrote very freely about everything he was doing and telephoned quite often besides. Then his letters began to get shorter—he didn't even say anything about going out to see Chess. And I haven't had a telephone call from him in several days. Probably he's stationed this minute at the Fouchard Bridge, where the boys used to end up their bootleg races, gazing into the sky with the hope of spotting a parachutist, and commanded by a very dashing young officer who's carrying a riding crop under one arm and wearing white gloves."

"I haven't a doubt of it. And I'm thankful you're not worried about him, Connie."

"No, I'm not worried about him. After all, the E.A.R. are just youngsters, much younger than the normal student body, and they've hardly begun their training. I'm sure they'd make very faithful and vigilant sentinels and that they have tremendous loyalty to their school and pride in its standards. I know they'd always strive to maintain these standards, but it's unthinkable that they should have to prove this by getting into any real fighting, whatever happens. It's Nick I'm worrying about just now."

"Not Tristan?"

Again Constance tried to smile. "I promised Tristan I wouldn't worry about him. I'm trying hard to keep that promise. But I didn't make Nick any such promises. He didn't ask me to."

"No. . . . Well, Connie, I'll drift along and see what Margot's up to."

It was the day after this that the *maire* had come to Malou to say that Nick had been killed at Dunkirk.

Inevitably, for the next few days the shock of these tidings and the sense of overwhelming tragedy that came with them obsessed the minds of everyone at Malou. Temporarily, the German onrush became focalized in personal loss. And with their many sad preoccupations, the various members of the family could not spend the accustomed amount of time listening to the radio. Besides, Constance had been sincere in saying that she had not worried about Bruno in the same way that she worried about Nick, and as she tried not to worry about Tristan. She missed Bruno, but for some strange reason she had not missed him so much since he went to the Cavalry School as she had when he was at the seminary and at the Centre Préparatoire; he actually seemed nearer to her at Saumur than he had at either Bayeux or Rambouillet. When Gerd von Reden and his fellow officers forced their way into her home on the very day of the Memorial Mass for Nick, one ray of comfort pierced her grief for her elder son, her shame for France, and her indignation over the outrageous intrusion to which she had been subjected: Since Marshal Pétain had asked for an armistice, it could be only a matter of days, perhaps of hours, before this would be granted. She had lost Nick, but Tristan and Bruno would both be saved to her. . . .

Then, little by little, she learned from the British broadcasts that on the fifteenth of June the cadets of Saumur had been informed by their officers that they would have the honor of holding a section of the Loire against enemy advance, and that on the seventeenth Colonel Michon, the Commandant of the Cavalry School, had proudly announced that having received no orders to lay down arms, he should proceed with the defense as if the Field Marshal had not asked for an armistice. She also learned that shortly afterwards a two-day battle had taken place, in which the cadets had made a sacrificial offering for the honor of France before they had been overwhelmed by the enemy. How many of them had been killed she did not hear. Nor who. . . .

She made frantic efforts to find out, yet a month went by and still she did not know. But one evening when she was sitting on the garden bench exhausted by a hard day's work, Chess came bounding in through the archway and leapt about her, barking loudly. She arose, with a cry she could not stifle, and looking past the dog saw a stocky, bespectacled priest, wearing a travel-stained cassock and carrying a large suitcase. His shoulders sagged under the weight of his burden, but he held his head high, and she was aware of wise kind eyes looking straight into her own. He set down the suitcase and hurried towards her.

"Madame," he said courteously. Then he added, compassionately, "My daughter——"

She did not need to have him tell her who he was or why he had come.

She sank down on the bench again, engulfed in waves of darkness like those which had eddied around her when she learned of Nick's death, and hoping that the horrible vertigo would pass, she covered her face with her hands, so that everything before her would be black in any case. Chess continued to leap about, but he had stopped barking, and was trying to reach her shielding hands and to lick them. The priest stood very still, close beside her, and gradually the steadfastness of his presence and the prodigality of his pity prevailed over the dark waves. She took down her hands, quieting Chess as she did so, and spoke to the priest in a muted voice.

"Tell me about it."

"I have come here on purpose to do so, my daughter. I assume that you know very little, so far."

"Almost nothing. Only that the Commandant decided to defend the Loire, in spite of the Field Marshal's appeal for an armistice."

"And in that decision, madame, he had the wholehearted support of every officer and every cadet in the Cavalry School."

The priest's statement was permeated with pride. He drew out a small stool from under the table where the milk pails were sunning, and sat down, facing her. Chess looked inquiringly from one to the other and then settled himself between them, his head on his paws.

"I shall try to be as brief as I can, with clarity," the Abbé Souillet began. "But in order that you may understand the part which your son played in this great drama, you must also understand something of the part played by others. The entire line of defense extended from Montsoreau on the east to Gennes on the west—a distance, as I do not need to remind you, of nearly forty kilometers. I shall not try to describe the action on the east —perhaps you will hear of that later from someone who was an eyewitness there. I shall only try to describe what took place in the west. I was very close to this part of the action myself. My own little village, Milly-le-Meugon, was selected as a center for the supporting forces of the defense area at Gennes. On the afternoon of June 18 a squadron under the command of Captain Foltz arrived at Milly. Your son was in that squadron."

The priest paused for a moment, awaiting a possible question. As none was forthcoming, he went quietly on with his story.

"Of course I knew your son already, since he had done me the honor of entrusting his fine dog to me. Until the watches by the river began, and the freedom of the cadets necessarily became restricted, he visited Chess and me fairly frequently." At the sound of his name, Chess pricked up his ears, and again looked inquiringly from his late guardian to his dead master's mother. But as both seemed to have forgotten about him, he closed his eyes and stretched out his legs, taking his ease; it was good to be home again.

"I grew greatly attached to your son in the course of these visits," the priest went on. "We talked freely together while we sat in my study and walked among my lilies. The boy told me that he intended to become a priest, and I encouraged him in his wish to resume his theological studies at the earliest possible moment, because I admired both his gentleness and his perseverance—essential qualities in the service of our Saviour. Of course I admired his scholarship and his spirituality even more. He was very learned for one so young. And I believe that he must have been blessed with the Grace of God from his birth."

"Yes," Constance said. "Yes, Father, I always felt that way about him too."

"So when he came to Milly-le-Meugon in the Squadron Foltz I welcomed him as an old friend. And though his companions were strangers to me in the beginning, I quickly became acquainted with all of them too. I am not an old man myself, as you see, madame. But these boys seemed very young to me—very young and very untried and very scantily prepared for battle, except through their brave spirits. In the way of arms they had only the muskets and such machine guns as they used for drill. Indeed, the lack of arms throughout the battle was pitiful almost beyond belief. On the entire battle line between Montsoreau and Gennes there were altogether only approximately eight caterpillars, two dozen cannon of various types, and two hundred and twenty machine guns, mostly light. Besides, much of this equipment was out of date, while the Germans, of course, were amply supplied with every instrument of modern warfare."

The priest paused again, not as if he were expecting an answer this time, but as if he were again watching that overwhelming advance and the futile, heroic resistance to it. He looked away from Constance, and she knew that he was not seeing the neat rows of thrifty vegetables and flourishing flowers that lay at their feet, but a battle line along the Loire. At last he gave a slight start.

"Forgive me, madame," he said. "As I was telling you—those boys seemed very young to me. A number of them brought me their belongings, which they had carried with them when they came to camp, and asked if it would be a nuisance to keep these for them. They had packed very hastily, with only an hour's notice to leave the school for the camp. But in all, seventy valises were entrusted to me. I stacked them up in my rectory and kept a watchful eye on them." Again he looked away and this time Constance knew it was the stacks of chocolate-colored suitcases, so different from American Army equipment, and so typical of the French, that he was seeing. Once she had thought those chocolate-colored suitcases rather absurd. Now she regarded them differently.

"About ten days ago, seeing that everything was calm, at least for the moment, in our unhappy country, and learning that trains were running more or less on schedule again, I secured a cart from one of my parishioners and took most of these valises to the station at Gennes for shipment," the priest went on. "Since then I have had a number of horrified letters. It seems that many of the boys, in their haste, had left their personal revolvers, for which they had no cartridges, in their valises. If the conquering Germans had searched my premises and found these revolvers, I might have been instantly shot, for as you know, madame, it is now a crime punishable by death for a Frenchman to have arms in his possession. The poor boys would have run a similar risk if any of the valises had been opened en route—which fortunately they were not."

"If there is a revolver in that suitcase you brought here——"

"Yes, madame, I can see that our thoughts are the same. And in this case, I brought the valise instead of sending it, for several reasons. I wished to talk with you instead of merely writing you. I felt closer to your son than to any of the other boys, because of those intimate visits he and I had together, and also because he intended to become a priest. And then there was the question of Chess. A valise may now be entrusted to a baggageman with a reasonable degree of assurance. But a dog like Chess—no, no, I could not have done that!"

Once again Chess raised his head at the sound of his name, and this time the priest stooped over and patted him.

"It was very thoughtful of you," Constance said. "Thoughtful and infinitely kind."

"No, madame, it was only natural. A few well-meaning but timorous persons warned me not to attempt the journey. They reminded me that according to the rules laid down by the Germans, a priest may only go from one village to the next. Well, that is what I did. I went from Milly to La Fourche, and from La Fourche to Gennes, and from Gennes to Trèves, and so on. Just from one village to the next, you understand. Entirely in accordance with the regulations."

"All the way to Lisieux!"

"Yes, all the way to Lisieux—or rather all the way to Le Breuil. I walked to Malou from Le Breuil. Until I reached Le Breuil I was fortunate enough to find small local cars stopping at every village along their route, and connecting with others which continued farther—sometimes after a slight delay, *bien entendu!* Ordinarily I should not leave my little parish to make such a journey, but I talked the matter over with my parishioners, and they were all agreed that in this instance I should absent myself. They knew that a priest from a neighboring village would come to them for Mass and to administer the rites of the Church, in the event that I were delayed or that there was a case of urgence. And they themselves all have a strong feeling about your son—about him and about all the other young men who kept their vigil in our little church. It now has a significance which will last through the ages."

"The cadets kept a vigil in your church?"

"Yes, madame. I am coming to that. It does not annoy you, does it, to have me tell you this story in my own slow fashion? I feel that perhaps I can do it better that way."

"I am sure you can. You are right in thinking I have to know something about the other boys, too, in order to understand about Bruno."

"Well then, since you have reassured me, I will go back a little. By early evening on the eighteenth, the Squadron Foltz was encamped at Milly, and about seven o'clock a message arrived from General Headquarters, which the cadets stood at attention to receive. It read: 'The enemy must be prevented from crossing the Loire and resisted to the death in order to save the flag and protect the gradual withdrawal of our armies towards the south.' This message was received quietly. Everyone who heard it recognized its meaning, and everyone was ready to die for the flag and for the school and for France.

"Almost immediately after dinner, the curfew rang, and all cadets not needed for guard duty were required to lie down. Lieutenant Bonnin, in giving the order, said: 'Tomorrow will be a hard day. That is why I am ordering you to sleep. What good will it do for you to be brave if you are exhausted?'

"He had no time to lie down himself. After giving the order, he left for a conference with his superior officer. At midnight he came and sought me out. 'Headquarters has just alerted us,' he said. 'That means that the Germans must be very close. We may be needed in Gennes at any moment. You have seen what we have for arms. You must realize that we have no illusions about what is ahead of us. Nearly all of us will fall. Would you be so kind as to go to your church and remain there? I will announce in camp that a priest is available for confessions.'"

"And you went?"

"Of course. Immediately. I could not help noticing as I walked over to the church what a beautiful night it was. The air was warm and soft and the sky was a strange color. The bursting shells from the German bombardment gave a vivid tinge to it, yet the moon and the stars were shining too, and their radiance was mingled with this red glow. The church was shaking when I went into it. The shells were already bursting all around it. Naturally we were without electricity, and until I lit the candles for Mass it was dark, except for the sanctuary light and the glow coming in through the windows.

"On my way to the confessional I could see the boys gathered in little groups, some praying, some talking quietly with their friends. They were coming and going all through the night. I knew that one detachment started into Gennes about two in the morning, but I did not see it leave, because I remained in the confessional until it was time to celebrate Mass. I heard more than a hundred confessions, and they were all made very calmly and quietly, though the shellfire was getting worse every minute. Most of the boys handed me letters as they finished confessing. I have one for you. Would you rather read it now or after I have gone?"

"I think I'd rather read it after you've gone."

"Yes, I believe that will be best. But I will give it to you now."

The priest put his hand in his pocket, and this time drew out a soiled limp envelope. After all, he had had it a long while. He saw the expression in Constance's eyes as she looked at the address written in her son's handwriting, but he did not try to express his sympathy again. He knew it would be better for him to go on with his story.

"Since they were already alerted, all the young men in the church were obliged to remain armed throughout the night. I could hear the arms clicking as I left the confessional and went to the sacristy to prepare for Mass. My little altar boy was there ahead of me. He had come trudging through the village as usual, in spite of the bursting shells. While I was commending him for his courage, I heard a knock at the sacristy door, and when I opened it I saw that two of the cadets were standing there. They had come to ask if they might act as servers. One of them was Bruno."

"So Bruno served at Mass that morning?"

"He served through the greater part of it. I had just taken Communion myself, and given this to my servers, when another alarm was sounded. Lieutenant Bonnin quickly came forward and took Bruno's place. My own little altar boy took his friend's. Other boys were filing forward, kneeling at the rail, there was that constant click of arms. I did not hear or see Bruno when he left the church."

"And you never saw him again?"

"Yes. I saw him again. I will tell you about it. But you must ask God to give you strength, for you will need it while you listen—and afterwards.

"The hardest fighting on the Saumur battlefront took place at Gennes. It became a furnace of artillery fire. Lieutenant Roimarmier, the young Supply Officer whose company had been the first sent out, was killed there. Lieutenant Bonnin, who took Bruno's place at the altar, was mortally wounded there and died two days later. Lieutenant Desplats, who defended the outlying island with twenty cadets and thirty Algerian soldiers, was killed there. Fortunately Captain Foltz was unharmed; he walked calmly about among his cadets, quieting and encouraging them. But one by one they fell, and finally the last of the few pitiful munitions gave out. On the evening of the twentieth the Germans took over the town. Later they said that if all of France had fought like this handful of boys they could never have conquered it.

"I realize that you are acquainted with the Barrau Inn at Gennes, that you have been there many times, so you know its character and its location. It was badly damaged by shellfire, but the Barrau sisters, who run it, stubbornly remained there until the night of the nineteenth, when they were ordered out by the military and turned it over to the cadets. They saw Bruno feasting on *pâté maison* in their kitchen before they reluctantly left to take refuge in one of the natural caves across the road, which like all the caves along the line of defense provided such shelter as there was for women and children. They told the boys to help themselves to anything they could find to eat, and the E.A.R. ate better that night than they had in their camp at Milly, for the larder of the inn was still well stocked.

"The next day the Barraux managed to get out of the cave and returned to their battered inn, where they were immediately imprisoned by the Germans, who were by that time in full possession. But on Sunday they were released, for the enemy moved on, leaving behind it a village almost totally destroyed and almost totally deserted—in fact, the only persons left in the upper section were the Barraux and three decrepit old men. After taking stock of the damage within, those indomitable sisters went out into the street to survey the wreckage, and instantly became aware of untombed dead.

"There were not many such. Desplats had been buried on the island, before the firing ceased, by the cadets who adored him, and many dead and wounded had been brought back from there in skiffs, under the direction of a young liaison officer who, though seriously wounded himself, went steadfastly back and forth between the various sectors. His feeling about military burial was very strong. He kept saying, 'When a man falls, we must rush to his side. Those who give a worthy sepulcher to soldiers will have one themselves when they die.' All through the night skiffs carrying their sad burden had slipped silently back and forth over the smooth waters under the bursting shells. But part of the *coteau* above Gennes had been completely cut off from the rest by the barrage. Climbing along the trunks of the uprooted trees slanting from the street to the summit of this isolated spot, the Barraux reached the top of the hillside opposite their house. Lying among the rocks and ruins were the bodies of two cadets who had been trapped there."

"And one of them was Bruno?"

"Yes, one of them was Bruno."

Again Constance bowed her head and covered her face with her hands. It was a long time before she trusted herself to speak. Finally she asked, "And afterwards—was there 'a worthy sepulcher'?"

"Yes, my daughter. I buried him myself. Where he had fallen. As he would have wished to be buried. As you yourself will feel most meet when God has comforted you in your grief and time has done its healing work."

"Can any mother be comforted who has lost both her sons within a few weeks of each other?"

"Yes. Through God's goodness and the merciful healing of time, as I have just said. But I did not know you had lost your elder son too. Surely Bruno did not know it either, or he would have told me."

"No. I'm thankful he didn't. I'm thankful he was spared that."

"He has been spared a great deal—perhaps as much as he has given. And he has given unstintingly, not only in his death but throughout his life. Perhaps the day will come, madame, when you can take comfort in that too—in that and in the knowledge that he and his comrades did not die in vain. Do not think of Saumur, madame, as marking the end of the French defeat. Think of it as marking the beginning of the French resistance. If you reflect, I am sure you will see I am right in calling it that. Meanwhile, is there nothing else that will give you solace?"

He waited patiently for her answer, knowing it would be hard for her to find one. But at last she said haltingly: "Yes. I have not heard from my husband in a long while, but the last time I did hear, he was still safe and well. And my daughter-in-law, my elder son's widow, has hopes of a child."

"You see. I do not minimize the reasons for your grief, my daughter. But I beg you not to minimize the reasons for your thankfulness either."

The priest rose and carefully replaced the little stool where he had found it, under the rustic table. Then once again he put his hand into his capacious pocket, and this time he kept it there while he went on talking to her.

"Now that I have told you my story and delivered your son's belongings safely into your hands, I must leave you, madame," he said. "But before I go I should like to make you a small present. I learned from Bruno that you have no lilies in your garden, and he seemed to take great pleasure in mine. I have brought you some bulbs of *Lilium regale* and also some of *Lilium pardalinum*. I should have liked to bring you a Charles Tenth also, for it is very beautiful. But it is one with which beginners have the least success because it does not pollinate easily. Besides, the *Lilium pardalinum* seems to me especially appropriate for a gift to you, as it is American of origin. According to Woodcock, an authority I often consult, it is the popular lily of Oregon and California, where it is called the leopard lily or panther lily." He pronounced the English words slowly and carefully, repeating them for emphasis. "I had planned to produce lilies from these bulbs out of season, for my altar, by planting them in pots," he went on. "But instead, I should like you to have them for your garden. Put them in the ground during October, and next June or July you will have a profusion of beautiful lilies. Perhaps they will be a symbol to you."

He withdrew his hand from his pocket, and once more he placed a packet in her hand, this time one that was knobby and somewhat earthy, though it too was carefully wrapped. Constance looked down at it with misty eyes.

"I don't know how to thank you," she said brokenly. "For these and—for everything. But you don't have to go right away, do you? Why, you haven't been to the house at all! Surely you'll come there with me, you'll let me offer you some refreshment after your long journey."

The priest shook his head. "I must lose no time in starting on my village-to-village journey," he said. "My people were glad to have me come here, but they will be needing me back. I would have gone on to the château, of course, if I had not found you here. But Chess bounded through the arch, and I followed him. It is probably better this way in any case. I understand that you have 'guests' at Malou, and it is just as well that they should not see me. Of course I have obeyed all regulations to the letter. However, I should not care to invite an argument on the subject."

For the first time he smiled slightly, and his hands strayed to the dog's head. "I shall miss Chess very much," he said. "But I know he should be at Malou with you, and not at Milly-le-Meugon with me. I am afraid there may be troublous times ahead before the France your two sons have died for again proves herself worthy of such sacrifices. You may have need of a good watchdog, madame. A village curé can always look out for himself."

Chess had ceased to doze and risen to his haunches, his head uplifted, his eyes fixed on the priest. "You will stay here, Chess, and take good care of your mistress," the priest said quietly, as if he were speaking to a human being. "Your mistress and her aged aunt and her young daughter-in-law and the new baby when it comes. Of all her household too, and all her lands. I am depending on you to guard them until her husband's return. And someday I myself shall return, to see that you have done well." He took his hands off the dog's head and raised them in benediction. "Let me give you my blessing, my daughter, before I leave," he continued. "In my prayers I shall remember you always."

Chess had watched the priest out of sight, but he had not attempted to follow, and in the weeks that had elapsed since then, he had hardly left Constance's side. Today he had been peacefully dozing for a long while, but now he stretched out his great paws languidly and lifted his head. He did not growl or bristle this time, he seemed only to be alert and attentive, and presently he began to wag his tail. It beat back and forth on the bricks, making a cheerful sound. Constance looked in the direction towards which he had turned his head and saw that Margot had come through the archway and was sauntering down the walk in the general direction of her mother-in-law.

Nothing about her approach suggested urgency. She was smoking a cigarette, flicking the ashes into the flowerpots as she came along, and stopping to inspect the wide strawberry beds, now well covered with a golden thatch, and the espaliered peaches and pears ripening against the mellow wall. She looked very lovely. Her hair was lightly confined in a shoulder-length net attached to a fillet, which hid none of its beauty, but gave the impression of deft and careful arrangement which her disordered curls had formerly lacked. The brilliant color in her cheeks glowed beneath her tan, which she never appeared to lose, and which tinted her neck and arms to a warm and delicate brown.

Though she walked so slowly, this manner of progress seemed the result of pleasant leisure rather than a burdensome lassitude. Her figure showed no change as yet, except that her hips and bosom were a little more rounded than they had been when she married, and this slight fullness was very becoming. She was dressed completely in white, which she had worn about the house and grounds for some time now. She went to Mass in her widow's veil and the other somber garments which were considered suitable, and she returned all formal visits of condolence attired in the same way; her appearance and bearing on such occasions had been impeccable by all French standards. But though she had not discussed the subject, she had obviously decided to make no further concessions to traditional mourning customs, and Constance was secretly glad that this was the case. She would have liked to tell Margot she too felt that a girl who had been Nick's bride and who had conceived his child must, even in bereavement, be still so impregnated with his vitality that she could not appropriately shroud herself in crape.

"Good morning," Margot said pleasantly when she was close enough to speak without raising her voice. "It's a very nice day, isn't it?"

Constance, who had not previously noticed the weather, agreed, with some surprise, that it was. Margot sat down on the bench beside her, patted Chess, and went on smoking quietly.

"Were you doing anything special?" she asked at length. "Or were you just sitting here thinking?"

"I'm afraid I was just sitting here thinking."

Margot opened her large dark eyes a little wider. "Isn't it all right just to sit and think sometimes?" she inquired with evident interest.

"Yes, of course. But there's so much to be done——"

"Maybe you'll feel more like doing it after you've sat still for a while. . . . Were you thinking about Bruno?"

"Yes, mostly. I was trying to do what the Abbé said—to think of Saumur not as the end of the French defeat, but as the beginning of the French resistance. It's been easier since I've heard De Gaulle's great challenge on the radio. I know now what the Abbé meant. Besides, you see, Chess came and got me. . . . But I was thinking about Nick too, and about their father. I used to say that the bond between us was so close that it couldn't be affected by silence or separation. I thought it was true when I said it. Now I try to think so, but I don't always succeed. If I could hear something, Margot, from my husband, no matter what——"

Margot nodded. "I know. I felt that way about Nick. And then when I did hear something, I heard he was dead. As long as you haven't heard that——"

"My husband told me before he left not to believe it even if I did hear he was dead."

"And you wouldn't?"

"I'd try not to."

"Well then, as long as you believe he's alive——"

"Yes. Yes. I have a great deal to be thankful for, being able to believe that he's alive. I know that, Margot."

Neither of them added, aloud, that as long as she could believe Tristan was alive, she should be able to live with greater resignation to her lot than Margot, who knew that Nick was dead. Margot continued to smoke in silence for a few minutes more and then she asked another question.

"You said Chess came and got you. You meant just the way he always does, don't you?"

"Yes. But when we got here, I found one of the soldiers at the *lavoir* with Aylette. They were very much preoccupied—though not with laundry work. And it was just as if Chess had tried——"

"Well, perhaps he did. Not that he'd know they were whoring. But probably they'd been up to something else—pilfering maybe."

"Perhaps. I hadn't thought of that. I ordered them both out of my sight, and I told Aylette that henceforth the washing would all be done in the laundry at the château. That's as far as I've gone for the moment. Of course I'd like to get Aylette off the place, but I don't see how I can, for several reasons. Even taking the laundry away from her is going to make things pretty hard for Blondine and Nicole. However, I can't have this garden used for—well, I think the word you used is the only one that expresses it."

"Whoring?" Margot repeated unhesitatingly. "No, I can see how you'd feel about that. It probably goes on in the commons all the time, and naturally you wouldn't be very happy about that either. But after all, a bitch is a bitch, and what she does in her own little bitch house is a shade more her business than what she does elsewhere about the premises." Margot paused and smiled faintly. "Of course your generation thinks all the girls in this generation are more or less bitchy, don't you? But you'll grant there are degrees. And even I think Aylette is very, very bitchy. She isn't even choosy about it either."

Constance looked at Margot with increased attention, in which a strange new tenderness was oddly mingled.

"It will be very tough on Pierre when he finds out," Margot went on. "Of course he will find out, sooner or later. He might even be getting home before long. Dad told me the last time I saw him that the Germans had decided to release a certain number of *cultivateurs* among the prisoners, because they wanted farming to go on, for their own sakes, and of course Pierre would come under that classification. If he walked in unexpectedly some night, there would be all kinds of hell to pay. As I just said, Aylette isn't even choosy. And it is very tough on Lucie already. She is a nice little kid. It seems as if we ought to be able to dream up something to do for her, if we put our minds to it. Not that I ever had much of a mind. But I ought to have that much."

"I have never thought there was anything the matter with your mind, Margot."

"Really?" inquired Margot. "I felt you thought something was the matter with everything about me." She spoke entirely without animosity, simply as if she were stating a mildly interesting fact, and the vague impression, which had been slowly growing on Constance, that Margot's antagonism to her was a thing of the past suddenly acquired new force. "Not that you were so very far wrong," Margot continued. "I was a brat from the beginning. I can't imagine why Nick should have been so crazy about me. But he was," she concluded triumphantly.

"I know that, my dear. I know he loved you with all his heart and soul."

"Well, I was crazy about him too. And he knew that before it was too late, even if he didn't know about the baby. . . . Listen, why should we be so sure he doesn't know about the baby? No one's ever found out, for sure, how much dead people know, have they?"

"No, my dear."

"Well, then I don't see what's to stop me from believing he knows, any more than I see what's to stop you from believing Commandant de Fremond's still alive. I'm going to believe it. I do believe it. . . . What do you think I found this morning?"

"I can't imagine. Were you looking for something this morning?"

"No, I found this without even looking. I went up to the attic, you see, to make sure the portraits were all right. I met that stuffed shirt of a colonel as I was coming through the fort, and he told me, in a very pained way, that you had declined to go and see what beautiful care he was taking of your prized possessions. I told *him,* in a slightly different way, that I could understand why the mistress of Malou might feel she was entitled to be consulted about the *kind* of care he was taking of her things, and that her natural resentment might make an exploring expedition under the eaves distasteful to her. However, I said that I would be very pleased to go to the attic with him. I checked over all the portraits, and really it is just as he said—they've all been nicely propped up and protected with wadding. As far as I can tell, Commandant de Fremond's papers are all in order too. I took the cartons into my dressing room. I thought maybe you'd come there and go through them some evening. Perhaps I could help you."

"Thank you, Margot. Thank you very much—for everything."

She was tremendously moved. She did not dare try to say more at the moment. But she stretched out her hand and took Margot's, and as she did so, she noticed how the two betrothal rings, the old and the new, which were identical in design, glittered alike in the sunshine. They were also now wearing two other rings which were identical—the gold signet rings, called *chevalières,* engraved with the de Fremond family arms, which had belonged to Nick and Bruno. Bruno's had been among the personal possessions which the curé of Milly had brought to her, and Nick's had been sent to Margot in the same packet which contained the letter from the captain of his regiment, telling her that Nick had been among the two hundred drowned when the *Douaisien* was bombed and sunk in the retreat from Dunkirk.

"You haven't asked me what I found, Mother."

It was the first time that Margot had ever called her Mother. She was even more moved than before, but this time she managed to answer, quietly though briefly. "No, I forgot to, because—— What did you find, Margot?"

"I found a cradle, a beautiful old carved cradle. And a funny little old wooden trunk, painted with apples and birds and stuffed full of baby clothes—queer little caps, ridiculous linen shirts, dresses with long lacy ruffles. Didn't you know they were there?"

"Yes. I knew they were there. But I never used them. You see Nick and Bruno weren't born at Malou. Nick was born in Saumur and Bruno was born in the American Hospital at Neuilly. So they had modern things— iron cribs, practical clothes. Except for the christening dress. We did use the old christening dress. That isn't with the other things."

"I'm going to use that and all the other things too," Margot announced. "After all, my baby is going to be born at Malou. Modern things wouldn't be suitable here. I don't think Nick would want me to use them. I've taken the cradle and the little trunk into my dressing room too. I hope you don't mind. I thought we could look the things over together and plan. It would be fun. I never saw anything like them before. And of course I didn't know they were there. Probably St. Anthony helped me find them. You know, I've just had another thought. I'm doing pretty well for me, two or three thoughts all in the same day, besides finding the clothes and the cradle. I might name the baby after St. Anthony, in gratitude—Antoine de Padoue de Fremond. We could call him Padoue for short. That would be a nice name for a baby, don't you think so, Mother?"

CHAPTER XXX

"*Grand'mère* writes that wolves have already been seen in the forest at Fontainebleau. That means a long cold winter. We're lucky, having so much wood."

"Yes, but we're using a good deal too. Or rather our guests are. If they keep on at their present rate, I don't know how we'll manage."

"We'll let the furnace fire out and have us one airtight, in your study.

There are plenty of airtights, such as they are, in the cellar. I presume you put them there when you opened up the fireplace and installed the central heating, as you call it. Of course not any one of them's big enough to make a hall bedroom really comfortable, but that's how we'll manage, at least till Margot's time comes, and if we start in saving right away, we won't have any lack then."

Margot, Connie, and Aunt Bertha were just finishing their supper, lingering over it a little according to the pleasant habit which they had striven to maintain. To Constance, the absence of Tristan's desk was still an aching void, and the knowledge of the use to which it had been put added perpetually to her pain. But to the others, the little sitting room still seemed cozy and homelike. With her characteristic skill in such matters, Constance had achieved an attractive rearrangement of the furniture. For the stationary center table, which Colonel von Reden had lauded to her in vain, she had substituted one with gatelegs and drop leaves, which was among the heirlooms Aunt Bertha had brought with her from Winchester; when not in use, this was folded against the wall, thus leaving enough space for the three women to sit and move about at ease. With determination, she had also continued a semblance of the evening's occupations which had been customary to Tristan and herself. She and Margot took turns in reading aloud, and they had both learned to knit. Aunt Bertha made buttonholes and did endless featherstitching on the baby clothes which, as far as seams were concerned, she "ran up" on the faithful Singer during the day. She had admired Margot's "find" no less than the girl herself, but she had insisted that for everyday something more practical than the yard-long dresses must be supplied, and the others had agreed with her, Constance readily, Margot reluctantly. She was now making "gertrudes" to her heart's content, and secretly counting the days before she would see these put to use.

"Those men make a sight more noise than they did before Colonel von Reden left," she now observed, holding her latest creation nearer to the light to get a better look at it. "Does it bother you, Connie? Do you want I should go in and say something to them?"

"No, it wouldn't be any use. Remember what happened with the radio."

None of them had forgotten, nor was likely to forget, this episode. When the Germans took over the large drawing room, they installed a radio there, supplementing the one in Tristan's office which they had already appropriated, and made use of this new instrument not only while they were eating their meals, but long afterwards, and not only for the reception of news, but for all sorts of noisy and raucous programs. Constance was making a more and more definite effort to avoid encounters with her unwelcome tenants, and to a greater and greater degree was successful in this; but inevitably she ran into them from time to time, and on one such occasion Leinmeister had asked her whether she objected to the new radio.

"Naturally I have no objections to a radio as such," she had replied frigidly. "I miss my own very much. But apparently you get more enjoyment out of it, over long periods, than I do, and apparently you do not care for the same type of music. Yesterday the new radio was turned on, uninterruptedly, at high volume from seven in the evening until one in the morning. As you know, my bedroom is directly over the large drawing room which you have appropriated. Naturally I was not able to get any sleep while there was such a racket. I would be most appreciative if you would turn the radio off before midnight."

Leinmeister had bowed in the usual formal fashion, and assured her that her wishes would have every consideration. The following evening the radio was turned on at six and kept on all night, and the Germans sang in accompaniment to the brassy music and guffawed with laughter at every vulgar joke in the comic dialogues. Also, for the first time, women's voices were mingled with the men's, and from then on such schedules had been the rule rather than the exception.

Aunt Bertha was right in saying that conditions had been much worse since the departure of Colonel von Reden. On Constance's return to the château after the disgraceful scene she had witnessed in the garden, she had sent word to him by Léon that she would like to see him immediately, and he had responded without delay to her summons. After listening gravely to her complaint, he assured her that disorderly conduct was not tolerated in his command, that the guilty soldier would be punished, and that this punishment would be sufficiently severe to serve as a warning to all the others. As for Aylette—— He had not finished speaking when Constance noticed that his voice was more than formal, it was abnormally repressed; and looking at him more attentively, she saw that the ruddy color had been drained from his face, leaving an unnatural grayish pallor, and that he was gripping the back of a chair against which he was leaning.

"Colonel von Reden, are you ill?" she asked, startled into reluctant concern.

"I beg your pardon, Baroness. I did not mean to mention it. But within the last few days I have had several attacks which, knowing something of such matters, I believe to indicate appendicitis. When you sent for me, I had just been seized with another attack, considerably more severe than its predecessors."

"But if you're ill——"

"I beg you not to let the incident affect you in the least, Baroness. I have already sent to the Clinique de la Providence in Lisieux, which, as you know, we have now taken over, for an ambulance and a surgeon, and I have also telephoned to General Headquarters for an officer to replace me, in case the surgeon confirms my suspicions and I myself am temporarily obliged to turn over my command to someone else. Nevertheless, you may be very sure that before I leave Malou I shall see that the conditions concerning which you so justly complained are rectified. I also assure you that I shall leave here with regret, and that at the earliest possible moment I shall return to assure myself that my policies have prevailed during my absence."

Within half an hour the ambulance had arrived, and shortly after Lieutenant Leinmeister reported to Constance that the surgeon had more than confirmed the Colonel's suspicions, and that the latter was in a serious condition, as the appendix had burst before it was possible to operate. The Colonel's aide-de-camp and orderly had left in the ambulance with him, but late that same evening Leinmeister returned to the study and said he had been apprised that the new command would be arranged by the following day, and that meanwhile he himself had been placed in charge. Neither his first visit nor his second seemed to present an appropriate moment for the discussion of discipline, and Constance decided that she would await the arrival of another superior officer without making further complaint. When this functionary arrived, however, she immediately regretted her procrastination. He was a captain named Pfaff, with a face which was both weak and vicious, and a manner so insolent, even when unprovoked, that she realized instinctively the extreme unwisdom of irritating him. After all, if von Reden made a reasonably quick recovery, Pfaff's tenure of authority might be comparatively brief. It would be better to go on temporizing. . . .

Though Pfaff had no aide-de-camp and no orderly, he brought with him, for some unexplained reason, two more lieutenants and several noncommissioned officers, and after a brief inspection of the château, stated that it would be necessary to take over the third-floor suite in order to supply sufficient sleeping accommodations. Accordingly, Aunt Bertha and Margot hurriedly vacated this, and from then on all three slept in Constance's bedroom, with Chess beside them, and all three used her study for ordinary daytime activities. So far, they had managed to reserve the little downstairs sitting room for their hours of relaxation, and except for the noise which invaded it from the large drawing room, its atmosphere remained peaceful, while in spite of its lacking space it seemed agreeably uncluttered. But the Germans were growing noisier and noisier all the time, and the disturbance was becoming more and more nerve-racking. The three women themselves, all deprived of accustomed privacy, were finding it harder and harder not to get in each other's way and to avoid being annoyed at times by each other's continual presence.

"Perhaps they won't be here much longer," Margot said, trying to speak hopefully. She had noticed that Constance winced a little every time the noise became suddenly and inexplicably louder; the girl had observed the same silent flinching whenever a formation of British bombers, presumably bound for Italy or Germany, went roaring over the château. Since August this had occurred at frequent intervals, and the French had coined a new word for the sound the bombers made; they called it *vrombissement*. Margot was intrigued by the word and she exulted in the sound; but she guessed that, for some reason, these phases of the occupation were among the hardest for her mother-in-law to bear. "I overheard something about Yugoslavia as I was going through the fort yesterday. This detachment has been here more than two months now—that is, the original part of it. Don't the Germans make a practice of moving the various units around from one part of their occupied territory to another?"

"I don't know. Let's hope so. Except that if this detachment left, another would probably be quartered on us. And we don't know what that would be like. The additions and replacements to this one are certainly a lot worse than the original group. Colonel von Reden was a martinet, but on the whole we benefited by that. Pfaff is just a——"

Before she could complete her sentence, her words were drowned out by shouts, clapping, and stamping in the adjoining room. She pressed her lips together without trying to go on. Again Margot looked at her searchingly.

"Why don't you go to bed, Mother?" she asked kindly. "You've put in a big day. You must be awfully tired."

"I can hear the noise almost as clearly upstairs as I can downstairs. Besides, we haven't done any reading yet. If we once stopped, we'd find it all the harder to go on."

"We could read upstairs. You could get into bed and I could sit beside you and read."

"Yes, we could. But it always seems more natural to me to read here. Besides, the fire's going so nicely it seems too bad to start another, and we'd be terribly cold without one."

"I guess I'm going to side with your mother-in-law this time," interposed Aunt Bertha. "We've got to think of the fuel. What's more, we've got to think about not losing our gumption. Once a body starts losing gumption——"

"I haven't lost my gumption, Aunt Bertha. I'd like to stay here. I was just thinking that if it would be any easier for Mother——"

Margot rose and went around the table. She still looked very lovely; her color had remained bright and clear and her carriage assured. She put her arm over the back of Constance's chair and then let it slide down until it rested on her mother-in-law's shoulders. Aunt Bertha took off her glasses and wiped them carefully. Afterwards she put them back on again, adjusting them with precision.

"I never said you had," she remarked with her slight snort. "It doesn't look to me as if you were going to either. I just said we mustn't, that's all. It wasn't you I had in mind. Lie still, Chess. Do you want I should find your place for you, Constance?"

There was certainly no doubt about it, the gatherings in the drawing room were getting noisier and noisier. Moreover, women's voices increasingly mingled with the men's, though the women themselves were nowhere in evidence around the place during the day and Constance had no certain knowledge of who they were. But there were other signs, beside the uproarious parties, that discipline was relaxed. The transformed dining room, which had formerly been kept in such a spotless state, was now disorderly in every sense of the word. Official documents were scattered haphazardly over the table, cigarette stubs and wastepaper littered the floor, and extra armchairs had been brought in so that the office workers would be more continually at their ease. They would not permit any of the house servants to come in and clean, saying they preferred to have their own men attend to that part of the work; but their own men, it appeared, were always otherwise occupied. Constance dreaded to go through the dining room on her way to the kitchen, and she did so

285

less and less, summoning Blondine to her instead; but there was also less and less she needed to say to Blondine.

They were not going hungry, but their meals increasingly lacked variety, and one by one the delicacies which had made these distinctive and appetizing were disappearing. If the men of Malou had been allowed to use their guns, game would have been forthcoming, and this would have been most welcome; however, the use of every sort of firearm was still strictly forbidden to the French, even for purposes of supplying provender, and the Germans apparently did not care for the type of sport the Norman countryside afforded, or mind monotony in their diet. Blondine worked early and late without complaint, and she accomplished wonders with what was available; but she was losing her buxom looks and bustling manner, her jovial earthiness and garrulity. She was beginning to seem like an old woman. Constance did not know her age, for Blondine was peculiarly coy when approached on that subject; nevertheless her mistress felt that she could not be far from seventy. Of course Aunt Bertha was much older than that, and Aunt Bertha, who had always been wiry, was beginning to look withered instead. Constance worried about the two aged women, wondering how well their lessened vitality would withstand the long grim months that lay ahead.

For it was already getting very cold, and this was only November. Wood from Malou's own forests had long since been the only fuel on the place, and the Germans were using this recklessly, keeping huge open fires going in every part of the house which they occupied. Constance watched the diminishing supplies with apprehension. At the rate the Germans were using the wood, it would be all gone before February—and in February Margot's baby would be born. Mindful of the results of her mild protest about the radio, Constance was uncertain whether or not she should attempt another on the subject of the fuel; but at last she did so, feeling that she must take a desperate chance because the need for conservation was so urgent.

Pfaff hardly listened to her. All the time she was talking he kept making irrelevant remarks to Leinmeister, who was seated across the dining-room table from him, and drawing designs on the topmost paper of the untidy pile sprawling in front of him. Once or twice Constance paused, thinking that if she stopped abruptly, the interruption might serve as a signal for more attention. Pfaff did not appear to notice the difference, but continued his sketching and his small talk. At last, with a yawn which he did not attempt to conceal, he told her she had better take up the subject with his successor; he himself had just received welcome orders for a transfer, and, with his officers and men, would be leaving Malou within the next day or two.

She watched the preparations for departure with rising spirits. Blondine, coming to confer with her mistress about the simple family meals, which required no consultation, added that orders had been given for a feast in the drawing room that night—the turkey she had been saving for Christmas and which was not yet even properly fattened, a great pastry which would deplete the fast-diminishing supply of white flour, a charlotte which would use up the cream they needed for butter. She spoke about these different dishes belligerently, and ended by saying that the *cave* would suffer even more than the larder and that it was a sin and a shame.

"Well, after all, Blondine, if it's the end of the occupation—— We can be thankful for that, anyway."

Her thankfulness that this was the end increased as the hideous night wore on. The farewell celebration began with the early dusk and continued until the late dawn, and the usual sounds of hilarity, which had been growing steadily louder and grosser, were punctuated by other noises, even more ominous and alarming. Every now and then there was a loud crash, indicating that china or furniture was being broken, and occasionally this was preceded by a pistol shot which suggested that deliberate aim was being taken at some object singled out for destruction. Constance managed to suppress the scream which tore at her throat every time this happened, but she could not control the feeling of mounting horror and dread for what the daylight would disclose. She had hardly slept at all when a loud rap on her door roused her abruptly from her first drowsiness. She leapt up, flinging a dressing gown about her, and speaking in a soothing voice to Chess, who had immediately begun to bristle and growl. Before she could cross the room, the knocking began again, with redoubled violence, and accompanied by a stern command to lock up the dog in the bathroom.

"You've got to mind what they say," Aunt Bertha muttered warningly. "If you don't, they'll batter down that door and they'll shoot Chess. I'd say different if you could stop them from coming in. But you can't."

"I know. I'm trying to be as quick as I can."

Constance was obliged to drag Chess bodily into the bathroom; for the first time since his adoption he violently resisted her orders and struggled against her. She had hardly bolted the door which confined him when the other gave way under the blows rained upon it. The ancient locks of Malou were massive and imposing, but they were rusty and cracked with age; for a long time they had been ornamental rather than serviceable, and since the recent need for greater security had arisen, replacements had been unobtainable. Pfaff and Leinmeister, both unshaven and disheveled and both obviously still under the influence of liquor, now burst into the room.

"We have come to bid you farewell, *gnädige Frau,*" Pfaff announced in a high falsetto voice. "You and your charming daughter-in-law and your venerable aunt." He made a mock bow, very different from the customary stiff salute, in the direction of each, tittering as he did so. "It is not our intention to prolong this leave-taking," he went on, with another silly giggle, "but I must ask you to comply with one slight formality. I am sure you will be delighted to do this, considering how little we are asking of you."

"I'm afraid you'll have to tell me what it is first."

For greater warmth, Constance and Margot were now sleeping together in the alcove, with Aunt Bertha in the day bed, which had been drawn up close beside it. Margot had the place next to the wall, and she was lying on her side, facing this, when the Germans came in. Constance did not know whether the girl was really asleep, or whether she was only pretending to be, but if the latter were the case, the pretense was a good one. She herself had hurried back towards the alcove, and was now standing beside it, with as much dignity as she could command under the trying circumstances. Aunt Bertha was already sitting bolt upright in her narrow bed, a grim figure in her drab flannel nightgown, her thin gray hair drawn away from her scalp in short tight little braids. She peered intently first at her niece and then at the drunken officers.

"Something very slight, I assure you," Pfaff hiccoughed. "Merely to sign a paper saying that we are leaving your charming château in the same state of excellent order as that in which we found it."

"But you aren't. You're leaving it in very bad order."

"*Gnädige Frau,* I am surprised that you should make such an unjust charge. Surprised and greatly pained. Are you not also greatly surprised and pained, Lieutenant Leinmeister?"

The Lieutenant attempted an affirmative reply, but it was swallowed in a convulsive gulp. After several such gulps he began to retch, and presently he vomited on the Aubusson carpet. Without paying any further attention to him, Captain Pfaff extended a soiled paper in the direction of Constance.

"I have made everything very simple for the *gnädige Frau,*" he announced. "The place where she is to sign is designated with a check mark. I can even lend her a fountain pen, if that will facilitate matters."

"If you will leave this room, I will dress and join you downstairs within ten minutes. Then I will go with you through the rooms you have occupied and see exactly what condition you have left them in. Then I will sign a statement describing this."

"I am desolated, *gnädige Frau,* but it would be impossible for me to wait so long. We are already a little later than we planned in getting started."

"Would ten minutes make such a difference?"

"*Ach,* but it is not only a question of the time it would take the *gnädige Frau* to dress! Not that I have ever known a lady to dress in ten minutes, above all a French lady, or one French through choice and adoption. That '*toute petite seconde*' of France, how well we have learned to recognize it as representing long, wasted hours!—hours which, *Gott sei dank,* facilitated our victory. . . . I am referring also to the length of time it would take us to make a tour of this extensive château. I assure the *gnädige Frau* that I myself have made a careful inspection, and that everything is in perfect order. If she will sign now it will save us both time and trouble. Or, if that is not agreeable, suppose she rouses her lovely daughter-in-law. If the young Baroness will accompany us in her present déshabille, we will agree to delay our departure for the sake of having her as our cicerone."

Aunt Bertha's gimletlike gaze was now fixed full upon her niece. She had not spoken again, but Constance knew what her warning would have been if she had. And she herself did not need this. She took the soiled piece of paper which Pfaff had continued to flutter in her face all the time he was talking, and signed it in the place where he had made a wavering indication. He pocketed it and, with a lingering leer, moved away from the alcove, linking his arm through Leinmeister's. Together they lurched out of the room, walking straight through the foul mess which Leinmeister had made on the floor. When the door finally closed behind them, Aunt Bertha swung her lean legs over the side of the day bed and rose.

"This is the first time in my life I ever advised anyone to submit to browbeating from a brute," she said, and her voice was shamed and sad. "Let alone as good as told a truthful woman to commit perjury. But there wasn't any choice. You know that too, Constance. You did the right thing, but I know it was the hard thing. You get back into bed and lie still for a minute, you and Margot the both of you, while I get me a cloth to clean up this filth on the floor. No, don't say a word. I'll feel better for getting some of the spleen out of my system. Afterwards we'll all have a cup of something hot before we look around to see how much lying those Huns have made you do. I've got some coffee, if you can call it that, here in the thermos, same as usual."

She would rather go alone on her tour of inspection, Constance said, and Aunt Bertha and Margot both understood. After all, this was her home, far more essentially than it was theirs; it was she who had rescued it from desuetude and made it a dwelling place of light. They had come later, profiting by her love and her labor; their grief over its desecration could not be as deep or as poignant as hers. They sat in the study and tried to talk to each other of inconsequential things while she went on her desolate pilgrimage.

In Margot's quarters, and in the boys' room and the guest room, which she visited first, she found nothing worse than dirt and disorder, battered chairs overturned, pictures askew on the walls, small ornaments broken, misplaced, or inexplicably missing. The bathrooms were inexcusably foul, but fresh air and scrubbing would remedy that in a few days. (Fresh air there was, of course, in plenty. But soap for so much scrubbing? Well, she would have to see. . . .) She was indignant, she was revolted, but there was nothing in these sections of the château nor in the dining room to turn the knife in the wound which had long throbbed with a dull ache. However, when she opened the door of the drawing room, which some warning instinct had made her leave till the last, she recoiled, unable this time to stifle the cry which rose to her lips. Then she entered it slowly and sank down, looking about her with increasing anguish.

To serve half a dozen persons, nearly all the precious porcelain of Malou had apparently been pressed into use—the dinner sets which Tristan's mother and grandmother had brought there as brides, and which had been carefully kept intact; the much older pieces representing similar equipment for several preceding chatelaines; the service plates which Constance herself had assembled a few at a time; the priceless Capo di Monte which the Craigs had given her on the twentieth anniversary of her marriage. And all of it had been smashed into thousands of pieces. The ruin did not represent accidental breakage, it represented wanton destruction. Generous platters, fragile cups, delicate epergnes—all had suffered the same fate. The jagged bits, the crumbling scraps, which constituted their pitiful remains were scattered over the stained tablecloth, ground into the carpet, strewn about the hearth, among cracked bottles from which vintage wines still dripped, showing that they had been cast aside from sheer repletion.

But this was only the beginning of the wreckage. The glass doors of the cabinets had all been shattered and so had their contents; each ornament lay in a small separate heap, suggesting that it might have been the target at which the pistol shots, reverberating through the night, had been aimed. The exquisite "lace"-clad dancer which Gwen had sent from Vitoria, the bibelots and bonbon boxes which generations of de Fremonds had cherished, were only little pieces of coarse powder now. The Sèvres vases which had stood on the mantelpiece, their graceful necks snapped, were propped up together, in a grotesque position, between the folds of a brocade curtain. A marble statuette of the Virgin had been hacked to fit a magnum of champagne.

The systematic destruction of the porcelain was reflected in the general condition of the room. The petit-point upholstery had been ripped open; the draperies had long jagged cuts in them; the portraits depicting French officers had been cut from their frames and laid on the floor in a manner intended to simulate corpses. The women's portraits had suffered still greater indignities. In some instances mustaches and beards had been added to the faces, apparently with a blackened poker, for there were signs of scorching too; in others the eyes had been gouged out, the décolletage outlined to a point of indecency, and obscene words scrawled across the hips.

For a few moments Constance sat looking about her, the feeling that she was in the grip of some dreadful nightmare growing stronger and stronger as she gazed. Finally, feeling that the very act of remaining in such surroundings was too loathsome for endurance, she rose and walked towards the kitchen. There, at least, would be warmth from the hearth and work going on and a vigorous reassuring presence, not the cold and emptiness and terrible futility of a room which for centuries had epitomized culture and hospitality and gracious living.

On the threshold of the great folding doors, she stopped short. For the first time in all the years she had lived at Malou, the crucifix was missing from the mantelshelf and the fire beneath this was dead. The black andirons rose above gray ashes, and at their base lay the stark forms of four cats. Blondine was sitting alone at the great table, her stocky form shaken with sobs, the apron which covered her head muffling but not silencing these. Her stout spirit had not been strong enough to surmount her sorrow; she was not only bowed by grief, she was engulfed by it. She did not even hear the approach of her chatelaine.

"Blondine," Constance said brokenly. "Blondine, *écoute*."

The old cook whipped down her apron and struggled to her feet. Her hair was in wild disorder, her round face bloated from weeping, her blue eyes bleary with tears. She swallowed hard and looked from her mistress to the empty place on the mantelshelf where the crucifix had stood, and then down at the bodies of her dead pets.

"The wicked men defiled our Lord," she said in a strangled voice. "Oh, Madame la Baronne, if you but knew! . . . And then they said—they said that one of my cats had scratched a soldier and they shot him, my poor Minette, my poor Nanine, all of them, one after another!"

"But the wicked men are gone, Blondine. Let's try to think of that. They won't do us any more harm. I'm terribly shaken, terribly unhappy too. When you see the drawing room—— I want you to come there with me presently, and help me with it. But first, let's sit still, side by side, for a moment and try to comfort each other."

She pulled out a second chair and seated herself, drawing Blondine down in the one beside her and holding fast to the old woman's gnarled hand. She did not try to speak immediately. But her thoughts were coming more clearly now, her courage was returning. When she did find strength to go on with what she wanted to say, it was not hard to find the words after all.

"Listen, Blondine," she said. "Mademoiselle Berthe is very old, almost old enough to be your mother. She does not realize that she cannot work hard any more, that she is failing very fast, and when I try to tell her so, I hurt her feelings without doing any good. And Madame Nick is getting near her time. She is strong and she is eager; but she must not be overtaxed either, or it may harm the little one whose coming is to bring us all such joy. Nicole will do her best, and Lise. But their hands are full already elsewhere. We cannot count on them to help us overmuch. So it is you and I who should share and surmount the work here. And we can do it if we help each other. I know you will never fail me and I will never fail you either. You know that too, don't you, Blondine?"

"Yes, Madame la Baronne, I know that all you say is true. I know we must work together and share the burden, and I know you will never fail me. The knowledge means much to me. But it does not bring my poor cats back to life. Perhaps you will tell me that it is better the cats should have been killed than Chess, and I know that is true too. A cat is not an important animal like a dog, and especially is there no comparison between cats that have belonged to me and a dog that belonged to Monsieur Bruno. But my pets were such company to me! They gave such *cachet* to my kitchen! They looked so beautiful, all black against the red flames!"

Blondine's voice was firm when she began to speak, but now it had begun to quaver again. Constance pressed the gnarled hand hard.

"It is very sad," she said tenderly. She did not minimize Blondine's grief; she shared it. But she also strove to relieve it. "Let us cover these poor kitties gently until we can take them out and bury them in garden graves," she said. "Four of them are dead, as you say. But, Blondine, Frou-frou is not among the victims! She must have eluded the killers, with the cunning that comes to all mothers when they need to defend their young. Some day, very soon, she will come to us proudly, bringing her new family to show us."

Blondine looked again at her dead cats, more searchingly this time, and then back at her mistress with a new glimmer in her old eyes. "*En effet,* Madame la Baronne, Froufrou has escaped," she said. "And to think it was you who noticed that, not I!"

"She will teach the new kittens to bask in the good firelight which must never die down again," Constance said encouragingly. "Let us get some sticks and rekindle the flames, before we do anything else. And let us start soup simmering, so there will be something to eat by and by when we are hungry again. After that we must go to the *grand salon* and start cleansing it. Who knows? The master of Malou might return this very night. We must at all times be in readiness for his coming. As for the Christ, He is with us always, even unto the end. The Germans could defile the crucifix that stood on your mantel, Blondine, and I know your grief for that is great, for it was very precious to you. But I will get you another to put in its place. Meanwhile, we do not need the symbol of His suffering to assure us of His presence. We have His own word for that."

CHAPTER XXXI

IT WAS HARD WORK, harder than any she had done in the garden. No weeding, no digging and spading could compare in backbreaking effort with this endless and monotonous scrubbing, into which all the greater effort must be put because the results were dependent so largely on what Aunt Bertha called elbow grease. Soap was getting scarcer and scarcer all the time; they were able to make a little of their own, but they also had to conserve the fats from the farm for cooking, and therefore they did not have much leeway. Though the shelves in the storerooms at Malou had been well stocked with reserve supplies, these had dwindled to almost nothing. It was necessary to scrub very hard in order to get the soiled surfaces clean, and, long before the gigantic task was finished, Constance felt as if she had been so thoroughly bruised and beaten that no fiber of her body had escaped punishment. With every stroke of her scrubbing brush in a foul toilet, with every cautious separation of one piece of broken porcelain from another, surges of hate rose again from her heart to her throat, strangling and suffocating her.

She did not work alone. Everyone helped. But what she had said to Blondine was all too true. Aunt Bertha's zeal for cleanliness, which had always been such a dominating characteristic, was no longer strong enough to overcome the waxing infirmities of her advancing age. She would scrub intensively for half an hour, only to be obliged afterwards to rest nearly all day, chafing and fretting under her enforced idleness. It required great tact and tenderness to keep her from rebelling against this. But fortunately her eyesight was still remarkably good, her skill with the needle still undiminished. Eventually Constance was able to persuade her that if anyone could repair the ravaged petit point she could, and after that she worked contentedly for hours at a time, using an embroidery frame and a magnifying glass, and viewing the results of her handiwork with pardonable pride every evening. Encouraged by success in this direction, Constance made a similar suggestion to Margot regarding the portraits. The offending beards and mustaches, the obscene inscriptions, could all be removed with care and turpentine. Probably only an expert could replace canvas that had been scorched or gouged out; on the other hand, where portraits had been cut clean from their frames, as in the case of the prostrate officers, perhaps these could be put back by pasting some supporting supplementary material underneath. Margot was no less pleased and proud than Aunt Bertha at being entrusted with so delicate a task, and with the results which she achieved. Every morning she began her cleansing and pasting with renewed enthusiasm; every evening she had something gratifying to show as a result of it.

None of this, however, lessened the labors which fell to the lot of Constance. Blondine protested at the sight of Madame la Baronne on her hands and knees, plunging and replunging a scrubbing brush into a pail of hot water, and bearing down harder and harder on the brush she moved over a soiled surface. She worked early and late, sturdily and willingly; but though the reasons for diverting her labors were different from those governing Aunt Bertha's and Margot's, they were none the less sound.

Within a fortnight after the departure of Pfaff and his minions, the interior of Malou had resumed a more or less normal appearance. Gerd von Reden, announcing himself one day in early December, was ushered into a drawing room which was very cold and completely unornamented, but which was orderly to the point of precision and immaculate to the point of asepsis. Léon, who admitted him, did so in surly silence, but this was nothing new; no German had ever succeeded in exacting servility, much less civility, from the independent old peasant.

Von Reden had ample time to become thoroughly chilled and also to take cognizance of the changed appearance of the drawing room before Constance entered it. Her acknowledgment of his presence was quite as frosty as his surroundings. He bowed without betraying his consciousness of this.

"Good afternoon, Baroness. I regret that my return to Malou has been so long delayed. Unfortunately my case presented some complications. Otherwise you may be sure I should have been here sooner."

"I take it that you have now fully recovered?"

"Yes, fully. That is to say, I am still hampered by a certain amount of weakness, but that is to be expected and will soon pass. I trust that you are well?"

"Quite well."

"And your aunt? And your daughter-in-law?"

"They are also quite well."

"I am very glad. . . . You are not finding this extreme cold unbearable?"

"No. We are keeping two fires, one in the kitchen and one in my study. But we are trying to conserve as much wood as possible, so that some will be available in February, when my daughter-in-law expects to be confined. We did not have as large a supply as usual this year, and unfortunately a great deal was wasted during Captain Pfaff's occupation."

"*So!* I am extremely sorry to hear that. I understood from him that you had no complaint to make whatsoever of his command—indeed, he showed me a paper you had signed, stating this categorically."

"A paper which he brought to my bedroom at daybreak, when my daughter-in-law was in bed with me, and which he offered me no alternative but to sign immediately—or rather the alternative he offered was one with which I could not comply."

"*So!*" von Reden repeated, with obvious interest. "And what was that, Baroness, if I may ask?"

"That my daughter-in-law should be roused to accompany him on a tour of inspection—just as she was. He declined to retire and wait until I could dress and go with him. I may add that he had obviously been drinking very heavily, and that he was still intoxicated when he battered down the door and forced his way into my room. Also that in the course of the preceding night's revels he and his companions had damaged or destroyed almost everything in this room and everything which they could bring here from the china closet. And that as a final outrage they amused themselves by shooting my cook's harmless pets, which were sleeping on the hearthstone, and desecrating the treasured crucifix on the mantelshelf above it!"

"But, Baroness, all this is a complete surprise to me! And a most painful one! I must beg you for more details!"

"I cannot see that anything would be gained by giving them to you. Unless you have some other reason for seeing me—some new order to enforce, or the announcement of some further occupation, for instance— I will ask you to excuse me."

She was already halfway towards the door. He stepped quickly in front of her.

"And I must ask that you do not leave until I have made myself quite clear," he said. "I have no new orders to enforce and though Malou will probably be occupied again some time in the future, no date has as yet been set for this. I called today wholly from courtesy, before starting for Poland. But after listening to your story I see that it will be necessary for you to report this destruction to the *Kommandantur* in Lisieux, where I shall go myself direct from Malou to make a preliminary complaint. Very shortly you will receive an official notice telling you when to appear and make a formal claim for damages."

"And then?"

"And then of course an order for restitution will be issued."

"Restitution? Of priceless heirlooms?"

"Of course sentimental attachment cannot be taken into account but——"

"I am not speaking of sentimental attachment. The Sèvres vases on the mantelpiece were alone valued at a million francs, and there were several complete dinner services for twenty-four persons, made of Sèvres porcelain, in which not a single piece had even been chipped. The de Fremonds have never been wealthy, but they have taken good care of what they had. The same is true of my own family. My aunt's ancestral china, which she brought with her from Massachusetts, was destroyed along with the porcelain that belonged to Malou. So was the set of Capo di Monte that my friends the Craigs gave me at the time of my porcelain wedding, as well as a Dresden china figurine given me by another friend on the same occasion. I do not know the exact value of the Capo di Monte, but I did happen to learn, by chance, what Miss Foster paid for the figurine, because the director of an art museum, also among my acquaintances, tried to outbid her when she bought it. She finally secured it for five thousand dollars because he could not go that high."

"I remember it very well and with great admiration. It stood in a cabinet over on the east side of this room, a cabinet which no longer seems to be there. But unfortunately it was very fragile, and ornaments of that type are particularly subject to accident."

"Yes. Especially when they are used as the target for pistol shots. The cabinet which stood on the east side of this room—not to mention the one which stood on the west side—is no longer there because the glass panels and shelves were also shattered in the course of all this careful aiming, and therefore could no longer serve their purpose, even if everything they contained had not been destroyed. I have had them removed to the attic where you put the portraits from the dining room. Incidentally, I thank you for removing those. In this way they escaped the mutilation of several here and the obscene inscriptions scrawled on others."

Von Reden's own eyes had never been colder, his own voice never more contemptuous than hers were at this moment. Years of training in lofty and arrogant speciousness were insufficient to supply him with an immediate and plausible retort.

"Perhaps I might also remind you that it is ten kilometers from Malou to Lisieux, which makes twenty for a round trip. That is a fairly long walk to undertake, in winter weather, to no purpose."

"No one would dream of suggesting that you should walk to Lisieux, Baroness."

"Perhaps not. But when Captain Pfaff left here, he found it convenient, for some reason, to do so in my car. Lieutenant Leinmeister found it equally convenient to leave in my daughter-in-law's. We have never been prodigally supplied with automobiles at Malou, and at the time these two were 'borrowed' they were all we had. Horses, as you know, have been more our specialty. And, as you also know, none of our own horses are left here, because their removal had been considered expedient before you went away yourself. Nothing would induce me to use one of the pilfered horses Captain Pfaff left in my stables, probably because he did not think

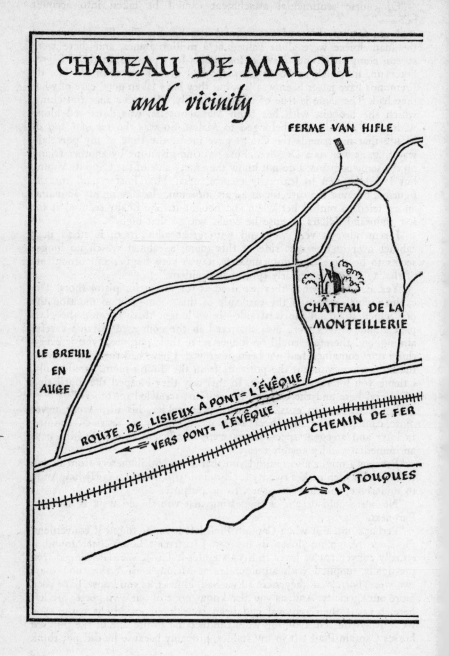

CHÂTEAU DE MALOU
and vicinity

FERME VAN HIFLE

CHÂTEAU DE LA MONTEILLERIE

LE BREUIL EN AUGE

ROUTE DE LISIEUX À PONT= L'ÉVÊQUE

← VERS PONT= L'ÉVÊQUE

CHEMIN DE FER

← LA TOUQUES

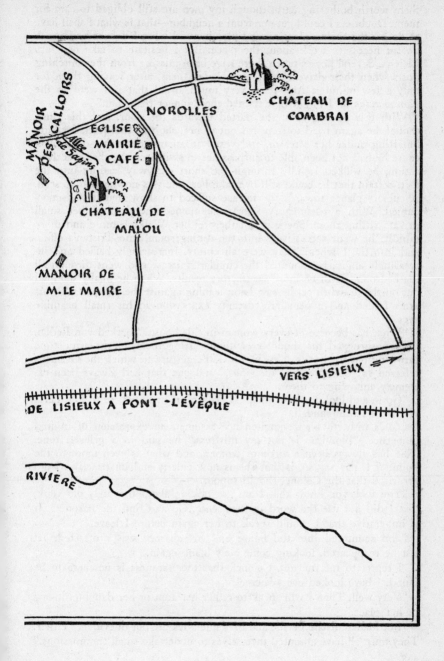

them worth bothering with, though my men are still obliged to care for them. Doubtless I could get one from a neighbor—that is what I shall have to do for the spring planting and plowing and what I do not hesitate to do for necessary work about the place. But I hesitate to take one into Lisieux. Several horses taken there have been missing from their hitching posts when their drivers went to look for them, after leaving them for only a few minutes. And I am very much afraid that if I went to the *Kommandantur* I might be detained there longer than that."

With this parting shot, she darted towards the door, and this time, though he again tried to step in front of her, she was too quick for him. Smarting under her sarcasm, and vexed to an unaccountable degree because he had not been able to surpass her in swiftness of either speech or action, he walked rapidly through the short entryway leading into the fort, certain that he could still overtake her. She was nowhere to be seen. A cursory glance towards the terrace sufficed to show that it was unoccupied. With a perfunctory knock, he opened the door of her small private sitting room. She was not there either. Walking more and more rapidly, he went successively into the dining room, into Tristan's office, and into the kitchen. They were all empty. Increasingly baffled and increasingly angry, he mounted the circular staircase and went through all the bedrooms with no more satisfactory results. When he finally stamped out on the drawbridge, he saw Léon leaning against the parapet with his arms folded and a peculiarly dreamy expression in his small beadlike eyes.

"What has become of every woman in this house?" barked von Reden.

Léon shrugged his shoulders without lifting them, at the same time throwing out his hands. This was a Gallic gesture to which the Germans referred as "the spreading of wings," and one that had always been extremely annoying to them.

"Go in and look for your mistress. You must know where to find her!" von Reden commanded.

Léon's hitherto blank countenance assumed an expression of injured innocence. "Blondine is not my mistress," he said in a grieved tone. "She has always been a virtuous woman, and what is even more to the point, if I may say so, is that she is now elderly and unattractive. I am surprised that the Colonel should suppose——"

"You fool, you know that I am not talking about that ugly old cook, that I did not use the word in that sense. Go and find the Baroness. It is imperative that I should speak to her again before I leave."

Léon sauntered into the house and his absence was protracted. At last he reappeared, looking completely blank again.

"I regret to inform you, Colonel, that the Baroness is nowhere to be found. I have looked everywhere."

"Very well. Then I will speak to either her aunt or her daughter-in-law in her place."

"But Mademoiselle Berthe and Madame Nick are not in evidence either. They must all have absented themselves to undertake small commissions."

White with anger, von Reden strode across the drawbridge, got into his car, slamming the door after him, and told his orderly to drive on. The meaning of the expression, *faire une petite commission,* as Léon had used it, was now clear to him; he had heard it so used before, and he cursed himself for a dolt and a dupe because he had not realized what had happened. The Baroness must have slipped quickly into the tiny downstairs lavatory, which had no outlet except through her small private sitting room; similarly and simultaneously, Margot de Fremond and Miss Bertha Slocum must have locked themselves into two of the upstairs bathrooms. Unless he battered down the door to these, abandoning not only his careful pose of complete "correctness" but every last shred of decent and civilized behavior, like Pfaff and Leinmeister, he could not get at them that day. They were all quite capable of indefinite self-incarceration. The more he thought of the manner in which he had been outwitted, the angrier he became. . . .

Two days later, Constance received an official notice, ordering her to appear at the *Kommandantur* in Lisieux.

She really did not mind the prospect of the twenty kilometers. She was still a very good walker, and moreover she knew that someone was sure to offer her a ride, for at least part of the distance she had to cover. Though gasoline was now strictly rationed, farmers still circulated freely in the high, hooded carts drawn by large powerful horses, except in the cases where their precious Percherons had been requisitioned. Constance was hardly outside her own driveway when one such cart pulled over to the side of the road and stopped.

"The Baroness is going into town? If she would do me the honor to mount in my cabriolet——"

Constance recognized the driver as Mesnil, the old gardener from the Monteillerie, who had been with the Carnots almost as long as Bernard had been with the de Fremonds. She thanked him and accepted the horny hand he offered to help pull her up to the high seat beside him.

"A pretty pass we have come to when the mistress of Malou goes about on foot while two hundred stolen horses are stabled no further off than Cambrai! What is in their evil minds to do next, do you think, Madame la Baronne?"

"I don't know. But I suppose we should be thankful that we still have plenty to eat. I hear that in some places food is now getting very scarce."

"*Hélas!* It is all too true. My wife's sister, who lives in Paris——"

The old man entered upon a long recital of the hardships his sister-in-law was enduring. Then he lowered his voice and looked cautiously about. The road was empty except for his cart, but he seemed to suspect that the very hedgerows might have ears.

"We are slaughtering tomorrow night," he whispered. "A fine fat pig. My grandchildren have grown attached to him, he is almost like a pet to them, and there will be a great outcry the next day. But what will you? They must be fed, and so must others. Pass the word on to Bernard and tell him to be on hand, not later than ten o'clock."

"I will tell Bernard. But let me thank you now for myself and for everyone at Malou."

"*Mais, Madame la Baronne, il n'y a pas de quoi.* You will be doing as much for us next week or the week after. And at Malou, it may well be a sheep or even a beef that will be divided. Then we shall be the gainers, not you!"

It was true. There was a tacit understanding that at frequent intervals whatever animals could best be spared from any given place should secretly be slaughtered, and that the neighbors should be apprised of this beforehand. They all shared willingly, even gladly, with each other. In this way, none of them wanted for fresh meat, in good variety. With any other method, there would have been an appreciable lack.

"But I have heard from Blondine that the Huns ate your Christmas turkey," the old man went on. "Fortunately we were fattening two at the Monteillerie, so I will send one to Malou. It must never be said there was none for the *réveillon* at any house on this hill. But it will be more than good fare we shall miss. It will be the good company to share it. *Hélas,* those two brave boys of yours! And there is still no word from the Baron?"

"No, not a word. I am thankful, Mesnil, that you have not had cause for mourning at your house."

"Yes, we have much for which to be grateful to the good God. And you, Madame la Baronne, have one happy hope ahead of you now, I think. It is in February that the little one will be coming, is it not? That is not long to wait now."

They were almost in sight of Lisieux. The approach from the east, made from level roads that merged easily into the suburban streets, had none of the breath-taking loveliness of the steep descent from the Paris highway, even in summer; and in wintertime, when the gray houses rose to meet a gray sky and the trees and shrubs were bare, it had a bleak, almost a dreary look. Little gusts of wind were blowing leaves over the pavements and spiraling dust about in small flurries, while the few drab pedestrians who were in evidence all seemed to be scurrying away from something towards something else which held out very little hope of betterment. Even the children looked subdued. They did not shout or run in riotous pursuit of each other, but formed shivering, uncertain little clusters and then separated, wiping their noses with their sleeves as they too went on their forlorn way.

"You do not have to go as far as Paris to find people who are beginning to be hungry," Mesnil said soberly. "They are hungry here in Lisieux too. One sees it in their faces. And they are very cold. That was to be expected. Perhaps those of us who live in the country, and who are better off, can get together and do something to help. . . . Is it to the Hôtel de l'Espérance that the Baroness is going?"

"Yes, to the *Kommandantur.* Thank you again for the ride, Mesnil. And as for these poor hungry people—you are right, we must see if we cannot help a little."

They turned from the Boulevard Herbet-Fournet into the Boulevard

Sainte-Anne, and with clumsy goodwill Mesnil helped Constance to alight before the hotel which, for some years, had enjoyed a reputation for excellence unsurpassed in Lisieux. A German sergeant major was seated at the desk just inside the door, and Constance showed him the notice she had received and asked him where she should go to acknowledge it. Nonchalantly rather than rudely, as if it were hardly worth while answering her, the sergeant major told her that Colonel Lauer's quarters were on the second floor, and that the military police in the outer office would let her know whether he was at liberty.

She found the designated suite without difficulty. Obviously it had once consisted of two fair-sized connecting bedrooms, and no effort had been made to disguise their former character, which was realistically evident from their plumbing. Four or five German gendarmes, greatly bebadged, were sitting in the outer office under an immense portrait of Hitler, and, when Constance had shown her paper a second time, one of them rose and strode into the other room ahead of her, motioning that she was to follow. A colonel was seated at an antiquated and rather battered desk. He looked up with a curt nod and, without making any gesture suggestive of rising, nodded in the direction of a straight-backed chair standing opposite his own. The gendarme who had come in with Constance did not leave, but the only occupant of the room, besides the Colonel, when she entered it, was a young and pretty woman dressed with noticeable smartness, who now left a typewriter beside one of the dingily curtained windows and came towards Constance, bringing her chair and a notebook with her.

"I am the official interpreter, madame," she said in faultless French. "Please believe that I will do my best to make your complaint clear to Colonel Lauer. You wished to enter a protest against certain damages that have occurred at your residence, did you not, and to claim restitution for them?"

"No. I did not have any idea of doing such a thing. I came simply because I was summoned and, in an occupied country, it is generally wise for the citizens to obey such a summons."

"Ah! Then you feel you have nothing to complain about, after all?"

"I did not say that either. I have already explained to Colonel von Reden that practically all the porcelain and some of the most valuable ornaments, paintings, and furniture at Château Malou were wantonly destroyed. Also that when the officers who perpetrated, or permitted, these outrages left the premises, they did so in my car and my daughter-in-law's. I could hardly be expected to make these statements as if the facts on which they are based were pleasing to me. But I realize it is quite useless to protest against the treatment given by an Army of Occupation, just as I realize it is unwise to disregard an official summons from one of its representatives. Also that it is useless to expect reimbursement to the extent of millions of francs."

Meticulously the young and pretty woman translated what had been said. While she was doing so, Constance observed her more closely. Everything she had on was new and stylish; her suit was made of well-tailored dark-green wool, her handmade white blouse was trimmed with fresh lace frills, and she was wearing sheer silk stockings such as Constance had not seen since the beginning of the war, and high-heeled, beautifully polished shoes. Though it had a slight telltale darkness near the roots, her brass-colored, burnished hair was beautifully dressed, her slim, carmine-nailed hands expertly manicured. The contrast which she presented to the shabby, shivering creatures whom Constance had seen on the street was not only striking; it was appalling. When she had finished interpreting, she turned to Constance with a dazzling smile, revealing white and even teeth.

"Colonel Lauer is very displeased to learn that there should have been the slightest lapse in the strict discipline which it is the policy of the High Command to maintain at all times," she said in a conciliatory tone of voice. "Unfortunately, in one or two instances which have been called to his attention, junior officers have regarded their last evening at a post which they have found in some respects tedious as the occasion for a celebration. You seem to have been inconvenienced by one of these regrettable episodes. Nevertheless, the Colonel ventures to recall to you that you signed a paper stating that you were entirely satisfied with the treatment given your château throughout the time of Captain Pfaff's occupancy."

"I have already explained to Colonel von Reden the circumstances of this signature. I shall be glad to do so again, if this is necessary. However, I should like to say in passing that it would never occur to me to designate a middle-aged captain, in a responsible position, with two lieutenants, several noncommissioned officers, and ten men stationed under him, as a 'junior officer.' I should reserve such a term for someone like my elder son, for instance, who was a second lieutenant, just twenty years old, when he was killed at Dunkirk. I am surprised to learn that the usage in the French and the German armies is so different."

Again the stylish young woman interpreted meticulously and politely, and, upon request, Constance again related, as dispassionately as possible, the recital of the disgraceful intrusion upon her privacy at dawn. When she had finished, Colonel Lauer designated some elaborate forms which the interpreter told Constance represented claims for damages that she should sign.

"Very well. But this time you may be sure that I shall read them first, with the utmost care."

"I assure you, Madame la Baronne, that it is not necessary. I can indicate the general purport to you in a few words."

"And I assure you, Mademoiselle l'Interprète, that I shall not permit the same reproach to be made me a second time—namely, that I must have known what I was signing, when actually this was rendered impossible. Not that I doubt your powers of translation. Indeed, you must permit me to compliment you on your marvelous French. I have never heard a language which was not a native tongue spoken so idiomatically and with such complete absence of accent. You put me to shame, and I have been speaking French for twenty-two years, besides studying it for several years before that. If I had not known to the contrary, I should certainly have taken you for Norman-born—indeed for a Lexovienne. But that is so ridiculous on the face of it that I am surprised at myself for having mentioned it. Of course no Lexovienne would be acting in a confidential capacity at the *Kommandantur.*"

The girl reddened to the dark roots of her dyed hair, and, for the first time, made no facile rejoinder. Constance read and reread the forms, striking out a word here and there, and in other places adding a few in pencil. On the line left blank for the amount of damages claimed, she wrote in ten million francs. Then she looked up.

"If Colonel Lauer will accept these amendments and this estimate, I will sign the form."

Speaking stiffly this time, the interpreter translated again. Colonel Lauer remarked coldly that the changes in the text were irregular and that the sum the Baroness was claiming was fantastic. She rose and walked past the portrait of Hitler towards the door leading to the outer office. He called her back, peremptorily.

"*Gut, unterzeichnet,*" he said in a gruff tone, making a motion with his pen.

Constance turned. "*Herr Oberst,*" she answered, "*ich glaube dass wir uns verstehen, ohne Dolmetscher.*"

She signed the form and left the room, conscious of the interpreter's increasingly flushed face and malevolent look and of the Colonel's grudging respect. Then she went downstairs and out into the windy street. Nobody stopped her, but nobody paid any attention to her either. She did not recognize a single face she saw. It seemed impossible that this was the city which for fifteen years had been her shopping and social center, where she could count her friends by the score. The hands of the clock in the tall tower of the Bureau des Postes pointed to twenty minutes of one, and it suddenly occurred to her that she was hungry, that she should not attempt the long walk back to Malou without anything to eat. But she did not feel in the mood for going to the Coupe d'Or or the Petite Marquise or any of the other restaurants where she and Tristan had enjoyed such gay and cozy meals together, and she also shrank from the idea of ringing the doorbell at one of the houses which had acquired so blank and strange a look and asking the friends who lived there if she might share their midday breakfast. Then she had a sudden inspiration: She would go to the Abbaye des Bénédictines, ask Gertrude to scramble some eggs for her and serve them with convent-made pâté, then arrange for a little visit with Marie Aimée. Afterwards she would start for home both physically and spiritually refreshed.

As she continued along the narrow winding streets leading to the Abbaye, she noticed that these too seemed increasingly unfamiliar. Instead of resounding with the customary clatter, they were even emptier than the street by which she had entered the city, and the few people she did see looked vaguely frightened as well as cold and hungry. Several small shops were placarded at the side with rectangular yellow signs which Constance had never before seen displayed and she stopped to read one of these; it was an announcement stating that the proprietor was a Jew. Nothing in the brief wording was ominous in itself; but the mere fact that the signs were posted seemed somehow disquieting. She had not heard about them before, and she realized afresh how isolated she was at Malou. She must make a definite effort to keep in closer touch with trends and events, she told herself resolutely, and she must also manage to go to the Abbaye more frequently, despite the difficulties of doing so.

The Benedictines, like everyone else, had undergone upheaval as a result of the invasion and the occupation, and some of them had judged it wise to vacate their ancient cloister. One of these, herself a Nantaise, had been offered the loan of a friend's château near there and, through the good offices of relatives occupying positions of power in the Saint-Nazaire shipyards, had secured a chartered bus, which conveyed the Benedictines who wished to leave Lisieux to their chosen haven, in advance of the enemy. But the experiment proved no happier in their case than in that of other desperate refugees. The Germans had soon overrun as much of the country as they pleased; and as Mark Mullins had predicted, it was the French who had stubbornly stood their ground who fared the best in the end, not those who had left their property unguarded and gone blindly forth in search of shelter and safety elsewhere.

Seeing what had happened to many estates in the vicinity of Malou, Constance realized afresh every day how great Tristan's wisdom and foresight had been in making her promise never to leave it. Much as she had endured, her basic security had not been jeopardized; and though the stable at Malou had suffered, and the equipment of the château had been abused and destroyed, the fundamental structure had never been threatened. In like measure, the nuns who had refused to leave their venerable cloister, Marie Aimée among them, were the ones who had suffered least from the invasion. The Germans had not molested them as they passed rapidly through Lisieux to more important points. On the other hand, the nuns who had gone to the château near Nantes had been ordered to vacate it, on a few hours' notice, because the invaders decided to take it over in its entirety.

Several Benedictines had been arrested in Saint-Nazaire as parachutists in disguise, and had suffered the indignities of arrest and disrobing before they were released; and as a final calamity, the driver of the car which was taking them from the borrowed château had accidentally hit and killed one member of a German motorcycle escort, and the nuns had been dragged from the car and detained amidst cries of "Shoot them, shoot them all!" This time their detention had been even more perilous and their release even harder to arrange, and shortly afterwards the refugees had returned to their Abbaye, thankful to escape with their lives, to find the rest of the community mentally tranquil and physically undisturbed.

Constance was hardly inside the great door when Gertrude, whose timid soul had been one of those most sorely tried, began a long repetitious account of the community's misfortunes; and though Constance listened patiently for some time, partly because she was truly sorry to think that even the poor little portress had not escaped such vicissitudes, and partly because it was literally impossible for her to get a word in edgewise, she finally managed to interrupt. Could she not have a snack of some sort, she asked, and hear the rest of the story while she was eating her *casse-croûte?* Gertrude now began interpolating apologies in her recital, but she could not be persuaded to interrupt it altogether until Constance actually propelled her in the direction of the kitchen; and the hungry guest was obliged to remain there while the *casse-croûte* was prepared, for it was obvious that the old woman was far too addlepated to do anything without supervision and direction. At last, pushing aside the plate which had been but meagerly supplied and interrupting again, Constance told Gertrude to announce her to Mère Marie Aimée.

"Yes, yes, Madame la Baronne. But first I will conduct you to the *grand parloir.*"

"Why, I know the way, Gertrude! Remember I've been coming here for a good many years now. It will save time if you send a message to Mère Marie Aimée at once."

The old portress was not to be dissuaded, however. With continued chatter and redoubled apologies, she scurried ahead of Constance, turning to nod and beckon as she always had. When they passed behind the hidden refectory, the sound of voices singing in trustful unison came clearly through the convent walls. The nuns had just finished their midday meal, and were standing in a circle, according to their custom, to invoke the protection of their patroness, Notre Dame du Pré, before resuming the day's activities. Constance also paused, in order to listen:

" '*Je mets ma confiance,*
Vierge, en votre secours!
Servez-moi de défense,
Prenez soin de mes jours:
Et quand ma dernière heure
Viendra fixer mon sort,
Obtenez que je meure
De la plus sainte mort.' "

Constance had heard this song before, when she happened to be at the Abbaye near mealtime, and she had always found it extremely appealing. She knew very few of the nuns by sight. The Mère Hôtelière, a forceful, energetic woman, who looked after the aged pensioners, and for whom the cloistral rules were somewhat relaxed on this account, was always a good deal in evidence; and the Mère Prieure, a very different type, reserved, remote, and distinguished, had occasionally received Constance, through courtesy, in the *petit parloir* set aside for her own use. A few years before the outbreak of the war, the Carmelites had presented the Benedictines with the statue of Sainte Thérèse which the latter had placed in their courtyard garden, emerging themselves in their entirety from their cloister for the dedication ceremonies. They had invited a few visitors to these, and Constance had been among those favored; but the guests had all been informed that they were on no account to speak to the nuns or even approach them. So Constance had seen the picturesque procession from a respectful distance, and only two or three forms and faces stood out distinctly in her memory. But somehow she had always seemed to see the singing circle with great clearness, partly, perhaps, because Marie Aimée had described it to her so vividly, and partly because its symbolism had made such an impression on her. Now as she stood and listened, she felt as if she herself were mysteriously linked with it.

The corridor was frigid, and she moved on in the direction of the *grand parloir*. But the great apartment was no warmer, and she sat there shivering while she awaited the arrival of Mère Marie Aimée. The Benedictines had never heated any part of the Abbaye except the chapel, the chapter house, and the infirmary even before the war, and seemed impervious to its glacial atmosphere. When Marie Aimée finally arrived, her serene countenance did not appear in the least pinched, and the fingers she put through the grille for Constance to touch were firm and warm.

"How glad I am to see you, after all this time!" she said cordially and unreproachfully, seating herself with her usual quiet grace. "I hope you have come prepared to tell me everything that has been happening at Malou. You have been constantly in my thoughts and of course in my prayers. But it is a long time since I have seen you."

"I know. I am very sorry. I should have managed to get here somehow. But we have no motorcars and no horses any more, and besides, I have not felt, for some time, that it was wise for me to leave Malou. The officer who was at first in command of the detachment there had a personality which was offensive to me in many ways, but I do not think he was either dishonest or destructive. However, he left abruptly for an emergency operation, and his successor was a cat of a different color, or, if you will forgive me for saying so, a skunk of a different stripe."

"I knew the horses had been 'removed' but I did not know about the motorcars. Or about—may I venture to say it too?—the extraordinarily striped skunk. Please enlighten me."

"But I came here to be enlightened myself. I want to hear about you."

"About me? There is nothing to tell you about myself, dear Constance. I live along from day to day, quietly following our rule, and finding complete happiness in doing so."

"I know you do, personally. But what about other members of the community? Gertrude has been giving me a lengthy and grueling account of their trials and tribulations."

Marie Aimée smiled. "Gertrude is a good faithful soul, but she is inclined to be *un peu bavarde*—a little garrulous," she said. "It is true that some of our community have undergone trials. However, these are now happily over and the nuns themselves are back in their beloved cloister. We even have several new postulants, one or two of them extremely promising. It takes more than an enemy occupation to disturb the quiet tenor of conventual life. . . . You still have no word from Tristan?"

"No, none whatever."

"And that, of course, is harder for you to endure than anything else. But you have not lost faith that you will hear?"

"No. I'm sure I shall. Of course I don't know when, but sometime."

"It is a great blessing, that faith of yours," Marie Aimée said earnestly. "Many pray in vain for such a gift through endless years. It *is* a gift like any other that comes to us through the Grace of God. . . . Have you seen much of Jacques and Stéphanie lately?"

"No, very little. As I said, I have felt for some time I should leave Malou as little as possible. And of course Margot shouldn't undertake long walks or ride in a jolty cart now, so since the automobiles were 'borrowed' she's been hampered too. She talks with her mother nearly every day, though—we've had very little interruption in the telephone service since the occupation has been actually established, though of course we realize that usually someone is listening in." She paused in her turn, struck by the unusual gravity of Marie Aimée's serene face. "Was there some special reason why you thought I should try to go to L'Abbatiale?" she asked.

"I thought perhaps you might give Stéphanie some comfort and reassurance if you did. I'm afraid that she needs both. . . . Of course Mark Mullins's absence makes everything much harder for her."

"Yes, but I think she's adjusted herself to that. It isn't as if there were much valuable stock left at L'Abbatiale. You know how clever Mark was about getting the best horses off to the Craigs. And after all, it's nearly six months since he was interned. She's had time to get used to doing without him. And she isn't worried about him. Apparently the British civilians at the camp in Caen are being very decently treated."

"Yes, that is my understanding too. But I must confess that when I said Stéphanie needed both comfort and reassurance I was not thinking primarily of Monsieur Mullins. I do not know whether she has told Margot over the telephone, or whether you may have heard it otherwise; but Jacques has been required to take his *carte d'identité* to the *mairie* to have it stamped *'Juif.'*"

"Indeed I hadn't heard! How could he be required to do such a thing? He isn't a Jew!"

"His mother is a full-blooded Jewess. You know that. And you know that his paternal grandmother was a Jewess too. It seems that anyone with three Jewish grandparents——"

"Well, I didn't know that."

"Unfortunately, it is true. Probably you didn't know either that Madame Bouvier *mère* and Madame Solomon are both at L'Abbatiale now, installed in the *petit manoir.*"

"I certainly didn't. Since when?"

"They came just a few days ago. It seems that Madame Solomon's great palace on the Avenue Foch was requisitioned for an office building almost immediately after the fall of Paris. So she went to stay with Madame Bouvier at the maisonette in the Faubourg Saint-Germain. That is so small and secluded they hoped it might escape. But the day after their cards were stamped with the word *Juif* they were visited by the police and asked to show these cards. Then they were told they would have to move out. Fortunately there is plenty of room at L'Abbatiale."

"Yes, of course there's plenty of room. But they must be dreadfully unhappy there! Madame Bouvier always hated the country; she wouldn't come to L'Abbatiale, even for short visits, if she could possibly get out of it. And I don't think Madame Solomon's ever been there at all, except for Margot's wedding. And now to be forced to stay there because they've been driven out of their own homes! . . . It will complicate things for Stéphanie too, won't it, having them on the place? You didn't finish telling me about that new ruling, Marie Aimée."

"According to the latest *affiches* all persons having three Jewish grandparents are now obliged to report this. Jacques and Stéphanie stopped in to see me on their way back from the *mairie*. Naturally this regulation cannot touch Stéphanie herself, but she had accompanied Jacques because he was much too lame to go alone. I notice a great change for the worse in him. And I can tell that Stéphanie is very much troubled. About his physical condition and now about how he may be affected through this new regulation. Not that it entails any hardship in itself. But it may be an indication of future hardships. . . . You have noticed that the Jewish shops are now all placarded as such?"

"I did, for the first time, today. Of course there are very few of them in Lisieux."

"Yes, and the law requiring those might be regarded as the first arrow pointing towards disaster, the one concerned with the *carte d'identité* as the second. . . . Well, we must trust in our Saviour, as always, not to make our burdens heavier than we can bear. But I do think if you went on, now that you are this far——"

"I shall, of course, after what you've told me. But that means I must say good-by to you at once."

The early twilight of winter was already closing in by the time she reached L'Abbatiale, and she realized she must telephone as soon as possible to avert worry on her account at Malou. She had been offered a second ride, which took her as far as La Bosquetterie, but beyond there she had been obliged to walk, and she reached the *grand manoir* chilled and weary. However, the warmth of the welcome she received restored her almost instantly. Stéphanie and Jacques were overjoyed at seeing her, and while they were installing her by the fire and mixing a hot drink for her, the talk and the atmosphere were both cheerful. But Constance immediately noticed that what Marie Aimée had said about both was true: Jacques moved with far greater difficulty than ever before, and Stéphanie's affectionate cordiality did not wholly mask the anxiety of her manner and expression. After they were all settled in easy chairs before the pleasant blaze, steaming glasses in hand, the conversation gradually took on a more serious tone, especially after Constance found that her efforts to reach Malou by telephone were futile.

"I'm not surprised," Stéphanie said. "Margot tells me that she has no trouble getting through to me, but several times lately when I've tried to get through to her the line seems to have gone dead. It looks as if calls originating from Malou got more attention than those originating from L'Abbatiale."

"It's probably just accidental. Or perhaps, since Malou was used as German Headquarters for two months——"

"Yes, probably."

Stéphanie tried to answer casually, just as Constance had tried to offer the suggestion casually, but neither one was wholly successful. There was a short silence.

"I'm afraid I ought not to stay long, since I can't let Aunt Bertha and Margot know where I am. They knew I was going to the *Kommandantur* when I left this morning, and they haven't heard anything from me since. They may begin to think I've been incarcerated at the Hôtel de l'Espérance because I made so bold as to complain about the broken china."

"We'd love to have you stay all night. You could have the rose-colored room and we could sit here and visit and gossip. It would be like old times." They all knew it would not be like old times, because Tristan was not there too, but none of them said so. "I suppose they would worry at Malou, though," Stéphanie went on. "Not that the Germans really would incarcerate anyone on such a flimsy excuse."

"No, of course not. . . . Speaking of incarcerations, do you still have good news from Mark?"

"Why, we still see him! The British civilians interned at Caen are allowed out on parole one day a week, within the city limits, and we've managed to get over there twice lately. He says he can't complain about anything."

"Well, that's one piece of good news anyway, and I'm relieved to hear it. I didn't worry about Mark at first, any more than you did, but lately I haven't felt so easy in my mind about him. It seems to me the Germans' 'correctness' is wearing a little thin here and there. And then they're beginning to dream up things, as Gwen would say."

"Have you heard from Gwen lately? How is she and where is she?"

"She's fine and she's becoming quite an Anglophile. She's still making her headquarters in London, and she says life is more or less normal, both there and in the country, in spite of the terrific bombardments. Every letter I get from her is loud in its praises of England and the English. She and Eileen have visited some bombing bases in Lincolnshire and taken part in a flying-boat patrol. You probably didn't know that Eileen's got credentials of her own now, from *This Month.*"

"I certainly didn't know. She must be awfully good, Connie, to have made a grade like that."

"She is good. If I had known I was coming here, I'd have brought you her article about 'Invasion Week End.' It comes pretty close to being a masterpiece."

"I don't see how she gets all this stuff through to you."

"Well, of course an American diplomatic pouch still goes to Vichy. And so does Duncan. He gets a certain amount of mail there and he manages to find ways of sending it along to me, together with his own letters."

"And he's all right too?"

"Oh yes! He's completely absorbed in his work with the war wounded and he looks and acts like a different person. He says he may be able to get down for Christmas, but that he'll be here the first of February anyhow."

"Well, that's another piece of good news."

"Yes, and he gave me still another. He said he'd run into Abel on the street in Vichy the other day and that he'd never seen the boy looking better."

"Yes. Yes, I believe he is very well."

Stéphanie spoke with unusual constraint, and glanced across at Jacques as she did so. Neither of them had said much to Connie about Abel lately, and she had attributed their silence to delicacy. He had not been called out until late the previous April, and had seen only a few weeks of warfare, through which he had passed unscathed; his parents might very logically feel that frequent or extensive mention of this would prove painful to a woman who had lost both her sons. Connie did not know that he had not been demobilized, that after the armistice he had been promoted, and that he now held the position of aide-de-camp to one of the generals on Pétain's staff.

"Of course he can't write very often or very fully," Stéphanie went on after a slight pause. "And he's intimated that it's pretty hard to get letters through, even in his position. Duncan must be on mighty good terms with the Underground. The Germans are drawing the lines between Occupied and Unoccupied France tighter and tighter all the time. And as you say, they're beginning to dream up things. You've heard about the latest requirement, haven't you?"

"I hadn't until Marie Aimée told me today. I haven't had the use of my radio since the Germans came to Malou, because it was in Tristan's office and they were using that. And they left it in pieces. Léon's good at tinkering with such things, he thinks he may be able to fix it up. But he hasn't been able to yet. So I don't know whether the B.B.C. had any announcement on the subject or not. But Marie Aimée said——"

Stéphanie tried to laugh, not very successfully. "You know the old saying, 'If you want to find out what is happening in the world, go to see a cloistered nun.' The advice seems to be as sound as ever. But of course this new ordinance doesn't amount to anything. It's a nuisance, that's all, having to go to the *mairie* in this weather."

"Yes, that's all."

Constance rose, reluctantly, and reached for her coat. "Give my love to Ghisèle. Where is she?"

"She has started a Red Cross course to qualify as an *infirmière* at the hospital in Lisieux. She didn't want me to tell until she was certain she'd be accepted, and it wasn't until yesterday that she found out for sure she was."

"Why, she isn't old enough to be a nurse, is she?"

"Of course she wouldn't be considered old enough in normal times. But as your German friend reminded you on the occasion of his first call, these aren't normal times."

"Don't you dare call that man my friend, even in fun, Stéphanie!"

"I have an idea he's in love with you."

"Don't say that, even in fun, either."

"I wasn't saying it in fun, Connie. But I was giving you a hint, in case you needed it. You hadn't ever thought that he might be, yourself?"

Constance hesitated uncomfortably. "I've been aware of something once or twice that made his presence even more hateful than usual," she said slowly. "Something like a small strange spark, struck from flint. No, that isn't it exactly. Something evil and darting, like a snake's tongue. But I hoped it was imagination. I thought it must be."

"Why did you think it must be? Neither of those is an astonishing way for sex attraction to betray itself in a man like von Reden."

"I suppose not. But it's a long time since I've associated anything evil with love, Stéphanie, though I've associated it with almost everything else. Besides, I'm over forty."

Again Stéphanie laughed somewhat wryly. "Don't be absurd, Connie. You look very tired and you're getting too thin again. But you're still very beautiful—very desirable. Tristan still found you so, didn't he? *Mon Dieu,* I believe you are the only woman left in the world who still blushes! But I also believe von Reden would give a good deal to get you, and Jacques agrees with me. In fact, it was he who first put the idea into my mind. Well, don't let's talk about it any more. I'm sorry if I've upset you. . . . Do you really have to go? Wait a minute, I'll call one of the 'boys' and have him take you home in Mark's car. I can do that for you anyway. Of course the Germans have 'borrowed' all of ours, the way they did yours, but no one wanted that one and it doesn't use much of any gasoline. Do try to come again soon, won't you? Our best love to Margot!"

Constance found the drive home far more trying than the one she had taken into Lisieux that morning. She had not been afraid of going to the *Kommandantur;* in fact she had thought, like Aunt Bertha, that she would feel better if she got some of the spleen out of her system, and she had been determined to do so; her resolution and her pride had upheld her. Now she was very tired, she was very cold, and she was a prey to anxious thoughts. Jacques was certainly looking very badly. If he did not have the strength to surmount both his physical ailments and his bitter humiliation, what would become of Stéphanie, whose life was so bound up in his? And what would be her own wisest course in view of the harrowing suspicions Stéphanie had raised? To be sure, von Reden had just left for Poland. But he would be coming back, probably before very long if Stéphanie were right. It would be easy enough for him to find pretexts to do so, and she could not deny him the hospitality of her house. Somewhere, somehow, she must beg, borrow, or steal new locks. And there was that hidden pistol of Bruno's. How could she get cartridges to put in it?

She was relieved when they finally arrived at the drawbridge of Malou. There was a light in the fort, and the great ironbound door opened at her approach. Evidently someone was watching for her, anxious over her absence. As the door swung wider, she saw that the watcher was Margot.

"Oh, Mother, *hurry!*" the girl called to her.

Constance hastened forward, asking herself what new calamity could have occurred during her absence. Then she saw that Margot's face was alight with joy.

"Look, Mother, look!" she exclaimed.

She was holding a battered post card in her hand, and now she thrust this into her mother-in-law's. Constance held it to the light, scanning it excitedly. It carried no postmark, and except for three printed lines and a blurred signature it was completely bare. One of the lines read:

No. 415.   OFLAG C–7.

Above this were two lines which read:

I am wounded.
I am well.

The line reading "I am wounded" had been crossed out. The blurred signature was "Tristan de Fremond."

CHAPTER XXXII

WHEN VON REDEN again returned to Malou, accompanied, as he had been on the occasion of his first visit, by Lieutenant Nolte, he found that the room he had previously occupied, and which had been very much to his liking, was not available, and that it would not readily become so.

He arrived—as usual without previous announcement—one evening in early February, and his displeasure was instantly aroused by the sight of Léon, whose insolence he had by no means forgotten. He still smarted at the memory of their last encounter, when the surly Norman had so successfully defied him. He rapped out a curt order to take the bags up, and himself started across the fort towards the stairway.

"Where shall I put the bags after I have carried them upstairs?" Léon inquired.

"In the same room where you have put them several times already, of course."

"I think perhaps it would be well if I should inquire from the doctor whether this will be agreeable to him."

"The doctor? Is the doctor here already?"

"Yes, Colonel. He has been here for two days."

"I did not expect him so soon. But of course it would be agreeable to him. He could not have been aware that he was occupying my room. He will move to another at once."

"That will naturally be for you and him to decide, Colonel. But I still feel it would be more prudent to consult him."

The Colonel strode off, Nolte at his heels, without troubling to prolong the argument. Léon picked up two or three of the smaller bags which he could carry without much effort, and hastened after them. Nothing could have been further from his wishes than to miss the encounter which he foresaw, and which he felt confident he could observe to great advantage from the corridor. This was very cold but it was reasonably well lighted.

Without knocking, the Colonel opened the door of the room which had once been Nick's and Bruno's. But he stopped on the threshold and Nolte halted behind him. Someone was inside and it was not the person he had expected to see when Léon told him the doctor had already arrived.

"There has evidently been some mistake," von Reden said coldly.

"Obviously. Are you in the habit of making them?"

The retort came from within. Léon suppressed a snicker as he heard it. He set down the bags and leaned back against the wall, folding his arms and preparing for further enjoyment.

"I am not," von Reden answered, still more coldly. "Nor am I making one now. This is the room which I habitually occupy."

"Then I'm afraid you're doomed to disappointment. For it also happens to be the one which I have occupied for a good many years. And I seem to have got here first this time. Moreover I have a deep-rooted dislike to sharing a room with anyone. Indeed, I make it a strict rule to sleep with no men and comparatively few women."

"The occasion does not lend itself to jesting," von Reden said severely. "May I ask with whom I am speaking?"

"My name is Duncan Craig. I take it that you are Colonel von Reden?"

"I am. And apparently you place me more easily than I place you."

"I shall be very glad to help you out. I served as a captain in the American Army during the First World War, and until last June I was with a French Ambulance Unit behind the Maginot Line. At present I am a consultant in several military hospitals run by the French Government. My errand here is purely personal. The Baroness is a very old friend of mine. Some months ago I promised her that I would try to be here for her daughter-in-law's confinement. It is not as easy to secure competent medical attention from Lisieux as it used to be."

"Perhaps you will permit me to say that you seem to have considerable freedom of movement."

"I should be the first to agree with you. And perhaps you will permit me to explain it. Last summer, when General von Kittwitz, whom I believe you know, was suddenly in need of expert medical attention, I was fortunate enough to be on the spot. You see, during my absence he had requisitioned my suite at the Ritz and after that I couldn't find the civilian clothes I had left there, though I went several times to look for them. It was on one of these occasions that I found General von Kittwitz in the midst of a seizure and was able to relieve him. Possibly you did not know that he is an epileptic—this has not been given as much publicity as some of his other attributes and he is very unwilling that it should be, so I am sure you will regard this information as confidential. He was rigid on the floor and foaming at the mouth when I arrived and in another moment he would have chewed his tongue to pieces. His aide-de-camp, who hitherto had treated me with great disdain, hailed my arrival as a godsend—as indeed it was for the General. Since then he has been extremely courteous and co-operative as far as I am concerned. He has even located my missing clothes. And he has been good enough to help facilitate the freedom of movement to which you just referred."

There was a brief pause, during which Léon waited expectantly. Then von Reden spoke again, somewhat less coldly and much more civilly.

"I will repeat that there has been a mistake, Dr. Craig, and this time I will acknowledge that I seem to have made it. But perhaps I can explain my intrusion better than by merely saying that this is the room I habitually occupy at Malou. I might add that a week ago I requested a friend of mine who is a distinguished German physician, and who is now attached to the Medical Corps in our Army of Occupation, to meet me here tomorrow and to make arrangements for remaining as long as his presence seemed indicated. When that stupid servant told me the doctor had already arrived and was installed in my room, I took it for granted that he referred to my friend. I think you will grant that the mistake was a natural one."

"Quite natural. I shall be pleased to explain to your friend, on his arrival tomorrow, why he is not needed at Malou."

There was another brief pause. This time Craig broke it.

"I appreciate your thoughtfulness in arranging to have a distinguished physician come here," he said pleasantly. "No doubt you were prompted, as I was, by the realization that it is very hard for such French doctors as are left in Lisieux to take proper care of their patients who live in the country, now that their movements are so greatly restricted. And of course you had no way of knowing that one of the de Fremonds' oldest friends was a doctor. But now that you find me here, I am sure you will agree I am the logical person to take care of Margot. She has known me ever since she was a child and we have always been good friends. It would be natural for her to feel more at ease with me than with a stranger, especially as I speak her language."

"My friend is also an excellent linguist," von Reden interposed.

"No doubt. But I was lapsing into colloquialism. I meant not only that I have a fair command of the French language, for an American, but also that I like and understand French people. The Bouviers have been my friends almost as long as the de Fremonds. I am extremely fond of both families. I believe they are extremely fond of me. And I doubt very much if this distinguished physician, who is also an excellent linguist and a very good friend of yours, would like and understand Margot de Fremond. Nor do I think she would be predisposed in your friend's favor. After all, her husband, with whom she was passionately in love, was killed at Dunkirk eight months ago. Since then she has been with her mother-in-law, to whom she has grown greatly attached, throughout your various visits here, and has found them rather trying; and she has seen her father, whom she adores, and who is a pitiful cripple old before his time, humiliated and abused. She is too young to regard any of this objectively or impersonally. She is an extremely healthy young woman, I am happy to say. But I think we would be inviting trouble if we permitted her to have a German for a doctor."

Léon was beginning to anticipate the pauses. He was also beginning to wonder how long it would take before von Reden, who had all this time been standing on the threshold of a room which he had not been invited to enter, would find himself firmly turned away from it.

"Incidentally," Craig continued, "you will be shocked to hear that no restitution has ever been made to the Baroness for all that porcelain and furniture which was destroyed. I understand that one of the technicalities which seems to prevent a settlement was her inability to give the exact value of a service I gave her. I'm pleased to be in a position to tell you, and you can pass on the information to the *Kommandantur,* that it cost seven thousand dollars. I think I could still produce the receipted bill if you would care to see it. I am very methodical about such things."

"I will pass on this information," von Reden said impatiently. Until now his annoyance had been fairly well curbed; but his self-control was beginning to crack. "Naturally there are some unavoidable delays in the settlement of such matters. However, this is perhaps not the best time to take up that subject in detail. I am willing to concede, after what you have said, that possibly it would be better if you officiated at the accouche-ment. But I also feel that after the effort this eminent physician has made to come here, he should be received with suitable hospitality and that I should be here to welcome him. You must have gathered that I was in-tending to remain here myself. I have only my aide-de-camp with me tonight, but very shortly——"

"You surely do not intend to stay here at the time of a confinement, Colonel! *You* must have realized that you would be most uncomfortable during the inevitable confusion of such an event, even if I had not fore-stalled you by using up all the available space. I have brought two nurses with me from Paris, and they are already installed in the large guest room. Margot's own quarters have been transformed into a nursery and a delivery room. And just now she herself is sleeping in Miss Slocum's room, so that she will be near the nurses and me if she should want us for anything. So you can see that there is literally not a free bed in the château at the moment."

"Very well. We will go to the Monteillerie until after the confinement. Since the owners are absent, there will be plenty of room there. But as there are no servants there either, we shall be obliged to come here for our meals."

"You'll consult the Baroness about that, of course. But I hope you won't feel it necessary to do so this evening. She has been looking very tired lately and I persuaded her to go to bed early. Miss Slocum is with her. We had a light, early supper—really no more than a *goûter*—and I am afraid that by now it has all been cleared away. But naturally the Baroness would not wish you to leave without any refreshment whatever. I will go downstairs with you and help Léon forage for something. You are still there, aren't you, Léon, with the Colonel's bags? I suppose his own orderly has been looking after the car all this time. But you may take the bags downstairs and turn them over to him again."

"With much pleasure, Monsieur le Docteur," Léon responded with alacrity.

In spite of his promise to von Reden, Duncan Craig did not personally receive the distinguished physician when the latter arrived the following afternoon. Léon, looking much less surly than usual in the presence of a German, admitted him and ushered him into the cold drawing room, where after a few minutes Constance came to greet him.

"You were very kind to come," she said almost cordially, "and it was very kind of Colonel von Reden to arrange for your services. But after all, they are not needed. My little grandson was born about two hours ago, and my daughter-in-law was ill only a short time. She had wonderful care —we were fortunate in having an old friend, who has been our doctor for years, and two excellent nurses with us for her confinement. But she was wonderful herself. Dr. Craig said he had never seen a girl who took child-birth so calmly and courageously. And she has a beautiful boy, the image of his father. I am sorry Dr. Craig cannot see you himself just now. But I am sure you will understand that he does not feel he should leave my daughter-in-law yet."

There was very little that the visitor could say except that he understood perfectly and that he congratulated her most heartily. Constance offered him coffee and Calvados, and these he drank gratefully, for he was chilled to the bone. Then, having learned that von Reden was expecting him at the nearby château of the Monteillerie, he took his leave. Constance sent a message by him to von Reden, saying that she would expect the Colonel and his aide-de-camp and the doctor for a light supper that evening, and that beginning the following noon, she would do her best to provide two adequate daily meals. But von Reden replied with a stiff little note, which was delivered by his orderly. He would not trouble her, he said; the wife of the old gardener at the Monteillerie had her niece staying with her; between them they would cook and clean for the two officers as long as it was necessary for them to stay there; the doctor would return to his own unit the following day in any case. Von Reden would, however, be grate-ful if the Baroness would advise him when he could return to Malou without inconveniencing her unduly, since it was much more suitable for his headquarters than the Monteillerie. He assumed that Dr. Craig's other duties would not permit a long sojourn, that after a week or so one nurse would be sufficient, and that the improvised delivery room would soon be restored to its former state. He could understand that the young Baroness would need to reoccupy her own quarters with her nurse and her child; but he would expect the north wing to be available for himself and his aide-de-camp again within ten days, unless there were unexpected com-plications.

Scrupulously, Constance sent him word when the north wing was vacant again. Her heart was still so full of thanksgiving that there was tempo-rarily no room in it for personal animosity, and after all, von Reden had never failed to conduct himself with "correctness," as he understood this; it was only after his departure that his underlings had got out of hand. The prospect of renewed occupation was naturally unwelcome, but she was not unduly apprehensive about it. And when she encountered him in the fort on her return from the baby's christening, she did not hesitate to go towards him with the child in her arms, and lift the light veil that covered its face, so that he could look at her grandson.

The presence of the Germans had of course made it impossible to plan for a celebration at the château after the ceremony in the church, even if this had been practicable otherwise, under occupation conditions. But Jacques and Stéphanie and the four younger Bouviers had all managed to come over from L'Abbatiale in Mark Mullins's wreck of a car; while, greatly to their rejoicing, Mark Mullins himself, who had just been released on parole from the internment camp at Caen, had come too. Margot had made such a quick recovery that she was able to go to the church, and everyone living in the village and on the surrounding hillsides had somehow succeeded in getting there. The *maire* acted as godfather and Ghisèle as godmother, and it had been such a mild day for February that it had been possible to linger a little on the porch of the church and let all the good friends see the beautiful baby as they came outside. For he *was* a beautiful baby—it was not merely Constance's imagination which made him appear so. His head was covered with fine black hair and long black lashes swept down over his blue eyes. His chubby cheeks and fists were firm and rosy, and he was already so sizable that the ancestral christening robes fitted him snugly, revealing the shape of his plump little body. To make everything perfect, he had been as good as gold throughout the baptism and the reception, and he was still cuddled contentedly in his grandmother's arms when she came into the fort. She walked over towards von Reden, holding the baby proudly.

"Wouldn't you like to see Antoine de Padoue de Fremond?" she asked, her pride ringing through her voice.

"Very much."

The Colonel bent over the baby, scrutinizing it critically. Padoue blinked his blue eyes, and for a moment his rosy lips parted slightly, disclosing a small pink tongue; but his infantile serenity remained untroubled by the prolonged inspection. At last von Reden raised his head and looked straight at Constance.

"Yes," he said. "Yes, that is a very fine specimen of the human race. It would be most unfortunate if I should receive an order to shoot him. Because naturally, if I did, I should obey."

CHAPTER XXXIII

CONSTANCE, CARRYING PADOUE, had been the first to enter the fort after the christening. Now the great door swung open again and Margot and

Aunt Bertha, who had lingered for a few moments on the drawbridge, came in too. Von Reden turned from his hostess and bowed ceremoniously.

"The Baroness has been good enough to show me the baby," he said. "Permit me to repeat the compliment I have just paid her on his appearance."

"Thank you," Margot said briefly. Her voice, like Connie's, was very proud, and because of this ringing pride, she did not sound curt. "Perhaps I'd better take Padoue now, Mother," she added. "He's certainly been on his good behavior so far, but I don't know how much longer it will last." She transferred the baby expertly from her mother-in-law's arms to her own, and when she had reached the stairway, looked back at Aunt Bertha. "Don't you want to help put away the christening clothes, Auntie?" she asked.

"Well, I'd just as lieve," Aunt Bertha answered. Unlike the others, she could not voice her joy; but they both knew how she felt about Padoue, and strove to share him with her.

"You're coming too, aren't you, Mother?" Margot went on.

"In just a minute. But don't wait for me. I've got to attend to something else first."

Nothing in her manner suggested distress. She was still smiling as she watched them out of sight. Then she looked back at von Reden.

"I'm not quite sure why you said what you did," she told him evenly. "Perhaps you thought that if you threatened to shoot my grandson I would try to bargain with you, and promise to submit to some new outrage in return for a promise of his safety. I shall do nothing of the kind. I know what your promises are worth. Perhaps you are trying to drive me away from Malou, so that swine like Behr and Leinmeister can defile it still further. I shall never leave it and I shall never take its heir away from it either. I know that if you were determined to destroy him, you would find him wherever I tried to hide him. Perhaps you are only trying to frighten me, to break my spirit by making me wonder every time I look at the baby whether I shall see him alive the next day. But I am not afraid of you or anything you can do to me, and I am not going to torture myself with thoughts of what you can do to a defenseless child. I am only going to remind you that one murder not infrequently leads to another."

He made no immediate reply, and as they continued to look steadfastly at each other, Constance realized that far from antagonizing him, her defiance had roused his admiration. Again she was aware of the flint-born fire between them and knew that this time she herself had struck the stone with steel. But she also knew that she must stand her ground, that it was now too late for compromise or retreat. She waited unflinchingly for the answer that was so long in coming.

"Your reasoning is bold, but it is not wholly sound," von Reden said at last. "Referring only to the first point you made, I might remind you that your great friend, Dr. Duncan Craig, has obtained very special privileges as a result of favors rendered."

"Yes. But that was a case of two men dealing with each other, not a man with a woman. And it was a case of a man who had something to conceal and a man who could betray the secret. No kind of bargaining is possible, Colonel von Reden, between a man like you and a woman like me, especially as neither of us has anything to conceal. At least I have not, and I assume you have not either. Certainly you are very outspoken, even on such a subject as shooting a child."

"No more than you in saying that one murder leads to another."

"I was only trying to match you in candor. And I was not threatening, I was stating a fact. If anything happened to Padoue every man left in this region would rise to avenge it. The French are not as cowed as you like to think. And even if you have taken away all their firearms, they still have powerful hands which could throttle a child's murderer, and strong arms which could swing a club. I know these Normans better than you do, Colonel von Reden. If you value your own life and your men's lives, I'd advise you not to invite trouble by provoking them too far."

As if there were nothing more to be said, she moved quietly away from him and mounted the stairs without haste. Von Reden did not seek to detain her and he did not speak to her again; he was looking out towards the valley when she left the fort. But Constance did not go on up the second flight of stairs to the nursery, as she had promised Margot she would do; instead she went into her own bedroom, locking the door after her.

Her assumed calmness had served its purpose, but now her knees were trembling, and realizing they could no longer support her, she sank down in the nearest chair. She knew that she had spoken the truth in saying that flight could not save Padoue if the High Command desired to destroy him; but she had been less truthful in saying that von Reden could not torture her with daily dread. From that moment on she would have to live with this dread; it would permeate her waking thoughts and haunt her dreams. She would never escape from the torture. She would have to submit to it. For days, for weeks, for months. Perhaps for years. . . .

She bit her lips, for these were trembling too now, and she bowed her head. But she did not cover her face with her hands, as she had when she heard of the boys' deaths, for this time there was no one to see her, and she did not need to fear that she would betray too much. Gradually she was able to raise her head again, and her blurred vision cleared quickly because she had kept her tears from coming in a torrent, though for a moment or two they had overflowed. She looked across the room towards the alcove, and her eyes rested on the blue handkerchief fastened above the footboard of her bed; then involuntarily her gaze shifted from the starry surface to the crucifix over the headboard.

For years it had continued to hang there only because Tristan expected it to and wanted it to. She had left it there for this reason and she had long since ceased to resent it. But after her distaste for its presence in such a place had passed, she ceased to consider it. It was only when Blondine had mourned over the desecrated kitchen that Constance had known, for all her brave words, that she too would have missed the crucifix of her own long association. Now, for the first time, she knew her need of it. She rose and crossed the room, walking steadily again, and knelt beside the bed, her eyes uplifted to the symbol of faith and salvation.

For the next few weeks, life at Malou remained tranquil. The baby throve undisturbed, and both Margot and Aunt Bertha were rapturously preoccupied in caring for him. A small detachment of soldiers had again been placed in the commons, but these men were orderly; von Reden's excellent discipline was as effective as ever. He himself had become more and more unobtrusive. He had never reclaimed the *grand salon,* and the dining room was no longer cluttered with files and papers; he and Nolte ate their meals and did their work, which no longer seemed to be very extensive, in Tristan's office. Beyond the briefest of greetings when he and Constance met accidentally, he had spoken with her only once since their encounter on the day of the christening, and this had been on the subject of the radio.

He had not brought one with him, he explained, because he distinctly remembered there were two at Malou, the one he had found there when he first came, in the Commandant's office, and the one he had installed himself, in the *grand salon.* Now both were missing, and it was, of course, essential that he should keep abreast of the news. Perhaps the Baroness could tell him——?

Leinmeister must have taken the new large radio away when he left, Constance replied; at all events it had already disappeared when she went to the *grand salon* the morning after his departure. His men had wrecked the little old one, which had been in her husband's office, long before this. She had scrapped it in the course of her housecleaning.

"It was really so badly damaged that it could not be repaired?"

"I am sorry to say that I have no mechanical ability."

"But perhaps someone else could have fixed it. My orderly, Klietsch, is very clever at such things, for instance."

"No doubt. But you will recall that Klietsch had left sometime before this and I had no special reason for expecting him back, or for caring whether he had a radio or not."

"It is of course unimportant that Klietsch should have a radio. In fact, he is probably quite as well off without one. I was thinking of my own convenience. And it is not necessary that you should remind me, Baroness, that this is of no importance to you either. That has been made quite clear already."

"Then you didn't wish to speak with me about anything else?"

"No thank you, Baroness. I will send for a new radio at once, but I promise that you shall not be disturbed by it, as you were by the last one. Indeed I doubt if you will ever hear it at all, from the other end of the house. Probably I could keep its existence a secret, if I wished to do so. But then, as you have been good enough to tell me, I am the soul of candor."

Their meeting, as usual, had taken place in the fort, since this was the only part of the house they were both obliged to use, and after the inevitable bow, von Reden left it immediately. Constance herself lingered for a moment, looking out at the bleak landscape beyond the terrace without thinking about this, except for the passing concern, which the sight of it always aroused, as to how they could cultivate it that year, with the scarcity of men and machinery, and no horses of their own. It was quite clear to her from his parting words that von Reden suspected her of an untruth, and his suspicions were justified. Léon had tinkered, patiently and at last successfully, with the damaged radio, and it was now installed behind her bed in the alcove. Every evening before she went to sleep, she lay and listened to it, and Aunt Bertha and Margot, who never both left Padoue at once, took turns in coming to her room and listening with her to the broadcasts from London which began at quarter after nine. The High Command had already forbidden the audition of this program, and had confiscated radios, imposed fines, and even resorted to imprisonment in order to enforce the ruling. The only programs heard in public places now were those emanating from Vichy, which were censored by the Germans, and those coming from Radio Paris, directly controlled by them. But all over France little hidden groups were listening secretly, and the women at Malou knew that they were part of a great unseen company as they waited breathlessly for the words, *"Ici Londres. Les Français, parlant aux Français, aujourd'hui ——iéme jour de la lutte du peuple français pour sa libération."*

From time to time, General de Gaulle spoke himself, encouraging his faithful adherents; more often there were commentaries on the news by Maurice Schuman, Jean Marin, and Pierre Bourdon. Occasionally the proceedings of a meeting held by the Free French were broadcast, or a great ceremony at Westminster Cathedral, led by Cardinal Hinsley, in which the French were taking part. Military marches and old war songs were revived. Sometimes these were preceded by the warning, "Lower the volume of your radio so that it will not be overheard." At other times, "Tipperary" sounded to the accompaniment of the challenge, "Presently you will be hearing this in your streets again."

Recently a thrilling interpolation had been added to these British programs. Immediately after the announcement "This is London. The French speaking to the French on the ——th day of their struggle for liberation," came another: "We will now give you a few personal messages. Jean, the son of Michel, has arrived safely in England. . . . Suzanne's brother André has had a comfortable journey. . . . Bernard, baptized on Christmas Day, has joined his brother. . . . Remy, the Norman recently living in Paris, has escaped from Hamburg and has just reached London."

To the Germans, whom not a word of these broadcasts escaped, these items were as baffling as they were infuriating. They could not tell which of the Jeans and Andrés and Bernards had eluded them, among the thousands so named whom they had imprisoned and maltreated. But families of these men, who knew their birthdays and their baptismal days and the names of their brothers and sisters, joyfully identified them and thanked God that they were free. For more than a month now, ever since Léon had succeeded in repairing the radio and Constance had listened to these programs, she had been straining her ears for the news that Tristan too had escaped from bondage and joined the forces of liberation.

Often, as they lay waiting for the program to begin, she and Margot played a guessing game about the form that the announcement would take. "The Commandant never had any brothers and sisters, did he? Well then, they can't word it that way." . . . "Tristan isn't a very common name, and his father and mother didn't have common names either. His father's was Gabriel and his mother's was Monique. I don't believe they'd use those. He could be traced by them, and who knows what torture might be visited on some hostage?"

Torture was no longer a mere word to Constance, as it had been before the day Padoue was christened. Every morning when Margot brought the baby to her she wondered whether she would see him killed before night; every evening when she gave him his good-night kiss she wondered whether she would be wakened before the next morning with the horrible news that he had been slaughtered. Well, that was how she had known it would be, at the very moment she was telling von Reden it would not, and she had neither broken nor faltered under the strain of this knowledge. Night after night, when the broadcast was over and she was alone again, she had risen and knelt and prayed, as she had never prayed before in her life; and as each day passed without tragedy, her faith in the literal answer to prayer became stronger.

Now, as she stood in the fort looking out at the bleak fields which she might not be able to cultivate that year, it wavered for the first time. Perhaps von Reden had only been waiting for a pretext which so far had been lacking and which at last she had given him: she was listening regularly, with her daughter-in-law and her aunt, to a forbidden program. Thousands of other women were doing this too, and in cases where they had been caught, they had been punished. So far the penalties had not been sufficiently severe to curb the disobedience, and sterner measures had already been threatened. There was no telling what these sterner measures might be. She must not take the slightest chance of precipitating disaster. She must give up listening to the broadcasts, she must forego the thrill of hearing the stirring messages and the inspired voices, and the hope of learning that Tristan had escaped. She must find a safer hiding place for the radio or scrap it.

She did not make the decision without a passing pang. Except for the news which Craig managed to bring her from time to time, the radio represented her only reliable source of news, almost her only contact with the outside world. The daily papers were suppressed or controlled; letters were few and far between; she had not been in Lisieux since her summons to the *Kommandantur*. More and more, her existence was isolated, comfortless, bleak as the landscape which lay before her. Except for the baby. The baby was nearly two months old now. He still lay contentedly in his crib for hours on end, but he no longer slept most of the time; instead he made little cooing sounds to himself. He was beginning to study his mother while he nursed, to turn his head when someone came into the room, to smile at Aunt Bertha and his grandmother. Every day in the course of his normal, healthy development brought some endearing change and revealed some fresh attraction. He was not only their future hope, he was their present joy. No sacrifice was too great if it would safeguard him for their sakes as well as his own. The outside world did not matter as long as their own little world revolved around him. Even the news from Tristan did not matter, if getting it would jeopardize the safety or even the welfare of this child. . . .

It was Margot's turn to listen to the broadcast that night. She came across the room buoyantly, eager for the guessing game which was about to begin and for the gay music and stirring speeches which would come later. The monotony of Malou must be harder for her daughter-in-law than it was for herself, Constance reflected as she watched the girl's approach. Margot had never lost her amazing vitality, even during the latter stages of her pregnancy, and now she seemed more animated than ever. Maternity became her, as it had become her mother, but Margot had other attributes which Stéphanie lacked; she was perhaps less close to the good earth and its creatures, but she was nearer other essentials; she had a keener mind and a more soaring spirit. And every day she seemed lovelier than she had the day before. It was a wicked waste that such beauty should be so immured. Constance wondered how long it would or could be, facing the fact that some day Margot might want to marry again, and that it would be natural and right that she should. But even if Margot married, she would not take Padoue away from Malou; that is, never for long. Padoue and Malou belonged to each other. At least they would if both survived. . . .

"I didn't dare tell you, my dear, where I thought someone might overhear us. But I'm afraid we ought not to turn on the radio any more."

"Oh Mother, why not? There can't be any real danger! Everyone in France listens secretly to that British broadcast!"

"I know. But 'everyone' hasn't a Gerd von Reden in the house. And I'm almost sure he suspects us."

"But if you don't listen, you won't hear those personal messages. You'll go on fearing that your husband is still in prison when perhaps he's safe and happy in England. You'll never know."

"Oh yes I will. I'll know sometime. And I'm sure it isn't best to antagonize Colonel von Reden, Margot, or to give him any pretext for reprisals. For one thing, we must think of your father."

"You mean you're afraid that if Colonel von Reden caught us listening to the British broadcasts he might——"

"Yes. Yes, I am afraid."

The night was very still, and Constance lay quietly, planning future lessons for Padoue, and slipping the rosary which Bruno had sent her from Saumur through her fingers. She did not use the rosary for the recitation of prayers, but she liked to hold it while she turned the problems of the present over in her mind and dwelt on the hopes of the future. Often she went to sleep with it in her hands. Once she had asked Marie Aimée if it were disrespectful to use a rosary in this way, and the nun had responded with her tranquil smile.

"Of course not. There's a charming legend to the effect that if one falls asleep with the prayers uncompleted, the angels finish them."

"But I don't even start them—at least not on a rosary."

"Well, it is blessed just to have it about you. I am sure the way you use your rosary is the right way for you."

Since then Constance had felt sure of it too, and now, as she lay fingering the rosary, she remembered that Padoue would learn to say his prayers on one, in the course of his other lessons, and decided she would give him for this very purpose the rosary Bruno had sent her. She also decided that she herself would teach him the prayers she had learned when she was a little girl, and that she had taught to Nick and Bruno when they were small boys. She had not said them in a long time. They did not voice the cry of anguish which was in her soul when she knelt before the crucifix praying that nothing should happen to Padoue. In fact they were not adult prayers at all; they were those of safe and sheltered children. But she repeated them now, recalling them to her memory, so that she would be ready to teach them to Padoue when the time came.

"Now I lay me down to sleep,
I pray the Lord my soul to keep,
If I should die before I wake,
I pray the Lord my soul to take,
And this I ask for Jesus' sake."

It was then that she heard the three shots ringing out through the stillness.

In her horror she did not even try to locate these. She flung a dressing gown around her and rushed up the stairs. The third floor was in complete darkness and not a sound came from any of the rooms. She switched on the hall light and opened the door of the nursery. Padoue was sleeping quietly in the cradle beside his mother's bed; their even, peaceful breathing was almost inaudible. Constance closed the door again and went down the corridor towards the servants' rooms on the other side of the house. The silence was broken by deep regular snores. As she went back down the stairs to the second story, she heard footsteps hurrying through the fort and German voices raised far above their normal guttural pitch. Then the great outer door shut with a clang and the footsteps resounded on the drawbridge while the voices grew higher and louder. She looked out of the window and saw that men were hurrying across the yard towards the commons with flashlights in their hands and that the commons were lighted, and presently a tumult rose from there.

She threw on her clothes, found her own flashlight, and sped along. But while she was tugging at the great door, it was opened from without and von Reden stepped in front of her, blocking her way.

"You had better go back to your room, Baroness," he said coldly. "There is nothing you can do at the commons. But perhaps it would be well that you should know at once what has happened there. Your gardener, Pierre, returned unexpectedly tonight. It was probably impossible for him to send word beforehand of his coming. Or perhaps he did not even try to do so because he wanted to surprise his wife. If that was the case, he succeeded. He shot her and the man he found with her, using the pistol that lay by the bed. Then he killed himself. So there has been murder at Malou tonight. And you spoke the truth when you said that one murder leads to another."

CHAPTER XXXIV

THE NEXT MURDER was not called that. It was called reprisal.

Bärenfänger, the soldier Pierre had murdered, was buried late in the afternoon, the day after his death. Von Reden selected a plot of ground on the far side of the garden, and had it neatly enclosed with some of the spare pickets which were kept on hand to repair the fences bordering the highway. When the committal service was over, von Reden sent word to Constance that it was imperative he should see her. He did not make a formal request, as he had always done before; he issued an order. He did not even ask where she would prefer to receive him; he said he would come to the small salon in ten minutes, and that he would expect to find her waiting for him. When he entered the room, he did not bow. He closed the door behind him and confronted her.

"I understand that you have made arrangements for the burial of your two dead employees tomorrow morning."

"Yes. There is still a hearse in the village. It will come for the bodies at ten o'clock. There will be short prayers here and of course a service at the grave. Under the circumstances it will be impossible to have more than that. But Monsieur le Curé has been most compassionate. He is with Lise now, trying to comfort her."

"Since a priest is on the place, and since these people set store by such things, it might be well for him to confess Bernard and his father, so that they will not also die unshriven. Their execution will take place at sunrise. That is what I came to tell you."

"Their execution——"

"Surely you do not expect me to let a crime like the one which has just taken place go unpunished!"

"But those two poor men have committed no crime. You cannot hold them responsible for what Pierre did. And Pierre himself is dead."

"Exactly. If he were still alive he would of course be the first natural *condamné*. But since he is beyond our reach, we must make an example of someone else on the place. We cannot permit the local population to suppose that German soldiers in an Army of Occupation can be murdered with impunity."

"Not even if the killer is a betrayed husband?"

"You are begging the question, Baroness. You know as well as I do that Aylette was not seduced. You yourself caught her with another man many months ago, and at your instigation that man was severely punished. I have regretted this for some time, because I came to recognize Aylette as a demoralizing influence among my men. In this case she was unquestionably the offender. To put it plainly, she was a whore. The place is well rid of her."

"Aylette was Pierre's wife and he loved her. Besides, there is an unwritten law——"

"We do not have unwritten laws in Germany, Baroness, or in the countries we conquer. They are all carefully recorded and rigidly enforced. Even if Michel had come home instead of Pierre, and killed a man whom he found with Nicole, whom I believe to be a virtuous young woman, some retribution would have been indicated. When one of our men is guilty of rape, we punish him ourselves. But we do not permit others to administer justice for us."

"And you call it justice to execute two harmless men out of revenge!"

"Not out of revenge, Baroness. I must insist that you keep to facts. If I had been bent on revenge, I should have selected Léon first of all, for he has lost no opportunity to be insolent and mutinous. I have been careful to explain to you that it is necessary we should make an example, and I have given careful thought to the manner of this. Under ordinary circumstances, we require the execution of at least five persons in reprisal for one. But I realize that this would represent a reduction of your limited staff which would leave you extremely shorthanded. It is also customary to wipe out the entire family of a criminal. But in this case, such action would involve the execution of a small child. As I told you before, if I were ordered to do this, I should obey. But I have received no such orders—and I have decided to be lenient. Lise will be severely punished, but she will not be put to death, because she is needed for manual labor, and Lucie will also be spared; but she will be placed in one of the orphanages that we supervise."

"Bernard is needed as much as Lise."

"I have thought that over, and I have decided that with four other men on the place, they should be able to do his work among them until Michel's return, which will doubtless take place before long, since *cultivateurs* are being systematically released. On the other hand, if Lise were executed, there would be no one but Nicole to look after my men in the commons, since of course Blondine must remain at the château. As to Bernard's senile old father, there cannot be the slightest question about him. He is a burden to everyone, including himself. In Germany, his death would have been expedited long ago."

Constance had been standing near Tristan's desk, with her back to the window, when von Reden came into the room, and she had remained absolutely motionless throughout the interview. Now she put her hands behind her, gripping the desk. But she continued to look von Reden full in the face while she groped for the right reply. This time, she knew, defiance could not save the day. Probably nothing could save it. But she must try. Perhaps there could be partial salvage.

"I would not advise you to seek communication with anyone on the outside, at this juncture," von Reden went on. "In fact, I shall take every precaution to see that you do not, as I have been unable to trust you since a certain prevarication which we will not discuss just now. One of my men will remain beside the telephone, another on the drawbridge, and another at the gate, while two others will patrol the grounds. If you wish to go over to the commons, I will accompany you there now, or you may send for the priest and speak to him here in my presence. The latter plan will perhaps be the less painful for you. However, if you wish to make known my decision to your employees yourself, I shall permit you to do so."

"And I shall certainly avail myself of your permission. Do you think I am such a coward that I would send a message like that through a priest to people who have given their lives to the service of Malou?"

"No. You are not a coward, Baroness, whatever else you are. And lest you do not ask me to tell you what else you are, I will do so on my own initiative: you are a very beautiful woman."

The evil, darting thing was between them again, in all its hideous force. But it was not strong enough to draw them closer together, as it had once threatened to do; it was only strong enough to widen the breach between them, to stiffen the resistance of the woman while it unleashed the passion of the man. In her new-found rigidity, Constance did not even need the support of the desk any longer.

"I must let my daughter-in-law know that I am needed at the commons," she said quietly. "And I must send word to my aunt to come here and stay with her, before I go over to the commons myself. Of course she has been there all day." Constance sat down, drew a piece of paper towards her, and wrote a brief message in a firm hand. Then she offered the sheet to von Reden.

Dear Aunt Bertha,
I think I had better relieve you now. Besides, Margot is asking for you. Suppose you bring Lucie over to the château with you. She could watch you and Margot put Padoue to bed and it might help.

                                Love,
                                   Connie

"You see I am also taking it for granted that you are not going to commit Lucie to the model orphanage tonight," Connie remarked, still quietly. "You would hardly have the means of sending her, with so many men on guard duty."

"You are right in that assumption also, Baroness. And there is nothing objectionable in this note. I will have it delivered at once."

"Do you wish to come with me while I speak to my daughter-in-law?"

"No. But I do wish to remind you that if anything you say to her can later be construed as a warning to the *condamnés,* the results will be very serious."

"Then I think it is better that you hear what I say, so that I can take full responsibility and nothing will be blamed on my daughter-in-law. Please ask to have her come here at the same time you give orders for delivering the note."

"Very well."

Von Reden went to the door and opened it. Klietsch was standing directly outside. The Colonel spoke to him briefly and gave him the note. Then he closed the door again.

"It will be a moment before your daughter-in-law and your aunt arrive, Baroness. In the meantime——"

"In the meantime we have nothing further to say to each other."

Constance went back to the place by the window where she had been standing when von Reden came in, but this time she stood facing it. She did not turn until Margot appeared, ushered by Klietsch. The girl was carrying Padoue over her shoulder.

"I'm going back to the commons, Margot. I think I may be there some time. I didn't want you to worry if I should be delayed about getting back."

"All right, Mother. I won't."

Margot did not appear to think it was in the least strange that Constance should have sent for her to come over two flights of stairs merely to make this simple statement in the presence of an alien.

"Is that all, Mother?"

"I've written a little note asking Aunt Bertha to come back. I said you were asking for her. I thought I'd better tell you because she might refer to this."

"Well, of course I would have asked, if I'd seen you. She ought to come home. She's been there a long time. She'll be exhausted."

"Yes, that's what I thought. . . . I suggested that she should bring Lucie with her."

"And that's a good suggestion too. I wish I'd had the same idea myself. I'll keep the poor kid in the nursery until it's time for the funeral. I suppose she has to go to that."

"I suppose so."

The door opened again, and Aunt Bertha came in, Lucie clinging to her hand. The old woman's extreme fragility, more and more apparent during the last months, had suddenly become submerged in her old look of wiry endurance. She spoke with indignation.

"If you think I was tuckered out, Constance Galt——"

"No. Of course I know you weren't. But I thought there were some things Lise and Bernard would want me to take up with them myself, as their chatelaine. And there are some things I want you to do here for me, as my aunt."

Constance bent over little Lucie, smoothing back her straight fair hair. She must have been crying hard for a long time; her pleasant little face was mottled and swollen and her mild blue eyes were red-rimmed. She was quiet now, but she was still bewildered and frightened. Constance drew her close and kissed her.

"You are going to have your supper over here, Lucie," she said. "Mademoiselle Berthe is going to give it to you, just as she used to give me mine when I was a little girl. It will make her very happy to do this, because she has not had a little girl in a long time now, and she has missed that. After your supper you will go upstairs with her, and watch the baby while he is getting ready for bed. Then you will get ready for bed yourself. You will sleep tonight beside Mademoiselle Berthe so that she will not be lonely. I will explain to *grand'mère* that I have asked you to stay at Malou tonight, and why. She will be glad to have you stay with Mademoiselle Berthe and keep her company. You would be glad to do that too, wouldn't you?"

Rather doubtfully, Lucie nodded. Constance patted her thin little shoulder.

"I think that in Mademoiselle Berthe's bottom bureau drawer there is a doll that was mine when I was a little girl—a beautiful big doll that opens and shuts its eyes. Mademoiselle Berthe has kept it for a long time, hoping that some little girl would come and play with it. Can you think of a little girl who might do that, Lucie?"

Lucie looked mutely from Constance to Aunt Bertha and back at Constance again. Then she drew a long breath.

"Oui, madame," she whispered, almost inaudibly.

"I hoped you would. The doll's name is Carol. You will take good care of her, won't you?"

"Oui, madame," Lucie said again. And this time, though she said it softly, she did not really whisper, and her voice did not tremble as she spoke.

Everything was very quiet in the quarters above the stables, where Bernard and his family lived and where the German soldiers were billeted, when von Reden and Constance entered. The steep little staircase led directly into the kitchen, and Joseph, the senile old grandfather, sat nodding, as usual, in the corner of the wide chimneypiece where his chair was always kept. The guard who was also there saluted automatically, and immediately froze again into immobility. Nicole looked up from something she was stirring over the fire, but she looked quickly down again and did not speak until Constance spoke to her.

"Monsieur le Curé is still here, isn't he, Nicole?"

"Yes, Madame la Baronne. He is still in there praying."

"And your mother-in-law is with him?"

"Yes, Madame la Baronne."

"It will be all right for me to go in?"

"But yes. You are expected."

Constance led the way into the adjoining room. Early evening was already closing in, and the dormers admitted little light. But tall tapers were burning at both the head and the foot of the wide bed where Aylette and Pierre lay side by side. Their hands had been crossed on their breasts and rosaries placed between their fingers, but the beautiful composure of natural death was lacking from their haggard white faces. The priest and the bereft mother were both on their knees near the bed. Constance went over and knelt briefly between them. Then she rose, touching each lightly on the shoulder.

"I am sorry to interrupt your prayers. But I must speak to you both."

The priest rose easily and instantly, as from accustomed practice. Constance addressed him while Lise was still struggling clumsily to her feet.

"Can you stay with us through the night, Father?"

"Of course, Madame la Baronne, if you need me."

"We do. We must be able to swear you have given no message or alarm to anyone, and we could not do that if you went away. Moreover, we must ask you to hear confessions. Last confessions. Of condemned men."

Lise was on her feet now. The flickering candlelight fell on her face, exposing its terror. She clutched wildly at Constance's arm. Von Reden leaned against the wall, his arms folded, watching her.

"What men?" Lise asked hoarsely.

"I have a dreadful thing to tell you, Lise. If I could save you from it, I would. But I can't. So I must share it with you."

"What thing?"

Constance looked over at von Reden and he shook his head. "The Colonel says his soldier's death must be avenged, Lise. Usually the Nazis take five lives for one. This time only two will be taken. But those two are your men."

"The Nazi swine, the assassin——"

She was already charging across the room, her back bent, her fingers clawing the air. Constance and the priest caught her and held her while she lashed out at them. Von Reden stood regarding her in contemptuous silence as the others tried to quiet her.

"Let me go! Let me go or I will kill you before I kill him!"

"That wouldn't help, Lise. That would only mean more murder and more and more. Stop striking at me and listen to me!"

"My daughter, if we cannot change this verdict, we must pray that God will give you strength to bear it."

"Pray? To a God who has forsaken us? Or to the Devil and this man, who are the same?"

"Shame on you, Lise, for brawling in our son's death chamber! What is this all about?"

Bernard had come into the room, his feet in their woolen socks making no noise on the paved floor. His wooden shoes, according to tidy habit, had been left side by side outdoors, so that the soil from the stable would not dirty the clean floor. But his garments smelled of the cows he had just milked and the sheep he had just herded. He pulled his wife away from the priest and shook her.

"Have you no decency? Look at that bed over there and tell me, have you none at all? Your pardon, Monsieur le Curé. Your pardon, Madame la Baronne. This is not like Lise, you know that. But it has been hard, bitterly hard, losing the boy, and in such a way, when we had waited so long for his home-coming."

"Hard! You do not know yet what that means! Wait till you hear——"

"And what shall I wait to hear then?"

"That the murder goes on. That the poor simple old one, who has not even wits enough left to know about last night, must die to pay for it. And that you—that you——"

She slipped from his grasp and to the floor beside him, clasping his knees. Then she buried her face in his baggy homespun trousers, her body shaken by sobs. He stooped over, the anger gone from his face, and stroked her unkempt head.

"There," he said. "There. So that is it. Well, we have had many good years together, Lise. We will not spoil them at the end. I have grieved, you'll never know how much, because I was too old to fight this time. Instead I can think that after all I can die for France. As for old soldiers like me, perhaps—— But it is too late to think of that. The old one, what will he know? Only that he is led out into the sunshine as he has been so many mornings. And after that will begin the long sleep, which would have come soon in any case."

He bent lower and by slow degrees lifted her up. "There," he said again. "It goes better when you think of it that way, doesn't it, Lise? Now we will go to our own room and talk for a while, because there are many things I must tell you before morning. About the stock, for instance. You know something of caring for it already, but you must learn more, to keep it as it is. Never have I seen it look better than it did tonight." He paused for a moment, thinking of the cattle he had just left, safe in their stalls. "Madame la Baronne and Monsieur le Curé will watch by our dead for us while we are gone," he went on. "And after we have talked with each other, we will come back. There are things I must say to them too. But you have always been first with me, Lise, you know that. And see, it is so to the last."

With one arm still around his wife, he stretched out a rough red hand, first to the priest and afterwards to the Baroness. Then he led Lise out of the room, his unshod feet still moving silently over the paved floor. He did not once look in von Reden's direction.

One by one the men and women of Malou learned what had happened. Each in turn came to watch by Pierre and Aylette, and the priest and Constance, who stayed there all night, told them. Then they all went to the office in the château, where von Reden had finally retired, after doubling the guard at the commons, and each in turn offered to die instead of Bernard and the old one.

They all gave a good reason for doing so: Denis because his eyes were so bad that he could hardly see anyhow and therefore was not much use, whereas Bernard had good eyes, which were needed. Martin because his back hurt so badly that he wanted to be put out of his pain, just like a crippled horse. Benoît because the army doctor had told him he had not long to live anyway, and he had never relished the idea of a lingering death—a quick shot and everything over, that was the way he had always hoped it would be. Léon because he had been insolent to the Colonel and now the Colonel was punishing Bernard for what was really his, Léon's, fault. The women had equally cogent reasons: Blondine had outlived her usefulness. Nicole was a member of the family too, now. Lise had shared a bed with Bernard for thirty years; well, now she wanted to share a grave with him.

It was all futile, of course. Von Reden received the first two or three and told them so, harshly, himself. Then he locked the door of his office and left Nolte to deal with them. They went sadly away, returning to the commons, and since Monsieur le Curé was still there anyhow, they all confessed to him. Very early in the morning, he told them he could celebrate Mass in the kitchen, or in the empty stable, if they chose; he had come prepared. Constance offered the fort, but von Reden would not let the condemned men leave the commons. So it was decided to use the stable, because when all came together, the little kitchen was not big enough to hold everyone. And everyone was there except Margot, who was taking care of Padoue, and Aunt Bertha, who was taking care of Lucie.

There was an old battered table in one of the stalls which could serve as an altar, and in another there were several old benches; it was a long time since the stables had been used for anything but storage, and that was how these things happened to be there. Constance sat at the end of a bench, beside Lise, who did not sit with Bernard, because the women remained on one side and the men on the other, just as they always had. But they knelt together when they went up to the altar and Constance sat alone on the bench. She was the only one who could not go to Communion that morning, but she knew that never again would she be left behind when all the others were going.

After Mass, the women went back to the kitchen, Constance with the others, and sat holding fast to Lise's hand, waiting for the shots. Afterwards she went to the cemetery. The sun had been shining when Bernard led his father out to the garden wall just as he had so many times before, and the old man had gone quite happily, exactly as Bernard had said he would. But now it was raining hard and a cold March wind was blowing. Everyone was wet to the skin and chilled to the bone long before the prayers were finished and the graves filled. It took longer because Aylette and Pierre could not be buried with the others in consecrated ground, whereas Bernard and the old one were buried near the *anciens combattants* who had fallen in the First World War. Also because all of Norolles, from Monsieur le Maire down, whom the news had reached some way though no one knew how, exactly, had flocked to do honor to Bernard and the old one. They had remained apart while Pierre and Aylette were lowered into their lonely graves, but after that they clustered around. And when the religious service was over and the *charitons* and the surviving *anciens combattants* started the *"Marseillaise,"* the others, including Lise, sang it with them:

> " 'Nous entrerons dans la carrière
> Quand nos aînés n'y seront plus.
> Nous y trouverons leur poussière
> Et la trace de leurs vertus.
> Bien moins jaloux de leur survivre
> Que de partager leur cercueil,
> Nous aurons le sublime orgueil
> De les venger ou de les suivre.' "

Constance and Blondine left Nicole and Lise at the commons and went on to the château to change their dripping clothes. When Constance was reclad, Aunt Bertha and Lucie came to her study together. Aunt Bertha was carrying a little tray with hot coffee on it and Lucie was carrying a big bisque doll.

"There!" Aunt Bertha said, when she had set down the little tray. "While the Baroness eats her breakfast, Lucie, you tell her what you and I decided after we went to bed last night."

Lucie looked at Constance without fear and answered without hesitation.

"We decided that I am going to stay right here and keep on being Mademoiselle Berthe's little girl until *maman* gets well and comes back from the hospital," she said. "Unless *grand'mère* should get lonely of course. If she does, I'll go and stay with her. But I'll take Carol with me when I do."

Eight months later, when Duncan Craig came to tell Constance that he was going back to the United States, the first person he saw was Lucie, who was wheeling Carol across the drawbridge in a little cart which had once belonged to Bruno and which Aunt Bertha had found under the eaves. Nothing more had ever been said about the model orphanage.

CHAPTER XXXV

DUNCAN CRAIG was fond of children, and he had never come to Malou without bringing Lucie some small present which she treasured with a fervor out of all proportion to its value. When she recognized him, she snatched Carol from the little cart and dashed forward to meet him.

"Why, hello there!" he exclaimed, tossing her up in the air and giving her a hearty kiss as he set her firmly on her feet again. "What have you been doing with yourself since the last time I was here? You've grown so much I wouldn't have known you if it hadn't been for your pigtails."

"I've had lots to eat," Lucie explained proudly.

"Oh, you have, have you? Well, I wish there were more little girls in France who could say that just now. Who gives you all these juicy tidbits? The Baroness?"

"No. The Baroness gives me my lessons. Mademoiselle Berthe gives me the tidbits. And Blondine. And sometimes Aunt Nicole. But mostly Mademoiselle Berthe."

"I see," Craig remarked, though he was not quite sure he did. Evidently Lucie was spending more time at the château than she was in the commons, and there must be some special reason for this, perhaps a sad one. "Run along and tell the Baroness I'm here." Lucie raced back across the drawbridge, her blond pigtails flying, and Craig, following at a more leisurely rate, had time to notice numerous signs of change around the place. The *Lastwagen,* which so long had cluttered the sloping area between the château and the outer gates, were all gone, suggesting that Malou was no longer being utilized by the Germans. On the other hand, the absence of the *Lastwagen* could not completely account for the neglected and deserted appearance of this area. There were alternate patches of bare ground and long rank grass in it, and a few untended and unkempt animals were straying over it at random. Its prosperous, well-ordered look was completely gone. Farther off, in the fields, two or three bent figures were vaguely visible, one of them apparently a woman. But Martin was not sunning himself beside the stables, and Léon did not come forward with a flourish to say that Madame la Baronne would be delighted to see Monsieur le Docteur, and would he mount at once to the study? Instead, Constance herself appeared, alone and unannounced, in the open doorway.

The change in her was far more startling to Craig than the change in the place. She was so much thinner that her dark wool dress hung loosely on her figure, and when she gave the visitor her hand, he saw that the great sapphire ring had been shifted to her middle finger to keep it from slipping off. Her hair was still wound about her head in a heavy braid, but instead of giving the effect of a golden crown, it had a drab, lifeless look. Her face was so lined with weariness that the pleasure with which it lighted could not wholly efface the deep traces of this. But her voice rang with welcome.

"With one marvelous exception, this is the best thing that's happened at Malou since you came the last time," she said joyously. "And that was so long ago I'd almost decided you'd gone home."

"No, not yet. . . . It has been a long time, but it's been harder and harder for me to get around. My epileptic general finally went back to Germany, and since then I've had fewer favors coming my way. In fact, I'm afraid the game's about up, as far as I'm concerned. That's what I've come to tell you about—mainly. But first I'd like to know what the marvelous exception is?"

"The news that Tristan has escaped."

"God, that's wonderful! You're sure?"

"As sure as I can be of anything. You know those 'personal messages' that come through on the London broadcast?"

"Yes. 'Henri, born the tenth of August, embraces his wife Marie and his daughter Mounette.' And so on. Is that the way you heard?"

"I didn't hear myself. I listened every night for a long time to all those announcements. And then I stopped turning on the radio because I found out that von Reden suspected I was tuning in on forbidden programs. But some of my neighbors who haven't had Germans quartered on them have gone on doing it secretly. Monsieur le Maire was the first to bring us word. Of course when we saw him crossing the drawbridge, we thought he'd come to give us bad news again, because the last time—— But instead it was to say that the night before the first 'personal' had been, 'Tristan, cousin of Marie Aimée, has landed in Southampton.' Before the day was over, half a dozen other friends came to tell us the same thing."

"And that was how long ago?"

"Way back in April. Just when everything was hardest."

"Well, what else has been happening here? The place looks as if a blight had struck it. Except for little Lucie. She's blooming."

"Yes. She is. And so is Padoue. Wait till you see him! But come in and let's sit down while I tell you about the rest. You like the study best, don't you? Go up there and I'll join you as soon as I've told Blondine to kill the fatted calf."

She rejoined him in a few minutes, bringing a tray more sparingly supplied than in the old days, but still attractively set. Craig took it from her, abruptly and reproachfully.

"You ought not to carry things like that over those long steep stairs, and you know it. Why on earth didn't you call me? What's become of Léon?"

"Léon doesn't work in the house any more. He was needed too much outside. Not that he's very good in the fields, but he does the best he can. And it doesn't hurt me to carry a tray. I do lots of things that are harder than that without any bad results. Perhaps you've forgotten, but I'm pretty strong. And the tray isn't very heavy-laden, I'm sorry to say."

"It looks all right to me. But you don't. You look damn tired. And you've lost not only those ten pounds you put on a while back when you needed to, but at least ten more, unless I'm a mighty poor guesser. I don't like it. I didn't expect you to blossom exactly, under the Occupation, but you certainly were taking it in your stride the last time I saw you. Is the noise of the bombers getting you down?"

"How clever of you to remember that phobia, Duncan! No—I can't say I don't mind them, but I'm not letting them get me down either. I'm still taking the Occupation in my stride and of course that's been ever so much easier since I've known that Tristan was safe and sound in England. But striding's strenuous exercise. I suppose almost anyone would lose weight keeping it up for long," she retorted. "And we did have one tragic episode here that took a good deal out of all of us." Briefly she told him about Pierre's unexpected return and its hideous consequences. "We've done our best not to dwell on it," she continued. "Lise has been wonderful—she never speaks of it at all, or stops plodding along. She's taken over all the work in the barns and farmyard, except that Nicole does some of the milking. We've been able to keep nearly all our cattle so far—of course we've shared a few with the neighbors for food and a few have been requisitioned. But not enough to make much difference, and of course that's helped a lot. And Nicole's good at field work as well as dairy work—really better than any of the men. They're all more or less disabled in one way or another. And now that there aren't any soldiers billeted in the commons, and that Lucie is here so much of the time, the housework in the quarters doesn't amount to much."

"How soon after this 'episode' did the Nazis clear out?"

"Not for a couple of months. And that was pretty hard too. Because we'd stopped thinking of von Reden as a martinet and begun to think of him as a murderer. Not just on account of Joseph and Bernard. You see, he'd threatened——— And we never knew when the threat might be carried out."

Briefly and quietly, as she had told him about Pierre, she told him about Padoue. He shook his head understandingly, swearing under his breath.

"It's all part of the Nazis' devilish plan—to keep their victims guessing, when these threats are made, whether it's all done for effect or whether it's done in deadly earnest. Most of the time, of course, it's merely for effect. But it's in deadly earnest just often enough to keep France terrorized. Of course you know what happened in Nantes?"

"No! What did happen?"

"Fifty Frenchmen were killed in reprisal for the assassination of one German officer."

"In *Nantes*—you mean just in the city?"

"No, the order took in the outskirts too. I'm sorry to be the bearer of such bad news, Connie. But one of the victims was Robert de Fremond."

With the gesture that had always been so natural when she feared her face might betray too much, Constance shielded it with her hands. But after a moment's silence, she spoke with composure.

"The poor Countess! Of course she loved them all. But Robert was her idol."

"With good reason. He was one of the best there was, Connie. You'd better say poor France."

"I will. I do. But I suppose women always think of these things more personally. . . . Have you heard about the others at Sainte-Luce? Are they all right?"

"I've not only heard from them, I've seen them. I've just come from Chassay, Connie. It's a sad house. But it's still a great one and it's carrying on. The de Fremonds and all their branches live up to their motto. . . . Tell me—did von Reden ever say anything more about Padoue?"

"No, never. At least not to me. And I think I'd have known it if he had to anyone else. Margot has wonderful self-control. But I don't believe she could have helped betraying her fear if she'd thought Padoue was in danger."

"Of course we're not saying anything about your self-control in keeping your mouth shut and not betraying your fear. . . . Von Reden hasn't been back since he removed his detachment?"

"No. One or two other officers have stopped by and gone over the château to see if it would suit their purpose. But it hasn't. I gather that in most cases they prefer properties with absentee owners. Probably Tristan foresaw that when he made me promise I'd never leave. But it is a godsend to see someone from the outside world. I hope you'll talk to me most of the night, Duncan, about what's happening there. With time out for a little food and drink every now and then, of course."

"I'll tell you everything I can that I think may interest you. Do you want me to begin with the purely personal and work up to the international scene or do you want me to do it the other way around?"

"I'd like the purely personal first. I just reminded you that's the way women's minds usually work. But when you come right down to it, the two are more or less connected in this case, aren't they? I noticed you said 'not yet' when I told you I thought perhaps you'd decided to go home; and then afterwards you said you thought the game was about up, as far as you were concerned. Doesn't that mean——?"

"Yes, it does mean. I was going to lead up to that gradually. But since you've asked me straight out, I may as well tell you. There's not much more I can do in the French military hospitals. I'm too restricted, every way. I'm going to resign as consultant as soon as I get back to Paris."

"I'm sorry. And not just because of what your work's meant to France, Duncan. Because of what it's meant to you. You don't seem like the same man you were two years ago."

What she said was true. Craig had sloughed off all his excess weight and regained the clean-limbed look and ease of bearing which had set him apart from most other medical officers at Grand Blottereau. His skin had cleared too; the telltale traces of dissipation which had been increasingly apparent and increasingly disfiguring in the late nineteen-thirties were all gone. No one could have called his mouth weak or sensuous now. His hair had begun to turn gray at the temples, but this gave him an air of distinction rather than of age. The rigors of the life he had led and the spur of a definite purpose had done wonders for him.

"Don't worry. I'm no more anxious to turn back the clock than you are to have me. I'm not going home to take up again where I left off. I'm going back to try for the sort of a job that'll have me all set to come back here the minute something breaks. I don't believe it'll be long. After all, Roosevelt's already said that the shooting's started."

"Yes, I heard that—and his pledge that he and the American people would do everything in their power to crush the Nazi forces. Now that we have the house to ourselves again, I'm turning on the radio once in a while. . . . So you think——?"

"I don't think, Connie, I know. Of course I don't know when or where or how. But it's bound to come. If I could do anything for you by staying on in France, you know I would. But I can't. I can't do anything now and if I were still here after war was declared, I'd be interned as an enemy alien. So I better clear out before I'm shut up for the duration where I couldn't do anyone any good, except maybe a few fellow prisoners, and probably they'd all be turned over to eminent physicians who are also excellent linguists, like the one who came here when Padoue was born." He grinned, paused to pour out a drink of Calvados, and went on. "It's quite a chore, just getting from France to England, these days. I have to go all the way from Paris to Madrid, and then from Madrid to Lisbon, and finally from Lisbon to London. Comparatively speaking, the rest is easy. And I'm expecting congenial company on my transatlantic trip."

"Gwen and Eileen?"

"Yes. Couldn't you give me the satisfaction of surprising you, Connie? They've decided, just as I have, that the U.S.A. is the best springboard into the next scene of action, wherever that is. I may add that I had a little something to do with their decision."

"So you've managed to keep in touch with them? I'm very glad."

"Any specific reason?"

"Why, yes. I know you were worried about Eileen, at first, and I think the more you've seen of this association of hers with Gwen, the less it's troubled you."

"Well, that's correct. The kid's had a great time. And she's developed into a great person. Of course she probably would have anyway. She'd have broken loose from the confines of the Junior League sooner or later. But she did it sooner this way. Easier, too, than if she'd stayed with her mother."

"So you're giving Gwen a little credit at last?"

"Sure. I'm giving her all that's coming to her."

As he made it, the remark was cryptic. Constance might have asked how she was meant to interpret it if Margot had not come in just then. She was carrying Padoue when she appeared on the threshold, but she promptly put him down on the floor and watched him with doting pride while he crept rapidly across the rug to his grandmother, making gleeful sounds as he went. Then she rushed after him and threw her arms around Craig's neck.

"Where have you been all this time?" she demanded with mock indignation. "I'd begun to think Padoue would be grown up before you came back to look at him! See, he's practically walking already!" As a matter of fact, with comparatively little assistance, Padoue had pulled himself up to his grandmother's knees, and was now seated on her lap, bouncing up and down and chortling with triumph. "Don't you dare tell me he isn't the most beautiful baby you ever saw in your life!" Margot concluded.

"I wouldn't dare. Besides, as a matter of fact, he really is. And you're not too hard to look at yourself, Margot. I'd say that neither of you had any use for a doctor, as such. However, since I'm here anyway, perhaps I'd better look you both over. What's the best time?"

"This is, isn't it, Mother? Because pretty soon I put Padoue to bed and then I help get supper. Mother and Aunt Bertha like to clean, but I like to cook."

"Well, as I like to eat, we ought not to have much trouble combining forces. So long, Connie. Unless you want to act as office nurse?"

"No. I must go out to the dairy before it gets dark. Lise and Nicole will be waiting for me."

She picked up a shabby coat that was lying over the back of a chair and buttoned it closely around her. Then she drew on some clumsy overshoes. The step which had once been so light and quick sounded slow and heavy as she went down the stairs and Craig guessed that this visit to the dairy, on top of a hard day's work, represented determined effort. But he knew it would do no good to suggest that she skip it. She had accepted such supervision and doubtless some of the actual labor which went with it as part of her stewardship. She would be faithful to every phase of this to the very end.

"I'd say Blondine had a very apt pupil," he remarked a couple of hours later as they all sat companionably around the supper table; and for a few

338

minutes Margot's increasing skill and her zest for creating new dishes formed an agreeable topic of conversation. The meal had been pleasant and leisurely, and though they waited on themselves, the lack of service had proved no handicap to the ease with which it progressed. But in many respects the same sort of change was apparent in the house as on the grounds. Inevitably, it showed the effects of being understaffed; though it was not dirty or even untidy, it had lost its shining look. The brasses were dull, the floors unwaxed, the draperies dingy; and the old warmth, which had set it apart from all other Norman houses, was largely gone. The halls and the fort were frigid, and though Connie had lighted a tiny fire after she and Craig first went to the study, there were no signs that one had been there before, and the same was true of the dining room.

When she finally gave the signal to leave the table, Aunt Bertha bade Craig good night in such a way that he gathered it was now her custom to go to bed immediately after supper. Margot, on the other hand, moved automatically to the kitchen, and it was evident that she intended to help Blondine with the dishes. Craig went out to joke and talk for a few minutes with the old cook, and found that she had failed lamentably. Obviously the others were trying to save her pride by giving her the feeling that her reign in the kitchen was still supreme, while actually Margot was doing most of her work. When Craig and Constance were alone in the study again, he reverted to the subject of the girl's glowing health.

"No wonder von Reden said Padoue was a very fine specimen of the human race," he remarked thoughtfully. "Nick certainly was and Margot certainly is. I never saw a more glorious young creature. She ought to have a dozen children. Will it hurt your feelings if I say I hope she does?"

"No. I realize it too. But we can't look very far ahead just now, can we, Duncan? Until the war's over, I don't see——"

"Probably not. But someone might turn up, at that. After all, Margot's mother married a *grand blessé,* and until recently she's been happier in her marriage than almost anyone I ever saw. Except, of course, you and Tristan." He hesitated for a moment and then went on: "Speaking of being hurt and happy marriages and all that, I've something else to say to you that I hope you won't mind too much either. I think Tilda and I are about through, Connie. And I think we ought to do something about it, before I get tangled up in another war, instead of getting tangled up with any more women. She'd have the law and public opinion both on her side in every state of the Union except South Carolina if she sued for divorce now. But if I were off in a field hospital somewhere, it would be different."

Instead of answering instantly, Constance rose and, standing with her back to him, carefully mended the small fire. When she sat down again, she picked up her knitting, and for a few moments the crackling of fresh twigs and the click of steel needles made the only sounds in the room. However, now that Craig could see her face again, he noticed, with relief, that it was pensive rather than shocked or startled.

"You're not surprised?" he inquired at length.

"No. I've thought for a good many years that this might happen sooner or later. I wondered the last time you and Tilda were here together how much longer you could go on the way you were, just drifting farther and farther apart, without trying to get closer together, or without forcing a definite break either. On the other hand, I knew that Tilda didn't like definite breaks, because they're too much trouble. And I knew that you were——"

"Finding consolation elsewhere?"

"Yes, I suppose you could call it that. I'm terribly sorry, Duncan. And I'm sorrier for you than I am for Tilda. I don't think she's really suffered very much. And I'm afraid you have. You see, I've always known you married the wrong girl."

"That wasn't my fault."

"Oh yes it was. I'm not talking about myself, Duncan, when I say you married the wrong girl. I wasn't the right girl for you either. The only thing that surprises me is, you haven't found that out long before this."

"You're not going to drag Gwen in again, after all these years!"

"I didn't mean to. I know you don't like to have me. You brought up the general subject, Duncan, I didn't. Let's change it. There's something else I've been wanting very much to ask you anyway. Did you ever run into Abel again at Vichy?"

"Yes, I ran into him several times again, and then I made a point of seeing him and having a talk with him. He'd roused my suspicions in the course of those accidental meetings, and I'm sorry to say he confirmed them when I pinned him down. He's an out-and-out collaborationist, Connie."

"Oh, how horrible! When his own father——"

"He isn't thinking in terms of his own father. He began by thinking in terms of tanks and machine guns and airplanes, and now he's thinking in terms of their results. He saw what the Luftwaffe and the Wehrmacht could do against forces, if you can call them forces, which had no leaders and no discipline and very little equipment. He's seeing what an Army of Occupation can do in a country that's riddled with corruption. And he's convinced that might is right. He's completely honest and coldly logical in all his arguments. He's always prided himself that no one could make him believe in anything that couldn't be explained. Of course, when he began saying that as a youngster he was referring to religion. Now he's twisted his theory around and made it positive instead of negative, so that it fits into the Nazi doctrine. That has been explained to his complete satisfaction, so he does believe it. He's begun to explain it himself to other people, with results that are very satisfactory to his superiors. He's been promoted again."

"Every word you say makes it all seem more terrible. Do you think Stéphanie and Jacques have any idea——?"

"No, I don't believe so. I wouldn't have told you if you hadn't asked. This was a subject you brought up, remember. Theoretically, he's doing mostly office work—he's in some kind of a bureau that handles statistics about internment camps and prisoners of war and so on. Of course I didn't know you had heard from Tristan when I talked to Abel and I tried to sound him out on that subject, but I didn't get anywhere. He merely remarked that visionaries and idealists did their country more harm than traitors, as if we'd been discussing their relative merits impersonally. Then he started talking about Hitler's latest address, the one where the Führer said the Russians were 'broken.'"

"And did you try to talk to him about Jacques?"

"Not this last time. I did once before, and he shut me off then too. I think he's trying to forget about his Jewish blood. Very successfully too. After all, physically, he's not unlike the most admired Teuton type. He's a fine specimen of a Breton."

"A fine specimen!"

"Well, you know what I mean—big-boned and blond-haired and ruddy-skinned. Take that with his amazing ability to digest and adapt statistics and ideologies, and you've got a combination that's hard to beat when you come to pleasing the powers that be. . . . Look, Connie, you've accepted the fact that Margot's almost certain to go the way of all flesh and that Tilda's about to divorce me for adultery or anything else she pleases, and I think that's about enough for one night. Don't try to swallow Abel's derelictions along with all the rest. Let's talk about something else."

She agreed with him that this might be better, and they devoted the rest of the evening to what he had casually characterized as the international scene. But there was, it appeared, one more personal matter which he wished to discuss with her, and he brought this up the next morning as they paced up and down the brick walk in the kitchen garden.

He wanted her to join him in trying to persuade Aunt Bertha to go back to the States with him. He would guarantee to see the old lady safely across the Spanish and Portuguese frontiers himself; when they reached London, Gwen and Eileen could take over. He had already consulted them by letter, and they were both agreed that he was right in feeling she ought to go home without further delay. Connie's own position would be increasingly difficult after war was declared between the United States and the Axis. But after all, she was legally a French citizen; she could not be interned as an enemy alien, whereas Aunt Bertha ran the same risk of this that he did, with potential results that could be far more serious. She was very old and very frail. She could not possibly survive the rigors of imprisonment.

"You're right, of course," Connie said without hesitation. "We'll talk to her about it. Can you stay until she can get ready to leave and take her along with you now?"

"That's what I came for. Naturally I wanted very much to see you before I left and have a good talk with you. But we've got lots of other good talks ahead of us yet, and don't you ever forget it. On the other hand, if I don't get Aunt Bertha out of France now, I'll never see her again."

They had no difficulty in finding her. She was in her own little room, to which she had contentedly returned after the departure of the Germans, since it was then no longer necessary for her to keep unremitting watch over Margot and Padoue. She looked thoroughly at home, with her Victorian furniture around her, and she was comfortably seated in her favorite rocker, with an illustrated French primer, from which Lucie was slowly and painstakingly reading, spread out over her knees.

"Just a minute, Lucie," Aunt Berthe said. "I presume you've come to say good-by, Duncan?"

"No. As a matter of fact I haven't. Connie and I wanted to have a talk with you."

"Well?" she inquired, rather tartly.

Craig had lost none of his persuasiveness with the years. He argued his case earnestly and eloquently, and every now and then when he paused, Connie put in a few words that were equally earnest and still more tender. Aunt Bertha continued to rock while they talked, and she did not once try to interrupt them. But when they had both said everything they had to say, she rose, pushing back her rocker.

"I know you've got a friendly feeling for me, Duncan," she said. "And I'm much obliged to you. It isn't every man who would put himself out undertaking to travel with an old woman. Just the same, I aim to stay right here in France, as long as I'm spared. I'll be eighty-five years old on Decoration Day and it isn't to be expected I'll be spared much longer. But that's something the Lord'll have to decide. The Germans can't do it for Him."

"If we were sure you could stay at Malou, Aunt Bertha, it would be different," Constance interposed. "A long time ago, when Tristan and I suggested that perhaps you'd like to go home, you said this was your home now, and we understood. It made us very happy that you wanted to stay. But as Duncan's been explaining, the United States may be at war with the Axis any day now, and if that happens you might be sent to an internment camp. It would make me terribly unhappy if——"

"Well, I don't know as I'd jump up and down with joy myself if I was lugged off by the Nazis and clapped into one of those camps of theirs," Aunt Bertha remarked. "But that hasn't happened yet and maybe it won't. Anyway, I never was one to cross my bridges until I got to them. I haven't lost my gumption yet either. If a body's got gumption, most generally they know what to do when the time comes. The time's come for you to go back to America, Duncan, I can see that. The sooner you're on your way the better, if you ask me. And I'm glad you're meeting Gwen and Eileen in London. It will be nice for all of you, taking that trip home together. I presume Gwen'll keep in mind that you're a married man, even if you don't. So I can't see that you need me along."

"It wasn't that we needed you, Aunt Bertha, it was that we wanted you. And besides——"

Aunt Bertha looked at Craig. "I told you before I'm much obliged to you, Duncan," she said. "But it looks to me as if I was needed and wanted both, right here. I hope you won't forget to remember me to Gwen Foster. I always thought she had considerable character. I liked that girl Eileen, too, the little I saw of her. I presume they've both got their share of gumption. If you ever see a chance to get one through, I'd admire to have a post card telling me what sort of a trip you had going back to America."

CHAPTER XXXVI

It was not until the early fall of 1942 that Aunt Bertha was sent to the internment camp on the Cotentin Peninsula near Cherbourg; and in the meantime everyone had much more reason to worry about what was happening at L'Abbatiale than about what was happening at Malou.

To be sure, almost immediately after Pearl Harbor Aunt Bertha was advised by the authorities that she would be obliged to report every week at the nearest police station, a requirement made of all American citizens who had been so self-willed as to remain in France against the advice of both their own and the Vichy governments; and the weekly trips into Lisieux entailed by this requirement involved considerable hardship. It was quite out of the question for the old lady to undertake the long walk, and there were still no horses at Malou. But after considerable maneuvering, Constance succeeded in getting a little donkey, and a cart small enough for it to draw with ease. Aunt Bertha never complained about its slow, jolting motion or inadequate shelter. She bundled herself up in a strange assortment of mufflers, hoods, shawls, and other knitted articles, in addition to an ancient sealskin coat; and sitting bolt upright beside Constance or Margot, who took turns in driving her to town, stoically accepted the discomforts of the trip. The only remark she made in the course of it referred to some sight she saw along the bleak road or in the drab streets; and at the police station she betrayed no resentment of the ruling which required her presence there and answered the routine questions with terse civility. The police officers were never rude to her and they never detained her; five minutes after she had stalked into their presence she stalked out again.

After these brief formalities had been fulfilled, Aunt Bertha and her companion went on to the Abbaye des Bénédictines for lunch, which they took with the aged pensioners. Then they went to the *grand parloir* for a visit with Marie Aimée, to the General Hospital for a brief visit with Ghisèle, or occasionally on to L'Abbatiale. Margot decided that it would be practical to take Padoue to see her parents, and she amused herself by decorating the harness of the donkey, which she had named Flora, with ferns and apple blossoms for these expeditions. By spring, the cart actually had quite a jaunty air when it started out, and the stop at the police station had begun to seem like a mere incident in a day's junketing.

Then, one afternoon in early June, when the cart was going along at a good clip between the Abbaye and L'Abbatiale, Margot saw that Mark Mullins's old car was coming from the opposite direction and that her mother was signaling for her to stop.

She handed the reins to Aunt Bertha and, jumping down, reached for Padoue, who could now walk steadily on his own two feet. Margot looked down at him beamingly.

"Throw a kiss to Granny, Padoue," she urged proudly. "And say 'Hello, everybody!'" Padoue had been throwing kisses upon request for several months, but the salutation of "Hello, everybody!" was a new accomplishment. Margot had every reason to expect a delighted response to it. Instead, only her father answered the little boy. Her grandmother and great-grandmother, who were on the back seat, did not act as if they had heard. Stéphanie, who was at the wheel, looked straight at her daughter without even glancing down at the baby.

"You won't find anyone at home," she said tonelessly. "We're on our way to the *mairie* again."

"What for?" Margot inquired with her usual directness.

"They're not satisfied with stamping our identity cards. They're going to label our clothes now, too," Madame Bouvier said vehemently, answering for the group. "And after we're labeled, they won't allow us on the streets after nine o'clock at night, or in a café or a cinema at any time. Not that the ruling about the cafés and the cinemas will make any difference to this family—stuck off in a place like L'Abbatiale! But it will to almost every other Jew in France!"

"Whom do you mean by 'they'? What sort of a label?"

"The Nazi Military Command in Paris—the Militärbefehlshaber—and its local representatives. From now on, all Jews over six years old have got to go around tagged. With yellow stars. We've each of us got to get three to put on different garments. And just to have insult added to injury, we've each got to give up one of our textile tickets for them."

Madame Bouvier's voice had become increasingly vituperative as she spoke. Madame Solomon, who was still a remarkably handsome woman in spite of her advanced age, remained majestically silent, nothing in her face or manner betraying an inner tumult. Margot looked from the back seat to the front; her mother was crying stormily, but her father was smiling, the furrows in his lean cheeks deepening as they always had when he did so and his amber-lighted eyes crinkling at the corners.

"Go along to the house and make yourself and the others comfortable until we get back, Margot," he said, in his usual pleasant way. "I don't imagine we'll be long. I think after we get the stars we'll be allowed to take them home to have them sewed on. That shouldn't be much of a task either. I haven't seen them yet, but I don't imagine they're very large. Or very disfiguring, for that matter. A star's quite a lovely thing."

"Not when it's made of dirty cloth and worn as a badge of shame!"

"We don't know that the cloth is dirty, Mother. After all, it's probably brand-new. And the Nazis can't change the Star of David from an emblem of honor into a badge of shame merely by making us wear it. We've proudly put it on our soldiers' graves for a long time. Why shouldn't we be just as proud to wear it in our own lifetime?"

"I can't understand you, Jacques, when you talk like this! Especially as you yourself are no more Jew than Stéphanie is!"

"That's what I've been telling Jacques, Mother. I've told him that if he has to wear a star, I'm going to wear one too!"

"And I've reminded you too, Stéphanie, that whatever my religion may be, I can't change my heritage. And I don't want to. I'm immensely proud of it—as proud as you should be of yours. Don't let's pretend they're the same, though. And look, the longer we stay here arguing, the later we'll be getting back. Please go on, Margot, as I told you to, and let the rest of us get along to town. I'm sorry your Mother signaled you to stop."

He spoke with the same quiet authority as he had when she was a child, and she obeyed him as unquestioningly. For a few moments after she had climbed back into the cart, she drove along in silence. Aunt Bertha made no reference to their halt and no attempt to draw the girl out. At last, of her own accord, Margot spoke.

"I'm afraid we're in for trouble again, Aunt Bertha," she said. "It seems there's a new edict requiring all Jews to wear a star. The family's going in town now to get their allotment. Father doesn't seem to mind. He says a star's an emblem of honor. But all the others mind terribly. I think Mother minds most of all, though she isn't as violent about it as Grandma. She says if Father has to wear a star, she's going to wear one too."

"What good'll that do?"

"Of course it won't do any, and he's trying to make her see that. I don't believe he'll succeed, though. Mother can be awfully stubborn. She was about marrying him, you know. Her family tried for years to stop her, and the harder they tried, the more bound and determined she was to do it. Not that I blame her. But she's that way about everything, especially everything that concerns him. The rest of the world can just go hang."

Margot did not pursue the subject, or speak again until they were in sight of the first fences around L'Abbatiale. Then she remarked that since the family would not be back for an hour or so, they themselves might as well stop in for a little visit with Mark Mullins. The stud master was delighted to see them, brewed them some tea from his small remaining store, and compared experiences with Aunt Bertha, agreeing with her that the perfunctory visits amounted to nothing. The British were obliged to report, up to now, more frequently than the Americans; but personally he was glad to get to town for a bit of a change. There was not enough happening at the stud to keep a man busy these days. Hardly any mares were coming in from outside for breeding, because of transportation difficulties; and only ten of their own, none especially valuable, were left on the place. There was no telling how long the Nazis would leave these few unmolested and besides, it was almost impossible, without electricity or any satisfactory substitute for it, to assure them of proper care. He had to scrape around for a bit of candle to furnish light during foaling, and was mostly using any kind of fat he could find, with a piece of felt stuck in it for a wick. To his way of thinking, it would be better to send some of the mares back to Malou, though he had been in favor of having them all at L'Abbatiale when the Baroness suggested that arrangement. Now he thought a division of the little stock he had left might be advisable. Not that any of it was likely to produce champions.

"I don't know whether the Baroness would think it was a good plan to try having any at Malou again, Mark. You know that what we had was requisitioned."

"I'm not forgetting. But there've been more changes than one since '39. From what I gather through the grapevine, the Baroness stands in better with the Nazis right now than the Bouviers do. You won't mistake what I mean, Margot."

"No, of course not. I'll speak to the Baroness about it and let you know."

Then for a few minutes the conversation turned on Tristan's probable whereabouts. Finally, Margot proposed, since there were no signs of the family, that Aunt Bertha should take Padoue to the *grand manoir* for his nap, and that she and Mark should go through the stables and paddocks.

The old car came chugging up the drive just as the little group left the old infirmary under the clock tower, and Margot hurried forward to meet the family while Mark went back to his own quarters. Madame Bouvier and Madame Solomon got out first, and entered the *petit manoir* without indicating in any way that they would like to receive their granddaughter there. The omission of such a hospitable gesture made very little impression on her, however, for she was preoccupied with her parents. Her father looked terribly tired, and it required the joint help of her mother and herself to get him out of the car; never had his disabilities seemed so completely crippling. Stéphanie supported him ably and tenderly until he was settled in his favorite seat; then she left the room. After a protracted absence, she returned, wearing a black dress with a yellow star sewed on the folds which crossed over her breast.

"Oh, Mother!" Margot exclaimed, jumping up from the low stool by Jacques' side where she had been sitting. "What made you do that? You know Father didn't want you to!"

"I don't need to have you tell me what I ought to do or ought not to do, Margot. Nor what your Father wants and doesn't want."

"But he said——"

"Perhaps your mother and I'd better discuss this alone, darling. It's getting pretty late anyhow. You ought to be starting back to Malou. I'll look forward to seeing you next week."

The words were spoken with the utmost fondness; none the less, they constituted a dismissal.

Margot relayed Mark Mullins's message to her mother-in-law, and after consultation with Martin, Constance agreed that it might be wise to bring over five mares, three of them with foals, from L'Abbatiale. The replacement not only eased Mark's anxiety, but did a great deal to restore the strained morale at Malou. The horses did not entail extra work, for Mark sent one of his elderly "boys," a stocky little Piedmontese by the name of Alpy, with them, and Alpy took it for granted he was to remain, as Martin had done so many years earlier. Besides, all the men on the place were happier now that the stalls were no longer empty, and in the comparatively small stable, eight animals made a vast difference, whereas in the larger one they made no impression at all. Every evening Margot took Padoue to the paddock to see the foals with their dams, just as Stéphanie had taken her when she was a baby. Often Constance and Chess, more rarely Aunt Bertha and Lucie, went with them; the tranquil hour just before sunset became a pleasant interlude between the hard physical work of the day and the sewing and ledgers of the evening. It was during their evening walk that Margot spoke to Constance about Stéphanie, and that Constance, after listening gravely, commented guardedly and tolerantly on her old friend's defiant attitude.

"I don't believe we can lay it all to the yellow star, Margot. Of course I can see that in spite of everything your father's trying to say to the contrary, she still regards that as a badge of shame. That's the way the Germans are trying to make people feel about it, and succeeding in nine cases out of ten. Why, look at Madame Bouvier! And your mother has to listen to her all the time! That's warped her viewpoint, and besides she believes, with all her heart and soul, that she's proving her love for your father and her loyalty to him by sharing his badge. Nothing he can say will change her mind. She's convinced herself that he's just being brave about it. And nothing anyone else can say will make any difference either. The trouble is——"

"The trouble is she may actually do harm instead of good, isn't it?"

"Yes, I'm afraid so. She isn't the only person, by any means, who's taking this stand. You know that some Jews who've been converts to Catholicism, for instance, are wearing the Star of David with great pride. In other cases, Christians are doing it out of sympathy and affection, just like your mother. I hear there've been several instances of that right in our locality. Rumors are floating around already that in every case it's leading to persecution and arrest, and still the zealots and the sympathizers persist in their course. It seems to be part of the war psychology. That's what I was thinking of when I said I didn't believe we could lay your mother's attitude wholly to the yellow star. I don't think her frame of mind is normal anyway. It's hard to keep an even balance through years of occupation."

"You have."

"No, I'm afraid I haven't. Not always, anyway. And if I have, it's largely because you've helped so much, Margot."

"I should think if I could help you, I could help my own mother."

"Not necessarily. Please don't misunderstand me when I say that I really don't believe you and your own mother are as close together as you and I are, now. Your father's always meant so much to your mother that in keeping very close to him, she hasn't ever been especially close to any of her children. She loves you and your brothers and sisters dearly, Margot. But she loves you less as individuals than as the greatly desired result of an exceptionally joyous union."

"Yes, of course I've always known that. If Mother'd been more interested in us as individuals, I wouldn't have been so boy-crazy or Abel so book-crazy or Ghisèle so terribly shy. Of course it's worked out all right. Nick snatched me away from the pack, and Abel's putting all his theories into practice, and Ghisèle's become a ministering angel to a lot of men instead of going to bed with one. Of course it's too soon yet to tell about the others. But it mightn't have worked out so well for Abel and Ghisèle and me if we hadn't happened to have the breaks. And I still think Mother and Father would both be a lot better off if she'd felt the same way about us that you did about Nick and Bruno. After all, you care a lot for your husband too."

"Yes, I care a lot for my husband too."

Constance paused for a moment and, stooping over, pulled up a long blade of grass and plaited it between her fingers.

"There are thousands of women in France who think a lot of their husbands, Margot," she said. "I'm only one of a great company. And I don't believe any of us should blame any of the others for the way they react to the strain we're all under. We don't understand these different ways, we don't begin to, we can't pretend to."

Margot also stooped over and pulled up a long blade of grass. There was a heavy silence. When Constance spoke again it was about the mares and their foals, feeding quietly in the upland pasture.

She returned to the château to find von Reden waiting for her in the *grand salon*. He hoped she would not regard his call as an intrusion, he said. It had nothing to do with any future occupancy of Malou, since none was so far planned. But he had felt it would perhaps be a kindness to tell her personally that Monsieur Jacques Bouvier had been placed under arrest early that morning, and that his destination, with the usual preliminary steps, would undoubtedly be Auschwitz. The Militärbefehlshaber deplored the apparent severity of such a step; but the regrettable behavior of Madame Jacques Bouvier had left the Command no choice. As in the case of Bärenfänger, it had been necessary to make an example. He would tell her daughter-in-law, or permit her to do so, just as she preferred. But in any case, before he left he would like very much to see for himself that Antoine de Padoue de Fremond was making satisfactory progress.

It was because they all knew that Cotentin was only an internment camp and not an extermination camp, like Auschwitz, that they were able to accept Aunt Bertha's departure with comparative fortitude. She herself accepted it with gumption, and her last words before she got into the police car which took her away reminded them that she had not lost that sturdy quality, and that she hoped she would never be shamed by hearing that they had lost theirs. The final words which Constance and Margot spoke to her took the form of promises that they would not. And after she had gone they looked at each other silently, knowing they must keep their promise, whatever it cost them. They knew they must not prove unworthy of her by a lack of courage, as Stéphanie had proved unworthy of Jacques when she stabbed herself, after he had been taken away, through the yellow star she wore on her breast.

CHAPTER XXXVII

THE ATMOSPHERE at Malou after Aunt Bertha's departure was one of appalling emptiness. She had become so much a part of the place that there was a quality of unreality about her absence; instinctively everyone still looked for her, still listened for her, still awaited her. Lucie glanced up from her lessons; Constance knocked at the door of the little room crowded with ponderous Victorian furniture; Margot stood civilly by the dining room table for one more of her elders to be seated. And nothing happened. Aunt Bertha was gone.

At L'Abbatiale, conditions were immeasurably worse. For the second time, Constance was obliged to accept the verdict that a burial could not take place in consecrated ground; and in Stéphanie's case, this seemed infinitely harsher than it had after the murder and suicide of Aylette and Pierre. Stéphanie and Jacques Bouvier had themselves restored, with loving care, the beautiful little eleventh-century chapel which had given their property its name, and for years had gone there regularly to Mass. With Jacques, at least, this attendance had been marked with great faith and fervor; and though Stéphanie was less essentially devout, the intensity of her love for her husband had resulted in a burning desire to emulate his religious observances. Now they were divided in death as they had never been in life, and neither of them could rest in the churchyard where the one child they had lost lay buried, and to which they had given the same zealous care they had to the chapel itself. It was all too certain that Jacques' wracked and profaned body had been impiously flung into a trench at Auschwitz; a garden grave near the entrance to the hillside cavern was the ultimate accorded Stéphanie.

Alternately, during late September and early October, Constance and Margot drove to L'Abbatiale, sometimes behind one of the mares that had been brought over from there, but more often in the old donkey cart. Neither Margot nor her mother-in-law ever failed to visit Stéphanie's grave in the course of these expeditions; but they were not undertaken merely out of mournful sentiment, and presently it seemed best that Margot should make most of them. An immense amount of practical readjustment had been necessary at the stud farm, and she was the logical person to assume the responsibility for this. Nothing had been heard from Abel in a long while; Ghisèle had her hands full at the hospital; Guy had been conscripted for hard labor in Germany, but, like many another French youth under similar circumstances, had failed to appear at the designated railroad station at the designated time. Instead he had mysteriously disappeared, and no one knew where he might be in hiding; he had become one of the great hidden company of *camouflés*, moving secretly about in the densest forests, subsisting no one knew how.

Though Madame Bouvier *mère* and Madame Solomon had so far been unmolested by the Nazis, their position was extremely precarious; women as well as men were not infrequently sent to Auschwitz now, and Madame Bouvier's rebellious and hysterical behavior, which, no less than Stéphanie's, had contributed to Jacques' fate, might at any moment be used as the pretext for other arrests. Belatedly, she recognized this and strove to maintain at least a semblance of self-control; but it was more and more of a semblance, less and less of a reality. She was a terrified and unbalanced woman. The ravaged look on Madame Solomon's majestic countenance revealed her humiliation and grief, though nothing in her dignified bearing and reserved speech betrayed this; she regarded her daughter with contempt, and did her best to create and preserve something resembling a home for Yolande and Adrien. But the de Vallerins were disquieted at the thought of such insecurity for the young girl and the little boy, and unresponsive to an affectionate suggestion from Constance that they should come to Malou.

The Marquis and the Marquise managed to journey up from the Haras du Pin and made a rather ponderous visitation at the château during the course of a brief and inharmonious stay at L'Abbatiale. Malou, they reminded Constance, might become German headquarters again at any time; it was horrible enough that Margot should be subjected to the ordeal of living in the same house with her father's murderers; it was unthinkable that her younger brother and sister should undergo a similar experience. The de Vallerins did not actually say that had it not been for Stéphanie's rash, unsuitable marriage, they themselves might have been spared many severe trials, culminating in the present one. But Margot, who had never been on really fond terms with any of her elder relatives except Madame Solomon, was quick to interpret her maternal grandparents' remarks both as a disparagement to the memory of her beloved father and as a slight to the generosity of her hospitable mother-in-law. She lost her temper and retorted with considerable heat that she was living where and as she wanted to live, and where and as she wanted her child to live. She had no doubt the Nazis would be delighted if they could pry her and Padoue loose from Malou, on top of every other damn thing they had done; but that was one dirty trick they would never pull off.

Shortly thereafter, Madame Bouvier was committed to a French mental institution by order of the German military authorities, who forebore from sending her to Auschwitz instead, and whose attitude was that by their action they had shown almost unwarranted clemency. With her departure, Mark Mullins suggested that perhaps it would be handier all around if Madame Solomon would do him the honor of coming to live at his quarters until things got straightened out again—an invitation which the matriarch accepted with unfeigned gratitude and unimpaired dignity. It was now obvious that her health was failing fast; but her spirit was still unbroken. Margot's attitude towards her great-grandmother was marked by increasing pride as well as unswerving loyalty. She went frequently and faithfully to see the old lady, generally taking Padoue with her; and when she returned to Malou, it was always to talk of "the grand old girl" and "that good scout Mark" and never to mention the blankly boarded windows of the *grand manoir* and the *petit manoir* and the guest house, or the rows of empty stalls she was obliged to pass before she came upon the few aged "boys" fussily caring for the few remaining horses.

Often she managed to see Marie Aimée also in the course of these expeditions, and less frequently, Ghisèle. This was not only because, without knowing exactly why, she found the peaceful atmosphere of the Abbaye more congenial than the hectic one of the hospital; it was also because she sensed that the nun wanted her more than the nurse. As the mistress of novices and the cellarer of the *abbaye,* Marie Aimée's time was by no means unoccupied between her periods of prayer; yet she always contrived to give an impression of serene welcome. Ghisèle, on the other hand, was forever hurrying from one ward to another; she was trying to catch up with this or that elusive doctor; someone was calling her, or she had promised to relieve another *infirmière.* It was she, more often than Margot, who brought their brief conversations to an end; and Margot, herself supercharged with vitality, missed the quality of repose in her sister that she found in Marie Aimée. One evening, after a particularly unsatisfactory session with Ghisèle, she tried to explain this lack to Constance while they sat together knitting, according to their companionable habit, in the *petit salon.*

"Nursing must agree with Ghisèle," she remarked. "You remember how she was always shrinking off into corners? Well, now she's stepping right out. I wouldn't call her fidgety exactly—that's not the right word. But she's certainly up and coming. I'm sure she could qualify as Miss Efficiency in a contest any day. And all this high-pressure action doesn't seem to be wearing her down either, any more than the various family problems have. She's blooming like a rose. Our drooping little violet is no more. Now don't tell me I'm mixing metaphors. I know I am. At the same time, I'm trying to give you a good general idea."

"And I'm grasping it. I've noticed the change myself. Do you think it's because she's so interested in her work?"

"Of course not. No girl was ever all that interested in her work. I think she's probably in love."

"Well, we both know that such things happen, and the pleasant effect they have when they do." The two smiled at each other, with the mutual understanding based on happy memories. Then Constance added, "Do you suspect anyone special, Margot?"

"No, but I'm going to keep a sharp watch. I'd like to see what type could get her into such high gear. Why, she mooned around like a sick calf when she was in love with Nick! And he was exciting enough for anybody."

"I'd have said that too. But she couldn't have been really in love with Nick—I mean not the way you were, or—or the way I was with his father. She wouldn't have 'mooned,' as you call it, if she had been. She was just an infatuated little girl finding her first thrills rather frightening."

"Maybe. But if I hadn't snatched him just when I did, she'd have come out of her trance and grabbed him. One of the things I like about you, Mother, is that you've got such an enormously high opinion of human nature—always excepting Nazi human nature, of course. It's a very endearing quality. But it prevents you from being a realist, the way I am."

Margot rose from the red plush chair beside the fireplace where she had been sitting and stretched herself, clasping her hands above her head and yawning. The movement was one of unstudied grace.

"I guess it's bedtime. I still hate going to bed alone, don't you? . . . Well, to get back to Ghisèle for a moment. I'm glad we're not both after the same man again. She might win out this time. Though of course, as far as that goes, I'll probably never be out for any man again. I don't see how I could be, after having Nick."

Constance knew that Margot must be giving further thought to this conversation and its underlying theory when, two days later, the girl said she thought she would go into Lisieux again. Usually she still went only once a week. With her usual directness, she said she wanted to go to the General Hospital to see if, for once, she could not waylay Ghisèle and have a real talk with her. Then, without further ado, she set off.

Ghisèle was surprised to see her so soon again, but this time Margot had no difficulty in "waylaying" her. Ghisèle came rushing out to meet her sister, her cheeks brightly flushed. "Oh Margot!" she exclaimed. "I *am* glad you've come! I've been trying to get Malou on the telephone all morning and I couldn't—it's getting harder and harder all the time. I suppose the equipment's wearing out, and of course there's been no replacement. . . . Well, never mind about that now. Who do you suppose is here?"

"What do you mean, here? In Lisieux?"

"No, right here at the General Hospital. Of course the Hermitage would have been the logical place for him, but it so happened there wasn't any room there just now and——"

"Well, who is here?"

"Michel!"

"Michel! Our Michel?"

"Yes, our Michel. That is, Nicole's Michel. Anyway, Michel Dufour from Malou. He got into Châlons-sur-Marne in a hospital convoy from Germany last week."

"What's the matter with him?"

"Exhaustion mostly. Bad food and bad treatment and a bad climate. A small spot on one of his lungs too. I don't believe that'll amount to much when he's had rest and nourishment and care. He keeps saying he isn't the same man he was, but that's ridiculous. He'll be all right when——"

"How did he get all the way from Châlons-sur-Marne to Lisieux in this short time?"

"Why, one of the doctors at the repatriation center is from Livarot. He's nice—I'd met him last year before he went up there. And when he found out that Michel was practically a neighbor of his and how desperately homesick the poor boy was, he arranged somehow. He brought Michel back himself, along with some other *répatriés* from different parts of Calvados."

"You want me to go straight back to Malou and get Nicole, don't you?"

"Well, that's what you'd want under the same circumstances, isn't it?"

"Of course. So would you. I'll be back as soon as Flora can get us here!"

Afterwards Margot recalled that the flush on Ghisèle's cheeks had grown even brighter when Margot herself said, "So would you." But she did not give it much thought, because the idea that Ghisèle might possibly be in love had temporarily been driven from her mind by her excitement over Michel's unexpected home-coming. She had never seen much of him, because he had been away most of the time since she had lived at the château; but he had made a favorable impression on her at the time of his wedding, and she was genuinely fond of Nicole. She forced the placid little donkey to unaccustomed speed on the hasty trip to Malou and burst in on Nicole, who was making cheese in the dairy, with a peremptory summons to throw on the first thing she could find and come into Lisieux at once.

"What has happened now, Madame Nick?" Nicole inquired, laying down her cheese frame.

"Nothing bad. Something good for a change. I'd say it was about time, too. Come on, Nicole. I can explain as we go along. The main thing is not to lose a moment."

Nicole put the cheese frame carefully back in the row where it belonged. Her stubby fingers shook a little as she did so, but her voice was firm.

"So Michel has come back," she said. "That's it, isn't it, Madame Nick? I ask you to tell me now, before we start, so I can tell his mother. It is only fair that she should know too."

"Yes, he's back. I'm sorry I didn't think of Lise myself. Run in and spread the good news and then——"

"And he is—all right? How then does it happen he is back? You're not keeping something from me, Madame Nick? He is not—blind? Or—mutilated? Tell me the truth. It will be easier to bear in this first moment, when I know that at least he is alive."

"There isn't a thing the matter with him, according to my sister, but exhaustion and a little spot on one lung and—well, deep depression. Apparently, he keeps saying he isn't the same man he was before. But you're the best cure for him, Nicole. Or will be, if you'll only come along. Why, if it were my husband, I'd be halfway to Lisieux by this time!"

"Yes, Madame Nick. That is understood. But we do things differently, you and I. I am very slow of both speech and wit and you are very quick. Which does not mean that I am the less joyful or less thankful to the good God."

There was no immediate prospect that Michel would be able to leave the hospital, and in his debilitated condition lengthy visits, or several close together, proved exhausting to him. So Constance and Margot saw him only often enough to assure themselves that his progress, though slow, was satisfactory. But Nicole and Lise took turns in going daily to the hospital, walking back and forth between Malou and Lisieux. Lise contrived to make her absences fairly brief. She was a surprisingly good walker for a woman of her age and build. Since Bernard's death, she had become increasingly taciturn; she wanted to see her son rather than to talk with him, and after feasting her eyes on him for a few minutes, she was satisfied to leave his side. Nicole's trips to town, on the other hand, consumed a good deal of time from the beginning; and with every visit to the hospital she was gone longer than she had previously been. At last Lise, who seldom found fault with her, complained that Nicole had no right to neglect her work at Malou for the sake of staying with her husband.

"I am not with Michel all the while. I am also making myself useful at the hospital," Nicole replied imperturbably.

"Mon Dieu! Since when have you needed to go to a hospital to make yourself useful? Can you find nothing to do here?"

"I have spoken of the matter to Madame la Baronne and she is satisfied."

"No doubt she had expressed herself as being satisfied. Madame la Baronne is always full of kindness, and I have noticed that she has a soft place in her heart for those who are in love. But that does not excuse you for absenting yourself for hours on end when we are shorthanded at Malou. What is it you are doing at the hospital which makes you so useful there?"

"I run errands. The hospital is shorthanded also. It had no one to send out on its *courses*. Sometimes it is necessary to get extra ice from the abattoir, sometimes extra drugs from this pharmacy or that."

"This pharmacy or that! The hospital has its own pharmacy, I should hope!"

"Yes, but ill supplied. It is always running short these days. The same is true of the kitchen, the linen room, every department. I carry notes telling of these needs—sometimes to a shop where one would not expect much help, sometimes to one of the convents, sometimes to a private family. . . . Well, since there is so much to do everywhere, we must not continue to stand here talking. I will make up for the time which seems to you lost, never fear, Mère Lise."

Lise shook her head and watched her daughter-in-law out of sight. But her puzzled expression gradually faded, and she made no more complaints and asked no more questions. The following Sunday, in returning from Mass at Norolles the two took the short cut across the fields, as usual. When they were well out in the open, with no one else in sight, Nicole slid her arm through her mother-in-law's and spoke to her in a whisper.

"I have talked with the Baroness again, and she has given me permission to confide in you. But she has cautioned me to use the utmost care in doing so, and has reminded me that all walls have ears. I could not be sure, therefore. . . . These errands—those notes which I carry—

well, all that is good work for the hospital, just as I told you. But in the course of it I am to do other good work. I am to get information—and give it."

Lise nodded her head, though she continued to plod on without saying anything a few minutes more. Eventually she observed: "I figured that much out for myself, at last. I am sorry I spoke to you sharply. This information that you get and give—is there any you can repeat?"

"I have not given much of any value yet, because at Norolles all is so quiet just now. The idea is that sooner or later the Germans will return, either to Malou or to the Monteillerie, and then I shall be in an advantageous position. Which reminds me, if Michel should be detained at the hospital longer than seems to you reasonable, do not worry for fear he is not making a good recovery."

"Well, I had guessed that much too. After all, I'm not altogether a dunce. But you still have not told me——"

"I'm coming to that, Mère Lise. Slowly, as I do everything. That is one of the reasons I have been chosen for this work. Anyone can see at a glance that I am slow and stupid. Well, as to the information I have secured, that is not so much yet either. But I have been able to tell Madame Nick about her brothers. Not the little one, Adrien. Of course there is nothing to say about him, since the poor child is now forced to stay at the Haras du Pin, where he is entirely safe. I mean the others, the one who went over to Vichy and the one who is a *camouflé*," she continued.

"Of the first, it is my opinion the less said the better," Lise announced, sniffing in her turn.

"Ah! But he has repented, that one! When he heard what had happened to his own father, which he did soon enough, being in a position to learn such things quickly, those books which he kept so well ceased to be inscribed with cold facts and figures. He saw that instead these records were written in letters of blood—the blood of human beings. Not that his revelation saved his poor father, or thousands of other such victims. It was too late for that. Perhaps it may be too late for him to save anyone. That is his great fear. But at all events this young Monsieur Abel has now forsworn all his false honors and deserted his lucrative post. He has become a fugitive from the Nazis and he is not without hope that the knowledge he gained among them may yet be useful or give comfort. To a certain extent his hopes have been justified already."

"To the extent of getting in touch with his brother Guy, for instance?"

"That is what I was coming to, Mère Lise. These *camouflés*—it is wonderful what they are doing, from their forest hiding places! Yes, Monsieur Abel found means of reaching Monsieur Guy and Monsieur Guy found means of reaching an apothecary in Lisieux, and from the apothecary in Lisieux I have been able to hear in what manner Monsieur le Baron made his escape and tell this to Madame la Baronne!"

Nicole's voice had become more and more triumphant, but she did not forget to keep it hushed, in spite of its glad note. She pressed still more closely to Lise and went on with her story.

"It took place during a heavy snowfall," she whispered. "He and two fellow officers let themselves out of their barracks by means of sheets and, because of their own white coverings, crept unperceived over the grounds of the camp, which of course were white with snow. They had almost reached the barbed wire when a guard in one of the 'miradors' became aware of their stealthy movements; but before he could give the alarm, they had overpowered him and hidden his body in a snowdrift.'

"Ah-la-la! What resourcefulness, what ingenuity, what courage! How like Monsieur le Baron to profit by the circumstance of a snowstorm!"

"You are right. . . . These gallant Frenchmen, using care to keep halfway between the miradors, then cut through the barbed wire with shears they had secured by some secret means—Monsieur Abel did not know just how. Once outside, the officers must have successfully retained their white coverings until they were at a great distance from the camp. At all events, their absence was not discovered until the next morning, and then they had made such progress that they could not be overtaken. Monsieur Abel did not know how they reached England, either. Naturally his information was gleaned wholly from official records, and these gave no more than I have told you. It seems there are various ways in which the journey could have been made—through Switzerland to Unoccupied France and thence to Spain, for instance. But Monsieur Abel hopes it was not thus, as the Spaniards retain all refugees for months on end, in concentration camps even filthier than the German prisons."

"Myself, I have always looked on the Spaniards as a cruel race."

"But the Swedes are perhaps less so, aren't they, Mère Lise? It is believed that prisoners escaping from Germany have sometimes gone as stowaways on Swedish cargo boats which ply between Hamburg and Stockholm. Also that in Sweden they have been well received, and that from there the passage to England has been much facilitated. Let us hope that Monsieur le Baron went through Sweden. Well, it would be interesting to know, and doubtless we shall, all in good time, for there is reason to hope that soon letters will be coming through also. It seems that these Bouviers have relatives in Saint-Malo—one of poor Monsieur Jacques' cousins inherited a fine fishing fleet, and of course fishing craft are constantly in the Channel. Now that the contact has been established——"

Nicole left the sentence unfinished, but Lise had no difficulty in grasping her meaning. "You are a good girl, Nicole," she said. "I have never been sorry that Michel married you."

This was the highest praise which Lise could bestow, and Nicole knew it. Michel's home-coming had not been like Pierre's; instead of finding a faithless wife, he had found a loyal one. She had been able to look him full in the face and tell him, without falsehood, that she had always been true to him. And he had looked back at her with glad eyes and spoken in a glad voice, telling her he knew it. And having proved worthy of his trust, she could be worthy of other men's also, in other ways. Michel could lie still and get well with a tranquil heart because, in a sense, she would be carrying on his work. Even if the time came when he did not see her for several days on end, he would not repine. He would know that she was taking messages between the apothecary and the *camouflés*, and that the *camouflés* would be getting them to the coast, and that all would be safely delivered.

For some moments she walked along in silence, happily turning these things over in her mind. Then, realizing that she had not yet thanked her mother-in-law for the praise Lise had bestowed upon her, she did so, briefly and respectfully; and after remarking that her work would become more and more important as time went on, she began to speak of other matters, as if the first question had been closed.

Nicole was still talking when she and Lise, who had said nothing more, came up the last stretch of hill behind the commons and entered the archway through the justly praised garden. They would have gone upstairs at once, to prepare an early dinner, leaving the afternoon free for a visit to the hospital, if Lucie, who habitually went to a late Mass with Margot, had not come tearing up from the château just then, shouting as she ran.

At first the shouts were unintelligible. They sounded joyous, but Lise and Nicole could not help wondering, with sinking hearts, if these really were. They could see a German military car parked beside the drawbridge, and this now familiar sight always brought with it a sense of foreboding. Then they were able to distinguish Lucie's words and they ran forward too, meeting Lucie midway to the château.

"Mademoiselle Berthe is back! It was all a mistake! She is home to stay! She is never, never going away again!"

Breathlessly, they all rushed into the fort together. Aunt Bertha was standing there, neatly clad in her best black dress, and calmly cautioning Léon, who was grinning from ear to ear, to make sure the German orderly placed her bags in her own room. Lucie hurled herself against the old lady in a transport of joy. Aunt Bertha paused in her directions to put an arm around the little girl's shoulder and pat it reassuringly. Then she extended her free hand to Lise and Nicole in turn.

"That's right," she said dryly. "It was all a mistake. The law says no person over sixty-five years of age is to be confined in one of these internment camps for enemy aliens. It's a law the Germans made up themselves. So when I heard about it from a fellow prisoner—a nice woman from Omaha, Nebraska—I made a complaint and asked for an investigation. I'll say this for the Germans, there's nothing pleases them more than a chance to investigate something. And it seems one of those clerks down at the police office in Lisieux had made an error in his figures. He'd written down my age as sixty-five when it's eighty-five—at least he'd written the first figure so badly no one could tell which it was and somebody decided it was a 6. I'm sticking to my story that it was meant for a 6. I'm flattered I can pass myself off as twenty years younger than I really am. Any elderly woman in her right mind would be. Well, the long and short of it is, the clerk got discharged and I got an apology out of the authorities, and then Colonel von Reden came down to Cotentin himself to bring me back to Malou. He's in the *grand salon* talking to my niece right now. I suppose you don't want to see him and I don't blame you. Why don't you come up to my room with me for a few minutes, while I straighten out my things?"

CHAPTER XXXVIII

"Since your radio was so unfortunately destroyed during the early days of the Occupation, I suppose the news of yesterday's happenings has not yet reached you," von Reden remarked, sipping his Calvados. "That is, unless it has already been conveyed to you by some kind neighbor who is foolhardy enough to risk getting himself and his family into trouble by tuning in on forbidden broadcasts."

"I haven't seen any of my kind neighbors yet this morning. I was just getting ready to start for Mass when you and Aunt Bertha arrived."

"I am sorry to have been so inopportune. Your religion apparently means a great deal to you."

"Yes, I'm glad to say it does."

"Yet you were not born a Catholic and you did not become one at the time of your marriage."

"No. That isn't saying religion hasn't always meant a great deal to me though. New Englanders are essentially God-fearing and churchgoing people. They read their Bibles very thoroughly too."

"Largely as literature, I believe."

"I wouldn't say largely, I'd say partly. It's very beautiful literature—worthy of a divine revelation."

"Then if these God-fearing, churchgoing, Bible-reading habits meant so much to you, I am at loss to understand why you abandoned them."

"I didn't abandon them. I improved on them—at least that was the way it seemed to me. And those habits you speak of with such sarcasm still mean much to me. But I found a way of worship that meant more. A way of worship and an expression of faith and—and a very present help in time of trouble."

Von Reden took another sip of Calvados. "I did not intend to speak sarcastically," he observed. "As a matter of fact, I am very much interested. You have always struck me not only as a very charming woman, but as a very intelligent one. A good many women have charm, of a sort, but not many are intelligent, and fewer still possess a combination of the two qualities—especially if they are also devout. All the devout women I have known so far have been either very plain or very stupid or both. . . . Apparently you did not even receive so-called instructions at the time of your marriage. That would have been at least partially comprehensible. I gather that you were very much in love. It would have been natural for you take make every effort to please your husband."

"Not if it meant compromising with conviction. It was very clearly understood when I married that no effort would be made by anyone to coerce me into Catholicism. Not that my husband would ever have tried or wanted to do that. He set me a wonderful example, but he never discussed religion with me at all, unless I invited such a discussion. He wanted me to think things out for myself, which is just what I have done.

He believed I was perfectly capable of clear thought. But then his opinion of women is very unlike yours. That's probably partly a question of individuality. No two men could possibly present a greater contrast to each other than you and Tristan de Fremond. It's probably also partly a question of nationality. The French viewpoint and the German viewpoint are so totally different on the subject of women, aren't they? Frenchmen have always not only conceded that women have brains, but have instinctively regarded them as intellectual equals and have wanted their wives to be their helpmeets and partners."

"And have found with the mistresses, whom they take and keep as a matter of course, the pleasures which these well-informed, businesslike women, whom they marry on such a sound economic basis, could not possibly hope to supply."

"I am not willing to accept your unqualified statement that all Frenchmen have mistresses or to subscribe to your theory that no Frenchman's wife is personally pleasing to him. Both are untrue, and under the circumstances, both are insulting."

She rose and stood stiffly in front of her chair to indicate that the conversation was ended. It had already lasted far longer than she expected or intended when she reluctantly consented to receive him; but the reception was inevitable, considering that he had personally brought Aunt Bertha back to Malou. Then she had permitted herself to be drawn into an argument, first about her religion and then about her husband—two subjects which were sacred to her. She was very angry with von Reden because he had adroitly precipitated this argument, but she was still angrier with herself for having fallen into his well-set trap. He had risen, of course, as soon as she did, but he made no move to leave the room, and for a moment they stood facing each other, with equal inflexibility. Then he spoke more softly than she had ever heard him.

"I stand corrected, Baroness. I am ready to admit that there are some Frenchmen who cannot fail to find their wives so stimulating that they never need to seek other feminine society. And at the risk of sounding contradictory, I will venture to add that Frenchmen are not alone in— *occasionally*—wanting very much to become lovers, in fact as well as in feeling. However much they may differ in other ways, Frenchmen and Germans are greatly alike in this respect. For that matter, so are Englishmen and Americans."

"Will you please excuse me, Colonel von Reden? I have hardly spoken to my aunt yet, and I should like very much——"

"I can understand that feeling too. I shall not detain you much longer. But speaking of Americans reminds me that I have not yet told you the news which you were not able to hear sooner, because your kind neighbors have been prevented from passing it on to you, owing to my inopportune arrival just as you were starting for Mass. Yesterday, very early in the morning, United States forces landed in North Africa, and the indications are that it will not be necessary for them to engage in a long and arduous campaign for the control of Algeria and Morocco. I have good reason to believe that an armistice will very shortly be arranged through the good offices of that noble patriot and great strategist, Admiral Jean François Darlan."

As she pronounced her icy words of dismissal, Constance had started towards the door. Now she wheeled around with a fast-beating heart and an exclamation of joy which she could not wholly suppress.

"In which case," von Reden continued smoothly, "we shall, of course, immediately retaliate by taking possession of all France, except possibly a small semicircle of land around the harbor of Toulon, where the greater part of the French fleet lies at anchor. It will be a very fitting way in which to celebrate the anniversary date of the armistice at the end of the First World War."

"As if you didn't 'possess' all France now! As if the terms 'Occupied Zones' and 'Unoccupied Zones' were anything but a mockery! As if every move of the puppet government in Vichy were not pulled by strings in Berlin! There has been no freedom in France, as a country, for more than three years now, and you know it as well as I do. You Nazis have completely crushed it. But you still have not crushed the yearning for freedom in the hearts of the French people—or the will to regain it!"

"Why, Baroness, I did not realize you were an orator as well as a scholar!"

"There are a great many things you don't realize! And one of them is the difference between what you can and cannot conquer."

They were still standing very close together, confronting each other. Suddenly he took hold of her arms and gripped them hard. He had never touched her before, though she had felt more than once that he was on the point of doing so. Now that he had, she instantly recognized the formidable quality of his grasp. She made no futile attempts to release herself. Instead, she continued to look him full in the face and to speak in tones of measured fury.

"You can't conquer a country that believes in freedom if you try to do it by force. There's something about it that's unconquerable—something Germany hasn't got, because it never learned about freedom. Only about power. And power isn't enough. It isn't enough between nations and it isn't enough between human beings. Especially between men and women. Let go my arms, Colonel von Reden. I want to go upstairs to see my aunt and I want you to leave this house. The next time it is required for headquarters, send someone else in your stead."

It was only afterwards that she realized the full extent of her rashness; but even if she had realized it at the time, she would have acted no differently. Until von Reden took hold of her arms, she had managed to keep her hatred for him in check. Now it had burst all bounds. His touch had been more than an affront to her dignity; it had been an insult to her femininity. She felt no more repentance than fright because she had lashed out at him, except when she thought of Padoue.

Fortunately, nothing further happened to rouse either her wrath or her fear. Von Reden did not return to Malou, nor did he send any representative in his place; evidently there was no question of reoccupancy by the

Germans, for the time being at least, and life at the château fell back into much the same patterns as before Aunt Bertha's internment and Stéphanie's suicide. However, brighter threads were woven into it now. Constance still concealed her little patched-up radio behind her bed, and would permit no one to listen to it with her; but she yielded to the temptation of doing so herself more frequently after having missed the great news of the American landing in Africa. The neighbors also brought her news more boldly now that there were no Nazis in the immediate vicinity, and Nicole managed to cull many items from the outside world. Not all the tidings were good: the scuttling of the French fleet to prevent its seizure by the Germans; the assassination of Darlan; the recapture of the heights near Mateur—such episodes as these inevitably caused deep distress and roused anxious doubts regarding the approach of victory. But close upon them came other tidings which were more reassuring: the siege of Stalingrad was broken; Tripoli had fallen to the British Eighth Army; American paratroopers were reported to be landing in France. . . .

And then a letter came through. . . .

Constance had already gone to bed when Nicole brought it to her, for the girl's "usefulness" at the hospital detained her for longer and longer periods, and it was often very late at night when she returned to Malou. It was understood, however, that she was always to report on Michel's progress—not to mention anything else that might be of interest—no matter what time she came home; and very often she brought a *tisane* upstairs and sat excitedly telling her story while Constance sipped the drink and listened with equal excitement. Constance answered Nicole's awaited knock with genuine anticipation of creature comfort as well as spiritual stimulation. Then she saw that instead of the customary chipped china, the little tray was set with the beautiful old breakfast service, which had happily escaped destruction, and guessed that this must be meant to mark some special occasion. When she sniffed the now rare aroma of coffee, she knew it.

"Is this an anniversary of some kind?" she asked, with an effort at gaiety. "How stupid of me to forget!"

"Oh, madame!" Nicole exclaimed. "To think that at last—— This time the little fishing smack has managed to slip across. . . . And poor Monsieur Jacques' cousin at Saint-Malo has got through to Monsieur Guy and he has got through to me. . . . The apothecary gave me the letter tonight. And I remembered how it used to be when I brought the tray to Madame and Monsieur in the morning, set with this service, and how Monsieur would come out of the bathroom singing '*Café au lait au lit.*' So I thought—— I will leave you now, madame. This time you will not want the rest of my news. That can wait until morning. You will want to be alone with your letter."

She set down the tray on the little table beside the bed and hurried out. Constance snatched the small folded sheet from the napkin which enclosed it, remembering, just in time, that she must not tear it open in her haste—every inch of it would be covered with handwriting, to save space. She took the knife that Nicole had laid beside the coffee cup and carefully pried back the edges of the flap. Then she spread out the sheet and devoured the contents with hungry eyes:

Dearest:

 At last the chance has come to send you a letter. Probably it will take some time to reach you. In that case I shan't be in the country where I am now when it does. In some ways I'll be sorry to go, for no refugee has ever been more kindly treated than I have been here. In other ways, I can hardly wait for the signal to start. When it comes, this will mean I'll be fighting again, and in the best of company. More than that, of course I can't tell you.

 But there are many other things I must try to say on this small sheet. I want to remind you that I told you when I left home that if I were imprisoned, I would escape. And this came true. So please believe that all my other confident predictions will come true. I may be wounded, but I shan't be killed. I'll come back to you safely, and victory is now only a matter of time.

 Dearest, through the same trusty messenger who will bring you this letter I have learned about the boys, and about the tragic fate of many of our friends. I know what these losses have meant to you. But you haven't lost me and you never will. I hope this gives you some comfort.

 I have also learned that our home has been occupied and misused, and that you have shown wonderful courage and endurance in meeting the situation. Of course I knew that you would, whatever happened. I wonder if you realize how much this certainty means to me?

 And one piece of wonderful news has come through, with all that is sad and bad: so you and I are grandparents, and the little boy and his mother are both with you and both well! When I come home I shall find a child in the house, and it will seem almost as if he were my own. I expect to be there to give him his first real riding lessons myself. Meantime, you and his mother can do a great deal towards getting him ready for them.

 And now what more can I say, my darling, except that I love you with all my heart and soul, that I have since the first day I saw you, and that I shall until the day of my death? Nothing—except to remind you that the latter is far distant, and that before it arrives we shall have many years of happiness together.

Toujours à toi,
T.

P.S. I hope our special stars are still shining for you.

Constance read the letter over and over again, at first through misty eyes, with a catch in her throat, then with clearing vision and a deepening smile. The letter was written in English, except for the last line, and the wording reminded her of Tristan's own comment when she had first told him he talked to her "formally"—"That's still the way it comes to me most easily, because that's the way I was taught to speak English. When I'm very much in earnest, I lapse, quite unconsciously, into stiffness." She knew how earnestly he had written. Her husband was revealed

362

in every line of the cramped handwriting. How like Tristan to remind her that he had been right in what he said about his imprisonment and his escape, and that therefore he was justified in saying that all in good time he would come home again safe and sound! This unshakable assurance, permeated with both bravado and faith, had always been one of his outstanding characteristics. How like him also not only to tell her of the big things, like his imminent departure for the war zone, but to say he hoped Padoue would be taught to ride and to inquire about the handkerchief! And finally, how like him to reiterate that he loved her with all his heart and soul, as if he never tired of telling her this, any more than she ever tired of hearing it.

She knew the letter by heart when at last she put it down. But she picked it up and reread it, over and over again, while she was writing the answer to it. She set the coffee service on her dressing table and, turning the tray upside down, used this for an escritoire. Paper had become very scarce, but she had salvaged every scrap which the Germans tossed aside, and she did not lack necessary writing materials. But she knew the letter should be very short, both because details might be dangerous and because the paper must not take up too much space hidden inside a shirt or a shoe. And she wanted to say so many, many things! She had always maintained that there were three ways by which a woman could tell that she was in love with a man: first, when it seemed natural to be with him; second, when she wanted to touch him and be touched by him; and third, when it was instinctive to confide in him. Just as she bitterly resented the compulsion which had forced her to answer von Reden, so she now longed to pour out her heart to Tristan.

All night long she wrote, destroyed, rewrote. Daylight was filtering in through the drawn curtains when she finally folded and sealed the one closely covered sheet. She turned the tray over and laid the letter down on it; Nicole would return to fetch it, she knew, before anyone else in the house was up. Then, tardily, she remembered the untouched coffee. She must never let Nicole think that the gesture in bringing it had not been appreciated. She rose and, going over to the dressing table, poured the coffee slowly, watching its graceful flow from the Sèvres *cafetière* to the delicate cup beneath. She added milk freely, sugar sparingly, and, getting back into bed, began to sip the drink. It was stone-cold now, of course, and it had the flat taste of all coffee which has stood too long and which has not been made strong enough to begin with. But she drank it to the last drop, and before she finished she had begun to hum the half-forgotten tune of *"Café au lait au lit."* This drink was the forerunner of those which she and Tristan would some day be sharing again.

Several weeks later Nicole brought Constance word that another little fishing smack had slipped through, but that when it reached "the other side," the skipper had found that her letter, though safely delivered as far as he was concerned, would have to go on "much farther." Apparently neither he nor Nicole doubted that eventually it would reach its destination in safety, and Constance shared their hopefulness, though months went by in which she received no answer. The nature of Nicole's work was changing, for Michel had been brought home from the hospital, and this could no longer be used as a center from which to "do errands." His convalescence had been slow, but his improvement had been steady, and the time came when it was obviously unfair to permit his occupancy of a bed badly needed for a sicker man. Besides, planting had begun again at Malou, and even if he were not strong enough to do much work, a little would help. He was overjoyed at the prospect of getting back to the land: just to feel good Norman earth under his feet again, just to scoop up a handful and let it sift through his fingers—that would go a long way towards bringing his strength back for him, he insisted. And to sit at his own table, watching his mother ladle out the soup from the *pot-au-feu,* to lie in his own bed with Nicole there beside him—ah, then he would know he was a man again, even though it was not the same man the *sales Boches* had taken into captivity!

Margot and Nicole went together to bring him home, and, while Nicole was packing his few belongings, Margot succeeded in getting Ghisèle into one of the small, musty reception rooms, on the pretext of needing further directions about the convalescent's diet and care. Though Michel's return to Lisieux had temporarily diverted her from her purpose, she had never ceased to insist she was sure Ghisèle was in love, and that someday she would find out more about it. But Ghisèle had been extremely adroit in evading the issue. She pretended not to understand veiled hints and indirect questions, and when Margot attempted a blunter approach, Ghisèle flared up and said with equal bluntness that it was none of her sister's business. Afterwards, she was sorry she had lost her temper; it was much less characteristic of her to do so than it was of Margot; and, though still noncommittal, she relented to the extent of indicating that someday she might have interesting news to impart. Now that the time had come for Michel to leave her charge, she agreed to do this.

"I don't suppose you'll be coming to the hospital so often from now on, Margot, and as long as you've been bound and determined to find out, I may as well tell you. I'm not exactly engaged, but——"

"What do you mean, you're not *exactly* engaged?"

"Well, it's just sort of an understanding. There never was a chance to speak to *papa* about it, so it didn't have his sanction, and later, when one awful thing after another was happening at L'Abbatiale, I didn't feel like saying anything to anyone else. I still don't feel like talking about it. Anyone but you would have gathered that and stopped pestering me long ago."

"Oh, I gathered that all right, but I wasn't just curious; I was really interested. After all, you are my sister, and we're the only ones left of the family here now, except good old Grand'mère Solomon. I know it would cheer her up to have a love affair to think about, too. Is this man a Lexovien? Have I ever met him?"

"N–o–o. But he comes from near by, and he's got relatives here. We may settle here later on. He's doing some special work farther north right now."

"I wouldn't say you were bubbling over with information, even yet. What kind of special work? What's the man's name?"

"The patient is ready to leave now, Mademoiselle Bouvier. If Madame de Fremond can come conveniently——"

One of the supervising nurses was standing in the doorway, speaking civilly but decisively; it was evident that she wanted to get the Malou group off with the least possible delay. It was also evident that Ghisèle was pleased rather than annoyed at the interruption. She could very easily have given the desired information to Margot in a whisper as they went down the corridor. Instead, she hurried forward and busied herself with several details about the departure to which someone else might easily have given attention. Afterwards Margot spoke, with irritation, of her behavior to Constance.

"I don't know why she should make such a secret of it. You'd think she was having an affair, or that she was ashamed of something else. Perhaps she's fallen for some kind of a cad."

"It isn't that, Margot, I'm sure it isn't. She's just shy. This means more to her than anything has ever meant before, and she can't talk about it to anyone. I know all about that feeling. Probably if you saw her and this suitor of hers together, with other people present, she'd choose a seat at the opposite end of the room from him, and hardly speak to him unless he spoke to her first."

"Yes, and it would be a dead giveaway, as far as I'm concerned. That kind of self-consciousness simply shrieks to high heaven, 'I'm in love, head over heels in love!' Besides, there's something electric in the atmosphere when two people who are crazy about each other haven't had a chance to do anything about it yet. Haven't you ever noticed? . . . Well, I'm not going to 'pester' her any more, as Ghisèle puts it. Why should I care, anyway? She 'doesn't suppose I'll be coming to the hospital so often from now on.' Well, she's right. If it wasn't for wanting to see Grand'-mère Solomon and Marie Aimée, I wouldn't bother to go into Lisieux at all. There's plenty to do here."

Constance was inclined to regard Margot's annoyance as rather amusing, and made light of it. But as time went on, she realized that there actually was a slight coolness between the two sisters. Madame Solomon died, later in the spring, and after that Margot went less and less frequently to Lisieux and threw herself with greater and greater intensity into the work at Malou. There was apparently no end to her energy.

She was no longer content with doing an immense amount of cooking; she could go into the fields, she insisted, just as well as Nicole, and she proceeded to do this too, effectually silencing the scandalized objections made to such a procedure. So the ladies of the *noblesse,* even the *petite noblesse,* never tilled the soil? Well, perhaps that was part of the trouble, both with the aristocracy and with the land! They needed to get closer together. Everyone admitted how greatly the garden had improved since Madame la Baronne had taken charge of it. If her mother-in-law could grow vegetables, she could help grow wheat and oats and barley, and she was going to do it. The *noblesse,* as far as she had observed, got just as hungry as the peasantry, and the day was past when one group had a right to live in laziness while the other labored to feed both.

The weeks slipped by fast, for the working hours were so long and hard that everyone was exhausted at the end of the day, and thankful to sleep until it was time to begin work again. But though laborious, the summer was, in many ways, more bearable than any since the beginning of the war. Malou was free from intrusion; Aunt Bertha and Michel were both restored to their families; Nicole was pursuing her Underground activities without discovery; the weather was fine, the crops abundant. The atmosphere was one of expectant waiting, unmarred by restlessness or disharmony. All the news from the outside world was good. The Allies continued to win victories in Africa; the French Committee of National Liberation was formed in Algiers; Italy was invaded; French troops landed in Corsica; the bombers above Malou increased in size and number, and their flights came closer and closer together; Nicole reported that more and more parachutists were landing safely in France. Everyone believed that very soon now, possibly before All Saints', probably before New Year, everything would be over.

And then, just when these hopes were highest and seemed most justified, Constance was abruptly summoned into the presence of two German officers who were complete strangers to her. They introduced themselves as Captain Jaeckel and Lieutenant Kremer and brusquely informed her that a large detachment of Storm Troopers would occupy her property.

At the first glimpse of smart black uniforms, her heart had turned over in her breast. Not until she was close enough to see the stylized twin lightning-flash *SS's* of the Schutzstaffel insigne did she face the realization that the officers she was approaching were not members of the Cadre Noir, miraculously restored to their old status of dignity and prestige, but leaders in the most feared and hated branch of the German Army, whose presence had never before been inflicted upon her. The thought that this was von Reden's answer to her repulse flashed through her mind. He had not returned himself; but he had arranged that these representatives of all that was worst in the forces of evil should do this instead, and he had chosen the time when he knew she must believe that the hour of deliverance was at hand.

Again cold anger consumed her, and she replied to the intruders with icy brevity. But she soon saw that they did not expect her to make comments; they were there to give orders and not to engage in conversation: she might reserve the apartments over the two salons for herself and her family; all the rest of the château must be turned over to officers of the Schutzstaffel by the following evening. Captain Jaeckel understood that twenty men could be billeted in the commons; but it was his expectation that this time as many as two hundred, very possibly more, might be quartered at Malou. It would be necessary to build barracks. The tennis court would make a good site for at least one such building. Probably it would be necessary to cut down some trees to make room for other buildings. . . .

The remainder of the day, and the day which followed it, had no reality for Constance, like the days which followed the orgies of Pfaff and Lein-meister; they seemed part of a hideous nightmare, from which she must somehow struggle back to the security of sound consciousness. Mechanically, she called her aunt and her daughter-in-law and all the men and women of Malou together, and told them what had happened and what they must do. They stood in the fort, listening to her, their attitudes and the expressions on their faces as unreal as everything else. Padoue, clinging close to Margot, stared at his grandmother, his big black eyes wide with puzzled fear; he could not understand her words, but he understood all too well that something frightening had happened. Five of them would be eating, sleeping, living, in two rooms now, one of these very small—a fragile old woman, a high-strung girl, two active children, herself. Dearly as they all loved each other, closely as they were bound by all sorts of ties, it would be very hard on all of them. Aunt Bertha was not physically fit to endure such confinement, Margot in no mental state for easy adaptation to it. Constance herself, having been keyed to high hope, was now fighting depression and despair. How could she continually be calm and patient in her attitude towards her aunt and her daughter-in-law? How could she remember to speak kindly always to Padoue and Lucie? She knew that she could not. She knew that sometimes, no matter how hard she tried not to fail them, she would inevitably do so.

It was agreed that they would all sleep in their own rooms this last time, and when Constance finally lay down alone in the alcove bed, it was with thankfulness for the reprieve which her brief solitude would give her. But she could not sleep. She turned on the radio, knowing she must not do so again—this time it really must be destroyed, and its pitiful remnants buried where no one could find them. The B.B.C. was announcing the resignation of General Giraud as cochairman of the French Committee of Liberation, leaving General de Gaulle in complete control, and ordinarily this news would have been thrilling and provocative. Tonight it did not seem to matter who headed the Committee of Liberation or even if there were such a committee. What happened at Malou was the only thing that mattered, and this was all a nightmare from which she still could not escape.

She hoped her head would be clearer in the morning, that she would not forget to tell Nicole to discontinue acting as a contact for the Resistance. Constance knew that, according to plan, Nicole was to do her most important work when the Germans came back. But, like the radio, that would be too dangerous now. With twenty enemies on the place, some secrecy of action might still have been possible. With two hundred it would be out of the question.

She did not sleep, but the nightmare persisted, and before the next evening the place was swarming with Storm Troopers. The sound of their heavy tread and harsh voices echoed through the château, and the areaway was a scene of even greater turbulence. However, rigid order was quickly established. Within forty-eight hours the soldiers had begun to build the barracks on the site of the tennis court with lumber they had hauled in, and trees at the fringes of the beautiful woods were already falling. The men shouted as these trees fell, and the noncommissioned officers shouted their orders; but the soldiers did not talk and joke among themselves as they went about their work. They were a grim group, functioning grimly. Only in the evenings, just before taps, they sometimes sang for a few moments, a song which Constance had not heard before:

> " 'Vor der Kaserne, vor dem grossen Tor,
> Steht eine Laterne, steht sie noch davor.
> So woll'n wir uns da wiedersehen,
> Bei der Laterne woll'n wir stehn,
> Wie einst, Lili Marlene, wie einst, Lili Marlene.' "

Eventually Nicole spoke to Constance about this song. The Germans sang it first in Africa, Nicole had learned; now the Allies were singing it too; there were French words and English words for the same tune. The Storm Troopers at the commons did not admit the Germans had been run out of Africa; Nicole did not believe many of them knew it, even yet— the officers, of course, but not the men. These men were no better than slaves, for all their big bodies and big talk; they said what they were told to say and did what they were told to do. They did not dare think or act for themselves.

"What are they doing at Malou, do you suppose, Nicole? Have you any idea why so many of them are here?"

"Not yet, Madame la Baronne. In time, perhaps I shall find out. Though not as easily as Aylette would have done."

There was a tinge of regret in her voice. The interruption of her Resistance work had been a bitter disappointment to her. She was naturally a patient girl, instinctively a good girl; but now Constance felt impelled to urge patience and rectitude upon her.

"Don't give up now, Nicole. You put up such a splendid fight, for so long. Don't lose hope. You kept saying all summer that you didn't think it would be much longer, that there was every sign——"

"I didn't. There was. But it would seem I was mistaken. It would seem the signs were misleading."

"I don't believe so. It's just that everything always takes longer than you think it's going to, beforehand."

She tried to sound convincing. But she was discouraged herself, more deeply discouraged than at any time since she could remember. The cold. The darkness. The crowding. The monotony. The intrusion. The arrogance. The destruction. She had managed to hide the carefully mended portraits, the few remaining ornaments and remnants of porcelain; but there had been neither time nor room to stow away much furniture. Every few days she saw a broken chair or a table which had been set out in the fort because it had become unusable through abuse; then it disappeared. This happened so often that finally she forced herself to speak to Captain Jaeckel about it, though up to this time she had not exchanged a dozen words with him. Her old servant, Léon, was handy at repair work, she said. If the Captain would have the damaged pieces assembled in one place, possibly the granary—— He cut her short.

"Those old sticks of furniture are not worth saving. They were decrepit long before we got here. Now most of them are wholly past repair. We are using the pieces for kindling wood as we discard them."

"Some of those 'old sticks' are very valuable antiques. They have been in my husband's family for generations."

"And have degenerated along with it."

She must not retort, she could not risk a rash answer. The consequences might be too dreadful. There was nothing to do but let the destruction go on, both indoors and out. Every tree that crashed to the ground seemed to crush some vital part of her as it fell. The beautiful beeches. The splendid oaks. The steadfast hemlocks. Between the areaway and the woods there was a strip covered with jagged stumps, and the strip was growing wider every day. One evening when the strains of "Lili Marlene" mingled with the strains of *"Tannenbaum, O Tannenbaum, wie schön sind deine Blätter,"* she felt like breaking into the barracks and demanding how men who wantonly hacked down beautiful trees could sit around a fire and sing that song. But she knew that such a foolhardy act would only subject her to ridicule—or worse. There was no connection in the minds of these men between the evergreens in Germany, of which they sang with such sentimentality, and the hemlocks at Malou which they were destroying.

Her mind reverted to that Christmas Eve of long ago, when she and Tristan had walked home together from Midnight Mass at Grand Blottereau. They had spoken of the hymns which had been sung at camp, and he had said, "Many different kinds of people, in many different countries, are moved by the same thoughts, in the same way, at a time sacred to all of them. Your hymn was written by a great prelate, ours scribbled by a lonely wastrel, the Germans' composed by a village choirmaster and a parish priest, striving together to overcome the handicap of a broken-down organ. We all celebrate the birth of the Prince of Peace as our supreme festival. And yet we go on from generation to generation striving against each other, killing each other. It is very sad." . . . He had sounded sad as he said this. But he had believed, and she had too, that there would never be another war, that in the years following the one which had just ended, the erstwhile enemies would somehow grope their way to a lasting peace which all could share, forgetting their differences, finding their common purposes. And it had not been like that. Some people had earnestly desired peace and had striven towards it. Others had been content to take it for granted, to slip back into easy and slothful and corrupt ways. Others had deliberately sought to undermine it. And now, for the fifth consecutive year, the birthday of the Prince of Peace would be celebrated in the midst of war.

No, that was not the right word. How could there be a "celebration" marking any holy day or happy feast under such conditions? Constance would have infinitely preferred to let the day go by as others were passing —a day lived through somehow, with an outer show of dignity and endurance and inward prayer that the dignity would not diminish or the endurance fail. But with children in the house, and the spark of faith to keep alive, there must be some observance of the day, even if there could

369

be no rightful celebration. Lucie still believed that Père Noël came to fill good children's sabots on Christmas Eve, and Padoue, though he had not fully grasped the meaning of the pleasant custom, already prattled about setting out his shoes with hers on *mémère's* hearthstone. So Margot went to L'Abbatiale and searched through the blank cold houses for something that would serve to fill the sabots. She found a few dilapidated old toys which had survived the onslaughts of herself and her brothers and sisters, brought them back to Malou with her, and turned them over to Léon for mending. She also extracted a promise from Mark Mullins that he would not stay alone for *réveillon,* or skip it entirely. There was no turkey this year, she admitted, but there were still two geese; the table would not be bare. He promised her that he would come. He did not mind sleeping with the "boys," in the hay; in fact such a bed would seem quite fitting for Christmas!

His acceptance gave an added incentive to make *réveillon* as cheerful as possible. Besides, Monsieur le Curé would expect a full attendance from Malou at Christmas Mass, and Constance would play the organ in the village church, as she frequently did now that no regular organist was available. That was why she had first done it at Grand Blottereau. Life was a series of strange cycles. Somehow you completed them.

She was astonished as she and her companions started for Norolles through the snow to see that several of the Storm Troopers were walking ahead of them, giving their customary effect of a military formation. She was still more astonished when she saw them turn off the highway into the narrow road leading towards the church. She had a vague recollection of hearing during von Reden's first occupation that one or two of his men had gone to Mass at Norolles or Le Breuil, but she had not done so herself regularly in those days, and she had never seen a German there. Aunt Bertha had also reported the presence of one or two others at the Protestant "Temple" in Lisieux; but for a long time now the old lady had spared herself the strain of attendance there. Instead, she sat reading her well-worn Bible and leafing through her battered book of *Gospel Hymns* every Sunday morning; so her impressions of the "Temple" were considerably out of date.

Constance had been prepared for the installation of numerous small decorated trees—trees which had been cut from her woods—in the château, the commons, and the barracks; after all the Nazis could, and doubtless did, claim that there was no religious, or at all events no Christian, significance to these. But she had never thought of the Storm Troopers in connection with the Christmas Mass—the strains of the beautiful old hymns coming from the barracks had seemed inconsistent enough. Her astonishment grew as she saw the black-clad officers walk stiffly into the church and take possession of front seats, across the aisle from the fauteuils occupied by Monsieur le Deputé and Monsieur le Maire. They were all wearing their side arms, and they did not remove these; and again, through a sudden trick of memory, the past seemed to merge with the present as she recalled Abbé Souillet's story: "Since they were already alerted, all the young men in the church were obliged to remain armed through the night. I could hear the arms clicking as I left the confessional and went to the sacristy to prepare for Mass. My little altar boy was there ahead of me."

It was fantastic, it was almost sacrilegious, to think of those doomed cadets in connection with these disciples of the Antichrist. Constance had not yet been able to form a conjecture as to the meaning of the Storm Troopers' presence. But at all events, this was no consecrated vigil on their part. They were not going gallantly forth from the church to a sacrificial death. That much was certain. And they had not confessed, they would not receive Communion. Or had they? Would they?

To her ultimate astonishment she saw them rise as soon as the priest had communicated. Would he pass them by when they knelt before him, rebuking them in the face of God and this congregation? No one else approached the altar rail. The *charitons* in the choir stalls, Monsieur le Deputé and Monsieur le Maire in their fauteuils, the stunned occupants of all the pews behind them, remained motionless. Constance lifted her fingers from the organ keys and clenched them in her lap. An unnatural hush had fallen on the church. Only the side arms resounded.

The priest stood at the altar holding the Host. For an instant he too was motionless, and the hush took on an electric quality. Then he made the sign of the cross and went swiftly down the steps. Before the eyes of his thunderstruck people, he was offering the sacred wafer and the Storm Troopers were accepting it. Then they rose and went rapidly down the aisle, staring stonily in front of them, the clank of the side arms marking the time of their march. The church door closed behind them and the priest continued to stand at the altar rail. For another portentous moment no one stirred. Then, slowly and dazedly, his people went to him.

They were a reverent group. It had never been their habit to leave as soon as Monsieur le Curé had communicated, even if they were not doing so themselves. Nor did they leave immediately thereafter if they were, as the Storm Troopers had just done. That, as Lise had once said to Constance, was the same thing as turning one's back on the good God, in their opinion. Now, in spite of their agitation, they waited reverently for the last gospel, the benediction, the withdrawal of Monsieur le Curé to his little sacristy. Constance played the recessional through to the end. Then, as the people rose and moved quietly towards the rear, the church doors were thrown open from without, and a sharp order clove the still air.

"*Halt!*"

The Storm Troopers were standing on the little porch, two on either side, the fifth directly in the center, blocking the entire passage. They had all drawn their pistols. Captain Jaeckel, who was the one in the center, began to speak—sharply, concisely, with dreadful impact.

"There have been signs of restiveness under the Occupation in this village; they must cease. There are rumors of Resistance; they must also cease. If at any moment a rumor becomes a reality, the death penalty will be executed in payment of the rebellious crime. And to make sure there is no repetition of it, the entire family of the criminal, as well as his close associates, will likewise be put to death. That might well mean every person here present. This is the only warning which will be given. Reflect on it."

His thin lips closed, forming a narrow ruthless line in his hatchet face; but his evil gaze did not shift from the victimized people, and he still held his great pistol steadily in his outstretched hand. Again a hush had fallen, and this time it was one of horror and not of amazement. No one was sure that the threatened shooting might not begin there, at the church portals, on Christmas Day; many listened, sick with fear, for the shot to ring out. Then, very slowly, the Captain replaced his pistol in its holster and wheeled about. His fellow officers followed suit. They stepped down from the porch almost jauntily, and went up the narrow road leading to the highway. Their shining boots crunched through the snow. Their side arms continued to clank.

None of the people left behind were able to say *"Joyeux Noël"* to each other. For the most part, they slunk away to their homes in stricken silence. Nicole clung to Constance and wept.

"They have found out," she whispered in a choking voice, as soon as they were alone. "They will kill us all. Oh, Madame la Baronne, I have brought death and destruction to Malou! And I meant to help bring about its deliverance!"

"Its deliverance will still come," Constance managed to answer. "There, Nicole, you mustn't leap to conclusions. I am sure this is just another threat."

But she was not. All that day she found herself watching and listening, as she had found herself watching and listening after von Reden made his first threat. At her feet, Padoue and Lucie played excitedly with the toys Father Christmas had brought them.

All that day and the next and the next. Through the cold. Through the darkness. Through the crowding. Through the monotony. Through the destruction. These went on and on. But the sounds for which she waited did not come, though each day that she listened for them, the dread of them seemed to grow.

And then, almost as abruptly as they had come, the Storm Troopers were gone.

The day before they left, the entire detachment drew up in parade formation in the areaway. Padoue, who had heard the military music, ran to the east window of the big bedroom, closely followed by Lucie, and both called excitedly to their elders to come and see. The window was open, for spring was in the air at last, and they grouped themselves about it, watching the soldiers goosestep into place. When Captain Jaeckel had reviewed them, one of them advanced slightly and read at endless length from a long scroll of paper. Something in his bearing and intonation suggested that in civilian life he might have been an actor, and after Constance had succeeded in quieting the children, she gathered that the man was delivering some kind of a fulsome ode. Then Captain Jaeckel himself began to speak and she grasped what was happening.

"You'd think the Knights of Pythias were celebrating their fiftieth anniversary or something," Aunt Bertha said acidly. "Can you make out what it's all about, Connie?"

"They're celebrating *Hitler's birthday! At Malou!* The pompous fool who spoke first was reading a long poem singing the Führer's praises! And that was the Horst Wessel song the men were singing when Padoue called us."

"Well, I've got so I'm familiar with that, after all these months. But what was that jackal saying to them in the long-winded speech he reeled off?"

Aunt Bertha had never referred to the Captain except as "that jackal" after first hearing his name. Constance had spelled it for her once, but she had never corrected her a second time and she did not do so now.

"I couldn't hear all of it, and of course there were some words I couldn't understand. A lot of it was apparently just the same old stuff: an expression of unbounded admiration for the great hero who has led the thought and will of Europe into new channels, and nullified the boundaries set by the shameful conference at Versailles." Constance seldom spoke sarcastically; but there was sarcasm mingled with the anger in her voice now. "That jackal actually did admit that the victorious armies of the Nazis had recently suffered some setbacks," she went on. "But he said that was because the Allies had secured a technical advantage with new weapons, while the Nazis—only temporarily of course!—continued to use the old ones. But now they are devising new weapons also. Terrible ones."

"Do you believe it?" Margot asked quickly.

"I don't know what to believe. So much of it is just lying, or intimidation. At the same time——"

"At the same time Joseph and Bernard were executed. And fifty Nantais, including Robert de Fremond, were killed in reprisal for one German. And my father was sent to Auschwitz. And the last we knew, the Nazis were still hanging on in Italy, besides 'possessing' all of France," Margot answered. "And they're up to something new, right here and now. We've known they must be, ever since November, and still we haven't been able to find out what. Personally, I don't think we're very smart."

"Don't say that in front of Nicole, Margot. You know how upset she is at what she considers her failure. And yet how fearful she is about bringing harm on us."

Constance's voice sank to the lowest of whispers as she spoke. Margot replied in the same hushed way. Nevertheless, the whisper had an inflexible ring.

"Anything would be better than going on like this any longer. One more such winter——"

One more such winter and we'd all be at each other's throats. One more such winter and we'd all be raving maniacs. One more such winter and we'd freeze and starve. One more such winter and there won't be anything left of Malou but bare walls and stripped grounds and empty barns. One more such winter and there'll be treachery and desertion where we're least looking for it, perhaps right here in our midst. The words were unspoken, but Constance knew they had been on the tip of Margot's tongue, as they had already been, time and time again, on the tip of her own. It had been hard to bite them back for a long while now. And once they were spoken, once the imminence of defeat were acknowledged, it would be upon them.

"Let's get outdoors for an hour or so," she said resolutely. "It's really a beautiful evening. The children won't be so restless after they've scampered around a little, and it will do you and me both good to stretch our legs, Margot. You don't mind being left alone, do you, Auntie?"

"I'd admire to be."

Aunt Bertha spoke with unaccustomed weariness. The lack of privacy and rest was telling on her too. She leaned back in her rocker, closing her eyes. Taking the children by the hand, Constance and Margot went as quietly as possible from the room. Just outside, they were accosted by one of the junior officers.

"Captain Jaeckel has sent me to say that he wishes to speak to the Baroness."

"Did he say where and when?"

"In the fort. Immediately."

So she would not get out for a breath of air after all! She told Margot to take the children and go on without her, and she herself stopped at the foot of the stairs and stood stonily beside them, waiting for the Captain to speak. As usual, he did so without preamble.

"The time has come for me to move to other headquarters, accompanied by most of my officers and some of my men. A certain number of soldiers, in charge of noncommissioned or junior officers, will remain in the barracks for a short while longer. Then these may temporarily be vacated. But at some period in the summer they will be occupied again, probably by the Wehrmacht the next time, as previously. You should be prepared for such occupation at any time."

Constance did not answer. The Storm Trooper rapped out a curt question.

"Did you hear me?"

"Yes, I heard you."

"Then why did you make no answer?"

"It did not seem to me there was anything I could say."

"I advise you not to speak that way in addressing an officer of the Schutzstaffel. You are not dealing with Gerd von Reden now."

"I have been well aware of that, Captain Jaeckel, for more than six months."

"And you will continue to be aware of it. The fact that I am leaving here to take up more pressing duties elsewhere will not prevent me from keeping myself informed as to what is happening in this locality. I suggest that you remember that."

"I have a very good memory, Captain Jaeckel."

"You are an extremely insolent woman. But you will not be insolent much longer. Neither you nor any of your breed."

There was a sneer on his thin lips now. He wheeled about in his usual mechanical fashion, and stalked into the dining room. Constance leaned against the wall, closing her eyes, as Aunt Bertha had done, in utter exhaustion. She had but one conscious wish at the moment: to throw herself on her bed and turn her face to the wall. But she did not know how she could summon the strength to get up the stairs.

She did not try. After a moment she opened the great door and went across the drawbridge, joining Margot and the children on the other side of the moat.

Following the tumult of the Storm Troopers' departure, the château was uncannily quiet again. This quietude, like the new spring mildness, brought hope and healing with it; but it did not signify relaxation. Seedtime was upon them once more, and this meant long hours in the fields for everyone able to work there, and equally long hours in the garden for Constance. She knew that she could not slight this, much less leave it unplanted. The vegetables she raised were now the mainstay of their meals; but she shrank from the galling realization that the more time she gave to the garden, the less she could give to the château, and this was in the same state of dirt and disorder as after the departure of Pfaff and his minions. Indeed, certain conditions of unspeakable filthiness were worse than they had been then; and though destruction had not been wrought in the same way, during the course of one night's unbridled carousing, it had gone on steadily for months. The abuse and wreckage of her precious possessions confronted her at every turn. She could not cope adequately with these conditions even if she gave every moment of her waking time to them.

Nevertheless, she tried. Aunt Bertha was still able to help her a little, Lucie was beginning to do so. She set stints, saying to herself that she would not go to bed any night until she could see at least a slight improvement in a given room. It took several days to make much of an impression on the larger ones; in the smaller ones, she could get visible results in less time. She did not make the mistake of rushing. Indeed, though this meant getting to bed still later, she stopped systematically once in so often and sat for a few minutes at the piano, running her fingers over the keys, or in an easy chair, leafing through a book. For some inexplicable reason, the Storm Troopers had thrown the contents of the bookcases in the small salon into the *cave*. As she salvaged the treasured volumes and got them back into place, a few at a time, Constance asked herself, over and over again, why the Nazis should have done this. After all, there were highly educated men among them, and the little library contained a variety of excellent literature. It would have passed the time on the long winter evenings to delve into this, as she had so happily discovered for herself.

She had no leisure for delving now, and the evenings were not long any more. But she read a page here, a poem there, a chapter somewhere else, often making the selections from the books Tristan had given her in Nantes, and rose, refreshed, to go on with her work. After achieving elementary cleanliness everywhere in the château, she strove for more com-

plete order in the *petit salon* first, because that was where they all most
enjoyed sitting; the satisfaction Aunt Bertha and Margot showed the first
time they were able to reoccupy it in a condition somewhat resembling its
normal state more than rewarded Constance for the drudgery through
which she had achieved this transformation. She next turned her attention
to Tristan's office. The Storm Troopers had left their own "literature"
there. They had received an enormous number of periodicals during their
sojourn, far more than any of their predecessors, and she was genuinely
curious to find out what was in these papers. As she went through them,
she had reason for renewed satisfaction because she read German so
easily. There was a blue-bound handbook, adorned with a silhouette of
Frederick the Great, containing a dissertation on the traditional bearing
of the German officer, and a pamphlet comprising brief biographies of the
Führer's officers. There were comic papers containing vicious caricatures
of the French, and army journals featuring fake photographs of heroic
achievements. There was an explanation for every setback, a justification
for every act of aggression; pomposity and vainglory permeated every
page. "If the entire Führer hierarchy is ordered in accordance with prudent principles, how can it be explained that for some time now success
has remained unfulfilled for us?" she read. "I can only point out that no
newly risen military commander has ever been spared powerful opposi-
tion, not even though his name was Frederick the Great or Napoleon."
And, a little farther on, "When, in prosecuting a great design, one does
not break a few things across one's knee, one will never amount to anything in this life."

Two of her discoveries especially intrigued her. In a militaristic magazine she found sandwiched in between "A Challenge to the Family in
Wartime" and "A Warning against Betrayal" an exquisite love poem with
the verse:

> *"Ach, ich ahn' es wohl, Geliebte:*
> *Heut' in tiefer Nacht*
> *hat Dein Herz nach mir gerufen;*
> *einsam, einsam wie ein treuer Stern*
> *hast Du fern um mich gewacht."*

She separated this magazine from the others, with the thought that
some day she would show this poem to Tristan; it bore out his contention
that many different kinds of people, in many different countries, could be
moved by the same thoughts, in the same way; and she herself visualized,
for the first time, a woman in Germany who was faithfully and patiently
waiting for her husband to come home, and a distant soldier comparing
his beloved to a star. . . .

Still dwelling on this strange revelation, Constance picked up the rotogravure section of a Cologne paper, and saw that its lead article was entitled, "KAMPFMITTEL DER KRIEGSMARINE: *Deutsche Ein-Mann-Torpedos
Werden an den Feind Gebracht."* Underneath this title were captions in
three languages, French, Spanish, and German, and she ran through these
quickly before studying the photographs to which they referred: *"New*

Maritime Weapon. German one-man torpedoes are put into action. The above photograph shows the new weapon. It is a combination of two torpedoes in which one carries the other destined for launching. As a reward for having sunk an English cruiser with this human torpedo, Corporal Gerhold, the first to put the new weapon into action, is decorated by the Führer."

Having read the captions with care, she gave the same attention to the photographs. These showed long, slim cigar-shaped tubes, one on top of the other, the upper surmounted by a globular excrescence, not unlike a huge inverted goldfish bowl. The longer she looked at them, the more deadly they appeared to her. She set the rotogravure section aside also, and the next day she showed it to Nicole.

"When you still had contacts with the Resistance, Nicole, did you ever hear anyone speak of weapons like these?"

Nicole studied the text and illustrations carefully. Then she answered with such hesitation that it was plain she did so guiltily.

"Before the Storm Troopers came, no, Madame la Baronne. But lately——"

"Nicole——"

"Madame la Baronne, I beg you not to blame me! It is something I have to do, just as there are certain things you have to do. And I have been very careful. There are no more soldiers at the commons now, you know that, and very few in the barracks. And it is still necessary for me to procure medicine for Michel; he does not have his strength, even now. So usually I go openly to Lisieux by the main road. This creates no suspicion if I do not do it too often. If I have reason to believe that I am needed at other times, I slip out through the back way late at night, and creep along the hedgerows in the fields. Thus by one route or another, I reach the apothecary's."

"And at the apothecary's——"

"Yes, at the apothecary's I have heard of these *hommes torpilles*. Enough to make me feel I had to hear more. Please, Madame la Baronne——"

"I'm not angry, Nicole. I understand what you mean when you say this was something you felt you had to do, just as there are certain things I feel I have to do. I want you to tell me what you've heard where you've been. But I don't dare have you do it here. It should be safe now. But we can't be sure. Wait till next Sunday. I'll walk across the fields to church with you then, and you can tell me, the way you told Lise."

"Yes, that will be better. On Sunday I will tell you—a great deal."

Suddenly she scuttled away as if she feared that by lingering she might say too much then and there; and in the next few days, Constance thought that she saw a change in her. And not only in Nicole. Somehow there was tension in the air. Day after day the sense of some great stirring force became intensified. Night after night, the planes flying over Malou continued to increase in size and number. Constance lay listening to them, trying to guess at their numbers and their portentousness. She did not sleep. Her apathy, her discouragement, her depression, had all left her.

She was keyed to high pitch again, and it was in this mood that she started across the fields on Sunday with Nicole.

She could see that the girl could hardly wait to speak. Constance shook her head slightly, controlling her own impatience, until they were out of all possible earshot. Then she put her head close to Nicole's.

"About the *homme torpille,* madame," Nicole whispered. "It has been used, yes, against the Allied ships in the Channel. There is a plan to use it more. It is not a secret weapon. On the contrary, the Nazis boast about it so openly that in some quarters it is felt they are purposely exaggerating its importance. As to that, I do not know. It must take courage to man these *torpilles,* for their missiles are released at only sixty meters from their target, and the explosion of these missiles comes too soon, in most cases, for a man to save himself. Or so it seems. Indeed, we are told that the Japanese are using these same weapons, and calling them 'suicide torpedoes.' In France, they are concealed in the woods and then taken to the coast on open trucks. It is my own belief, which is shared by many of my coworkers, that they might do a great deal of damage. But there is another new instrument of war, madame, which it is thought will prove far more deadly still. It is known as the *bombe volante.*"

"The *bombe volante?*"

"Yes. Because it flies through the air by itself, without any pilot at all. It can be launched from a great distance and do great damage where it falls. It is filled with high explosives. And the Nazis are planning to launch it from emplacements in France, aiming at the supply depots in England. In this way there will be less question of destroying ships; the supplies will be stopped before they ever start. That is, if the wicked plans of the Nazis are carried out. But perhaps they never will be."

"And did you find out all this at the apothecary's in Lisieux, Nicole?"

"No, madame. I have been much farther than Lisieux now. I am a good walker—I can cover as many as thirty kilometers, sometimes forty, going through the woods in the night. Even without shoes. So now, when there is need, I do not stop at the apothecary's. I go among the *camouflés* themselves. And then I find the contacts with the Resistance which they, in turn, indicate."

"I see. And what did you mean when you said, 'But perhaps there never will be'?"

"I meant that other plans might be carried out first."

Nicole had stopped and was standing still, her head raised as if she were listening. She was only a squat little peasant, dressed in ill-cut, shabby clothes, and her drab hair, loosened by the wind, blew untidily across her weather-beaten cheeks. But somehow, standing there, she gave the effect of a beatified sibyl. Startled by the strangeness of this apparition, Constance raised her head and listened too. Not a single sound penetrated the complete quietude. Nicole lifted a roughened hand and brushed away the long strands of hair. Then she looked at Constance with a smile which transfigured her plain little face.

"Presently," she said.

CHAPTER XXXIX

For nearly twenty-four hours they had been hearing it, distant but monstrous. It was less a perception of sound, something to which they listened, than an awareness of force that somewhere was filling a vast shuddering space with violence; and the unbroken tide of its fury bore no kinship to the roar of the bombers now streaking through the starlit void above the Vallée d'Auge. The sky was full of planes, and their thunder was inescapable from any point at Malou. Nevertheless, when Margot found Constance sitting on the terrace long after midnight, she put her hand on her mother-in-law's shoulder and tried to remonstrate with her.

"Why don't you go to bed, Mother? It doesn't do any good to stay here. And the noise doesn't seem quite so bad inside."

Constance reached up for the girl's hand and clasped it in her own. "I suppose you won't believe me," she said slowly, "but I haven't been thinking half so much about the noise while I've been sitting here as I have about what it means: that at last the invasion's begun."

"Yes. The Allies must have landed. Maybe not so very far from here, either. Maybe at Arromanches. Or maybe at more than one place. And they'll be bombing all over the shop. They may reach Lisieux any moment."

"Lisieux—and Malou, Margot."

"I don't believe they'll waste their bombs in the country. If I did, I'd be mighty anxious about L'Abbatiale. But I think they'll strike straight for key cities."

She had hardly finished speaking when the low wail of a released bomb became a rising shriek. For a moment the whole earth seemed to leap and cry out in pain; then the convulsion passed, only to be followed by others, coming in swifter and swifter succession. Margot did not try to speak again. She stood quietly, her hand still on her mother-in-law's shoulder, listening to the screaming missiles and watching the great fountains of turbulent fire gush upward beyond the encircling hills which separated the valley from Lisieux. The sky was all alight now. Red and orange tracer shells arced lazily aloft, shrinking into pinpoints of radiance as they soared and died out. Far above the crisscross pattern of the tracers, heavy antiaircraft shells were bursting in vicious crimson.

"Margot, you mustn't stay here," Constance said, when at last she could make herself heard. "You ought to be with Padoue."

"Padoue's sound asleep in the *cave*. If he's safe any place, he's safe there. Aunt Bertha and Blondine are both with him. There's nothing to worry about as far as he's concerned—at least, not right now. But I'm damned worried about Ghisèle and Marie Aimée. For all we know, they're in the thick of this."

Margot was still gazing in fascination at the multicolored flashes which danced across the sky. But these were now diminishing and the ripping, shattering explosions were farther and farther apart.

"I think this particular preview of hell's about over," she said. "I wish we knew exactly what's happened. Perhaps someone on the hill has a radio or a telephone that hasn't gone dead. I'll strike off as soon as it's light, and try to find out."

"Please don't, Margot. I'm worried about Ghisèle and Marie Aimée too. But let one of the men go, or Nicole."

"I'll be just as safe, Mother, on the road or in one of the other houses, as I am here. I don't suppose any place is going to be entirely safe from now on until the last Nazi is cleared out of Normandy. Not that it's been particularly safe anywhere around here for nearly four years now. It seems funny, doesn't it, to stop worrying about what the Germans are going to do and start worrying about what the British and Americans are going to do? The show here seems to be finished for the time being, though. Let's go in and snatch a little sleep ourselves. We're going to need it."

"I suppose we are. You're right, as usual. But, Margot, when I asked you to let one of the men go for news, or Nicole, I wasn't thinking only of your safety. Of course that means everything to me—at least it would if I could only ensure it. But I know I can't. And I was being selfish. Not just because you're so gay and gallant that you make everything bearable. But because I've come to care so much for you that I hate to be parted from you."

"Don't worry, Mother. You couldn't get rid of me, for long, if you tried. I happen to like you a lot too."

They moved slowly across the terrace, arm in arm. The distant, monstrous tide of something which must be sound, but which bore no kinship to the roar of the bombers, pursued them into the fort.

With the coming of daylight, it seemed to deepen rather than lessen, and it had a stronger quality of foreboding. The men and women of Malou went about their accustomed tasks mechanically, their ears cocked for reverberations of the sounds which had riven the night. Early in the morning old Mesnil came over from the Monteillerie, bringing news; rumors of all sorts were flying in every direction. But yes, it was certain that the Americans and the British had landed on the beaches at dawn the previous day. Caen was already a mass of smoldering ruins. Lisieux was also half destroyed, if what he heard was true: everything had been tossed about and turned upside down, partitions had fallen in, doors and windows had been torn out, even solid walls were rocking. The smell of sulphur was said to be stifling. Smoke, plaster, and dust filled the eyes, the ears, the noses; no one could see or hear or breathe. He would try to get there later in the day and see for himself. Some of the roads were probably gutted out. But others must still be passable. When he had anything else to report, he would come back. . . .

About noon Nicole slipped across the fields to the *mairie* and the *bureau de tabac* and came back with fresh gleanings: no one had been killed or injured and nothing had been destroyed in the vicinity of Norolles, but in Lisieux, alas! all was different. It was the British who had come over during the night, aiming at the railroad. There was talk of torn and twisted trains and locomotives lying on their sides like dead horses. But these Britishers had hit a lot of houses too, which were still crashing to the ground. And more than horses were lying dead. Nicole had not been able to find out just who or where. But if Madame la Baronne were willing, she also would go to Lisieux that afternoon. She and Mesnil had different sources of news; it would be well to tap them all. . . .

Constance gave her consent reluctantly. But after all, as Margot had said, one place was probably as safe as another; and not only Malou, but all Norolles, was in need of news, for inevitably the villagers would have friends and relatives among the victims; and among the survivors would be many requiring succor and shelter. Nicole sped off, but within the hour Constance had reason to regret her decision. The planes swarmed back over the valley, and presently the bombing began again, with redoubled force, while thick clouds of smoke billowed upwards in the distance. In midafternoon, the sight lacked the deadly and spectacular quality of the night assault, when the darkness was furrowed by sinister light. But the noise was even more deafening; doors and windows shook with the terrifying vibrations that rocked the solid structure of the château violently. Michel and Lise refused to leave their cattle, Martin and Benoît their horses; but Alpy, Denis, Léon and Blondine went willingly enough to the *cave,* where they made a half-hearted pretense of joining in the game of hide-and-seek which Padoue and Lucie played among the old casks, while Aunt Bertha sat erect on the lowest step, industriously knitting. Constance and Margot remained on the terrace as before; and again, though they spoke only in short, disjointed sentences, they drew closer and closer together in spirit.

"Those are American planes this time, Mother."

"Your eyes must be better than mine, Margot. I can't see the insignia."

"Neither can I. But I can tell a Flying Fortress from one of those fat British Lancasters. Can't you?"

"No. And besides, I still have to brace myself against these loud noises, Margot. I suppose, subconsciously, I concentrate on doing that. Anyway, I don't distinguish among them. They're all horrible to me."

"No one would ever guess that you were bracing yourself against anything, Mother. You've got as much 'gumption' as Aunt Bertha."

"I'm afraid not. But I'm glad it seems that way to you."

"You don't mind too much about this bombing, do you, Mother? I don't mean the noise. I mean because Americans are killing French people and destroying their homes."

"Of course I can't help minding dreadfully. But if it's the only way——"

"It must be, or they wouldn't do it. We'll find out why they did sometime. . . . Meanwhile, it's pretty grim business waiting around to find out just what's happened. I'll feel a lot better when I know Ghisèle's all right. And Marie Aimée."

"Mesnil told us the British were aiming at the railroad. They wouldn't try to hit hospitals and convents!"

"They wouldn't try to, but they might just the same. They can't be all that accurate. Well, I'm glad you're not worrying too much. There's no one else in Lisieux, is there? I mean no special friends?"

"No. I'm overwhelmed with the realization of the mass destruction of life. But Ghisèle and Marie Aimée are the only persons in Lisieux I really love. Of course I have lots of pleasant acquaintances there. But I've never been very close to any of them. If your father and mother were alive, that would be different."

"Yes, that would be different. And my mother might have been, if only——"

"You don't think hardly of her, do you, Margot? After all, everyone can't face——"

"No, I don't think hardly of her. But I don't think of her in the same way I think of people who can face things, either. I hope to heaven Padoue'll be that kind."

"I'm sure he will. He couldn't help being. He's a de Fremond and a Bouvier."

"And a Galt and a Slocum. Put that in too, Mother."

The roar was gradually subsiding to a rumble, as it had the night before. Margot rose, pulling down her short, shabby skirt.

"I think this is an afternoon we have to drink coffee, Mother. Coffee and Calvados both. I've still got a cache, you know. I'm going out to the kitchen to start things. And I'm going to give an 'All clear' signal to our refugees in the *cave*. Then, after we've had our heartening refreshments, if you don't mind too much, I'm going to range around and see what I can find out. After all, we haven't heard anything but rumors yet, and this shooting started thirty-six hours ago. We can't go on indefinitely without knowing what it's all about or whether anyone we know's been hurt."

"Nicole ought to be back any moment. That is, if she's all right."

"Of course she's all right. Don't start worrying about her now. But as she told you herself, this is the time to try different ways and means of getting news. We can't tell which one will work best."

Margot rose and sauntered towards the kitchen. It was quiet and pleasant there, and she decided that if the "refugees" did not come up from the *cave* of their own accord, they might as well stay where they were until she had finished making the coffee. Even Blondine had never been able to discover the whereabouts of Margot's "cache," and extracting the precious beans from their hiding place, she smiled at the thought of her well-kept secret. Blondine had carefully banked the fire before descending to her shelter, and it was no time at all before Margot had it burning brightly again. Then, having ground the coffee, she sat down while she waited for it to drip. Never in her life had she felt more restless and disturbed; never had she been more determined to remain outwardly calm and collected. One of the black cats which had been dozing by the hearthstone jumped up in her lap and, tucking its paws contentedly under its breast, began to purr loudly. Margot stroked it, and hummed the air of a half-forgotten song:

" 'Je t'attendrai toujours,
Je t'attendrai la nuit et le jour . . .' "

Yes, that was probably to be her life. She would wait for Nick always. But this waiting was not the same as when she had first sung the song, in Paris, during the *"drôle de guerre."* She had felt sure then that he was coming back to her, as sure as he was that he would be killed; and though she had known too that this might happen, she had never feared it would do so before they had their share of joy together. Now she knew he was never coming back, that her waiting would be in vain, and sometimes the days were very long, and the nights were longer still. While her grief for Nick was fresh and piercing, while she was carrying and nursing his child, she had not felt like this. But Nick had been dead four years now, and Padoue was a hearty rollicking boy who needed her less and less every day. And she was only twenty-four. . . . She wondered if her mother-in-law, whom she dearly loved, as she did her child, realized that love like that was not enough for her any longer, that she wanted desperately. . . . But of course she would wait. She would wait always. . . .

She set the purring cat quietly down on the hearth again, tested the quality of the coffee, and finding this satisfactory, finished arranging her tray and started back to the terrace with it. As she entered the fort, she saw that a stranger was standing just outside the great door, on the drawbridge. The door was open, precluding the use of the old iron knocker, and there had never been a front doorbell at Malou. Margot set down her tray and went forward.

"Good evening," she said pleasantly. "Can I do something for you? Won't you come in?"

"Thank you, mademoiselle. The matter is very urgent, and I could not seem to make myself heard. I was beginning to fear that I should be obliged to come in uninvited, and call out or walk around until I found someone."

"I am very sorry. The Baroness is out on the terrace, and the house servants are down in the *cave* with the children. I have been in the kitchen making coffee. Won't you have some while you tell me your errand?"

He glanced past her at the inviting tray, and she could see from his expression that her suggestion was tempting. He was a slight man of medium height, greatly in need of both a shave and a haircut; his shirt was dingy and his suit shabby. But in spite of his unkempt appearance, he was far from unattractive. His tired face was kind, and he had a fine head; beneath his pale, drawn skin, the structure of his brow and cheeks was beautiful, and his manner had dignity and distinction. When he shook his head, smiling, there was something about his expression which reminded Margot of her father.

"I really should hurry back to Lisieux, where, unfortunately, I am very badly needed," he said diffidently. "Excuse me—I should have introduced myself at once. I am a doctor and my name is Gérard Lutaud."

"Then please, Dr. Lutaud, let me give you some coffee! I'm sure you must need it dreadfully. And besides, while you're drinking it you could tell me not only why you came to Malou. You could tell me what's happened in Lisieux. I'm terribly anxious to know." She began to pour the coffee while she was still speaking and he did not decline it. As he gratefully took the brimming cup from her, Margot was again reminded of Jacques Bouvier. *This doctor's the same kind of man my father was,* she said to herself. *Very sensitive. Very—well, very refined. I've always hated that word. But I don't any more. It's the only word that describes him. And he's a wonderful person. I don't know why I'm so certain of that when I never saw him until about three minutes ago, but somehow I am. . . .* She waited silently for him to go on.

"Lisieux is almost totally destroyed," he said, speaking with quiet intensity. "The attack came from three squadrons of airplanes and these modern bombs pulverize everything within a set radius. Reinforced concrete crumbles like plaster and hangs from its steel cables like dirty linen on the line. The city—what there is left of it—presents a dreadful sight after this avalanche of flame and iron. We accept the bombing as inevitable, part of the price we are to pay for liberation—both the bombing by the English last night and the bombing by the Americans this afternoon. However, it was not inevitable that all the morning the Germans should go about setting fire to buildings which had so far escaped. The result is a holocaust. I must not stop to tell you about it now. But it is necessary to understand that more have been injured than can possibly be cared for at the hospitals. The civil authorities of Lisieux have therefore decided that they must requisition every château available in the vicinity as a hospital. Malou is naturally among those designated. I have come to say that the first six patients will be here within an hour and that the Baroness must somehow arrange to lodge them, feed them, and help care for them. Also to inquire how many more she can arrange to receive by morning. I am sure it is superfluous to add that the need is very great."

"Of course the Baroness will arrange to care for your first patients immediately. As to how many more she can receive—wouldn't you like to come and talk to her?"

"You couldn't give me an idea yourself, mademoiselle? It would save time if you could."

Margot made a swift calculation. "Twelve?" she hazarded.

"Twelve! Why, mademoiselle, it will be necessary to put as many as twelve in one room. If it should be as large as many of those at Malou must be! I was about to suggest fifty."

"Then it will have to be fifty. I didn't realize. . . . You know we wouldn't have that many beds."

"This will not be a question of beds, mademoiselle. It will be a question of floor space where grievously wounded men and women may at least lie in comparative safety. And you must be prepared for many deaths."

"We'll try to be prepared for everything."

Impulsively, she stretched out her hand. He took it, looking at her gravely and attentively.

"I have told you my name, but you have not told me yours," he said. "Would it be indiscreet if I asked this, mademoiselle? We shall inevitably be seeing much of each other in these next days, and perhaps it would be more convenient——"

"Yes, naturally. I'm Margot de Fremond."

"Margot de—you don't mean Madame Dominique de Fremond?"

"Yes."

"And I have been calling you mademoiselle all this time!"

"I didn't think it mattered. Does it?"

"No," he answered, "it doesn't matter. Though I should have guessed immediately who you were. But you look so young I didn't. So young and so——"

He stopped, and for a moment he stood motionless, looking at her. He was no taller than she, and his eyes were on a level with hers. She returned his gaze steadily and without embarrassment. His error was natural enough. He had seen her carrying a tray, and he had mistaken her for some capable young neighbor, probably a girl from one of the prosperous independent farmsteads scattered among the more pretentious *manoirs* and châteaux of the locality, who was lending a helping hand to the Baroness in an emergency. But as she stood quiet under his scrutiny, she realized he was thinking less of his mistake than of her beauty, and that for the first time in four years a man of her own age and class was looking at her with ardent admiration. Suddenly a little forking flame crept through her, filling her with strange unexpected warmth; and though she did not turn away, she knew that in that moment something had happened which neither he nor she had sought, but which could not be undone, because the flame within her had been kindled from another that was stronger still. . . .

"If you are Madame Dominique de Fremond, you must be Ghisèle Bouvier's sister," Gérard Lutaud said at last, slowly and rather lamely.

"Yes, I am. But how did you know that?"

"Because she is one of my best nurses, and——"

"Is she all right? We've been frantically trying to get news about her."

"Then I am happy to be able to tell you that she is unhurt. It was something of a miracle, for the hospital was hit this afternoon, though it escaped the bombardment last night. It was in part demolished, and ignited. But not one of the physicians or nurses was injured. The patients were less fortunate, and that is why it is so urgent to set up emergency accommodations for the care of the injured."

"Mother will be so relieved. We have all worried about Ghisèle."

"I will tell her I was able to reassure you, and also that everyone here at Malou is all right."

He moved towards the door, picking up the battered hat which he had laid down beside the coffee tray. "In an hour, then," he said. "You will tell the Baroness for me? *Au revoir—madame.*"

"*Au revoir—Monsieur le Docteur,*" Margot replied.

The linen closet on the third floor at Malou contained a seemingly inexhaustible supply of sheets, pillowcases, towels, tablecloths, and napkins. The first time Tristan had showed them to Constance, he asked her laughingly if even the famous Craig mills could have done any better for her, as far as linen was concerned; and she had answered, in all honesty, that she did not believe they could have done anywhere nearly as well. The sheets were enormous, wide enough to tuck in a foot on either side of the biggest beds, long enough to double over an eiderdown. Many were handwoven and all were heavily embroidered with the crests and initials of countless de Fremond brides; and as they had been accumulating through the years, there were so many of them that even during the largest house parties of happier times, or the most taxing days of the German Occupation, no visible impression had been made on the supply. Everything else was proportionately large and proportionately plentiful. Now, with Margot's help, Constance dragged down from the shelves pile after pile of the great linen sheets, of the *traversins* that covered bolsters and the huge square cases for pillows. Every bed in the house was freshly made; and, in addition, sheets were folded crosswise before they were restacked, in order that they should be ready to receive immediately the patients who must be laid on the floor. It was agreed that the right wing should be used as a male ward, and the left wing reserved for women. Aunt Bertha moved her most personal belongings back to Margot's dressing room, and for the first time Constance prepared to vacate her own bedroom and share her daughter-in-law's. The extra flight of stairs would be a handicap in caring for so many injured; as far as possible they must be nursed on the lower stories. . . .

Aunt Bertha and Constance and Margot were all in the fort, eagerly waiting to be of service, when the first car drove up; and as it stopped, they hastened across the drawbridge. Apparently no ambulance had been available, for this was an ancient limousine, creaking and cumbersome. An elderly, rather uncouth man, obviously unaccustomed to its idiosyncrasies, was driving it and brought it to a jolting halt. The two women who had been on the front seat with him clambered hastily down. One of them, the waiting group saw with amazement, was a nun wearing the habit of a Benedictine novice; the other was Ghisèle, in a uniform so torn and bloodstained that it was hardly recognizable as that of a Red Cross *infirmière*. Ghisèle came quickly forward and pressed her cheek first against Constance's and then against Margot's. They could feel its wetness, and knew that theirs were wet too. For a moment none of them tried to say anything. Then Ghisèle broke the poignant silence.

"I've come to stay," she said, steadily but a little huskily. "We'll all be working together. We can talk by and by. There isn't time now. Except that I must tell you one thing before we start taking the wounded out of that car. Dr. Lutaud didn't realize how much it would mean to you—he's a comparative stranger here. But the Abbaye des Bénédictines was totally destroyed in the bombing last night. At least twenty of the nuns were killed outright. Most of the others must have escaped, but we don't know yet where they are or how badly they may be hurt. Six of them were brought to the hospital on improvised stretchers. Of course we couldn't keep them there after that was bombed too. We have them here now, and I think they all have a fighting chance. But before you see them, Aunt Constance, I ought to tell you that one of them is Mère Marie Aimée."

CHAPTER XL

CONSTANCE DID NOT MOVE from her own bedroom to Margot's after all. She was too greatly needed for the care of the wounded. Ghisèle, who shared the alcove bed with her, was the only Red Cross *infirmière* who could be spared for Malou; most of the nursing was necessarily done by eager but inexperienced volunteers. Ghisèle and Sœur Paula, the novice who had been with her on her arrival, looked after the most critical cases and assumed the responsibility for the others, directing the amateurs. Sœur Paula had taken a nursing course herself before entering the convent; she was strong and skilled, while Ghisèle had a more profound sympathy for human suffering and a more tender touch. Together they accomplished wonders. But tireless as they were in their ministrations, they could not do much more than supervise and direct, except in actual emergencies. Dr. Lutaud, who had been assigned to Malou as resident physician, explained this briefly to Constance and asked that she and her aunt and daughter-in-law should each undertake a specified part of the hospital work.

He suggested that Constance might, for instance, have charge of the allotment of linen and the distribution of food on trays, of such superficial bathing as could be done, and of the simpler bandaging, which he would show her how to do; then he added that she would also probably have to circulate with bedpans, or anything that would serve as a substitute for these, in the women's wards. Mademoiselle Berthe could sit beside the patients, watching them attentively, and call the nurses if their presence seemed urgently required; she had better keep little Lucie, who seemed an exceptionally intelligent child, near her, and Lucie could run minor errands and summon aid. As for Madame Dominique de Fremond, the doctor believed she would be most useful in the kitchen; it would be no small task to feed sixty mouths, more or less; obviously, someone more vigorous and alert than the old cook—Blondine, was that her name?—was needed at the helm. He hoped that within a few days, they could have more help from outside. Possibly one or two Sœurs de la Providence could be brought out from town, though this would be impossible as long as the intermittent bombing continued; and possibly the Baroness herself could suggest some source of service, since Lise and Nicole, as well as the men of Malou, were needed in the fields.

Constance shook her head. Every farm in the vicinity was understaffed and overworked; if all the helpless and injured were to be fed, the normal labors on the land must go forward. A couple of weeks later, however, as he was leaving the women's wards after making his rounds, she joined him in the upper hall and asked if she might speak with him for a moment. He nodded, his expression indicating that he hoped she would be brief, and she handed him a small piece of printed paper.

"Léon picked that up in the lower pasture early this morning and a little later Mesnil came over with one like it that he had found at the Monteillerie," she said while the doctor was scanning the paper. It was a small printed notice, evidently dropped from the air, warning the Norman farmers that they must attempt no more planting and cultivating. The Allied bombers would be obliged to attack anyone they saw in the fields, because the Germans were using farm implements as a means of defense, concealing cannon in haycarts, machine guns in tractors, and hand grenades in smaller utensils.

"This means we won't have any harvest," she said quietly. "And if we don't have any harvest, we won't have much food by next winter. However, I didn't stop you to talk about that. I only wanted to tell you that as no one can go into the fields any more, you can count on having more help in the hospital from now on."

"Well, Lord knows we need it. One of those two deaths we had last night might have been avoided if Ghisèle hadn't been obliged to leave a desperately wounded man to go to another who was even worse off. How many extra helpers will this mean?"

"Four. Nicole for the women's wards, Léon, Denis, and Alpy for the men's."

"What about Nicole's mother-in-law? Lise, is that her name? Couldn't she be spared from the farm work too?"

"Lise is doing all the laundry, besides helping Michel look after the cattle and the poultry. Martin and Benoît are taking care of the vegetable garden, now that I can't do it any more, but they aren't much good in the *bassecour*. And I've felt it was necessary to keep Lise where she was, because the milk and eggs are so important to the patients. But of course you must decide where she's needed most."

"I'll think it over and let you know. Meanwhile, get the others into the house right away, will you? Have them report to Ghisèle. She'll tell them what to do first."

He was already moving away from her, in the direction of the men's wards. She knew he had been delayed and harried that afternoon by a visitation from the German medical and intelligence officers who periodically called at the hospital to satisfy themselves that no fugitives or spies were camouflaged among the patients, and this tedious and disagreeable formality had interfered with his regular routine. Obviously he had hardly heard what she said about the impending scarcity of food; he was too beset by the more pressing problem of caring for the wounded. But after she had called Lucie and told her to send Nicole, Denis, Léon, and Alpy to Mademoiselle Ghisèle, Constance stood looking out at the fertile fields, no longer bare and bleak as they had been when she first regarded them with anxiety because she lacked the means to work them, but fresh and green and shimmering under the summer sun. Somehow she had managed, year after year, to find the necessary manpower for tillage; but she could not send men out to almost certain death. Two or three planes were circling slowly over the valley now; at the slightest sign of forbidden activity below, they would release their deadly projectiles. For the first time in the history of Malou, none of its crops would be harvested. . . .

She closed her eyes for a moment, shutting out the sight whose very beauty gave it added poignancy; then she walked slowly back towards her own room. The curé of the village church, who now came regularly to Malou, was just leaving this. There was a priest among the patients who had been wounded in the bombardment, but not seriously. So far he had been able to say Mass every morning and administer Extreme Unction in sudden emergencies. But his strength would not permit him to do more than that, and though Dr. Lutaud was trying to arrange for a resident chaplain as well as additional nursing Sisters, none had as yet been secured. Constance had never wholly understood or entirely forgiven Monsieur le Curé's denial of consecrated burial or his bestowal of the Host on the Storm Troopers; but he and she had always been on friendly terms, and since their shared vigil the night before the execution of Bernard and Joseph, and her own further rapprochement to the Church, they had seen more of each other, in an increasingly personal way. Both stopped instinctively now. There were always matters which they wished to discuss.

"Did you find everyone as well as you hoped, Monsieur le Curé, in there?"

"Yes—or perhaps I should say as well as I expected. I was troubled yesterday about Mère Marie Aimée. I am more troubled today."

"I know that Dr. Lutaud is troubled too. He felt encouraged after the operation he performed last week. But she has not seemed to rally so well from the second one."

"This last operation was really the third, wasn't it?"

"Yes, that's true. For a moment I had forgotten the one in the crypt of the basilica, where the nuns first took refuge after the bombardment of their Abbaye."

"She has been talking to me about the destruction of that. Of course all the nuns do. It will naturally be their main topic of conversation for years to come." The priest smiled faintly, as if he suspected that the excitement of the bombing might have mitigated the sufferings of a few who were not severely injured themselves, and who had not happened to witness the worst agony of others. "But Mère Marie Aimée is not dwelling on the wreckage of the convent," he continued. "She is dwelling on the idea of its restoration."

"Its restoration! Why, it is completely in ruins, isn't it?"

"Yes. But she has so much faith that she believes it could be rebuilt. She has even drawn a little sketch, with a detailed plan for such reconstruction. I do not know much about such things, but it looks to me like a very practical plan. I think she would like to show it to you and talk to you about it, if you have the time."

"And I'd like to have her—if I had the time. I haven't had, so far. But perhaps I shall have a little more now." Briefly, she told the priest, as she had told the doctor, about the warning which had been dropped from the air and he shook his head gravely. He was country-bred himself, and his parochial work had always kept him in a small village; more clearly than Gérard Lutaud, who was the product of a provincial city and had always practiced in one, he knew what this unavoidable order would mean not only to Normandy but to the less fertile parts of France which this rich region supplied. With gratitude, Constance sensed his sympathetic understanding. "As a matter of fact, I think I could take a few moments right now," she said. "It isn't quite time to start on the supper trays."

"Then go to her, by all means. It will encourage her. And keep up your own courage, madame, in spite of this new difficulty about the land. You will find a way to meet it, as you have in the case of all the other hardships. And the rest of us need the example of your fortitude. It sustains every one of us."

They parted with as little formality as they had met. Constance heard someone call out to the priest as he went nearer the men's wards, and was aware that he quickened his pace in response to the summons. But she knew that Ghisèle was on hand and that she herself could do the most good by keeping to the tasks that had been set for her.

Most of the cases which were under treatment here were for burns, in varying degrees of severity, and among these were three nuns. Marie Aimée's injuries and those of her two closest companions, Mère Claire and Mère Martina, were different, however. Mère Claire had tripped over the corpse of another Benedictine while stumbling down the great central staircase in the darkness; then she had fallen the rest of its immense length and had cut her right hand so badly that it had been necessary to remove one of her fingers. The floor of Mère Martina's cell had received a direct hit, and she had been hurled through the hole thus made to the library far below; when she was dragged out from under the debris, one of her arms was found to have been crushed. Mère Marie Aimée, who was also in her own cell when the bombardment began, had been struck by bomb fragments while trying to put on her shoes, and one of her feet had been horribly torn. Two unsuccessful operations sought to remove the bomb fragments. Then it had been necessary to perform an amputation; now it appeared that all the doctor's endeavors had been vain. She had borne the pain heroically, and during the earlier stages of her stay at Malou had even made little jests, saying that her disability was less annoying than Mère Claire's or Mère Martina's because she could use both her hands; this enabled her to write letters, to knit, and to hold a book, whereas they could do none of these things with ease.

During the last few days, she had not been able to do them either, because she was too exhausted by pain; but the fiction that she could if she wanted to was still maintained. She was lying back on her pillows when Constance approached her, dressed in a plain, long-sleeved white gown which Ghisèle had managed to procure, her head covered with a soft linen towel, which had been draped to form the semblance of a veil. Small bright spots of feverish color, very different from the healthy glow which had once suffused them, burned on her wan cheeks; her pale hands were clasped loosely over the counterpane and her translucent lids were closed. As usual, Mère Claire and Mère Martina were seated on their pallets next to her bed, watching her as they talked in low tones about their harrowing experiences. Mère Claire was a round-faced, rosy nun, whose solid frame and cherubic expression had hardly changed at all; her eyes twinkled and her mouth turned up at the corners while she recalled her most lurid experiences. Mère Martina was a tall handsome woman with noticeably fine teeth and a commanding presence; she had endured more than Mère Claire, both spiritually and physically, but she too seemed to Constance essentially unchanged. It was Marie Aimèe, who had looked enough like Tristan to be his twin, who wore on her calm brow the unmistakable stamp of what had already happened and what was still to come. . . .

"May I break in for a minute? Monsieur le Curé thought that Mère Marie Aimée would like to see me, and presently I must go down to the kitchen to look after the trays."

Constance had been circling the room, checking on the condition of the women who were the worst burned. Now she came up and put her hand on Mère Claire's solid shoulder. Would this comely nun, who so far seemed almost unaffected by the ordeal she had sustained, still be so plump and placid a year hence, Constance wondered, with a passing pang at the thought of the uncultivated fields. But this was no time to dwell on that. It was of Marie Aimée that she must think, and of ways, if any there were, to mitigate her anguish. She had opened her eyes now, and was smiling in her old inimitable way; at least that had not changed—that and her clear direct gaze.

"Yes," she said softly, but clearly. "Yes, my dear Constance, I do want to see you, if you can spare me a few moments. You have done such wonders with Malou that I am sure you could tell me whether you think the little plan I have drawn is practical. I should place great confidence in your judgment."

"Where is your sketch, Marie Aimée?"

"Here, by my side, under the coverlet, where I can reach it quite easily."

The nun felt for it, found it instantly, and handed it to Constance, who studied it carefully. Though her knowledge of conventual requirements was necessarily limited, she thought she recognized in the plan an intelligent and comprehensive effort to meet these. Moreover, she could actually visualize a new structure rising from the ashes which would retain much of the charm and dignity of the ancient Abbaye, and at the same time prove far more sanitary and commodious.

"I haven't had any architectural training, you know, Marie Aimée," she said. "What I did here at Malou wasn't structural. But as far as I can judge, you've drawn a very good plan. I'm not sure though that I understand just what you want me to do with it."

"I want you to keep the little piece of paper I have given you in some safe place—where you keep your will and Tristan's most important documents, for instance. And I want you to pray, every night, this plan may be a reality—that a new Abbaye may rise where the old one has fallen, to serve as a symbol for rebuilding wherever there is devastation in France. I want you to promise me that you will do everything in your power to see that the land given us by William the Conqueror never falls into impious hands, that the Community over which his cousin presided as first abbess is not scattered and disbanded. Most of all I want you to reflect that the place where our little Sainte Thérèse passed her school days and made her first Holy Communion is too sacred to pass into oblivion, but should be restored as a monument to her grace and glory."

"Marie Aimée, I promise you that I will do everything I can, but I have no way of knowing how much that will be. It may be very little, even after the war is over. And the war may last for a long time yet. Just now, I do not think you should tire yourself with talking about all these details, in any case. I think you should rest and conserve your strength. Then by and by, when you are better——"

She stopped, halted by the expression in Marie Aimée's eyes. Then she knelt down beside the bed. Marie Aimée put out her hand and stroked Constance's hair.

"You must not grieve," she said. "But you must not admit obstacles either. This is something that can be done, that ought to be done. I have tried to tell you that more than this one building is involved, since its restoration could serve as the incentive for so much other work. And you can help to do it. Hundreds of your compatriots will help too. Was it not an American who rebuilt the Cathedral at Reims, after the First World War? Are not the Americans again with us now? Destroying for the moment, it is true, because they must. But afterwards they will restore. You can help to make our need known to them. Not that you can do this work alone. All France should help in it. And those of our Order who have survived must do their share. That should not be too hard either. We must be worthy of our own past. Not only the past of which I have already spoken, the past of William the Conqueror and his cousin, the Countess Lescelines. But of our great Abbess, Louise de Créqui."

"I know about the Countess Lescelines but not about the Abbess Louise de Créqui. I'd like to hear about her—some other time. But Marie Aimée——"

"She was elected to office immediately before the French Revolution," Marie Aimée continued with determination. "She and her nuns suffered untold hardships and persecution during the next dreadful years, and finally they were driven from their Abbaye and imprisoned. They were obliged to flee as refugees, in different little groups, as we have done now; these groups did not see each other nor hear from each other, just as at present. It was nearly twenty years before Madame de Créqui was able to return to her convent, with a few of her spiritual daughters. And how did she do it? First by renting it and then by purchasing it from a hostile government! The Community's own property! It was *thirty* years before this was entirely reassembled! But our Abbess had the joy, before she died, of seeing it living in peace and harmony again under the shadow of its ancient cloister. Is what we have to face now so much harder than what she faced; can some of our survivors not dwell among the ruins and hold them for our own?"

A silence had fallen on the room as the nun talked. The whispering and grumbling, the sharp cries of pain and low smothered groans which usually sounded through the ward, had all ceased. By intent, Marie Aimée was speaking only to Constance, and her voice, always soft and low, was further muted by weakness and suffering. But every woman in the room was listening to her now, and her words were clearly audible.

"When I speak of those who will help," Marie Aimée said, "I am thinking not only of our great allies, your compatriots, or of our many friends in France, or of our own Order. I am thinking also of our own little Sister, Sainte Thérèse. You know what our *poilus* said during the First World War when they were told to invoke the help of the Maid of Orleans, Patroness of France—'The Little Sister seems nearer to us.' She seems very near to me now. Shall we pray to her, all those of us who are in this room together? A great prayer asking for the victory of right and the liberation and restoration of France? And then afterwards a little prayer, asking that the place sanctified by her presence while she was on earth shall not vanish from among the sanctuaries of the world? I believe that she will hear and heed both prayers."

The room was still very silent when Constance left it and, blinded by her tears, groped her way to the kitchen. The evening was extremely warm, for Normandy, and though Margot had thrown every door and window open, despite Blondine's protests about currents of air, the leaping flames on the great hearth and the sun streaming in through the west windows combined to make the kitchen very hot. Blondine was arranging the trays neatly on two long tables, a second one, for the greater accommodation of these, having been added to the normal kitchen equipment. She was growling to herself as she did so; apparently her present grumblings arose from the fact that one of the soldiers had stopped her when she went to the woods to gather mushrooms, and had told her this was now *verboten*. It was understandable that she would be provoked because the guard had halted her and disturbed because she could not get the mushrooms which were needed to eke out other diminishing supplies. But Constance did not take her grumbling too seriously, or indeed pay much attention; it had become Blondine's habit to complain about trivialities, while bearing great burdens with fortitude.

On the other hand, there was something abnormal about the haste and clamor with which Margot was rushing back and forth. She nearly always moved quickly, but her speed was characterized by efficiency rather than noise; now it seemed as if she were actually banging her pots and pans about on purpose. Her eyes were snapping too, and bright spots were burning on her cheeks, larger and redder than those on Marie Aimée's. Constance suddenly realized that Margot was very angry, angrier than she had ever shown herself since the night she had ragingly informed her mother-in-law that it was not her fault because she had failed to conceive a child during the first weeks of her marriage. That she might be utterly exhausted by the hard work she was doing, or moved, almost beyond endurance, by the sights and sounds of suffering with which she lived surrounded, was easy to understand; but what could possibly have roused her to sudden violent fury was a mystery.

There was no time to attempt a soothing gesture now, or tactfully to seek the source of the trouble. Marie Aimée's impassioned plea in behalf of the Abbaye had detained Constance in the women's ward far longer than she expected; she must begin, immediately, to circulate with the trays. Lucie carried some of the lighter ones to the second and third floors, Aunt Bertha some equally light to the ground floor; but Constance had been carrying most of the heavier ones herself. Tonight she would have help with them, and she was thankful for it. She was very tired, so tired that when Nicole, Denis, Léon and Alpy all appeared, prepared to assist her, she did not remember, for more than a moment, that they would not be there if they had not been compelled to quit the fields. With the evening meal more easily and quickly served than at any time since the installation of the hospital, she forced herself to put more time into making the patients comfortable for the night.

Ghisèle had everything well under control in the men's wards, and there seemed to be no further cause for immediate alarm among the patients there— After all, with two deaths only the night before, it was certainly to be hoped not! Sœur Paula had joined the other nuns grouped around Mère Marie Aimée. Her face, habitually somewhat severe of expression, was sterner than usual tonight, and her white veil and wimple, instead of softening it, seemed to accentuate its deep lines. Because another vocation had preceded the conventual one, she had entered the Abbaye later than most nuns did, and she still retained the bearing and mannerisms of the *clinique* rather than the cloister. But her eyes behind her large glasses were very wise, and her strong square hands were unerringly skilful. Her fingers were against Marie Aimée's wrist when Constance entered the room, and she shook her head sorrowfully at their hostess' unvoiced question. Marie Aimée's eyes were closed again now, and she did not seem to be aware of Constance's approach; but her fingers were slipping over her rosary, and her lips were moving, as if she were trying to join in the old familiar song which the others were softly singing:

> " 'Je mets ma confiance,
> Vierge, en votre secours!
> Servez-moi de défense,
> Prenez soin de mes jours!
> Et quand ma dernière heure
> Viendra fixer mon sort,
> Obtenez que je meure
> De la plus sainte mort.' "

Marie Aimée's death would be a blessed one, there was no doubt of that. But the tragic waste of it was overpowering. Why should this quiet and holy woman, who had never harmed anyone in her life, be the victim of a war in which one evil man had possessed the power to embroil the whole world? There was no answer to this, of course, any more than there was an answer to the deaths of Bernard and Joseph and Jacques, and to the threat of death which still hung over Padoue like a menacing sword.

Constance left the women's wards with the intention of going straight to the nursery. But for the second time that day she stopped to speak to Dr. Lutaud in the upper hall, and on this occasion it was he who took the initiative.

"I'm on my way to see Mère Marie Aimée," he said. "Not that I believe there's anything that can save her now. But of course we have to keep on trying to the end."

"I'm afraid she overtaxed herself talking to me so long. But she was so determined——"

"Yes, and her mind's more at rest now that she's done it, however it affected her physically. And after all, a day or two more or less won't matter at this point. But it's hard seeing a woman like that die so needlessly, and not being able to stop it. I haven't been able to get her out of my mind all day. . . . I'm afraid I was pretty abrupt when you spoke to me this morning about the extra help. I know what it means to you, in other ways, letting me have it, and I ought to have said so. It's bad enough for you to be faced with what you are, without having the people around you act as if it didn't matter. I want to tell you I realize it does matter, even if I'm doing it hours too late. But the truth is, I've been pretty well shot to pieces myself today. About Mère Marie Aimée and those prying German inspectors—and one or two other things. Well, there, I feel better now I've apologized. I know you believe the apology's sincere and that I don't need to say anything more."

He was gone, with the smile which had reminded Margot so forcibly of her father the day the girl first met the doctor, and of which she had spoken to her mother-in-law.

She paused for a moment, looking out on the fields; in the moonlight they were almost as clearly visible as they had been in the shimmering sunshine. Then she went on up to the nursery. To her amazement, she found Margot there before her.

"My dear, are you ill?" she asked in quick solicitude. "I noticed, when I went down for the trays, that you didn't seem quite yourself. Is there anything——"

"Yes, there is something. Not that I'm ill. Or pregnant either. History repeats itself, doesn't it? I seem to remember another scene in this same room."

"I remember it too. But Margot, you must be terribly unstrung. You're overworking. Some of this extra help that's available now will have to be transferred to the kitchen—I think perhaps it better be Denis, because he already knows how to make himself useful there. No one could possibly go on the way you've been doing without paying for it."

"Stuff and nonsense! I'm as strong as an ox. I can carry all the work there is with one hand tied behind me. I'm in love, that's what's the matter with me. And I've had a frightful row with Ghisèle."

"You're in love! You've had a frightful row with your sister!"

"Yes. After all, I'm only twenty-four. And Nick's been dead a long time. I loved him, I loved him a lot, whether you believe it or not. But I can't go on any longer just loving a memory. I want to love a live man, and I want him to love me. I want Gérard Lutaud. I fell in love with him the first time I ever saw him, and he fell in love with me, the same way, at the same time. Only it seems that before that happened, he was more or less committed to Ghisèle. More, rather than less. In a mild sort of way."

Without answering, Constance sat down on the nearest chair. Unconsciously, she looked from Margot, standing defiantly in front of her, to Padoue, sleeping peacefully and untidily in the nearby crib.

"We weren't thinking of an affair, if that's any comfort to you," Margot went on. "To begin with, this isn't the time nor the place for one— we've both got sense enough, and decency enough, to realize that. Of course I'm not saying that sometimes things don't happen awfully quickly, when you least expect or intend to have them. After all, that's the way we fell in love. If Gérard came up here some night because he couldn't seem to help himself, I might not throw him out. I'm only saying that sort of thing wouldn't be part of our plan. We'd like to get married, with your blessing, and with Padoue for a ring-bearer—all that sort of thing. After the war's over.

"And if that infernal noise, which doesn't seem like a noise at all and which seems to be getting closer and closer, keeps up, I'd say that wouldn't be so long that it would put too much of a strain on our moral standards. But that's where Ghisèle comes in. She was planning to marry Gérard herself as soon as the war was over. And I'm bound to confess that her plans had some basis. I've tried, as pleasantly as I know how, to tell her that these things aren't anyone's fault, and that it'll be easier all around if she'll just step aside instead of hanging on like grim death. And she says she's done that once already, that she did it when I decided to marry Nick, and that she's damned if she'll do it again. Or words to that effect. Of course Ghisèle never swears."

"Margot, darling, please don't feel that I can't see your side. And I've realized for a long time that someday—— But if Dr. Lutaud and Ghisèle——"

"Please, Mother, don't start talking to me about Gérard being a 'man of honor,' the way you'd have talked to me about 'eating for two' that other time if I hadn't stopped you. And don't talk to me about 'someday,' either! I'm not going to wait for *someday!* I'm going to marry Gérard as soon as peace is declared. Just as I married Nick as soon as I knew war was going to be declared. I'm going to leave Padoue with you. He belongs at Malou, I know that, and I'm going to come back, ever so often, to see him and you. But I'm going to have a husband and a home of my own and a lot more children. A baby almost every year, the way my mother did. Only I'm not going to be a coward and a quitter, the way my mother was. I'm going to see this thing through and then I'm going to see the next thing through. But neither you nor Ghisèle nor anyone else is going to stop me from marrying Gérard."

Margot spoke the truth when she said that neither Constance nor Ghisèle could stop her from marrying Gérard Lutaud. But none of them foresaw what would stop her.

Marie Aimée died peacefully soon after dawn. It was as though she felt, having poured out her heart to Constance, that there was nothing further to detain her on earth and that she was ready for heaven. The other nuns whom she loved, Mère Claire and Mère Martina and Sœur Paula, were grouped around her bed when she died, and Constance and Ghisèle joined them. Earlier Constance and Ghisèle had gone to bed in the alcove, because, as Gérard Lutaud had said, there was nothing more they could do. But neither of them had slept. Constance had lain wide-eyed in the darkness, gazing towards the starry handkerchief, even though she could not see it, and Ghisèle had smothered the sobs which rose in her throat from time to time, no matter how hard she tried to suppress them. They were both apparently calm when Sœur Paula called them, and when Marie Aimée, who was conscious to the end, bade them good-by. The wounded priest who was not too badly injured to administer Extreme Unction did this, and afterwards he recited the Office of the Dead.

By this time Marie Aimée had been robed in her habit and crowned with pink roses from the terrace garden and white lilies that had grown from the bulbs the curé of Milly had given to Constance. And she had been moved from the room where the women who were so badly burned were still lying crowded together, and placed on a bier in the fort, awaiting the time when she would be taken to the little cemetery and buried beside Joseph and Bernard. No one could be spared to watch beside her, but Padoue, ranging around as usual, came and looked at her in wonderment and stayed beside her for a while, because she was so lovely to behold; he had never seen anyone who looked like that before and the sight intrigued him. Then he heard a sound which intrigued him still more, and rushed out on the terrace to watch the plane that was circling overhead.

He had never ceased to gaze at the passing planes with fascination, no matter how often he saw them in the sky. This time, to be sure, there was only one, which was not as thrilling as when there were a great many; but still it was well worth watching. It circled round and round, as if someone high, high up were looking for something. And then as if this searcher, whoever he was, had seen what he sought, he sped away down the valley. But as he went, there was a loud wail which became a rising shriek, and a strange missile dove deep into a nearby field. With a mighty noise, its splintering fragments flew far and wide, carrying great sections of earth and rock with them. One of these fragments landed on the terrace of Malou. But it did not touch Padoue. For Margot had heard the low wail too, and had rushed through the fort and seized Padoue, forcing him down into the embrasure formed by the angle of the high stone railing. Then she quickly knelt and with her own body formed a third protective wall. As the great rock fragment struck the railing near her bent head Padoue felt her sag down upon him and struggled desperately to free himself from her inert weight.

At last he succeeded. When Constance reached the terrace, a moment or two later, she found him crouching down beside Margot, shaking her and calling to her, his cries mingled with little frightened sobs. This battered, bloodstained form did not look like his mother any more, and it did not move or answer.

CHAPTER XLI

SHORTLY AFTER the middle of July, von Reden appeared at Malou. Constance had neither seen him nor heard from him since their volcanic parting the day after the American invasion of Africa, and he made no reference to this scene, nor to the subsequent occupation of Malou by the Schutzstaffel, for which she still felt he was responsible. He immediately explained that he would need to occupy the château again, and that the hospital would have to be evacuated. He added that he wished to be as considerate and helpful as possible. He would allow forty-eight hours for the evacuation, and a certain number of German army trucks could be available for the transportation of patients.

"Transportation where?"

"That, of course, is something for the resident doctor and the civil authorities to decide. After all, it was the latter who designated Malou as a hospital. They should now be able to designate a substitute. There are several smaller châteaux which, so far, have not been utilized. Moreover, there is nothing to prevent a return to the General Hospital in Lisieux, or rather to that part of it which your compatriots and their noble allies were considerate enough to spare during the bombardment."

Constance attempted no retort to this sarcasm. As a matter of fact, the evacuation order did not come as a surprise. The barracks which had been run up on the grounds during the previous autumn had never been available for patients because, beginning in early June, German soldiers had again been quartered in them. Lately the numbers of these had been so substantially increased that there was not room for them inside and many were sleeping out of doors—*à la belle étoile,* as the Normans called this. These fresh detachments had made no demands on the château or the commons; they had their own cooks and kitchen police and kept very much to themselves. But during the last few weeks a general air of increasing activity had pervaded the place, and it had been easy to surmise that before long accommodations for senior officers would once more be required. She had already braced herself against the demand.

"I know that you feel very bitterly towards us, Baroness," von Reden continued, after allowing a sufficient interval for the reply, which had not been forthcoming. "I also realize that your personal losses have been so crushing that it must be very difficult for you to evaluate current conditions objectively. I think I have heard you say that the feminine viewpoint is always more personal than the masculine viewpoint—an admission very few women would be fair enough to make. All in all, it must be hard for you to reason logically. But if you will make an honest attempt to do so, I am sure you will grant that though the Occupation has imposed certain hardships and restrictions on Normandy, it has at no point been destructive. On the contrary, it has sought to establish and maintain much needed order and discipline."

"Really? I seem to remember that property to the value of several millions of francs was destroyed right here at Malou, at the end of the first Occupation."

"There have been a few unfortunate episodes, of course," von Reden said with a touch of impatience. "Such isolated instances are unavoidable, no matter how hard we try to avert them. What I meant, as I believe you know, Baroness, was that no historic monuments and places of worship have been attacked. No defenseless invalids and nuns have been slaughtered. No young mothers have been wantonly murdered on the terraces of their own homes. The difference between our methods and those of our enemies must by now be horribly clear to you."

"Margot was the victim of a terrible mishap," Constance replied. "But she was not wantonly murdered, and I know that as well as you do. The bomb which killed her was aimed at some of your own men, who were concealing their antiaircraft guns in our farm implements. The aim accomplished its purpose, unless I am very much mistaken. If your tactics had been different, if you had not so misappropriated and misused the utensils which represent our very livelihood, no such attack would have occurred; and Margot would still be alive."

"I see that it is as I feared, Baroness. You are in no condition to argue logically."

"I do not wish to argue at all. If I did, I might ask you to explain the execution of Joseph and Bernard, the deportation of Jacques Bouvier, the wholesale reprisal at Nantes, the——"

"I should be very glad to explain them all, Baroness, on the most reasonable grounds, if you will stay and listen to me. But you have just said that you do not wish to argue. Perhaps on my return you may feel differently. Therefore I will take my leave of you now. I understand, do I not, that it will be possible to receive me and my staff by the twentieth?"

"I don't see how it will be possible to remove all the patients as soon as that. Some of them are still in a very critical condition. But I'll talk to Dr. Lutaud about it and let you know. Perhaps you'll send your aide-de-camp ahead of you for information before you actually prepare to move in again yourself."

The Colonel extracted the small pad, which he still habitually carried, from his pocket and made a careful memorandum. "I shall be very glad to do so," he said, replacing the pad with precision. "And remember, our ambulances are at the disposal of your patients if you wish to use them. Perhaps you will let Captain Nolte know about that too. I am sure you will be glad to hear that my former aide is still with me, though he has received a well-deserved promotion. Now if I might say good day to my friend Padoue before I leave——"

"My aunt has him with her. And she is with the patients, as usual. I shall have to look through the wards to find him and then fetch him."

"I shall await your return with the fine little boy, Baroness."

Since Margot's death, a great change had come over Padoue. Instead of rushing boisterously about the place, he clung, more and more persistently, to Aunt Bertha and Constance. After the first few days he had never cried, and he asked less and less often for his mother. But he did not want to be alone, either by day or by night, and he did not want to stir out of the house. As Aunt Bertha sat still for longer periods than Constance did, he was with her more during the daytime; but he slept beside his grandmother, and somehow she contrived to give him the bedtime care he had so long lacked. She had moved to Margot's room at last, after all, leaving Ghisèle in sole occupancy of the alcove bed. There was less need of her constant presence among the patients now: many had died; a few had recovered and returned to what was left of their homes; and two nursing Sisters had belatedly been added to the slender staff. Except for the more and more pressing problem of food, the situation had eased in many ways, as far as its material aspects were concerned. But with Margot's death, something warm and vital had gone from Malou, leaving a chill emptiness behind it. Others were doing her work; no one could supply the missing spark. . . .

As she had expected, Constance found Padoue with Aunt Bertha in the women's ward. He was sitting on the floor near her, playing solemnly with a canton-flannel lamb. He had been warned, when he first began to cling to the old lady, that he must be careful not to disturb the poor sick people, but the warning had been more or less superfluous. He did not seem inclined to make any noise. Even the toys he chose were not the small clattering railroad trains, the whirring tops, and mechanical music boxes in which he had once delighted, but tamer things, like the lamb, which he had formerly tossed aside. Constance held out her hand to him, and he got up, unquestioningly, and took it.

"Colonel von Reden is downstairs," Constance said in English to Aunt Bertha. "He's just told me that the hospital will have to be evacuated in forty-eight hours. Everything seems to be all right here just now. Perhaps you'll find Dr. Lutaud for me and tell him, so that he can start thinking up ways and means right away. I'll see him myself, as soon as I can. But von Reden's asking for Padoue, as usual, and I don't dare refuse."

Aunt Bertha nodded without answering, glanced around the room to make sure that everything was indeed all right, and rose to go in search of the Doctor. Padoue, still unquestioningly, trotted along beside Constance, holding the canton-flannel lamb under his arm. Von Reden bent over and shook hands with him.

"Good afternoon, Padoue."

"Good afternoon, Monsieur le Colonel," Padoue replied without prompting. He was used, by this time, to the little ceremony that had so often been repeated.

"I hope you are well."

"Yes, thank you, Monsieur le Colonel."

"Isn't that lamb you have there something new? I do not remember seeing it before."

"It isn't new. Before, I didn't like it much, that's all."

"Do you like it now? Wouldn't you rather have some nice bright tin soldiers to play with?"

The Colonel spoke with the manner of one awaiting an enthusiastic response. Padoue answered with unexpected indifference.

"I don't like soldiers much either. I don't see why they stay around all the time."

"Have any of my men been unkind to your little grandson?" von Reden inquired, switching to English in his turn and addressing his hostess.

"No," Constance said honestly. "In fact, I think some of them would have made much of him if he'd have let them. But he won't have anything to do with them."

"You haven't said anything that would prejudice him or frighten him, have you?"

"No. I've been very careful not to."

"Ah—that was wise. Because he will be seeing more and more of them from now on, and so will you. In fact, the time is not far distant when you will probably think of them as your defenders. . . . Well, we shall have to overcome this childish dislike in some way, and we shall have to find some toy that will please Padoue. A lamb is certainly not a suitable plaything for a boy. Perhaps I can bring a substitute for it on my return. . . . Good day, Baroness."

"Good day," Constance said mechanically.

She watched the military car out of sight, and then stood for a few moments looking beyond the open slope of land towards the barracks and the woods. Certainly something was going on there, though at this distance she could not see what it was. Later she would walk out there and inquire. While she had been preoccupied with hospital work, she had been obliged to forgo her customary evening strolls, so she was not as well posted as usual. All sorts of rumors had been filling the air during the past few weeks, few of them substantiated, for it was hard to get reliable news from any source. But it seemed certain that Cherbourg had fallen to the Allies several weeks earlier, after a terrific siege, and now reports, apparently authentic, indicated that Caen had done so too. If all this were true, the invading forces were now only fifty kilometers from Lisieux. And fifty kilometers was only thirty miles. Whatever the Germans were planning to do at Malou, or elsewhere in the neighborhood, their time was running short. They could not do much harm before the Allies traversed thirty miles. Or could they?

She was still standing on the drawbridge, looking out towards the woods and wondering what was going on there, when Gérard Lutaud joined her. Both of them had striven not to let the thought of Margot complicate their relationship, and because they had done this with honesty and without animosity, they had succeeded to a remarkable degree. The Doctor now broached the subject of the immediate emergency without preamble.

"Mademoiselle Berthe tells me that we have an order to evacuate within forty-eight hours."

"Yes. Can you do it?"

" 'If it is possible, it can be done; if it is impossible, it must be done,' " Gérard quoted ruefully. "I must start out immediately, to see where I can find other quarters for the patients. Naturally, I can't begin moving them until I have secured those. But I think by tomorrow——"

"Then you wouldn't wait for the German ambulances? Aunt Bertha told you they would be available, didn't she?"

"Yes, she told me. But nothing would induce me to use them. For all I know, once my patients had been loaded into them, they would be driven off to concentration camps. Well, I must not linger now. When I get back, I will let you know what success I have had."

"Is there anything special you want me to do while you are gone?"

"It would perhaps be well to let the convalescents know what is about to happen. Some of them might even be able to help in the preparations for departure, and the whole idea will be less of a shock to them if it is not sprung on them too suddenly. The less said the better, of course, to those who are very ill. By the way, I've already told Ghisèle, so she can help you spread the news."

Yes, Ghisèle would do that very well, with great care and tact, Constance reflected, walking back into the fort. Ghisèle was a wonderful nurse. Except for that smothered night sobbing, she had never betrayed desperation in any way, at any time; the long hours, the hard work, the inadequate equipment, the smells and sights which made a hospital revolting as well as sad—all these she had accepted and surmounted with cheerfulness and courage and tranquillity. She had never referred to Margot since her sister had been buried, and this, perhaps, was the greatest example of self-control which she had shown. Margot's death must have been a terrific shock to her, coming as it had with such suddenness and violence, when the two were estranged by a bitter quarrel over the man they both loved. If they could have been reconciled, if there had been time to retract some of the unjust, angry words that had passed between them, if the departure from life had been calm and beautiful like Marie Aimée's, the tragedy of it all would not have been so overwhelming. As it was, nothing seemed to mitigate it.

Yet, even while she told herself this, Constance found herself wondering. If Margot had lived, she would have robbed Ghisèle of her heart's desire. Constance had no delusions about that. Nothing except death itself would have stopped Margot from marrying Gérard once she had made up her mind to do it; and Ghisèle might well have become a bitter frustrated spinster, distrusting and despising all humankind because she had been given cause to distrust and despise her sister. As it was, she would continue to minister to the maimed and helpless as long as the greatest need for this endured, and later she would marry the suitor she had so nearly lost, and make him a devoted and tender wife. She was much more suited for the role that she would play as helpmeet to a provincial doctor than Margot would ever have been. Jacques had been right in saying that doves and hawks were never fit mates; and Margot would have had a soaring spirit to the end, whenever the end might come.

During the next two days Constance dwelt on this thought, in her rare moments of respite from active work, with lessening grief and increasing resignation. Gérard Lutaud had shown himself astonishingly resourceful in finding havens for the patients from Malou. Some of them had surviving relatives who agreed to take those who were well on the road to recovery; to be sure, the quarters they could offer were mean and cramped, but such as they had they would share with goodwill. Those Benedictines who had escaped the bombardment unscathed had found shelter in the stable of a friendly farmer, whose property, hidden away in the green countryside between Lisieux and Saint-Julien-le-Faucon, had not been damaged. Mère Claire and Mère Martina would now be able to rejoin the rest of the Community there, and the injured nuns belonging to other orders could be similarly restored to their own sisterhoods.

The most critical cases, which it would be dangerous to move far, were to be received at the nearby Manoir de Cailloirs, belonging to the de Lavarande family, and the *manoir* of Monsieur le Maire, which was adjacent to it. Sœur Paula would stay in one of these houses, Ghisèle in the other, and both would have help with the nursing. Besides, Nicole and Léon and Alpy could go back and forth between these *manoirs* and Malou, if need be, since the distance was so small. The German officers would have to do with limited service this time. Indeed, it was probably all they expected. With the closer and closer approach of that unbroken tide of fury, whose thundering violence had never stopped day or night during six weeks now, they could hardly ask for meals served in five courses or clean towels every time they washed their hands. . . .

It was Blondine who put the matter thus succinctly, as the task of evacuation neared its end. Surprisingly, because everything had worked out with such unexpected smoothness, this had actually taken less than the allotted time. When Captain Nolte appeared, in accordance with the previous understanding, he found the château already vacated, except for its normal occupants, and preparations for the enforced reception of the German officers already well under way. It was difficult for him to conceal his amazement beneath his usual frozen mask. It would give him pleasure to report to Colonel von Reden how efficiently everything had been done, he told Constance. He regretted, of course, that Dr. Lutaud had not seen fit to accept the Colonel's offer of the German ambulances; but that was like the French, they were always biting off their noses to spite their faces. The Colonel had charged him to tell her that it would not be necessary to dislodge her from her own apartments; her study and bedroom, and the connecting bathroom, would be left completely at the disposal of herself, her aunt, her small grandson, and Lucie, if she cared to include the little girl. No doubt it would seem doubly agreeable to occupy these comfortably again, after she had been obliged to submit to their conversion into a crowded hospital. Captain Nolte was also entrusted with the message to the effect that the officers would be able to bring two very capable menservants with them this time, so that the household staff at Malou would be but little inconvenienced. *Ach—* there was one thing more. The Colonel had sent a present to the little boy, which he hoped the Baroness would permit him to accept in the spirit in which it was offered.

Constance knew that she could not decline to accept it, but she took the package from Nolte with a mental reservation bracketing modern Germans with ancient Greeks as bearers of gifts. Padoue also received the package without visible enthusiasm. But when the wrappings were removed, disclosing a small horse on wheels, covered with real hide and splendidly saddled and bridled, his face lighted up. He insisted on fastening the horse to the table while he ate his supper and to his crib when he went to bed, and several times in the course of his preparations for the night he broke away from Constance to stroke it and move it about. It was a long time before he could be persuaded to lie still. When he finally went to sleep, a look of deep contentment, bearing no resemblance to the puzzled and troubled expression that had stamped it for so long, settled over his face.

"Padoue finally dropped off like a drowsy cherub," Constance told Aunt Bertha as they were finishing their simple supper. "But he was so excited about his horse that I thought he never would. It really is a beauty. And it's hard to keep on being angry and suspicious about something that's given him so much pleasure."

"I don't say but what it's hard. As far as that's concerned, I wouldn't know what to call easy these days," Aunt Bertha remarked dryly. "Just the same, I don't admire the idea that von Reden and all that crew of his will be back here tomorrow."

"Neither do I. But I'm ready to give thanks that they're not here tonight. How quiet it is, except for the distant cannonade! How different from what yesterday was—and what tomorrow will be!"

Constance leaned back in her chair, looking around her with the nearest approach to contentment she had known in a long time. Aunt Bertha regarded her shrewdly.

"Why don't you go take a look around the place, Connie, now you can do it with no one pestering you? I'll listen for Padoue. Fact is, I'd like to get to bed in good season myself. It's a long time since I've had a real night's rest. But a breath of air'd do you good."

"I've been thinking of that. Thanks, Auntie. Blondine can do the few dishes there are alone. I'll stroll for a while."

Chess, who had been lying quietly under the table while they ate, stretched himself and stalked after her stiffly when she rose. There was no doubt about it, he was getting very old and feeble. But Constance felt younger and happier than she had in a long time. The hospital was moved, the greatest need for it over; the Nazis would not be in the château until the next day; the Allies were coming closer, hour by hour. Meanwhile she could survey the domain as its chatelaine. And she would not think, she would not let herself think, that when the next winter came there would not be enough food there unless the liberation came first.

She went up the slope of the areaway and into the garden through the arch that bisected the commons. Here, too, everything was quiet. Lise and Nicole, Michel and Benoît, Martin and Alpy, must all have gone to bed early. Well, she did not begrudge them their rest; they worked hard, early and late, and they had all put their shoulders to the wheel so that the patients could be transferred to other quarters without harm to injured persons and without the delay which would have angered the Nazis. Besides, she liked to have the garden to herself; it was still a peaceful plot and it gave every sign of thrifty growth. The strawberries had passed their prime and their beds were well covered with straw; but the espaliered peaches and pears were already beginning to ripen against the mellow walls; peas, beans, lettuce, radishes, onions, young beets, and carrots were all abundant, while cauliflower and brussels sprouts were coming along well and would be plentiful later on. Fruits and vegetables were doubly important now, with meat becoming scarcer and scarcer because so many animals had been requisitioned, and because it was risky to slaughter many of those that were left—the cows were needed for milk, the poultry for eggs, the sheep for wool. And the bread was getting worse and worse. For some time now, its quality had represented the greatest hardship, as far as the palatability of food was concerned. It was made of barley, corn, rye, and wheat, not mixed in equal quantities, but according to the available supply. Often Padoue pushed it away, and the patients turned from it with aversion, leaving it on their trays, when their appetites were fickle. But such as it was, there had been enough of it until lately. The last few weeks, however, it had been scarce. Next winter it might be lacking entirely.

Resolutely, as she had done many times before, Constance closed her mind to the realization of this and tried to think of other things as she went up the slope. Somewhere overhead a purring drone became audible and she peered upwards, hoping to locate it. She could see nothing, yet the drone persisted for a time, as if the unseen plane were lazily circling above the Vallée d'Auge. Then it was lost in the distance. The barracks as well as the commons were in darkness now. But from within, she could hear the voices of men who had not heard her quiet footsteps, and who were talking to each other unguardedly.

"The war's been as good as over ever since the Yanks landed. What's the use of all this? The game's up."

"Man, what is that for talk? We'll still invade England. Don't forget that secret weapon of ours. Not to mention that little gadget right here in these very woods."

"Shut your dirty mouth. How many times must I tell you there was never yet built a wall which did not have ears?"

Constance crept forward, more stealthily now, but with a new incentive. As she approached the woods beyond the barracks, she discovered that barbed wire had been placed around these. In the last light of the gloaming she had not seen it until she was actually upon it. Its erection was obviously still incomplete. But while she stood considering where and how she could best pass this new barrier, a harsh challenge sounded from the dusk beyond.

"*Halt! Wer geht da?*"

"I am Madame la Baronne de Fremond. Am I forbidden to walk about my own property?"

There was a brief pause. She could hear two guards talking in undertones together. Then one of them came forward, a big blond awkward boy—they were mostly very young or rather old now, she had noticed, these Nazis around Malou. The youth spoke almost apologetically.

"Forgiveness, *gnädige Frau*. But we have orders that no one should pass beyond this point."

"I knew that you stopped my cook, but I did not suppose you would stop me. Have you done so much damage to the woods that you do not want me to see it?"

The question was unfair and she knew it while she was asking it. The woods had been somewhat mutilated at the time the barracks were built, but after all, the damage was not great, and in any case this blond boy was in no way to blame for it. He had not even been at Malou when it occurred. Now he spoke even more apologetically than before.

"No, *gnädige Frau*. We have done no damage that we could avoid. But until the Colonel arrives——"

She could sense his embarrassment and his distress. Suddenly she felt sorry for him. It was a strange sensation, this sympathy for a German. But it was there, mingled with her aroused curiosity. What was in those woods that neither she nor anyone else must see? What did these swarming troops, massed in the face of a great advancing force, really mean besides natural resistance? Why had there been an order to evacuate a harmless hospital on forty-eight hours' notice? She stood for some time asking herself these questions and pondering on their possible answers before she turned back to the château. And in the gloaming which was now deepening into darkness, she saw, or thought she saw, strange shapes among the trees which bore no relation to the men of whom she was also aware.

She went back to the château deep in meditation. Its quietude had deepened rather than lessened since she left it. Both doors of the fort stood open, and after bolting the one which gave on the drawbridge, she walked across the paved floor and stepped out on the terrace. It was one of those perfect nights when moonlight bestowed on the valley that touch of supernal beauty at which she had never ceased to marvel; and as she went out, it was with the idea that she would sit for a few minutes tranquilly gazing at this beauty and, for the time being, dismiss from her mind every sad and disturbing thought. Then, as she leaned over the parapet, she saw in the garden below something extraneous and startling: a shapeless white mass, vaguely suggestive of a tablecloth which had been carelessly flung down, overlay one of the boxwood shrubs, almost concealing it.

She felt, rather than knew, that she should investigate this cloth immediately. There were no steps between the terrace and the terrace garden, so she went back into the fort and through the darkened and silent rooms to the outer stairway leading from the kitchen to the slope beneath. She was breathless with both haste and excitement when she reached the hooded shrub, and it was not without some inner qualms that she raised the white cloth. A box with a latticed lid was attached to it by long cords, and she suddenly realized that the strange covering was a miniature parachute. Letting this fall, she lifted the box and, unfastening the clasp at the side, opened the latticed lid and peered within. A fluttering bird looked up at her with shining, beady eyes.

She closed the lid hastily and picked up the box, wrapping its strange white draperies around it. Then, even more breathless than she had been before, she sped up the stairway with it. This must be a carrier pigeon, she understood that now, and what a chance, what an almost miraculous chance, that it had come just when it did! The night before, preoccupied as she had been with the removal of patients, she would not have gone out on the terrace, she would never have seen the parachute. The following night the Nazis would be at the château, and they might have seen it first. In that case, if it had come from Allied sources, they would have killed it and its mission would have remained unfulfilled. Worse still, they might have seized on its presence as another pretext for reprisal, for it was strictly forbidden to harbor a carrier pigeon under any circumstances. And this time, the reprisal might have taken the form of fulfilling the long-delayed threat to Padoue.

Constance did not dare stop in the kitchen for fear of the cats, apparently slumbering, but easily enough roused, as she knew, by the prospect of securing such a prey. She hurried on to Tristan's deserted office, deposited her precious burden on the floor, locked the door, and closed the window shutters. Then she groped her way towards the electric switch, and after turning on the light, bent over and took the pigeon from its box, tethering it to a chair.

A tiny metal tube was attached to each of its legs by a small band and she unscrewed these tubes and opened them. The first one contained a blank scroll. The second one contained a similar scroll, covered with microscopic writing. Constance took an old magnifying glass, which had belonged to Tristan's father, from a desk drawer and scrutinized this writing carefully. The first few sentences were devoted to instructions regarding the pigeon: it must be given water and fed with the grain contained in the tiny pouch on one side of the box. This grain, if sparingly used, would suffice for two or three days; but if humanly possible, the pigeon must be started on its return journey sooner than that, both because its detention might be dangerous to the finder, and because there was vital need of the information it might carry. The finder was urged to report, at the earliest possible moment, any unusual activities which might have been observed in the locality, or any comments made by the enemy which might have been overheard.

Constance unfastened the pouch, scattered a little grain on the floor, and stood thoughtfully watching the pigeon while it eagerly pecked this up. Her first instinct was to seek out Nicole and ask for information about the girl's latest gleanings. But Nicole had gone into Lisieux that afternoon on "errands" and had not yet returned; she probably would not do so before morning. Constance could of course send the pigeon back at once with the message that she had heard men muttering from the barracks on her own grounds that an invasion of England was still being planned, and that a secret weapon was still in reserve. But there was nothing new or startling about these statements. Doubtless they had been made over and over again already. She could also say that the civil hospital which had been installed, without objection on the part of the Nazis, in her house six weeks earlier had been evacuated on forty-eight hours' notice and that there must be some reason for it; but without giving a reason the news would still be indefinite. She could say she suspected that something was concealed in the woods of Malou, but until the statement was based on something more than suspicion, roused partly by further mutterings from the barracks and partly by what she thought she had discerned in the gloaming, it would have no strategic value. Somehow she must find out exactly what was happening, and she must do it before daylight of the next day, because otherwise the pigeon might be seen when she dispatched it. She must hide it and she must return to the woods; and this time she must get close enough to identify the vague shapes among the trees.

It was nearly eleven now. This meant that day would break in about four hours. She had always rejoiced in the expansive summer days, with their long twilights which lasted until ten in the evening and their rosy dawns which began to flush the sky with their first faint streaks of radiance soon after three. Now this unbroken length of light, which had never ceased to be a delight to her, took on aspects of a menace. The sooner she went the better. It would probably be wisest to go down the steep slope below the terrace and approach the woods from the pasture rather than from the upper driveway; there was always a chance that they might not be fenced in yet where the undergrowth was thickest and most impenetrable; and they might not be so well guarded there either. She would put on her disused riding breeches—in these it would be much easier to move through the underbrush and she would not so readily be seen. Of course she might not be recognized in them, she had worn them so little in recent years, and if she were not, she might well be shot as a spy. Well, after all, that was what she would be. And as for getting shot, that was a chance she must take.

She brought some water to the pigeon, which drank as eagerly as it had pecked at the grain, and then she locked the door of the office after her again and went up to her room, seated herself at the desk in her study, and scribbled a note to Aunt Bertha saying that something unexpected had arisen and that she would not be coming to bed until early morning; Aunt Bertha was not to worry if she were not there. She pinned this up above the basin in the bathroom, shed her own regular garments, put on the old riding habit, and tiptoed past the day bed and the crib where the old lady and the little boy were peacefully sleeping. Then, already halfway across the room, she turned back and knelt beside the alcove bed, between the starry handkerchief and the crucifix.

She could not see either one clearly; though the moonlight streamed in through the open windows, it did not penetrate to the far corners of the room. However, this dimness was soothing to the tumultuous sensations which, at first, precluded all articulate petition. No words, not even coherent thoughts had come with the realization that this was supremely a time for prayer. She had learned to accept with calmness—and endure with courage—privation, grief, and suffering; but these had been inevitable. She had never before deliberately courted danger. Her pride, her dignity, her inherent self-control, were not strong enough to support her now. She needed other mainstays which she knew she had always lacked: Gwen's inflexible determination, Margot's defiant intrepidity, Aunt Bertha's grim fortitude, Marie Aimée's sublime faith. She was not a daring woman in the sense that they were daring women. Yet now she must act the part of one and, if she were to do it worthily, she must have help from on high.

"Dear God, this is something I must try to do. So far, you have shown me the way to everything else I've had to do. Show me the way this time. I know it's got to be hard. I know it's got to be dangerous. But if this is my greatest trial, don't let me fail. No matter what it costs, let me succeed. For Christ's sake. Amen."

For some moments after her lips had ceased to move, she continued to kneel. Her thoughts were no longer confused, her sensations no longer chaotic; when she finally rose, her spirit was both tranquil and uplifted. She went quietly out of the house and down the terrace steps. She could feel her way, easily enough, zigzagging along the slope to the valley pasture beneath; then she would be at the lower edge of the woods ready to creep in if she were not stopped before that. Sentries might already be posted around the château by this time if her unexpected appearance had disturbed the guard with whom she had spoken early in the evening; such a measure would be entirely logical. But evidently the blond boy had felt more concern over his unavoidable incivility than anything else and it had been obvious the installation of the barbed wire was still incomplete. So she could hope for the best.

The steep descent was accomplished without incident, except that once or twice she slipped in the mud. That, after all, was to be expected; there had been heavy showers late in the afternoon, just after the last patients were evacuated, and this dampness would mean that the branches of the underbrush and bushes would not crackle, that they would be limp and dripping—another piece of luck. Every foot of the way was familiar to her. These were the grounds over which she had wandered with Tristan when they were newly married and when, more than once, some secluded bosquet had been the scene of passionate love-making. These were the thickets in which she had romped with Nick and Bruno when they were little boys, delighting in long daily rambles. These were the woods over which she had zealously watched as their guardian for five long years.

Lately she had also been alert for lurking danger—bombs that might have fallen unexploded, desperate men who might be seeking sanctuary. But she had never thought before of the danger which actually existed—a peril not only to Malou but to the forces that had come to save France.

Her guess that the lower part of the forest might still be unfenced and unguarded proved well founded. She had already made her way past the fringes of it, but she was still on the lower part of the slope, where nothing could conveniently be located or hidden. With the utmost caution, knowing that a single snapping twig or misplaced footstep might betray her, she made her way slowly up the incline. Then, when her eyes were level with the crest of the hill, she stopped.

At first she could discern nothing more clearly than she had that afternoon. But as her vision adjusted itself to the moonlight filtering in through the trees, she saw, or thought she saw, a long platform, gracefully inclined, which stretched out from a small hut that was evidently its base, and that rose to a height of about twenty feet at the end. Ranged alongside this were some twenty-odd objects which looked like miniature aircraft. The moonlight glittered on their steel flanks and fins and on the protuberances which surmounted them in piggy-back fashion. Beside them, with rucksacks and rolled-up overcoats for pillows, several men were sleeping, while two, with rifles over their shoulders, walked up and down, turning their heads from side to side to look about them as they patrolled.

For some moments she gazed at the strange aircraft uncomprehendingly. They were not like any she had seen before. Then slowly the awful realization of their nature and purpose crept over her. These glittering shapes must be the deadly *bombes volantes* of which Nicole had told her —the glider bombs on which the Germans were still counting to knock out the supply bases of the Allied Armies in England; the platform extending from the hut must be the ramp from which they were to be launched. The installation was indubitably not complete as yet, for surely she would have heard the noise of the bombs' release above all other noises, and surely every approach to the forest, and not only the ones most accessible, would have been guarded if operations had already begun. But obviously preparations were already well under way.

She ducked quickly. Now that she had the knowledge she sought, she could take no further risks. Still more cautiously than she had made the ascent, she went down the slope. Once or twice, as she moved she was aware that she had been unable to avoid a faint rustling; but such sounds as these were made by small animals, hares and squirrels, in which the woods abounded. They need not, and probably would not, cause suspicion among the guards. . . .

She was back in the office, the door locked behind her again. The pigeon was still nestling quietly in the corner; it cocked its head, revealing the sheen of its iridescent feathers and the brightness of its beady eyes; but it did not otherwise move until Constance again scattered a little grain on the floor for it. While it daintily ate this, she took the tiny blank scroll from its metal tube and painstakingly wrote out a brief message:

At least twenty small aircraft, apparently glider bombs, concealed in woods of Malou, château near village of Norolles, halfway between Lisieux and Pont l'Évêque, fifteen kilometers inland from Deauville in straight line. Château serving as German headquarters for locality with large force occupying adjacent barracks and grounds. Owners of property Commandant Tristan de Fremond and his American-born wife. Latter in residence with aged aunt and small grandson.

The final sentence might serve as a safeguard—or it might not. After all, Margot had been killed because bombers were aiming at antiaircraft guns; Malou might well be destroyed because they were aiming at glider bombs. And she had sworn to preserve Malou. . . . Well, now she must run the risk of breaking that oath. It was no longer a question of shielding her own home and saving Padoue's heritage; it was a question of averting disaster from the liberators of her husband's country. Of her country. . . .

She turned the scrap of paper over and, for greater clarity, sketched a little map on the back. Then she replaced the scroll in the tube and attached this again to its band on the pigeon's leg. For a moment she stood clasping the bird against her breast, and still more briefly she bent her head and pressed her cheek against its soft plumage.

Carrying the bird tenderly, Constance mounted the stairs to the attic and went to one of the west windows. Then she held out her hands, releasing it with an upward fling of the arm. Unhurriedly it rose and circled slowly three times above the château, gaining altitude with each circle, then, with incredible swiftness it sped off, and presently it was only a speck in the distance. She closed the window and went slowly down to her own room.

Aunt Bertha and Padoue were both sleeping soundly. They did not look as if they had moved since she left them. Her note was still pinned above the bathroom basin. Constance tore it up and threw the fragments away. Then she slipped out of her old riding habit, put on her nightgown, and lay down, thankfully and wearily, in the alcove bed. But before she composed herself for sleep, she looked up at the crucifix and prayed again, a prayer of thanksgiving this time. Then she turned towards the starry handkerchief and smiled.

"*A la belle étoile!*" she whispered triumphantly.

CHAPTER XLII

THE NEXT BOMBS that fell on the grounds of Malou did not miss their mark.

Constance, who had been watching for them, saw the planes come over and the swift descent of the bombs; then the dense clouds of smoke rising from the woods, followed by thunderous detonations. She heard men shouting and saw them running, and afterwards she saw others whose faces were covered being borne on stretchers towards the enclosure in the upland pasture which von Reden had fenced off three years earlier. She saw still others whose faces were not covered, and she averted her own, for one had a crushed head and a second a shattered jaw, and a third a gushing wound where his ear should have been. She had become accustomed to dreadful sights at Grand Blottereau a quarter of a century before, and though the memory of them had grown mercifully dim with time, her training there had stood her in good stead during her weeks of work at Hospital Malou. But though nothing in her bearing betrayed the way she was affected by such sights, she still shrank from them inwardly, just as every nerve in her body still quivered with the reverberations of the bombing. Besides, this time she herself was responsible, or believed she was, for those still forms on the stretchers, that crushed head, that shattered jaw, that gushing wound. If she had not sent the carrier pigeon out with a minute message in the tiny tube attached to its leg, there might have been no more bombs at Malou.

Nothing indicated that what she had done was suspected. Twenty-five Germans were now quartered at the château and in the commons, besides all those in the barracks and in the woods. But in spite of their numbers, they managed to be much less in evidence than the smaller detachments during the early days of the Occupation, and their manner was much less arrogant and assured. Not only von Reden, but every officer on his staff, treated Constance and Aunt Bertha with the greatest courtesy and consideration, and went out of his way to make overtures to the unresponsive Padoue. After the bombs had fallen in the woods, German ambulances —doubtless the same, Constance assumed, that had been offered for the evacuation of the French patients—appeared with amazing promptness and removed the wounded; the dead were buried in the improvised cemetery, with no religious ceremony, that same afternoon.

Within the next few days the character of the activities about the place seemed to be undergoing a change. The barbed wire which had already been strung up around a portion of the woods was not removed, but neither were its lines extended, and no one appeared to be formally on guard before it, though the place still swarmed with soldiers. When Constance went past them they said, *"Guten Tag, gnädige Frau,"* very respectfully, and then went on with their work. She did not see the blond sentry among them, and she wondered if he were one of those who had been borne away with a covered face. Somehow she hoped he was not.

When she reached the kitchen garden she found the fruit and vegetables covered with thick white dust from the laden air. She was not sufficiently informed about the effects of smoke on such growth to know how harmful it would be, and a fresh anxiety rose in her mind. For several days now they had been entirely without bread of any kind, and this lack had made her realize how dependent they were even on the miserable substitutes for the crusty loaves, which, to the French perhaps more than to any other people, actually constituted the staff of life; but as Constance had told herself the last time she visited the garden, they could live on vegetables for a long while. That is, they could if this fine white powder did not affect the thrifty plot.

She remained, working her way up and down the long rows, as long as she could see. She had put Padoue to bed before she started out on her rounds, and she knew that he was sleeping comfortably in his crib, with his beautiful horse tied securely to it, and Aunt Bertha in the day bed beside him; once he was settled for the night, Constance had no further pressing duties in the house. Chess stayed with her all the time she was dusting and weeding, and stalked sedately along when she started back towards the château. His attitude towards the German soldiers was disdainful; if one came close to him, or to his mistress, he growled; otherwise he did not appear to notice them. A few of them were still scattered over the grounds, but they were not working. Evidently they were on the point of going back to their barracks for the night. A small group of officers had gathered near the drawbridge, von Reden among them. He detached himself from the others and came towards Constance.

"Good evening, Baroness," he said with his usual formal courtesy. "As you see, we have been busy here and there removing some—ah—installations from your grounds. I do not think we have done much damage, at least so far. I hope there will be none later on, either. At all events it is doubtful that there will ever be as much as has already been done in the woods."

"Is it so very bad? I had not seen it, of course. I started to take my customary walk through the woods about ten days ago, and was stopped by a sentry. And the woods seemed to be at least partially enclosed by barbed wire. I thought I would speak of this to you the first time I saw you. But the occasion has not arisen before."

"You know you have only to send for me, Baroness, at any time. I shall always be delighted to come." She made no answer, and von Reden went on, "The exigencies of the situation seemed to indicate the temporary use for barbed wire. But the need for it now appears to be over. I will not bore you with tedious technical details. Temporarily, it also seemed best to issue a general order that no one should be permitted to wander through the woods. If you had told me that you especially wished to go, the order might have been modified. As far as I am concerned, you may now go there whenever you wish. But I should warn you that there may still be Allied bombs that have not yet exploded. I think you would be much wiser, for this and other reasons, to keep fairly close to the house for the present, though of course we have no way of knowing that the liberators will not aim at that next."

"They may *hit* it at any moment. I realize that."

"I accept your correction, Baroness. I did not wish to seem to cast aspersions on their marksmanship. . . . Are you really in a great hurry? There are two or three other things that I should like to speak to you about."

"If they're really important, of course I can take the time to listen."

"I will permit you to be the judge of their importance, Baroness. I will, however, assure you in advance that none of them is personal in character." Again he waited for a rejoinder that did not come. Then he continued: "Besides doing the work of removing certain fixed installations, we have, within the last few hours, brought into position mobile artillery pieces some distance west of the château. They are fairly well concealed, and will be still better camouflaged by tomorrow, so the chances are that you might not see them in any case. But I do not wish you to be unduly alarmed if you should. I assure you that they are there for your protection. The same is true of the machine guns that you will now find at nearly all the west windows of the château."

"Then you're actively preparing for an attack?"

"For an attack of sorts, yes. Listen for a moment. Can you not tell how much closer the sound of cannonade is than it was? Tomorrow it will be closer still. But the château itself is not an objective. The Allied advance is not even in this direction. But your liberators are following our von Schlieffen plan in reverse, sending out a strong right column, and leaving us here to be encircled, if we were fools enough to stay."

"I don't understand. At first you said there would be fighting, that artillery had been brought up. Now you talk as if you were planning to leave."

"That is true. We will remain here until the last possible moment, harassing any patrols or reconnaissance groups that attempt to pass this valley. Do not forget there are other secret weapons which will turn the tide of battle sooner or later. When that time comes, we must be ready to strike back. We shall do so from here, if we are still here, or from the prepared positions to which we shall withdraw, if that becomes the proper course, as now seems likely. But let me spare you the particulars."

"And what is likely to happen to the château in the fighting that will take place, in the battle that will not be a battle?"

Von Reden smiled in his usual mirthless way. "That is in the hands of your liberators, Baroness," he said coldly.

Constance made no reply. In the silence that fell between them she gave her attention to the roar of artillery fire. As she had confessed to Margot on the night of the first bombardment, she had never tried to distinguish between the different types of tumultuous sound, because all were so horrible to her that she spent her strength in bracing herself against them. Now, consciously attempting to tell the difference between what was near and what was distant, she recognized that the present relentless thundering was not the same as that to which she had listened for over two months. Her face betrayed what her lips would not confess.

"You see," von Reden said quietly. "And there is another detail which I should perhaps mention, though there is nothing alarming about this one. I have given orders that all our horses, except those which are in actual use with the *Lastwagen,* should be placed in the moat. There have been times when I regretted that the water had long since gone from this —a Norman château which does not have water in its moat certainly loses much of its character. Now I am very glad there is none there. This declivity will afford protection which the stables do not give. Thus we can have replacements for those horses that will be killed."

He spoke quite dispassionately. She knew that he would speak in exactly the same way about the disposition of his men, because he would feel exactly the same way about it.

"I think that is all, Baroness, for the moment, unless there is something you would like to say to me."

"Yes. There is one thing. I would like to thank you for not sending Lucie to an orphanage. I know that it rested with you whether this should be done, and it was not."

"There is something else that has not yet been done either, Baroness. I have hoped that one of these days you would thank me for that."

"I shall, if it has not happened when you leave for good."

"Then you still do not trust me?"

"No. And besides, you said if you had the order——"

He bowed. "That is true. And the order might still come through. Any day. At any hour. Good night, Baroness."

From the dreamless sleep of utter exhaustion into which she had sunk two nights later, Constance was jarred into confused wakefulness by a welter of conflicting sounds. A distant thunderous rumble was punctuated by the crash of closer explosions, and in the crib beside her Padoue was screaming at the top of his lungs. Deafened and still dazed, she turned quickly towards him and drew him into bed with her, murmuring vague words of comfort; but these were drowned in the din of the detonations. The solid structure of the château seemed to be rocking, and the big room was in total darkness except for far-off flashes of dull flame. As one of these briefly illuminated the room, Constance saw that Lucie had crept up to the day bed and was clinging to Aunt Bertha, who was sitting bolt upright and had managed to drape a wrapper over her gaunt shoulders. Her lips were moving, and though she could not make herself heard, Constance knew that she must be trying to reassure the terrified and trembling child. She herself tried to signal and to shout, but without success. The darkness had engulfed them again and the din was more deafening than ever.

As abruptly as it had begun, the cataclysm came to an end. The sudden silence was broken only by the sound of harsh voices, muffled by doors and walls; of heavy feet hurrying about the lower floor and speeding up the stairway. Lucie was still crying softly, but Padoue's screams had subsided into choking sobs. For a moment Constance held him closer than before. Then she tried to free herself gently from his clinging arms.

"There," she said. "There, darling. It's all over now. Let go of *mémère,* so that she can get up and dress."

"But if it's all over, why do you want to dress? Why don't you try to go to sleep again? It isn't time to get up yet. It's night. It's dark."

"I think it's almost morning, darling. I think it's going to be light pretty soon. Anyway, we can make it light, just the way we always do."

This time she succeeded in detaching herself from him and reached for the switch of her bed lamp. She snapped it vainly several times. There was a small flashlight in the drawer of her night table, and she felt for this, found it, and turned it on, shielding it with her hand. Padoue would have liked to argue with her some more, but she did not give him a chance. She went very quickly into the little bathroom on the other side of the fireplace, and he sat up, solemnly, in the big bed, awaiting her return with anxiety. He had found, long before, that he could always depend on *mémère;* when she said a thing was so, then it really was. But this time he did not feel quite sure. He had seen Aunt Bertha, who was dependable too, shake her head when *mémère* said it was all over and heard her mutter something that sounded doubtful. He was relieved when *mémère* came back and said she would dress him now too while Aunt Bertha and Lucie went into the study to dress. Then they would go down to the kitchen and see if Blondine was up and whether she could give them all some breakfast.

It was dark going down the stairs, for *mémère* had now tied something over the top of the flashlight so that it gave out only a tiny glimmer; yet one of the Germans whom they met growled under his breath and said they had better be careful how they used it. In the kitchen all the shutters were closed, and blankets had been tacked over the windows too. It would have seemed gloomy except that the fire was still bright. Blondine was up, and so were Léon and Denis, and they talked very excitedly to *mémère* about the terrible noise and strange shaking, and nothing more was said about breakfast for some moments. At last Padoue reminded *mémère* that was what they had come downstairs for, and she said oh yes, of course, and Léon brought him some milk and a plain boiled egg, which was one of the things he most hated. There was no jam, there was not even any bread, and he did not see how anyone could talk about breakfast when things were like that.

However, he drank the milk and ate part of the horrid tasteless egg and then *mémère* said they would all go back to her room for a while. He took his horse and went over to the window, hoping to see something which would make all the strange things which were happening clearer to him. There was a little light in the sky now, pale and gray, but nothing showed that he had not seen many times before. A single plane was droning past without making much noise; it did not snarl or roar, and it was not very high above the ground. From some place nearby there came a single brief outburst of noise, but this was not frightening, like what had happened earlier. It sounded the way he thought a giant probably sounded while gargling, and Padoue put back his head and tried to imitate it. Then Lucie tried to imitate him.

"No, no!" he said. "Not like that, Lucie. Like this!"

They both gargled until they began to giggle and had so much fun that Padoue did not look out of the window again right away. When he did, he saw that the valley was not empty any longer, that something was moving on the other side of it. It was a queer gray thing, monstrous and ungainly, with a big tube sticking out in front of it, and it was waddling across one of the fields beyond the Touques. Then it went through a hedgerow and disappeared. But another just like it came out from behind another hedgerow and followed after it, and so did a lot of small trucks. Then a shattering roar seemed to shake the hill where Malou stood, and something screamed swiftly across the valley and burst in the field the gray monster was crossing. A moment later there was another roar and another screaming missile went hurtling away from their own side of the valley.

The distant field was now spouting fountains of earth and smoke amidst which the gray monster vanished. When the fury subsided Padoue could see the monster quite motionless, and it looked different, as though parts of it had been torn off. And he could see tiny figures dart from the hedgerows with what appeared to be stretchers, like what had been used when the hospital was at Malou, and lift forms from the ground and carry them back to the shelter of the concealing trees.

Then more things began to happen. From other hedgerows here and there came light puffs of vapor, and missiles that streaked towards the hill of Malou. Just above the ground they burst with the same crashing fury that had awakened him that morning, and *mémère* came quickly and snatched him and Lucie away from the window and hurried them to the farther side of the room.

The din was different now. There was the same light noise made by a small plane that Padoue had heard earlier, but there were more planes. As these passed across the panel of light framed by the window he could sometimes see as many as three at once: small khaki-colored planes, some with circles on them and some with a black star on a white field.

Padoue watched them with fascination. He was no longer terrified, for somehow the daylight seemed to make a great difference; it was not like being trapped in the darkness. He wanted to go back to the window, but *mémère* would not let him, and suddenly there was another note in the bedlam, making it louder than ever. This was the *vrombissement* he had heard so many times before and with it came long wailing sounds and the château and the earth shook again. *Mémère* clutched Padoue tighter and tighter as the noise grew worse and worse and she was still clutching him tightly when it stopped. She did not even seem to know it had stopped. He was wriggling to get away from her and asking her why she did not let him go when there was a knock at the door and Captain Nolte came in.

"Colonel von Reden desires that all civilians withdraw at once to the cellar," he said quite calmly, though the gargling sound had just started again from somewhere downstairs.

"At once?" *mémère* asked, and Captain Nolte nodded curtly.

"For how long?"

Captain Nolte shrugged. "That's as may be," he said shortly, and turned away.

Padoue did not mind going to the *cave*. He had enjoyed himself when he was there before playing hide-and-seek among the old casks with Lucie, and he thought he would have a good time doing this again. Besides, he could not see much out of the window any more; there was such a lot of smoke in the air, and this was beginning to make his eyes smart and give him a choking feeling in his throat, something like the choking feeling he had had when that dreadful thing happened to Mummy, but not quite. *Mémère* said it would be all right for him to take his horse with him to the *cave* if he wanted to, and he did. He was quite contented for a while, arranging to stable it there and so on. But after a while there was not much to do. It had been early in the afternoon when Colonel von Reden sent word they would have to go to the *cave,* and when night came they were still there, and *mémère* said they would have to sleep there. Of course he had slept there before, but not when he had stayed there all day too. It was beginning to seem very dull to him in the *cave,* though *mémère* did not seem to think so. She kept urging everyone to keep quiet, so that she could listen to the telephone between the gargling sounds that did not keep up all the time. Padoue heard her tell Aunt Bertha that she was sure this was a short-wave radio-telephone, and that it was being used to send and receive messages. She said that if everyone would only keep still, she could tell what these messages were; and Padoue thought this was probably true, because *mémère* understood the Germans' strange talk, as well as the strange speech Aunt Bertha used sometimes. *Mémère* knew lots of things, besides being very kind and very nice to look at. Only, of course, not wonderful to look at, the way Mummy had been.

If there had not been so many people in the *cave,* it would not have been so hard to keep them all quiet at once. Everyone was there this time. Martin and Benoît had not wanted to leave the horses, and Michel and Lise had not wanted to leave the cows, any more than they had before. But the Germans had made them. So with Léon and Denis and Blondine and Alpy and Nicole and *mémère* and Aunt Bertha and Lucie and himself, that made a great many people. Padoue counted them up to ten, and then he had to stop, because that was as far as he knew how to count. But he saw there were only two more than ten, so he asked Lucie what did two more make, and, very importantly, she said twelve. That way he learned twelve and then he asked her some more numbers and pretty soon he could count up to fifteen. This helped pass a little time, but not much. It did not take long to learn to count to fifteen.

Finally Michel said he was going up to milk the cows. Whatever happened, the cows had to be milked, and anyway, there seemed to be a little lull between attacks right now. Lise said she would go with him, and he said no, she mustn't, but she did just the same. Then Blondine and Léon said they would go up to the kitchen and bring down some supper. They were gone only a few minutes, and when they came back, they did bring a little food, but nothing you could really call supper. Just a few horrid little vegetables. Padoue did not care much for vegetables. He liked juicy red meat, lots of it, and big red strawberries, and sweet things, plenty of them. There had not been any juicy red meat at Malou in a long time. There had been strawberries, big red ones, earlier in the summer, but that was when the poor sick people were there, so they had eaten most of the berries; and there had been some jam and some bread before Mummy went away, and now there was no jam and no bread either. It was as if she had taken them with her when she went, as if being hungry were part of the dreadful thing that had happened to her.

When Michel and Lise came back, they brought some milk with them and Padoue drank it thirstily. He heard them talking about the smoke in the yard, which was now so thick that they could hardly see to get through it to the dairy, and he heard them say that the château had not been hit. Then he heard *mémère* tell Aunt Bertha, very excitedly, that while there had been fewer people in the *cave,* she had managed to overhear what was being said on the telephone, and unless she was very much mistaken, the moment of retreat was drawing near. Presently she took Padoue and cuddled him in her lap, and said she would tell him a story and hear his prayer now, and after that he went to sleep.

He waked up two or three times in the night, partly because he was not as comfortable as he would have been in his crib, and partly because there were more sudden noises and some of them were very near and sounded very frightening. But every time he waked up, *mémère* was there, with her arms around him, and she told him everything was all right, that he must be a good boy and go to sleep again. Then at last she said it was morning, and that he could get up if he chose.

He would not have known whether it was morning or not, because it was so dark in the *cave,* and he did not know what he could do if he did get up. He was hungrier than he had been the night before, and *mémère* had not said anything about breakfast or even anything about milk. He hoped that Michel and Lise would say again that they must go to the cows whatever happened, but apparently they were still asleep. There was no reason why they should not sleep, as far as the noise was concerned. That seemed to have almost stopped.

Mémère said again that he could get up if he wanted to, and because she seemed to expect it, he did. She got up too, acting as if it hurt her to move. He asked her and she said she was just a little cramped, because she had been sitting still so long, that she would be all right in a minute.

While he was trying to decide what to do next, the door at the top of the stair leading into the *cave* opened and Captain Nolte came down. He went up to *mémère* and saluted.

"Colonel von Reden presents his compliments to Madame la Baronne de Fremond," he said. "He asks me to inquire whether it would be convenient for her to come to the fort. He and the officers of his staff are on the point of leaving Malou, and he would like to say good-by to her. The battle is over."

CHAPTER XLIII

He still looked almost exactly as he had when she first saw him. With the inescapable realization of how much she herself had changed, this was the first thing that struck her: how could any human being go through five years of war and emerge from it the same person, spiritually, physically, or mentally, as before? Yet, to all appearances, this was what von

Reden had done. His skin had not lost its fresh ruddiness or his eyes their cool, clear blue; he still held himself proudly and erectly; everything about him still suggested a superb physique and unconquerable power. Even the arrogant tone of his voice had not changed; only the words were different.

"Our sole purpose in remaining here as long as we did has now been accomplished," he said. "We have held up the British for two days. It is now necessary for us to occupy the points from which our counterattack will be launched after our V bombs have done their work. I hope you will give my compliments to the commanding officer of the British upon his arrival at Malou."

He held out his hand. Constance, who had not attempted any rejoinder to his stilted speech, ignored the gesture.

"There is something I should like to give you, Baroness, as a memento of my stay here. I hope you will not decline to take it from me."

Involuntarily, she glanced down and saw that he was holding a piece of folded paper in his outstretched hand. She extended her own, hoping to accept the paper without more than touching his fingers. But she did not succeed. He slipped it between hers and grasped them firmly before raising them to his lips. Then he released them slowly and saluted.

"There will probably be a little more intermittent firing, so it may be well for you to return to the *cave* and keep the others there for a short time longer," he said. "I am taking some of my men with me, but leaving a cordon of others here to safeguard my withdrawal. As soon as that is assured, they will follow. There will not be time for them to bury our dead or remove our wounded. But I know I am leaving these in good hands."

"I will see that they are cared for," Constance said, speaking for the first time, and slipping the piece of folded paper into her blouse without looking at it.

"I shall count on that. You are most dependable. *Auf Wiedersehen,* Baroness."

"Good-by," she said mechanically.

He saluted, his bearing still that of an officer reviewing troops. Turning, he marched across the drawbridge, followed by the members of his staff, who had been standing at attention, and who now also marched as if they were on parade. They went through the littered yard and up the slope to the outer gate in the same formation; then they disappeared in the avenue of pines. The cordon to which the Colonel had referred held their position near the gate, beyond the overturned *Lastwagen,* the dead horses, and the fallen men. Constance looked down into the moat, and saw that some of the horses there were also dead, and that others were writhing about in agony. In the direction of the commons the smoke was still dense, but it looked to Constance as if these had been hit above the arch, for they seemed to be caving in towards the center, forming a triangle. The drawbridge itself was so clear as to suggest that men who had fallen there might have been moved to make way for the Colonel's dramatic departure. But several soldiers were scattered about the fort, in grotesque positions. Some were silent, but two were groaning. Constance approached the latter and spoke to them.

"I will do what I can to make you more comfortable," she said. "But first I must get help. I will be back in a minute." She hurried through the chaotic dining room, and as she reached the stairway to the *cave,* she heard another discharge of artillery, but it did not sound as near as the earlier salvos. She thought the firing was coming from farther south. The tanks and other vehicles on which the Allied cannon were mounted must be pushing on swiftly now that the German fire from Malou had been silenced. In any event she was resolved that she would not stay in the *cave* any longer herself, and she knew that all the others were eagerly awaiting a signal of release. She opened the door, letting in air and light, and sped down the stairs. Padoue ran to her and flung himself against her, catching her around the knees.

"Oh, *mémère,* I'm so hungry!" he sobbed. She drew him closer to her, bending over to kiss his tousled head.

"I know you are, darling. But you're going to have lots to eat very soon now," she said soothingly. *"Mémère* wants you to stay here with Aunt Bertha and Lucie. But she wants Léon and some of the others to come up with her now and she'll send you down something."

"Not vegetables?"

"No, not vegetables. Or not just vegetables. We'll find something else too. Be patient just a little longer. . . . I need all of you men now. Denis, come to the kitchen with me. Michel, please see if the rear guard has left and report to me. Then go to the dairy and start milking. . . . Martin, I'm afraid the commons have been hit. If any of our horses are injured, put them out of their misery—the ones in the moat too. You can take a gun from one of the dead Germans. We must see, right away, how many of the men who are lying around the château and grounds are just wounded, and get them together in one place. Benoît, you and Alpy can do that. And Nicole, you can start giving first aid. I'll be with you as soon as I can."

"Please, Madame la Baronne, permit me to go too!"

Blondine and Lise had spoken simultaneously. Constance made a swift decision.

"Lise may go, because this will enable Michel to get through the milking more quickly. But Blondine must stay here. It is not best that Mademoiselle Berthe should be alone with the children. She might need help too. We must divide our forces, so that no one will be without assistance in an emergency."

The artillery sounded again, though even more briefly and distantly than the last time. No one questioned her judgment or authority. Without wasting words, the men and women of Malou began their appointed tasks. The rear guard had left and most of the soldiers lying in the fort and on the grounds were dead. One who at first appeared so proved entirely unharmed; he had feigned death because he preferred to remain and become a prisoner rather than to take part in the retreat. He said he would be glad to be useful in any way he could until the British arrived, and it was suggested that he might start digging graves. He found a shovel and set sturdily to work. Alpy and Benoît, having cleared a space in the cluttered dining room, ranged the wounded side by side, and Nicole gave them water to drink and bandaged them as well as she could. With characteristic resourcefulness, she tried the telephone, found that it was still working, and succeeded in reaching Ghisèle at the Manoir des Cailliors. The Britishers had just passed by there, Ghisèle told her, and there had been no sign of the Germans for several hours now. Perhaps later in the day she or Dr. Lutaud could get through to Malou. Meanwhile, Nicole had evidently done a good job herself. Was everyone in the household all right? Nicole answered with a swift affirmative and hung up.

Then she went on to the kitchen, where Lise had already arrived with the first pailful of milk and three chickens which had been killed in the battle. Denis promised to dress these directly and get them onto the fire. Nicole, seizing the pail and some mugs, hurried down to the *cave,* while Lise returned to the dairy to go on with the milking, calling back over her shoulder that a lamb had been killed too, and that they would soon have *pré-salé* for dinner. Martin had come back from the commons with a report that Madame la Baronne's fears in regard to these had been all too well founded; the central portion was entirely destroyed, two of their own horses had been killed, and he had been obliged to shoot two others, as well as several in the moat. He would remind her that horsemeat could be used for food. Michel was already dressing the lamb. One of the small reconnaissance planes was still circling the area, but that was all. It was marked with a white star on a black circle. There was nothing else to report. What should he, Martin, do next? Whatever he thought best, Constance told him. She was going back to the *cave* to urge further patience on the remaining refugees, because she still did not feel it was wise for them to come upstairs. But while she was talking with Martin, a jeep came bucking down the slope; in it were two officers whose sleeves showed shoulder crescents on which the word "Canada" was lettered.

"*Pardon, madame, pouvez-vous nous dire——*" one of them began, speaking with a strong accent. Constance interrupted him quickly in English.

"Don't bother to try talking in French. I'm an American. At least I was. I'm Madame de Fremond now. What can I do for you?"

"Well, bless us all, a proper lady!" exclaimed one of the officers in obvious delight. He flung himself out of the jeep, saluted smilingly. "I'm Lieutenant Carnahan, and this is Lieutenant Joe McKenzie. We'll not trouble you more than a moment, ma'am. Perhaps you'd be good enough to tell us one or two things. First, are there any British or Canadian wounded about?"

"None that I know of. Perhaps across the valley." . . . She pointed to the fields, patterned with hedgerows, beyond the Touques.

"They're all accounted for. Next, any Germans left?"

"Only the dead and wounded. And oh yes, one prisoner who is waiting to surrender."

"Right. We'll take him with us. As for the wounded, we'll have a cadre of medics back here as soon as possible to take them off your hands, and a detail to bury the good ones. How long since the rest of them pulled out?"

"Not more than two hours or so. If you hurry——"

The young Canadian chuckled.

"They won't be going anywhere except into a pocket. No use chasing single detachments, ma'am. We're cutting off whole armies of 'em, and rounding 'em up wholesale. Saves time and trouble. . . . By the way, is this the captive of our bow and spear?"

The German soldier who had been put to gravedigging was approaching the group uncertainly, hands clasped at the crown of his steel helmet. Sensing that the officer was referring to him, he stopped, tried to stand at attention without lowering his hands, finally gave this up as a bad job, and saluted.

"Chuck it, Fritz," the Canadian told him, and jerked one thumb at the back seat of the jeep. "In there, *versteh?*" The soldier complied, stopping only to salute the second officer, still hunched under the wheel of the jeep.

"And now, ma'am," Lieutenant Carnahan continued, "if you'd be——"

He stopped, looking in astonishment to something beyond Constance. She turned and saw Padoue pelting towards her as fast as his little legs would carry him.

"Reinforcements at the double, eh?" grinned the young Canadian. "Your young 'un?"

"My grandson." And then to Padoue, in French: "What's the matter, darling?"

Padoue gripped a fold of Constance's skirt in his small fist.

"I want you. Nobody would tell me where you were, and I thought maybe you would go away too. So I was going with you."

"Of course I wouldn't leave you. But everything's quite all right." She ruffled his hair and explained to Lieutenant Carnahan: "He's been through some pretty dreadful experiences, you know. Not only these last few days, but before, when we had a civilian hospital here after the bombings, and when his mother was killed."

"His mother? Gosh, that's mighty tough! I hope——?"

He left the kindly question unfinished, but Constance understood and completed it for him. "His father—my elder son—was lost at Dunkirk before this little boy was born. My younger son was killed at Saumur. I haven't seen my husband in five years. But he escaped from Germany to England, and I still believe——"

"Well, so long as you can do that—— But I know it's been mighty hard for you, ma'am. You won't misunderstand when I say it's been even worse for the youngsters, though. Like in England during the Blitz. This kid's probably terrified of any stranger in uniform. So we'll be off directly in a cloud of dust. Only two things more. Can you tell me how many wounded Jerries you've got on the place, so that we can send back enough ambulances and so on?"

"I think there are about twenty, but I'm not sure. We've just been getting them together as best we could, and trying to make them comfortable."

"No matter. I'll check."

He reached into one of the pockets with which the baggy trousers of his British battle dress seemed to be supplied in all sorts of ordinarily unexpected places, and drew out a notebook in a stiff binding.

"Where are the casualties, ma'am?"

"In the dining room. If you walk across the drawbridge, you'll find them just beyond the fort."

"Right. Meanwhile we'd take it kindly if you'd give Lieutenant McKenzie directions for getting to Lisieux by the shortest and best road from here. I'll be back by the time you've finished, and then we'll not be bothering you any longer. Carry on, Joe!"

McKenzie started to extricate his rangy frame from beneath the wheel of the jeep, making an awkward job of it.

"Oh, please don't bother to get out of the car," Constance urged. "I can show you very easily. . . . . Go up the avenue of hemlocks—the same one you came down. If you turn right when you get to the end of it, and then right again when you see a little cluster of houses—all there is to the village of Norolles—you'll strike the main road to Lisieux after you've gone about three kilometers. That's the shortest way, but it may not be the best right now. I imagine the stretch between here and Norolles may be pretty badly shot to pieces. If you think you'd have trouble getting through, then turn left instead of right at the end of the avenue. That'll take you into Le Breuil, where you turn left again for Lisieux."

"That's all clear enough. Well, thanks a lot and the best of luck to you!"

Carnahan had already returned and they were off, bucking out of sight among the pines, and whistling the tune of "Lili Marlene" as they went. Padoue looked at Constance in bewilderment.

"Aren't they going to stay here, *mémère?*"

"No, darling. These soldiers are not like the others."

"No one's going to live at Malou except us?"

"No, Padoue. Just us."

"And we don't have to stay down in the *cave* any more?"

"No. We can all sleep quietly in our own rooms tonight. We can go and sit quietly on the terrace now."

He hung back. The terrace was still a place of horror to him, and Constance knew it. But she also knew that she must teach him to overcome this horror, to accept one part of the château as naturally as he did another. After all, it had all been a battleground now. As if she had not noticed his reluctance, she held out her hand.

"Come, Padoue. *Mémère* wants to sit down while she's thinking over what she ought to do next. She's very tired. But she'll read you a story, if you like."

"Any story I want?"

"Yes."

"May I bring my horse?"

"Yes, if you want to."

424

She would much rather not have seen the horse. But she did not wish to complicate matters after finally having persuaded Padoue to accept the terrace. He went off to get his toy, and while she waited for him to come back, she took from her blouse the paper which von Reden had given her that morning and unfolded it. She had forgotten about it until that moment. Now the horse recalled it to her.

It was dated March 11, 1941, and bore the letterhead Oberkommando der Wehrmacht. The clipped military phraseology presented no difficulty; but as the full import of the words was borne in upon her, a deadly coldness overcame her and she caught at the shattered section of the stone balustrade for support. Then she began once more to read the text of the message typed on the sheet which she held in trembling fingers:

WFSt/WPr
N° c–45–X–769
From: Feldmarschall Helfrich zu Habichtshorst
To: Oberst Gerd von Reden, im Feld
Subject: Execution of Antoine de Padoue de Fremond

1. The French prisoner, Commandant Tristan de Fremond, quartered with other officers at Ofstalag W–III, *escaped on Sunday morning from the custody of the detachment charged with the administration of this* Lager. *In effecting his evasion, he took the life of Oberleutnant Erich Reiniger, to prevent him from giving the alarm. The crime was not discovered for some hours, for the prisoner de Fremond hid the body of Lt. Reiniger in a snowdrift during the night.*

2. When recaptured, the prisoner de Fremond will be dealt with according to the laws of war.

3. Records compiled by the Central Bureau indicate that de Fremond was the father of two sons, one of whom was killed in the victory of Dunkirk, the other in the skirmish near Saumur. His only surviving male descendant is a grandson, living with his grandmother at the Château of Malou where you have established your Kommandantur *as commanding officer of the district forces of occupation.*

4. It is directed that you take the person of this grandson, Antoine de Padoue de Fremond, and put him to death, without making the fact generally known in your district.

5. It is further directed that compliance and proof of death be furnished this headquarters at the earliest moment, so that the other prisoners at Ofstalag W–III *may be in no doubt about the consequences of any rash step they might contemplate in emulation of Commandant de Fremond.*

Braeuer, Adjutant   *(signed) Habichtshorst*

Penned at the bottom of the sheet, in a calligraphic script which might have been beautiful but for its mechanical, copybook precision, was the following message:

Notification of compliance was sent to Berlin within the week, and was accompanied by proof in the form of a bloody baby garment, appropriately bullet-torn, and marked with the embroidered initial "P." But you

had showed yourself to be a very brave woman, and I did not feel you
should be forced to endure more. I add that you have also caused me to
respect, however reluctantly, the quality against which I could not prevail
except by force, and the only one against which I did not wish to use
force in order to prevail. I wanted to be your lover. I shall always remem-
ber with regret and admiration that you accepted me only as your enemy.

Gradually the cold fear which had gripped her relaxed its deadly hold, and she slowly refolded the sheet of paper and put it back in her blouse. But she continued to lean against the shattered balustrade, staring off into the distance, her thoughts still chaotic. In one sense, Gerd von Reden had gone out of her life with his dramatic farewell; she knew that she would never see him again. But in another sense, he would always be a part of her existence. She had lived in the same house with him, off and on, for five years, and he had left his imprint on the place and on her; henceforth it would be inescapable. He was not intrinsically bestial, like Pfaff, and he would never deliberately profane a church, like Jaeckel; but he was the most arrogant, unscrupulous, and ruthless man with whom she had ever come in contact, a militarist, a martinet, and a torturer. More than that: he was the embodiment of an evil system, a cruel occupation, and a score of wicked purposes. His character was one of strange contradictions; he had taken meticulous care of family portraits and private documents, but he had not hesitated to order the execution of a helpless and harmless old man. On the other hand, he had been unable to resist the temptation of threatening to shoot Padoue; but he had loftily disregarded an explicit order to do so, over a long period of years, and no doubt at considerable risk to himself. So his armor of inhumanity was not complete. He was neither a fool nor a weakling, and in his warped, unfathomable way he had loved her enough to refrain from forcing himself upon her, because he respected her more than he desired her. . . .

His message not only provoked deep and bewildered thought; it impelled absolute honesty. He had written "I wanted to be your lover." He had not added, "And under somewhat different conditions, I might well have been." But she knew that this was true, and that in writing, he had known it. She had not been insensible of his strange magnetism; if she had not intensely hated him, she could perhaps have been constrained to love him with equal intensity. The margin between hatred and love was dangerously narrow sometimes.

The unwelcome thought was driven from her mind by another: von Reden's statement that he wanted to be her lover was unequivocal. If he desired her, then she must still be desirable, in spite of the changes wrought in her through hardship and neglect. It was a long time since she had considered this possibility. And suddenly she knew it meant a great deal to her. If Tristan—when Tristan—— She put her hand to her hair, feeling the great braid which still wreathed it. She could not remember when she had last thoroughly brushed it, much less when she had last washed it. She must find soap somewhere, she must dry her hair in the sun, she must let the cleansing wind blow through it before she dressed it carefully in front of a mirror. Her hand, in sliding from her braid, rested on her face. This was still smooth to the touch, and a little thrill of pleasure went through her as she realized this; but she knew there was no color in it, she could feel it curving in from the cheekbones instead of out from them. Well, perhaps now that the Germans were gone—perhaps now that there might soon be more food—— Her hand slid still further down and she saw it, resting on her lap. Its skin was not like the skin on her face; it was rough and reddened, and the nails were broken and discolored. She no longer had the hands of a lady—that is, by her old standards. But after all, the original meaning of "lady" had been "giver of bread." And she had managed to give bread to many during five long weary years. Only within these last weeks had she failed to do so, and within a few more weeks she would succeed again. At least, so she hoped and believed. And by that time, too, she would have managed to do something to her hands. They slid away again, and spanned her waist. That was slimmer than ever. When she could remodel her shabby old clothes—— She thought there was still one blue dress, folded away in a chest.

"*Mémère,* you promised to read to me. I've brought *Chicken Licken.*"

She looked up with a start. Padoue was standing before her, holding fast with one hand to the string attached to his beloved horse, and with the other to a tattered book which had once been bound in brightly colored cardboard. She held out her arms to welcome him.

"That's right, darling. I did promise. Come sit on my lap, and we'll read all about her."

Still clinging to his horse, Padoue snuggled close to her and handed her the book. She opened it at the first torn page and began to read. It would not have mattered if the page had been missing instead of torn, for she knew the story by heart, and so did he. Padoue could have prompted her, wherever she stopped.

" 'One day as Chicken Licken was walking through the woods, an acorn fell on her head.

" ' "Dear me," she thought, "the sky is falling. I must go and tell the king."

" 'So Chicken Licken hurried off——' "

"*Mémère,* the soldiers must have come back after all."

Padoue was tugging at her skirt. She looked down at him in surprise. Mercifully, the fairy story had carried her away from grim realities and she did not immediately return to these.

"What makes you think so, Padoue?"

"Because I can hear Léon shouting and Chess barking. Can't you?"

"I do now. I didn't until you told me. But I'll go see what's happened."

"Can't I come with you, *mémère?*"

She had succeeded in luring him out on the terrace with a promise of fairy tales, but she saw that he was still unwilling to stay there alone, and she did not want to press her first advantage too far. After all, there could be no danger at the outer door now. Again she extended her hand. But before she and Padoue could cross the fort, the shouting of Léon and the barking of Chess came closer, to the accompaniment of a resounding

American voice. And before she could cry out herself, she was imprisoned by the strong arms of Duncan Craig and felt his rough cool cheek against her own.

"Connie," he said huskily. "Connie." Nothing else for a moment. Then: "Thank God you're all right. I got here as soon as I could."

She was not sure whether his cheek was wet too, or whether it was only her own tears, glad ones this time, that she felt. Such joy welled up in her heart at the presence of this faithful friend that she could not speak and she did not even try. It did not matter for the moment whence he had come or how. The only thing which counted was that he was there.

"Let's go and sit down somewhere, shall we?" he said presently. "There's a lot I want to tell you and a lot I want to have you tell me. We might as well be as comfortable as we can while we're doing it. Léon's unloading some stuff I brought along with me. I thought some American Army rations might taste good to you. I remembered you used to like them pretty well and we get special ones for 'hospitality' right now. . . . Padoue, why don't you run along and see what's in those baskets? Maybe you'd like a snack."

"He's hungry, Duncan," Constance said, speaking for the first time as Padoue fairly dove from the fort. "Terribly hungry. It hasn't been so bad until the last few days, but——"

"Don't fib, Connie. What's become of the girl who couldn't tell a lie? It's been damned hard for five mortal years. Do you suppose I don't know? Oh, you haven't been hungry that long, of course. But to begin with, you've had the infernal noise to endure—that alone would have turned most women handicapped with your special phobia into raving maniacs."

"I did think at first I wouldn't be able to stand it. But I found I could."

"Exactly. You found you could because you made up your mind you were going to. But it's never ceased to make life hideous for you. Don't you suppose I know that too? Besides, you've been bullied and humiliated, you've been cold and lonely, you've lived face to face with battle, murder, and sudden death."

"Margot——" she began.

"Yes, Léon told me right away—that is, the bare fact. It's a dreadful thing. But you've still got Padoue. Try hard to think about that, instead of thinking what you've lost. And you're not going to lose anything more. The war's over, as far as Malou's concerned. If I'm not terribly mistaken, it'll be over mighty soon as far as Paris is concerned. And while we're talking about that—— Look, where did you say we could go and sit down?"

"I didn't say. Shall we try the *petit salon?* That's nearest. And there must be something left in it we can sit on."

"Bound to be. Or if there isn't, I can always drag in something from the *grand salon*. The main thing's to get you off your feet and give me a good chance to look at you."

With his arm still affectionately around her, they crossed the fort and Craig flung open the door to the little sitting room. The windowpanes had been blown in and mirrors and pictures lay on the floor in piles of broken glass. One bookcase had toppled over, and its contents were strewn across the rug; but the plush-covered chairs were still in their usual places. Craig straightened the bookcase, pushed the fallen books aside, and dusted some of the fine white powder from the furniture with a large handkerchief, which looked incongruously clean in the midst of the disorder. Then he motioned Constance to a chair and sat down opposite her, lighting a cigarette.

"Suppose I begin by giving you a brief case history," he suggested. "The last time we had a heart-to-heart talk, I told you I was going home to try for the sort of job that would have me all set to come back here the minute anything broke. Well, I got it. I went to England as a surgeon with the first of the sponsored university units. It happened to be a Harvard unit, but I don't really hold that against it." He grinned in his old engaging way, and Constance found herself smiling in return. "Our headquarters were in Salisbury, but of course I had my eye on Normandy from the beginning, so I asked the commanding general of the section for a transfer and eventually I got it. I've been in Cherbourg ever since it fell—nearly two months now. And believe me, we've got some hospital there—room for a thousand patients and a hundred nurses and seventy-six medical officers on duty. The hospital's used primarily for the evacuation of patients to England and the United States. But lots else goes on there too. For instance——"

Léon appeared in the open door, proudly bearing a tray. The chickens which had been among the casualties of the attack had already been stewed, and part of this stew had been converted into an excellent soup, rendered doubly appetizing by a little of the rice which Craig had brought with him; moreover, the bowl containing it was flanked by a plate piled high with toast made from white bread and liberally buttered. A pot of jam, a halved grapefruit, and a cup of steaming coffee completed the spread. Craig salvaged a small table from the general wreckage and set it in front of Constance.

"I have a hunch Padoue's not the only person on this place who's hungry," he observed. "Anyway, I suggested to Léon that he and Blondine had better get busy. You go ahead and eat while I talk—I'm full of food myself." And as she sat staring at the tray without immediately touching anything on it, he added, "That's an order, Connie. Don't tell me I've lost my job as your 'personal physician.'"

"You know you'll never do that. It's just that I still feel so choked up I——"

"That's why I ordered broth to begin with. Later on, we'll have steak." Then, as she took up a spoon and began to sip the soup slowly, he went on: "I get nearly all my evenings off and most week ends. So while I've been waiting for the roads to clear—that is, to the point where they'd be passable—I've taken someone else's week-end duty and let my own time off pile up. It's also understood that I'm to have occasional leave. All that means I can stay a week or so right now, and come back good and often. I shall, too. . . . That soup's pretty good, isn't it?"

"It's wonderful soup. But it's much more wonderful having you here, Duncan. . . . Then we don't have to hurry? I mean, we can just tell each other things gradually, without any sense of pressure at all?"

"None at all. In fact, after you've eaten that soup, if you really want to show me how glad you are to see me, you'll go to bed and try to sleep the clock around. After that, we'll begin at the beginning and cover all the ground there is. But as I started to say once before, I have one news item that won't keep. A lot of new troops landed in France around the middle of the month. And those troops aren't just British and American, Connie. They're French too—what we've been calling Free French for a long time. And among them there's an armored division under General Le Clerc."

She put down her spoon, resting her hand on the tray so that it would not tremble.

"He put on a magnificent show in Africa," Craig went on. "All the way from Lake Chad to Tripoli—well, you can hear about that later, probably from someone who'll be able to tell it to you a lot better than I can. This armored division of his was finally routed to France via England and got a great send-off when it left Southampton—military bands playing and all that sort of thing. Bates Hammond, one of our new orthopedic men, came over in the same convoy and gave his men proud of them! Apparently he's got about the slickest outfit there is. The last I knew, he'd been operating around Alençon, before heading for Paris. And the report is that one of the officers on his staff is a Colonel de Fremond. I haven't been able to check on his initials yet, but—— There, let me get that damned tray out of the way. Just hang on to me for a minute and let the world go by."

She was constantly reminded during the next few days of the week Craig had spent at Malou after Nick's death. To be sure, that had been a period of black despair and this was one of reawakened hope; but Constance had the same sense of understanding and support, the same long-denied opportunity for quiet and confidential talks, which on the previous occasion had relieved her mind and restored her spirits. She spoke of Margot, of Ghisèle and Gérard, of Marie Aimée, and of von Reden. Craig went to the cemetery, carrying flowers, and talked with Monsieur le Curé and Monsieur le Maire about memorial services; but later he dwelt on the splendor of Margot's life and not on the tragedy of her death. What a gorgeous creature she had been, he said musingly, as if the memory of her charm and daring were not mournful but glowing. How much ecstasy she and Nick must have crowded into their brief and passionate union—more than most married couples did in a lifetime! And what a heritage of vitality they had given their son! If Margot had not conceived before Nick's death, if she had not borne and nurtured this beautiful boy, if she had not succeeded in saving his life—that would have been calamitous. As it was, there had been a crescendo of glory about her being to the very end. . . .

When Craig saw that Constance was beginning to accept this theory, he dealt, one by one, with the other matters which were disturbing her mind. He created an early opportunity of going to the Manoir des Cailloirs, and returned to voice unqualified approval of the work going on there and immense goodwill towards its supervisors. The patients could not be in better hands, to his way of thinking, than those of Gérard and Ghisèle. He had never met a more likable Frenchman or seen a girl whom he thought better qualified to be a doctor's wife. He believed they were hesitating to get married for fear Constance might resent this; in his opinion, it was the only sensible thing for them to do, and the sooner the better. . . .

He looked over Marie Aimée's sketch, inspected the ruins of the Abbaye and visited the refugee nuns at the farm near Saint-Julien-le-Faucon, where he talked at length with Mère Claire and Mère Martina. Of course a new Abbaye must rise from the ashes of the old, he told Constance heartily; there were Communities of Benedictines all over the world, which, as far as he knew, might be a good thing; but only these had a heritage of such immense historical and religious value. Besides, the new Abbaye would not only preserve the great traditions of William the Conqueror and Sainte Thérèse; it would be the most fitting possible memorial to the twenty nuns who had lost their lives in the bombardment, and especially to Marie Aimée, who had visualized its restoration not only with great faith, but with great practicality. If fifty thousand would represent a good nest egg for a building fund, he was prepared to offer it; of course that would be just a starter. . . .

He was thankful it was von Reden who had chosen Malou as head-quarters, and not any one of several other high-ranking German officers he might mention. Things had been really bad where these were. But they would not talk about that. At least not now. Meanwhile, wouldn't she like to hear what was happening at L'Abbatiale? Not that she would believe all of his tall tale, though every word of it was gospel truth. But he was so near there when he got to the site of the Abbaye that he decided to go on. Ghisèle had intimated that she was worried about Mark and that had influenced him also. Well, she needn't have worried too much. A battalion of Gordon Highlanders had taken the place over temporarily, but before their arrival, while the fighting in that area was still going on, Mark Mullins had retreated to a cave. Did Constance know there was quite a large cavern near the chapel? Oh, she did? Well, Craig had never known it before, but one of the canny Scots had directed him to a narrow slit in the ground and he had squeezed through it somehow. Then, after he had crawled along it for some moments on his hands and knees, towards a little glimmer of light, the passage opened up before him and he was able to stand upright, and presently had come to a huge chamber where there were nearly a hundred refugees, divided into little groups of five and six which he supposed were dispossessed families. In the midst of them whom should he see but Mark Mullins sitting on a divan (of horse blankets!) like an Eastern potentate, and peering grimly about him through his thick spectacles!

He had been delighted to see Craig and had promptly produced a bottle of excellent champagne and two bottles of well-aged Calvados, not to mention a cold roast chicken, from some mysterious hiding place. It was all fantastic. But then, Mark had always been fantastic. He had got the last of the horses away to small obscure farmsteads in the nick of time, and they were apparently all safe, though some of the cattle had been killed and some of the buildings bombed. Best of all, Guy had managed to make his way home and was there in the cave with Mark. He had lots of tall tales to tell himself about his experiences as a *camouflé*. But those were ended now. He and Mark were going to get the horses back and start all over again as soon as the Highlanders were gone. Meanwhile, there were trenches around the yard and rough boxes, mortars in the stallion's paddock, and the command post was dug deep into the manège. But all that would soon be in the past, and Craig knew Constance would want to help Mark and Guy carry on. It would be her turn to facilitate an *haras* now. Incidentally, Craig had already told all this good news to Ghisèle. It seemed she knew about the cave too. He hated to have his thunder stolen like that. . . .

Craig did most of the talking and he contrived to do much of it in the same light vein as when telling Constance about L'Abbatiale. He could see that it tired her to speak even of her most vital concerns, and when she had unburdened her heart of its heaviest load, he gave her to understand that he was gradually securing general information from others at Malou, and that there was nothing more she needed to tell him unless she felt so inclined. He insisted that she should rest a great deal, trying to convince her that if she did, she would be able to work all the harder in the end. She protested against lying still while everyone else was toiling early and late to restore the first semblance of order indoors and out; but Craig, aided and abetted by all the others, succeeded in silencing these protests. She might hear from Tristan any day now, he kept saying; what was even more to the point, Tristan might suddenly appear on the scene, without any previous notice. It would be quite in character. Possibly he would have difficulty in dispatching a message because no wires were going through yet; but if he could not get himself sent down to Normandy from Paris on some kind of a liaison mission, he was not half the strategist or half the husband that Craig gave him credit for being. For the present, Constance must follow the orders of her personal physician and lie still, sleeping as much as possible.

Between naps, she could contemplate the starry handkerchief, which he noticed was still hanging where they had tacked it up five years before. It was pretty dingy-looking, to be sure, but he did not suppose she minded that; probably it had even more meaning for her than when it was fresh and new. The very fact that she had managed to keep it would give it this; and besides, every one of those little stars must have more significance than when Tristan had offered her his parting present; while she was in bed she could plan what she would say to him about that—and many other things. Then, as soon as she was a little stronger, she must resume her usual walks. They would do her good, if she did not undertake them on top of a hard day's work. And some evening when she was strolling along she would probably see Tristan approaching through the avenue of hemlocks, and they would come home together, just as they had when he first brought her to Malou. . . .

Craig made all this sound so plausible and vivid that Constance soon began to visualize it herself, and it was the easier because she eagerly desired to do so. His strongest argument was the contention that if she rested now, she would seem like her old self to Tristan on his return. But Craig had other good arguments too. He kept her quiet because he kept her interested and happy. He had brought a special service radio with him, and they listened regularly to the American networks and the B.B.C., of which she had been deprived ever since the destruction of her own hidden instrument. They also heard the first broadcast of Radio France after the fall of Paris, and learned from all these sources of the Allies' triumphant entry into the capital, and later of their drive as far as Troyes. And eventually, in the midst of these thrilling tidings, Craig reminded her that as yet they had said nothing to each other about Tilda or Gwen or Eileen.

"No, we haven't. There have been so many other things. Besides, you didn't mention them of your own accord, and I didn't like to ask prying questions. Tell me."

"Well, I'm now more or less a free man."

"What do you mean, Duncan, more or less?"

"The divorce went through like a breeze. Tilda didn't really care about having a husband any more. A man can be an awful nuisance around a house, you know—at least some women seem to think so. Not that there aren't others who rather like the idea. I've turned the Park Avenue apartment over to her. I never cared much about it anyhow, so that wasn't a particularly generous gesture. But I've kept the stud farm in Kentucky. By the way, all the horses Mark Mullins sent over there were in the pink the last I heard, and there are a number of new foals. You ought to realize quite a lot on them, sooner or later. I could give you some figures now if you like."

"No. Tell me about that some other time. Go on about Tilda now."

"Well, just before the decree was final, so that it would still be perfectly proper, I gave her one more pearl necklace. A knockout. She was tickled to death with it."

"Duncan, you're incorrigible. . . . Did it have the usual connotation?"

"No, as a matter of fact it didn't. That wasn't what I meant when I said I was only more or less free. I never wholly subscribed to the idea that when a woman makes up her mind she's going to marry a man, he hasn't a fighting chance of escape. But when two women make up their minds that he ought to marry one of them, and settle on the same one, the game really is up. Or so I tardily seem to have discovered."

"What on earth are you talking about?"

"Didn't Gwen and you both decide, twenty-five years ago, that she was my predestined bride?"

"Oh, Duncan!"

For the first time, except when she had spoken about Tristan, her voice rang with genuine joy. He made a gesture which was intended to be deprecatory, but which lost its effect because of his broad grin.

"As a matter of fact, I'm rather pleased myself," he remarked. "I suppose I can say, more truthfully than most men, that I've never loved but one woman. That is, in a special way. And you know who she is. Don't let's pretend about that, Connie. That or anything else. But I've loved lots of others in lots of other ways. Most of them not so good. But this is good. It's very good. I'm admitting this a great deal too late, but put it down to my credit that I am admitting it. Gwen's got guts—as much so as any woman I ever saw, not even excepting you, Connie. She's got brains and character and looks too. Well, she has what it takes. Incidentally, she's seen a lot more of this war than I have. She got to Africa with the first contingent of WACS. She and Eileen both. I don't mean as WACS, of course; I mean as regularly accredited reporters—they even got out a daily newspaper on the transport going across. And did they tell the world afterwards! Just wait till I show you some of those pieces! The best one's about stumbling into the Kassarine Pass break-through. I don't know, though—another piece is about visiting the inner sanctum in the palace of some great Moroccan dignitary and came out with the caption, 'The Story No Man Could Get.' Of course, Gwen was wearing her WAC uniform and the Moroccan lady who received her was seated on a satin pillow, and so loaded down with jewels and gold ornaments that she couldn't get up from it without a struggle. Gwen stressed the fact that they probably looked equally queer to each other."

"Have you got that piece with you, Duncan?"

"Sure. I've got them all. Eileen's are almost as good as Gwen's. She went on to Italy after a while. You can count on her to head for Rome, just like a homing pigeon, on the least provocation, and to get there about as easily. But eventually she and Gwen joined forces again, in England. They're planning to keep right on working together most of the time, which suits me down to the ground. Just now, Gwen's a lap ahead. She's in France and Eileen's still in England."

"Gwen's in France right now!"

"Yes," Craig said with elaborate casualness. "She and a few other correspondents were flown across by the Ninth Air Force Service Command on D-Day 12. Two fighter planes went out to meet them and escort them in. They were the first women journalists to get to the invasion beaches. But it's a still bigger feather in Gwen's cap that she was the *only* correspondent, *man or woman,* present when the first American casualties were brought ashore in England from the Smoky Joes on D day itself."

"The Smoky Joes?"

"Yeah, the mine-sweepers. Nobody seemed to notice there was considerable action on the English coast as well as the French coast that day until Gwen wrote it up. I'm not surprised that when she was sent over here her instructions read, 'You are hereby attached to the staff not only to cover women's angles, but to take other assignments as you did particularly well last week.' She's done particularly well since then too. She doesn't mind bombs a bit. On the other hand, she's quite allergic to spiders. She refused a nice safe foxhole on Utah Beach because she saw one in it. She slept in a tent instead."

"Duncan, you're not making this up as you go along, are you?"

"It's all gospel truth. The last time I heard from her she was in Saint-Lô, diving in and out of craters, but still mostly right side up. She said to be sure to give you her love. I thought maybe the next time I came down I might bring her with me. We even played with the idea of asking you to let us get married at Malou. After Eileen gets here too. We rather thought we'd like to have her for a bridesmaid. How would that strike you? It wouldn't complicate things for you, would it, to have a wedding at Malou?"

"Of course not. At least, I don't think so. But anyhow———"

Anyhow, she was delighted and excited beyond measure, and eagerly asked for permission to pass on the great news to Aunt Bertha, who was unfeignedly pleased too. Since Craig's arrival, the old lady had apparently taken on a new lease of life, which he insisted was not due to the honor of his company, but to the animating effect of the "hospitality" rations he had brought to Malou. With considerable spirit, she denied this.

"I hope I'm still so I can miss a few meals without being any the worse for it," she informed him loftily. "I haven't got any complaint, if I am getting on in years. But I never thought I'd live to see the day when I'd know I wasn't clean, me, nor the house I lived in, nor the young ones I took care of. If you want to know what's making the difference, Duncan, it's that soap you brought along with you."

Duncan laughed and told her he would guarantee to keep on stealing soap for her. There had been no laughter at Malou in a long time, but now it began to ring out again. Padoue and Lucie laughed as they went rollicking through the woods, chasing each other. Nicole laughed when she looked into Michel's eyes and told him he must have spoken the truth when he said he was not the same man as before the war, because that one had never got her with child. Even when there was no actual laughter, there were approaches to it. Blondine chuckled in her old hearty way instead of grumbling as she went puttering around her kitchen; Lise made cheerful sounds as she called to her chickens, Martin and Benoît as they watered their horses. And then there was the sound of Alpy and Michel shouting to each other above the clatter of the mowing machine. For the men of Malou were back in the fields again, and there would be a harvest after all.

A harvest and a home-coming. With certitude and joy, Constance awaited them both.